The Stormcrafter Chronicles

Scion of Lightning and Blade of Lightning

J.T. Moy

CENTAURUS
PRESS

Contents

Scion of Lightning

Blade of Lightning

N
W
E
S
VOROS
Dunberrin
Finstaf
Dunberr
Tillidor
Irin
Kilanae
Hera
Sanford
to RANILA

FAUCONY
to PIHAAT
STROCK
Jurn
ELLIPTA
to ZURA
ASCORIA
HUSVAN
Cerik
NERA BOA

Scion of Lightning

Book 1

Chapter 1

The Frostbear

A dozen conscripts stalked between massive giantwood trees as a storm exhausted itself over the forest. They hoped for the return of birdsong and insect chirrups, but heard nothing but the squelch of their boots on muddy leaves.

The young men edged forward with arrows nocked to their hunting bows. Swords swayed at their hips, and their gazes turned to every flicker of movement as they sought their prey.

A thirteenth man, a king's ranger, led the way.

He stopped and listened.

Forest sounds returned to their rear, but not ahead.

The ranger fanned out the fingers of his left hand and gestured for the less experienced men to spread out. He resumed the advance.

Jaks Rauhalik was at the back of the group. Tall with a head of brown hair, he bore the square jaw and aquiline nose of a nobleman's son. On any other day, his eyes would have drifted as he daydreamed of great battles and heroes, but today his gaze focused on the hunt.

Determined to impress Ranger Cromer, on this week of survival exercises at the end of their two-year mandatory conscription, he couldn't make any more errors. All his hopes of joining the army as a career soldier depended on it. For protecting his kingdom, as his older sister did, was the noblest of professions.

But yesterday, unfortunately, he'd taken a fall, just before a squad mate loosed an arrow at a deer. The sound of him skidding down a muddy slope had scared the animal off and earned Jaks an admonishment from the ranger and the inglorious position at the back of the squad.

They had been tracking a frostbear all morning; that is, the *ranger* had been tracking the bear, and the inexperienced conscripts were following like lion cubs learning to hunt.

Without the deadly archer, a frostbear would have been completely out of the conscripts' capabilities.

Twelve-foot tall and two tons in weight, it was a formidable beast that required at least a squad of experienced soldiers to bring down—or a master ranger who could shoot unerringly for the heart. Yet, its size was not its greatest strength. Silence was. Frostbears were arcane predators with an innate ability to magically absorb sound. They were massive, silent killers of the forest whose victims never even heard them coming.

The beast had come from the much wilder northern mountains to this tree-felling region and had already slaughtered seven woodsmen over the past several months. It was the conscripts' training exercise to assist the ranger to kill it. Nothing like a giant bear to challenge one's survival skills.

They had not yet seen the frostbear, relying on Ranger Cromer's tracking skills to follow its lumbering path over the mountains. But it had been three hours now, and the rain had hindered their progress significantly.

Another half hour passed, and the forest grew thicker. The full sounds of the forest had returned, and the conscripts' formation loosened, their postures less anxious and eyes less vigilant. Surely, the master ranger would call a rest break soon.

Jaks was tired and bored. He un-nocked his arrow and returned it to his hip quiver. Far easier to walk without the arrow knocking against underbrush and branches.

His only friend in the squad—and friend since childhood—Minto Piccaton, had also lost interest in the hunt. A foot shorter than Jaks, but of stockier build, he had a square face dotted with freckles and a head topped with a scruff of brown hair. A carefree spirit, he was the jollity that countered Jaks's earnestness. As they tramped behind the rest of the squad, Minto hissed at him and veered closer.

"I've been thinking. Could your father help us get into the King's Rangers? Is it worth asking him?" questioned the freckled youth.

The question froze Jaks in his tracks. "My father would rather spit on me than help," he replied through gritted teeth. "You would not want anything to do with him. I can assure you of that." He felt bad being so blunt with his friend, but thinking about his father sent chills through his body.

"His lordship looked pleasant enough at the Royal Parade last year. Why are you so foul of him?" he said over his shoulder as he clambered over a rotted tree trunk.

"Would a pleasant man do this?" Jaks stopped again and raised his left hand, baring the stub of his little finger for Minto to see. "Forget about him. Our only path forward is if we can get a commendation from the master ranger." He gritted his teeth at the thought of their trainer's disapproving glares.

Jaks's attention drew to the empty woods in front of them,

devoid of any sign of their fellow conscripts. "Oh, hell—we've lost them again. We need to find the trail, quick."

"I thought they went that way?" Minto pointed toward a patch of dense forest rising ahead of them. He looked up at the sun through the thick canopy of branches and leaves.

"But aren't those their footprints?" Jaks pointed in the opposite direction, toward a muddy clearing. He cursed and pulled on the buckles of the pack that were always slipping because of his bony shoulders.

They milled around the clearing for a couple of minutes, looking for a clear trail.

It was then that Jaks noticed there were no birds or insects to hear.

The forest had gone quiet.

"Don't move," Jaks whispered to Minto.

His friend froze in his steps. "What—"

"Shhh . . ." Jaks slowly reached for the arrow he'd returned to the quiver, cursing himself for letting down his guard.

A flicker of movement caught his eye. There, forty yards to his left, a huge, brown-furred beast lumbered between the bases of two giantwoods, crushing bushes and undergrowth beneath it, but astonishingly without making a sound.

Crouching, hoping the knee-high undergrowth would camouflage him, Jaks trembled in his attempt to nock the arrow.

The frostbear raised its snout and sniffed the air. Its head was massive, as big as one of the army's warlions, with jaws that could certainly bite his arm off as a snack.

"*Grafuk*," swore Minto in a panicky voice. "We've got to hide."

He was right. The two of them alone couldn't take it out. The ranger's plan had been to surround the frostbear and pepper it with arrows—individuals running away if it came for them—enraging it into rearing up on its hind legs, where the ranger would kill it with a heartshot.

Sniffing the ground, the bear ambled closer and behind another giantwood. It paused, its backside and two rear legs still visible.

"Quick, move." Jaks jogged in a crouch in the opposite direction.

Around enormous trees and through dense underbrush they fled, dodging low branches and leaping fallen trees until they ran out of breath behind a gray boulder.

Silence still embraced them.

"Did it follow us?" asked Minto, puffing and sweating heavily.

Jaks peeked over the boulder.

Thirty yards distant, the frostbear had its nose to the undergrowth, coming their direction. It was tracking them.

A wave of panic flooded over Jaks. Desperately, he looked around—and then upward.

The giantwoods were notoriously difficult to climb. Their wide bases were more like cliff faces than regular trees and their lowest branches thin and weak, if they could even be reached.

A stand of ironwood trees rose nearby. Yes, their narrower trunks and wider spread of branches were reachable and more likely to take their weight. Although nowhere near the height of their majestic cousins, if he could even get halfway up, Jaks was sure he'd be out of reach of the twelve-foot-tall bear.

He tapped Minto on the shoulder and pointed at the gray-barked ironwoods.

Running to the closest tree, Jaks threw away his pack and bow—they would only slow him down—grabbed the lowest branches, and shoved his foot between two of the sturdiest. Then the next ones, and again and again, he climbed.

Fearing to look down, he pulled and pushed his way up through the branches, not stopping until the branches were too thin to climb any higher. Minto was in the tree next to him, but having chosen a taller specimen, he was up higher by two yards.

Jaks's tree shook violently. Gasping in fright, he stared down.

The bear was pushing against the ironwood, its giant front paws pressed against the waist-thick trunk. Evil-looking claws dug into the bark. Dark eyes stared up at Jaks and the beast opened its mouth, baring rows of triangular teeth.

A deafening roar blasted at Jaks's feet. Its arcane powers allowed the frostbear to stalk in silence, but also, if it chose, to terrify with loudness.

The tree shook again. A branch broke in Jaks's grip. A foot slipped from between a fork of branches. He wrapped his arms around the upper trunk, paralyzed in fear, and unable to do anything but scream in terror.

The beast rose higher on its hind legs, front paws clawing up the ironwood.

Minto yelled at the frostbear from the other tree and threw arrows from his quiver—having also abandoned his bow to free his hands—trying to distract the frostbear.

The tree swayed sharply. Branches snapped and cracked. Jaks's grip slipped. His foot swung wildly.

The bear swung its paw and a claw hooked Jaks's boot and tore it from him.

A warhorn blared from the forest and shouts surrounded the stand of ironwoods. Almost a dozen men encircled Jaks's tree from a range of twenty yards and began loosing arrows at the frostbear. The ranger and the conscripts had come to the rescue.

Arrows thudded into the animal's back and legs. Some,

unable to penetrate the thick fur and hide, bounced off and fell to the ground along with Minto's thrown ones. Others bounced off its thick skull or missed completely and thumped into nearby trees. The few that penetrated angered the giant and distracted it from its tree-bound prey.

Bellowing, the bear dropped to all fours and charged toward a hapless conscript with a spent bow in his hands.

The youth screamed and ran.

Hiss. Another flurry of arrows. Only two stuck but were enough distraction that the bear turned again and charged toward another conscript. The unfortunate youth tripped as he turned to flee and fell with an anguished cry.

Twang. A single arrow zipped through the air and into the bear's eye.

Half-blinded and fully enraged, the frostbear rose to its full height, searching for the archer to tear apart.

Twang. A second arrow thudded into the beast's chest. As the bear roared and staggered clumsily, a third shaft followed and embedded in the same spot.

Two heartshots—the frostbear collapsed into the undergrowth, moaning.

Two final breaths and the brown-furred chest never rose again.

Cheers broke out and the conscripts filtered out of the woods to examine their conquest. Several nudged it gingerly with their swords. Declaring it dead, they whooped and hollered.

Jaks descended, shivering at the sight of the deep gouges in the trunk as his hands passed over them. His torn-off boot rested at the foot of the tree, a large hole in the sole, a reminder of the bear's deadly claws. As he pushed it back on, he trembled, knowing that with another shake of the tree, he would've fallen and been torn apart.

"You all right?" Minto asked, down from his own perch. "Almost got you, it did." He gestured at Jaks's boot.

"Nah. Would've kicked it in the nose," replied Jaks with faked confidence.

Nodding, his freckled friend picked up his arrows from around the base of the ironwood. Finding Jaks's bow undamaged, he handed it back to him.

A voice called out from the conscripts around the dead bear.

"Nice view from up there, ladies?" spoke a thick-necked thug named Baden, as he swaggered over to Jaks and Minto. "You're good bear-bait, I have to admit. He was gonna eat you up." He lunged at Jaks, gnashing his teeth, prompting an outburst of laughter from the other conscripts. In their squad called the "Thorns"—to demark them from the other dozen or so conscript units active around the kingdom—Baden ranked as the senior conscript.

"Shut up, Baden." Jaks squared off against the smirking youth. "You would've done the same."

Ranger Cromer stood up from behind the bear, where he'd been studying his marksmanship, and strode through the circle, silencing the group. He was a cutting figure in weathered black leather and an arrow-thin beard. Female conscripts swooned after him as though he were a dashing pirate, but his cold demeanor kept all but the most brazen from his attention. But none of that mattered to Jaks as the ranger descended on them with flaring nostrils and blazing eyes.

He stood before Jaks and Minto. "A few minutes later and you idiots would've been dead. You're lucky I realized it'd circled back behind us as soon as I did." He pointed his bow tip at them and scowled. "Stop getting separated from your squad. It is not that hard."

"Sorry, sir," Jaks said with his eyes downcast.

"Sir, the underbrush got really thick and we couldn't see anyone—" Minto started.

"Don't give me excuses." The ranger loomed over them. "You two are the worst conscripts I have ever been cursed with in these forests—that's twice you've gotten lost now. Now, after we get this thing buried, you're going to get your weedy asses over that ridge and lead us south until sundown. Go off course, and you make your own way back to Dunberrin."

The master ranger returned to the main squad and began snapping orders. Shovels were produced, and a grave was dug. Jaks and Minto went to help.

Two hours later, the bear, minus a few body parts taken as tokens, lay beneath a pile of dirt, and it was time to return to base.

Minto led the way, Jaks a few paces behind, and Ranger Cromer tracing their steps. There were a few more jibes and jokes from the other conscripts at their expense, but the scowling ranger shushed them and they walked in silence.

A while later, they came to a rocky stream, wide but shallow, running down from the mountains ahead. The cold water soaked through Jaks's boots—especially quick in his left through the hole at its base. He followed his friend across the stream and then climbed the opposite bank to find him staring into the sky.

Minto pointed upward. "Look at that."

Jaks followed his gesture and saw a bright yellow speck trailed by a long tail falling through the clouds toward the distant mountains.

"Meteor," he said. "Make a wish and get moving."

He pushed Minto's hand away and walked on, not wanting to be chewed out by the ranger again.

"It looks close . . . really close. Like it might land near us," Minto said, adjusting his sword belt and striding to keep up with Jaks.

They made their way back into the forest edge, which was on a slope getting higher and colder toward the mountains.

Jaks and Minto continued to catch glimpses of the bright meteor through the speckled canopy overhead. It seemed to be getting closer to them. The speck turned into a large burning glow.

Then it dimmed—the front glow first, then the tail disappeared. He heard a distant hissing sound from its direction and glimpsed an object disappearing into the shadows of a distant mountain.

Minto waggled a finger. "It's just over there! Probably no more than a day's trek from here, I reckon."

Ranger Cromer caught up. "Stop gawping. Nothing to get excited about. It's just a lump of rock," he said and pushed past them. The trees had thinned into a clearing with a small crag of rocks. "All right. This'll do. Stop and set camp."

The Thorns spread out around the area to set up their shelters and a campfire. Subdued chatter about the meteor went around, but everyone soon lost interest.

That night, Jaks woke to the sound of water splashing against his makeshift tent. Two feet were planted by his shelter and their owner was urinating against the oilskin near his head. Jaks scrambled out, cursing and swearing at the vandal. Baden grinned at him in the moonlight.

"Didn't see you there, bear-bait," the senior conscript said.

"Hell, you didn't," Jaks forcibly whispered back, not wanting to wake anyone. "Don't push me. You'll regret it one day." He kicked the tent and splattered the brute with his own urine.

Baden stepped back in annoyance and hiked up his breeches. "Your watch now, city-boy," he said, as he walked to his own shelter. Then over his shoulder he added, "Better guard your back."

Muttering in disgust, Jaks slapped on his sword belt and went to clamber up the crag of rocks overlooking the campsite. Other cohorts of conscripts were fast friends who played, drank, and stood loyally alongside each other. But Jaks's group was rude and cruel toward outsiders—and Jaks and Minto had been outsiders to them from the beginning.

The only two city-born recruits in the Thorns, they were assumed to be privileged and haughty, despite Jaks's efforts to befriend the rest of the squad. He always had a supportive word or a lending hand if anyone stumbled or needed help with their training exercises or duties. However, the city-country split and Minto's unhelpful reminders to the others of Jaks's father's status as a lord castellan—even though he'd been disowned— kept them excluded. The crux had come when they'd expressed disgust at Baden's vile game where he'd cajoled the other conscripts into kicking a dead cat back and forth like a ball. From there, the senior conscript had taken extra efforts to ostracize the two. Fortunately, Jaks and Minto were strong friends from childhood and continued their shared interests in heraldry and ancient stories of lore, regardless of their status in the group.

As he sat, Jaks's anger soon turned to wonder as he gazed up at the night sky and saw two more glowing white streaks blast across the black. They flared and faded but far more distant than the meteor from earlier that day; however, they were still spectacular to behold.

Over the next two hours, he sat with knees pulled up and wrapped under his fur jacket, listening to the rustle of the trees and snores of his campmates as he stared into the abyss, hoping to see more of the mysterious phenomena. However, none else appeared but the stars and moon.

Eventually, he slid down and prodded the next watcher awake.

Fatigued, he went to his sleeping mat and dragged it away from the urine-stenched canopy. Lying down, images of the frostbear shaking the tree and its shark-like maw gaping at him flashed through his mind. He stared into the dark, worried the beast would come back.

Hours later, he finally succumbed to sleep—and dreamed fitfully of a giant bear who transformed into his father and then chased him through dark woods until he fell down a staircase in the middle of the forest; catching him, it proceeded to devour him. He half-woke, and the dream began again.

The next morning when they had broken camp, Ranger Cromer called the squad together for the day's survival exercise.

Jaks rubbed his eyes, poorly rested from a disturbed night.

"Pair up. From here to the White Cliff is an easy eight hours. Get yourselves to the base cave there." He pointed at a far-off mountain with a sheer white cliff face to the south. "If you're not at the base by tomorrow midday—you had better be dead, because that is the only excuse I will accept."

Baden stood up. "Sir, I'll be there this evening," he said, greasing favor with the ranger.

"But I know who probably won't." Cromer glowered at Jaks and Minto as the group readied to leave.

Jaks stared at the ground, riled up by the ranger's words; the man was expecting them to fail.

He would show Cromer he wasn't a complete failure.

Chapter 2

The Meteor

Jaks and Minto were the second pair to be sent off, ten minutes after Baden and his partner.

Tall trees enveloped them as they left the clearing. A pair of fantails fluttered after them, darting over the forest floor, spearing beetles and worms unveiled by their footsteps. The sky was clouding over and threatening another downpour.

"Let's not get lost today," Jaks said. "We really need a win to get the ranger on our side."

"Don't worry about it." Minto grinned cheerfully. He slapped Jaks on the back as he brushed past. "There's always second chances. If we get to the base on time, he'll forget about yesterday."

"Yeah, we'll be fine." Jaks nodded.

Minto widened his steps and sweat glistened his brow. "And . . . that meteor landed in that valley over there. I have never seen one before. We should have a quick look."

"Not sure that's a good idea," said Jaks, intrigued with the concept but conflicted by the need to do well on their trek that day.

"We've got heaps of time," said Minto. "If we don't get to the cliffs by tonight, I'll take the blame, okay? Okay."

He smiled at his friend's boundless optimism. Jaks had to admit, after seeing the meteors in the sky last night, he would love to see one up close.

Two hours later, the threat of rain clouds had passed, but Minto's curiosity had not.

"This way. I'm sure the valley is over here. Looks like something circling over it," said Minto. He pushed his thumbs into his belt and walked faster.

"Carrion birds?" Jaks hurried to catch up.

By midday, they had climbed steadily to where the trees thinned and were much smaller than their sisters below. Jaks looked back over the lower forest and then searched for the White Cliffs but could only see jagged outlines of mountains. He did not know where they were.

Less than a mile away, the flight of dark wings continued to spiral and swoop.

"We really should go back down. I think we're lost." Jaks grabbed Minto's elbow to slow him.

"It's just over this crest, I think." Minto pulled away from him and gestured rapidly. "I don't think they're birds."

At the top of the ridgeline, they looked into the next valley and gasped at the sight below.

On the valley floor, a pod the size of a giant boulder rested against a shattered tree stump. Its gray surface was smooth and symmetrical, and a huge orange sail, with thin black tethers, lay tangled over nearby trees.

He saw that the dark wings belonged to a thunder of dragons. A half dozen bronze-colored ones, bodies the size of a dog but wings measuring six times their width. Two other dragons perched on top of the bulbous object; one of them slid to the ground, its claws unable to grip the surface, whilst the other twisted its head around and flicked its forked tongue over the object.

Minto crashed down the slope. He yelled and drew his sword, slapping it against its sheath. The startled dragons jumped into the air and took flight to join their packmates overhead.

Jaks hurried to join his friend beside the mysterious object, pulling out his sword and keeping a wary eye to the sky. Hopefully, the dragons would fly off back to their roost. Although they were smaller than the army's trained war dragons—and not red fire-breathers nor black acid-spitters—all dragons were dangerous, especially if they attacked in unison.

But seeing the dragons spiraling higher, Jaks gingerly prodded the boulder-like object with the tip of his sword. "This is no mere rock. It looks metal." His eyebrows furrowed. "I wonder if it's dangerous?"

Minto walked around from the other direction, caressed it, and then pushed against it. "Do you think it's valuable? We could be rich, Jaks! I bet some merchant or forgemaster would pay a cartload of gold for this." His eyes were wide and darted about.

"What's this?" Jaks lifted part of the sail that still draped the top part of the object and uncovered a dark opening to the inside of it. He swept aside the rest of the orange material and stooped to peer inside.

Minto came up and gave a low whistle.

The midday sun illuminated a small interior. Inside, Jaks could see an empty padded seat with straps and clasps on either side of it. To its left, square and round inlays marked by nonsensical symbols indented the internal surface. And to the other side of the seat, a glass panel clung to a thick metal arm. Some leaves blew into the otherwise empty vessel.

He touched his fingers to the cold exterior. The surface vibrated. Surprised, he quickly withdrew. He could have sworn it responded to his touch. *Is it alive?*

Minto dropped his pack and weapons, and then threw a leg over the edge of the entrance and straddled it.

"What are you doing? You can't climb in there," said Jaks. "I have a bad feeling about this. We should get back to the forest."

Minto grinned at him as he crammed himself into the tight space and lay in the upward-facing seat. "Bit cramped . . ." He poked some of the inlays, which depressed, clicked, and rose. He moved the panel back and forth. Finally, he reached over his head and thrust an arm into an alcove above the seat. He brought down his hands, pulling out a thin blue tube. He studied the end of it and squeezed—a stream of liquid spouted from the nozzle into his face. Spluttering and wiping his face, he dropped the tube and it stopped flowing. "Water." He laughed.

"Looks like it was made for a person," Jaks remarked. He stood back to cast his eyes around the sparsely wooded mountainside again and briefly up at the circling dragons.

The orange sail stretched from the metal object and up the slope to wrap itself around the bases of three speckled trees. The material bore an emblem repeated several times over the sail, a white circle crisscrossed with lines cradled in a basket of branches. "Is that the symbol of Ranila?" he asked Minto, a self-proclaimed expert of country flags and heraldic symbols.

Minto climbed back out of the vessel and shrugged. "I've never seen that emblem before. I'll get some of it to show Ranger Cromer." He drew his dagger, attacked the thin material, and remarked that it was much tougher than it looked.

Jaks heard several screeches from the dragons overhead and breathed a sigh of relief as they peeled away and winged toward the mountain peaks. The tension eased in his shoulders, and he began to pace the landing site, examining the ground for tracks.

Amongst their own footprints, he found a drag mark heading up to the speckled trees.

"There might be someone here," he hissed to Minto. He hefted his short-sword. The small ashes could easily hide a person beneath the folds of orange fabric covering them.

Minto tucked the cut square under his belt as he kneeled beside Jaks and squinted at the disturbed ground.

They stood and crept forward, their weapons waving unsteadily before them.

In a high-pitched voice, Jaks called out, "Is there someone there?"

He stepped around to the back of the trees and found a woman.

She sat on the ground on a crinkled silver sheet with her back against a tree trunk. The material hanging from the branches cast an orange hue over her. Her dark-blue clothes were tightly fitted and embroidered with emblems and words on her shoulder and chest. An open satchel lay on the ground, and her lower body was blanketed by a second sheet. A bandage circled her forehead and short, raven-black hair framed a face that was unnaturally narrow but bewildering to behold. Wide lips thinned, and huge, brown eyes dilated as she stared at the intruders.

Jaks's face reddened and his heart raced as he drew in a quick breath and drank in her exotic features. Her skin was pale as though not sun-touched for months but flawless, suggesting a similar age to his own. He could not identify her country or race, but he knew that she was beautiful.

She shouted and pointed an object at them, weaving it back and forth between them like targets. Jaks thought it must be a weapon; the way she was pointing it at them was threatening and it looked hard and evil. Although she held it like a crossbow, it was much shorter and had no string or limbs, but despite that, it looked dangerous.

"We won't hurt you," Minto said in a controlled voice, putting his sword back into its scabbard. He nudged Jaks, who sheathed his sword in response and raised his hands.

Still pointing the weapon toward them, she struggled to her feet, favoring her left leg, and slid up against the tree. The silver blanket fell away and Jaks saw that her right lower leg was wrapped in a blood-soaked bandage. She grimaced as she moved.

The three of them stood frozen for several seconds. Again, she shouted some words at them, but slower this time.

"I do not know what you are saying," said Minto, intoning each word clearly. "Put the weapon down." His right hand lowered and patted the air.

Forehead wrinkling, she squinted at them as though reading their thoughts. After a minute, she sucked in a deep breath and pointed the weapon at the ground. She uttered a few more words and placed a hand on her injured leg.

"I can help you," said Jaks. He moved toward her a few steps, taking confidence when she remained unflinching.

Then beside her, he grasped her arm, and she sat with a groan.

Up close, she seemed delicate and small. His gaze lingered on her face.

She glared back at him fiercely.

A hard object prodded him in the ribs. Her weapon against his chest.

Jaks backed away. Ears burning, he retreated and joined Minto outside the shelter.

"Hell's breath. We have to let Ranger Cromer know about this," Minto said and then looked up to position the sun. "Maybe four or five hours of light left. We can get her to the base by night."

"Not with her leg like that. We have to bring back help so we can carry her on a stretcher. Also, he'll want to see this vessel," said Jaks.

After a short debate, they decided Minto would continue to the base cave, as he had better navigation sense, and Jaks would stay with the woman in case the dragons returned to harass her.

It was midafternoon, and rain clouds were rolling in again, when Minto eventually shouldered his pack and weapons and started his trek to find Ranger Cromer and the rest of their conscript unit.

Jaks stared out around the mountainside for several minutes after Minto had left, then shook out his hands, swept back his hair, and went back over to the woman, intent on trying to talk with her.

She was sitting, shivering, with her silver blanket around her shoulders but with her right hand resting atop the material, gripping her unusual weapon. She gazed at him suspiciously, but despite her wariness, her eyes mesmerized him with their size and exoticness.

"How is your injury?" he said slowly.

She stared at his mouth as he spoke but did not respond.

"How is your head?" he tried again, pointing at the dirty bandage. She reached out from under her blanket to touch it and said a few words in lilting, musical tones. The sounds made little sense to him, and his face creased in puzzlement.

She shivered again. Her thin blanket seemed inadequate to keep out the chill, so Jaks removed his fur jacket and held it out to her. The woman looked surprised but pushed aside the crinkly wrap and reached out with her left hand to accept the coat. She rolled up the sleeves, far too long for her arms, and pulled on the garment.

She looked up at him and smiled, then pointed at herself. "Meila," she said.

That must be her name, he realized. Jaks crouched at the shelter entrance, looking at her, and repeated her name carefully, but unable to replicate the lilt associated with it.

She smiled and nodded.

He then said his own name once and mimicked her actions by pointing at himself.

"Jaks," she copied without hesitation.

They repeated the exercise with different objects. The woman led, finding greater ease at pronouncing his words than he at hers. Eventually, she stopped trying to teach him her language at all and simply pointed at objects for Jaks to tell her the names of in Ascorian. Her memory was remarkable and her pronunciation of the words concise but with a slight musical lilt. A pleasant and melodic voice.

At one stage, her forehead creased in concern, and she waved her hand around and said, "Voros." He had not taught her that word and was surprised to hear her say the name of the foreign country far to the west.

"Ascoria," he repeated several times and made a broad sweep with his arms.

She nodded, and her face relaxed.

It became more difficult when they tried to extend beyond naming objects, to explaining things. She was able to extract from him words for "yes," "no," "come," and "go," but after that, they stopped—both exhausted from their awkward efforts.

She yawned and said to him, "Go." Lying down, she pulled the hand weapon into the overlong sleeve and tugged the fur closer around herself like a blanket. She stared blankly over his shoulder and appeared lost in thought.

Jaks left shelter and paced the mountainside, gazing up often for any sign of dragons. Without his coat, he shivered, but navigating the slope soon warmed him. Putting himself to task, he gathered dry branches and steepled them, preparing a campfire for sundown.

Later, he turned to strengthening the makeshift shelter. He rearranged the orange sail, fully covering the three small trees and weighting the edges with large stones but leaving an opening to the front. The material was plentiful and tough, making for a perfect cover.

As the sun faded, he lit the campfire and sat to bask in its warmth.

The woman shuffled to the opposite side, dragging her pack. She lay against it and stared into the flames.

"Ahh," she said, face brightening, minutes later. She rummaged around in her pack, gave a cheerful yelp, and drew out a handful of small bars. She threw one over the fire at Jaks and landed it deftly in front of him. She held up another and pulled at it; a thin wrapper tore away and revealed a brown block. She put it to her mouth and bit. Chewing enthusiastically, she gestured at the bar in front of Jaks.

He picked it up and copied her motions. Sweet flavors flooded his mouth. Sticky, delicious tar clung to his palate.

The woman laughed and smiled when Jaks stuck his finger in his mouth to unstick his teeth.

He chuckled in return and offered her his waterskin.

The rain started an hour after nightfall and drenched the valley. The campfire collapsed and steamed out. Jaks dashed to lend an arm to the woman as she hopped back into the shelter.

Inside, she propped herself against the tree trunk again and said a word he guessed might have been in thanks.

Rain drummed against the sail material and wind blew through the opening. Jaks released a rolled section, weighing the edge down with his backpack, and sealed the entrance against the elements.

The woman pulled the hood of the oversized coat over her head and, with her hand gripping her weapon within the depths of its sleeve, shut her eyes.

Jaks feigned rest as well. When her breathing slowed, he opened his eyes. Although too dark to see, her exquisite features were burned into his mind as though it were daylight. He longed to touch the outline of face, but knew that if he tried, he would learn what that dangerous-looking weapon could do.

Hours later, the rain stopped and Jaks slipped into a fitful sleep, dreaming of dragons and a winged woman soaring over him.

The next morning, the woman recovered a long branch with a Y-shaped end and crooked it under her left arm. As she hopped clumsily around the campsite, the fur coat brushed the ground, further hindering her progress. However, her eyes were full of determination, and she pushed ahead despite the obvious pain from her injured leg.

His conscience told him to help her, but his mouth went dry, and the pit of his stomach fluttered. He was bewildered that she had such an effect on him; he had been around extraordinary women all of his life. In fact, they did not get any tougher than his older sister, Vixhana, a captain in the Order of Nightwraiths, nor more talented than his younger sister, Karisa, who crafted illumancy for spectacular performances before audiences of thousands.

Yet, this foreign woman with a limp disconcerted him completely with her sheer willpower and intensity.

***

Midmorning, the pack of dragons reappeared. Three patrolled the air while the other three landed to investigate the metal pod again, hopping onto, into, and around the object curiously. Jaks and the woman, resting under their shelter, peered out through the opening and spied on the reptilian beasts.

"I'm sure they know we're here. Hopefully, they're not looking for food." Jaks nocked an arrow to the string of his hunting bow. Wild dragon attacks were rare on the plains, but here in the mountains, they had no fear and preyed on all creatures, including humans. He had never shot at one before. He hoped he would not have to today. Their quickness, scales, and sinuous bodies made them hard targets.

The woman clearly read Jaks's anxiety. She nodded to him and held her weapon in front of her with both hands.

Several minutes later, the three bronzes screeched at one another. One snapped at the others until the other two scraped their chins to the dirt. Then, as though they had made a decision, the dragons turned away from the pod and started toward the improvised shelter.

A beat of wings and one hurled itself through the air, landing several yards from the entrance. The other two followed with a flurry of wings and could be heard landing on either side, but out of sight, hidden by the walls of the shelter. And behind them, a screech and a thump announced a fourth dragon: one of the overhead beasts completing the encirclement.

With wings extended and claws scratching at the ground, the lead dragon snarled and hissed at the two humans.

The woman made a coarse utterance and raised her weapon at the beast.

Jaks whipped about as light filled the shade behind them. A dragon was twisting its neck under the orange sail and had raised the edge. Trembling, he drew his bowstring to his cheek. The end of the arrow wavered over the torso of his target. The dragon's head weaved back and forth like a snake with a gaping mouth of daggers.

Thuck. Jaks released the bowstring. *Zip.* The arrow missed the dragon's head. But piercing the tent, it passed through and struck the body of the beast. With a screech, it recoiled and flailed out of sight.

Hands still shaking, he nocked another arrow and turned toward a tent wall where a set of sharp teeth clamped the orange sail outside and pulled at the material.

Squelch. A queer sound drew Jaks's attention to the shelter entrance.

Blood and gore stained the mountain outside the entrance to the tent. Two disembodied wings and a decapitated dragon's head remained; the rest was a smear of red and gray turned inside-out, as though the beast had been squashed by a giant's foot.

The woman cried out. Her weapon arm swung toward Jaks. A dragon had collapsed the tent wall and was now rearing up on its haunches, ready to lunge.

The beast exploded.

A second splatter of muscle, scales, and bone pasted the mountainside. No hammer, no missile, no visible effort he could see—yet the beast was obliterated.

Jaks recoiled in horror. The arrow fell off the string of his bow and flipped to the ground, but he did not need it any longer —the screeches and the sound of retreating wings indicated that the remaining dragons had taken flight.

"How . . ." His question faltered as he stared at the weapon in the woman's hand. A chill ran along his spine. He backed away from her. The same weapon had been trained on him less than a day before. She could have killed him and Minto in less than a blink. *What manner of magic is this?*

She replied with some soothing noises as though he were a startled puppy, and she tucked the weapon away into a pocket of the fur coat.

He lowered his bow and forced a twisted smile. If she had wanted to harm him, she could have already at any time that day.

A distant screech carried in the wind, tailing the fleeing dragons. With two of their kind dead and another injured by Jaks's arrow, surely, they would keep their distance for some time. Some species were vengeful for their dead, but Jaks could not remember if dragons were one of them. They would need to stay vigilant.

For the next hour, Jaks dug a shallow hole using a small shovel that conscripts carried, mainly for latrine duty, and buried the remains of the dead.

Later that morning, a loud moan emanated from the now-repaired shelter. Jaks discovered the woman slowly unwinding the bandage around her leg, pain etching her face.

Without a thought, Jaks dropped the bow from his hands and kneeled beside her. He hesitated as he reached for the edge of the bandage.

She nodded, and he began peeling away the rest of the sodden material.

She followed his every movement, wincing and grimacing.

Jaks cringed, empathizing with her pain. He stretched his mind for a way to distract her from staring at the wound.

He started singing.

In his childhood, his mother would sing quietly whenever she tended his, or his sisters', grazes and cuts. Her soothing song calmed and said everything would be all right. Although far less dulcet than his mother, he hoped his singing might help Meila.

It was a children's lullaby about a baby crying and being rocked to sleep. A song that every child had heard, that had existed forever.

He immediately felt like an idiot and was about to stop.

She lifted her head and stared at Jaks. Her breathing slowed, and her face relaxed. She nodded encouragement and curled a little smile.

When the song finished, Jaks began a repetition—and Meila also began to sing.

She sang exactly a verse behind, but instead of words she sang in las. She had an acute musical ear. They sang in rounds, his baritone voice and her alto dancing and weaving, as though they had sung together for years, perfectly partnered in pitch and tone.

Jaks smiled and laughed in delight as they completed their song.

Meila's gaze was warm and grateful.

They looked at each other, unsure what to say, then murmured and uttered a few words. Eventually, they stopped altogether when she winked at him and laughed.

His hands had paused during their song. Resuming his task, he unraveled the last of the bandage with a couple more turns.

Beneath, the wound was raw. A blood-crusted vertical laceration exposing the bone on her shin.

Meila took charge again, clearing the blood and clot from the wound with a flask of water and then covering it with a square of material with a gelatinous blob in the center. She topped it with a second, thicker pad, and proffered a new bandage to Jaks.

Jaks wrapped the wound pad into place as she held still.

With their task done, Meila sat back and studied him. A minute later, she began singing again and raised her eyebrows at him to join.

This time, she sang in her own language. Another lullaby? Although unfamiliar to Jaks, he too had sharp ears and picked up the melody well enough to repeat it the second and third time she sang it.

She clapped her hands, smiled, and motioned for him to take a turn.

For the next hour, the pair shared simple songs and counterpoints. They laughed at their mistakes and paused to teach other trickier verses and phrases. So entranced, Jaks forgot his worries of the future, and the woman never flinched to her injury.

Eventually, his singing companion blinked with fatigue and

sought to lie down. She pulled the blanket to her neck and closed her eyes.

He left her to rest, picked up his bow and walked outside to stand watch over the camp. He hummed to himself, thinking he could not remember the last time he'd known such joy as today.

Later that day, as the sun dipped low, and Jaks was readying another fire, several voices called out from the ridgeline of the valley.

A dozen familiar-looking figures angled down the slope. Jaks smiled as he caught sight of Minto. However, his relief evaporated as he realized that the ranger and other Thorn conscripts came with danger in their eyes and their bows half-drawn with nocked arrows.

Ranger Cromer cast an expert eye over the mountainside. He immediately took control, ignoring Jaks's explanation of recent events.

The woman was declared a foreign spy, disarmed, and ordered to be tied up.

The training exercise was over. The ranger ordered that they would return to the City of Dunberrin the next day and hand over the captive for interrogation.

She did not fight but looked pleadingly at Jaks while two burly conscripts forced her up by the arms and a third approached her with a rope. Her face contorted in pain and then anger. The feeling of betrayal was clear in her eyes.

Jaks protested to the Ranger, arguing her innocence. She was no spy. He didn't know what she was doing here, but had he detected no malice in her.

However, the superior officer refused to hear his arguments.

Though she did not understand his words, Jaks turned to her and said quietly, "I'll help you. I'll make sure they don't treat you like a spy." For the path of a spy was execution.

His promise, though, was of little use when they tied her hands and trussed her up to a tree. The anger in her voice displaced all of its musical tones as she then spat what could only be obscenities or curses.

Baden, grinning maliciously, took it upon himself to stand guard over their new prisoner.

Chapter 3

The Siblings

A week after the conscripts returned to Dunberrin with their captive, Jaks battled a troubled mind as he sat amongst a throng of soldiers within the city's massive cathedral.

"Quit fidgeting. It's almost over," Minto whispered next to him.

He stilled his leg—difficult when the droning voice of the Bishop of Dunberrin gnawed inside his ears. He cursed the poor luck of their unit being "privileged" with attending this week's Faithday cathedral service. Wasted time that could otherwise have been spent tracking down the prisoner he knew as Meila.

He was obsessed with her, unable to stop thinking about their short time together: the most exhilarating experience of his eighteen years. And what was more, he had made an oath to aid her plight.

His dead mother's words harangued him: "A broken oath will plague your soul." Her warning against childhood lies and a warning he used to think ridiculous. But since her death, the phrase, like a curse, honor-bound him to his promises.

But despite his inquiries, he could find no rumor or sign of what had happened to her. After the ranger had handed her to the city guard, she had simply vanished.

After this religious tedium was over, perhaps he could get his eldest sister to help locate her? Jaks began jigging his leg again.

Finally, a gong reverberated through the building and the assemblage groaned to their feet as the bishop gave his final blessing.

The cathedral took prominence in the city's cultural district; the magnificent stone building, along with its expansive gardens and cemeteries, cultivated a sense of importance to the area. Although it was commonly thought that the kingdom's official religion was nothing more than a method to harvest money from the populace, as a piece of architecture, it could not be denied that the cathedral lent great beauty to the city.

Beyond the religious grounds, nearby streets sheltered opera houses, theaters, galleries, and taverns that contrasted starkly to the hallowed structure but were the true center of Dunberrin's cultural wealth. Festooned with banners, streamers, and colored lanterns, the district was a spectacle at night.

"I'm off to the tavern. You coming?" Minto asked Jaks as they followed the throng of soldiers tipping into the streets to celebrate the rest of the day of rest.

"Go without me. I've arranged to meet my sisters."

"Your gorgeous sisters! I could go throw dice later . . . I'll join you."

"No, I don't think they would welcome your hellos and come-ons at the foot of our mother's grave." He laughed.

"Well, at least pass on my greetings to them." Minto waved cheerily as he departed with the crowd. "I'd marry either of them in a second. Tell them that?"

"I won't," said Jaks, shaking his head at his friend's boldness.

Over the few minutes it took to walk around the cathedral, Jaks's mood deepened. He stepped onto the short grass of the east cemetery and paced down a solemn row of gray headstones —one of the many that stretched out to the distant low boundary wall. On the other side, two stall-keepers rolled their carts noisily along a wide, cobbled street.

At the center of the graveyard, his sisters stood by their mother's grave. He called out a greeting, and they turned to his voice.

Karisa, only sixteen, looked like a woman several years older than she was. Even though as tall as her brother and more shapely than her sister, it was the haunted depths of her eyes that betrayed her lost innocence. She hid herself that day in a dowdy, gray shift with a sash tied at the waist and a cape with a hood over her head. Only her opal-blue eyes and a curl of golden hair could be seen.

She carried a small, shaggy dog under her arm. Lowered to its paws, it wandered off to sniff flowers and potted plants along the row of headstones.

Jaks gathered his younger sister into an embrace. "Karisa, how I've missed you," he said.

Her hood slipped and revealed her face lit up with a smile.

He loved his little sister dearly. As children, they had been inseparable: monkeying backstage at their mother's performances, mimicking the actors, and leaning against one another as they listened to their mother sing. A more caring, gentle sibling he could not have had. For her true gift, he knew, was not her beauty or her illumancy magic, but her compassion. Even as they grew older, they still shared an unbreakable bond.

Vixhana was ten years older than Jaks, tall and masculine, with the hard, stern face of a career soldier. Deep-set eyes with heavy brows offset a long, aquiline nose, and a small scar—one of the few injuries she had taken in numerous battles—etched her square jaw. A fur-lined cape covered a suit of black leather armor. Her left hand rested on a longsword at her hip, and in her other hand, she held a bunch of white flowers. She locked her brother with her steely eyes and thrust out her sword hand.

He stared at it momentarily, then grasped her hand. She pulled him into a full embrace, knocking some petals off the flowers.

"What a proper little soldier you make," she said, looking him up and down. "Still scrawny as a lightning rod; even a uniform can't hide those twig legs." She smiled as she let go of his hand and stepped back; in contrast, her own tight-fitting armor undulated and bulged.

Vixhana gave Karisa the bunch of flowers, and the girl knelt beside the headstone to lay them down.

Her fingers trailed over the delicate white blossoms as she whispered quietly to herself. A tear dropped onto the flowers. "I miss her so," she said eventually. "But I can't even remember her face anymore."

"She was beautiful, Karisa," Jaks said hesitantly, wanting to comfort her. "You look so much like her."

"I don't know. I wish I could see her again."

The tiny dog sensed her distress and placed its front paws on her leg and gave her a querulous look. She stroked its head until it dropped away to sniff at the bunch of flowers.

The cathedral bells tolled noon. The streets around the sacred grounds now throbbed with citizens and soldiers, walking at pace between riders on horseback and the occasional horse-drawn carriage.

"Let's eat," Vixhana said. "I know a soldierly tavern where we won't be disturbed." She led the way to a large establishment with a swinging wooden placard marked "The Beer and the Boar."

On entering the tavern, the barkeeper gestured to an empty booth in the furthest reaches of the hall. Men and women, mostly in military uniforms, sat at tables and booths, eating, drinking, and talking; several stopped to nod at the tall captain of the Nightwraiths as they wound their way through the busy eatery.

At the table, Vixhana shouted an order of ale, bread, and stew to the serving boy. He scurried off with a "Yes, ma'am."

"It's only a month until Summer Solstice," said Vixhana as she turned to her siblings. Her eyes alighted on Jaks. "What are you going to do when you complete your conscription? Regular infantry?" she demanded.

"I don't know. Minto wants me to apply for the Rangers with him, but I don't think any of the army units will want me," he said, fiddling with the sleeve of his tunic. "I hear that the magistrate's office might have work. Maybe a job as a clerk?"

"Sounds dull," Vixhana said. But compared to her job, everything was dull. Following her conscription, she had qualified for, then rapidly advanced through the army's elite Order of Nightwraiths—battlefield assassins that terrorized the enemy in their camps and ambushed army lines.

Jaks spun the conversation toward his dilemma, spluttering a question back at her. "Could you find a prisoner for me?"

"Prisoner?"

He leaned forward and detailed his encounter with the mysterious woman in the mountains. Vixhana's brow rose as he described the otherworldly Meila and then furrowed as he outlined the carnage delivered by her weapon.

"Extraordinary," replied Vixhana, tapping her chin with an empty fork. "If I hadn't heard some rumors of a recently caught spy, I would have thought the fluff between your ears had finally got the better of you."

"You know where she is? Where? Can you get me to see her?"

"Sit down. I only know a little about your prisoner," she replied, and then glared at a curious cavalryman at a neighboring table until he averted his eyes. "But I have to agree with your ranger. She does sound like some sort of spy. What else would she be?"

"She's not," he said. "She's lost—"

"In the middle of Ascoria? I think not." Vixhana shook her head, shutting off his defense. His frustration must have shown on his face, as she paused and then sighed. "I'll see what I can find out, brother. But there will be nothing you or I can do if the king decides she's a spy."

Jaks nodded his thanks, hope renewed with his sister's offer.

The serving boy then thumped mugs of ale on the table and returned with a platter of food.

Vixhana turned her attention to the youngest of the three siblings. "You're quiet . . . How are you, little sister? Ready to start your conscription next month?"

Karisa, her dog at her feet under the bench, sat opposite Vixhana. Silent while Jaks and Vixhana had been speaking, she looked up and pulled down her hood. Tresses of golden hair tumbled about her shoulders. The sunlight adored a face blessed with jewel-like eyes that sparkled blue against a sculpted brow and cheekbones. Heart-shaped lips lent to a delicate chin.

A sigh arose from a nearby table.

She ignored the rising pitch of voices around the tavern and said, "I'm not going to do it. My acting troupe is going on tour to Faucony after the Summer Solstice. Ella and I are going to go with them." Her voice was defiant. "You know I would die in the army. The girls are cruel, they cut off your hair, and they scar you."

Vixhana leaned forward, glancing around. "You can't shirk conscription, Karisa. They'll track you down. You know the Pact Countries all have agreements to send back deserters." She scowled and leaned back. "And, if you fled, I would have a duty to report you."

"The only way out is to petition the king. But I hear he doesn't exempt anyone," Jaks added.

Several pairs of eyes around the hall were focused on Karisa, hungrily fixed on her like spectators at a play.

Vixhana leaned forward and returned the stares with a flinty glare. Their attention withered away from the challenge.

Karisa's hair abruptly changed to a mottled gray and shadows contoured her face to a gaunt and sickly appearance. It was as though a gnarled peasant woman had taken her place.

With the magical ability to control light and dark, she was a gifted illumancer able to augment her already natural beauty with ease. But, targeted by obscene attention from admirers— particularly after her portrayal of a dryad princess in a popular play, *Nereen and the Forest*—she had recently taken to obscuring her features.

Jaks frowned momentarily, taken aback by his sister's transformation. But returning to her outburst, and wanting to reassure her, he continued, "The conscription is not that bad. They make up stories like that to scare new recruits. The male and female conscript units may be kept separate, but I can tell you that the girls I do see still have their hair and bear nothing more than a few scratches."

"The two years go fast. When you finish, you can do what you like and go back to live with your troupe," Vixhana said.

"I promise, no one will hurt you," said Jaks. "I made an oath to Mother to look out for you." He tried not to wince as he said the words. Even to his own ears, they sounded weak.

"I don't need you to protect me. I can look after myself." Karisa flared her nostrils and locked in a haughty look. A look not unlike a noblewoman admonishing a feckless servant.

Jaks sighed. Both of his sisters could be as stubborn as mules. *She'll come to her senses.*

But Karisa continued to glare. Defiant.

"Come on, this food isn't going to eat itself," Vixhana said to break the tension and grabbed a bowl of the stew.

They ate and drank in quiet for several minutes.

When the last of the food was gone, Vixhana thumped the table. "I know something that will do you both some good," she said. "Follow me." She threw some silver coins onto the table and strode off as though certain her younger siblings would follow.

Jaks and Karisa exchanged looks of curiosity and followed their sister into the busy streets.

The City of Dunberrin covered a giant finger of land at the northern tip of Ascoria and, as the largest center of commerce and politics in the realm, the most important. A fortified wall sealed the main city from the mainland to the south, and a busy harbor dominated its east coast. Boats and ships ferried passengers and cargo to the Pact Countries and other nations.

Fishing boats brought in their catches to sell in the city's celebrated markets, and merchant carts delivered a constant supply of everything else. Avenues, streets, and alleys of cobblestone sectioned the metropolis into districts of commerce and residence.

Beyond the fortified wall, the "Grand Avenue" reached out toward the pastures and farmlands of the south. On either side of the thoroughfare, though, just outside the main gates, a worker's town of manufactories, iron smelters, and other industries billowed smoke and steam—and spawned waves of stench and dust.

The Rauhalik family were long established in a noble district within the main city, where two generations had been born and raised. Jaks's grandparents, self-exiled from Voros, had brought wealth with them when they arrived in Ascoria and bought a minor title. Their estate consisted of a three-storied manse, stables, and servant quarters, at the base of the city wall.

But since the death of the siblings' mother, it lay abandoned. Jaks had started his compulsory conscription period; Karisa had been sent to live with a Matron in the market district—but instead ran off to join a local theater group; Vixhana continued in the army barracks, as she had been for the past ten years; and their father departed for a distant province.

It was to that estate that Jaks suspected his elder sister was taking them. The final clue revealed as their path turned onto "Rose Row" with its characteristic stretch of red and purple blooms.

"Vix, I can't go back there," he said, stopping in his steps and his face turning pale.

She stood to the side of the road. A horse and carriage clattered past. Glaring at Jaks, she said, "Get a hold of yourself.

It's been two years now. You'll be fine." She slapped him lightly on the back.

Karisa stepped up beside them. Her face hidden under the hood, she clutched her tiny dog to her chest. "No, Vix. It's horrible. I never want to go back inside that place," she said.

"What if Father is there?" Jaks stammered. "He said that I should never return." After Lady Rauhalik's funeral, Lord Rauhalik had thrown Jaks a coin pouch and torn the family insignia from his tabard. Then, as though to a flea-ridden stray, he instructed him, "Be off with you. You are worthless to me." Had he possessed Karisa's charisma or Vixhana's physical prowess, he might have earned his father's respect. But with neither, he was discarded and disowned.

Vixhana pulled her siblings into an alleyway and spoke sharply. "This needs to be done. You must find closure one way or another. Trust me, you need this. Besides, Father's attentions are in the far south now, not here."

Karisa opened her mouth as though she were going to say something but pursed her lips and switched Ella the dog from one arm to the other.

Vixhana placed a hand on each of their shoulders and turned them to face her. Her face softened. "You both have to move on. Mother's accident was years ago and you act like it was just yesterday. You'll see that it is just a dusty, decrepit building, and then you will be able to close that part of your life off—and then get on with the rest of it." She was well-meaning, from her gruff take on life.

An iron-spike fence surrounded the Rauhalik's city estate. *Surely, it did not always look like a prison,* Jaks thought as

Vixhana creaked open the rusted main gate. In its prime, four horses could ride through those gates side-by-side. But the barricade, like the rest of the grounds, was a decayed remnant of its stately past. Weeds overran the foreyard, and a pair of unruly willow trees smothered the cobbled promenade. The stables along the far boundary were a shuttered and empty shell. And far from the street, the three-storied main building, covered with ropey vines, stared at them through a dozen dark windows.

Although Jaks had last lived here with Karisa and their mother just over two years before, it looked to have aged a century.

Vixhana disappeared behind the stables and returned with an iron key. She unlocked the main door of the manse and led them inside.

As the last to follow, Jaks closed the door and paused as his eyes adjusted to the dim interior. Sunlight filtered through two opaque windows in the foyer. It was as he remembered: wood-paneled walls covered with artwork and frames, capes and hats on wall hooks, and hallways leading off to a maze of corridors and rooms within.

But as he turned to the foot of the stairs, it hit him.

Images flickered and battered at a wedged door in his mind.

Dark hands and a flash of light.

A metallic taste in his mouth. A scream.

Jaks's mind spun, forcing the memories back. *Stay away. Not now.*

Breathing rapidly, he braced himself against the wall.

That dark night when his mother died. Too gruesome, too terrible to allow into his consciousness. He did not want to remember.

Not now. Not ever.

He stumbled out of the foyer, away from the crime.

"Jaks, what's wrong? You look like the breath of a wraith," Karisa said as he entered the main reception hall. She rushed to him and laid hands on his waist.

"I'm fine . . . just wasn't what I expected." He slowed his breathing and sealed his thoughts, forcing a smile to reassure her. "I shouldn't have come back."

"Nonsense. This was your home for sixteen years. Walk around. Get it out of your system," said Vixhana. She paced the length of the far wall and drew aside a velvet curtain.

A long panel of frosted glass illuminated the hall, revealing the carved whirls and rosettes that decorated the ceiling and the crystal chandelier at its center. Padded wooden chairs surrounded several low stone tables in this reception hall where officers, nobles, and dignitaries once smoked cigars and lounged about with glasses of heady liquor.

Karisa put down her little dog. It yapped twice and scampered off, wagging its tail and sniffing about the hall.

The girl then went over to a table and touched the runestone lamp sitting at its center. It sprang to life with a steady, pure light. She pulled back her hood and dropped the cosmetic enchantment from her face and hair, reverting to her normal appearance.

Picking up the light, she walked over to one of the many paintings on the wall. Tears welled in her eyes and rolled down her face.

The oil painting had hung in the exact same spot since Jaks was six years old. Years of dust had gathered on its wooden frame, but it still imbued the essence of their once idyllic family life. Lady Katerin Rauhalik sat on a carved wooden seat, smiling. Wavy blonde tresses framed an aristocratic face and highlighted eyes as blue as the northern sky. At that time a lauded actor and singer on the theater circuit, she wore an embroidered crimson dress for the portrait. Little Karisa smiled, snuggled in her mother's arms, and small Jaks leaned against their chair. On the other side, Vixhana stood in her formal conscript blues, a scowl marring her face. And behind them, their father stared out of the frame.

Captured in the painting, Lord General Sicaro Rauhalik—dark-haired and bearded below soulless eyes—towered like a bear. The corners of his eyes drooped and curled in toward a mouth that never smiled. One gloved hand capped the top of a six-foot warhammer whilst the other gripped his wife's shoulder, possessively. A fur-lined robe draped his massive shoulders and obscured a black breastplate beneath. But despite the fine brushwork and detail, it did not show that Sicaro Rauhalik was a troubled man.

A career soldier, he thrived in wartime and maddened in peace.

After the Unifying Wars, his glory years stalled as the soldiers of his army retired to farms and mines or were amalgamated to other corps—General Sicaro was a general with no army.

A general who festered while the king then played at populist and builder.

And then, the most insulting of acts. On the death of an elderly custodian in a distant, southern province, Sicaro Rauhalik was installed as his replacement: royal castellan over Castle Sanford and a garrison of a mere two hundred soldiers. No matter what fancy titles the king made up, he was little more than the caretaker for the remotest and poorest of provinces in Ascoria. A poor reward for decades of service.

Jaks stared at the painting across the room. His father stared back, eyes demanding an explanation for his intrusion. Fleeting memories returned. Shouts, blood, and dark hands. Always dark hands.

Knees weak and sweat beading his forehead, Jaks collapsed onto a seat. *Not now.* Quicker this time, more prepared, he hummed the first tune that came to his throat and ground a fist into his leg.

Vixhana placed a hand on his shoulder. "It's okay, brother. You need to let it go."

"I tried to stop him. But I couldn't," said Jaks. "You don't know what he was like in those later years."

Her hand went rigid on his shoulder. He could sense her conflict. She had outright denied Jaks's accusations on previous occasions. Refused to believe that their father had pushed their mother down the stairs, repeating the magistrate's conclusions like a parrot. "It was an accident," she would often say to finalize the subject. Jaks suspected she believed him, but her blind adherence to the kingdom's laws prevented her from denying the summary of a king's official.

Vixhana turned her attention to her sister. "Karisa, bring down that painting. You can take it back with you."

"I don't want a picture with him in it," the girl replied.

"He doesn't have to be in it."

Karisa and Vixhana lifted the heavy frame and leaned it against the wall. The nightwraith slipped out a boot-knife and sliced the canvas, leaving the bearded monster alone in the frame.

Chapter 4

Reunited

Karisa's little dog had wandered back into the foyer. It started yapping again. Karisa apologized and skipped out to find her excitable pet.

Vixhana ejected a breath. "We should go anyway, we've done what we needed to do here. You go ahead," she said to Jaks and went to close the wall-length curtain.

Jaks joined his younger sister in the foyer. She had a leash in her hand and bent down to scold the animal. "Shhh . . . Ella. Stop being silly. What's wrong with you?"

The door opened, and a gush of wind swept over the siblings.

Three large figures loomed in the door frame.

Karisa gave a startled cry and stood. The leash fell to the floor. The dog leapt in front of her and started yapping and growling at the intruders.

Jaks froze on the spot and gasped as his father strode through the entrance.

Lord Sicaro planted his feet squarely and stared at his two

youngest children. He wore a chain hauberk and a steel chestplate emblazoned with the Sanford Crest—a falcon with two heads. Battle-scarred boots, built to stomp skulls and wade through blood, adorned his feet, and a longsword hung at his waist. At fifty years old, he stood the size and stature of a bear and towered over them.

"Look at this one," he said, glowering at Jaks, and laughed. "The little runt. Should have drowned him in the horse trough." He walked up to his son and shoved him aside.

Jaks stumbled and fell onto his backside.

The two other men, dressed in similar armor and livery, laughed as they stepped inside the foyer.

The bearded giant's gaze roamed and settled on Karisa. He smiled broadly. "There you are, my love. I've been looking for you everywhere."

Karisa's face twisted in fear. Her dog suddenly gave up its brave face, whimpered, and ran behind her legs.

Chills ran down Jaks's spine. He retreated into the shadows toward the closest door, scuttling backward. *Dark hands. They mustn't find me. Hide.*

Sicaro reached out to take hold of Karisa's chin and tilted her face to appraise it.

"A merry hunt, you've led. The matron said you ran off to the theater, and that dandy of a theatrician refused to tell me a thing until Bako parted him with an ear," he said, gesturing at a balding man behind him. "But what a joyous reunion."

He ran a hand through her thick blonde hair, placed it behind her neck, and pulled her in intimately. "You've grown even more beautiful. I have ached for you, my darling."

Karisa, terrified, pushed at him ineffectually.

Her father tightened his grip until her face contorted in pain.

"Take your hands off her. You're hurting her," Vixhana shouted as she stormed into the foyer.

A henchman dashed forward and imposed himself before her. Her equal in size, the man smirked at her.

Vixhana stared at him and, in an instant, transformed into her nightwraith form. Her features lost all definition, and her outer appearance went black as though dissolved into a swamp of darkness.

If Karisa was unusual in abilities, Vixhana was exceptional. Both gifted in illumancy, the older sister focused her magic on camouflage and distraction in combat, making her an evasive foe. And, in addition, she was a skilled gravmancer, manipulating the weight of any object around her, enabling her to wield enormous swords, hammers, or axes that no ordinary soldier could.

Where Karisa was beauty and grace, Vixhana was stealth and destruction.

There was an explosion of violence as a dark arm picked up the warrior by the throat and threw him across the room in the way that only a gravmancer could. Rendered as light as a puppet for seconds, he hurtled through the air and recovered his full weight just in time to smash heavily against the wall. Several wall hangings fell around the stunned man.

The room danced with shadows.

The darkness that was Vixhana slammed into the second henchman, magically manipulating him and launching him hard against the other wall, where he slumped to the ground with a grunt.

Vixhana coalesced from the shadows and returned to her normal form, an arm's length away from her father.

Sicaro spun his youngest daughter around and wrapped an arm around her neck. Elsewhere, it might have looked like a father tenderly embracing his child, but here the hold was sinister.

Karisa's eyes darted around frantically. She looked at Jaks imploringly, as though willing him to do something.

"Let her go," Vixhana commanded, her hand resting on the pommel of her sword.

"That was unnecessary," their father replied.

His injured henchmen, groaning and cursing, dragged themselves to their feet.

"What do you want?" Vixhana addressed her father, her eyes flitting between all three of the dangerous men.

Sicaro stroked Karisa's golden hair with his free hand. "I've come to take my darling to her new home."

"No, no, no . . ." Karisa cried out in a feeble voice and struggled against his grip. The rolled painting fell to the ground from where she had tucked it under her sash.

"Leave her be. She is her own person. She doesn't want to go with you." Vixhana walked slowly until her back was to the main door. Sicaro twisted to follow her movement, keeping Karisa in front of him.

A tense minute followed as father and eldest daughter stared each other down. Karisa was pale and rigid in her father's arms.

Jaks was behind his father now. He should draw his weapon. Attack unseen. His hand fell to his dagger but he couldn't draw it. His arm was paralyzed with fear. Instead, he could only stare at his father's massive hands. He was a child again, regressed and quivering in the corner.

"Step aside. She's coming with me," Sicaro said calmly and changed his grip on Karisa to drag her by the arm.

Vixhana slowly held up the palms of her hands to him, as though resigning to his will.

"Good girl," he said.

However, surrender was not her intention—a brilliant light, an illumancer's invocation as bright as the midday sun, beamed from Vixhana's palms directly into Sicaro's eyes.

Instinctively, his hands raised to shield his eyes from the blinding light.

Karisa fell from his grasp and scrambled away toward the gaping door. With outstretched hands, she grasped the frame, hurtled through, and sprinted across the foreyard.

Her little dog, bereft of a hiding place beneath her skirts, panicked, and with blunt claws scrabbling against the wooden floor, it fled deep into the house.

Vixhana lunged forward and rammed Sicaro with both fists. The moment before the strike, her gravmancer powers rendered him as light as a doll, negating his massive build and armor. However, just as her knuckles connected, her father invoked his own gravmancy—reversing the weightlessness to normal.

Instead of the potent, magically-augmented blow she had expected to deliver, Vixhana's attack was mitigated to that of a muscular warrior striking another powerfully built warrior— Sicaro staggered sideways and fell heavily to a knee.

The henchmen had recovered, and snarling, started toward her with bared swords.

"Get out!" Vixhana yelled at Jaks, drawing her sword.

He leapt up, charged the closest man, and shoved him as hard as he could. The man stumbled and careened into the bannister of the staircase.

Jaks then ran and fled out the door, only pausing when he reached the estate gates to look back for his older sister.

Vixhana faced the soldiers as they reformed their fighting stances. She brandished her sword, hunched low, and mutated her appearance into a hideous demon form: illumancer magic elongated her face, sprouted vicious teeth and horns, glowed her eyes red, and cast flames around her body.

The men backed away. With faces full of fear, their weapons went limp in their hands.

Sicaro lurched back to his feet, his eyes clearing from Vixhana's blinding flash. "It's just an illusion, you fools," he shouted, and his sword rasped from its scabbard.

Confronting Vixhana in her demonic guise, he met her glowing eyes.

Vixhana invoked again and melted into a writhing shadow that sucked at the light in the foyer, then vanished out the doorway.

Sicaro stormed to the door. "You can't keep her from me. I will find her," he boomed at the retreating shadow. "Then I will kill you, bitch!"

Several people on the street nearby stared at the source of the shouting for a moment and then hurried away in fright.

Jaks spun from the gate and ran.

Chapter 5

Fleeing the Manse

Jaks and Karisa wound their way through the streets and stumbled into the market district, hand in hand, neither knowing where to go. Midafternoon, and people were shoulder to shoulder, intent on stocking up on vegetables and fruits, haggling with butchers, or perusing knickknacks from stands of artisan crafters.

Going back to Karisa's theater was not an option, nor was taking Karisa back to Jaks's conscript barracks. Their father might be on their heels, still intent on his youngest daughter.

They both breathed a sigh of relief when Vixhana caught up with them. She materialized out of the shadows without warning, startling a young mother with her baby. The woman squealed and hurried away.

"Come with me, you'll be safe in my quarters. We need to figure out what to do with you," Vixhana said to Karisa and marched off toward the army district, beckoning them along.

The district sheltering the barracks and half of the military ranks of the kingdom ran along the western bay of the city. A ten-foot wall segregated the military compound from the rest of the city and housed many thousands of professional soldiers, a few hundred conscripts, and a naval base.

Vixhana vouched for Karisa—the only of them without military attire—to the Gate Sergeant and passed into the drill area. Being a rest day, the massive field of compacted dirt was empty but for flagpoles around the circumference flying the yellow and blue of Ascoria.

Although Karisa was new to the district, she commented that it seemed eerily quiet even for a Faithday. Vixhana informed her that four regiments of soldiers had recently vacated and marched west to reinforce the coasts of the Hera and Finstaf provinces against increasing numbers of Vor raids. "That'll be why," she explained.

The nightwraiths' quarters were tunneled deep beneath the barracks of the regular army, hidden and protected by a runestoned maze of magical shadows and darkness. Although their father, as a royal castellan, could enter the army district, he only had control over the garrison troops at Sanford and no longer held power over regimented soldiers as he once did.

In Vixhana's personal chambers within the underground base, Karisa breathed a sigh of relief as she sat down on her sister's cot, removed her cape, and pulled a blanket around her shoulders. Her older siblings sat at a small table in the center of the room, next to a rack of knives, swords, and a single shield. Several shelves of clothes and wooden boxes lined the walls.

"What was all that about? Why is he looking for you?" Vixhana asked her sister, her face stony and hard.

Karisa stared at the ground, shuffling her loose shoe about on the floor. Eventually, she said, "Father has been asking after me at the theater for the last few days, but . . . I wanted nothing to do with him. I hoped he'd just go away."

"Okay, but what does he want of you?" Vixhana leaned forward.

Jaks shifted uncomfortably in his chair.

Karisa sank lower onto the bed, looking exhausted and spent. She tucked her knees up to her chest and wrapped the blanket tightly around herself.

She spoke in a small voice. "You weren't there when he came back from the war. He was always drunk, and he would accuse Mother of terrible things—you know she wasn't like that, she'd never do anything like what he accused her of. He wouldn't let her leave the house and dismissed everyone except for the guards to keep us in." Tears formed in Karisa's eyes. "That one time you came home for the weekend, he was so nice for a while, but after a few days, he started accusing her again and beat her . . . it was awful." She sniffed and wiped her eyes.

Vixhana rested her arms on the table and wrung her hands.

Karisa suddenly glared at her. "Why didn't you come back? You were away for years. You could have stopped him—you only came back when she was dead!"

"I couldn't. They needed me on the border, my unit needed me . . ." Vixhana started, then more softly, said, "I'm sorry, I didn't know it was like that."

Jaks frowned. A wave of guilt battered at him. He had been there. He had done nothing.

Karisa glared at her sister for several seconds and then slumped to her side, the anger retreating. Lying on the cot, she stared at the opposite wall with glazed eyes.

"All I could do was try and distract him," said Karisa. "Remember when I was little? I did silly dances and made up stories to make him come away and play with me. He loved the disguises I made up. Angels, sylphs, fairies."

She paused and took a deep breath. "Well, in the last few

years, it was the only way I could get him away from her. He used to beat her so much, she lost some teeth and couldn't eat properly for weeks. She always had so many cuts and bruises. I had to protect her. I . . . I just had to."

Jaks had some idea of what she was going to say. For some reason, the knowledge had always been there but sequestered and repressed amongst other shuttered doors.

"He liked me most when I pretended to be older—like one of those painted women." Karisa started gently rocking on the bed. "So, I did. I did those things . . . for him. I used the magic to make myself desirable. I would say things I didn't mean . . . promise him things I didn't have. I lowered my clothes to show him what he wanted." She went quiet for a while and collected herself. "He brought me gifts. Flowers, jewelry, and then clothes of frills and lace. He would make me dance."

"Did he touch you?" Vixhana asked.

Karisa was quiet for a long while. Tears spilled down her face. Her silence answered their sister's question.

"From then, it was only me he came home for. I let him do what he wanted to me—so he wouldn't beat Mother anymore. She couldn't take much more." The girl stopped rocking, closed her eyes, and pulled the blanket over her head.

Vixhana and Jaks stared at the stone floor, not making eye contact or talking, but sinking in their own shame as they tried to comprehend the vile abuse that the youngest and most vulnerable of their family had traded for the protection of their mother.

From her woolen refuge, Karisa's voice became thin and high-pitched as she said, "It was the only way I could protect mommy . . ."

"The filthy bastard. I should have killed him." Vixhana's

chair scraped back as she stood, clenching her hands. She pounded a fist into the wall.

"I'm so sorry, I should have tried to help," Jaks said, ashamed of his own inaction and naivety, knowing that at all those times he had simply run to his room and hid. And although he suspected evil, he had never talked openly with Karisa about their father's visits—cowardice and shame had dug the deepest of holes to bury secrets.

Vixhana ground the knuckles of her fist into the table, and her face stormed with rage.

A knock at the door broke the tension, and a servant brought in a bowl with ham, cheese, and cobbled bread, and a jug of water. When he spilled some of the water—trembling at the sight of the furious nightwraith—Vixhana simply waved him out and threw a cloth square over it, then poured the remaining water into cups.

She then looked at Karisa, who had sat up after the servant left. "This is the safest place you can be. He can't come here. It's only a month until Summer Solstice, and then he won't be able to bother you once you're a conscript."

Karisa remained silent and sipped from her cup.

Jaks had an idea. "After basic training, maybe you could apply to be a signaler for the regular army instead of doing the full conscription. A recruit from my unit did that after the first six weeks, and his illumancy wasn't anywhere as good as yours."

Vixhana's eyes rose as she thought on this. "Not a bad idea. Signalers keep back from the heavy combat. In fact, you could have it easy. Once you're in the regular army, you only need to stay in for one year, instead of the two if you stayed a conscript. You would just have to learn to signal, of course." She reached for the bread and tore off a chunk. "And, if you were regular army, he wouldn't dare touch you, as one of the king's professional soldiers."

Karisa brightened at the idea, and after eating some bread and half a pear, agreed to stay within the regimented order and protection of the army.

But whether she was fully accepting of the idea, or simply agreeing to please her older siblings, Jaks was unsure.

"I promise you, Karisa. It'll turn out fine. I'll always be there for you," said Jaks, affirming the oath his mother had implored of him.

Chapter 6

The Creatures of the Forest

Two days later, the conscripts of the Thorns unit returned with Ranger Cromer to the northern mountain range of Ascoria. This time, however, they approached from the east, many leagues distant from their encounter with the foreign woman.

With no further word about Meila, Jaks's last hope was with his eldest sister and her military connections. The only indication she had even existed was a sketch he'd made of her lying in his pocket.

They set up camp as the sun dipped toward the end of the day. Around them, giantwoods, some as wide as castle towers, stretched up to the clouds. A family of squirrels scurried around a nearby trunk and knocked bits of bark to the forest floor in their hunt for nuts and bugs to eat. The leaf-strewn gaps between each of the mighty trees spared plentiful ground for the conscripts to spread out their camping gear.

Jaks noticed Baden and a few of the other men glaring at him as he gathered firewood around the campground. He was glad their conscription period would be over in a few weeks. After two years of shoves and putdowns, he would be rid of these ruffians when the Summer Solstice arrived.

"This is all your fault," a voice interrupted his thoughts. "If you'd just killed that spy, or just left her to die, we wouldn't have to be doing this all again." Baden shoved him in the back. Firewood spilled from Jaks's arms as he stumbled.

Jaks turned to face the senior conscript and raised his fists. "You shouldn't have done that."

"Go on. Take a jab," the brute said, raising his chin and sneering at him.

"You're not worth it. I'd probably kill you and end up court-martialed for it." Jaks said, his voice trembling with false bravado. He lowered his fists.

"You couldn't kill a gnat," said Baden. "Weakling." He spat at the fallen firewood and stalked off.

Minto rushed over. "You can't keep letting him get away with that sort of thing," he said, glowering at Baden and his cronies.

"It's only a few more weeks. I'm used to it," Jaks said.

But Minto was right. Jaks was tired of bullies. Instead of keeping it bottled up; instead of looking away; instead of thinking everyone else was better than him, he needed to stand up for himself.

The next morning, once the conscripts had downed hardtack and dried fruit, Ranger Cromer gathered the Thorns for the day's assignment.

"Leave your packs here. Hunting gear only," the gnarly woodsman said from his perch on a fallen log. He whittled away at a stick with swift slices of his knife as he spoke. "Hunt, fish, or forage—but do not steal. Use your wits and find some food. Prepare me a dinner feast."

They were to go out individually to hone their lone-wolf skills. Baden and a few others headed toward denser forest for deer; the majority, including Minto, toward a river or stream; and Jaks remained in the giantwood forest. He did not want to get lost. He would stay near the camp to forage and hunt.

Dappled sunlight shimmered through the trees as Jaks walked through the forest of red and gray trunks. He was off to a good start when he stumbled across a couple of thorny bushes bursting with small, juicy berries; unfortunately, they were so delicate that they mushed to a pulp within his leather pouch.

He sighed. He needed something more substantial.

Alone in the forest, his spirits calmed, and his head cleared of the hostility of the previous day. He listened to the wind rustling through the leaves, trees creaking and groaning as they swayed, and watched the birds and insects darting about, but found no trace of larger game.

His fantasy was to bring down a deer or boar. The ranger could not help but be impressed if he saw Jaks roasting a haunch over the campfire that evening. But whether lacking in luck or stalking skill (or both), animals always seemed to be aware of him and dashed away before he could bring his bow to aim. Even rabbits and squirrels seldom dallied long enough to give him the chance of loosing an arrow. It was as though he emitted some energy that warned them of his approach.

He circled in wider and wider arcs from the campsite, keeping watch for forest dragons—protective of their tree groves and liable to attack humans who strayed near their nesting sites —and listened out for the furtive shufflings and flaps of lone wyverns, who, more vicious and fearless than their dragon cousins, would stalk down their prey over many hours or even days.

Jaks stumbled upon a small creek burbling with water from molten snow high up in the mountains. He followed it to a point where he found deer tracks beside a natural ford. There were no animals around, but he did find a spot to hide and wait—a giantwood that had grown irregularly into a steepled recess at its base, big enough to back into and stack up branches to create a hunting hide.

As he scanned the forest for signs of a deer or boar, growing bored, his mind drifted to imagining a battle scene that Vixhana had told him of from the Unifying Wars. She and a swarm of nightwraiths, each hidden by their lightvoid invocations, charged across a field fought over for days before their arrival. In his mind, she leapt the wall of pikemen and landed behind the enemy formation—he'd forgotten whose army they had been; it didn't matter—then cleaved through their rear with a giant double-bladed axe. She would materialize to strike, then vanish, only to reappear dozens of yards away to smash her axe through more hapless soldiers. As she, and others, reaped confusion from the rear, even more attacked from the other sides. He was grinning as the images ran through his mind—but then something caught his eyes.

A small brown face across the creek.

The face stared at him.

Alarmed, Jaks blinked and narrowed his eyes to focus. He had been daydreaming again and was caught unaware.

Beady, brown eyes peered at him from a thicket of shrubs.

The bushes quivered, and the face disappeared.

Jaks rubbed his eyes. Were they playing up, or was that a dryad—a guardian and watcher of the forest? He had never seen one before, except for his sister performing as one on stage.

However, he doubted they really looked as enchanted and svelte as Karisa's "Princess Nereen." *Something* had been there. If it had been one of the rare forest folk, might it warn game animals away from his hunting hide?

Jaks decided that he still had a chance of game at the water crossing, and staying in the hideout was safer than wandering about.

A few hours later, the sun reached its peak. Boredom and the gentle babbling of the creek lulled him into a doze. Images of the beautiful foreign woman filled his mind. He dreamt of rescuing her from whatever prison she was in and running off with her to some exotic land.

A tug at his belt snapped him out of his nap.

Startled, he stood up, knocking away most of the branches that he had stacked up in front of his hide.

His hunting bow and an arrow clattered to the ground.

Again, the tugging at his waist. A doll-like creature hung by the handle of his shortsword, both of its tiny hands gripping the sheathed weapon.

"Get away from me!" he yelled as he stumbled out of the giantwood shelter, knocking the miniature thief away from him.

The creature fell on its back with a small cry. Empty-handed, it scrambled out of sight.

Jaks returned to the shelter to grab his hunting bow and quiver, then backed away from the tree. He looked up and down it, but there was no hint of the creature.

Rattled, Jaks jogged away from the creek with his bow in hand and a nocked arrow at the ready, throwing back glances for signs of pursuit.

When he reached a small clearing, he stopped. He listened to the forest as he had been taught: the chirruping of insects returned and the songs of birds sounded brightly. The danger was gone.

But, oddly, amongst the sounds of branches swishing and leaves rustling, a distressed mew carried in from the east. A sound like a wounded cat.

Puzzled and curious, but wary from his encounter with the forest creature, he walked toward the cries, keeping his bow tense and gaze alert.

It was another forest creature, similar to the one that had tried to steal his knife. This one, however, was hanging by the wrist, a noose ensnaring its limb. The rope was taut and tied to the top of a strong sapling that bent slightly with each of the creature's struggles.

Knee height, the creature had wild brown hair, mottled bark-colored skin, and what seemed like a dress of leaves. Its face was rounded and smooth, with brown eyes and a lipless mouth.

It pulled and gnawed at the rope around its wrist with little effect, but stopped at the sudden appearance of the human and whimpered.

Jaks felt sympathy for the trapped creature hanging by its wrist.

Two more of the creatures appeared. Partially obscured by a tree, they all stared wide-eyed at him.

He put down his bow. "I won't hurt you. I can help." One of the creatures stared at the sword on his belt. He unsheathed it and placed it on the ground in front of him.

"You can use it to cut the rope."

The tiny creature slid out barefoot, looked around cautiously, and reached for the blade. The sword fell from its claw-like hands several times. It was too heavy for it to hold.

Jaks took a step forward and slowly reached for the sword.

The small creature retreated and sheltered behind the bough of the tree.

Jaks picked up the blade and advanced on the ensnared creature, who trembled and pulled at the noose a few more times, looking pathetic with its tiny arm drawn taut above its head.

He reached up and sliced through the rope. He thought that the animal trap would have been easily noticed by intelligent creatures such as these, and wondered whether it had been accidentally triggered while they had tried to defuse it.

Freed, but with the knotted noose still around its wrist, the creature ran off behind a tree.

"Wait," Jaks called out, "I can cut the rest off."

All three of the creatures disappeared. When he searched the area for them, all he found was a half-eaten red apple lying on the ground next to the trap.

The rest of that afternoon, Jaks returned to roaming the forest armed with his bow. He loosed two arrows off at rabbits but missed both times.

He was desperate. He needed to salvage his standing with Ranger Cromer. Had to prove he had at least some skills and capability if he was to have a chance of a proper job in the king's pay. Minto had a good chance of getting in, as did Baden and all the other recruits in their unit. It would be shameful if everyone received a commission and he did not.

Even his claim that he might gain employment as a clerk in the magistrate's office was doubtful. His last coppers would not stretch far before he would be forced to beg in the streets or indenture himself as a covenant-slave to a plantation owner in a Pact Country.

By midafternoon, Jaks had only a pouchful of squashed berries and another of tree fungi that he wasn't even sure were safe to eat.

He started walking back to camp, biting his lip and cursing his poor take, when he heard a mewing sound again. This time it came in long bursts and was melodic like a song.

One of the forest creatures stood near a particularly wide redwood, hopping from one foot to the other and gesturing at him to follow. It appeared to be calling him. Maybe another of their kind was trapped?

Jaks shrugged and followed the creature. He was late already, so another minor diversion would not make much difference.

The creature ran from tree to tree on graceful legs, as though it slid on ice. Sometimes it climbed a few yards up a trunk and leapt to the next, pausing episodically to glance at Jaks. They ascended a hill, and the trees and bushes thickened considerably. When Jaks was puffing heavily and questioning the wisdom of following this creature, they reached the top of the incline and walked onto a grassy plateau.

At the center of the level clearing were several apple trees planted in a neat circle. Red fruit dotted the trees, amongst branches lush with green leaves.

There were hundreds of ripe fruits on the trees and lying on the ground. Jaks picked one up and smiled at the pleasing weight and glossed surface.

The forest creature began running back and forth, heaping apples at Jaks's feet, emitting happy mewling sounds as it worked. Laughing, Jaks filled a large sack with fruit and crammed every pocket he had.

Weighted down but grinning, Jaks was indebted to the little forest guardian—he could return with pride from this survival exercise.

"Thank you," said Jaks as he crouched and looked at the creature obscured by a tree trunk.

Its ethereal face curled a smile in return. It scooted up into the leafy recesses of a tree and sat on a large bough, where it dangled its legs.

He had not eaten all day since leaving camp and crunched into an apple, delighting in the sweetness of the white-fleshed fruit.

Jaks hefted the heavy sack, wiping apple juice from his chin, and marched back to camp.

Chapter 7

The Bully

Jaks arrived back at the campsite at sunset to discover the other recruits' preparations and cooking were well advanced. Several fires roasted animals on cooking spits—several fish, rabbits, and a small boar—wafting delicious aromas around the area.

Only Minto acknowledged his return by giving him a cheerful wave.

"Have a look at these beauties," said Jaks, walking over to where Minto was tending to one of the cooking fires.

He dropped his sack next to Minto, noting his two roasting fish, and pulled an apple out to offer to his friend.

Minto examined the apple, bit into it with a satisfying crunch, and nodded his approval with a smile on his face.

"Ranger Cromer isn't back yet," said Minto between munches of apple. He reached out to rotate his spitted catch. "I only got these two pathetic things all day at the river. Apparently, there was a pond further down that had some handsome wigglers." He flicked his head at one lad beaming with his catch of four fish, each the length of his elbow to fingertips.

The other conscripts had brought back at least a fish or rabbit; however, Baden—of course, thought Jaks—had trumped them all with the boar and two rabbits. Bringing back fresh fruit was acceptable, but far less soldierly in their eyes, given the snide comments a few made as they walked past Jaks's collection.

Night fell, and they waited for their instructor to return. But after an hour tiring of their rumbling bellies, Baden started eating, and the others followed. When they'd finished, only the senior conscript, the fishing prodigy, and Jaks had any food left over.

"Here. I'm going to share these around," said Jaks, giving Minto another fist-sized apple.

"Don't waste them on those idiots. If you think you're being nice, think again; they don't care."

Jaks thought of the forest creature in her leafy dress bringing him fruit that afternoon and decided it would be selfish to keep the apples just for himself. The fruit was a gift from the forest itself.

He told Minto about his encounters with the forest folk, the snare, and the apple orchard. But feeling protective of the little people—who they decided could only have been dryads—he asked his friend to keep the proximity of the dryads secret. It wouldn't take much for a malicious soul to take sport and hunt the gentle beings—something that Baden and his cronies were likely to do if they knew about them.

He stored a few leftover apples in his own pack and took the remaining ones to the middle of the campsite, leaving them sitting in the open sack. He called out to two of the less surly conscripts and told them the apples were for everyone.

A few of the other recruits ambled over to the apples and took up his offer. One even held up an apple and nodded thanks to Jaks.

Baden sauntered over to the sack of apples, picked one up, studied it closely, and walked over to Jaks and Minto.

"You've been messing around with my traps." Baden glared at Jaks, holding the apple accusingly in front of him. "I found one half-eaten at my last one. Some dumbass cut the rope."

Ice ran down Jaks's spine and his mouth formed a circle as he realized it was probably Baden's snare that the dryad had been caught in.

"It was you, wasn't it?" the heavyset youth challenged him, his eyes protruding and lips flat.

Fear coursed through Jaks like frost. He couldn't tell Baden about the dryads, but he couldn't deny damaging his snare either.

"I had to cut it. Got my foot caught in it," he said, thinking fast. "I didn't see it until it was too late."

He got to his feet, his shoulders stooped and head held low.

Baden closed the gap between them. His nostrils flared, and he pointed a finger. "You thought you'd have a laugh and wreck my trap, is what I think." He shoved Jaks in the chest with both hands, causing the taller youth to fall onto his backside.

Jaks sat bewildered for a moment, then fear surged as Baden advanced on him again. Baden's gang gathered around to watch the spectacle.

Not this time. He wouldn't let this thug bully him any longer.

Thoughts of the brave forest creatures, the verbal insults, name-calling, and being pushed around pumped fiery indignation through Jaks's veins.

It was time to take down this brute.

Jaks gritted his teeth and rose to his feet. Anger burned down his back.

Staring directly into Baden's eyes, he stood tall and tensed his shoulders, but his confidence was shaky. He knew he would get flattened by one of the thug's huge hammer hands if he didn't strike first. He raised his fists in front of his face.

"Fucking weakling. I'll smash you." Baden snorted and pulled his fist back.

Summoning the resolve to launch an attack, Jaks imagined hitting the brute in the face and willed himself to attack.

Suddenly, a flash of brilliant light blasted from Jaks's knuckles, accompanied by a sharp crack of sound.

An arc of white struck Baden and exploded in a dazzling ball of fury. The huge conscript was slammed off his feet. Flat on the ground, his arms and legs twitched several times before he went limp and lifeless.

Smoke wafted from a black mark on Baden's face and the cloth tunic over his chest, and a metallic odor cut through the air.

There was a sudden clamor of voices as several of the conscripts swore and shouted in astonishment.

Amazed faces flitted glances back and forth between the immobile body and Jaks, who still stood in a boxer's stance. Minto looked to the sky as though wondering whether a passing storm had been the source of the lightning strike.

Two of the senior conscript's closest associates gingerly approached the body.

Jaks stood rooted to the ground, staring at his hands. The lightning imprint on the backs of his eyes had dissolved, but the memory of the sharp forked lines tracing from his clenched fists to Baden's twisted face was etched in his mind. He stared down at his victim's unmoving body, confused by what had happened. Had he invoked an illumancer flash similar to what Vixhana had used against their father? No, it was much greater than that. He had knocked a grown man down without touching him. He had produced the same energy that traveled with storms. Energy that crackled, burnt —and destroyed.

He staggered a few steps as the enormity of his actions fell heavily on his shoulders. He had killed Baden.

He turned and fled into the darkness.

Branches whipped at his arms, and roots and bushes grabbed at his legs as he ran. The shouting voices of the conscripts trailed off, and the forest became an army of accusing giants as he rushed through.

A thick bough flicked out of the night and bashed him in the face. Pain exploded, stars spun, and he was slapped to the ground, knocking him unconscious.

When he came to, his forehead throbbed. No blood, but a definite promise of a days-long headache. His breathing slowed, and he listened for the mood of the forest. It slept, with the rustling of leaves and the creaking of trees his only companions.

His eyes adjusting to the night, he sat up and stared up at giantwoods silhouetted by the dim light of a clear, starry night sky. The camp was far behind him, and the chilly air embraced him.

Was Baden dead? If he had killed him, he would be tried and executed for murder. Perhaps he could flee to another country as a fugitive to start a new life.

He held his hands to his face. Black fingers in the night. There was no doubt to him that arcs of lightning had come from these hands. But *how*? Up until today, he had never generated even the slightest sign of magic. Karisa had instructed him how to invoke simple illumancer tricks and illusions when they were younger, but his efforts to mimic her conjurations had always failed.

She would have him recall a happy moment—patting a puppy or watching their mother perform on stage—then encourage him to imagine a light forming on his fingertip. "Then *will* it to happen," she would say as though it were the most natural thing. Then the magic was supposed to begin. She would demonstrate by dancing colored lights along her fingertips. But then all he could do with his fingers was make shadow puppets to her scintillating show.

Jaks stood. His head throbbed harder, feeling like it was going to burst. Hands fumbling along a fallen tree in the dark, he sat.

He had visualized . . . striking Baden. And he had certainly wanted it to happen very strongly, so maybe that counted as willpower. But it was fear that had filled his being, not joy or happiness, and it was forks of lightning, not a simple light, that had channeled through his fists.

Jaks sat in the dark woods for another hour and came to a decision.

"There you are! Ranger Cromer is back," said Minto, after Jaks returned to the camp. He had crept in quietly, evading the sleepy recruit on watch, and had shaken Minto awake under his shelter. "You'd better go see him."

He found the Ranger by a firepit, staring into the embers. He had a cloak wrapped around his shoulders and was poking a stick at the dying fire. As Jaks approached him, he looked up, his eyes pinpoint despite the dark but otherwise unreadable in a face like granite.

Jaks stood at attention and stammered out a few words, but they spilled out in a jumble.

"Shut up. Start again," Cromer directed him, his voice gravelly.

Jaks took a deep breath and told the Ranger about the altercation between Baden and himself, describing the initial shove from Baden through to the lightning strike when the senior conscript was about to attack him a second time.

"Where did it come from . . . this lightning?"

"I don't know. He was about to hit me. It just came out when I was trying to defend myself." Jaks trembled in anticipation of his fate. "Am I under arrest, sir?"

Cromer looked at him hard and threw the stick onto the glowing firepit.

"He isn't dead, boy. Whatever you did knocked him out but didn't kill him." The grim man rose to his feet and kicked dirt over the campfire.

He then pierced Jaks with his intense eyes in the darkness of their sockets. "You're no soldier, boy. You cause too many problems to be a part of my army." The ranger leaned in close to Jaks, his breath sour in Jaks's face. "In a few weeks, you'll be on your backside on the street. Get out of here."

With a dismissive flick of his hand, he sent Jaks slouching back to his shelter.

The rest of the week, Jaks kept to himself, staying at the back of the Thorns when they marched or performed their duties, and keeping his distance during their off time.

Baden, the morning after their clash, was marred by an angry burn on his right cheek and shot Jaks a baleful glare.

Whether fearful of Jaks or planning a delayed revenge, neither Baden nor his gang bothered Jaks or Minto for the rest of the week.

When Minto questioned him about the lightning, Jaks would say he could not remember and did not want to talk about it. Thinking on it too hard sent him breaking out in a sweat and grinding his teeth. There was something more to it than just the brief fight with Baden. Something buried deep in his memory, threatening to claw its way up with dark hands. Yes, it was best to forget it and push the incident to the back of his mind, he told himself.

But despite his reprieve from the bullies and time alone, Jaks was miserable. For after the Summer Solstice, he would be homeless, an outcast.

Chapter 8

Conscription Ends

F ive days until the end of conscription and Jaks would leave the army. The problem was that he had nowhere to go.

That morning, the Thorns unit was posted to sentry duty on the city wall of Dunberrin. Staggered out along a length of the twenty-foot-wide fortification between two catapult towers, the conscripts sagged under the weight of their armor and weapons as the day rose to its promise of clear skies and damning heat.

Over the battlements, the wall dropped fifty feet to the green waters of the outer canal, and on the other side, a mosaic of buildings, streets, and alleys stretched out for a mile and thinned away to countryside. A dozen pillars of smoke blew across Jaks's view, spewed from manufactories that produced half of the realm's iron goods, leather, cloth, and other basic goods.

Perhaps there, he could find work.

Jaks placed his wooden shield on an embrasure gap in the wall and pulled at the neck opening of his steel breastplate. The leather doublet underneath was rubbing his skin raw, and the sun didn't help his discomfort, either. In his other hand, he held a spear with a polished iron point. Beside him, Minto had laid down his own spear and shield and was crouched over, tightening a bootstrap.

"I hear that the Den of Warlions are looking for apprentices," Minto suggested as he straightened and picked up his gear. Minto had been refused by the Royal Rangers, but he had scored his second choice—apprentice to the Heraldic Corps. A profession that started him out as a simple errand boy for the royal palace, but that could advance to royal representative around the country and, ultimately, a chance to become a diplomat to one of the Pact Countries.

"Absolutely not! I'd rather stir a tanning vat than end up as a lion's breakfast." Jaks's flippant reply hid the fact that he had already applied to the Den and been rejected because of his "inappropriate temperament during conscription." In fact, the leather works were looking to be his best chances for a job, for even the desperate could find work breaking their backs over stinking vats of hides and urine—they just never lasted long at the miserable job.

"How about that clerk's job at the magistrate's office then?" asked Minto, twirling his spear by its blunt end on the stone underfoot.

"Maybe. I haven't heard back from them yet. I think my scribing exam was satisfactory, but they haven't decided how many clerks they're going to take this year," Jaks said. "I really hope I get in. If I were a magistrate one day—"

"You'd be filthy rich and get to execute whoever you like," Minto said with a grin on his face.

Jaks's face turned solemn, his forehead creased, and he stared into the distance.

"No. I'd petition the king to change the justice system." He turned to look at Minto and held his gaze. "I'd make it so that anybody can have a fair say during a trial, so everyone can get justice—not just lords and ladies." He was thinking of the inquest into his mother's death, where only their father had needed to give his recollection of events. He and Karisa had not even been allowed to be present in the magistrate's proceedings.

Minto was quiet for a while, gazing at the far-off mountains that lay beyond the workers' city and farms and pastures below.

"How about that magnificent sister of yours, do you think she'll be impressed when I'm a master herald?" Minto asked, puffing out his chest, trying to turn from the somber direction the conversation had taken.

Jaks grinned and said, "Honestly, I don't think Vix would care whether you were a herald, a governor, or the Emperor of Zura. I don't think she's interested in men in that way." He laughed as Minto's face crumpled with disappointment, and his thoughts turned to Karisa. "You *are* talking about Vixhana, aren't you?"

"Hell yes, even I know that your other sister is beyond my fair charms."

"And barely sixteen," Jaks added. He hadn't seen either of his sisters for three weeks, since he had gone on the second survival exercise. In a few days, he could visit Vixhana and Karisa. He hoped Karisa was coping with the underground bunkers of the nightwraiths and had not changed her mind about her conscription: she had threatened to run away with her acting troupe; he prayed she had not.

And perhaps Vixhana had news on the whereabouts of Meila. He had not forgotten his promise to her, too.

Although he lacked any genuine power or authority, maybe he could help the foreigner argue against her charges of spying. She would need someone who spoke Ascorian. He brightened with hope. If he got that clerk's job at the magistrate's office, he might discover an even better way to help free her.

"Oi, you two get back to your posts, proper like!" a man-at-arms sergeant yelled at them from further down the battlements. Jaks and Minto hurried back to their assigned positions with their spears. Standing eight merlons apart, they stood at attention and stared at the countryside.

At midafternoon came the Changing of the Watch. A new shift of conscripts led by another man-at-arms replaced Jaks and Minto's section of guards. Wearily, the two youths and the rest of the Thorns trudged down a tower stairwell and marched through the army district to their barracks.

The army district felt even emptier than when Karissa had commented on it weeks before. The deployment of four thousand troops to the west coast of the realm, followed by another four thousand a couple of weeks later, had reduced the city's garrison to a ghost town. The chatter and gossip amongst conscripts said that coastal raiders were so frequent and well organized that King Silas was preparing a defense against a Vor invasion.

However, as they neared the central drill area—a huge field that took up almost a quarter of the entire army district and could stand ten thousand men and women at attention—they were greeted by the shouted commands and war cries of ranks of infantry drilling for battle. Three battalions of Royal Pikes practiced defensive maneuvers against fast-moving sections of close-melee soldiers armed with swords and shields. The Pikes maneuvered to counter flanking efforts and bristled their formations with unwavering polearms.

Jaks was impressed with the discipline and coordination of these professional soldiers and felt disappointed at failing to meet the required standards to join them.

The conscripts followed the cobblestone boundaries of the grounds and kept on marching.

Their barracks were in an ancient keep at the end of the army district and had once been the Royal Castle over six hundred years ago. Built without the benefit of magic in its building or maintenance, the keep was now run-down, dark, and damp—nothing like the gravmancer-crafted and purpose-built barracks of the professional soldiers.

Jaks sighed with relief back in their twenty-bed dormitory, having relieved himself of his armor and spear at the foot of his bed, and happily anticipated the thirty-minute break until his section was due in the kitchens for dinner prep.

On his pillow, an envelope awaited him.

His excitement grew, seeing both his addressed name and the wax seal of the Royal Magistrate's Office on the rectangle of paper.

Flicking it open, he unfolded a letter. As his eyes darted from sentence to sentence, his shoulders drooped and his head sank.

He had been rejected.

Minto, seeing him with the letter, asked him the result and gave his commiserations.

Across the room, Baden smirked as he overheard Jaks's rejection. He rubbed at his scarred cheek. Menace lurked in the thug's eyes, but with his imminent transfer to the Royal Lancers—a legendary division of heavy cavalry—following conscription, his opportunities to return the injury were running out.

That night, retribution was delivered in the form of a pillow and fists.

Jaks woke to a smothering pressure over his face. Blinded and unable to breathe, his reflex was to pull the obstruction away; however, his arms and legs were pinned. Iron hands gripped his wrists and ankles.

Pain exploded in his belly. An onslaught of heavy jabs struck his unprotected abdomen. Unable to breathe, he struggled his best, but numerous attackers held him to the cot.

Muffled voices arose near his covered head, but he could not make them out.

The attack renewed and continued for what seemed forever. The face covering stifled his breathing as fists and elbows struck him over and over.

His mind retreated, as it did from time to time. Aware of the physical blows but detached from pain or response.

A shout roused him an unknown time later. The pillow fell from his face and Minto was standing at the side of Jaks's cot with a bared sword. "Get away, you fucking bastards," his friend shouted around the dark dormitory. He waved the blade with one hand and shone a runestone flashlight at a group of retreating shadows with the other.

Jaks rolled to his side and gulped in air. The act of breathing stirred a wave of nausea, and he dry-retched.

The soft front of his body was in pain. From his chest down to his groin, it felt like he had been stomped by a horse. He curled into a ball and moaned.

"Damn whoresons . . ." said Minto. He placed the sword on the ground and gently examined Jaks's injuries. Finding numerous bruises but no blood, he laid a calming hand on the youth's arm and returned to glaring around the room.

Baden's voice rose from beyond the reach of the torch. "Oops, didn't see him there," he said, and laughed.

The next morning, Jaks remained in his cot, nauseated and aching from the beating. Minto covered for him when the man-at-arms queried his absence from sentry duty, blaming food poisoning for his infirmity.

Later that day, as the Thorns returned from their duty, an errand boy employed by the Captain of Conscripts trotted up to his bedside and handed him a summons to present himself to the captain in his tower. *Oh, God, more trouble?* Had Baden contrived further devilry, using the commanding officer to exact further revenge?

Midriff aching, Jaks struggled into his uniform and lurched after the waiting messenger.

Jaks had only spoken with Captain Buik once over the past two years. In the initiation week, the short, well-dressed officer had given Jaks his condolences, saying that he had heard that his mother had fallen to her death. "A fine actress. Saw every play she was in. She was so splendid. Such a tragedy," he had said in a clipped and precise manner, and then added, "And your older sister—yes, she was an excellent swordfighter. A nightwraith now, I hear." Fortunately, he had not mentioned his father, for Jaks would have had no reply. Since then, he had only seen the captain from afar: on the drill grounds, on march, or on parade.

The boy led Jaks through the keep to an anteroom and knocked. A voice sounded in reply.

Pushing open the timber door, the boy announced Jaks and

stepped back. Unsure of proper protocol, or the reception which he would get, he marched in and stood at attention in front of the captain's huge wooden desk.

Captain Buik sat in a tall carved chair, dressed in an officer's formal uniform decorated with gold tassels over the shoulders and bronze clasps down the front. Partially bald, he had carefully plastered a few strands of hair across his head.

Curiously, another man sat in one of the over-padded armchairs to the side of the room. Attired in a nobleman's clothes—well-cut and tailored with sharp straight lines in the latest fashion—he rested a clipboard and stylus on his knees.

"Conscript Rauhalik, this is Master Cranbrook from the Academy." The captain nodded to the other man. "He is here to evaluate your . . . power."

"Power? I have no powers, sir," Jaks stammered.

The mage stood and walked over to Jaks with an inquisitive look on his gaunt face. He had deep-set eyes as though he neared death, and a scar that ravaged his neck from ear to ear but was partially obscured by a rounded collar. "You look ill, young man," he said.

"Just a sour stomach . . . my lord," replied Jaks, unsure of how to address a member of the Academy. The Academy of the Arcane harbored the elite of mages. Renowned as the center for inventing new implementations of magic and creating powerful artifacts, only the most brilliant and powerful of gravmancers, pyromancers, and suchlike dwelt there. Whilst the army trained battlemages in offensive magic, the Academy trained magesmiths and mancers in everything else.

"Reports are that you invoked lightning." The master sat on the captain's desk, placed his clipboard and stylus down, and folded his arms. "If that is true. You would be the first electromancer since Grandmaster Vinton—the first in over eighty years."

Jaks's stomach churned and his face went pale. *Electromancer?*

"I'm going to need you to do exactly what I say. If I find you're just a common illusionist or trickster, I'm not interested in you," said the wraith-like mage. "But, if what the Ranger reported to Captain Buik is true—then it would be a waste not to explore your powers somewhat more."

The errand boy took Jaks and Master Cranbrook up to the captain's solar, a sun-soaked room filled with potted plants spilling out sweet scents and cascades of color.

They sat on two wicker chairs at the center of the round tower room. The mage pulled at his collar, leaned forward, and looked intently at the young man. Jaks stared at the man's nose, avoiding the temptation to glance at the scar, wondering how close to death the mage had come.

"Feel. Visualize. And then, will," said the master, flicking each word through the air with his writing stylus. "This is how you harness magical power. Summon the emotion, create a picture in your mind of what you want to do, and then push your willpower into making it happen." He sat back in his chair and looked expectantly at Jaks.

"Wait." The master waved his stylus toward the other end of the room. "Go over there, by that watering can. I don't want to be in the way if something happens."

Jaks faced a metal watering can and tried to recreate the sequence of events from his encounter with Baden. For a few minutes, he ran the scenario over and over, stretching his hands in front of him at the watering can, but nothing happened. He recalled and followed Master Cranbrook's instructions, and nothing happened.

"No, no, no," said the mage. He sighed, tapping his chin with the stylus, and then walked over to Jaks.

"You need to incite and hold your fear." He stopped a few steps from Jaks, placed his hands on his shoulders, and turned him back to face the metal bucket. "Electromancy draws on the feeling that your life, your very existence, is under threat. It comes when you are being chased or attacked by a great evil. Electromancers in the past manifested their greatest invocations when in battle and wounded."

Jaks had never heard of a mage drawing power from fear. It sounded wonderful, but impossible. Fear was the opposite of power. It was what he felt under the heel of someone else's power—like last night in the barracks.

Master Cranbrook continued, "This is not happy, joyous illumancy or anger-driven pyromancy. It is fear, dread, terror. It rips at your deepest being. Tears at your soul." He spoke so passionately, spittle flew from his mouth. "Think of times you have been attacked or felt you might die. Falling from a tower . . . the dread of a bear staring at you . . . the terror of—" He paused, searching for an example.

But Jaks had his own: the terror of his raging father hammering down a heavy gloved fist, sweeping past his head, and smashing a kitchen table to splinters. The terrifying mask of anger stretched over his father's face. The horror of seeing the dark fist descending toward his mother's head.

Jaks breathed rapidly. Couldn't get enough air into his chest fast enough. He felt as though he was suffocating, as though a pillow smothered his face again. His heart raced and his mind spiraled—and then the room abruptly closed around him and he collapsed to the floor.

For the second time that day, Jaks revived from blacking out. This time, he found himself lying on the ground in the captain's solar. A half-empty bag of dried sheep manure cushioned his head. The side of his head ached and was tender to touch. He had been injured so many times in the past week, he was losing count. He sat up groggy and nauseated.

"You took a bit of a knock as you fell," said Master Cranbrook, examining a hanging plant with conical yellow flowers.

"Sorry, sir. I don't know what happened."

He turned from his botanical study and looked at Jaks. "A panic attack. Something threw your mind into a whirlwind, by the looks of it. Common with battle veterans or torture victims, but sometimes a dire memory can trigger emotions that consume and engulf a mind completely, propelling you back to re-experience your trauma again." He pulled his round collar up higher around the pale scar curving around his neck.

The mage signaled for Jaks to return and sit with him in the wicker chairs. "It may take a while to elucidate whether you have any magic power. Today, your anxiety and . . . indigestion, appear to have won the day."

"Sorry, my lord. The—"

The mage held up a finger to interrupt. "Learning to harness your emotions will give you the best chance of unveiling the presence of magic. If you have the power of electromancy, it will be in the Academy's best interests to help you develop and explore its potential. Grandmaster Vinton documented the use of his lightning power on the battlefield. Indeed, Ascoria would not be here today if it had not been for him. But we know little of the nature of electricity and whether it has other practical uses as well."

Master Cranbrook reclined in his chair, lost in thought for a while, and then finally slid his stylus into a holder on his clipboard.

"Grandmaster Mulgrave needs a clerk at the Academy. He will continue from where we have got to today. And, in turn, you will assist him in his research and administration. It will be up to him to further evaluate your power. Who knows? One day you might apprentice at the Academy."

Master Cranbrook looked at Jaks and arched his eyebrows questioningly.

Tingles of excitement radiated through Jaks's neck and shoulders once he realized he was being offered a second chance at making a difference of some sort.

He nodded.

Despite two dismal years of conscription and two rough weeks at the end, his future had flipped from bleak to bright. He wouldn't have to sleep on the streets and scrape coppers from the gutters, or sell himself in servitude; instead, he had a job and income—and had been given hope to possess the rarest of magical powers.

Chapter 9

The Archway of Perpetual Night

The Summer Solstice festival, heralding the start of the new year, had begun in the City of Dunberrin. The week-long festival summoned provincial nobles to deliver their tithes to the King, brought household retinues and guards, traveling troupes of performers and minstrels, crafters of jewelry and trinkets, and rich and plain country folk wanting to join in on the most exciting event of the year.

Several festivals, markets, and outdoor performances were taking place centered around the market and cultural districts of the main city. However, the usual festivities seemed more subdued than other years, and rumors of war with Voros led to smaller audiences and crowds coming to attend.

Summer Solstice was also when every youth in Ascoria who had reached sixteen years was brought, voluntarily or not, to be sworn into the Royal Conscripts during the Ceremony of Age. Tearful families waved off their sons and daughters to join the army.

However, those new conscripts would not arrive until

tomorrow, for today was "The Outgoing," for those who had finished their two years of service. Jaks, along with the rest of the outgoers, would be branded with a completion mark on his arm, given a small stipend, and handed his identity papers.

His last morning in the barracks, Jaks threw his last few possessions into a sack and relished the comfort of being back in comfortable civilian clothes: woolen leggings, a cotton tunic, and an armless leather jerkin.

"Watch out for all those princesses," he said, coming up to Minto, who was closing the trunk at the foot of his cot.

"I wish," replied his mop-haired friend, who then laughed and slid his coin purse into a pocket inside his jerkin.

"Hells, this hurts." Minto rubbed the skin around the Shield and Crossed-Pikes emblem that had been burnt onto his upper arm earlier that morning. "Well, this is it then," he said, and threw Jaks a tense smile. "You'll keep in touch?"

"I'll write you," Jaks replied.

"Write? Hell no, send me a messenger to tell me when your master lets you off duties and we'll meet at the tavern! I might even be able to visit you when I'm on messenger duties."

"I might get Faithdays off?" Jaks said, not even sure how to get to the Academy, how much he would be paid, or where he would sleep. At the end of his meeting with Master Cranbrook last week, he had simply been told to report to Grandmaster Mulgrave at the Academy on this day, then sent away.

They walked to the district gates amongst the hundreds of other outgoers. A few parents waited for their now-adult children on the avenue outside the army district barbican and sentry post, but most of the conscripts simply walked out and made their own way to their various destinations with excited goodbyes to one another.

"Farewell, old friend. See you again soon," said Minto, and

then jogged over to meet with another novice who had also joined the Heralds.

A pang of loss struck Jaks as his friend was swallowed into the crowds.

He sighed and prayed that his next two tasks for the morning would be more satisfactory—for, once he reported to his new job at the Academy, there was no telling when he would have more free time like this.

Jaks heaved his carrysack and headed to the military prison in another attempt to locate the foreign prisoner Meila. He pestered the guards there and then at the three city prisons for word of her. They had none. Again, he had exhausted his limited avenue of inquiry and slumped away.

He wondered whether a palmed coin was needed to loosen their tongues and gain their cooperation; he knew little of these things.

Vixhana would know. She might have even uncovered the foreigner's whereabouts already.

He swore to himself, shaking his head as he walked toward the nightwraiths' barracks. On reflection, he should have visited his sisters *first* that morning.

The nightwraiths' arch was an enigmatic landmark in the army district near the city wall. A gigantic curve of granite connected two large buildings. At the apex of this archway stood a statue of a warrior raising a greatsword as if to plunge the blade onto anyone who dared to pass below. But most remarkable was the arc below called the Archway of Perpetual Night, a wall of impenetrable darkness where light could not pass or escape. Rumors told that the mysterious complex was filled with this same magical dark and that the elite soldiers crept about with magical night vision and performed bizarre rituals and sacrifices. Nonsense and mystery, Jaks knew from his sister, created to keep curious regular soldiers away.

It was this arch that Vixhana had brought them through after their encounter with their father over a month ago.

At midday, he stepped into the blackness under the arch and felt his way along the wall of the left building. Several steps, then he followed a gap leading down five steps. Light returned as he entered an enclosed alcove lit with a runestone globe above an ironwood door and barred window. He gave it a sharp rap with his knuckles.

A small slot slid open behind the bars and beady eyes peeked out.

"What do you want?" asked a raspy voice. But before Jaks could answer, the voice continued, "Oh, it's you. What are you doing using this entrance? Shouldn't you be in the kitchen?"

What a curious greeting, thought Jaks.

There was a heavy clank, and the door opened, revealing a gray-haired sentry armored in chain mail and bearing a sheathed shortsword. "Well, get in, lad," the sentry said.

Jaks entered a square guardroom and saw several unmarked doors and passageways.

A second wrinkled guard, with an eyepatch over his left eye, sat at a small table in the middle of the room and was staring at a hand of cards.

"Why don't you use the servants' entrance?" The rough-looking guard frowned at him. "You got lost in the Dark?"

"Oh, I'm not a servant. I just came to visit my sister."

Both of the guards stared at Jaks, the seated one placing down his cards to squint at him.

"Your sister? Who is that, then? You're just that serving boy, you're having us on," the first guard said.

"No, I'm not, not," Jaks stuttered and felt his heart quicken. "She's Captain Vixhana Rauhalik. My other sister is here too, staying with her a short time."

The sentries gaped at Jaks for several seconds, then looked at each other and roared in laughter.

"You said your 'other sister,' you dolt. You meant your *brother*, of course, you two look so alike. Twins, are you? Never mind." The eye-patched guard sat back down, wiping his eyes and still chortling. "You've missed Captain Vixhana. She was deployed several days ago. Sent to the provinces on one of their covert missions," he said, tapping the side of his bulbous nose. "But your brother should be here, of course."

Baffled, Jaks couldn't think of anything to say and simply stood with a puzzled look stuck on his face.

The first guard ducked his head into one of the many doors, and a girl with a cheerful smile came running out after him.

"Take this lad to his brother," the guard instructed the girl and sat down to pick up his hand of cards.

"What brother, sir?" The girl then looked Jaks up and down and a flash of recognition appeared over her face—although Jaks had never met her before. "Oh, I see. He'll be in the kitchen."

"Of course, you dolt. Off you go. I have some coins to win back."

The girl led Jaks through a maze of doors, stairs, and magically darkened passageways he knew would be impossible for him to remember in finding his way back. How did this child navigate the tunnel complex so easily? He would have to ask his sisters whether illumancers could actually see in the dark.

Finally, they entered a large dining hall filled with long tables and benches, but only a quarter of the seats, at the far end near the servery and kitchen, were occupied by black-armored men and women eating what seemed to be bread, beef, and corn. A few other nightwraiths returned tin trays and dishes to the kitchen and headed into the hallways.

Jaks followed the girl into the kitchen, where two men tidied the servery benches, and several workers out the back were washing dishes and utensils in tubs of soapy water and then stacking the items in piles.

"Oi, your brother is here," the youngster yelled toward the dishwashers.

The workers stared up from their tasks to Jaks.

One tall youth stood up, brushed his hands on his apron, and walked over to him.

The young man's face looked oddly familiar. A moment later, he backstepped and gaped in surprise. The man was his mirror image.

"What?" Jaks blinked several times.

"Jaks, it's me, of course." Karisa dropped part of her illusion for a second and revealed her normal face. "It's just easier like this," she said, and re-invoked her illumancy to complete the mimicry.

A coarse matronly voice called over from the washing area, "Boy, get back to work. Talk to your brother after breakfast." Jaks looked over to see an old woman stacking dishes and glaring at Karisa. He was dumbfounded as his sister scuttled back to her chore.

Jaks waited, rubbing his arm below his newly branded mark of a conscript, and stood awkwardly outside the kitchen. A quarter hour later, Karisa came out drying her hands on her leggings.

Back in Vixhana's quarters, Karisa fell onto a chair and kicked off her shoes. She dropped the mirroring illusion and restored the appearance of her face and hair. But even without magic, the siblings looked similar: noble, refined features and generous lips and eyes. Only Karisa's blonde hair, blue eyes, and the swell of her chest—inherited from their mother—significantly marked her different from him.

"Sorry, Jaks, you must have caught a fright," she said. "After I got here, Vix didn't want any soldiers to bother me, so we decided I should cut my hair, strap my chest, and use an illusion. It's tiring keeping it up, but it's better than fighting off stupid men. I hope you don't mind?"

He laughed and shook his head, then went to sit in another of the chairs beside the round table at the center of the room. He looked about.

Vixhana's bed was tidily made, and they had set another bed up against the opposite wall since the last time he had been here. As he had expected based on the guard's information, his older sister was absent, as were the weapons and shield from her equipment rack.

"You must be excited for tomorrow," he said. "Don't take too much of your own gear. The quartermaster'll supply you a uniform and boots when you get to the conscript's barracks."

He then frowned as a small brown mouse climbed up the table leg and ran over the top to Karisa. It rose on its hind legs, waggled its front paws, and sniffed at her. The teenager took out a small nub of carrot and offered it to the mouse. The rodent scrambled onto her palm and nibbled the vegetable. Cradling the tiny animal, she smiled.

Jaks loved to see his sister happy and didn't press her for a response.

A minute later, however, she lifted her eyes to him and replied, "I've changed my mind. I'm going to run away in the morning." She shot him an anxious look. "You won't tell Vix, will you?"

"What? What do you mean?"

Karisa stroked the mouse a few times, then placed it on the ground. It skittered away beneath Vixhana's cot.

"I found some money that she left in a jar. I'm going to borrow it and buy a berth to Faucony and wait for my troupe." She smiled and looked at him with a sly look on her face. "I'm going to disguise myself as you. You just said you didn't mind."

"That's not what I meant," Jaks said, his voice almost a shout in the small room. "You can't run away. I thought we had a plan. You were going to report for conscription tomorrow."

Karisa continued as though she had not heard. "Father would never leave Ascoria to find me. If I leave the country, he will give up searching for me," said Karisa. "You could come with me. We would be twin brothers on a voyage!" Her face brightened with a smile.

"No. It's not just Father you should worry about. The army would trial you as a deserter and hang you, Karisa." Jaks rose from his seat and stared at her. "You know what Vixhana said about the Pact Countries—they would only need one look at your identity papers and they would send you straight back. If you don't turn up for conscription, you will be marked a wanted criminal. You can't hide forever." He threw his hands up in the air, exasperated.

"I could," Karisa said in a petulant tone of voice. "They would never hang me," she added with less certainty and put a hand to her throat.

"Father can't force you to do anything anymore—it's not your fault he did those things to you, so don't let him make you a criminal and steal your freedom. Do the right thing." Jaks reached out and grasped her arm gently. "When you're in the army, he can't get to you. He only commands his garrison. He is not a general anymore. So, if he tried to take you or hurt you, he would have to answer to King Silas himself." Jaks released her arm and sat down.

She persisted with her stubborn look, a child not getting what she wanted. "I thought you would want me to be happy after all we went through."

"I do, but you will never be happy, running and hiding for the rest of your life." Jaks's eyes dropped to stare at the table. It was difficult for him to look at her with what he was about to say. "Karisa, I am sorry I was such a coward when we were children. I was so scared of him. I should have done more for you and Mother."

"It wouldn't have made any difference. He would have just beat you even more," she replied. He needed no reminder of the beatings he'd received.

"I promised Mother that I would look out for you if she died. She seemed to know she wouldn't live to an old age."

Karisa's eyes misted and her face softened at the mention of their mother.

The siblings sat in silence for several minutes.

Finally, Karisa found Jaks's hand atop the table and gazed at him. "You are right. It is not our fault how things turned out. It was his fault. He is the criminal, not me. I won't hide. I need to get through this. Running away seems the easiest thing, but you are right, it would be the *worst* thing—I could not live as an outlaw."

Jaks smiled and patted her on the hand. "You are far too pretty to be an outlaw."

"You're so nice, Jaks. You and Mother are the only people who say things like that and don't want something back from me in return."

"That's the way it's supposed to be in families. Here, I brought you these." He reached into his carrysack and extracted a folded document and a small book. "It's a signalers' application form and a signalers' code book. I asked Captain Buik for them before I left. You just need to give him your application before you finish basic training, and he will process them. He will know you; in fact, he said he saw you in a play last year and thought well of your performance."

Karisa drew the objects toward her and looked at them curiously.

"You will be fine tomorrow—you are tougher than me—and if I survived conscription, you certainly will," Jaks said, feeling pleased with himself for averting this disaster. Then, putting on a deep voice, he added, "If anything happens to you, I'll come and set things right. Your big brother will take care of you."

They both laughed.

But even as he made light of his oath, an unusual heaviness fell upon him. A premonition that some mystic cyclone had been triggered and his words would drag him into its perilous path.

Perhaps she was right. Perhaps she would be better off absconding offshore? Their father was seldom denied, and the army was no place to be if a war broke out . . . No. He gritted his teeth. The honorable path was the best path. Vixhana had also wanted this for their sister. *Karisa will be fine.*

Jaks looked over his shoulder to see if anyone had entered the room, but on finding no one, he shivered as though the night itself had laid her fingers upon him.

Chapter 10

The Academy

The midafternoon sun sweltered over Jaks's head as he farewelled Karisa outside the Archway of Perpetual Night. He welcomed the warmth, a stark contrast to the cold subterranean tunnels of the nightwraith barracks.

As he walked away, he cursed his luck that his other sister was away on deployment. Not that he doubted Karisa would follow through with their agreement, but for another reason: Vixhana was his last chance to find Meila.

Already, he was wondering whether the entire escapade in the mountains had been a dream. It was almost as though she had never existed, it was so hard to find any information about her.

But unable to do anything more about Karisa or the foreign woman, he bit his lip and steeled himself for his last destination that day: the Academy.

Make a good impression with his new master, and he could prove he could do something right.

He wiped the sweat from his neck and headed into the

foundry district. The narrow streets were lined with workshops of crafters and fine artisans of materials and magic. A horse-drawn carriage, attended by a steely-eyed guard, waited outside one goldsmith's shop. Outside another, a nobleman and his mistress gazed through the barred windows of a jeweler. The beautiful woman pointed a finger at a gem-encrusted bauble and the shop guard unlocked the door to allow them in.

Jaks squeezed past a cart laden with coal bound for one of the many smithies and almost fell over a beggar sitting in the shade of a runestone-hewer's shop awning. The one-legged man rattled a wooden cup at him. Jaks frowned. *There go I but for the grace of God*, he thought.

Jaks dropped a brass coin into the cup, then as an afterthought, he asked the beggar for directions to the Academy.

The man pointed a crooked finger at one of the many chimneys to the south. Taller and wider than any of the others in the district, it spewed a thick column of smoke from its tapered top.

Guided by the landmark at the tip of the peninsula, Jaks came to the harbor's edge.

A prison-like building squatted on a small island connected to the mainland by a land bridge.. Windows dotted the bleak stone exterior, and battlements and parapets lined the roof. However, the only sentries that Jaks saw guarded the main gates at the end of the bridge.

Several blue dragons with bodies the size of hawks—less aggressive and smaller than the bronzes that he had fought in the mountains—soared and screeched above the square building. A few others perched on its walls, preening and sinuating their necks to gaze over the area with possessive arrogance. One dived off the rooftop and swooped toward a pair of seagulls beating over the wharves. The birds cried out and winged away. The blue then looped back over the harbor and dove into the sea; a minute later, it dragged up a struggling fish in two of its claws and flew back to the roof of the Academy.

Jaks returned to examining the famed building. This was the closest he'd been to it, despite living in Dunberrin all of his life. Unlike the children's picture-book drawings, or how his mother had described it after taking six-year-old Karisa there to be assessed, it did not look like a majestic castle overlooking the ocean; instead, it appeared dark and grim.

But it was here that the Grandmasters researched and discovered new methods of using the magic energies, and here, in the runic forge, that the most powerful artifacts in the realm were crafted.

Two huge archways greeted his approach. Wooden signs marked one "in" and the other "out." Three guards stood with bored expressions on their faces. When asked the whereabouts of Grandmaster Mulgrave, the middle guard shrugged and pointed at a map panel fixed to the wall behind him, detailing the three floors of the institution: enormous squares with a wide courtyard. He tapped a ground floor area of the map marked, "Metals Laboratory."

As Jaks took his leave from the guards, a man in coal-blackened rags trundled two horses and an empty coal cart out from the exit arch. A clattering of hooves from the other direction saw another carter approaching, his cart full of the black nuggets.

Jaks walked through the archway, along a double-laned tunnel, and out to a dirt courtyard. He had expected the area to open to the sky; instead, a bronze dome roofed the enormous space. The great chimney that had led him here rose from the middle of the courtyard and pierced the dome at its center as though it were the rounded handguard to its blade.

The bottom of the chimney was encircled by workshops stationed by leather-aproned smiths, striking a rhythm with their hammers against anvils. Each station fed on a roaring flume of blue and white fire within a single enormous furnace.

Despite a breeze blowing in through a giant portcullis overlooking the sea and out through the archways behind him, the courtyard sweltered in the heat of the furnace and the acrid smell of molten iron.

"Out of the way," a voice called out. Jaks jumped aside as the carter's horses snorted at his back and passed him on their way to coal bins by the furnace.

Recalling a mental image of the Academy map, he weaved his way across the courtyard through stacks of sheet metal, cages of metal bars, piles of chiseled stone, spools of wire, and curious machines with moving cogs, levers, and rollers—some so peculiar that they looked like torture devices.

He skirted the furnace workshops, through an area with several wooden tables laden with books and documents. At one desk, a group of crafters appeared to be in a heated argument with raised voices and gesturing forcefully at various papers in front of them.

Grandmaster Mulgrave did not look pleased when Jaks found him in the Metals Laboratory.

The mage's lab was a maze of desks and benches that staggered the mind. Every flat space was covered with a plethora of partially constructed machines, machine parts, and tools. In addition, over-stacked bookcases and shelves partitioned the room into uneven sections.

Jaks had never seen a room like this before, and it took

several moments to realize that at least half a dozen people were busy around the giant room, tapping, wrenching, and examining their contraptions or reading tomes and scribbling notes.

"What do you mean, 'new clerk'?" The bald mage glared at Jaks. Grandmaster Mulgrave had come from the back of the laboratory, after Jaks's inquiry had passed through several of the lab workers. The man now stood in front of him and studied him from head to toe.

Below his shiny head, the grandmaster's face continued as sharp as a knife down to a wild beard that covered his jaw and chin but left his neck bare. Threadbare eyebrows hovered above penetrating green eyes. A head shorter than Jaks, his chest and arms bulged with muscles. Dressed in an armless tunic and leather leggings, the old mage resembled a blacksmith of horseshoes and pots.

Jaks shifted from foot to foot. "Master Cranbrook said to come here today. I have just been released from conscription," he said.

"I don't need a clerk; I have a new apprentice already."

Jaks was lost for words for a moment. "He said . . . Master Cranbrook said that you would be able to help me with my magic, and that you needed help with your writing."

"I can write quite adequately, thank you very much—young whippersnapper." Mulgrave's face soured. "What's so special about you? Why would Master Cranbrook think I would help you with magic?"

A young man with ears that stuck out through sandy-colored hair ran up to the mage and handed him a plain leather-bound book embossed with silver lettering. "Here is the Navindi book, Grandmaster."

The mage took the book wordlessly but continued to ponder Jaks.

"I can't control my magic. Actually, I am not sure if I even possess magic," Jaks said.

"What? Preposterous! What is Master Cranbrook up to? Does he think I'm a nursemaid, taking care of any young pup who runs up to me? Why are you so special that he would have me teethe you?" Mulgrave demanded from Jaks.

Jaks felt the itch of many pairs of eyes on him from around the lab. His tunic was stained with sweat. Had he misunderstood Master Cranbrook last week? He searched for an explanation that might please the mighty mage, but all he could stammer was, "Electromancy?"

Mulgrave stepped closer, his expression unreadable. A vein on his temple throbbed like a pulsating worm. "Electromancy . . . that is a remarkable claim you make. Master Cranbrook is one of the least stupid administrators around here, so he must have seen something in you. Show me what trickery you can do." Mulgrave placed the book atop a pile of others and leaned against a workbench.

"Sir . . . my lord . . . I have only ever been able to invoke it once. I was under attack and there was lightning. I think it was lightning. It struck Baden and knocked him to the ground. It burnt a scar into his face."

"What makes you think it was not a fire invocation? You may have burnt him and he staggered backward and fell over."

"Master, I don't know, but it was incredibly bright and cracked like lightning in a storm. I'm sure it wasn't flames."

"There are many types of flame, not just what you see under your mother's cooking stove." The mage put a finger to his chin. "What I want to know is what can you do with your conscious will?"

"Sorry, Master. Since that time, I have not been able to invoke again." Jaks described his failed session with Master

Cranbrook and the subsequent panic attack at the Conscripts' Keep.

Mulgrave creased his forehead and began pacing a path between two rows of benches.

Big Ears, whom Jaks guessed to be the grandmaster's apprentice, lost interest in the conversation and meandered off to tinker with some tools.

The grandmaster stopped mid-pace and turned to Jaks. "Are you afraid of lizards?"

Jaks blinked rapidly, not sure he had heard correctly.

"What about spiders?" the mage continued, smiling broadly. "I think we will set up an experiment. I love a good experiment. Tavis!" He clicked his fingers at the apprentice, who scrambled over to his master.

Jaks looked at Tavis properly for the first time and was surprised to see a handsome face, solid chin, and a hawk-like nose, only spoiled by his forward-pointing ears. A couple of years older than Jaks, he dressed tidily with his tunic buttoned to the top and tucked into his pressed cotton trousers. He narrowed his eyes at Jaks.

"Well, are you, lad?" Mulgrave repeated.

"Yes, I'm afraid of them," replied Jaks.

"Which ones, lizards or spiders?" Mulgrave opened a desk drawer and shuffled the contents around noisily.

"Both, Master. And caterpillars and worms and . . ." Any critter with the wrong number of legs sent shivers up his spine.

"Hells, we don't need a zoo. Tavis, go find a spider and meet us over by the portcullis." He handed the apprentice a glass container stoppered with a wide cork.

The portcullis was a frame of rusted bars blocking a short tunnel that opened out to a neglected wharf and the harbor beyond. A salty breeze blew through the grilled barrier. Jaks welcomed the cool air dampening the furious heat of the courtyard behind him.

Seaweed covered the slimy green surface of the wharf outside, giving it the appearance of having been unused for years. Jaks imagined that if he tried to walk along it, he would end up sliding its length instead.

At the tip of the boat jetty, a couple of blue dragons squabbled over a fish: hissing, lunging, and swiping at each other with their front talons. And past them, waves undulated with creamy white tips and floated several boats traversing the city's port.

"Boy, what is your name?" Grandmaster Mulgrave was at a wooden bench dwarfed by the portcullis. He pushed aside empty beer bottles, cups, and dishes to clear a space.

"Jaks Rauhalik, Master." He turned away from the dragons, who had ripped the fish in two and were now eating their uneven halves.

"Rauhalik . . . name sounds familiar." Mulgrave removed his leather apron and draped it over the bench. "Anyone I would know?"

Jaks told him of the illumancer powers running through the female side of his family and Vixhana's additional gravmancer abilities, but he faltered at mentioning his father, simply staring at Mulgrave with his mouth opening and closing soundlessly, his mind and emotions swirling in a confused maelstrom of indignation and fear as he tried to think of how to describe him.

"Ahh, your father . . . General Rauhalik, yes? One of the king's old favorites, a shrewd strategist. Castellan now, I understand?" the bald mage interrupted, filling in the words that Jaks could not say. "From what I recall, also a gravmancer. It would seem that you have a fine lineage of magic. But let's see about you—and my experiment."

Jaks disliked the idea of being experimented on but said nothing.

"When that nice juicy spider gets here, it is going to help you." Mulgrave slapped his palms to the bench and grinned. "Hairy, leggy one, I hope. Ever eaten a spider?"

Jaks's face twisted in fear at the mere thought of a spider near his face. "No, Master, please don't make me eat it! This is too much. I'm not sure I want to do this . . ."

The grandmaster's face suddenly turned serious. "Fear like that sweeps from an arc of simple worry and concern through to horror and terror. It is the fuel to electromancy, much like anger is to firemancy." The mage's lips thinned, his nostrils flared, and in his upturned hand, a ball of flame ignited and rolled in his palm. The heat reddened Jaks's face but seemed to have no effect on the mage.

"Fear is your reaction to threat of harm." He pushed the sphere of fire closer to Jaks, causing the youth's eyes to blink rapidly against its heat. He stepped back.

As quickly as it had ignited, the fireball was gone, and the mage looked up at Jaks. "Anger, though, is your reaction to an injustice."

A pinch in the arm surprised Jaks, then several more followed as Mulgrave pinched his arm repeatedly; he moved away, but the mage followed him with his pincering fingers. His face flushed again, but this time in anger at the irritating mage.

The bald mage ceased his assault when Jaks backed up against iron bars. "What starts out as one emotion can lead to the other. It depends on how you choose to perceive danger . . . a threat, or an injustice."

Jaks nodded. The words made sense, but he was too annoyed to think on their meaning.

The mage continued, "Electricity is the most elevated of the energies we know of, so complex that we do not understand it well—so when Grandmaster Vinton died, our knowledge of it going forward also died. So, you could be our next chance of expanding on that knowledge."

"I don't think I am a grandmaster," Jaks said. "In fact, I'm probably nothing." The desire for magical power was not as appealing to him, with such a legacy laid on his shoulders. Better to stay unnoticed and out of danger.

"Yes, most probably nothing," sighed Mulgrave.

Tavis jogged up and clunked his jar on the bench, looking pleased with himself. An almond-sized spider with a green line down its back reared up against its glass-walled prison. "Found a good one, Master. I think it might be poisonous!"

"Well done, apprentice! Have *you* ever eaten a spider?" Mulgrave said and then laughed at Tavis's shocked expression.

"Emotion the fuel, imagine the goal, willpower the trigger, and power will go," intoned Mulgrave like a children's rhyme. "What my dramatic friend Master Cranbrook failed to do was to guide you in generating an appropriate level of emotion that you could control. He thought to dump a cartload of coal on a match and expected a bonfire; of course, you wouldn't be able to trigger anything."

The stocky mage nudged the glass jar toward Jaks. "Go on, open the jar and stick your hand inside. That will likely cause you a good amount of fear but should not be overwhelming."

He pushed it closer when Jaks hesitated, and continued,

"Once the fear is strong, create a picture in your mind of lightning from your hand striking the spider. Then, the hardest part . . . you will need to *will* the lightning into being, all the while continuing to hold the image and your fear. That is the trinity of power." He bounced on his toes eagerly and drummed his fingers together.

Jaks looked at the jar. The spider disgusted him. He wanted to throw the jar into the furnace rather than open it. Even putting his hand on the outside of the jar sent a chill down his back, and he shivered.

"Okay, here goes." He plucked the cork from the mouth of the jar and placed it on the bench.

The spider skittered about but could not climb the slippery wall. He stared at it for a minute, his heart pounding and his hand trembling.

His hand slowly moved into the mouth of the jar and started to shake more coarsely, bumping the sides of the receptacle.

He visualized a white lightning bolt crackling into existence from his hand and held the image for several seconds and then, recalling Mulgrave's instruction to turn his mind to commanding the image into reality, he focused on cajoling, pushing, and building his expectation that the deadly bolt would trigger.

He closed his eyes, hoping it would help him focus.

Nothing happened.

Jaks opened his eyes and saw that his hand had drifted away from the jar, well out of danger.

"Try again," Mulgrave said.

Five times, he tried again.

Each time, the mage's face drooped further and further in disappointment.

After the sixth attempt, Mulgrave sighed. "Put the jar

down, let's see if you can make a fire." He beckoned his apprentice closer and ordered him, "Tavis, start pinching the lad."

When the apprentice looked confused, he added, "Like this," and pinched Jaks in the arm.

"Ow . . . I don't think that is necessary . . ." Jaks said, pulling his arm away in pain.

"Nonsense. This is the second part of the experiment. Pinch him, apprentice," Mulgrave commanded with renewed fervor.

Tavis approached Jaks with an outstretched hand and pinched him in the arm.

Jaks yelped and backed away from him.

The older youth began grinning and chased Jaks around the bench, taking to his task with evil delight. He had surprisingly strong fingers when he could land a pinch on his target—an arm, leg, or buttock.

Jaks's temper brewed, and he turned to face Tavis, preparing to slap his hand away the next time he lunged. "Get away from me!"

"Imagine a wall, a wall of fire, boy. Between you and Tavis. Burning hot flames as high and wide as you are tall."

Jaks followed Mulgrave's visualization. The anger lingered in the peripheries of his attention as he willed the flame wall into being.

Nothing happened.

Tavis lunged forward and pinched Jaks on the arm where he had scored twice already and roared with laughter. "Gotcha!"

Jaks jerked away, feeling bullied and desperate. He was tired of being toyed with.

Tavis came for him again.

Jaks scooted backward and smashed into the wooden bench. Bottles, cups, and plates flew through the air and crashed around him. He fell heavily against the upturned edge of the bench, and pain lanced through his back. He cried out and slid to the ground. Face scrunched in pain, he closed his eyes.

A creeping sensation on his shoulder drew his attention as the back pain subsided. *Was I cut?* He felt for blood, but instead his palm found a hard, round object.

He drew his hand away to find a green-backed spider clinging to his wrist.

He yelled in fear, willing the monstrosity gone from his arm. Suddenly, a sharp, needle-like pain barbed his arm and his yell turned into a cry of agony. His arm flexed in response and brought the persistent spider close to his face.

An abrupt crack sounded like a tree branch bent beyond its limit, and a brief flash of white sparked at Jaks's wrist.

The spider's fried husk fell from his arm and landed on its back with its legs curled up, dead.

Grandmaster Mulgrave froze mid-breath and stared back and forth between Jaks's arm and the dead spider for several moments, then exhaled. "Well, that was something."

Jaks did not hear, gasping at two fang marks and his swelling wrist. *I'm going to die.*

The mage ordered Tavis to fetch some ice and an aid kit, then turned to Jaks and grabbed his hand to extend the spider-bitten arm above his head.

"Stop being dramatic. The greenbacks aren't poisonous. I just needed you to think it was."

Chapter 11

The Meeting in the Bay

Lord Sicaro—Province of Sanford, Southern Ascoria

"Take down those damn banners." Lord Sicaro gestured at the pennants of the Ascorian king draping the throne-room walls of Castle Sanford.

The massive hall accommodated gatherings of several hundred people and was crafted by gravmancer masons so that no columns or supports were needed for its immense arched ceiling. High up the walls, stained-glass windows cast a dazzling palette of colors and patterns over the marble floor. Intricate engravings of battle scenes covered the west wall and holy scenes depicting The Creation were etched into the east.

Sicaro had glared at the pennants all morning as petitioners poured out their problems to him, as the castellan and surrogate governor for the province. The queue was longer than normal, following a long absence. A month lost to travel to the other end of the country and back, delivering the king his taxes at the Summer Solstice. A month lost to find and then lose his daughter.

He ground his teeth at the sight of the wall hangings, a

reminder that he was a mere caretaker of this province and not its owner. A mere titled lord, not a landed lord as he should be. King Silas owed him this. This very land that General Sicaro had conquered for Ascoria only fifteen years before.

Instead, he was a general with no army and a lord with no land. *An affront that must be corrected.*

Two guards scurried off to pull down the banners, using the blunt ends of their spears to lift them off their hooks and then kneeling to roll them up against the wall. Several minutes later, they returned to their posts by a clerk and his small desk at the foot of Sicaro's dais.

A small white dog sat at Sicaro's feet, staring up at its new master with droopy brown eyes. He'd named it Kat in a twisted memorial to his dead wife. His henchmen had found it whimpering under a kitchen bench in the Dunberrin estate, and Sicaro had brought it back with him. As a reminder of his favorite daughter, it was pampered. Any who maltreated the dog spent a day in the stockade, and any who so much as smirked at their master's uncharacteristic tenderness was whipped and salted. However, much like how he should have kept his daughter close, the dog was on a tight leash and locked in a metal cage when unattended.

A royal herald entered through a side door to the throne room and bowed to Sicaro. "My lord. Commander Lytton insists on an audience with you this afternoon. He repeats his desire to speak to you about the disposition of his troops, in particular, allowing him to position some of his battalion inside the walls."

Sicaro regarded the herald with dispassionate eyes. He disliked the fop immensely. Although every soldier in his garrison had been hand selected by him, this herald had been appointed by the king.

The man, as his role required, was pristinely dressed: tailored trousers, silk shirt, a vest emblazoned with a two-headed falcon crest. However, it was how he wore his feathered herald cap—jauntily tipped to one side—that made Sicaro want to crush the man's skull. But, for all his finery and dandyism, he was yet another agent that the Ascorian king used to keep a rein on him. He mentally shifted the herald's order of termination up on his list of people who needed to be purged in the coming months and smiled at the thought of the man's head mushed in his hands.

"What say you, my lord?" asked the herald.

"I'll see him tomorrow at afternoon court." He saw some potential in meeting the commander, even though he resented the presence of the newly arrived battalion. When the king had offered to send more soldiers to Sanford, Sicaro had been adamant that his heavily fortified town was already fully defended and had no need of the king's troops in his region. The Vor raiders were only striking the regions on the west coast of Ascoria, he'd argued. The battalion was an additional five hundred bellies to feed. Their encampment trampled two good pasturing fields, and Commander Lytton was another of the king's lackeys to challenge Sicaro's rule of the region. An unnecessary aggravation. He had been stuck in this rut for too long, stagnated, stalled, and underappreciated—it was time for a shift in power.

"I shall inform him, my lord," the herald genuflected and retreated.

Sicaro beckoned to his clerk. The twitchy man shot up from his chair and scampered up the throne steps.

"How many more?" the castellan said.

"Just one citizen awaits, my lord. Publican Unraster from

The River Thistle tavern. He requests a month's reprieve from taxes." The clerk scratched at his thin mustache.

"Last month, he was complaining about the alcohol levy. The idiot should be increasing his beer and food prices to raise his income."

The clerk nodded like a drowning man keeping his head above the waves.

"Send him away. Halve this month's tax, but he must make up the amount next month," Sicaro said, and waved the man away. He was merciful to the Publican. Taverns dulled the masses and kept them happy, but he would not allow his coffers to suffer. Especially now that the coins would fill his personal coffers and not the Ascorian king's.

"Feed the dog, then lock it up," he said to a servant girl waiting on the side. She scooped up the animal in her arms and dashed off to the kitchens.

He looked to the back of the hall and gestured to a man with blue rings tattooed around his neck and curved shortswords swinging at his hips.

His constant shadow and chief enforcer was a bronze-skinned ex-gladiator named Craeg Vesenira. From the Isle of Ellipta, he had joined the army in Sicaro's regiment many years ago. Truly a mercenary at heart, he had not intended to contract long with the Ascorians, but the man had a quality too useful to lose to another banner. A shadowdancer and skilled swordsman, Vesenira was a formidable assassin.

"Prepare the horses," Sicaro instructed the man.

At midday, Sicaro rode out of Castle Sanford on horseback, accompanied by Vesenira and six others of his personal guard, all veterans from his days as their commander. He informed the garrison captain, as he trotted past, that he was visiting villages along the coast and would return late in the evening.

The royal castellan wore a black cloak over a carapace of black steel-plate armor embossed with gold. Across his lap rested a giant warhammer: six feet of titanium topped by a huge fist holding a steel stake—pointed at one end and flat at the other—so tremendous in weight that only he, or another battle-trained gravmancer, could wield it in battle. Claimed in war, as it had been several times in the centuries since its creation, the weapon, called "Sorrow," was an apt symbol of the result of Sicaro's fighting powers.

They rode over Sanford Bridge, shadowed by the high walls of the castle and under the curious eyes of his soldiers on guard duty. If an enemy were to traverse the bridge, or sail the river, they would come under a hail of arrow, catapult, and ballista fire.

He had ensured that Castle Sanford was the strongest bastion in the region, and perhaps the entire realm.

The castellan and his retinue passed through two villages that afternoon, each time stopping to test a call to arms. A bronze bell would ring at the center of each settlement and summon every conscript-trained, able-bodied adult within earshot. Simple pastoral folk, both villages rallied a paltry twenty fighters armed with either a rusty sword, blunt spear, or frayed-string crossbow.

Inadequate fighters but obedient workers. *They will make good slaves.*

"My lord, the grain stores are filled to the brim. May I have your permission to sell the excess to the produce markets in Irin?" asked the mayor of the second town. A lanky, tough woman who bore too many opinions for Sicaro's liking.

"Build another silo if they are overflowing, Mayor Worten. You have done well with the crops this summer. I have a new market . . . overseas that I am working on. The returns will be far greater than what we would get locally. In the meantime, keep stockpiling," Sicaro said and flicked her a coin. It landed at her feet. She scowled at it as he departed.

At the last village, they supped early at a local inn on lamb and potatoes. As the innkeeper brought ale to his lord's table, he voiced his concerns that Vor raiding ships might spread to their region.

"You need not worry, proprietor. The only ships that touch this coast are the ones I invite," replied Sicaro.

As the sun touched the horizon, Sicaro and his men departed.

"What if the Vors are full of betrayal and break their promise, my lord?" asked one of Sicaro's henchmen once they had ridden several miles clear of the last settlement. The man was Kyle Halwoth, often called "Sneer" because of a left-sided facial droop that stretched his mouth in a permanent veil of contempt. A sycophant, he often rode close behind his lord, leveraging favor with flattering words and comments. Today, however, his words were full of worry.

Sicaro replied, "Never. Even after they land and have a foothold, they still need me to open the way north over the Reynford River. And besides, Harek knows he only has a moderate advantage in numbers. They need me if they are to anticipate and outwit Silas." The goal to replace the latter king relied on a successful war campaign, but his importance and station with the Vor invaders depended on making sure that they were forced to rely on him to win.

Since Sicaro and King Harek, the Vor ruler, had first met over a year ago, their initial distrust had settled to a mutual wariness. Their plan for the Vor invasion of the Kingdom of Ascoria had matured as Sicaro leaked valuable information piecemeal to the wily Vor in exchange for the promise of a dukedom over lands of his own. With final touches, their plan would be well-oiled and faultless.

The invasion would launch in two months' time. It would be early autumn and the conditions ripe for war: mild weather, summer harvests stored, and autumn produce ready for the horde of Vor warriors, dragons, and the monstrous *gargantors*.

"Fields will be toiled and turned with the changing of the crop." Sicaro spoke a metaphor of the upcoming invasion. "Our place is as the plowmen, and only I know how the machinery works. Harek needs me and will deliver his promise. You will all be richly rewarded, I can assure you." He spoke confidently and loud enough for all of his henchmen to hear.

He turned to Sneer as they directed their horses down a junction into the forest. "I have tasked Craeg with a task for the night of the invasion, but the signaler's tower on Dustun Cliffs needs to be taken care of. What do you suggest?"

Sneer flicked his reins to bring his horse alongside the castellan. "My lord, with the full moon and a wide field around, Arlo and I could sneak up on the tower around midnight. Two of us is risky but easily done with a silencing runestone to muffle our approach. We climb to the first floor and kill the sleepers, and then go up the internal stairwell to take out the night guard on the roof."

"Agreed, but not with Arlo. You just need muscle . . . take the brothers instead," said Sicaro. Sneer assented and nodded to the two red-haired siblings at the rear guard.

"Arlo is too important to risk this close to the invasion. The

Vor king has agreed to take him into his retinue as an advisor whilst I am gone." Sicaro turned to the man himself: a fellow Vor emigrant who had fled their homeland as an orphan and later joined the Ascorian army as a mercenary—well before the Vor ships had begun raiding. A square-faced man with a braided beard who was the most loyal of Sicaro's men, and so entrusted to the most important of tasks.

The path ended at an abandoned woodsman's hut, but they continued through the small clearing and back into the swaying boughs, their horses pushing toward their meeting point with the Vor king.

By the time they had left the forest and descended to the edge of a sheltered bay, the sun had disappeared, but they still had a few hours to wait.

The twin brothers built a fire on the stony beach, although the evening was warm and the moon was full.

Staring out over the calm, moonlit ocean, Sicaro said a private word to his blue-necked enforcer. "Craeg, how fares your kinwife? How many months until her confinement?"

"Four months. She wishes to return to her mother and my other daughters in Ellipta soon. Which, in these turbulent times, might be a good idea, do you think, my lord?" Craeg had four wives, three of which were his daughters, a large family by Ellipta standards.

"By all means, send her off. Better she labor and birth in peace amongst her sisters. I hope to visit your enlightened country someday." Sicaro admired the progressive nature of Elliptan culture. Though most other societies found the island nation's practices repulsive, he saw much to appreciate. There were no barriers to who could consort with whom: cousins married freely, aunts married nephews, brothers married sisters, and fathers married daughters. And further fueling the liberal practices, polygamous families were the norm. The Royal Family of Ellipta, themselves, were a result of generations of inbreeding—the current king and queens were three siblings. That their religion involved the ritual sacrifice of physically defective children, of which there were many, meant they could breed strong pedigrees.

"Any word from Bako, my lord?" Craeg asked, referring to the one of the men Sicaro had left back in Dunberrin to continue searching for Karisa.

"He's found neither hide nor hair of her since the manse," Sicaro said levelly. His anger at Vixhana, after she interfered with his reunion with Karisa, had been fierce, and a week of further scouring the city had him think that the she-bitch had stolen his beloved out of the city against her wishes.

He had had no choice but to leave Bako and another man behind to continue the search, for he was needed in Sanford for this very appointment.

"She will come running to me at the first chance she has of escaping that devil. Bako will help her return when she re-surfaces." Sicaro returned to scanning the ocean.

A lantern flared in the bay, revealing the prow of a Vor longship. Rhythmic slapping of water soon followed, as oars dipped and pulled the boat toward the beach.

Several more lanterns lit up, and when the boat crunched onto the shore, a score of fleet-footed warriors leapt from the ship to take positions around the fire.

Another two ships slid onto the pebbles and spat out even more armed men and women. They disappeared into the surrounding forest in groups of ten. Armored in leather, chainmail, or steel plate, they wielded swords, shields, and shortbows—except for several who carried the enormous double-bladed axes of gravmancer warriors, and a few who bore nothing but the sun-symbolic facial scars of firemancers.

Sicaro was impressed by the Vors' military operations, even at this small level. Seeing them in action gave him a respect for Harek's capability as a military leader. He had known that King Harek Raukela had been unifying Voros at the same time that King Silas had been unifying Ascoria; however, he only now saw the prowess required to subdue and diplomatize the fragmented country into one nation.

"Come join me, brother," Harek called from the deck of the longship.

Sicaro made an effortless jump onto the ship with his gravmancer powers, making him feather-light. Then, as he cleared the edge of the vessel, he steadily returned his weight to normal and landed gently—a graceful maneuver that was impossible for a plate-armored man of his immense size without similar magic.

"Bravo." Harek slapped him on the back and laughed. He had a face made for it, a broad smile and bright green eyes that glinted whenever he was in good humor, as he seemed to be that evening.

Slightly shorter than Sicaro, the king of Voros was more sinew than muscle. He was dressed plainly in battle leathers, with steel plates around his chest and arms, and wrapped in a finely woven gray cloak. But despite his fine garb and features, Harek was a renowned warrior—as were all Vor kings—for ascension to leadership was only by duel and fight to the death.

I could kill him, thought Sicaro. But this was not the time nor place. He would be seen as an assassin, not a contender.

They exchanged pleasantries and went to stand on either side of a thwart covered with maps.

He looked at the clean-shaven monarch. "As expected, Silas has spread himself thin along the coast of the western provinces in response to the raids. Word is that he has about a quarter of his army along the coast of Finstaff and another quarter along Hera. But, unfortunately, I was not able to convince him to leave the south completely unreinforced. Five hundred Ascorian soldiers arrived in Sanford a week ago."

Harek stiffened. "That is not many, but we'll need to amend our plan."

"I am meeting the commander tomorrow. I will get him to spread his force along the coast in small groups, which can be dealt with more easily; although, I expect most will lose heart and surrender when the head is chopped off the night before the landings—my man will deal with the commander directly."

Harek appeared happy with the idea. A smile reappeared. "My warriors will be better off for it if they can get their teeth into a few good fights. They will want some blood to begin with. Give me the location of each post and I will assign *torgues* to visit each of them," he said, referring to the battle groups of fifty warriors that his army was based upon.

Sicaro nodded. "We'll signal you the locations before you land."

They spent the next three hours poring over maps, running through the invasion plan, and fine-tuning their ultimate strategy for the weeks and months that would follow. Their scheme was meticulous, with a contingency for every eventuality.

"Another thing, Lord Sicaro," said Harek, as they were

about to conclude their meeting. "We found a man recently. A hermit living in the jungle."

Sicaro waited in silence for the Vor king to continue.

"He had an artifact. With it, he killed half a torgue, even though he was physically weak and diseased."

"He lives?"

"Captured," Harek replied.

"And you have this weapon now?"

"Yes, but we cannot make it work. I saw the results of what it could do—it put a hole the size of my fist right through a breastplate . . . from a distance an arrow flies. It is unlike anything I have seen." Harek refocused his gaze on Sicaro. "I need someone who can make it work for me."

"The hermit cannot?"

"He is of limited help . . ." said Harek.

"And you think I can?" he said, confused at Harek's train of thought.

"The man reminded me of the spy you asked me about last time. The one found in the mountains. You asked whether she was one of mine," said Harek. "Of which, she was not."

Sicaro nodded.

Harek continued, "You described a vessel that had been found with her." He took a breath and stared at Sicaro as though about to reveal a secret. "Well, the man we found was near a vessel the same as what you described to me—silver with orange sails."

"Fascinating," Sicaro said, his mind churning through the ramifications of the two events.

"Is she still alive?" asked Harek.

"The woman? I think Silas has her locked away somewhere. The last I heard, she was in the Royal Infirmary with a broken leg."

"You must bring her to me . . . I would be very appreciative." Harek raised his eyebrows again.

"You want her?" Sicaro asked, his mouth agape. Why would Harek waste his time on a prisoner when they had a sea-born invasion with over a thousand ships to worry about? Was a single weapon that important? There was more to this than the Vor king was revealing.

"Alive. She is no use to me dead," said Harek.

If she was so valuable to Harek, and Sicaro could secure her, he could use her for leverage. For what, he did not know yet, but definitely something he could use as future capital.

"I have a couple of men in Dunberrin. I'll have my man Arlo signal an order when I return to the castle."

While Harek changed the subject back to the invasion, Sicaro could not help but puzzle over why the foreign woman could be of such importance.

Chapter 12

There Can Be Only One

Jaks—The Academy of the Arcane, Ascoria

The day after the spider experiment, Grandmaster Mulgrave examined Jaks's wrist. "It's fine. It'll be no more than a lump in a week. Those greenbacks have a painful bite, but no venom," he repeated. "Can't go killing you off yet, can we?"

They were in a spare clerk's office that Mulgrave had given Jaks to use as a bedroom. One of a dozen such vacant rooms along a cob-webbed corridor, filled with dusty shelves of documents and lined from floor to ceiling with ancient, yellowed books. A set of folding wooden panels bisected the room. A desk and chair on one side of the room divider, and a small bed on the other.

Jaks sat on the bed while Mulgrave inspected his wrist.

"But without a writing hand, you are not much use to me as a clerk," said the mage, releasing Jaks's limb.

"I could dust and clean," offered Jaks. He had noticed that the mage's quarters were in dire need of a brush; some rooms, like this one, had been unused for several years, or decades even, and were cobwebbed and cluttered with junk.

"Or, I could help Tavis set up experiments?" He looked at the apprentice leaning against the doorframe and noticed the young man roll his eyes at Jaks's suggestion. Tavis had some issue with him.

He had to find a way to befriend the apprentice.

Mulgrave stroked his beard for a moment. "Actually, I was thinking you could do some research in the library for information about an object that the palace has passed on to us. Come with me."

A door at the furthest end of the corridor opened into Mulgrave's private library.

Bookshelves marched in darkened rows around the octagonal chamber. Several desks were scattered around the room. Chairs surrounding a large, round table formed the centerpiece of the room and lead-lined glass windows looked out over a blue-green expanse of ocean.

One particular desk stood out amongst the others. It was covered with piles of letters, stacks of books with bits of leather poking out, stray styluses, and a taxidermied ginger cat. It was a wonder anyone could find anything on it. This was Grandmaster Mulgrave's desk.

On the opposite side of the library, a doorway led to a short corridor that housed the private quarters for the grandmaster and a smaller one for his apprentice. And through another door out of the library lay the main hallway and the rest of the Academy.

The fortress-like Academy was a continuous square building with a central corridor on each of the upper levels, linked by staircases.

Down into Mulgrave's laboratory and through the empty

Metals lab, Jaks followed the bald mage to the main courtyard of the institute.

The giant furnace was quiet today, and they encountered only a handful of people, all of which were on their way out to spend the day off with friends and family or were rushing off to visit the city markets.

"Foolish love," Mulgrave said in a judging tone when two young women, an apprentice and a journeywoman, sped past them, hand in hand and laughing. "If those two devoted as much time to the lab as to each other . . ." he said to Jaks, shaking his head and returning to his path.

As they came to the outer ring of the courtyard, it surprised Jaks to discover it was a museum.

Where the main central area was dominated by the runic furnace, workshops, and their associated paraphernalia, the outer part was laden with old artifacts and relics from distant lands and countries. The objects rested on wooden platforms, some encased in glass cabinets and others not. Signs notified anyone would want to read about each object and its history.

At one curious object shaped like a chariot with a sail on it, Jaks read that it was a "Zuran Flyer" used by gravmancers over two hundred years ago to levitate and fly around in.

Further on, an intricate machine of mirrors stood on rotating rods controlled by an array of levers and dials. "Howe's Signal Device – prototype" for long-distance communication between illumancers.

There were so many odd and fascinating devices that Jaks could have spent the entire day examining them. But Mulgrave came to a stop and stood with both hands on his hips and stared at one peculiar object.

Jaks joined his new mentor and gasped in surprise.

It was the metal pod from the mountains.

The capsule looked in even better condition than when he had last seen it over two months ago in the valley. Someone had taken a cloth to it and brought out a silver sheen to the surface.

"I know this!" Jaks stepped forward and touched the pod.

"Ridiculous. How could you?" Tavis challenged him. "You've only been here a day."

"We found it after that meteor storm last month. I was in the mountains on training and saw it come down. Minto and I found it the next day. It had an orange sail with it."

Mulgrave stepped up onto the stone platform beside Jaks. "Quite right. The material has gone to Grandmaster Hazeldine to examine in her lab."

Tavis's expression curled into a scowl.

"But I am sure anyone could have found it, if they had been around," Jaks said, downplaying the discovery, feeling that he had offended Tavis in some way.

Mulgrave pulled a sunken handle and a small door swung open to reveal the capsule's interior with seat, wall inlays, and glass panel—nothing had changed from how Jaks remembered it.

"Do you know anything about how it operates?" Mulgrave asked.

"No, we didn't really look at it very hard. I know there is a water pipe up there." Jaks pointed above the seat.

"Yes, which is why we think it was built for a long journey." Mulgrave rested a hand on the pod. "A ship of some kind, advanced beyond anything I have ever seen. I have not yet tampered with it except to take a piece of the internal frame that was loose. The alloy was incredibly strong and composed of materials I know not. Even more than that, that panel there is astonishing, but again, none of us can fathom its design or purpose."

Back in the mountains when Jaks had touched the object for the first time, a queer vibration had assailed his fingers. He touched it again now, and the buzzing sensation returned to his fingers. He jerked his hand away.

Mulgrave continued, "What I need you to do, my boy, is to find information about the machine. I want to know the significance of those inlays causing images to appear on the panel. You might find some references in the Academy library—"

"There was a woman," Jaks said in a rush. His heart thumped as he recalled the woman in the mountains, his emotions a mixture of guilt and excitement. "Her name was Meila."

"Remarkable." Mulgrave focused his eyes on Jaks as though seeing him in a new light. "So, you know of the prisoner, then? You spoke with her? Learned her name?"

"She did not speak any Ascorian at first, but I taught her some words."

"Was she able to tell you anything about this ship?"

"No. We were only together for a brief time. Our ranger arrested her and handed her over to the city guard. He thought she was a spy." Jaks pressed his lips together for a moment. "But she's not. I know she's not."

"An expert on spies now?" The grandmaster raised an eyebrow.

Jaks continued, ignoring the mage's sarcasm. An opportunity was forming. "I've visited the city's prisons. But I can't find her. I need to find her. Perhaps . . ."

"Why do you care what happens to her?"

"I promised her I would help. She saved my life." Jaks described encountering her on the mountainside. Wide-eyed, the grandmaster and his apprentice listened. But after he described the fight against the bronze dragons, they both looked skeptical.

"If she had a weapon of such power, why did she not escape capture by simply killing the ranger?" Tavis snorted and crossed his arms.

"Don't you see? If she *was* a spy, she *would* have. It proves she is not." Jaks waved his hands excitedly and gave Mulgrave an eager look. "Grandmaster, we could ask permission from the king to talk to her. I could teach her Ascorian. And she could tell us all about this ship . . . and far more, I bet."

"Spy or not, only the king decides." The mage pulled his beard to a point. "I have not met this prisoner, but apparently no one has made sense of her except for a few basic words. However, it was Silas himself who ordered the investigation into this ship." He tapped the shell of the unworldly pod. "It shan't hurt to ask him for permission. Good idea, young man."

Again, Tavis's face crumpled, the way one defeated would on seeing an opportunity slip from his grasp. "Master, if the king gives us permission, perhaps *I* would be better to liaise with the prisoner. I have some skill with languages. I learned how to speak Pihaatian," said the apprentice.

Mulgrave nodded and turned to Jaks. "Oh, and how is the new lad with tongues?"

"My grandparents were from Voros. My sisters and I speak Vorosian, and I know some Fauconian," replied Jaks.

Tavis glared at him.

"And, you also already have some connection with her," Mulgrave said to Jaks and stepped down from the narrow platform around the ship. "Let's go back to the lab and we'll write a request to the palace."

Tavis scribed the letter that Jaks should have written but for his injured arm. The apprentice threw another dark look at him as he passed the completed letter to Mulgrave.

"I have some business with Master Cranbrook now. I'll have his office deliver the request to the palace in the morning." The mage pulled on a plain brown cap over his bald head. "You two can have the rest of the day off. We will start busy tomorrow."

The two young men watched the Grandmaster close the library door behind him.

Jaks was about to retreat to his corridor when the apprentice grabbed him by the elbow. His arm dropped, and he staggered as the weight of his forearm suddenly felt as heavy as stone. Tavis was using gravmancer powers on him.

"I can see what you are trying to do, and I'm not having any of it." Tavis glared at Jaks, whom he had magically dragged down to his knees. Flecks of spittle flew from his mouth as he spoke. "It took me four years to get this apprenticeship, four years of petitioning the Academy and breaking my back as a coal-hauler. If you think you're going to walk in and take my apprenticeship, you better think again, because I will fight you with everything I have."

Jaks had no intention of stealing the apprentice's job away from him. He hadn't even known that he was a threat.

"I can see you're trying to prove you are better than me. All you city boys think you're better than us from the farm. You're just some stupid clerk straight out of conscription. You can't even control your pathetic magic. So, just do your scribbling and keep away from my apprenticeship or else I'll hurt you, do you hear?" Tavis's hand tightened around Jaks's arm.

Jaks winced in pain. Hand cold and numb from lack of blood, his arm was on the verge of breaking.

A small blast of light—brief, sharp, and white—erupted, along with a cracking sound, where Tavis held Jaks's arm.

The apprentice jerked his hand away and cried out in pain. He tottered backward and careened into a shelf of books, knocking down several. Righting himself, he then emitted a chain of expletives and curses. "You'll regret that," he said, rubbing his hand.

"I'm sorry. I didn't mean to, it just happened." Jaks reached forward to help the apprentice regain his feet. The invocation had been unbidden: he had not attempted to visualize or will the magic into being. Why was it so erratic?

Tavis shoved his way past Jaks. The apprentice augmented the push with magic and hurtled Jaks across the floor. The younger man slid into a chair and under a desk. "Get away from me. Stay away from my apprenticeship!" Tavis yelled and then stormed out the door to the main hallway.

Hyperventilating, Jaks crawled out from beneath the desk and slumped against a bookcase to calm his nerves.

He'd already made an enemy within a day of arriving at the Academy, and the job he had been promised was on tenterhooks.

It was apparent that rather than simply coming to work as a clerk and being trained in the arcane arts, he had been thrust into a bizarre contest for an apprenticeship.

To win, he had to remove the existing one and impress the grandmaster.

Could he displace Tavis by simply attaining control of his magic—electromancy was certainly rarer and more precious than Tavis's powers—or would he have to defeat Tavis through some form of duel? This place was turning out worse than conscription.

Chapter 13

The Wall

The next morning, the grandmaster and the two young men met in the private library. The stocky magesmith and Tavis, both dressed in little more than a leather apron and leggings, would be at the runic forge all day.

"Two tasks for you today, lad. First, go through that section"—Mulgrave pointed a stubby finger at several bookcases—"and record anything that might relate to your friend's vessel in the museum. Second, I have some exercises for you to practice."

Mulgrave instructed him on several exercises to invoke magic. Each targeted one of the three steps, and if Jaks could isolate and identify each separately, the mage told him, he might be able to bring his electromancy under control. However, the mage had his doubts.

"Unfortunately, some candidates with great potential are incapable of learning how to control all three aspects. Whether it be labile emotions, a weak mind's eye, or poor focus, no matter how hard they try, their fledgling magic remains nothing more than a gimmick," said the grandmaster.

"I can do this. Don't worry, grandmaster, I won't fail you," replied Jaks.

"Focus on the three aspects. Don't attempt a full invocation yet—I wish my library intact." Mulgrave then slapped his bare arms as though warming up and departed into the main hallway.

Tavis followed, but not before throwing a glare at Jaks. If the apprentice's stare had been a knife, Jaks was sure his neck would have been severed.

He gulped. He would need a breakthrough today to keep up his chances of staying.

He drained hours into the invocation exercises that day, dragging up fearsome memories until despair blocked him, painted mind images until they grayed with boredom, and concentrated willpower until he was drained of any.

But disallowed from attempting any actual electromancy until he was supervised by the grandmaster, Jaks exhausted his progress and stared at the books.

At least a hundred books padded the "Vessels and Vehicles" section that Jaks thumbed through. Although full of intriguing machines and designs—gigantic sailing ships, wheeled monstrosities, and more gravmantic flyers—nothing resembled the silver pod from the mountain.

So, it was with great relief when Grandmaster Mulgrave and Tavis returned that evening and the aging mage waved a torn envelope at Jaks. "Good news, boy! The king has signed a permit to interview the prisoner."

"Thank you!" Jaks leapt to his feet and reached for the letter —his hand pausing only a moment until his eyes gained permission from the mage—and read. Indeed, the document granted access to the prisoner for research. *I've finally found you.*

Additionally, it stated that any spy-like activity that the prisoner performed should be reported to the warden immediately.

"Let's hope she can illuminate us on the object," said Mulgrave as he rearranged the stuffed cat on his desk to weigh down some other papers.

"I'm sure she will, Master. She is very smart."

"If we can get her to talk and if she is willing to learn more of our language, I'll draw up a list of questions that you must ask her. If she can show us how to create machines such as this, the potential is staggering—perhaps even a revolution in technology."

"She knows me. She'll want to talk," said Jaks, hiding the uncertainty building in his mind. *What would be her response at their reunion? Will she believe I didn't intend to have her arrested? Might she still be bitter and see me as an enemy?*

"We'll visit this prisoner of yours tomorrow," said the mage. "This evening, though, after I get changed out of these leathers and get something to eat, let's go down to the 'burn room' and see what you have gained from your exercises today."

That evening, the lab was dark when they reached the bottom of the staircase.

The mage carried a staff topped by a bronze eagle claw grasping a bright lightstone and led the way between cluttered benches and shelves of tools to a large room at the far end of the lab.

Mulgrave propped the staff up in a stand to cast a steady light throughout the cavernous room. A low stone wall stood close to the door and salty ocean air breezed through a barred opening in the far wall. The walls and ceilings were black with soot, and the acridness of smoke lingered in the air.

Jaks needed no explanation for why it was called the "burn room."

"Tell me about the exercises today. Which did you find easiest?" the mage asked.

Jaks explained that the easiest exercises had been conjuring the images: visualizing electricity discharges ranging in size from little sparks on a fingertip through to mighty forks of lightning arcing from his hands. He had never had trouble daydreaming and imagining fantastical settings. He had spent much of his childhood with his mind reeling with images of the stories his mother told him of immense battles of great armies of warriors, warlions, mages, fireballs, siege machines, and dragons combating the skies. To visualize magic was not difficult.

Mulgrave held up a finger and disappeared from the room. A minute later, he dragged in a burlap-sack dummy that he leaned against the far wall. "And the other two aspects?" he then asked.

"The willpower exercises got boring . . ." Jaks said. They were an extension of the visualization exercises and meant long periods of holding and intensifying the images in his mind.

"As an exercise, it might seem easy, but it gets harder when you meld all three aspects together in an invocation." The grandmaster rested his hands on the chest-high wall. "How about the exercises to control your emotion?"

Jaks shifted uneasily on his feet. "Difficult, Master. My

feelings just seem to come and go as they please. Sometimes I think of a frightening memory, like you taught me, and my head feels like it's going to burst, my heart is jumping out of my chest, and the fear is so strong that it feels like it is happening again."

He was referring to an experience that he often tried to block but had, twice now, willed himself to re-experience: witnessing his mother's crushed head in his father's hands.

Occasionally, the flashback was triggered by some insignificant sound or sight. Like the time he was stirring a pot in the conscript-barracks kitchen and Baden lifted up the brain of a lamb he'd butchered and then, grinning, squished it in his hand—the squelch and mushed tissue had sent his mind reeling back to that bloody night and the sight of his murdered mother. Sometimes, the fear so overwhelmed him, he would blank out and rouse minutes or hours later lying on the ground, soaked in sweat and stinking of his own urine.

However, he did not tell Mulgrave the details of the flashback, fearing that just speaking of it might trigger a spiral of panic.

"And other times, I think of a terrifying memory, but all I get is a wall. I don't feel anything. My mind goes numb," Jaks continued. That day, he had reached a block in practicing the mage's exercises. He'd battled his emotions, trying to hold a constant level of fear. But his feelings had abruptly shut off and he'd stared at the bookshelves for an hour. "I admit, Master, that I cannot control my fear well . . . but I will keep practicing, though." He looked at the grandmaster, hoping for some empathy, but was met with a blank expression.

Mulgrave stroked his jaw and gazed at Jaks. "You have had a troubled past, I think," he said in a quiet voice. "Some evil visited upon you." The mage sighed, and his face deepened. "You must confront the past; otherwise, your fears will always control you. For a mage, it must be the other way around." He rubbed his thick neck for a moment, then spoke again. "When you're ready, you must talk to someone about them."

"Yes, Grandmaster Mulgrave, thank you," Jaks said. He was grateful that someone wanted to help him. Tears welled in his eyes and ran down his face. "I really am trying my best, but I've failed at almost everything I've ever tried in my life. I'm scared that I'm going to fail you . . . I sometimes feel like giving up because it's so hard." The words spilled out in a hurry.

The mage stiffened for a moment and then slowly reached out to pat Jaks on the back. "Don't worry, lad. You'll be fine." After Jaks had recouped and wiped his eyes, Mulgrave stepped back and said, "Failures are learning tools . . . let me tell you a story few know.

"I was about your age when I discovered my firemancy powers. I was excited and did tricks and showed off to everybody. One day, I was visiting my friend, Davik, and I showed him the 'burning man' invocation that I had just mastered. It creates a skin of fire. I had practiced it by the lake, but I didn't think what would happen if I did it inside, in a house. I proudly invoked the burning man, and then the flames ignited everything around me. Rugs, cushions, chairs, curtains—the entire house burnt down. We escaped, but we didn't realize his little brother had been upstairs . . . he died in the flames."

The old mage shook his head, reliving the past. "It was a small village and his mother wanted blood justice. Wanted me dead—even though it was an accident. My father rode me out in the middle of the night and we came to Dunberrin, where he left me to find work on the dockyards. In my grief, I didn't use firemancy for two years after that, but when I did come back to it, it was with much greater awareness of and respect for my surroundings."

Mulgrave arrived at the point of his story and said, "We all make mistakes, we all fail, but it's learning from them that is the important thing. The worst thing you can do now is give up and go on thinking you're a failure."

Jaks stared at the ground for a while, then looked up at the mage. "I'm scared I might kill someone. Sometimes the urge to kill is so strong, it frightens me." He averted his eyes in guilt as an image of electrocuting Tavis flitted across his mind.

"We all do, we all do. But it is always our choice whether we act on those impulses or not. We're not animals controlled by bestial drives. Again, it is about control," Mulgrave said. "Keep at the exercises, but instead of starting big, start small. Focus on controlling little things like . . . worrying about talking to a pretty girl and being rejected, or teetering at the top of a staircase, or worrying that you are going to fail me . . ." The mage grinned.

After that, Jaks attempted a full invocation several times, visualizing a spark on his fingertip. But the magic would not invoke.

A half hour later, Mulgrave sighed one last time. "That's enough for today. Keep trying, boy. You'll get there."

Jaks prayed that was true. Tavis had a lengthy head start on him and wasn't going without a fight.

Chapter 14

The Prisoner

Meila—City of Dunberrin, Ascoria

The rattle of keys at her prison-cell door roused Meila Tahn from her meditation. She opened her eyes but remained cross-legged on her cot, waiting to see which of her captors was interrupting her.

For a prison, the cell was more comfortable than she had hoped to expect from these primitives. Larger than the ship cabin that she and her husband shared on the *UWFS Mendhelsson*, and furnished with a bed, table and chair, and sink and toilet-hole, it possessed the basic necessities.

But it was still a prison and she desperately wanted out.

After she had been captured and dragged from the crash site seven weeks earlier, they incarcerated her in a prison infirmary. There, she was strapped down, broken leg immobilized and splinted in a contraption of metal bars and leather braces. A series of interrogators then visited her: some gentle, with soothing voices; others evil, who tortured her with thumb screws and thrust hard fingers at her injured leg. Of course, she could not understand their words, but she guessed their accusations—spying on their country.

If she replied in her own language, it angered them. And using the few words she'd learned from the young man in the mountains seemed to anger them further. But eventually, the interrogators had relinquished and transferred her to this cell.

The prison surgeon, a white-haired man with a stoop, had been surprised to find that after only a month, her leg was perfectly healed. He was not to know of the medigel that infiltrated the hematological system and bone matrix for rapid healing.

The only visitors that came nowadays were the prison guards to deliver a tin-tray meal and a pail of water each day. The rest of her time was spent on calisthenics, meditation, and staring out her window, which overlooked a grand cathedral and its manicured grounds.

She had no support, no advocate, no defender. She must find a way to escape.

They suspected she was a spy already. *If only they knew . . .*

Seven thousand years ago, the Virgo-Supercluster Wars had destroyed the dimensional portals that allowed the first seeding of planetary colonies—of which this was one. And only in the past three centuries had the United Worlds Federation (UWF), led by old Earth, finally developed stardrives that allowed them to revisit distant galaxies and begin offloading their overpopulated and resource-depleted home planets.

She and her eight-person crew had been orbiting this planet, designated "Maya-four," for over two years, and were in the last months of their mission. Their data collection, on this planetary oasis of natural resources and habitable land, was almost complete.

On arriving at Maya-four, Meila's crew were not surprised

at the devolved human civilization, given that most other Old Colonies had also regressed or gone extinct after the schism from their motherworld all those millennia ago. Maya-four, having barely clawed its way back to a pre-industrial age, was ripe for a UWF battle fleet to sweep in and remove the existing inhabitants, making way for a colony fleet to follow.

If they knew my mission, they would torture and execute me, and be fully justified in doing so.

She inhaled and exhaled.

It was a scenario that Meila and her husband—the mission's physician and geneticist—had witnessed on three out of the four planets they'd analyzed together. Only Old Colonies that had achieved specific criteria of civilization were eligible to continue alongside the new.

With their starship soon to return to Earth, the final report would have been straightforward: the humans of planet Maya-four were substandard. Feudal governments, archaic technology, and unusual genetic heterogeneity led to one conclusion: "Cleanse and repopulate."

She was not only here to spy, but to make a summary judgement of life or death for the entire human population of this world.

The sound of the cell door opening interrupted her thoughts.

Two men dressed in civilian garb and a guard walked in.

Meila surged to her feet. This was not a simple water-and-rations delivery.

New interrogators were here. The older one looked harsh. She vowed she would put up a fight now that her leg was healed.

The old man was bald and had a neck and arms like tree trunks. Although muscular and solid all over, his eyes gleamed with intelligence and guile. He wore brown leggings, a blue overshirt, and an armless cloak with frayed edging. He stood in front of Meila. Although he was short for the men here, she was shorter still and was forced to tip her head to meet his eyes.

He said something to her, and she understood it as the Ascorian introduction, "Hello, I am . . ." The rest of the sentence she heard as garbled syllables of their foreign language. However, she picked up his sentence when he said, "And this is . . ."

The other man stepped forward. He was far younger and taller than the bald interrogator. He looked familiar, with tousled brown curls and an innocent, slender face.

"Meila . . ." the young man said.

". . . Jaks," the old man finished saying.

She stared at Jaks. On many occasions during her captivity, she had retrieved recordings from her memory implants to review her interactions with the handsome youth at the crash site and knew his face intimately. But what was he doing here? He wasn't dressed as a soldier like the last time she'd seen him, but in plain gray leggings and a tunic that made him look like some form of servant. Was he now a lackey to this bald, evil-looking brute?

The young man said a few more words. When her stony expression made it clear to him that his words made no sense to her, he started gesticulating and acting out a scene: he made flapping-wing motions with his arms, talons with his fingers, and mimicked the actions of drawing a bow and arrow.

Amused, she could see he was trying to communicate his memory of their time together fighting off the dragon attack. She restrained a smile.

He finished by mouthing words and making large, round sweeping motions with his arms. Yes, they were here to interrogate her again, but it seemed they wanted to use someone familiar to her. He was a nice boy. Gentle and kind in their first encounter. When he'd sung to her, trying to distract her pain, she had laughed at first. But when she'd recognized the compassion of his act, she had been touched by the tender gesture. Her recall of them singing together almost brought tears to her eyes. However, she reminded herself, hardening her resolve, he had ultimately been one of the team that had incarcerated her. *It's either me or them.*

Perhaps she could manipulate him into helping her escape.

She had some influence over him—she remembered his yearning eyes over the campfire. *I can use that to my advantage.*

She thought quickly. Yes, here was an opportunity to exploit his youthful desires and manufacture a situation where she could escape from this prison.

She gave him what she thought was an appealing look, based on how her cousin Lezal, back on Earth, used to act around young men when they were that age. Although, that was a long time ago.

"Jaks. Hello. We fight dragons," she said in a stilted attempt at the Ascorian language, using words she'd snatched from what he had just said and from what she had learned earlier.

He gaped at her for a moment and then gave her a charming smile, and in doing so reminded her of Anton, her husband, with the same ability to melt hearts. So reminded, a pang of worry about Anton and the other crew tore through her. She triggered the emotion-regulation implant in her amygdala and quickly stifled the worried thought.

The bald man appeared surprised at her response but then nodded a few times, as though identifying something in her voice. He spoke to the younger man and then gave instructions to the guard. The latter left and returned with two wooden stools for the visitors.

The rest of the morning panned out similar to their campfire lesson many weeks ago: Jaks pointing at objects and associating them with Ascorian words for her to repeat. It appeared his orders were to teach her their language. Did they expect her to learn it, just so they could interrogate her and force her to declare herself a spy?

She shrugged imperceptibly. Whatever their motives were, she would play along and turn the situation to her advantage. She'd survived worse imprisonments before. She'd get out of this one, too.

The bald man left after two hours, leaving Jaks with her, while the bored guard took the vacated seat and nodded off.

Without the older man there, she went to work. Sitting at the table next to Jaks, she leaned forward and touched his arm, laughing, breathing deeply, and staring into his eyes. She was disgusted with herself, but the young man was her best chance of escape, and she would do anything for her freedom.

Chapter 15

Defending the Village

Karisa—Province of Finstaf, Ascoria

Damn you, Jaks. Damn you, Vixhana. I shouldn't have listened to either of you, thought Karisa as she watched her company of soldiers line up on the crest of the hill. They were about to charge down into the village of Triserly, swarming with warriors of a Vor raiding group. *I could be safe in Faucony or Pihaat now, hundreds of leagues away from this stupidity.*

Karisa peeked over the hill. The village was one of a dozen farming settlements along the coast of the Finstaf province and housed about two hundred families. Tile-roofed wooden buildings—homesteads, barns, storehouses, and workshops of simple peasants—clustered around a village square.

Vor warriors, with green and brown war paint streaking their faces, darted in and out of buildings carrying armfuls of loot or dragging out screaming villagers. Variously armed with axes, warhammers, or swords, they were clad in steel breastplates, pauldrons, and greaves, with chain or leather in less exposed areas.

Elsewhere, dead bodies littered the streets. Smoke poured

out of a storage silo at the far edge of the village and flames leapt from building to building—the fires needed to be put out soon or they would destroy the entire village.

It was the pillar of smoke that had alerted them to the raid. Arriving within a half hour by horseback, they had left their ponies with handlers at the back of the hill before grouping to advance. As mobile infantry, they only used their mounts for transport and fought on foot, where their tactics and training were at their most potent.

She looked to the captain for a signal.

Captain Vale was a battle-scarred veteran and as hairy and ugly as a boar. He lifted his arm and pointed forward. A roar of voices and the clamor of armor and weapons crashed past him as one hundred and ten soldiers charged forward as one.

The mass of steel and blades accelerated away from Karisa, and she walked to the crest, where she and the senior signaler were ordered to hold and await further commands from the captain with his retinue of ten reserves. The captain took a vantage point nearby, placed his hands on his hips, and watched the charge explode upon the disorganized Vor warriors. The raiders had been too preoccupied with ransacking the houses and toying with the surviving villagers to notice the Ascorian infantry until they poured down the hillside like a thunderstorm.

The enemy called out in panic and ran in all directions. The most confused were impaled and sliced where they stood in the streets. Others scrambled to the village square and were joined as their companions spilled out of the buildings and surrounding streets.

"The bastards are rallying. Send a signal to pincer the village square," Captain Vale said to the senior signaler, a small man named Osiru who had a weasel-like face and breath like carrion.

"Yes, sir," Osiru replied, before lifting a horn to his mouth and blowing a trill of notes. He then stood steadily at the hilltop crest with both hands held in front of him and concentrated for several seconds. It annoyed Karisa that the man was taking so much time to formulate the invocation pattern; she could have flashed the message out in half the time. Finally, strobes of light flashed from his palms, signaling the message downhill. Osiru repeated the illumancy pattern two more times and then said to the company leader, "It's done, sir."

Skirmishes had broken out around the settlement as the outnumbered Vor warriors stood their ground against squads of soldiers. Most were just shot down with crossbows, but a few put up valiant fights despite bolts piercing their armor and trickling the life-force out of them.

However, Karisa was slack-jawed at a melee that defied the odds.

On a side street, five Ascorian sword-and-shield soldiers had surrounded a Vor warrior. The man wore a skirt of scalps and braids and brandished a giant double-bladed axe. Karisa expected he would fall after a brief clash like many of his other countrymen, but it became apparent that he was of an entirely different class.

Surrounded, the axeman ran forward and leapt into the air —three times his own height—and landed behind the three Ascorians who had been facing him; he then clove his battleaxe in a two-handed sweep and sliced through the chainmail-covered thighs of two of the infantrymen. They screamed as they collapsed to the ground, surrounded by their severed, bloodied limbs.

The third soldier turned to face the axeman gravmancer

and steadied her shield while staring aghast at her fallen colleagues, grabbing at the stumps of their legs as their lifeblood pumped away.

The axeman advanced on the soldier, lifted his axe overhead, and then swung it as though chopping a piece of firewood. Her shield rose to block the blow, but it was not enough. The battleaxe split the wooden shield and continued down to cleave her iron helm in two—blood and brain splattered and the body crumpled under the magically augmented attack.

Karisa bent over to retch as a wave of nausea struck. Morbid fascination compelled her to return her gaze to the Vor warrior and the remaining two soldiers.

One of the pair dropped her sword and shield and grabbed a crossbow from her back while her companion stepped in front of her with his sword and shield, trembling.

The Vor gravmancer yanked his axe out of the dead body, then sprinted a few steps and leapt into the air, hurtling out of sight over a weathered barn full of hay.

Karisa, from her hilltop vantage point, followed the axeman's trajectory to see him land on the other side of the building. The Vor gazed about for new opponents, but finding none, he jogged around the barn back to the blood-stained street.

The two soldiers were back-to-back, looking skyward, as though expecting the gravmancer to return over the building. The one with the crossbow pushed a bolt into the dorsal groove.

As if time had slowed, Karisa watched in horror as the Vor charged around the corner of the hay barn. He gained sight of his victims and leapt with his axe raised above his head, targeting the nearest.

The swordsman dodged, barely evading the executioner's strike, and stumbled to the side. The Vor followed up, sweeping his axe from the left, knocking aside the shield and chopping the soldier's head from his body. The decapitated corpse tipped to the ground as the head flew a short distance and splashed into a muddy puddle.

Karisa screamed and put her hands to her mouth, but her eyes remained glued to the melee below.

The last soldier, looking over her dead companion, raised her crossbow and shot the gravmancer in the chest.

He staggered back, staring at the crossbow, then lurched a few steps toward its owner—but thankfully, his legs buckled and he collapsed to the ground on top of his dreadful axe.

Even though the Vor was surely dead, the woman dropped her missile weapon and took up her sword. She stabbed the facedown body again and again. Four of her unit dead. She was lucky she wasn't the fifth.

Still nauseated by the horrific fight but relieved the gravmancer was dead, Karisa turned her gaze to the rest of the battle—and found the remaining Vors surrounded in the village square.

The few that had shields protected the rest behind them. A volley of crossbow fire dropped a few more Vors as bolts flew through unprotected legs or gaps in the shield wall. The remaining twenty or so warriors wavered and looked ready to break.

A movement from the woodland edge to the west caught Karisa's attention. The captain saw it too and cursed as a mass of Vor warriors spilled out of the forest and ran toward the village, their war cries loud enough to carry across the fields to their hill.

"It's a setup. They were hiding!" shouted Captain Vale. He then spat out orders to Osiru for another signal message.

There were several shouts from behind Karisa. She turned

and looked down the slope. It was the horse handlers pointing and shouting at a second band of ambushers who were ascending the hill toward the captain's retinue. The captain was such an obvious target on the hilltop. Arrows whistled as some of the Vor archers targeted them, but at this distance and uphill, the arrows flew wild.

The captain drew his sword and ordered his soldiers to form a shield wall against the approaching warriors.

The rat-faced signaler kept at his job and sounded his horn; this time, he signaled his message without hesitation to the troops below, warning them of the Vors racing toward them from the forest.

Karisa was terrified and looked around desperately. She had been with the infantry company only a few weeks and, prior to that, had had just six weeks of conscript basic training. Although she had easily passed the proficiencies for fitness, crossbow, and spear—and to the surprise of her instructors, displayed heightened prowess with the sword—her illumancy had been her ticket out of conscription. Fast-tracked to specialist training, she had expected this signaler's job to be easy: staying back from the fighting and perhaps lazing up in a signaler's tower for the rest of the year before resigning and returning to her acting troupe. Fighting off a Vor ambush was not what she'd had in mind.

A second flight of arrows whistled toward them. Most flew overhead but several thunked against the shield wall. The captain barked some orders, and the squad shuffled into crescent formation with the captain and the signalers behind them. Osiru drew a shortsword and a dagger. "Get behind me, lass. Get your sword out," he yelled at Karisa.

Moments later, there was a roar and a crash of metal as the Vor warriors threw themselves against the soldiers. The shields of the Vors smashed against the Ascorians' shield wall. Swords slashed and jabbed between gaps while warhammers and axes smashed at the wooden barricade.

The Ascorians were fresh, unlike the Vors, who had charged uphill. And with their added height advantage, they struck three of the attackers dead or incapacitated from wounds in the initial clash.

However, the shield wall parted in the center when two Ascorians fell to longsword thrusts and more Vors arrived to throw themselves into the fray.

Several of the war-painted warriors flanked the Ascorians, and the organized defense crumbled before the orgy of violence. The defenders were outnumbered and falling one by one.

Captain Vale entered the fray, striding toward a Vor who had struck down one of his sergeants with a warhammer and had raised it for a deathblow with its spiked end. He swung his longsword, striking the Vor with an upward sweep to the pit of his raised arm. The blade impacted chainmail. Although it did not slice through, the impact knocked the hammerman to the ground. Without hesitation, the captain dropped his shield and shifted to a two-handed grip on his sword. The Vor rolled to his front and began to rise with his hammer in one hand. Vale struck the man again: a diagonal overhead cut to the neck. The runic-forged blade severed the chainmail, enough for the edge to slice into the artery beneath. Blood spurting, the man fell to his knees, and the hammer dropped from his hand. The captain reversed his blade and plunged the sword tip down through the gap and into his thorax. The man spasmed in his death.

Three Vor warriors moved toward the two signalers cowering at the rear.

"Girl, listen to me. Focus a light blast to the right. I'll focus on the left." Osiru lifted his left hand up and concentrated.

Karisa raised both palms toward the snarling warriors. Despite her pounding heart and shaking hands, she was so practiced with invoking magic that it took little effort to trigger an emotion for illumancy—the memory of her little dog, Ella, sitting on her lap and staring up at her with big brown eyes sparked joy and happiness—where it mingled with terror. Armed with hatchets and shields, a stocky woman and two men advanced toward her.

She visualized and willed her palms to explode with light. It was as though a sun had suddenly birthed on the hilltop. So bright was the radiance, all three warriors brought up their arms to cover their eyes in reflex; the shields slipped from their grips and they stumbled around blindly.

Altogether, a dozen war-painted warriors, and one Ascorian, had been facing the signalers and were blinded by the light blast. They staggered and lurched. Some slid or fell down the steep hillside. And others, defenseless, were stuck down by opponents nearby.

Osiru ran forward and stabbed a blinded swordsman in the back, then turned toward another stunned Vor further along the hill.

One of the blinded hatchetmen continued staggering toward Karisa, but then tripped a few yards before reaching her. She watched in horror as he struggled to push himself back up, swearing and cursing. Although she had not spoken Vor in several years, she clearly understood his angry words and savage intent.

She had to do something before his sight returned.

She jabbed her sword at his heart, but the desperate attack merely scraped his breastplate and tipped him off balance. She cursed herself for not targeting his exposed face instead.

"You little shit! I'm going to rip your fucking arms off!" the man shouted as he staggered a few steps downhill. He fixed his gaze on her.

His threats angered her. She was not scared by his rant; he was just a pathetic man stumbling around. She had never killed anyone before, but she knew that, even against the burliest of warriors, a sharp blade in the right place would kill anyone.

With her sword in both hands, she lunged on her right foot and swung the blade at his face.

His eyes opened wide, seeing her intent. Unable to lift his shield in time, he flicked his head away from the approaching blade.

The attack clanged against his helmet and knocked him senseless.

Her opponent splayed before her, Karisa grimaced, but she knew no mercy in that moment and sought her finishing blow.

She slipped the sword tip beneath his chainmail skirt and pushed the three-foot blade upward with all of her strength. The weapon pierced his groin, his abdomen, and then his heart.

The Vor screamed and thrashed as her sword plunged in up to the hilt. Blood poured from the groin wound, and he sputtered bloody foam.

Karisa extracted her blade in a swift movement and then stepped back to stare at the dying man. A sense of exhilaration filled her.

She considered stabbing the man again but was distracted when Osiru came hurtling down the slope and knocked her down.

The weasel-faced signaler was lying on top of her and she saw that he was dead. A cut from the corner of his neck down into his chest opened up his internal organs to the air. Revolted at the mangled corpse, she writhed and pushed to escape the dead weight.

A warrior with a crocodile-hide cloak stood several yards uphill from Karisa, holding a double-bladed axe in both hands and sneering at his handiwork. He saw Karisa struggling under Osiru's corpse and walked over to her.

One leg was still stuck under Osiru when the killer grabbed her by the hair—although it was far shorter than when she was a civilian, it was an easy handful—and pulled her up; she screamed and grabbed at his wrist with both hands, having lost her sword somewhere during the tumble.

In a frantic motion, Karisa extended one hand toward the man's face and invoked another light blast—much less powerful this time due to her lack of focus—but he merely grunted at the bright flash and stunned her with a slap to the head.

In the Ascorian tongue but with a Vorosian accent, he said, "Where you going, darling?"

It was the term of endearment her father used.

That one simple word cut deep and rattled her, leaving her even more powerless than the strike to her skull had.

He dragged her up to her feet, let go of her hair, and then punched her in the stomach, and Karisa buckled to her knees. "That's for killing Ritter, even though he was a hell-born sack of crap."

The brute tipped her onto her back with his boot and stood on her forearm. The blood-stained edge of his axe pressed against her neck.

From the corner of her eye, she saw at least a dozen dead Vors. But also dead were the Ascorian command group, including Captain Vale and the senior signaler. Only she and one other captive, a terrified-looking soldier, had survived.

On the rear of the crest of the hill, she could not see the village, but her intuition told her that the battle there was just as bad.

Blood dripped from Karisa' brow and she ached all over from the beating she'd been given.

The Vor lifted his boot off her arm. "Watch out, she's a witch. Make sure she doesn't get up to any trickery," he said to two other warriors as they bound Karisa's wrists together, pulled her up, and then threw a bag over her head.

She sent her angry thoughts into the ether. *Damn you, Jaks, look what you got me into.*

Chapter 16

A Songbird in a Cage

Jaks—City of Dunberrin, Ascoria

Jaks entered Meila's prison cell and thanked the guard who had unlocked the door.

Immediately, a missile flicked into his vision, coming toward his face. He flinched, but not in time. The object struck him in the nose and bounced to the ground.

The cell filled with laughter as Meila grabbed for another ball of rolled up paper from her table. "Right on the nozzle," she cried out, then bounced another missile off his chest.

Jaks frowned at her, admonishing her playful antics. She was supposed to be his student. When he had been at school, infractions like this were punished with a swish of the cane, often several.

"Lighten up. It's not as though it hurt or anything," she said in a melodious accent.

He grinned, threw a ball back at her, and joined her at the table. How could he think harshly about anyone locked in a prison cell as small as his little room at the Academy? For her, this space was her entire existence: she slept, exercised, and idled away in this box of stone, surrounded by hundreds of similar cells throughout the prison building. A songbird in a cage.

Jaks vowed silently, he would do whatever he could to win her freedom. He would challenge her wrongful imprisonment, stop running from conflict, and right the injustice. ·

It was late morning, and her playground attitude promptly turned studious.

"Read this," she instructed him, pushing a children's picture book from a pile he'd brought a previous day.

He read her the story of a man chasing a mouse and destroying the house as the pursuit unfolded. As he spoke, she wrote quickly in a notebook; Jaks thought her writing looked strange, with too many curves and dots.

"I use this when you are not here. Practice," she said. Her accent was thick, with a lilt and rhythm that was both confusing and intriguing. "I like these pictures. Paper books are . . . What is the word? Not many? Not common? Rare? In my world."

He had visited her every day for the past three weeks and barely kept pace with her ability to learn. It turned out that she had already acquired many of the Ascorian language sounds from listening to the guards and possessed an astonishing, precocious talent for languages—she did not forget any word or grammatical construct that Jaks had explained.

She had quickly taken over the instruction process.

Instead of waiting for Jaks's lead, she used her blossoming Ascorian to direct the instruction how she wanted. He was glad for her decisiveness once he learnt that teaching a language was very different from just being able to speak it. She told him that she already spoke eight other languages—none of which he had heard of before.

And most bewilderingly, later that day, she told him she was from a different world.

"The stars. Some of them are planets like the one we are on —but very far away," she explained and pointed to her caged window. "I am from one of those planets."

He did not believe her. She was teasing him. The stars were light stones planted in the sky by God, or so he had been taught. He had never heard of planets.

Certainly, she looked exotic, different from any other person he had ever seen, and she once possessed items and a weapon of foreign manufacture, but it was madness to believe she had come from the stars.

They did not speak for a couple of minutes while Meila flicked through the picture book looking for material, the rustle of paper the only sound in the room.

They were alone in the cell. The prison guards had decided a week ago that their interactions were so dull that they would stop sitting in on the language sessions and let Jaks come and go as he pleased. Since then, Meila had relaxed and would sometimes brush his hand or forearm with her fingers; he thought the touches were by accident but wasn't sure.

Jaks took the silence as an opportunity to confess to her. So far, Meila seemed pleased with his visits and had not expressed any resentment or anger toward him about her capture. In fact, they had spoken twice about their first encounter, and she had complimented him on his bravery facing the dragons.

"I am sorry you are here. I did not want you to be arrested and put in prison." His remorse spilled out. "They think you are a spy. I want to help prove you are innocent."

"A spy?" she asked, her eyebrows creasing together.

"A thief who steals secrets," he explained further.

"And what is 'innocent'?"

"Someone who is not a thief."

She shifted her chair and faced him directly. "Why do you think I am *not* a spy?"

"Because you would be a terrible spy . . ." he said, waiting to see if he caused offense. She did not react. "You had no disguise. Your face is unlike any in Ascoria, it is so . . . delicate and strange, and your hair is so dark, it would stand out like a pillar of obsidian. Your clothes were peculiar, and people would have stared at you. Also, what use is a spy who could not understand our language? And lastly, why would you be in the mountains, in the middle of nowhere?"

Meila swept back a lock of hair behind her ear and quirked the corner of her mouth. "Maybe I am a terrible spy."

Jaks was distracted for a moment—seeing the exposed nape of her neck seemed peculiarly intimate to him—and then he coughed and gathered his thoughts.

"If you were a spy, you would have killed me and Minto when you saw us, in seconds. I saw what it did to the dragons." The memory of the monsters dismembered by the violent blasts appalled him.

She leaned toward him, suddenly concerned. "What happened to my weapon—my *handgun?*"

"I don't know. All of your items were thrown into a sack and brought back with us. I guess they're locked up around here somewhere." *So that was what it was called,* he thought, visualizing the deadly object she had shoved in his chest at one stage. He couldn't blame her in the circumstances.

Meila reclined and stared at the door, lost in thought for a few minutes. "What if we told the judge . . . magistrate, that I can prove my innocence based on the items I had at the campsite."

Jaks was shocked and thought that she meant to trick the

magistrate into giving her access to her weapon. "You can't mean to fight your way out—"

"You believe I should be free, though?" she said.

"Well, yes, but not by committing a massacre. It would be wrong. There must be another way." Jaks tensed. He wanted to help her, but not by evil means. "Is there anything else you could do, or show them, that'd prove that you are not a spy? What *were* you doing in the mountains?"

She stared at Jaks for a long minute, her face wracked by unspoken thoughts. Finally, she looked like she had come to a decision and laid her hands on the table.

"I crashed in an escape pod, the metal ship—I came from a starship," she said levelly.

Jaks sat stunned as Meila then elaborated on her claim that she came from beyond the sky, from a civilization of so many people that they were forced to live in gigantic buildings.

At first, he thought she was insane, even looking to the door in case her insanity was dangerous, but her earnestness and confidence in her descriptions kept him listening.

Over the next hours, in her broken Ascorian, she told him of concepts and technology that were truly alien to him, including the planets she had spoken of earlier, and ships that traveled between them. Although he understood little of what she described, the idea of an enormous universe with the possibility of life on other planets excited him. Somehow, it seemed right. If the night stars were suns like the one he saw in the day, then there must be millions of planets like the one they stood on. His eyes drifted as his imagination exploded with the possibilities.

Meila continued, her forehead furrowing as she drew drawings on loose bits of paper to accompany her descriptions: bulbous ships that housed thousands, buildings that covered miles of land, magnificent monuments, and bizarre animals.

There was great beauty to the clean lines and geometry of the objects created by her people. Her artistry could line galleries if patrons could look past the alienness of the content.

She stalled when she returned to where she started—describing her starship. "The *Mendhelsson,*" she said as she put down her pencil and stared at the drawing she had made of it. "It was a small ship. I commanded eight crew. We were . . . traveling between planets. It was home to me and Anton for many years."

"What happened?" asked Jaks, his elbows leaning on the table. He did not know who Anton was, but the sadness in her eyes told him that he was significant to her.

"A terrible accident . . . I cannot explain. I do not have the words," said Meila, leaving him hanging as her voice tapered off after speaking for almost three hours.

Dozens of questions arose at her vagueness, but it dawned on Jaks that he had made the breakthrough with Meila. The exact connection that he had promised Grandmaster Mulgrave. This was just the beginning. He had to find the mage and tell him of the incredible things she'd just told him, perhaps use it to prove she wasn't a spy.

"I have to go now, but I'll come back tomorrow," said Jaks. "Can I take these drawings to show my master?"

Meila nodded and rose from her seat. "You know, if I got my possessions back, or get back to the escape pod, I could show you real pictures from my world that I have stored."

"Yes, I'd like that." Jaks stood. He wanted to hug her but kept his arms to his sides on seeing the movement of a guard outside. This was still a prison.

The next day, Mulgrave came with Jaks to see Meila. The mage was so bemused by Jaks's report of Meila's claims and her drawings that he wanted to see her again. "She's been monkeying around with your head," he had said to Jaks.

She greeted them coolly as they entered her cell.

Mulgrave studied her.

"Hello, Grandmaster Mulgrave. How nice to see you again," she said, her diction perfect with a musical lilt.

She gestured to the chairs around the table.

The mage smiled and sat down. "Wherever you are from, you know your manners." He did not like to banter and got to the point. "What is all this mysticism you are telling the lad here?"

She sat down and opened her palms to him. "I do not know what mysticism is, but what I told Jaks is all . . ." She paused for a moment, searching for a word. "True."

Mulgrave studied her for a minute and then stroked his jaw. "Tell me about where you come from."

"It is a planet called Earth," she began.

Meila repeated what she told Jaks the previous day, but to a far more skeptical audience.

The mage regularly interrupted her and demanded more details for each of her claims and greater explanation of the concepts and places that she described. He stretched her nascent language skills. It was hard to gauge how much he believed, but after several hours, as the clattering of the meal cart sounded in the prison corridor, they both seemed to have exhausted their powers of speech and fell into a long silence.

The next morning, Jaks found the mage asleep at his desk, lying over copious notes that he had written overnight. "I don't know why I have a clerk when I do all the writing myself," Mulgrave said.

"Sorry, Master. If you'd told me, I would have stayed up—"

"Never mind." The mage's chair scraped as he pushed it back and stood. "She's not telling us everything. It may be the language barrier, but I think she is withholding something . . . maybe a lot," he said. "We're going back today. There is one more thing I need to know."

In the prison cell, Meila smiled brightly and thanked Jaks for the bunch of scented yellow flowers that he had plucked as he and the mage walked by the cathedral gardens on their way here. Guessing his intent, Mulgrave had scowled at him and scolded, "She's not your woman. She's a prisoner."

Jaks had blushed and sheepishly replied with a muted, "Yes, I know."

"Did you rest well?" Jaks asked her when they were seated at the round table. The flowers sat in her wooden mug in front of them.

Before she could reply, Mulgrave interrupted, "If you were freed, where would you go?"

They had not discussed her imprisonment the previous day, although Jaks had mentioned wanting to petition for her release sometime before. At that time, Mulgrave had dismissed the idea as ridiculous.

"Back to the mountains. To my escape pod. I need to be close to it if . . . when . . . the rescue crew arrives. It is the only way they can find me here."

Mulgrave looked at Jaks. "You didn't tell her the ship is at the Academy." It was more of a statement than a question.

Meila frowned and glanced at the younger man.

"How long until they come for you?" Mulgrave asked.

Meila sighed. "Many of your planet's years, unfortunately. Thirteen or more. This planet is very far from Earth. It takes many jumps and time to travel between each point. When our ship fails to return in seven years' time, the Agency may take a year or so to decide whether to send another mission. Then, if they do, it'd take a new ship about six years to find its way here."

"What'll happen if you stay in this prison here?"

"I would grow old. What else could I do?" She pursed her lips and stared at Mulgrave.

Keeping to his line of questions, he ignored hers and continued, "What do you know about the manufacture and materials of the vessel you were with—what you called your 'escape pod'?"

She was puzzled by Mulgrave's words and looked to Jaks, who took a minute to clarify the question for her.

"Why?" she asked.

The mage sat back, and his eyes flitted back and forth. It looked to Jaks as though the mage was trying to decide whether to reveal a hand of cards.

"You are either completely mad and what you say is just the ravings of a lunatic, or you are telling us the truth," said the mage.

"You think I am insane?" asked Meila, her accent thick and musical.

"If I had not seen your ship and the technology inside, I would not have believed you. But I have. And what you say is very convincing and explains a lot about why I can't comprehend its design." Mulgrave rubbed his chin. "So, how much do you understand about the manufacture of this technology and what can you teach us?" He leaned across the table. "If it is worth it, in exchange, we would petition your release—and you would come to the Academy and teach us all you know."

Jaks leaned forward. "Meila, the grandmaster knows the king personally—he could get you out of here," he said, louder than he should have.

Meila's look turned cold. She crossed her arms and furrowed her brow. "You will only help me if I help you?" Her voice became monotone, unlike her normal lilting voice, as though she were practicing the words for the first time. "I see things work here the same way they do back home."

Jaks hated the tension. He didn't know why she did not just say yes immediately. Surely, she could not be hiding something. "We are helping you. Please say yes?"

Chapter 17

Blackmailed

Meila—City of Dunberrin, Ascoria

Meila stood and paced the room. Indecision was a rare companion. It was not often that she was blackmailed for her freedom.

She needed to escape from this prison and had been willing to do anything—including murder—to escape. But the deal offered by the grandmaster contravened her code of duty. As a United Worlds Federation commander, she had vowed to never intervene with the politics of any colony that she was sent to evaluate; protocols dictated that no mission should contact or assist an Old Colony.

Violate her duty to the UWF and she would be court-martialed and decommissioned. Refuse Mulgrave's offer and she would waste away or die in this cellblock.

She paused mid-pace and looked at the mage. "What information do you want from me?"

"Everything. What metals make up this ship? What does the ship's machine do? How does it work? That would be the beginning." The bald mage paused. "Then, I would want to know, if the stars are planets, how do they stay up there? What keeps our world around the Sun? There are a thousand and a million questions I would ask."

Not difficult questions. Any UWF engineer could answer them. Her mission role, in addition to mission commander, had been engineering scientist, and she was as expert in that area as her husband in genetics and her other shipmates in their respective fields. It was not *whether* she knew the answers, but how sparingly she dished them out.

She was being offered a path to freedom. It was the best she could make of a poor hand. The only choice to take.

To hell with it, I'll deal with a court-martial when it comes.

She inhaled and triggered a memory implant. Reviewing information through her lens prosthesis she said, "The escape pod hull is an alloy of forty percent titanium, thirty-three percent lithtarite, seventeen percent xarcontate, and ten percent dothenide. I can tell you the alloying process and parameters and a million other details. But it won't help you, because you cannot recreate them here. The process requires elements and chemicals that do not even exist on this planet."

The old man remained silent and seemed to be waiting for more.

"That information is unhelpful to you, but I can teach you things that are far more practical and useful." She stood before Mulgrave and then said, "You do not know how *little* you know."

Chapter 18

Slave of the Vor King

Karisa—Magmatin Castle, Kingdom of Voros

Karisa did what she did best: act and play her part. Do it well and she would be a slave to just one man; fail, and she would be raped by many. The hungry gazes following her movements left no doubt of that in her mind.

She walked in a haze through the audience gathered in the throne room—blobs of shifting shadows and whispering shades held back by a lane of armored sentinels leading up to a dais.

Today, her performance was *The Seductress*.

Although trussed up like a child's doll in a tatty yellow dress, an uneven pearl necklace, and ragged slippers, her bearing was regal. She raised her chin high, squared her shoulders, thrust out her chest, and glided her steps.

The brute urging her along was the warrior in crocodile skin who had murdered her signaler-master and bruised her into submission: Hau Carric, a leader of a band of fifty warriors and a sycophant who made it clear to Karisa that she was a prize-mare to be offered to the Vor King.

After the ambush, and the raiding band had raised their

sails for the motherland, Carric had gone to reappraise his loot in the middle of the longboat.

He scrubbed her face with a rag soaked in saltwater and stripped her of her leather armor.

Standing naked and trembling on the deck, she had thought of running for the gunwale and throwing herself into the ocean but knew it would be suicide. She would get out of this alive. Nothing was more terrible than what her father had already done to her.

Carric cupped her face, fondled her breasts, and parted her buttocks and labia. He huffed a satisfied grunt, then pulled out a dagger and pointed it at his leering troops, men and women alike, and said, "This one is for the king. Not a hand on her."

He had then thrown her a thick robe to cover herself those several days ago.

And now, before the king of Voros, Karisa stopped at the foot of the dais.

Marble statues encircled her, a stone honor guard of chiseled animals: lion, bear, dragon, eagle, and some hideous tusked monster she'd never seen before.

Between each statue, living guards completed the circle: steel-clad warriors keeping the mob away from their monarch. The hall looked to hold a thousand comfortably, but that day swarmed with twice that number.

A dozen steps led up to a cushioned granite throne, on which reclined a long-limbed man adorned in silks and velvets and a plain circlet of platinum atop his head.

The crowd fell into a hush as she curtsied and bowed her head as she had been instructed by Carric.

"Sire. Along with killing over a hundred Ascorian soldiers and taunting the Ascorian on their coast, I present to you a gift from our raid," Carric said, an arm pointing at Karisa. "A beauty unlike any I have seen before." A sonomancy runestone in the mouth of the dragon statue magnified the volume of all sound around them, so although Carric only spoke to the king, his voice was projected throughout the hall.

Karisa was glorious, a nymphet slathered in sensuality. She had ripped the dress that Carric had given her to expose her long lithe limbs and elegant neck. Her face was perfectly symmetrical, eyes opal blue, lips bee-stung and ruby red, and her hair haloed in gold. She hoped she had not overdone her illumancer enhancements—too much and she could appear an over-painted whore.

But she need not have worried, because King Harek Raukela was clearly smitten.

"What is your name?" Harek leaned forward, his eyes wide and drunk on her.

"Karisa, sire," she replied. "My grandfather once lived in this very province—before you invaded it," she said, raising her gaze to meet his green eyes.

Harek laughed at her impudence and was soon echoed around the hall. "Rightly so. Magmatin would not join our union, so it needed to be forcefully . . . welcomed. But it has been all for the better. Isn't that so, Lord Magmatin?"

Karisa followed the king's gaze to a rusted iron cage to the side of throne room at his left—several listless forms huddled inside it—from which a crumpled man croaked out incoherently.

The king stood and strode down to her. Few men were taller than her, but the king loomed as tall as her father; however, unlike the latter's bearishness, Harek was a python: sinuous, smooth, and powerful with a crushing intensity. She drove back an impulse of fear and forced a smile.

He traced a finger from below her ear, down her neck, and

stared at her for several long seconds as he lingered in the hollow of her neck. "Well done, Torgue-commander."

Two women swept down the dais at the king's command and led Karisa out the back of the throne room.

Karisa imagined and visualized the welcome she would deliver to the king as she lay and waited for him in his private bedchamber under the watchful eye of a guard. She thought that the seduction scene from *Lord Porten's Lover,* a titillating play in which she had acted as an innocent housemaid, would be the perfect enactment to complete her seduction of the Vor king. After their introduction in the throne room, she felt supremely confident.

The bedchamber was high in a tower, she deduced from the view out of a window overlooking battlements below and then a city beyond.

She could see a crescent-shaped port with hundreds of ships bobbing under a sky dark with rain clouds, neighborhoods of gray buildings tangled with streets and alleyways, and in the distance, a peaked mountain with a craggy top.

Seduction was a tool demanded of her at the most desperate times of her life. The first time had been to stop her father abusing her mother—a trade: herself for her mother, one for one. The second was when she had run away and sought refuge with her mother's old acting troupe. The playhouse owner had been more than pleased to give her a roof over her head—as long as it was in his bed. And now, she was forced to seduce yet another man to prevent being sold as chattel.

Or have I been bought already? For a moment, her confidence wavered and a wave of sadness swamped Karisa as the bedchamber walls closed in on her. It was her prison. She was trapped, bound, and paraded like an animal.

Surely, there must be more to life than running, hiding, and being a plaything of men.

Footsteps approached the bedchamber door, and Karisa composed herself. She clambered onto the four-poster bed, arranged her yellow dress, and then leaned gracefully on one arm.

A guard pushed the door open and stood aside.

Harek entered the room and fixed his eyes on her.

Karisa looked up in simulated surprise and formed an O with her lips.

The king gestured at the guard to leave and went to a table of stoppered bottles to pour and then quaff a glass of amber liquid.

"Stand up," he commanded her, motioning her off the bed.

She stood before him and chewed on her lower lip, staring at his chest.

He reached for her face as though to caress her. Then his fingers were around her neck. He stared at her with cold, soulless eyes and squeezed.

She pulled urgently at his wrists, but his grip tightened, lifting her off the ground.

The strangle-hold suddenly loosened, and he threw her onto the bed, where she lay gasping for breath.

She felt the front of her dress rip from the neck down and then a sharp pain shear across her face.

He slapped her several more times, grunting with each blow.

It was then that her act plummeted into a nightmare of violence as the beast brutalized and violated her into the night.

In the morning, a guard dragged Karisa out naked into an adjacent chamber. Her mind was in a daze of fear and humiliation.

A silk-wrapped woman with red hair ushered Karisa to one of several velvet divans and snuggled a cushion beneath her head.

A moment later, a second woman appeared with a cloth and a steaming bowl in her hands. She tsked and tutted as she patted Karisa's face tenderly with the dampened cloth.

"You are strong, girl. You did not scream or cry," said the redhead. She grimaced at the black eye and red marks around Karisa's neck. "He is not a gentle man. Although he could have any of us, at any time, he is always as cruel as a lion toying with its prey. I don't know how you put up with it without making a sound. When he comes at me, I can't help but cry the whole time—I think he likes it the more I weep." She bent close to her ear and whispered, "He is a monster."

A third woman, also cocooned in silk, swept over and brought a mug to Karisa's lips. "Drink this. It is required after he gives his seed."

After a while, Karisa stirred from her daze.

The women fussed over her. They draped lengths of red and blue silk over her battered body and asked her which she preferred. They puzzled over her accent and asked her how an Ascorian girl knew the Vor tongue. They showed her the harem and asked which divan she liked.

But despite the courtesans' warm welcome, Karisa shivered in despair. *Damn you, Vixhana. Damn you, Jaks. What of your damn oath now?*

Chapter 19

The Ward

Jaks—City of Dunberrin, Ascoria

Seated at the table in her prison cell, as usual for their lessons, Jaks contained an annoyed expression as his student soundly demolished his opinion on what was turning out to be one of her favorite subjects: frogs.

His disgust for the slimy animals was as severe as that for any belly-crawling, bug-eyed creature—and he had said so. However, Meila's defense decried the reptiles as beautiful guardians of the swamps with glorious traits that put human beings to shame.

She was launching into the fourth minute of the wonders of frogs when there was a rattle at the cell door that caused her to pause.

Jaks sighed with relief.

A female prison guard walked in. Typically, she would enter yawning with a bored expression, but today she was twitchy and nervous.

"Er, well . . . King Silas wants to see you," said the broad-jawed woman, her face sharing the same surprise as Jaks's and Meila's.

It had been a week since Jaks had delivered their petition for Meila's release to the Royal Palace, and they had been losing all hope of getting a reply.

Jaks tagged along with Meila and her escort of three Royal Guards, unsure whether or not he had been invited.

They led her from the prison to the Royal Palace through an enclosed bridge he realized was the famous "Wailing Bridge." Fortunately, today they did not cross paths with anyone weeping and crying after being condemned to death by the king.

He got as far as the waiting room of the king's private offices before a Master Herald barred his way and pointed for Jaks to sit at the end of a row of citizen petitioners.

He lost sight of Meila as purple-robed sentries guided her into an antechamber of white marble and flowing banners, but not before glimpsing Grandmaster Mulgrave inside.

An hour later, the stocky mage exited the king's court room and pulled on Jaks's arm as he swept by. "Come. The king is following soon. We are to go ahead of him and reconvene at the Academy."

An impromptu visit to the Academy by the king was an event to be excited about, but Jaks was doubly excited to see that Minto was part of the Royal Entourage. The apprentice herald waved enthusiastically to Jaks from the back of the group of soldiers and officials gathered along the land bridge in front of the Academy.

The king and twelve gleaming knights dismounted their

horses while a throng of soldiers, advisors, and heralds, who had accompanied the entourage, waited on their king.

Meila was transported on a horse-drawn prison carriage by the same trio of guards who had escorted her from her cell. Her hands were cuffed in iron and her legs were in iron chains, heavy enough to cause her feet to drag.

Jaks frowned at the sight of the excessive bindings.

Along with Mulgrave and Tavis, he waited under the main gates of the Academy. Grandmaster Hazeldine, the Head of the Academy, and dozens of other mages had also stopped their work and had joined the welcoming party as word spread of the royal visit.

According to Mulgrave, the King had come to the Academy to see Meila reveal information in the escape pod to prove the existence of other worlds.

The entourage filed through the gate behind Mulgrave and the king; however, there was a pause when a raised word came from the king leading to Meila's leg bindings being hastily removed by an embarrassed guard.

Jaks moved to the side to let everyone pass. He'd catch up later; he was eager to speak to Minto.

Slightly plumper than when Jaks had last seen him two months ago, the apprentice herald was finely dressed in a blue-bordered uniform and short cloak.

They clasped hands and clapped each other on the shoulder.

"They must be fattening you up for the king's table. They've even trussed you up like a roasted goose," said Jaks, grinning at a triangular hat sitting atop his friend's head.

Minto grinned, plucked at his sleeves theatrically, and bowed. "I thank you for your gracious compliment, m' lord." He then laughed. "I didn't think you could get any taller . . . you'll be bashing your brains out on doorframes if you don't stop growing!"

"It's a family curse," Jaks joked and pulled Minto aside. "I've got so much to tell you. No, I haven't got the apprenticeship yet . . . but that woman in the mountains we found. This is all about her! I've been seeing her in the prison for the last month."

"I know, beanpole, I hear a lot of the goings-on around the place. But, listen . . ." Minto glanced around and grabbed Jaks's arms. "The Vorosian Empire is going to invade Ascoria."

"They've been saying that for years," said Jaks.

Minto shook his head. "This time, it's for real. Merchants and traders have been blockaded from Voros, and I heard a message read to the king with enemy troop and ship numbers. The king is sending even more reinforcements to the west coast as we speak." He paused, a look of concern crossing his face. "My master says there will be a call to arms. There's going to be a muster soon. You have to get a proper apprenticeship; otherwise, you'll get re-conscripted."

Jaks frowned as he considered Minto's warning. It was the king's prerogative to issue a call to arms where all fighting-age adults were summoned for active military duty. The only exceptions were people in essential jobs and their apprentices. At the moment, Jaks was a non-essential clerk and, likely in the eyes of the army, more useful holding a poleaxe or crossbow.

"No way. I can't go back to the army. To fight as a conscript against the Vors is a death sentence." Jaks faltered for a second. "Thanks for telling me, Minto. I have to work on it." *I have to get Tavis's apprenticeship. I have to get rid of him somehow.* His thoughts then turned to Karisa. *She was right. We should have run away to Faucony.*

"Look, we have to catch up with the group. We should try to meet again soon," Minto said.

In the covered courtyard of the Academy, the clang of anvils and thump of machinery continued at the hands of those who had been unable to stop midway through their creations to ogle at the king.

When the entourage arrived at Meila's metal ship, King Silas said a word and the rest of Meila's restraints came off.

She clambered in without hesitation.

A guard went to grab her, but the king waved him away, then leaned over the lip of the metal ship to watch her. The grandmaster joined him.

Saying to the guards that he was "with the grandmaster," Jaks pushed up on the opposite side of the ship's opening—and found himself face to face with the king of Ascoria.

King Silas Montras had a long face, firm jaw, steely eyes, and silver hair. There was no indication of his status other than a gold collar made of small interlinking shields embossed with major insignias of his realm.

"Oh, hello there," the king said in a reedy voice that Jaks did not expect from such a distinguished-looking man.

Jaks turned red as soon as he realized his gaffe. "Sorry, my king. I didn't mean to, to—"

"This is the boy I told you about—the tutor," Mulgrave said. "He is a bit excitable."

"Understandable," Silas replied and winked at Jaks. "Shall we get on with it, then?" He redirected his gaze into the pod.

Meila was absorbed with the panel suspended on the metal arm. Symbols and images lit up and flickered across the surface as her hands slid and tapped at inlays on the pod's walls. "This is the taskwall. I enter requests through the keys, and they go to the onboard AI under my seat and send images to the panel."

The images changed too fast for any of the Ascorians to comprehend.

"Here," she said a few seconds later.

The panel displayed a picture of her with eight men and women, all dressed in navy-blue uniforms, standing in front of a large window. On the other side was a sleek silver squid-like object with contours similar to the escape pod. It was completely enclosed and seemed to float in the night. "That's my starship, the *Mendhelsson*," she said. Behind the ship were huge extrusions and dark arms that Jaks couldn't make sense of. And, in the background, a glowing circle of large blue, brown, and white patches.

"This is a pre-launch picture. Those are my crew. Those are parts of the space station you can see there. And that is Earth."

She then showed hundreds of pictures including immense buildings, land and air vehicles, sophisticated objects, and sweeping views of cities that extended beyond the horizon.

Last, she played recordings that revealed minutes of life itself: people talking, laughing, eating, hugging, and living life on her planet and in her starship.

Once he saw the wondrous images, Jaks lost any doubt of the reality of Meila's claims. The amazed expressions on the faces of both the king and Mulgrave revealed they must have felt the same.

As Meila's eyes misted over as she watched the recordings, Jaks wondered what she felt, severed from her past life, stranded here in their world.

The next day, Mulgrave received a Royal Decree declaring Meila his personal ward. She was to be transferred to his guardianship at the Academy, where technically, she was to remain a prisoner. The letter stated that if she complied with the demands of the king and Grandmaster Mulgrave's to supply knowledge, and did not attempt to escape custody for two years, she would be freed and released.

Jaks read the document several times, then whooped and danced around.

Mulgrave chuckled, seemingly infected by his clerk's joy. "We did it boy."

Only Tavis was not pleased with the news and went back to his room with a soured expression.

Chapter 20

Confrontation in the Library

"You're no hero," said Tavis, sneering at Jaks from a dark corner of the library. "Just because you got her to talk, doesn't make you any better than me. I could have taught her Ascorian—faster than you did—if I hadn't been helping the grandmaster with real work."

Mulgrave and Jaks had returned that afternoon from the prison, bringing Meila back with them.

When they had told her that Grandmaster Mulgrave was now her guardian, and that she would move to the Academy, Jaks had expected a more exuberant response. But she had just blinked at them a few times and then picked up her notebooks and said, "Let's go."

Mulgrave had converted another office on Jaks's corridor for her use. "Guard her close," he had said, creating an awkward moment between Meila and Jaks, who wondered at his seriousness.

So when Tavis ambushed him in the library, Jaks was distracted by thoughts of his new neighbor.

"Never said I was a hero," Jaks said. Tavis's presence brought Jaks back to the present and reminded him of his bigger problem: how to wrest Tavis's apprenticeship away from him.

Although Jaks felt like a hypocrite for going back on his word—he had told Tavis that he would not steal his position—the circumstances had changed with the threat of re-conscription.

"You are wasting your time here. You'll never get my apprenticeship, you slimy bootlicker." Tavis sheathed his hands in flames, showing off his pyromancy. "I've seen kids like you before, with your little tricks. It's not real magic, it's a vagary of childhood. And when your pimples clear, you'll find that you are just as vacant of magic as your mother is vacant of life." The apprentice snuffed out his fire-hands and snorted derisively.

Jaks's face colored, his ears burned, and the hairs on his neck stood up. The reference to his mother was tasteless but hit a sore point with him. Tavis was trivializing his mother's death.

They faced off between two towering bookshelves.

The veins in Jaks's neck throbbed as he clenched his fists and glared at Tavis.

The apprentice wrinkled his nose and scowled. "I'm just telling you the truth. You should leave the Academy today and save yourself the embarrassment," Tavis said. "The grandmaster doesn't need both of us; it's obvious he'll keep me and get rid of you eventually. We don't need you here."

They were interrupted by a female voice from the center of the library, Meila's lilting accent. "Jaks, there you are. I have been looking for you. Oh, pardon me . . . ." she said, as though only just realizing the apprentice mage was also present. "I did not see you there, Tavis. Anyway, come here and help me now, Jaks." She turned from apologetic to commanding in an instant and gestured at Jaks to follow her back to their corridor.

Jaks glowered one last time at Tavis, then went to follow Meila.

The apprentice made a parting shot at his opponent. "Run to your mistress, slave boy."

Jaks slammed the library door behind him.

Meila stood in the corridor, waiting with folded arms. "What was that about?" she asked.

Jaks slapped the back of his hand into the palm of the other. "Tavis hates me and wants to get rid of me. He thinks I want to steal his apprenticeship."

"Is it true?" she asked.

Jaks pushed back from the wall as his anger waned. "It wasn't at first, but it is now—an apprenticeship is the only way I can avoid being re-conscripted."

Jaks told her of the incidents with Baden and Tavis, describing the dormant magic that had lashed out to defend him. "It's the rarest of magics, but I need proper training to use it."

He sighed and then told her about the history between Tavis and himself and his fears of a war. "Raiders from the Vor empire have been hitting the coast for years, but my friend Minto says the king expects they are about to invade."

"So, if the kingdom is about to be invaded, why are you so desperate to become an apprentice?" asked Meila.

"It's the only way I can escape a Conscript Legion; they'll be the first to be thrown to the dogs. Imagine a bunch of old men and bumbling draftees like me fighting together. We'd be slaughtered."

"And you think the grandmaster must choose between the two of you?"

"A mage only has one apprentice," he said. "That's how it is with masters and apprentices in every occupation."

She paced for a minute, then turned to Jaks with a frown. "I think your problem is not Tavis—it is you." She pointed a finger at his chest.

"Huh? Tavis has had it out for me right from the day I got here. Just this morning, he threatened me and told me to leave the Academy," Jaks said in a defensive tone.

"Your problem is that you can't even do magic properly. It is not you against Tavis. It is you against *you*. If you can show that you can use this magic . . . this electromancy . . . properly, the other master, Cranbrook, you say, has already said it would be the first time in eighty years that anyone has had it. You don't think they would throw away a once-in-a-lifetime opportunity to have a fully-fledged electromancer, do you?"

"Well, I suppose not—"

"If you can show that you have this rare power, they'll find you an apprenticeship. You don't have to steal Tavis's apprenticeship. You only think that because he thinks that. You don't have to worry about whose apprentice you might be. The fact that Mulgrave spent so much effort to get me . . ." Her voice drifted as she struggled for a word. "To *acquire* me, for a chance at my knowledge, tells me he would do even more to help you— if you can show him electromancy." Meila pointed a finger at Jaks. "You should stop worrying about Tavis and worry about finding out how to do magic."

Meila made a convincing argument. This antagonism between him and Tavis was a waste of time. He nodded reluctantly. "You are right. I need to focus on the magic."

But the realization did little to lift the dark shroud over him as he recalled the failures he had experienced with invoking.

Jaks then helped Meila finish rearranging her room. "We can move the junk you don't want into one of the other rooms next door," he said.

She paused and puffed away a layer of dust from a wicker basket. "This room is smaller than my prison cell."

"Well, at least you can go out and walk around whenever you like," said Jaks. "The grandmaster said that I can escort you if you want to leave the building and see more of the city. In fact, he said I *had* to accompany you if you wanted to go anywhere outside."

"Don't worry, I will not run away. I have nowhere else to go," she said to assure him. "But yes, show me around. It's nice having such freedom after months in prison." She smiled at him.

He led her on a tour of the hallways, libraries, and labs, sharing as much as he could about their common home; eventually, they ended up in the museum courtyard, standing at her escape pod.

"This is the only link I have left to my people," Meila said and clambered into the pod.

He peered in to see what she was doing and was curious to hear her speaking to herself in a foreign language.

"What are you doing?" Jaks asked, trying to make sense of the images flickering on the display panel in front of her.

She swept a wisp of hair out of her face but did not respond as she continued her tasks.

Jaks wondered if the pod itself could be used to escape. Was she about to fly away?

The pod did not move, and eventually, she sighed. "The emergency beacon is working perfectly—there is enough power to last three hundred years. If they don't come by then, I'll probably have forgotten about Earth anyway—or have been murdered by one of you barbarians."

"Three hundred years? You'd be dead of old age." Jaks wondered whether she had translated her words correctly.

She looked at him and smiled. "You pup! I'm already one

hundred and twenty of your planet's years old." She laughed at his astonished gape. "I hope to live a few hundred more yet."

"No. I don't believe you," he said. "You're jesting me."

But she was focused again inside the pod and busied herself with the panel screen. An image settled on the screen; it looked similar to the background of the very first picture she had shown the king and Mulgrave earlier. A beautiful round disc, blue and green, with white patches.

"That is your planet. We call it Maya," she said.

It was a stunning picture that undulated as he watched an overhead map of their world. After a minute, Jaks was distracted from the panel by a pained look creasing Meila's face—a tear rolled down her cheek and she wiped it with the back of her hand.

"What's wrong?" he asked her.

She stared at the panel for a while and replied in a deadpan voice, "Four escape pods from my ship made planetfall." She stopped to wipe her eyes. "But over the past few months, they've all disappeared . . . I can't find any life signs of my crew. Even Anton, I can't find his implant signal anywhere."

She climbed out of the pod and shuffled off in a daze.

Jaks glanced at the panel.

The display blinked a single lonely dot.

Chapter 21

Guns

Meila—The Academy of the Arcane

Meila awoke to screeches outside her window. Two blue dragons lashed about as a furious ball of teeth and claws on the rocks below. An injured fish flopped nearby, inching toward the waves. The size of hawks, the two creatures were far smaller than the bronzes that she and Jaks had encountered in the mountains, but seemingly just as loud.

She pushed the window open, leaned out, and yelled at them.

Ignoring her, they continued their struggle for several more seconds. One then snatched the fish and flew away toward the wharves as the other winged after it in pursuit.

There was a quiet knock at her door.

She pulled the window shut and waited.

Bony knuckles tapped louder.

So used to the prison guards entering without notice, she had forgotten the courtesy. "Oh, yes . . . come in," she said.

Jaks creaked the hallway door open and peered in. His eyes

widened and he pulled back. "Sorry, I didn't realize you weren't dressed."

In nothing but a clerk's shirt, she grabbed her leggings draped over a chair and pulled them on.

"What's going on?" she said as she pulled the door wide open and threw on a green cotton jacket similar to Jaks's own.

"Grandmaster Mulgrave wants us downstairs . . . he's going to give you a tour of the Academy," Jaks said, seemingly embarrassed at seeing her naked legs. She was amused. *So naïve . . . surely, he has experience with women?*

A half hour later, down in the Metals lab, Grandmaster Mulgrave greeted her and Jaks. Tavis stared at the floor glumly.

"I'll show you around some of what we do, and then you must tell me what you can contribute," said Mulgrave. "I expect great things."

The old man did not waste any time. Deliver or go back to the prison. What could she give them that would prove her useful?

They began with the grandmaster's own team of magesmiths: Master Samis, the bug-eyed forgemaster, and his apprentice, the pretty Olire; Master Ivaleen, the wizened firemancer, with her journeyman, Benny, who never made eye contact; and Master Randell, obsessed with creating the perfect signaling machine.

Last were Doeg and Shazair.

A honey-skinned man turned from his bench as they approached. The bench was so covered in hammers, chisels, files, rulers, pliers, clamps, stones, screws, nuts and bolts, and metal panels that Meila was sure everything would slide off if anything else were added.

A woman with tight curls and a round face sat opposite him and looked up from her task of polishing a runestone.

"Master Doeg and Journeyman Shazair have a special interest. Why don't you show us your project?" said Mulgrave.

The man nodded and picked up a small square of metal. "A multi-cell sourcestone storage unit . . ." He slid open a cover on the container. Runestones packed the interior. "It's part of a battle flamer that we're designing."

"Flamer?" she said.

Doeg grinned. "Blasts whatever you point it at."

Meila stared at the mountain of parts on the workbench but could not see a weapon in the making.

Doeg plucked two stones out of the container. Shaped and polished, they were perfect cubes. "There are only twenty master firemancers in Ascoria, and only four battle-trained. So, we research ways to allow pyromancy to be used more widely. We use sourcestone devices, but most stones are so small that they need frequent recharging and generate weak magic."

Sourcestones, or as they were more often called, "runestones"—Jaks had told her during one of their lessons—were commonly used as light sources. Streetlamps, ceiling lights, chandeliers, and hand torches held the magical stones that could be purchased in any market or luminary shop. Any of thousands of people who were gifted with illumancer powers could rejuvenate the stones—for a price, of course. It made sense for families to store dozens of the stones in drawers and cupboards, ready to replace dimming lights.

Although other forms of magic were sometimes used—firestones to start cooking hearths, gravstones to lift granite blocks on construction sites, and sonostones for the hard of hearing—those types were rarer because of fewer mages of the corresponding power.

Doeg flicked one sourcestone to Jaks, who clapped his hands

around it. The cold, gray stone was exceptionally well cut, highly polished, and barren of any lettering or marks.

The Fauconian offered another of the stones to the foreign woman.

"*Mayatite*," Meila said unexpectedly, as the runestone tumbled into her hand like a dice cube. "Unique to this planet alone. Either formed or deposited in a single event millions of years ago. Its properties are unlike any other known mineral . . . conducts like a metal but with an internal structure that changes dynamically like a living creature."

Master Doeg, Jaks, and Tavis stared at her as though she talked gibberish. Only the grandmaster followed her.

"You say it's alive?" Mulgrave asked.

Meila shook her head. She pincered the stone between two fingers and narrowed her eyes. "My geologist . . ." She stopped and sucked in her breath, eyes darting around the group.

"Geologist?" Jaks repeated the unfamiliar word.

"Never mind. Um," Meila said. Say too much and it would become clear that the *UWFS Mendhelsson* was doing more than just traveling past their planet. *They'll suspect we were observing them. They'll demand to know why.*

"How do you know so much about them?" Doeg looked at a runestone as though seeing it for the first time.

"Just general knowledge . . ." Meila said. Her eyes shifted quickly. "It's everywhere. The mayatite, that is. Dust particles. Pebbles. Boulders. Mountains of the stuff."

"Mountains!" Shazair interrupted, pausing her polishing to gape at her. "Where? No one has ever found a source that size."

"Beneath the sea," said Meila. Then turning away from the astonished woman, she said, "My hypothesis is that mayatite allows the creation and manipulation of energy out of nothing . . . what you call magic."

"The sea. I told you so," said Shazair, pointing a finger at Doeg.

Doeg continued as though hearing none of the last comments. "So, if you shape and polish the stones and then line them up in a row, they'll store far more magic. And here's the topper, if you stack them tightly together, they'll channel as much power as a master mage."

"If you don't blow us up first," said Shazair.

"Don't mind my wife—she's a killjoy," said Doeg, rolling his eyes.

"*Do* mind my husband—he's a daredevil," the woman replied, squinting at her partner.

"Come see our prototype," said Doeg, as he winked at Shazair fondly.

In the soot-covered chamber, a long metal contraption resembling a ballista with a steel tube but stripped of its limbs stood within an iron frame. Doeg inserted the sourcestone container that he had brought from the workbench into a cradle atop the device. "The full versions will be attached to frigates and shoot fire at attacking ships," he explained.

"Stand back," the master firemage warned. Meila joined the grandmaster and the two younger men behind a chest-high wall at the back of the room.

The Fauconian pointed the tubular end of the weapon at a sooty wall on the opposite side of the chamber and touched the sourcestone pack with his fingers. *Whoosh.* A fierce red flame shot out the front of the weapon.

A back-wave of heat smothered Meila. The fiery tongue scorched the far wall for several seconds.

"That's about half-power. A charged sourcestone pack will reach thirty yards and give about thirty seconds of flame," explained the pyromancer. "More than enough to set an enemy ship afire or burn down a dozen warriors."

Meila screwed up her face. "A flamethrower. Dirty weapon. So imprecise and short-ranged."

Master Doeg crossed his arms and raised his chin, clearly not pleased at her comment.

Don't be so critical, she thought to herself. *I need to prove my worth to them.* "However, I can see how useful it could be . . . at your level of technology," she added pathetically, doing little to repair her initial snub.

"Well, I think it's impressive," said Jaks. "I wouldn't want to be toasted by that."

"The design of the sourcestone pack is your limiting factor." Meila saw an opportunity to improve Doeg's weapon and pointed at the container. "If it follows the same principles as electrical battery cells, as it sounds like it does, I can help you calculate a setup that could double . . . triple the fire power? We'd have to develop a method to accurately measure mayatite power and start with some base calculations."

Doeg nodded his head and agreed enthusiastically. She could see none of them understood much of what she'd said, but they were open-minded. *Not too proud to take advice*, thought Meila.

"Good, good." Mulgrave took charge again. "But before you get ahead of yourself, come see what else we do here." Like an ambassador, he appeared keen to show off their feats, but the calculating look in his eyes betrayed his expectation for a trade that favored his needs.

The runic furnace glowered and roared like a caged beast at the heart of the Academy. Coal-shovelers fed the hungry beast and magesmiths worshipped with a chorus of hammers and anvils at its unholy maw. Blistering heat smothered anyone who dared go near.

Meila stopped as her eyes dried in the heat and sweat beaded her brow.

"Are there always so many workers here?" she asked Mulgrave as they neared the forges around the furnace. Dozens of men and women in leather aprons and leggings glistened with sweat and pounded away at lengths of glowing metal.

"A busy time. The Order of Nightwraiths put in an order for a dozen more whisperblade swords last week and requisitions from other divisions are coming in fast. There will be war soon. Damn Vors aren't happy with their own country, now they want ours," replied Mulgrave.

Five workshops encircled the runic furnace with a sixth space dedicated to the shovelers feeding the roaring inferno. The grandmaster stopped at the entrance of the closest workshop and nodded to the forgemaster.

The man looked up briefly between strikes of his hammer against a length of glowing metal. Another magesmith held the blade fast with a pair of tongs and was invoking a continuous wave of fire that spread over his bare hands and the steel.

Meila stared open-mouthed. "Why aren't his hands blistering?"

"Mages are not harmed by the magic they invoke, and if the tongs get too hot, he can dampen the heat in the metal. A mage can both produce and negate energy of their type." Mulgrave peered at the blade. "That particular blade has sourcestone dust crushed into the steel and will have a stone in the pommel. The stones can be invoked by anybody with training, even without mage abilities," he said.

"What about other types of magic?" Meila leaned into the workshop but retreated when the forgemaster snapped at her for getting too close. Moisture dampened her forehead, and she loosened her tunic.

"Any magic can be forged into an object. Flaming weapons, grav-balanced greatswords and hammers, blinding shields, and even armor that casts the wearer into shadows. Grandmaster Graywish once made a broadsword that invoked images of a dozen swaying cobras. When you held it, it looked like a handful of giant snakes poised to strike!"

At the next workshop, a handsome, muscular woman, near Mulgrave's age, came out to speak with them. She glistened with sweat, and ash smeared her face. "Mulgrave. What have you here?" She looked curiously at Meila.

"Grandmaster Arolee, meet my ward," Mulgrave said as he introduced the two women. To Meila, he said, "Arolee is the only triple mage in Ascoria."

The woman's gaze remained locked on Meila, and she reached out a hand to touch her face, as though she were a fragile object, but stopped and snatched it back mid-gesture. "You are exquisite. I wish I could cast you."

Meila frowned at the curious comment and responded instead to Mulgrave's statement. "Triple mage?"

Arolee gasped and stared at Meila's mouth with an incredulous look on her face. "Your tones are perfect. I bet you sing like an angel."

Mulgrave replied, "She commands fire, gravity, and sound. The only magics that she doesn't control are light and electricity."

Finally, Arolee snapped out of her reverie and stared into Meila's eyes. "Are you gifted?"

"We don't have magic where I come from."

"No magic. Ridiculous. There's magic everywhere."

"Not where I'm from," repeated Meila.

"I suspect you are gifted, though," persisted the female mage.

Mulgrave coughed and interrupted, "What is this you're working on?" He gazed at a suit of steel plate armor large enough for a horse.

Two of Arolee's assistants were working on the rear part of the armor, but it was the helm that demanded attention: a head cover molded to the face of a snarling demon complete with sharpened teeth, blazing eyes, and pointed horns.

"It's hideous." Mulgrave shook his head.

"Thank you," said Arolee. "It's also rune-forged to be as light and flexible as leather." She shifted her attention to Mulgrave and went to stand beside him.

"Is it horse armor?" Jaks asked as he and Meila moved around to appreciate the other side.

"Warlion armor. The beasts usually only tolerate leather armor, but this suit was commissioned for Pride Queen Kassindle by her rider. It even has a sonomancy runestone in the helm that augments her roar tenfold. Can you imagine a steel-clad warlion bounding toward you, screaming like hellspawn?" Arolee stroked the armor as though the beast were already inside it.

The last stop on their circuit took them from the forges to a fenced-off area of the courtyard. A flat-bottomed boat levitated several yards in the air at the center of the clearing, tethered by ropes to four granite blocks. The boat wobbled midair as Jaks and the rest of their group approached.

"Hazel?" Grandmaster Mulgrave called from the fence line.

The boat dipped backward suddenly, and a chorus of swearing and curses poured out from within. A voice shouted the others to order, and the rest of the vessel tipped down until it leveled off at chest height.

A woman with a head of wild curls and a heart-shaped face peered over the boat's side at the visitors. Three younger mages sat inside, the one in the front admonishing the two at the back.

"Shut up, you three," snapped the older woman, not looking so generous at that moment. "Put her down."

The wooden hull crunched to the dirt, and the mages climbed out. The younger three paced about, stretching their legs. The eldest came to the fence and picked up a clipboard lying there.

"Work in progress." Mulgrave offered a hand to the woman. She waved it away.

"Four gravstones aren't enough. Too vulnerable to incongruences in power. I'm thinking I'll have to double the number."

"Grandmaster Hazeldine's latest project. A reinvented grav-flyer." Mulgrave nodded at the plain-looking boat sitting abandoned.

"Previous flyers were limited by a single gravmancer and a sail," said Hazeldine. "With sourcestones and multiple gravmancers, I can get bigger ships into the air. And with more grav sources, I can propel the vessel in any direction without the need of a sail . . . theoretically. Getting it to work properly is proving more difficult." She pulled a pencil out of her wild hair and marked something on the clipboard.

"How do you coordinate direction?" asked Meila, climbing over the wooden barrier and examining the boat.

Hazeldine frowned. "I shout at them."

Jaks stifled a laugh.

Meila shook her head. "You'll need a better system than that. I could help you with a communication system for your boat. I used to design ships."

Hazeldine nodded approvingly but was interrupted by Mulgrave before she could question Meila.

"Later, later. One thing at a time, lass," said the bald mage. "It's time we sat down and talked about what you can do for me first."

Back in the lab, Meila, Jaks, Tavis, and Mulgrave gathered around a workbench next to a tall window. Rain pattered against the glass, creating tiny rivulets of water that dissolved the salt-crust on the outer surface. The sky was dark with storm clouds and the harbor swayed with several fishing boats urgently returning from sea.

"So, where do we start?" Mulgrave opened his hands as though to receive something. "You've seen what we do here. What can you do beyond that?"

"For your era, it's commendable that you can manufacture sheet metal, signaling machines, weavers, and printing presses . . . but disgraceful that you have little knowledge of chemistry, physics, engines, or even steam power." Meila got up and stood behind her chair. "You compensate for some of that with magic." She shrugged. "Maybe that's why those areas are behind." The sourcestones came to mind.

"Chemistry, physics?" said Mulgrave.

"Sciences that I could teach you but that would take years to benefit from. The question really is, what do you want from me?"

"Practical things. Weapons, armor, machines," said Mulgrave, steepling his hands in front of his chin.

"War machines," she said, "a warmonger." She shook her head disapprovingly.

"War is inevitable. In the likelihood that the Vors invade, they'll field an army far larger than ours. If we lose against them ..." Mulgrave said in a somber voice.

"I get it. I lose too. My fate is caught in yours," Meila said. She stared out the window as though searching for something. Eventually, she sighed, resigning to the most obvious technological advance she could think of, and said a single word.

"Guns."

Meila described and drew diagrams of muskets and cannons, the most basic of propellant-based weapons she knew of.

"You have the metal-working capability to produce the weapons, but you know nothing about propellants to fire them with," she said.

"Was it a . . . what did you call it . . . a *gun* that you used against the dragons that attacked us in the mountains?" asked Jaks.

Meila continued, talking over the apprentice's question. "Yes, it was a gun, of sorts. Similar idea, except mine used technology that is impossible to even consider making here." She twirled the pencil that she had been drawing with and tapped it on her drawings. "Gunpowder, however, requires only three chemicals. You already have charcoal sitting out there in the courtyard. It shouldn't be hard to source the other two."

"What do these guns do?" asked Mulgrave.

"Simply put, the explosive power of black-powder guns can shoot lead balls at extreme speeds that can penetrate even steel plate armor."

A doubtful look crossed Tavis's face. "Penetrate plate . . . not grav-forged plate." He shook his head. "Explosive. This powder sounds dangerous. Is it safe?"

"There are strict rules that we would have to enforce during manufacture and storage to make it safe," Meila said.

Mulgrave rubbed his hands together and grinned. "Yes, this sounds like just the thing. If it could be reliably used by common soldiers, it could change—"

"It *would* change warfare as you know it," Meila finished. She looked down at her drawings of the muskets and cannons scattered over the table and grimaced as if in pain. "If I ever get back to Earth, I'll be court-martialed for this."

"Where is the gun that you spoke of? That you fought dragons with?" Mulgrave looked at Meila and Jaks.

The pair looked at each other. Jaks replied, "Last I saw, it was taken away with her other possessions when Ranger Cromer arrested her. I assume they were all handed over to the prison."

"I'll see if I can track it down. It may very well still be there." Mulgrave looked back to the drawings scattered over the bench. "In the meantime, how long would it take to start making this gunpowder?"

"If we can find reliable sources for saltpeter and sulfur, we might be able to start mass producing quantities in a year or so."

"A year? We don't have years. The Vors already hound the coast and could invade at any time. The threat is high enough that the king is enacting a province cordon tomorrow," said Mulgrave.

"A province cordon?" asked Meila.

"No one will be able to travel out of a province except with a military permit. First step toward a call to arms. It prevents people from fleeing conscription. I know King Silas, and if he is calling a cordon, he will have strong convictions of an impending invasion."

"That might be so, but we won't be able to create workable guns overnight. It will take time," Meila said. "Time to find the chemicals and materials, time to develop a mass-manufacturing process, and time to perfect them. Ideally, we'd rifle the weapons but that would take even longer." She scribbled numbers on a new piece of paper as she spoke. "Solving the gunpowder recipe might only take a few months. But the whole process, mass gunpowder production *and* a safe weapon manufacture would take at least . . . twelve to twenty months."

She leaned over the table and stared at the bits of paper scrawled with diagrams and numbers.

"Are there other weapons like this that we could make faster?" Mulgrave asked, sounding deflated after his initial excitement at the gun concept.

"Gunpowder would be the easiest and fastest to get up and running. Unless . . ." Her face darkened, and she turned toward the window, tapping her chin. "I have another idea, but I need some time to think. I'll go back to my room for a while."

Mulgrave nodded and directed Tavis to gather up the papers.

Chapter 22

The Letter

Jaks—The Academy of the Arcane

After Meila wandered up the staircase, Mulgrave turned to Jaks. "Before I forget again, a letter came for you late last evening. It's on my desk; go get it if you like."

Jaks hurried after Meila, but by the time he caught up with her, the door to her room was swinging closed.

The letter had his name scrawled on the envelope and lay on the grandmaster's desk under the stuffed cat. He had hoped it was from Karisa, updating him of her experiences and to assure him that she was well; however, the handwriting looked more like Vixhana's messy scribble.

Back in his room, he tore the envelope's seal and unfolded the parchment inside. It read:

Jaks,

Karisa is missing. Her company ambushed during a Vor raid on Finstaf coast.

One hundred and three of her company are dead. Eight missing.

I am back in Dunberrin City on royal protection duty.
Will let you know if I hear anything more.
Vixhana

Meila appeared at his door. "What's wrong?"

Jaks had not realized he had called out, and only now heard himself saying, "No," over and over.

"My sister, Karisa . . . the Vors," said Jaks. Then, composing himself, he described the contents of the letter.

Meila replied in a placating tone, "At least she wasn't among the dead. There's a chance she might have run off or hidden somewhere."

"Oh, God, I hope so. It was me who convinced her to join the regular army. If she had stayed as a conscript instead, she would have been doing light duties or training away from the coast. I told her she would be better off as a signaler and then she could resign after just one year . . . what an idiot I am." Jaks leaned against a wall of empty shelves and placed his forehead against an edge.

Meila stepped closer. "It's not your fault—"

"She has been through so much already. She trusted me. I've already failed her so often, and I pushed her into danger again . . . and now she's gone. It *is* my fault." Jaks thumped a fist against the wall, shaking the shelves.

"I've got to help her. I've got to find her," he continued. "I made an oath to our mother that I would keep her from harm."

"Do you even know where she is?"

"I'll go to where she went missing and start from there."

"Sounds awfully dangerous. You might get captured too, or killed, and then you would be no use to anyone." Meila placed a hand on his shoulder. "Your older sister. Vixhana? It sounds like she is much closer to useful sources of information. There's no point throwing yourself into such an unsafe area with Vors everywhere."

"Yes, I suppose so," said Jaks.

"Until you know where she is, all you can do is prepare."

He turned to face her. "You're right. I need to prepare. I need power . . . magic . . . if I am to help her," Jaks said as he edged past her and then fled downstairs to the burn-room to coax his electromancy into control.

And when he failed yet again, his anger grew. Anger at his erratic magic, his failures to protect Karisa, his sister's captors, and his father's abuses. Unable to contain his frustration, he yelled and hurled himself against the uncaring stone walls of the chamber until his fists were raw, black and bloodied.

He sank to the ground in a crumpled heap and whispered a promise to Karisa, wherever she was: "Magic or no magic, I won't fail you again."

Chapter 23

Balance of Power

Meila—The Academy of the Arcane

How much power is too much? pondered Meila. After Jaks rushed out of the library, she welcomed the opportunity to stretch her legs. She kicked off the ill-fitting shoes the Academy had given her and ran barefoot through the hallways of the Academy.

She jogged and weaved through the hallways and stairs, leaving a trail of apprentices, clerks, and mages staring after her in surprise. Fortunately, she was fleet enough to escape anyone's lasting attention.

While she felt a burst of freedom from the running, her thoughts returned to the greater issue that hounded her. If she gave these people centuries of military advancement beyond any other civilization on this planet, would that be too much power? Would it create such an imbalance that the Ascorians would subdue or destroy every other nation? Was this King Silas a tyrant or a diplomat? An Attila or a Solomon? Her brief interactions with him told her little.

Meila's crew had not discovered the cause of this colony's

fall of civilization after it had been severed from contact with Earth. If she accelerated their military capability tenfold with advanced weaponry, would it tip them toward another apocalypse of civilization?

Did she care?

What she did care about was providing her captors with enough capability to defend themselves against a superior enemy; if they succumbed, the probability was that she would be killed or made captive by even crueler masters.

A pang of self-pity struck her as she took inventory of her situation: ship destroyed, captured by primitives, impending invasion, her husband dead, and rescue at least a decade away. *Stop feeling sorry for yourself and think.*

After two circuits of the building, she was back in Mulgrave's library and breathing hard; it had been a reasonable effort, considering the month it had taken to recover from her leg injury and the limited exercise she had achieved in the prison cell.

She began a set of calisthenic stretches and considered the powerful weapons that already existed here: illumancers, firemancers, and gravmancers. Adding firearms was not that much of a step beyond.

But what if she could limit the numbers they could make or use? Enough to defend themselves, but too few to contemplate world-wide dominance.

Even better would be if she could *loan* them a number of weapons.

To her, the answer was obvious now, but it could be a hard sell to get the old man to agree.

That afternoon, Meila found Jaks in his room, bandaging his hands.

He explained he had fallen down some stairs, then changed the topic. "Someone said they saw you running through the halls this morning. Was someone chasing you?" he asked.

"I just needed exercise. They locked me in a cell for a few months, if you remember." She helped him to tie up a bandage, but seeing his ragged knuckles, she looked up with concern. "You haven't been fighting, have you? Not Tavis?"

"No." He would not meet her eyes. "No. I just . . . fell."

She saw his evasion but did not challenge him; she would soon see for herself whether Tavis had injuries, too. "You want to come with me to find the old man? I've got an idea," she said.

Mulgrave and Tavis were in the ground-floor lab at a wide table mulling over blueprints and documents. The younger man had no obvious fight marks, Meila was pleased to note, and when the grandmaster asked Jaks about his bandaged hands, he received the same reply as she had. "Just a fall, Master." He then made a request to the mage. "The letter said my younger sister is missing. No one knows where she is. Could I go see my older sister in the evening?"

"I'm sorry to hear that. By all means—go now, if you want," Mulgrave said.

As Jaks left, Meila said to the grandmaster, "I have something to show you. Follow me." Without waiting for a response, she turned and walked through the lab to the Academy courtyard.

At the escape pod, she waited until Mulgrave and Tavis caught up with her. "What if we could get our hands on working weapons right now?" she said.

She put a hand on the hatch and pulled it open. "There are fractured sections of the *Mendhelsson* that crashed to the planet. It's possible that the wreckage will have weapons and ammunition still onboard." She climbed up onto the pod and slid inside.

"And you know where these sections are?" asked the old man, peering over the lip at her sitting in the one-person capsule.

She turned the panel screen to him.

A map of Ascoria flashed up in front of him, and his eyes grew wide as he absorbed the details.

"Amazing!" He traced a finger over the screen. "That's Ascoria . . . Ellipta . . . Faucony . . . Voros."

"Look at those three red dots. Those are some of the larger sections of the *Mendhelsson* that broke off and scattered nearby." She pointed at one dot near the middle of Ascoria, one in Voros, and another in the ocean to the south. "There may be weapon lockers in those sections, and if we can get there, I can unlock them and we would have guns. Not just any guns, but darkcore weapons that could easily kill any man or beast walking this planet."

"Which ones have these guns?" Mulgrave asked, still staring at the brilliantly colored screen.

"That, I don't know. There were two weapons lockers on the ship. One fore and one aft." Her memory implant inventoried each locker with two handguns and two rifles, along with twenty magazines. "That section's the closest." She pointed at the red dot at the center of the Ascorian landmass.

"What are the chances of salvaging weapons?"

"Reasonable, I think. To show up on the scanner, the sections would have to be at least one-sixth of the entire hull in size. The hull fracture was mid-ship, so both ends are likely to have remained intact." The suicidal blast, whether or not intentional, had destroyed a central reinforcing beam. Although protected from exterior attack, the ship was not designed to withstand a darkcore event from within.

"And what about those?" Mulgrave asked, pointing at orange dots on the map.

"Escape pods."

"There are other survivors? You should have told us," the mage said sharply.

"No . . . I'm fairly sure I'm the only one alive." Meila repressed the stab of grief brought on by the words. "See. The green dot is me. Either the others have wandered beyond the ten-mile range of their escape pod—which is against Rescue Protocol—or they're dead."

Tavis leaned into the capsule to look at the map. "If we get to those weapons, what's stopping you killing us all and running off?"

"Nothing. Maybe I will." She glared at him, annoyed at the apprentice's distrustful tone, and enjoyed the shocked look he gave in return. After a few seconds, she sighed. "Of course, I wouldn't. I need to be near this pod; it's a beacon for my rescuers to find me—it's my ball and chain. Killing you would not help me."

She grabbed the edges of the hatch opening, forcing the mages back, and pulled herself out with a lithe jump. "I'm not familiar with your modes of transport. How long would it take us to travel to the nearest ship section?" she asked.

"Well, the closest one is in the middle of the roughest terrain in Ascoria: the Jurn Highlands. By horseback, we could get to the foot of the mountains in perhaps a week or two, but navigating the mountains . . . we would need a ranger to guide us. It is dangerous territory." Mulgrave rubbed his chin. "Reputed for impassable mountains, sheer cliffs, and ancient forests. It is largely unmapped. Do you know the area, Tavis?"

The apprentice shook his head. "All I know is, the woodsmen say it's a common place for bands of wildmen and packs of wulverions and dragons. No one goes there but the desperate."

The old man nodded and crossed his arms. "This is no small endeavor you're suggesting. Dangerous, in fact. I would want to know more about these weapons before we think about trying to salvage them, young lady."

Meila laughed at the reference to her age. "I'm twice your age in years. I should be calling you 'young man'." She winked at the bald mage.

Mulgrave and Tavis stared at her, unable to resolve the incongruence of her physical youth and stated age.

She continued, "If you want to know the value of the darkcore weapons, the best way is for you to see its power for yourself. If you track down my handgun, I'll show you what it can do."

Tavis looked up quickly but held back the alarm that shaped on his lips.

"Excellent idea. Let me find out what happened to your possessions. I'd like to witness these wondrous things," said Mulgrave.

She smiled in response. *I like how this man works; he does not waste time.*

That evening, Meila encountered Jaks in the hallway, returning from seeking his older sister. She asked if he had eaten anything that day. He replied he was not hungry, but she ordered him to follow anyway.

In the mess hall, they sat at an empty table, away from the other diners, with bread and a bowl of fish stew each. Jaks picked at his food, holding his spoon awkwardly with a bandaged hand.

"How did it go? Did you get to see her?" Meila asked, dipping a bread roll into her bowl.

"It was pointless. Vixhana had nothing to add to what was in her letter. I asked her if Karisa might have escaped during the fight and gone into hiding, but it's been over two weeks now, so she thinks Karisa was undoubtedly taken by the raiders." Jaks stirred the stew around his bowl.

"I'm sorry, Jaks. You've done your best. I'm sure you will be the first person she tells if she hears anything new."

She then told Jaks about the crashed ship fragments and her idea for a salvage quest. She asked him if he knew anything about the mountains that harbored the wreckage, but he, too, drew a blank. "At school, it was just a blank area on the maps. Is it worth the trouble going all that way?"

"Remember the first day we met—the handgun I used on the dragons? That was the *least* powerful of the weapons onboard the *Mendhelsson*. It would be worth it."

What she did not tell him was she alone would have implant control over each and every weapon, including ammunition limits, power settings, and, most importantly of all, who could use them and for how long.

She would loan them weapons that could alter the course of battle, but only under the tightest of controls.

The next day, as Meila walked through the city, returning to the royal prison with Mulgrave and Jaks to seek the return of her possessions, she encountered a much-changed city to that of a few days before.

A somber mood hung over the crowds of people who all seemed on urgent business. In the market district, eyes followed her with whispers and pointed fingers—not curious this time, but suspicious. A group of urchins waved pretend swords and threw pebbles at her but gave flight when she boomed at them. Mobs jostled in the marketplace over food and supplies, with occasional scuffles breaking out in stalls and shops. Fresh posters depicting soldiers standing on duty were pasted to notice boards and walls of buildings; notices proclaiming the king's will for a province cordon. Dunberrin prepared for war.

At the prison, the Prison Magistrate admitted them immediately and greeted the mage with obsequious aplomb. "Welcome, Grandmaster. What an honor to see you again," he said as he bowed. "I see our lovely ward is doing well." His words acknowledged her, but his weasel eyes did not deviate from the mage.

After an exchange of pleasantries, Mulgrave requested Meila's possessions from the prison storage and the magistrate flicked his fingers at a guard to retrieve her items. While they waited a tedious quarter hour, the magistrate drew a reluctant Mulgrave into a conversation to whine about the prison's finances.

"Please accept this small donation to your facility," the mage said eventually and reached into his money pouch to place a gold coin on the man's polished desk.

The magistrate beamed and slid the coin into a drawer with a deft hand.

As they exited the prison, Meila remarked, "Greedy man. Is that the correct term?"

"You wouldn't believe how much that one slithers," Mulgrave replied. "Hopefully, he hasn't stolen and sold off what we are after." He looked at the prison sack that Jaks had accepted from the guard as they left.

An hour later, in Mulgrave's library, Jaks dumped the contents of the sack onto the central table.

Meila whooped in glee when she saw familiar objects in the pile. She pushed aside the bulkiest items: boxes of ration bars, silver insulation blanket, backpack with heat cells, medikit, and her old jumpsuit.

Picking up her handgun from the remaining small items, her implants confirmed that the black synthmetal weapon was still operational and had ninety-seven charges left in the energy cell. She checked both of the trigger locks, the first, a toggle above the grip, and the second, an internal lock activated by the implant in her forebrain through electrical impulses through her palm.

Satisfied, she looked up to see Jaks and Mulgrave staring at the gun. She flipped it around to offer it to the grandmaster. "Take it. It's locked."

Mulgrave cautiously took the gun, weighed it, felt the texture of the grip and barrel, looked down the muzzle, and then examined the details of the trigger in the sunlight. "Not much to it. Is this all?"

"Let me show you what it can do. We'll need somewhere safe to use it," she said.

"The battlements. Barely anyone goes up there, and if we stay away from the dragon nest, they won't bother us," Jaks said, and then led them through the hallways to a spiral staircase leading up to the top of the Academy.

The roof was a wide stone walkway surrounding a huge bronze dome. The chimney of the runic furnace pierced the center and spat a column of smoke into the sky. Merlons and embrasures ran along the top of the outer walls, and thin towers crowned each of the four corners of the building.

Several blue dragons perched along the battlements while a pair of the hawk-sized creatures curled around the top of the furthest tower. Long necks sinuated as they tracked the appearance of humans in their territory.

"I could clear some of those pests out." Meila gestured at the blues, four of which took to the air as she watched, diving from the wall and then swooping long, tapered wings until they circled the furnace above.

"No, don't do that. Master Cranbrook treats them like pets. He throws them leftovers from the kitchens. They're fairly harmless and keep the roof from being infested with filthy gulls," Mulgrave said.

"The ones in the mountains weren't harmless. But, it's your choice." Meila turned to gaze out beyond the battlements. To the north, the ocean stretched toward a thin line of clouds as a pair of warships carved the sea at full sail below. To the east and west, cliffs and stony beaches undulated along a craggy, gray coastline. To the south, a vista of rooftops was nobbled with chimneys and tall buildings, and in the center of the city, the triple peaks of the Royal Palace, the cathedral, and the army's main signaling tower—resembling a giant lighthouse—triumphed over the cityscape. She wished Anton were here to share the beautiful sight; it was a rare one to find on any planet of the United Worlds.

"Could you hit one of those gulls?" said Jaks, pointing at three gray and white gulls sitting sixty yards away at the end of the Academy's disused wharf.

The range would be an easy shot for her, but even so, she rested the butt on the battlement and magnified her right lens implant to train the gun sight onto the closest bird. As the small red dot hovered over the white of the bird's midsection, she paused her breathing and gently squeezed the trigger.

A capsule of darkcore matter energized and transformed a metal pellet into molten plasma.

The handgun emitted a barely audible hiss as the weapon spat the plasma out of its barrel.

The gull exploded into a cloud of feathers. Flesh and bone splattered the wharf. The water behind the bird erupted into a plume of water and steam.

Jaks and Mulgrave gasped in synchrony and leaned over the embrasure to get a better look at the remains.

The younger man slapped the stone and laughed. "Not even enough left for the dragons to scavenge!"

"What form of magic is this?" Mulgrave asked, staring at the handgun greedily.

"Not magic . . . science," replied Meila.

"May I try it?" Mulgrave nodded like a little boy eager for a new toy.

She had known he would ask, and although her professionalism screamed at her not to allow an untrained civilian to handle the weapon, she briefly touched the grandmaster's arm to read his neuronal signature, then signaled her implant to unlock the weapon to him.

"Careful. Don't point it at anything you don't intend to kill." Her nerves settled once she had Mulgrave holding the pistol properly with both hands and pointed at the water below.

"Use your thumb to slide off the lock. Now, slowly squeeze the trigger to shoot."

The mage followed her instructions, and the weapon hissed again; the shot created another plume of water in the distance. She could see he was breathing rapidly and told him to slow his breathing before his next shot.

Wanting a live target this time, the mage aimed at a seagull on the edge of the wharf below and squeezed off another shot. Miss. Too low. The tip of seaweed- and algae-covered wharf exploded in a ball of a fire. A loud boom startled nearby wildlife

—birds and dragons leapt to the air and scattered. Fragments of rock flew through the air and splashed far out in the harbor. The end of the wharf fractured and sloughed into the sea, leaving a jagged ramp of freshly revealed stone.

"Ahh . . . Hazeldine will be mad," said Mulgrave. "But dog's balls, that is power!" he added, grinning. "Several blasts with this could bring down a castle gate in no time. How many of these are there? With enough of these, our armies could repel the Voros with ease."

"There are four per locker. But with limited ammunition, they would need to be used sparingly."

"They would be a stopgap until we could start mass producing the gunpowder weapons you spoke of earlier?" He toggled the trigger lock and hefted the weapon again.

"Yes. But only if we find all the chemicals we need for the gunpowder," Meila said, but kept her deeper thoughts to herself.

I'll make sure we don't find them . . . Just a few darkcore weapons should be enough to neutralize the invaders and keep the peace until I can get off this planet.

Chapter 24

The Salvage Mission

Jaks—Royal Palace of King Silas, Ascoria

Jaks was running out of time. The king's cordon on the province borders was a tightening noose, threatening to end his clerk job at the Academy and thrust him toward a pointless death in a conscript battalion. He couldn't go into the army, he had an oath to keep, he had to rescue Karisa.

Despite the flurry of activity over the past couple of days, following Grandmaster Mulgrave's decision to mount a salvage expedition to the wreckage of Meila's starship, he fretted over his personal dilemma: his magic was a dead end, so if he couldn't be the mage's apprentice, how else could he stay off the front lines?

A nudge in his ribs interrupted his thoughts.

"Here comes the herald. It's our turn. Get yourself together," Meila said as she smoothed the sleeves of her tunic and picked up her backpack.

The two of them, along with Mulgrave and Tavis, were seated outside the Royal Court waiting to see the king. They needed a permit to cross the province cordon to pursue their quest.

Jaks hoped the herald would be Minto. It felt like a long time since he had seen his jovial friend.

Unfortunately, the red-capped official who called them out from the other petitioners was a middle-aged woman with a no-nonsense expression.

Expecting a majestic throne room, Jaks was surprised to enter an austere chamber plainly furnished with a row of chairs facing a long oak table. King Silas, adorned with a purple cloak and his gold monarch's collar, sat behind the table, talking with a clerk to his left. *Maybe I could get a clerk's job with the king? That would be important enough to keep me out of re-conscription.*

Armored sentries stood at each corner of the room, and Vixhana—fully armed and in nightwraiths' black armor—stood with crossed arms behind the king. She nodded at Jaks when they made eye contact, but her face stayed as hard and expressionless as a rock. Another nightwraith—older, male, and similarly battle-ready—stood to the side of the king's table and studied them as they approached.

A low growl sounded to Jaks's right—a sharp-snouted hound with bared teeth glared at him from the side of the chamber. The dog's handler pulled on a leash, and the animal sat back on its haunches but continued to menace Jaks with its eyes.

The silver-haired king looked up, over the maps and letters spread out in front of him, and smiled as the herald announced them.

"Mulgrave, my friend, please sit. All sit," Silas said. The clerk slid a document in front of him. "My apologies that I was not able to see you yesterday. As you can see, many call on the royal wax—and the situation with Voros becomes graver each day. I grieve for peace. Perhaps you have an invocation to summon it back?" The king grimaced, despite his joke.

"Sorry, my lord. If only I could. What news of the coast?" Mulgrave sat in the chair closest to the king.

"Five major raids on Finstaf over the past few weeks, each pushing further inland. The damned Vors appear to be searching for a beachhead." Silas looked down at a map for a moment and then continued, "Although I've reinforced the coast as much as I can, my generals predict a full-scale invasion within weeks. I will make a call to arms in the coming days."

Jaks tensed and his skin prickled at the king's mention of a call to arms.

"And ships?" Mulgrave asked.

"They outnumber our galleys and frigates, particularly after a heavy engagement some three weeks ago. Our navy still barricades the Gulf of Irin and the northwest tip of Ascoria, with the help of the Fauconians. But elsewhere, the Vors have free rein at sea."

"Can we count on the Pact Countries to send soldiers?"

"Strock promised troops, but they will not formally join an alliance. Faucony has promised more ships. But, Nera Boa has flatly refused." The king opened his palms to the air.

Mulgrave leaned forward on his chair. "My lord. It may please you that we might secure artifacts to greatly assist a war effort. May I show you something?"

He placed a cloth bundle onto the oak table and peeled back the layers to reveal the darkcore handgun.

They all stared at the alien object. King Silas and the clerk leaned forward with puzzled expressions. The two nightwraith soldiers looked on with the slightest of frowns.

"My ward brought this with her from her . . . planet," Mulgrave said, still grappling with the new concept. "Small as it may be, it is the most powerful weapon I have ever seen." He then went on to extol the destructive power of the gun with graphic descriptions of the dismembered seagull and the fractured wharf and then offered to demonstrate the weapon.

In the royal courtyard, a pole used for sword drills was mounted with a suit of steel plate armor. The better shot, Meila, received the gun from Mulgrave, but concerned over the confined area, she stood on the marble steps overlooking the courtyard to fire from.

Once the courtyard had been cleared of exercising guards and palace staff, she took a two-handed grip on the handgun, aimed, counted down, and fired.

The back of the mannequin exploded with a spray of molten steel and incinerated splinters. Several paces behind it, the ground erupted, throwing up dust and stone. What little was left of the armor spun down the length of the courtyard.

The crack of exploding wood and stone, the scrape of metal, and the pitter-patter of falling fragments resounded in their ears for a moment until the area settled into silence.

In the aftermath, pieces of mangled armor lay strewn about the courtyard, with just a splintered stump of the wooden pole remaining.

None of the guards or administrators seemed alarmed that a foreigner had destroyed a suit of heavy armor only yards away from their king. The only thing that registered on their faces was shock.

"Bravo!" The king slapped a hand onto Mulgrave's back. "Spectacular. Can you forge more of these things?"

"No, unfortunately. They are forged back on her homeworld. But we know where we might salvage more of these weapons." The grandmaster looked at Meila approaching, the handgun sitting in the hoop of her belt. "As you saw at the

Academy, her technology surpasses ours beyond imagination. I believe that with these weapons, we could repel any invasion force the Vors throw at us."

King Silas nodded. "Yes, yes, you must retrieve them. From where?"

"Damaged parts of her ship are scattered around the lands and may yield more of them. All we need, my lord, is free passage through the province borders," Mulgrave said.

"Of course. I'll have something drawn up. What are your plans?" Silas replied and directed them back to the audience chamber to continue their conversation.

Back at the oak table, the grandmaster and the king bent over a map as the mage traced a stubby finger over their planned route.

"Just the three of you?" Silas turned a critical eye over Tavis and Jaks in the row of seats. "You, my friend, can handle yourself—but these two lads are a bit green."

"I would take my ward too. I need her to access the weapons, as they may be locked away; also, she can identify any other salvage that might be of use."

"She is very . . . slight." The silver-headed king looked at Meila's svelte figure. "The Jurn Highlands are treacherous. You need more protection." He turned to Vixhana behind him and exchanged several words with her.

She nodded and returned to her position.

"The captain here will travel with you—she is a very capable warrior." The king gestured at Vixhana, who inclined her head to Mulgrave. "And you will need a ranger through those mountains . . ." He conferred with Vixhana again, then said, "We'll send a master to the Academy to accompany you. And, if you need anything else, let my quartermaster know."

Jaks smiled at the thought of Vixhana joining them on the salvage quest. He caught her eye again and received a wink.

———

A letter was signed by the king naming Mulgrave a Royal Emissary and granting him and his party ease of passage through the kingdom and special powers to request aid from any Ascorian forces they should meet.

Taking advantage of his new privileges, they entered the Royal Stables and flashed the letter at the stable master to requisition four palfreys and a pack mule—the most placid beasts available, knowing that none of them were confident riders except for himself.

Meila had never even seen a live horse before, and although she was quick for the challenge, she rode out of the stables lying flat over the saddle, clutching at the horse's bridle with white knuckles and gritting her teeth.

In the Academy courtyard the following day, they packed food rations and supplies into saddlebags, readying them to be loaded for whenever their ranger and nightwraith companions arrived.

It was while Tavis crammed a rope into a pack that he expressed his displeasure at the mission. He spoke to Mulgrave, who was rearranging some hardtack in a saddlebag. "Master. Perhaps my skills could be better used staying here in the Academy and helping one of the others . . . maybe Master Doeg with his work?" said the apprentice. "Traveling and the outdoors are not my strong point . . ." He tucked back his hair behind large ears and looked up uncertainly at the grandmaster.

"Have no doubt, you will learn far more afield than crammed

up here in this old keep. To be my apprentice requires more than forging and smithing—you didn't think your entire apprenticeship would have you stuffed up inside of here, did you?"

Tavis opened his mouth and closed it, then opened it again. "I just thought . . ."

"If I'm dragging my clerk along, you're coming too." Mulgrave laughed and returned to his task of packing hardtack into the saddlebag. A moment later, he said in a serious voice, "It will do you both some good. Maybe the two of you will learn to get along better."

Jaks looked up in alarm from the sack of dried apples he was holding and wondered how the mage knew of the conflict between Tavis and himself. He exchanged a look with Tavis; they both looked away awkwardly and hurried back to their tasks.

That afternoon, Mulgrave outfitted them from the Academy armory where weapons and bits of armor from the workshops were stored. Each piece was unique and often the result of magesmith experiments. Although the most valuable breastplates, helms, swords, and axes awaited distribution to the king's champions or generals, Jaks, Tavis, and Meila were free to arm themselves with whatever else they wanted.

Hanging from the wall, Jaks found a set of riding leathers that were as flexible as cloth but as strong as steel, and he grinned when he pulled out, from under a jumbled pile, a round, steel shield with a lightning bolt emblazoned on the front. A barrel of swords gave up an intricately engraved shortsword, and Mulgrave handed him a light crossbow that could reload itself from a magazine of bolts with the single pull of a cocking-lever.

Feeling suitably warrior-like, Jaks helped Meila carry the arsenal of knives that she was acquiring. She had a wicked gleam to her face that he had never seen before as she examined dozens of knives and daggers spread across a bench from which she selected a couple more. There had been no armor small enough for her diminutive form, so she had settled for a short riding cloak that Mulgrave had stabbed with a dagger, demonstrating it to be as tough as chainmail. "Interwoven layers of steelinium alloy and wool," he'd explained. And, of course, she had her darkcore handgun.

Mulgrave pointed out his own midnight-blue plate armor with runestones encrusted in the greaves of both arms. He claimed to have forged the suit decades ago and then campaigned in it during the Unifying Wars as one of King Silas's battlemages. His weapon was a flanged mace with a red runestone pommel.

Tavis, however, was in a fit of indecision. Between choices of armor ranging from a suit of full plate through to a mishmash of leggings, pauldrons, greaves, breastplates, and helms, whatever he tried always seemed better than the last.

After three hours, they abandoned him to his buffet of armor and descended to the mess hall for actual food.

The next morning, Jaks waited for Vixhana and the ranger to arrive. He sat on the wall of the land bridge, tapping his fingers on the sandstone blocks, excited about the salvage mission. In his mind, a quest to recover powerful artifacts was the stuff of dreams, or lived in legends and storybooks populated with mighty heroes. From his conscription experience, however, he knew the reality would be far less romantic and glorious: endless miles of boredom and trudging through wind and rain, over steep mountains and thick forests, and constant paranoia about snakes, wyverns, wolves, and other nasties. But, despite his worries, he took comfort that he was going in the company of a grandmaster battlemage, a nightwraith, and a ranger.

Jaks rose to his feet expectantly as two riders approached. The nearest sat atop a black courser and wore a traveling cape over black leather, while a bastard sword swung at the hip. Behind the rider, the haft of a massive axe rose like a flagpole, its double blades scabbarded in a riding holster attached to the horse. Jaks beamed at the sight of his sister.

Her companion rode a brown courser and held a recurve bow across his lap. Quivers of arrows were bundled into saddle bags, fletched ends sticking out like porcupine spines. The man was smaller than Vixhana but carried an air of immutable self-confidence, and together with his pointed beard, Jaks instantly recognized someone he had hoped never to see again—Ranger Cromer, his old survival instructor.

"Greetings, little brother," Vixhana said as she stopped and dismounted at the gates. In her nightwraith armor, she looked imposing; if it were not for the shape of her chest armor, she would be easily mistaken for a clean-shaven yet handsome man. "Set to go?" she said.

"Shouldn't be long. Let's go in," Jaks replied and glanced nervously at the ranger, who followed on his horse and stared blankly ahead. Perhaps he'd forgotten Jaks and his dismal failures during survival training?

In the courtyard, Mulgrave tugged the bridle straps on his horse and then popped an apple half into the eager animal's mouth and munched on the rest. As Jaks brought in Vixhana and Cromer, the mage welcomed them warmly and then pointed out the rest of their traveling party.

Vixhana nodded politely at Meila and then frowned at

Tavis, who was wearing a mishmash of armor pieces and resembled a dress-up doll with push-on, pull-off parts.

"It's all excellent armor," Tavis said to her and showed off a pair of white leather gloves.

The ranger slid off his horse and nodded an acknowledgement to Mulgrave. "Grandmaster, what route do you favor?" he then asked, slipping off worn riding gloves.

Jaks tried to read the man's expression but couldn't tell the ranger's normal impassive state from resentment or even annoyance. *One thing for sure, he can't be happy that I'm coming along,* thought Jaks. He then straightened his shoulders, annoyed at himself. *I don't need to prove anything to him, he's not my instructor anymore.*

A bench was cleared, and the ranger laid out a map. Their route would be direct and simple. Across the riverplains of Dunberrin and then south through the province of Jurn to the Highlands. Paved roads until Jurn, from where they would skirt the fringes of a grassland sea, wandered by herds of antelope, wild horses, and longhorns, and prowled by lions and wolves. A dirt road would take them down this border between the two provinces. Although they might glimpse inhabited ranches of cattle herders in the northern region of Jurn, there would be naught but wildlands further south. It was from there on that Jaks expected they would be most thankful for the extra protection of Vixhana and the ranger.

To traverse the lowland expanse and reach the central Highlands, if undisturbed, could take a little over a week. But how long it would take them to find the ship wreckage in the uncharted area—rumored to be inhabited by exiled tribes of savages and dragons that curled around the tips of frozen mountains—depended on the ranger's skill to lead them through unknown perils to where Meila had marked the wreckage of her ship.

Jaks shivered, both excited and anxious. If they returned alive from this madcap quest, with darkcore weapons, they would return as heroes. But even with his new armor and weapons, he didn't feel the least bit heroic.

At least Vixhana was here. She could handle anything.

Chapter 25

Rivertown

They rode out of Dunberrin in the late morning, a party of three war veterans, two novices, and a foreigner.

The Grand Avenue led out of the city and became the southern road as it cut through a patchwork of farmlands and cottages. Gray mountains in the distant south painted the horizon. Clear autumn skies promised a decent day for riding.

Jaks sat atop his brown and black palfrey, a gentle mare who sometimes fretted in the city streets but in the open roads calmed easily as long as he used a light touch with his reins.

Ranger Cromer led the group, followed by Mulgrave, and then Jaks and Meila. Behind them, Tavis rode a brown palfrey and led a pack mule laden with tents and supplies. Vixhana brought up the rear of the party.

Jaks wanted to talk with his sister, but at the moment, he coached Meila in horse-riding and some finer points of controlling her gelding with the reins and her knees. After a few hours, she had relaxed enough to stop grabbing at the saddle horn whenever she felt unbalanced and shifted her weight on her feet instead.

"I could see myself enjoying horse-riding . . . ask me again in a couple of weeks," said Meila, "but my thighs are killing me right now." Despite her complaints, her riding had progressed within hours beyond what Jaks had taken weeks to develop as a youngster.

"You're lucky you're small. It's worse for tall people."

Around midafternoon, a wind blew in from the east and brought with it high clouds. Further south, a thick gray layer capped the mountain range to the south, heralding rain in those distant parts.

Meila rode confidently now—as long as she stayed in a straight line—and she gestured at a paddock of sheep. "This countryside is incredible. I've never traveled through anywhere with so much open land that animals can walk freely and eat grass out of the ground," she said to Jaks.

"Your land must be tiny." He laughed at her wide-eyed amazement at the unremarkable farmlands spanned out from both sides of the road.

"The opposite, actually. Earth Prime has greater land mass than this planet, but with so many people living there, there is no space for pastures and fields like this. They manufacture most of our food on other planets because agricultural land is so scarce."

"Sounds awful. I wouldn't want to live somewhere like that," said Jaks.

She went silent and returned to gazing at the fields. "Butterflies . . ." she said quietly.

With Meila losing interest in talking, Jaks slowed his horse with a tug on the reins—ignoring Tavis as he plodded by—and pulled alongside his sister at the rear of the group.

Vixhana leaned her massive arms on the pommel of her saddle with the reins held loose in her fingers. "Your friend is a natural rider. I'm surprised. She hasn't the legs for it," she said, thrusting her chin toward Meila. Directing her eyes at Jaks, she continued, "You spend a lot of time with her. She is nice to look at."

"That's not why I—"

"Sure, it is," she said and laughed as a flush crept across Jaks's cheeks.

"She's new here and doesn't know our ways. So, I'm helping her," said Jaks defensively. "She's the grandmaster's ward. He told me to guard her."

"Remember your loyalties, brother—country before heart. I could have killed you the other day for allowing her to handle that weapon so close to the king. What if she had been an assassin?" Her face frosted for a second.

"But she wasn't," said Jaks weakly, only now seeing the danger to the king had she been false with her motives. He consoled himself that the grandmaster had also trusted her enough to support the demonstration.

"Be careful with her. She may not be all that she seems. You must tell me if she makes any plans, okay?"

"Plans?"

Vix looked at him closely, as though talking to a child. "Escape, run away, that sort of thing."

He had not seriously considered that Meila would think of running away, but now that he thought on it, he realized he knew very little about what she wanted or desired. "I don't think she would. She said she has to stay near her pod for her people to find her." Could she be lying? His heart told him no, but his head warned him otherwise. "I'll tell you if she says anything strange."

They continued in silence, following the ranger at a turnfork, and then east for several more miles.

Jaks summoned the courage to ask his sister a question. The reason he had dropped back to see her in the first place. "Do you hate him?" he asked.

"Who?"

"Father." He rubbed at the stump of his missing finger. "I want to hate him . . . I need to hate him."

"What are you talking about?" Vixhana frowned at him.

"The grandmaster said I should talk to someone about the past. He thinks my unresolved issues are holding back my electromancy powers."

"I don't think I'm the best person to talk to about that." Vix looked uncomfortable and shifted in her saddle, staring up the road. "I don't . . . do feelings."

A few minutes passed and then he asked again, "But, do you hate him?"

She looked at him squarely. "Do I hate him . . . Before you or Karisa were born, it was only mother and me. For ten years, I had her all to myself. Do I love her as much as you did? Do I miss her as much as you do?" Her eyes misted.

Jaks was shocked. It was the first time Jaks had ever seen his sister show any sadness, but then it flipped to anger.

"Of course, I hate him for hurting her. Of course, I hate him for molesting Karisa. I wish I could snap his filthy neck in my hands. I should have tried when I had the chance . . ."

Without warning, Vixhana stalled her horse to take up the rear and distanced herself from Jaks. Her face was granite and she sat upright, as stiff as a statue. He had picked at a scab covering his sister's emotions. She didn't approve.

She, too, had not dealt well with the past and obviously harbored bitter anger toward their father.

However, knowing that did not help Jaks with his torment about the same issues. He thought he wanted the anger that Vixhana had, but instead, he was mired in grief, guilt, and fear.

Later that afternoon, they rode into a picturesque riverside town nestled on the border of the river plains. White-washed cottages bordered with black beams were set back from the paved road by stone boundaries, apple trees, and gardens ablaze with summer yellows, blues, and reds. Bees hummed from flower to flower and several children, shouldering school satchels, returned home from school. An affluent township—inhabited by ancestors of the original gold-panners—was almost as cultured and wealthy as the Capital. However, unlike Dunberrin, the locals showed none of the anxiety and wariness that their big-city cousins had recently acquired.

The town center yielded several inns and shops, with most of the activity gathered around a few food and drinking establishments.

A group of local young men on the side of the road tumbled toward the closest inn, initially loud and jovial, but then quiet when they spotted the new arrivals. They stopped in their tracks and watched Ranger Cromer lead the others past them. A red-haired youth bowed his head toward Mulgrave, then stared at Meila—who, in response, pulled the hood of her cape over her head.

The ranger stopped at a traveler's stable and negotiated with the elderly stablemaster to attend and secure their horses and mule for the night.

The Drover's Inn, nearby, was a two-story stone building with a tiled roof and covered stairs running up the outside. The ground-floor tavern door stood open with a steady flow of locals going in and out. Wafts of ale, fresh bread, and roasting meat assaulted Jaks's nostrils as he followed the ranger inside. There was a brief lull in conversation amongst the bar patrons as the newcomers entered. A troubadour, however, playing in the corner kept up his strum and song.

A pudgy man in a beer-stained apron waddled up and bowed to the grandmaster. "Af'ernoon, m' lord. Will you be seeking lodgings and fare for the night?"

After agreeing to terms, the grandmaster and Tavis retreated upstairs to their rooms, with a serving boy running up some bread and stew soon after. Ranger Cromer joined a group of woodsmen who recognized him and called him over to a table on the other side of the tavern. Jaks and the two women huddled around a table by the wall and ordered a leg of roast beef, carrots, and mash.

As they waited, Meila quirked an eyebrow at Vixhana. "Jaks has told me a lot about you. You're some sort of elite warrior?"

Vixhana glanced at Jaks and then turned toward the dark-haired woman. "I've been in the nightwraiths since I finished conscription."

"King's personal guard?"

"No, not typically. But in wartime, we rotate royal protection duty with our regular duties."

"What do you usually do?" Meila leaned in.

"We observe the enemy and infiltrate behind lines to ambush or take out important targets," Vix replied in a bland tone.

Jaks, eager to impress with his knowledge, added, "The Order of Nightwraiths started two centuries ago, after Kilka Entme used illumancy to take the guise of an enemy soldier, then slipped into the Elliptan camp and assassinated Warlord

Ponti—ending the Battle of Bays. After she escaped, she gathered other illumancers and trained them as mercenaries to use stealth and camouflage in battle. Then decades later, the Order vowed to the king and have remained loyal ever since, mercenaries no longer."

"Quite so," Vixhana said, but keen to change the subject, directed her attention back to Meila. "And what is your purpose, where do you come from?"

Before Meila could reply, a serving girl with a hefty bosom glided up with plates and a platter of food and slid them onto their table wordlessly.

Vixhana grabbed a plate, spilling juices as she did.

As the young woman, he guessed of similar age to him, turned to leave, she laid an arm across Jaks's back and slid her hand along his shoulders. He looked up into her face and was captured by smoldering eyes full of invitation. She sauntered away across the tavern, leaving him hot under his leather armor and cape.

Jaks's attention snapped back to the table as Meila replied to Vixhana. Neither seemed to have noticed the serving girl's flirtation.

"I used to design and build engines for starships—but I got bored and wanted to fly them as well. Joined the navy and made my way up to ship commander," said Meila.

"It must be amazing to fly," said Jaks, interrupting her as his imagination took flight.

"Exhilarating. Is that the word?" She stabbed a carrot on her plate and then continued, "You feel like you can go anywhere and do anything. The ground pulls away beneath you. People and buildings become tiny, but the land expands below you like a canvas. When you rise through the clouds, the world turns into a white blanket, leaving just you and the sun. And, when you reach space itself, you forget your worries and want to disappear into it forever . . ." Meila's eyes glazed over. A few seconds later, she stared at the carrot and bit into the vegetable.

Vixhana stared at her. "And anyone can fly on your world?"

"Not anyone can fly starships. But skimmers are everywhere. You can fly anywhere on a planet if you have one."

"Did you have one?"

She nodded and stabbed a chunk of steak.

"You must miss your home; it sounds incredible," Jaks said.

"The only thing I miss is my daughter." She looked away briefly before continuing. "But other than her, I don't miss Earth —I certainly don't miss the crowds or the pollution."

"Why are you so keen to be rescued, then?" Vixhana asked, pushing away her empty plate and wiping her mouth.

Meila raised her eyebrows and sat back, frowning, before she responded, "I have no place here. I have no one. But most of all, I have a duty to uphold." The words sounded forced, but once out, she looked satisfied with her claim.

"Duty is important." Vixhana nodded appreciatively.

"Despite how much I hate the issues back on Earth, I have a vow to assist my homeworld."

Disturbed by the idea of Meila leaving, Jaks spoke up. "But if you stayed with us, you could find work here—you're very clever—and could have another family."

Meila laughed. "Maybe." She looked at him with a glint in her eyes. "If I ever get released. Although I'm not locked in a prison cell, I'm not completely free either."

The serving girl returned and cleared away their plates, but this time, she gave Jaks no further attention. He was relieved, as he did not want to field awkward remarks or comments from his stern sister, or Meila, about romantic liaisons with a serving girl, or any other girl, for that matter. In truth, he was shy with girls and probably would have embarrassed himself with her, fumbling as she laughed at his inexpert hands.

Their meal finished and at an hour past dusk, Vixhana announced she was having an early night and went upstairs to retire for the day.

Alone with Meila, Jaks noticed two men staring at them.

The first stood by a wooden column at the side of the room. Bald and clean-shaven, he dressed in riding leathers and had a scabbard at his side. The second, a short and stocky man, leaned against the wall.

Jaks glanced at them again. *Yes, they are definitely staring. Probably leering at Meila.* He glared at them as he'd seen Vixhana do.

The two men turned away.

Jaks felt a chill run down his spine and felt an undeniable desire to escape the room.

"Want to see the river? They pan gold from it," he said to Meila, keeping a sideways watch on the two men—but they seemed to have lost interest and spoke softly to one another.

Jaks and Meila stood and walked across the tavern toward the outside door.

A voice called out. "That one?"

A sharp-faced man with a crooked nose slid off a barstool from around a bench of several locals. He looked like a forester, one of the unkempt men who eked a living from hunting wild animals to sell as meat and furs.

Ranger Cromer sat with them, staring at Jaks, but made no motion other than to swig his tankard of ale.

"Wan' a dance, pretty boy?" slurred the man, his breath reeking of alcohol and rot. Slack-faced, he opened his arms to Jaks. "Come on, come on." He wrapped the tall youth in a crude hug and started to sway, rubbing his crotch against Jaks's leg.

Rough hands pressing against his backside and the stench of the man's wiry hair pressed into his face. Laughter erupted around him and everyone in the entire tavern looked on as Jaks was pawed by the drunk man.

He pushed the man away in revulsion, but the hands of the slobbering man came back at him grasping like leeches.

Suddenly, the drunk was twisted sideways with his right arm wrenched behind his back. The man groaned, and his face distorted in pain. Meila stood behind him, contorting his arm, and with a tug, she threw him to the floor.

She stood over him and kicked him once in the belly, causing him to double up and retch.

The onlookers clapped and pounded their mugs against tabletops in applause. The evening's entertainment had started out well by their accounts. The troubadour continued strumming his lute and sang.

Jaks stormed out of the tavern into the dark with his head low and buttocks stinging from the pinches and gropes.

He followed the main street until he got to a bridge. Wanting to hide from everyone, he stumbled down to the riverbank and trod along the side of the river over rounded stones and patches of grass. Soon, the bridge and the lights of the town were distant. Stopping, he sat on an uprooted tree trunk and stared out over the river. Even with a full moon, the other side was barely visible, but with the mood he was in, he didn't care about anything but the solitude.

Minutes later, he heard rustling from the bushes above him, and Meila angled down the incline toward him. She sat down on the tree trunk with him.

Jaks picked up a stone and splashed it into the river. He felt humiliated and didn't feel like company—especially with someone who had observed his embarrassment and rescued him from it as though he couldn't do so himself.

They sat listening to the river burbling past and harmonizing with nightsongs of crickets nearby.

"I can't count the times I've been groped," said Meila. "The first few times, I was embarrassed and did nothing either . . . but now if anyone touches me like that, they end up regretting it." She bent down to flick a stone out into the water. "Don't beat yourself up about it."

Several more minutes passed by, then Jaks replied, "Thanks for helping me. But I can stand up for myself. I was about to knock him down." He found another stone and ran his fingers over its polished surface. "But perhaps you could teach me that arm-hold? They didn't teach us things like that in conscription training."

"Sure. In the daylight, though."

Jaks relaxed, and he started to enjoy being with a beautiful woman on a secluded riverbank. He sensed her warmth beside him. *What would she do if I took her hand or put an arm around her? Would she wring my arm like she did the forester?*

Meila, instead, changed the topic. "How are your mage exercises going?"

It took him a few moments to realize she inquired about his magic practice. He had all but abandoned his efforts since he last failed in his attempt to invoke magic. He had bashed his knuckles bloody in frustration.

"Haven't had much time to do them. Been busy the last few days." He rubbed his hands. Although they were not bandaged any longer, they were still scabbed and hurt when he clenched a fist.

"To be honest, I've about given up on it all . . . I can't get it to work." Jaks dropped the stone to his feet. "I'm running out of time and there's no point continuing the exercises—"

"Running out of time?"

"When the king makes a call to arms, I'll be drafted back into the army." He pulled his collar against the cold. "I need to find a job where I can support the war cause but without having to carry a spear . . . I'm not a good soldier. Vix got all that."

"What choices do you have? I thought you wanted to be an apprentice?"

He shrugged. "I don't know now. Perhaps instead, I could reapply to be a clerk at the magistrate's court, or maybe even the king's court." He thought back to the clerk organizing King Silas's documents. That was an important clerk.

"Don't be so stupid," said Meila. She leapt in front of Jaks onto a pebbled strip right at the river's edge. "You can't give up. You've got this . . . power. This magic that no one else has. You have a chance to learn how to do amazing things." Her voice became heavily accented, as it did when she spoke quickly. "Who cares about writing letters and contracts and whatever? If I had a chance to do magic, I would do everything possible to make it work." Her empathy for him had disappeared.

"I have been trying. It's so evasive."

With hands on her hips, she stood silhouetted against the moonlight and slowly shook her head.

Eventually, her face softened. "Tell me how it is *supposed* to work," she said.

He took a moment to collect his thoughts. "You summon up an emotion, which acts as fuel for the magic. Then you imagine a picture of what you want the magic to create, and then you concentrate on pulling the magic into reality . . . that's what I have been told how it works." He spread his hands and shrugged in futility. "The three times I *accidentally* invoked magic, I didn't do any of that—didn't do anything but panic."

"Well, that's something consistent. So, what happens when you practice?" She sat back astride the tree trunk.

"When I try to induce feelings of panic voluntarily, I get to a point where something in my head slams shut and my mind goes numb. Thick and heavy like mud." Jaks bent over with his elbows on his knees. "Sometimes, I've practiced by putting myself in real danger. Once, I climbed up onto the battlements and hung my toes over the edge. But those times, I can't visualize or focus any willpower. I get overwhelmed and turn away. There is a point where I can't break past."

"What would happen past that?" asked Meila.

"A tornado. My mind would spiral and spiral without escape. There are things in the past that can't come out." He began rocking back and forth.

She paused for a minute, then said, "Being afraid of being afraid . . . is being afraid of paper tigers."

Jaks frowned. "Paper tigers?"

She placed a hand on his arm. "Every New Year's Day, my *gwama* would tie a paper tiger outside her window, to scare off evil spirits, she would say. It'd stay there, swinging around uselessly, banging against the glass, until the wind and rain blew it down." She dug her fingers into his flesh. "Although a *real* tiger can kill you and deserves to be feared, a *paper* tiger cannot and does not." She squeezed her fingers into his arm. "Fears of the past are just that."

"My fears are paper tigers?" said Jaks.

"Thoughts are just thoughts. And feelings are just feelings. They are not real. They cannot hurt you or kill you. When you stand back and see that fear itself cannot harm you, you can fold it anyway you wish."

Meila bent low, a hand on each of his shoulders, and caught his gaze. "Will you tell me what you're so afraid of?"

Jaks was quiet, considering, then said, "My father—" His voice broke and he coughed to clear his throat. "My father. I have nightmares of him coming from the darkness and crushing my head with enormous hands. Dark hands. The first few times that I tried to use that memory to invoke magic, I reached a point where I could almost feel my head bursting in his grip. But now when I try to use that image, a barrier smashes closed."

"Your mind is shielding itself," said Meila in a gentle voice. "Tell me more about your father." She sat back down on the tree trunk, half-turned toward him.

"My mother—" Jaks said.

"Your father."

"No, it starts with my mother." His eyes became unfocused. "We were happy when it was only her with my sisters and me. We were so proud of our mother. She was famous for her acting and singing, but she loved us fiercely." He paused for a breath. "Father rarely came home from the war when I was young, but when the realm was finally unified, he was back. He fired the house servants, drank all of the time, and he would beat her . . . accusing her of adultery. He kept her prisoner in the house for months at a time."

"Everything changed," she said sympathetically.

"Eventually, the beatings stopped. For a few years, at least. And we pretended to be a happy family. She even returned to acting for a while." Jaks could not bring himself to tell her the price of that peace—Karisa's sacrifice, her body for their mother's.

"Then, when I was about fifteen, he started beating her again and accusing her of sleeping with her patrons." He listened to the gurgling river for a minute. "One night, mother and I were in the upper kitchen when he stormed in. He started shouting the same accusations and waved around a play ticket as though it were some proof of her unfaithfulness. I cowered in the corner. I just wanted to get away. He is terrifying when he is in a rage. Then he started hitting her and hitting her. I can still hear her screams. She was telling me to run. He would start on me after he finished with her—but I couldn't. He crushed a table. He smashed the kitchen to pieces. She tried to run . . . the memories go blurry. I think he threw her down the stairs. The last thing I remember was his gloved fist. Her face destroyed . . . her beautiful hair . . ."

Jaks faltered as tears welled in his eyes. "Her neck was bent, and her head pulverized. There was blood everywhere."

"Oh, Jaks, I'm sorry. That's all awful." She touched his arm.

"He ordered me to clean up the blood. My mother's blood," Jaks said in a strangled voice and started shaking his head.

Meila slid over and wrapped her arms around him, holding his head to hers for a long while.

When his trembling stopped, she spoke quietly. "Fear and anger are lovers." She pushed him back gently. "They are entwined, and when danger rears its claws, they want to save their owner, but in different ways. Fear wants to run. But anger wants to fight. Fear says, 'We must escape the danger,' and anger argues, 'We must fight.' How can you *not* feel anger at your father? He has taken away your childhood, your peace, and your mother from you. You have a right to be furious at him—to want to shout at him, to hurt him, to want justice for her murder!" Spittle sprayed from her mouth onto Jaks's face; she wiped it away with a quick sweep of her palm and then grabbed his chin. "You are no longer a little boy. You have powerful magic, and you can stop him."

Jaks stared at her, wanting her words to be true.

"Embrace fear as it builds. Know you are strong, dwell on the injustice, and grasp your anger—there you will find courage." Meila pushed his chin away and sat back.

She was right. He had every right to be angry at his father, but for as long as he had known, fear was the only emotion he knew well. In the past, to have expressed anger at his father would have drawn attention to himself and thrust him into danger. He had been a coward. He should have been angry.

The monster had murdered his mother and abused his sister. Not only did he have the right to be angry, it was his duty.

Chapter 26

An Unexpected Journey

The evening chilled as Jaks and Meila watched the reflected moonlight on the river, preoccupied with their thoughts.

"It's getting late, we should—" Jaks was saying, when abruptly everything went silent around him. Even though he felt his mouth still moving in speech, his ears heard nothing.

Puzzled, he looked at Meila and saw a dark figure standing behind her. Its arm was raised above her head. He cried out in alarm to warn her, but, again, nothing came out of his mouth. Magicked silence. *Sonomancy!*

The arm descended and struck Meila in the head.

Her body slumped off the tree trunk onto the rounded stones of the riverbank, her face just inches from the water's edge.

Jaks jumped to his feet and turned to the attacker.

The watching man from the tavern.

Moonlight illuminated the bald man's face as he looked

down at Meila. A blackjack was gripped in his hand, half-raised to club her again.

Jaks reached for the attacker's arm and shouted to ward him off—silence.

A dark figure moved in the corner of his vision.

Whack. A brick-like fist smashed into Jaks's jaw, spinning him around. He toppled to the ground.

The slobbering face of the second watcher from the tavern loomed over him, mouthing soundless words, and spittle dripped into Jaks's eye.

Thud. A shadowy blur cracked into the side of his head.

Darkness.

Jaks roused with a throbbing head, his thoughts thick and muddled.

In the pitch of night, he found himself lying facedown over a horse's back. Wisps of long grass brushed his rope-bound wrists as the beast walked steadily through a wild field. Unable to move his arms or legs, he was trussed to the horse like a deer hunter's prize.

Next to him, Meila's legs hung close to his face, bound facing the other direction. He called her name but received no response.

Three horses traveled together. The middle carried the captives, while the other two—forward and behind—bore silhouettes of riders on both.

"The boy's a deadweight. Let me slit the shagger's throat. If we rid him here, the wolves and crows will clean his bones in a few days," the rear rider called out to his companion in a raspy voice.

"You know we can't kill him." The front rider turned around and replied in a cultured, city-born accent. "We'll dump him once we're far enough away that our trail will be cold by the time he makes his way back. We should get to the mountains by dawn. Then we can rest a few hours."

They continued all night through moon-lit paddocks, fields of corn and wheat, and at one stage along a shallow creek, as Jaks drifted in and out of consciousness.

At one point, he croaked a request for water to his captors, but they either did not hear him or ignored him.

He tried to rouse Meila again. She didn't stir.

Eventually, a rooster crowed in the distance, followed by another, and dawn sullenly reddened the sky.

The horses plodded single file through rows of ripening corn.

Jaks's hair was wet from brushing against broad, green leaves beaded with condensation. His back and head ached. Pain lanced through his jaw and temple whenever his head knocked against the thick, woody stalks of the corn plants.

Meila roused and began kicking at her rope restraints.

"Who the hell are you?" she called out to their captors. "Why are you doing this?"

"Shut up," said the rear rider.

"Untie me, now."

"Shut your mouth or I put a gag in it." He then yawned loudly.

She went quiet but struggled against her ropes for a while longer, and then eventually stilled.

The rear rider grumbled. "Damn it, we're nowhere near the mountains yet. I tell you, the boy's holding us up," he called out to his partner.

After a few minutes, the cultivated voice replied, "There's

some sort of shack in the middle of the field up ahead. We'll stop there and rest."

The shack stood in the center of a small clearing. The doorless shelter covered a rusty horse-drawn plow, a farmer's hoe, shovel, and several buckets.

Jaks and Meila, hands and feet still tied, were man-handled from the horse to the ground. They wriggled upright and examined each other.

A bruise reddened the right side of Meila's face by her ear, and a bloodied graze marked her chin. Her knives and darkcore gun were nowhere to be seen. Her furrowed eyes and thinned lips were fired up with anger. She glared at their captors.

With a clearer look at them, Jaks was certain they were the two watchers from the tavern.

The man with the city-born accent was bald, pale-skinned, and moved with the confidence of a hardened warrior used to giving orders. Leather straps and molded armor were visible beneath his overcoat. A sword with a well-worn grip rode at his hip.

The other man was stockier than the leader and nurtured an impressive mustache under a wide, flat nose. He bore a flanged mace and a blade with a wide knobbed pommel: a rondel dagger used to finish off plate-armored opponents by pounding it through helmet openings or gaps in their armor.

"Jop, water the horses. I'll get them some feed," the leader ordered the other as he walked to the edge of the clearing and broke off heads of corn.

There was something familiar in the man's face. Jaks wracked his memory to place where he'd seen him before but could not.

"Who are you?" Meila demanded again as the bald man walked back with an armful of corn ears.

He paused and looked at her. "No one you would know, nor that you need to know."

"Then what do you want from us?" she asked.

"I want you to just do what I tell you to do," he said, stripping the corn to the yellow and dropping them to the ground. "If you behave, I won't have to hurt you or your boyfriend."

"Where are you taking us? Are you going to sell us?"

"You've already been bought." He laughed, standing over his two captives.

Jaks plucked up his courage and shuffled to face the man. "You'd best let us go now. We travel under the king's seal with Grandmaster Mulgrave of the Academy. My sister is a nightwraith who could kill you both before you even saw her. And our master ranger will bring them right to us. If you let us go, you could get a head start—"

The leader laughed. "They won't have noticed you missing until about now." He gauged the dawn-lit sky. "And I think your *master ranger* will be sporting such a raging hangover from his drinks last night that he won't know a piss-hole from a pothole until midday." He planted his hands on his hips and leaned over Jaks. "I know how to cover my tracks."

"You have to let us go," Jaks implored.

"Be quiet. That's enough talking," said the bald man. He then returned to tending the horses and ordered his underling, "Jop, tie them back-to-back against the wall of the shack. I'm going to rest inside. Keep them quiet and wake me in an hour. Then we switch."

He untied a bedroll from his horse and disappeared inside.

The man named Jop dragged Jaks and Meila to the shack wall and dutifully roped them together. He then sat cross-legged under the cornstalks, several yards away, and stared at them. He muttered to himself and pulled out a cloth to rub the ridges of his mace.

A breeze shushed through the corn field and sparrows flew overhead as the sun arced higher into the morning.

After a while, Jop's hands slowed in their task and his head nodded and jerked up several times; after a few minutes, it slumped and he snored quietly—echoing louder snores came from inside the wooden shack.

By Jaks's estimations, hampered by night travel and an indirect path, they had only traveled fifteen or so miles from the rivertown. Their destination, the mountains that their captors had referred to, could only be the Northern Ranges Jaks knew well from his survival training. Their peaks were still twenty or more miles distant. But even so, he knew that Ranger Cromer would have a tough time even finding a lead from the tangential route of their kidnappers.

He found himself mired in defeat and hopelessness, in contrast to the defiance and anger he had seen smoldering in Meila's face. Although tied facing opposite directions, he could tell by the tugging movements and tension in her back that she hadn't let up—a wild dog who'd fight to the bitter end.

Defeatism wasn't going to help here; he needed to be more like her.

He needed to fight—and he knew the perfect weapon. *I can do it. I am not powerless. I can—I will—control magic.*

"Jaks, can you get at any knots?" Meila whispered, interrupting his thoughts. They leant back against each other, and her fingers brushed against his.

"No, how about you?" He bent his wrists and angled his fingers, but the rope was high around their wrists. "Are you hurt?"

"Just a pounding headache. I'm fine. We've got to escape. Do you have any ideas?"

Their guard emitted a loud snort and woke himself with a start. He looked up with groggy eyes.

Jaks and Meila desisted from testing their restraints.

He twisted his mustache and sat upright, blinking fatigue out of his eyes. "Did you say something?" he asked, smoothing out his mustache.

Jaks shook his head and stared at the ground.

A minute later, the man clambered to his feet, checked on the horses, and roamed around the clearing, looking for something of interest.

Thinking of her handgun and the half dozen knives and daggers she had armed herself with from the Academy armory, Jaks whispered to Meila, "Did they get all your weapons?"

"They got everything—even my boot knife."

"I can try to invoke magic. I might be able to electrocute them."

She paused before replying, "Not right now. Wait until either we're untied or you can get both of them at once. If you only get one, the other will end you . . . can you do it?"

"It's all we've got," he said, trying to sound confident, pushing away his self-doubt.

"You have to kill them, not just stun them." Her voice hushed as Jop reappeared. "I know you can do it, Jaks. Be brave."

Bored with his exploration, the mustached man settled back down to watch them while chewing on a piece of jerky. When he finished the meat stick, he wandered over and crouched in front of Meila.

Jaks twisted his head and saw the short man lifting her chin to appraise her.

"You're a sweet pie. Where are you from?" Jop brought his face in close to hers, the caterpillar of hair below his lip quivering. "I wouldn't mind a taste of you."

"Get away from me," she snapped at him, "or I'll wake your master."

"Bako's not my master," the man replied, but then released her and stepped back. "You play along, you hear? We got a long journey ahead, and I can be nice . . . or not nice to you." He settled back under the cornstalks, took out his dagger, and skewered fallen leaves.

With the sun angling over the cornfield, the captors and hostages left the shack and continued their ride south.

Jaks sat upright, alone on the middle horse—wrists bound and tied to the saddle, but feet unrestrained—leashed to the lead horse.

The bald man, who Jop had named Bako, rode with his arms around Meila ahead of him. Ostensibly, they looked like a father and child riding leisurely through the countryside; on closer inspection, an observer would see her tied up like the hostage that she was.

Jop took up the rear again and shot envious eyes at his associate's closeness to Meila; however, the other man had no physical interest in her other than to keep her upright in the saddle.

They emerged from the cornfields into a prairie of green grass and sped up to a trot, aiming toward the craggy mountains. A flock of starlings startled out of the long grass and flew off with caws and a thrash of wings. A farm building was several miles to the west, with what might have been cows or horses clustered near a barn house.

Over several hours, the prairie changed from crop fields to pastures of roaming cattle several times over as the mountains loomed closer.

Bako veered away from buildings or human contact but could not avoid a chance encounter with a farmer erecting a scarecrow.

They were traversing another cornfield when the stalks parted and revealed the man digging a hole with a shovel and a strawman nearby. Reflexively, the man yelled out, "Hey, you're damaging my crop."

Without a word, Jop cantered forward, whipping out his iron mace, his horse crushing cornstalks.

The farmer, seeing trouble, turned to run but was struck down by a single blow with the head-crushing weapon.

Jaks lost sight of Jop and the farmer as his horse continued in tow of Bako, but a few minutes later, the mustached warrior returned to his rearguard and winked at Jaks. "Unlucky fellow. Lucky crows, though, feeding on meat instead of corn for the next few days."

Finally, with the sun at one finger above the horizon, they rode into a valley climbing up to a tree line at the start of the mountain range.

Their captors visibly relaxed as they entered the forest, slowing their pace and joking about the unfortunate farmer.

The giantwoods were immense guardians of the forest, their boughs wider than some houses and their canopies so far overhead that only the most determined, courageous climbers could reach their leafy tops. The scent of the forest was familiar: sharp and crisp over a mustiness of decaying leaves and wood.

Beneath the creaking boughs, Jaks recalled the little woodland creatures he had encountered on the hunting-and-gathering exercise—seeming an eternity ago—however, no matter how much he wished it, he knew he would have to rely on his own wits, not the gentle dryads, for escape. They were far too small and docile to combat two human warriors.

Bako and Jop dismounted at a clearing with a pair of ten-foot-high ironwood trees at the center. Jaks and Meila were looped to one each.

After the horses were watered, fed, and secured at the clearing's edge, Jop held a waterskin to Meila's mouth and thrust a nob of bread into her hands, a task he then repeated with Jaks.

They ate hungrily—their restraints tied in a way that they could bring their hands to their mouths—and were surprised when Bako then dropped a thin strip of beef jerky and a carrot into their laps.

"Can you at least tell us where you're taking us?" Meila asked the bald man.

He looked at her with a wry smile. "Somewhere cold. You like cold?" he toyed with her.

Meila raised her eyebrows. "Look. You're a smart man. We'll cut you a deal. If you let us go right now, Jaks and I will head back down the valley and forget this ever happened. I can guarantee no one will even bother to look for you—we have better things to do. Deal?"

Bako smiled at her. "I'm not that stupid. You have no bargaining chits to offer; you'll do what I say, girly." He nodded to himself. "I think I'll keep ahold of you for the time being. Boy Rauhalik here, though, I will leave behind in the morning."

At the sound of his family name, Jaks spluttered, "How do you know who I am? Who are you?" Jaks asked.

The bald man frowned and flicked a hand at him. "Never you mind. Now, shut up, the both of you. I think I'll gag you both tonight."

After a simple meal over a campfire, they then bickered until Jop, resignedly, sat the first watch as the leader lay down and rested his head on his scabbard and was soon snoring.

Again, Jop proved a sloppy guard and nodded off as well, slumped at the edge of the clearing against a giantwood. The campfire cooled to a glow, and darkness settled in. A warm night, the forest sighed and rustled high above where the leafy foliage met the abyss of night.

Jaks could see Meila's silhouetted form against her tree, two yards away, but couldn't speak through the cloth gag in his mouth.

Now wasn't the time to attack.

But it was time to prepare.

Closing his eyes, Jaks reached into the depths of his mind for the invocation and awoke to the nightmare of his father's horrific hands and his huge, bearded face emerging from the dark. He flinched, even though it was just a mental image, anticipating the hands on his throat. He clenched his jaw and bit on the cloth in his mouth.

Fear swirled around him and rose like flood waters, enveloping him and about to drown him when a numbness descended—a protective mist to beat away the flood—but instead of succumbing to it, as he normally did, he pushed it aside and summoned the image of his mother lying at the foot of the stairs.

Anger ignited and flared, recalling his father ordering him

to mop up the congealing blood. Shoulders tensed and blood boiled.

Inner fire seared with the memory of being ordered to clean the carnage and the monster calling her "the whore."

With the Anger parting the mists of the Fear, he steadied the deadly emotions and held them ready. It was almost more than he could bear, but the anger spurred him to endure greater fear than he had ever felt before. *Courage.*

He cupped his hands and imagined a tiny ball of lightning nestled inside, pulsing blue-white like a miniature storm cloud firing out sparks every which way.

With the visualization vivid, and trembling with fear, he willed the lightning to be.

The hairs on his arm rose.

Acrid metal clouded his nostrils.

A white spark arced between his palms with a snap and then flicked out of sight.

Encouraged by the attempt, he renewed the visualization and channeled his fear again.

Blue and white flashed within Jaks's hand, but steady this time, gradually brightening. He tightened his fingers around a ball of scintillating sparks.

Through a gap between his hands, he stared at the magic he had invoked as if it were the most precious treasure he had ever found. Then his delight extinguished the fear and anger, and along with it, the electromancy.

Undeterred, he repeated the steps. And several times more, he channeled the ball of lightning.

Having forgotten to breathe while he magicked, he sucked in a deep breath and panted. Overjoyed at his accomplishment, he kicked his bound feet against the ground.

Meila grunted. She also kicked her heels, and the silhouette of her head nodded excitedly. She had seen his electromancy.

The mustached man, however, kept on snoring, having not seen a thing. Likewise, the bald man by the campfire lay unmoving, asleep.

Violent thoughts leached into Jaks's mind. *Come on, you bastards, untie me. Gather close. I have something for you.*

The giantwoods creaked and rustled their leaves as though to caution him. *Wait for daylight. Wait for dawn.*

Chapter 27

The Waterfall

The distant shrill cry of a wyvern woke Jaks, slumped against the ironwood. He shivered to throw off the chill of the night as a thin blanket of mist trickled down the wooded slope.

The bald man and Meila were already awake. Bako was crouched behind her and untying the rope that held her to the tree. With her wrists still bound, she groaned and struggled to her feet. Her eyes met Jaks's wearily—she hadn't rested well either.

"Give me some privacy," Meila said to Bako and disappeared behind some bracken.

The man followed, despite her request. The campfire was now just black ash and lumps, and Jaks could see Jop on the other side of it.

A few minutes later, Meila and Bako returned. "Sit back down," the man ordered. "I'm not having you wander around."

Jaks grunted and wheezed around his gag, drawing the attention of the senior man.

"I suppose you have to go now too?" said Bako, striding over to him. He removed the gag and released the knots behind Jaks's back.

After the rope fell slack, Jaks pushed against the tree to stand. It felt good to get to his feet. He ached all over from lying half-slouched all night, and his head still pounded from the whack it had taken a couple of nights before. He really did need to empty his bladder and stumbled behind the tree to tug at his breeches.

"When you're finished, get back there." Bako stood waiting with the rope in his hands.

Jaks hiked his breeches back up and turned to face his captor, arms tense and a bead of sweat forming on his brow. It was time. Even though his hands were still bound, he was on his feet and a lightning invocation would need only travel a few feet to strike Bako, then a second invocation against Jop. The second man had risen and stood yawning, arms outstretched. *I can take them out. Bako, then Jop—one, then the other.*

Jaks's and Meila's eyes met. She gave him a single nod.

"All right, sit down, boy. Haven't got all day. When we leave you here, I'll give you a blunt knife, so that you can cut yourself out of the ropes. It might take you a while, but you'll get free, and your daddy won't be angry with us. Well, I think so, anyway. Who knows with him?" Bako gestured with a finger for him to sit.

He gawped at the bald man and shook his head. "My father?" A memory flooded back. That was where Jaks recognized this man from. Back at his family's manse, months ago, one of his father's henchmen whom Vixhana had fought. Back then, the man still had some hair, albeit a mere crescent from ear to ear.

Bako placed a scarred hand on Jaks's shoulder and pressed

him downward.

"Did my father send you?" asked Jaks. His knees buckled and he sank to the ground, mouth still agape. His plan to attack faltered. "Why would he send you? I don't understand any of this."

"You're not meant to." Bako tied him back to the ironwood. "Just don't try to come after us. You won't have any chance of catching up on foot." He ambled off to check on the horses and gave Jop an order to ready the saddlebags.

Jaks struggled against his restraints. Now, Bako was too far away to attempt a lightning attack, and being fully restrained again, he'd lost his opportunity.

Meila called out, "Don't just leave him here tied up. Cut him free before you leave him. A bear or wyvern might get him while he's still bound."

"He'll be fine. Few of those around these parts of the woods," Bako replied. Then to Jaks, he said, "Just head back the way we came and follow the valley to the plains. You'll find your way back easy enough."

"Cut me free," begged Jaks. "I promise I won't follow you," he lied. He couldn't just let them flit away with Meila and leave him here trussed to the tree. He needed to take action now—but he needed to be on his feet, not tied up. *Could electromancy sever the rope?*

He curled his knees up in front of him and pressed his wrist binds against his legs. Bako and Jop were turned away. Meila's eyes jerked back and forth in fear.

He imagined a white blade of electricity against the loops of hessian, then summoned the fear as he had the previous night— his arms tensed, heart hammering to escape his chest. He *pushed* the mental image into reality.

A fine sliver of blue-white light appeared at his wrists, and the rope began to smoke. The pungent cloud filled his mouth and nose, startling Jaks into a spasm of coughing.

The blade disappeared, and he hastily blew the smoke away. The rope was blackened and singed, a few fibers parted by the brief invocation. He looked up at the two men, oblivious, busy with feedbags for the horses.

Meila's eyes were wide. She mouthed the words, *You did it.* She looked at their captors and back to Jaks, then shook her head.

It would create too much smoke. They would notice before he could sear through the ropes. *Unless I do it in short bursts while blowing the smoke away.*

He invoked the lightning blade two more times, burning a quarter of his wrist bind, until Bako and Jop finished fastening the saddlebags and walked back toward them.

"What's burning?" Bako peered around the clearing, and into the depths of the forest, but finding nothing, he shrugged.

A few minutes later, Jop had Meila untied and onto her feet.

It was all going too fast.

The bald man padded over to him and ran a thumb over a short knife. "It's even blunter than I thought, but you'll get there." The knife dropped to the ground by Jaks's feet.

He kept his knees curled up and wrists tucked low. Better not to say anything. *Just let them get out of sight, and I can sear through the ropes in a few minutes.*

Jop wrapped his meaty hands around Meila and pushed her up onto a saddled horse, then threw the tether to Bako on the lead horse. "Have a nice life, boy. If it'd been up to me—I would've slit your throat yesterday. Think of me having fun with your woman." He laughed as he clambered onto his brown gelding.

Meila and her captors rode into the forest. She cast back an agonized look as her horse was led away.

Jaks ignored the knife at his feet and looked down to his hands and once again invoked the lightning blade against the wrist bindings. He channeled a bright, thin edge. A swirling cloud of smoke and yellow flames rewarded his effort. Finally, the hessian fibers burnt through and he wrenched his wrists free. It had taken less than a minute.

Jop's back and his horse were still visible amongst the giantwood boughs and low-lying brush heading up the mountainside.

He didn't care if they saw the smoke now; he'd be out of the ropes before they could get back.

Hands free, he grabbed the knife and held it to the loop of rope binding him to the tree. He invoked lightning through the blade. Tiny arcs of electricity leapt and snapped over the steel, coming together where Jaks pressed it against the rope, and quickly burnt it through.

By the time the last strand fell away, Jop's horse had disappeared from view.

Each invocation of electromancy had fatigued him like a weight dragging on his head and shoulders. His emotions were frazzled, flagellating him like a whip. He needed a rest—but each minute was a minute that Meila and her captors got further away. *I've got to get them back in sight. I can't risk losing them.*

Jaks stumbled to his feet, stuck the knife under his belt, then began jogging through the forest in the direction he'd last seen the last horse.

A few minutes later, he paused to catch his breath.

No sighting of man or horse.

He looked to the ground for recent disturbance and

breathed a sigh of relief when, not too far away, he found fresh horse prints.

Master Cromer would be impressed.

He laughed at the random thought and shook his head; now was not the time for self-congratulations.

Eventually, Jaks caught a glimpse of a brown horse a hundred yards ahead. He sighed with relief and hurried forward, keeping the giantwoods between them. Now that he was tracking them, he wracked his brain for a plan to rescue Meila.

If he called out to them while they rode, Bako and Jop would turn back, and he wouldn't know what direction they would approach—it would devolve into a melee and risk getting Meila or himself killed. No. Better to continue tracking them until they stopped for a break. Then he could sneak to within a few yards, ambush one and then the other before they could defend themselves. A simple plan, or so he thought.

As he scurried after Meila and the two men, he thought back to his lessons with Grandmaster Mulgrave for a clue about which aspect of invocation would increase the power of an invocation.

Willpower, visualization, or emotion?

The difficulty came when he focused on the mental control part of the invocation. The more attention he gave to willing the image into reality, the less fear he felt; not that it removed the fear, but that it became distant and detached.

Meila's wise guidance on the coupling of anger and fear had allowed Jaks to achieve enough fear for the electromancy, but his lessons with Mulgrave had never passed a beginner's level— he could play random notes of the instrument, but he couldn't play a melody.

Willpower, visualization, or emotion? He suspected it was all three—he would have to find out by himself.

Bako and Jop continued in the same southward direction as yesterday and skirted the inner edge of the mountain forest. Even so, the ground undulated across valleys and hills until Jaks's legs burned and his breath labored to keep up with them.

Thoughts of the grandmaster turned him to wonder whether the mage and the others were close by. His boast about Ranger Cromer's tracking skill had been fantastical, but it was possible that the eagle-eyed mountaineer might have picked up their trail by now. Despite his anxiety about his ex-instructor, Jaks respected the man's sharp mind and experience. However, with the situation as it was, it came down to just him.

If he failed to act, Meila could be lost to Bako's payman forever. He shook his head at the idea that his father was involved somehow. What interest could he have in her? How did he even know of her? Maybe Bako had a new employer, someone who wanted Meila for some inscrutable cause.

The riders stopped up ahead at a dark pool beneath an outcrop of rock. A waterfall fanned water from a crest several yards up and collected in the center of the pool with a churn of fine mist. Flat rocks lined the fine-looking pool. The horses dipped their heads to drink.

Jaks scrambled to within earshot of the group, colossal tree trunks hiding his approach.

One rider dismounted and crouched at the water's edge; the stocky figure of Jop cupped his hands, dipped them into the pool, and drank.

Bako looked down the wide stream feeding off the pool, as though searching for its end.

Meila flicked a look at Jaks, and their eyes met briefly. She knew he was there.

He slunk back behind the tree. Was she sending him a warning that he was too obvious?

"What a beautiful place." Meila's voice sounded in the distance. "Bring me some of the fresh water to drink."

Bako grunted. "You're a little princess, aren't you . . . yes, your majesty—would you like a slice of lemon with that?" he said.

Jaks dared another glimpse. Bako had dismounted from his horse with a flaccid goat bladder in hand, and now bent to plunge it into the rushing water.

"I need a few minutes," Jop said to Bako, then unbuckled his belt and walked behind a clump of ferns well away from the water. He dropped his trousers and crouched out of sight.

Bako lifted the full waterskin out of the stream and walked over to place it into Meila's bound hands.

She balanced on the saddle and drank deeply.

She passed the waterskin back to Bako and said, "Many thanks." It slipped from her fingers and bounced against Bako's chest and onto the ground with a thud.

Water drenched his front and poured over his boots.

"Oops. I'm so sorry," Meila said as he jumped away. At the same time, her horse scuttled sideways, obscuring Jaks's view of the man.

Had she fabricated the distraction on purpose? It didn't matter. Jaks scrambled up to and behind the giantwood closest to them—only ten yards from Meila.

Jaks's chest pounded. His mouth was dry as he pressed against the coarse bark and listened.

"Like I said, it just slipped out of my hands," Meila was saying. "That disgusting animal skin was slimy and slippery. Where I come from, we have bottles. Maybe you should look into it. Don't blame me." An imperious tone that Jaks had never heard her use before.

Bako replied in an exasperated voice, "You're acting like a child. This kidnapping business is ridiculous. The sooner I'm rid of you, the better."

Jaks took two breaths and stepped out from behind the tree.

"What . . . how in seven hells are you here?" Bako froze mid-dab with a cloth and gawped at Jaks.

"Let her go," Jaks said. He had hoped to sound commanding, but his voice quivered, and his throat tightened. "I don't want to hurt you, but I will if you don't let her go."

Bako laughed loudly, silencing the cicadas and insects nearby. "You won't . . . *hurt* me. That's a rare one. What are you going to do? Fight me with that dulled knife I gave you?"

The warrior dropped the cloth, placed a hand on his scabbard, and tilted his head at Jaks.

"What's happening?" Jop's head poked up from behind the bushes.

"Wipe your arse and get a load of this," said Bako.

Jaks raised his right arm and pointed outstretched fingers toward the bald warrior. "Stand back, I'm telling you." His words were authoritative, but his soul was fearful. He retreated a step when Bako sauntered toward him with a grin on his face.

At that moment, Meila dug her heels into her horse's sides as Jaks had taught her a few days earlier and kicked her horse into motion. The animal whinnied, then leapt and trotted forward. She tilted dangerously in the saddle and gripped the saddle horn with her hands.

"Damn it. Get her!" Bako yelled and ran after the startled mare.

The horse hurtled past Jop, who stumbled to his feet and then lumbered after it. He struggled with his breeches and tripped after a few yards. Up on his feet, he buckled his leggings into place and returned to his pursuit—well behind the escaping equine and its rider.

"I'll get a horse." Bako stopped and turned to the two remaining horses.

Jaks stood in his way.

"Get out of the way. This has gone far enough, no matter whose son you are." The warrior strode toward Jaks. His longsword rasped as he pulled it from the scabbard.

Jaks planted his feet and thrust a trembling hand toward Bako, but didn't have time to recall the practiced invocation involving his brutal father—the swordsman was almost upon him.

A hand reached forward to shove Jaks's arm aside; the other raised the longsword, preparing to strike.

Terrified, Jaks fought the instinct to flinch and instead straightened. Anger rallied his fear into courage. *How dare he attack and bind us like animals? How dare he dismiss me like a child? Die, you bastard.*

"Damn you to hell," yelled Jaks.

A fork of white electricity skimmed the air to Bako's hand.

Electricity channeled into his body. Excited tendrils of magic danced over the man.

A brilliance illuminated the area, and the crack of lightning shattered the tranquility of the forest.

The explosion lifted Bako off his feet. His limbs and torso arched, muscles contracted, and he was thrown back several yards.

The acrid smell that followed each invocation of electromancy filled Jaks's nostrils. Although its harshness made him wince, his lips curled and he welcomed it as a mark of a successful invocation. His arms fell to his sides, and he stared at the motionless body lying beside the stream. Smoke wafted from the man's blackened hands and boots. *Was he dead?*

The smell of burnt flesh hit him with a wave of nausea; he pursed his lips and clenched his throat to calm his stomach. He walked over to the body and picked up Bako's longsword. A well-balanced weapon, its grip was blackened but otherwise undamaged. He prodded Bako's body with the tip of the sword and dry retched at the sight of his burnt, peeled skin, and the man's melted eyeballs—congealed pulpy ooze in their sockets.

I killed him.

He staggered away from the corpse and squatted with his head low as he battled with the guilt of killing a man. *He deserved it. It was either me or him.*

He shook his head, remembering his purpose, then stood and gazed into the forest for signs of Meila.

Nothing but the giantwood sentinels and their shadows.

He would need to search for her; on horseback would be best. The warriors' two horses had bolted at the sound of the lightning bolt, but the trained animals wouldn't have gone far. He would find them and go after Meila.

However, as he followed the horse tracks—going back to their original trail—a voice called out behind him.

"Grafuk! What the hell happened here?" Jop was half-way down the hillside, gaping at Bako's lifeless body. He was astride Meila's brown mare, while she herself shuffled on foot behind him on the end of a long leather leash around her neck.

A cut and bruise marked the left side of Meila's forehead, complementing the purple bruise on the other side of her head.

"Boy. Who did that to Bako?" The stocky warrior's eyes narrowed and he surveyed the forest, not knowing that the killer stood before him.

"Me. I killed him," Jaks said, his voice so confident that he surprised himself. "I killed Bako. And I will kill you, too, unless you get off your horse and drop your weapons." He raised his arm and pointed at the stocky warrior.

Jop harrumphed and stared back and forth between Jaks and Bako's body several times. "*You* did that? You're a mage?"

"Get off the horse and lie on the ground," commanded Jaks.

In a swift movement belying his rounded shape, Jop dismounted and tugged on the leather leash, pulling Meila stumbling toward him. "I don't think so."

The same height as her, he spun behind her and flashed one of his rondel daggers to her throat.

Meila's face twisted in anger.

"Listen to me, boy. You may have got Bako by surprise, but I've got the upper hand now, don't I?"

"You can't harm her. You have to take her to your master." Jaks's outstretched right hand wavered while the left gripped the blackened sword at his side, parallel to the ground.

Jop shoved Meila forward until they stood alongside Bako's disfigured corpse. "Nasty work. Never liked the bastard, anyway. But you try that on me and you'll burn the girl too."

Despite her peril, Meila laughed. "I haven't been a girl for over a century, you filthy pig."

Without warning, she snapped her head back into Jop's broad face. The dagger fell from his stunned fingers. As he reeled back, she half-turned and kicked her heel into his right shin.

The man fell to the ground. But with the leash still wrapped in his fist, Meila was yanked down too. Both of them rolled to within a few feet of Bako's dead body.

Swiftly, Meila grabbed the leash with her hands to ease the tension. "Get him, Jaks."

With a roar, Jop surged up to his feet, one hand pulling on

the leash and the other tugging on the mace at his belt. Crimson flowed freely from his nose and dripped from his chin.

Meila was too near.

The magic could kill her, even if the warrior was the target. He knew little of electromancy, but from his readings of Grandmaster Vinton's archives, he knew well enough that lightning could leap from victim to victim with indiscriminate lethality.

With magic out of the fight, Jaks grasped the longsword in both hands and raised the blade to a middle-guard position. During conscription, he had trained with the longsword but had never mastered the strikes and lunges, lacking the aggressiveness to react quickly or strike well. Now, he had no choice but to set sword against mace.

The mustached warrior sneered, released the leash, and shoved Meila away. "Yes, fight like a man."

She stumbled away from the warrior.

Nothing to protect him now, thought Jaks.

Jop hefted his mace over his right shoulder with both hands and lurched forward with a blood-curdling scream.

I won't fight like a man, I will fight like a battlemage.

Electricity hummed into being as Jaks visualized and bent his bristling fear. The blade sparked with crooked tendrils of the white energy as he intended—but a second later, stuttered and fled from the shining steel.

The mace smashed against the longsword, knocking it aside like a stick in a child's hands. The stocky warrior then charged bodily into Jaks and slammed him onto his back, knocking the wind out of him and causing the sword to spin out of his hands.

The warrior stood over him—face bloodied and contorted— and raised the mace two-handed over his head. The evil flanges of the mace would crush his skull easily.

Jaks threw a hand up to ward off the deadly blow and frantically mustered the three aspects of invocation together.

Desperate, he willed up a bolt of lightning.

Snap. Light leapt out from his hand; however, instead of a powerful bolt, three thin forks of lightning crackled.

They struck Jop in the chest, but weren't strong enough to blast him off his feet as with the first warrior.

Regardless, the man careened backward in pain and alarm. His mace fell from his hand.

"You little prick," Jop yelled as he bent down to the mace lying next to the water's edge. The waterfall, just a few yards away, spilled its foamy discharge into the pool.

Suddenly, Meila appeared behind Jop with a dagger in her hands. She raised her rope-bound wrists and plunged the needle-sharp weapon into his upper back—ramming it through leather armor, skin, and lung.

Once. Twice.

The brute cried and twisted toward her. Pain etched his face and blood spluttered from his mouth.

Turning sideward to Jop, Meila balanced on her left leg and brought the other to her chest. Her boot lashed out in a side kick and smashed Jop in the face with a satisfying crunch.

He fell backward and toppled into the water. His face mangled with a broken nose and split lip, he splashed about on all fours at the edge of the pool, blood pumping from his mouth and nose. He managed to stand waist-deep for several moments until his footing slipped and his knees collapsed. Weakening fast, he thrashed about, stumbling further and further into the pool.

One more step—and the downpour of the waterfall pummeled him down and held him under a frothy, blood-tinged embrace.

Breathing heavily, Jaks rose to his feet and walked over to Meila. They stared for a long minute at where the body lay submerged.

"Should we fish him out?" Jaks asked. Even though they had killed these men who had been their captors, human bodies deserved some respect. "Bury him?"

"We have nothing to dig a grave with. Besides, that one already has a watery one. The other . . . the carrion eaters can just feast on. Such are the cycles of life," she replied in a dismissive tone.

The forest had now dimmed into late afternoon. A light breeze murmured through the wooded canopy and fantails flitted from branch to forest floor around the waterfall, oblivious to the violence that had scuffed up the ground to expose the bugs and worms they eagerly plucked.

Soon, a pair of small green dragons winged into the boughs high above and clung to the trees, necks sinuating as they eyed up the meat on Bako's corpse. Greens didn't worry him; the smallest of the dragons, they never attacked live humans, but dead ones, he was sure they would.

Jaks cut the rope binding Meila's wrists. "Are you hurt?" he asked, looking directly into her bruised face for the first time since the fight began.

"Nothing major. How about you?" Her eyes softened and her tense lips smoothed to a line.

He minimized his aches and pains with a head shake and asked, "Why did they want you?"

"I have no idea. Other than being a curiosity, I don't know why anyone would want to kidnap me. Unless they know about . . ."

"Perhaps they're after the weapons on your ship. Someone found out about them or was told about them."

Meila shrugged, looking deep in thought. She extended her neck as Jaks fumbled at the knot tying the leather leash around it.

"That man," Jaks nodded at Bako's body. "I think he used to work for my father. But I can't think why he would want to kidnap you. He's an evil man, but it's beyond me why he would do this."

"Your *father* organized this? What has he got to do with it? I can't get my head around any of this. We need more information . . ." Meila walked over to the body and rummaged through the clothes but found nothing of interest. She sighed. "We need to find those other horses. They may hold clues, and I need my darkie back."

Unwilling to let the man be ripped apart and eaten by the dragons, Jaks grabbed the dead man by the legs and pushed him into the pool. The waterfall greedily welcomed the second body into its depths.

"You know, they'll most likely bloat up and float ashore downstream," the woman commented.

Jaks frowned but said nothing and turned to leave. With the mare in tow, they regained the sunken tracks of the other two horses and left the waterfall to its gruesome new inhabitants.

A quarter hour later, they spotted Bako's stallion and Jop's gelding nuzzling through the undergrowth around a cluster of boulders. The horses looked up briefly and returned to their grazing.

They searched the saddlebags. Meila breathed a sigh of relief as she drew out her handgun from a jumble of hardware, including Jaks's shortsword, her assortment of knives, and a couple of runestone lights. She holstered the darkcore gun and secreted the sheathed blades about her body.

Their kidnappers had been well supplied with rations,

blankets, and two tents, but nothing to reveal the identity of their employer.

"Is this a good place to camp tonight?" she asked Jaks, who was tethering the horses to a beech tree.

"Good as any. I'll get a fire ready. I've been in these parts of the woods before and there are wild animals we should watch out for." Green dragons were nothing, but a wyvern or frostbear sneaking up on them would be a disaster. He finished belting on his scabbard and then searched the area for sticks and branches.

"I suppose I'll go set up a shelter," Meila said.

As the last rays of daylight vanished, they sat beside Jaks's sputtering campfire in its circle of stones and ate hardtack biscuits from Bako's supplies.

A memory of him and Meila singing together the first time they met came back to him. He smiled. He would've loved to sing with her again, but now was not the time for noise and distraction.

She interrupted his thought, asking, "Where do we go from here?" She handed him a waterskin and he nodded thanks. "Back to the rivertown or Dunberrin?"

He wasn't thirsty but sipped a mouthful and gave it back. "I think we retrace our path back to the rivertown. If Vixhana and the others are on our trail, we'll hopefully cross tracks. If we don't find them along the way, we'll have no choice but to return to the Academy."

She nodded and after a few minutes placed a hand on his arm. "Thanks, Jaks. Thank you for coming to rescue me from those men. I know you didn't have to, and you put yourself in great danger to come for me." Her intense brown eyes bore into his.

"I had to." He looked aside as heat rushed up his neck. "There was no one else around."

Despite his earlier courage, he faltered from telling her that he couldn't bear a day without her, that she was his every waking moment, and that he would go to the ends of the world for her. It wasn't just her beauty—delicate features, lithe and graceful—it was her intensity and inner strength that drew him to her like a nail to a magnet. He revered and desired her. She was a goddess to him.

"I couldn't have done it without you. You stopped Jop when I faltered," he said and shuddered at the image of the man and his mace standing over him with murderous eyes.

"You killed the bald one—he was terribly disfigured. I'm guessing you used electromancy on him?"

He nodded. "What you told me the other night helped. It made sense what you said about fear and anger working together. Anger has always been an evil to me, I've avoided it. It was my father's domain, his rages, his beatings. But you made me realize that anger is neither evil nor good—it's just an emotion. I was able to draw on it when I was about to panic. And gathered the courage to complete the invocation against Bako."

"I'm glad you overcame the barrier. You did well." She picked up a stick and stabbed at the fire. After a long pause, she said, "That brute would have raped me eventually, even with the other one around. I know men; they're no different here than home. His eyes were always on me. He would have taken me when the other was asleep. I'm glad I killed the pig."

Her bluntness about murder, and that she had plunged the dagger so efficiently into Jop, sent a chill through him. She was callous sometimes. Regardless, he couldn't help but draw confidence from her self-assurance and grimaced at the memory of the violent thug receiving his comeuppance.

"You wouldn't understand . . . or maybe you would. When

that man in the tavern grabbed you and forced you to dance. What did that feel like?" she asked with the tip of her stick flaming like a candle over the fire.

"Filthy. I was as disgusted at myself for not being able to get away from him as I was at his hands groping me—he had such a strong grip. I felt violated." He shuddered at the memory.

"Exactly. That's how you feel after you've been forced . . ." Her stick burnt out and she threw the rest into the fire.

He thought about what she had said for a few minutes, realization brewing, and then asked in quiet horror, "You've been raped before?"

She rubbed at her right wrist. "This isn't the first time I've been a prisoner. Last time, my captor was someone I thought I loved. I was only twenty, and I was so naïve that I didn't see the warning signs. He had eyes like fire and a voice like thunder. I joined his colony on a station orbiting Mars. Long story short, over a year, I went from being his wife to being a pleasure slave for all the men in the commune. I only escaped when a government raid came and arrested him for fraud . . . I've said enough." She jumped up and paced to the other side of the campfire.

"I'm sorry, I didn't mean to open old wounds." He rose and stood awkwardly, not knowing how to retrieve the moment.

After a minute, she came to him beside the flickering flames and gripped his forearms. "It's okay, Jaks. It was a long time ago. Time heals. The scars are healed, and I've had much happiness and joy in my life since then. Even with Anton gone, I know that I'll find happiness again sometime. I'm pretty happy just to be alive right now." She smiled up at him.

He drank in oval eyes and wide lips, inviting in the firelight. Intoxicated with her nearness and the touch of her hands, he longed to embrace and devour her. Face filled with desire, he reached forward to wrap his arms around her and bent down to her lips.

"No, Jaks. Don't." She pushed him away and stood with a hand raised between them. "I'm sorry. I must be giving you the wrong signals. It's not right. You're still a boy."

He bristled at her words, wanting to reach for her. "I'm not a boy. I love. I love you."

"No, you don't," she said. "You're too young to know what love is. You're just infatuated with me. If I lay with you, it would be wrong. You should be with sweet things your own age—like that serving girl the other day." She crossed her arms, her face unreadable. "It's not going to happen." She retreated to the tent she'd pitched and huddled under a blanket.

The rest of the evening, Jaks toiled the fire and ruminated, rejection twisting like a knife. He shouldn't have just thrown himself at her. She deserved more respect than a rut in a forest. She was vastly more mature and experienced than he, and infinitely more knowledgeable. *What did I expect?* He would apologize in the morning and pray things returned to normal.

She woke around midnight, climbed out of the tent and over to the campfire—flames teased a dry branch that Jaks had thrown on just minutes before.

"I didn't expect you up so soon." He rose as she approached. "Meila, I'm sorry—"

"Don't worry about it, Jaks. It's not your fault. Sometimes these things happen when you're young. Let's just go back to how it was, okay?" She smiled at him, tugged her navy-blue cloak about her, and crouched by the fire. "Go get some rest. I'll keep the fire going. I'll wake you if I see anything."

He lay in the tent and closed his eyes, listening to her shuffle about the campsite for a few minutes; then, not realizing how tired he was, he fell asleep.

<h1 style="text-align:center">Chapter 28</h1>

<h1 style="text-align:center">Ascoria Invaded</h1>

Lord Sicaro—Province of Sanford, Ascoria

The sounds of battle were magnificent to Sicaro's ears. It had been too long since he had heard the clang of steel and the war cries of men and women hacking and stabbing each other to death. Grander than the ridiculous orchestras of the Ascorian king and sweeter than the screeching operas of his dead wife.

That morning, at an Ascorian encampment just five miles from Castle Sanford, he meandered amongst crushed tents, smoldering campfires, and dying Ascorian soldiers. He stopped at a man crawling through a pool of blood and kicked the man over to find he was, in fact, unwounded. Grimacing, he smashed down the steel tip of his six-foot hammer into the craven's skull against his shrill pleas for mercy.

Ahead of him, pockets of frantic Ascorian soldiers stood back-to-back as Vor warriors surrounded them and struck them down, one by one.

A young soldier broke out and ran across an open field, only for a broad-shouldered warrior woman to toss a spear at him that impaled him in the back. An impressive throw of sixty yards.

Elsewhere, other Ascorians had thrown down their weapons and were being trussed up into a slave chain—so many in number that Sicaro spat in disgust at the display of mass cowardice.

"Silas should be ashamed how low the army has fallen since I left command," he said to the Elliptan assassin shadowing his side, trailed by ten Sanford men-at-arms. "A clear reflection of the weakness of their leader."

"Aye, my lord. Quite so . . . Commander Lytton struggled pitiably when I strangled him. Couldn't command his bladder, let alone a battalion," Craeg Vesenira replied with his eyes fixed on the spear-thrower as she hefted an oversized battleaxe.

The woman clanked toward them, her plate mail pauldrons overlapping a chest plate emblazoned with the volcano crest of the Vor army. Taller than most Ascorian men, but average for women of the Burnt Lands, she threw her helm to the ground, planted her feet shoulder-width apart, and draped gauntleted hands over the end of her axe. Close-set eyes appraised him. "Lord Sicaro. I am *telsun* Cloete, leader of Zenith Torgue. We met briefly at one of your meetings with King Harek earlier this year . . . We are almost done with this camp."

"I see, telsun. How fared the initial assault?" asked Sicaro.

"They were forewarned. Probably by fires from the other assaults further up the coast. However, they didn't expect an ambush in their own camp. My torgue assaulted directly whilst Basalt and Granite Torgues attacked from the flanks. It was a massacre, my lord. A delicious bloodbath. We suffered one casualty to their hundred dead and captured." She delivered her report in a strong Vor accent—guttural and breathy—reminding him of his dead mother.

"Just make sure there are none feigning death to escape."

The woman nodded. "If the rest of the Ascorian army fights as poorly as these, we could be in Dunberrin by spring," she said, wiping her nose and sneering at the final prisoners being tethered to the slave chain.

"I admire your confidence, telsun. King Harek and I would be pleased if we could stretch so far, so quickly . . . but why rush? There is nothing more magnificent or beautiful than war. Would you not linger?"

Her gaze faltered and she pursed her lips. "Surely, my lord. I cannot say. That is up to the king to choose." She rotated her shoulders, moving easily despite her shell of steel.

"You are a griefmaster?" He used the Vor term for those gifted with gravmancy. He stepped forward and placed a gloved hand on her arm and *weighted* her elbow with his own gravmantic power. She staggered, her arm dragging her down under magicked weight, but within the blink of an eye, she recovered, standing tall as she countered his magic with her own.

"No match for you, my lord." She lowered her eyes, and Sicaro released her arm.

He stared at her and savored her deference, envisaging his defiant daughter Vixhana in a similar pose of submission. What he'd give to beat her down. Pummel her to a pulp for interfering with his reunion with Karisa.

"My lord, we should get moving if we are to receive King Harek at the castle at midday," Craeg said, interrupting his master's thoughts.

"Sergeant, have your men burn the bodies. Stockpile armor and weapons, but burn any Ascorian insignia—they have no place here anymore." Sicaro dismissed the woman and then returned to his destrier.

His armored retinue followed a cobbled road back toward his stronghold, a six-towered castle overlooking the town of Sanford. Pillars of smoke ranged up and down the surrounding coast, cleansing the Ascorian blight to make way for his Vor cousins and settlers to help bring this realm into a new era.

That his family, a generation ago, had been welcomed into Ascoria as refugees, was a great irony to him. For today, he had summoned war to its very shores.

His father had been a royal guard in one of the many fiefdoms of Voros—then known as the Burnt Lands—back when borders rose and fell by the year. He'd impregnated the king's only daughter and, suffering her father's wrath, had fled with her to Ascoria.

As a son of royalty, Sicaro could have had claim to some nameless region; however, it was all meaningless now that Harek had annexed and conquered all the Burnt Lands, claiming them under one crown. Harek had done all the hard work for him.

His thoughts returned to the task at hand as he entered the outskirts of Sanford. His eyes trailed over the two hundred village folk corralled into the market square by his troops. Ironically, the same troops who had, until the previous day, been responsible for defending and protecting them. He caught sight of the town's mayor and ambled his horse over to tower above the man.

"Lord Sicaro, how dare you treat us like this." The mayor looked up, straightening as tall as he could. "You're a traitor to Ascoria. King Silas will have your head for this treachery."

Two men-at-arms stood between the town official and their lord, swords and shields shoved into the man's face.

Sicaro admired Mayor Trentholm's bravery, a rarity in this sedate country. However, such men with passion and a righteous cause incited rebellions amongst the peasants and could not be tolerated.

"Alas, it will be King Silas's head that shall be kicked through the streets." Sicaro, adorned in gold-embossed armor and a black cloak, slipped from his stallion and thudded to the ground, clutching the warhammer Sorrow in one hand. "Down on your knees, man."

The two soldiers prodded the mayor in the back of the legs.

The man stared up defiantly at Sicaro. "Do what you want, but God as my witness, you will burn in hell for all you have done."

Cries of fear and anguished sobbing rose from the gathered villagers. Parents shielded their children's eyes and averted their own.

Sorrow rose above Sicaro's head, six feet of metal topped by a giant fist bearing a sharp steel stake. It descended in a blur. The fist smashed down into Mayor Trentholm's head, pulverizing his skull and ripping through his torso in an explosion of blood and gore.

Screams from the village folk accompanied the crunch and squelch of the grav-augmented blow. What remained of the mayor's body slumped to the ground. Burst bowels stenched the square, and smashed bones and internal organs smeared the cobblestones.

Sicaro righted his bloodied hammer and gazed at the horrified villagers. Nodding to the captain of his men-at-arms, he said, "As you were, Captain. Continue your orders for the rest of them. You should be at the slave camp by nightfall. March well. Don't let any of them escape. I will need as many as we can get in the coming years." He returned to his destrier and climbed into the saddle. Yes, he would need tens of thousands for the ambitious works he had in mind.

At midday, a column of warriors traversed Sanford bridge. The array of siege weapons brimming the castle at Sicaro's sides could have made quick work of the warband if he had wanted; however, these warriors were his welcome guests—and perhaps one day, his loyal subjects.

He stood on the ramparts of Castle Sanford and had been watching King Harek's retinue approach for the last two miles. Below him, the gates and drawbridge gaped open with two lines of his garrison waiting as an honor guard.

The Vor king arrived with six hundred warriors: half on horseback, armed with axes and swords, and the rest on foot with crossbows and shields. At their lead, Harek rode a huge stallion who wore a horse-helm spiked with a vicious horn. The tall, slender man himself wore a robe of bear fur over bronze-colored plate armor; and, in place of a helm, wore a simple golden circlet. A longsword hung at his hip.

Curiously, in contrast to the mass of intimidating warriors, three riders wearing colored lace and silk trailed on ponies a few yards behind the king. Sicaro was surprised that, on this critical day, the regent would bring his own courtesans; the man was so confident of success that he had brought along his harem.

In the distance, yet to cross the bridge into town, the tail of the column snaked forward and brought with it scores of circling and swooping flyers that glinted with green, red, and gold.

Wardragons. Not small dragons as found in the wild, but wolfhound-sized beasts bred for war.

Even a mile away, he could hear their cacophony of screeches and yowls. The damned creatures had caught sight of a cattle herd and were diving at the defenseless animals stampeding in every direction around their grazing field. The dragonmasters whistled and blew their trumpets to rally their beasts of war but were only able to summon back the dragons after they had downed dozens of cows and bulls. But not to waste good meat, the handlers then sent the dragons back to feast on their kills. Sicaro frowned, hoping the dragons were better disciplined on the battlefield.

The main Vor column stopped in the now abandoned town square below, while King Harek, his harem, and a torgue of fifty warriors continued up to the castle. Back in the square, a gray-bearded warrior shouted commands at the remaining warband to encamp.

Sicaro descended the battlement steps to greet Harek within the castle courtyard. "Welcome, your majesty. The gods of the sea cradled you like babes last night," he boomed in a deep voice.

The Vor king dismounted and strode over to grasp arms with and then slap the shoulder of Sicaro. "That they did, Lord Sicaro. I could not have dreamed of a smoother invasion. Tell me, are the Ascorian forces all so poorly organized and craven? My commanders report that when they assaulted the camps, the sentries tried to flee and over half of the soldiers surrendered. Shameful."

Sicaro nodded and walked the king toward the main hall. "The Ascorians are rigid in hierarchy. They fare well in orderly battle but are slow to react tactically. Silas believes that when it comes to leaders: the fewer, the better. He thinks of his army in large chunks—easier for him to command—but it is a weakness, these lumbering masses of soldiers, easier to confuse and divide." At the entrance to the hall, he looked back to see that half of Harek's guard followed, along with the three women in silk.

The two leaders abandoned the guards in the main hall and retreated to Sicaro's war room with a few select commanders and Craeg Vesenira, his forever shadow. In the center of the chamber, a large table was shaped with molded plaster, painted and covered in sculpted landmarks showing a god's-eye view of Ascoria.

Messengers reported to the doorway, running back and forth with messages and reports from the continuing boat and ferry landings along the shoreline—all positive and according to plan.

"And how go the preparations for the gargantors?" Harek asked one of his generals, a barrel-chested man.

"Six will start the crossing tomorrow. Unfortunately, two of the males were injured fighting each other and won't be able to make the swim until their wounds heal. The pridemaster estimates three to four weeks," the man replied.

The gargantors were fearsome beasts with a thick leathery hide, saber-like claws, and snouted jaws with dagger-like teeth—and could tear an armored warrior apart in seconds. Giant tigers the size of elephants, they were almost as lithe and fast as the Ascorian warlions, but at five times their size, they were the most formidable of the beasts of war. Fortunately for the Vors, the gargantors' intelligence made them tamable and directable as long as they were caught young and rewarded with a steady flow of cattle and pigs.

"The monsters can't be coaxed onto a barge?" Sicaro asked.

The general shook his head. "Interestingly, they refuse to stand on a floating platform but will swim enthusiastically. In the ocean, we guide and speed them from island to island by pulling them with ships."

Sicaro nodded in appreciation. He had heard descriptions

and stories of the monsters and was eager to see them tear into Silas's armies.

The king and his strategists spent the next several hours reviewing and revising their plans for the land campaign: troop movements, supply chain, harvest activities, and key engagements with the enemy.

At one point, two men-at-arms carried a large, padlocked chest into the room and placed it in a shadowy corner.

By late afternoon, light beams of green and red from a leadlight window slanted over the map table to illuminate motes of dust, lazy in the air. King Harek looked at the men in the war room. "Thank you, my friends. We are done for today. This evening, we banquet and celebrate our success. When you return to your warriors, assure them that there will be much bloodsong and victory to come. May the gods delight in our offerings," he said, clasping arms with each of his generals and commanders. "Lord Sicaro, stay a moment. We have one last issue to finalize."

The war room emptied, leaving just the two men.

The Vor king removed the circlet around his head and placed it on the map table. "My lord, I have been thinking on your mission," he said. "You have proved yourself invaluable so far. The landing could not have been easier." Harek picked up a pawn from the table and examined it. "Of course, as we agreed, Sanford is your fiefdom—settlers will arrive and it will grow into a city-state, I have no doubt—but I implore one thing more of you," he said as he replaced the pawn on the table.

The next phase of the conquest plan was for Sicaro to return "defeated" to the court of the Ascorian king and begin a mission of deceit. His man, Arlo, would remain as a strategic advisor to the Vor king, but the rest of his retinue would accompany him and a band of "survivors" to help sabotage the

Ascorian defenses. That was the plan. What else could Harek want of him?

Harek walked to the steel chest that his men had brought in. He bent down to unlock the padlock and then lifted the lid. "Have a look," he said.

Inside were several sinister-looking objects, one hand-sized and the others as long as his arm. Individually, they looked highly crafted—sleek, black, and menacing. Sicaro's warrior instincts recognized them as weapons, but of a curious design. "What are they?"

Harek wrapped a hand around the shortest artifact and held it up to a ray of light. "Weapons. Such as the one we found on the foreigner who killed my men."

"You have many now," Sicaro plainly stated, staring at the beautiful weapon. He reached forward with his palm extended. "May I see it?"

The weapon was as light as oak and smooth except for diamond-shaped hatching where the hand went naturally to grip it. It was expertly designed to sit in a hand and point at a target. He had seen one-handed crossbows before—little more than toys—and this weapon looked as though it was missing the essential bow-limbs and projectile groove that would be necessary for it to be an effective missile weapon.

He guffawed and looked at Harek. "This little thing killed your men?"

The tall king nodded and then extracted another weapon from the steel chest and held it to display. Similar to the first weapon, but longer and heavier—made to be handled with two hands. "*These* artifacts came to me by way of a merchant from Volkre City in southern Voros. He said that he bought them from a group of desert gypsies, who said they found them in a ruined temple of the gods."

Harek laid down the sleek object on the map table and reached under his breastplate to extract an exact copy of the weapon that Sicaro held in his hand.

"However, this is the exact one that killed my warriors . . ." The king caressed the exotic object. "The prisoner called it a 'darkcore gun.' This one is usable by any holder. However, he said the ones in the chest are 'locked' and was adamant he could not unlock them. He told the truth; my interrogators made sure of that."

"What is it you want?" Sicaro suspected the answer but needed the man to say.

"You see, I need the foreign woman that Silas has captive. They are of the same ilk, wherever it is they are from. Although he could not unlock these artifacts, she might." Harek stared at the gun gripped in his hand for a moment longer and then slipped it back under his breastplate to a presumable pocket. "I want her. I want these weapons working."

Sicaro placed the gun back into the chest. "My lord, the latest information I have on the woman is that they transferred her to the Academy of the Arcane. Still a captive, but I assume under interrogation by the grandmasters. Last I heard from my man Bako, a few weeks ago, he had not seen any opportunities to steal her away."

Harek pounded a fist onto the table. "I need greater action. When you go north, along with your primary task, you must personally take a hand at seizing the woman. I must have her. In the long-term, these artifacts could be even more important than the death of Silas."

"Certainly, my king. I may even be able to persuade Silas into giving her to me directly."

"Marvelous." Harek's demeanor switched in a heartbeat from commanding to affable. He grinned, locked the wooden chest, and walked over to the war room door, marking the conclusion of their discussion. "Let us go find some ale."

In the main hall of the castle, lines of banquet tables and benches had been prepared. Castle servants scurried about preparing for the banquet as the sun dipped into evening. Mouth-watering wafts of various roasting meats carried from the kitchens of the castle and the cooking pits in the courtyard. Sicaro's soldiers and Harek's warriors mingled like long-lost comrades, rollicking and jesting loudly about feats past and upcoming with the help of those who spoke both languages. The ale and beer had started to flow early, but Sicaro was not bothered in the least.

Four men-at-arms tagged along behind their king as he strode into the hall and met with a cluster of his captains.

At the arched entrance, Sicaro was accosted by his newly appointed chamberlain—an elderly, but efficient, man who was previously his head of coins.

Half-listening to the administrator, he was distracted by a woman sitting on the steps of the throne dais on the opposite side of the hall.

A courtesan from King Harek's retinue.

Draped in fine yellow silk, her long, willowy form and shapely legs were stretched out before her. But her face hid within the shadows.

He waved the man away and said, "That's fine, Master Feroz. Replace whoever you wish. I will be gone for a long while. Just make sure you keep my holdings well." He dismissed the chamberlain and gestured for Craeg Vesenira to follow him over to the throne dais, lured by his curiosity.

She leaned into a sun ray cutting across the steps. Sicaro's heart leapt as golden hair blazed in the light. He froze in his steps as he took in the features of the woman.

For a bewildered minute, he was looking at his resurrected wife: Katerin, the wife he married thirty years before. Aspiring actress, songstress, and dancer—liar, adulteress, and whore.

The woman's eyes grew wide and in the moment, he realized it was not his wife, but his daughter, sitting before him.

Karisa, his princess, his queen.

She gasped as their eyes met, and then quickly retreated to the shadows, clapping her hands over her mouth.

"Beautiful, isn't she?" Harek drew up behind as Sicaro continued to stare at Karisa. "Exquisite bone structure. A prize from a raid a few months ago. My captain has a good eye for slaves."

Anger surged at the king's objectifying comments about his daughter.

"I never grow attached to them . . . even though this one is a true pleasure. If you like, you can have her when you return," offered the king in an affable tone. He gulped from a mug of ale in his hand and nodded to himself. "Yes, I'll give her to you as a reward."

Outrage rose in Sicaro's gullet at the liberties Harek spoke of with Karisa, but it quickly dampened at the thought of his daughter finally returned.

She was the only woman he had truly loved, born of his own loins, trustworthy and pure. As beautiful as his deceased wife, but as virtuous as a child. He had given her life; she was his.

Karisa flinched when he walked up the steps and bent down to her ear. "My darling, it won't be long before we will be together again. I will come for you soon."

Chapter 29

The Call to Arms

Meila—Northern Mountain Range, Ascoria

The golden rays of dawn illuminated a carpet of mist seeping down the mountain.

Meila grinned as she watched the vapor caress the forest floor around her legs. The bare ground higher up warmed to the rising sun and generated the mist that then swept down the slopes. She delighted in the natural phenomenon that she had only ever seen once before—yesterday.

Her eyes clouded with tears of sadness as she thought of the decades, the century, that it had taken for her to see this beauty. Despite studying recordings of geo-atmospheric physics as part of her pilot training, actually being present in the mist harmonized her to nature in a way she'd never known before.

A selfish thought teased her. She could live on this planet for the rest of her life. Find some secluded island where she could live simply: stand with nature and breathe fresh air every day. She needed at least a few decades alone. Away from people. Away from responsibility.

Marooned, imprisoned, kidnapped, and rescued—the last

few months had been the most exciting she had experienced for a very long time. But also more than enough to last her for the next twenty or thirty years.

Her smile disappeared as she compared her memories of Earth with the spectacle of nature around her and felt a pang of sadness.

She ran a sensory recording of her birthworld; her intra-ocular and intra-aural implants overlaid her senses and took her back several decades to an outing with her daughter—only four years old at the time—and Anton. They played on the shore of a rectangular lake in a green field, several hundred meters wide, surrounded by sky-reaching towers and apartment blocks— looming like walls of an animal enclosure. Their daughter, Erin, in a toddler's bathing suit, looked at her and laughed, eyes full of mischief, then hurtled on tiny feet along a sandy beach into the artificial lake. It was a hot day, as was every day. Anton laughed as he stood ankle-deep in the clear water nearby and was caught by splashes from his errant daughter.

Hundreds of other children and families similarly frolicked and played in the water under a dying, red sun that was partially obscured by toxic clouds of brown and gray. Even at the center of highest society, purifiers were unable to cope with the fumes that enveloped the planet.

Sadly, it was the most cherished memory of nature that she had.

In the past, the memory recording had stimulated joy for Meila, but now it generated only sorrow. Sorrow at the thought of the cancer her homeworld had been and still was.

A noise within the campsite broke into her reverie. Jaks shuffled in the tent as he began to stir from sleep. He was a sweet boy, handsome with a noble face and a sweep of brown hair. If she were a hundred years younger, she would have bedded him without hesitation, but she was wiser now—and almost a species apart.

Although born human, her genes were spliced and augmented beyond semblance of anyone in the Old Colonies. Her implants and embedded technology systems made her a cyborg: part human, part machine. As such, she told herself that she shouldn't form an attachment to a sub-evolved human. For that, she was thankful for the implants that allowed her to turn her primal drives and libido on and off at will.

The youth clambered out of the tent and yawned. "Anything happen overnight? I didn't think I would sleep so deeply. Sorry, I should have woken to let you get some more rest," he said.

"That's all right. I'm rested enough," she replied, thinking of the metabolic rejuvenation cycle she had run over the past hour.

A thought occurred to her. "Do you think there are more men out there hunting for us? That there could be a bounty in place?"

Jaks paused in his task of packing away the tent. "Maybe for you, but not me. They only took me because I was with you. They didn't want me." Again, he puzzled aloud about Bako and Jop's connection to his father. But he soon diverged from the idea, talking himself into thinking that the men must have switched to working for a slaver or harem collector. Far shores, he explained to her, such as Ellipta and Nera Boa still thrived on markets of flesh.

As she listened to Jaks debating with himself, a movement in the forest distracted Meila. Wary of predators—or possibly bounty hunters—she magnified her lens implants to examine the area closer.

Identifying the source of movement, she pointed at a

giantwood. "Two or three animals over that away. Up in the trees. Can you see them? Monkeys?"

"Monkeys?" Jaks frowned. "What do you mean?"

"Little primates. Oh, of course, you don't have them here. Human-like animals that used to live in forests and jungles . . . before they went extinct." She palmed the grip of her darkcore pistol resting in its holster, reviewed its settings with her transdermal palm circuits, and adjusted the weapon to the lowest setting: one-fiftieth of full power—enough to kill any small animal.

"Little people." Jaks peered out into the forest. "Could be the dryads. Slender and about knee-high?"

She nodded. "Climbing around like squirrels. There's one there, halfway up. Whatever they are, their movements don't seem predatory." She took her hand away from her weapon and crossed her arms.

"It's probably them. They're peaceful creatures. I rescued one from a hunting trap once. They gave me apples in return." He smiled and stood beside her. "I hope they come out. I'd love you to see one up close." The youth looked at her, eyes flashing warmth for a moment, and then twisted back to stare at the trees.

Meila returned his smile, then brushed past him to the boulders where the saddle bags rested. Bako's stallion nudged at one of the bags. She opened it and extracted the feed bags, poured grain into each, and placed them on the ground.

Happy with her work, she dusted off her hands and foraged around in the saddlebags until she found some dried meat and fruit that she went to share with Jaks.

He was on the other side of the clearing, bending down. In front of him stood one of the small creatures with tiny clawed hands raised with an offering. A doll-like creature made from the forest, with skin the color of mottled bark, clothing of dried leaves, and hair of twigs and fiber. It turned to Meila with large green eyes, then skipped away to the trees on graceful limbs.

"Wait," Jaks cried out, staring after the dryad. A burst of mewling sounds followed in return, but the creature scampered up high into the overhead tree branches and away from view.

"Skittish," observed Meila. "Interesting little thing, though."

He held up a cluster of berries on a stalk. Crimson-colored, wrinkled, and the size of a grape, there were five of them, and they looked delicious.

"Are they safe to eat?" she asked.

"Only way to find out." Jaks plucked one fruit and tossed it into his mouth. "Mmm . . . tangy. Try one?"

She looked at it dubiously but popped the proffered berry into her mouth. Her tongue tingled and her lips puckered. "Sour. If you don't want them, hand them over. They're delicious." Mouth salivating, she crammed the last berries into her mouth and winced at the tartness bursting through her senses.

Jaks looked at her as though she had just grown a mustache and then laughed.

Meila grinned at him and wiped her lips. "All right, let's get going. Unless your little friend is bringing back some more berries."

They rode north, Meila keeping a steady direction as they retraced the exact same route from the previous day with the assistance of her memory implants.

"You have such good navigation sense," Jaks remarked to her after a few hours of riding through the wild woodlands. "I get lost unless I'm following a trail or something. Ranger Cromer said insects have a better sense of direction than me."

"He might be right. Some beetles, back on Earth at least,

have excellent navigation sense. Some even use the stars to find their way around," she said.

Jaks frowned and looked wounded.

"I'm not teasing. It's true. Don't worry, everyone is unique in their own way. Scarab beetles navigate by stars—and you can literally do magic. You did well yesterday."

He raised his hands, studying them like they were foreign to his arms. "I felt sick afterward . . . Bako . . . it was gruesome. His body was so disfigured. Like a pig seared over a fire. His eyes—"

"You did what you had to do, Jaks. One of them would have killed you. Him or the fat one. They were professional killers. You saw the farmer they murdered. You couldn't have fought them on their terms. You used what you had," she said, directing her horse down a gully lined with skeletal trees almost bare from dropping their summer leaves.

A few minutes later, she asked in a small voice, "What does it feel like when you invoke magic?"

"It's hard work getting all the aspects to work together."

"But what does it *feel* like?"

He grimaced and narrowed his eyes. "Powerful. Like destruction bottled up and trying to force its way out. But uncontrollable. You don't know what will come. Whether it'll be a trickle or a flood. I want to invoke it again right now, but I'm afraid it would hurt you or the horses. I want to test it. Maybe blast that tree and see it explode." His voice took on a chilling tone.

"Okay, calm down. Let's just focus on riding," she said, surprised at Jaks's turn of mind. "Leave the experiments for some other time."

Late that afternoon, Jaks whooped in delight when they broke out of the forest at the top of the valley. Below, pastures and plains, green and brown, spread out like a patchwork quilt.

Far to the north, through augmented eyes, Meila could see the city walls and smokestacks of Dunberrin; Jaks, however, despite his youthful eyes, reported he could see only clouds on the horizon.

Thankful that the rest of the forest had been uneventful, they set up camp within the tree line and rested for the night.

"What do you think's happening?" Meila asked the next morning as she and Jaks watched a great column of soldiers, horses, and wagons traversing a highway far off in the distance. They were just partway down the mountain slope and had caught sight of the organized mass. As far as she could tell, it began in the capital city and disappeared to the south. She magnified her intraocular implants with a thought and studied the constituents in detail.

"My guess is there's been more raids along the coast," said Jaks. "The Vorosians scare me. I was only a kid when the last war finished, and we never really saw the effects of it at home, except my father coming back now and then. News of it all seemed very remote—like an entirely different country." He pulled his horse up next to Meila, who was at a standstill, holding her hand against the glare. "I suppose it was because Ascoria was conquering other kingdoms . . . but it's now us who might be invaded."

"About four thousand troops, by my estimate. Forced march, some of the heavily armored soldiers are struggling to stay in formation," she told Jaks.

"Maybe they've *already* invaded," he replied, chewing on his lip.

"If they have, our time's running out. Let's get moving." She pulled her cloak tight around her chest and flicked her mare to descend the green vale.

A few hours later, a cornfield ranged in front of them. The heads of the plants looked full and ready to harvest, but there were no signs of harvesting. The only movement, in fact, was the breeze shushing through swaying rows of cornstalks.

Jaks pulled his gelding up next to Meila. "Is this where they murdered that farmer? Don't know if we should trample through their field again . . . and if his body is still there, and someone saw us, they might think we did it."

"We'll go around. I'm sure I can pick up the trail from the other side. There is a risk that the grandmaster and the others could be going through the field at this very moment and pass us by, but I think that's a low probability." She nudged the mare left to follow the field's edge.

Soon, a farmhouse came into view, built at the corner of the cornfield. Tidy with not a loose board in sight, a tail of smoke trickled into the sky from its brick chimney stack.

"Let's give it a wide berth. Best if we don't interact with anyone." Meila applied gentle pressure to her horse's left side. Her thighs ached with the past few days of riding, but her muscles were firming up fast.

As they ranged away, four people walked out of the farmhouse. Despite being a few hundred yards away, Meila could feel their eyes upon her. A woman waved an arm at them as though to beckon them and began jogging toward them, hollering as she came.

"Just keep going. Pretend we didn't see them," Meila said, staring straight ahead at the horizon.

A few minutes later, the shouts were too close to ignore. She sighed and turned in her saddle to see a woman and three youths puffing after them. "Excuse me, excuse me," the woman called in a screechy voice.

"We should stop. Sounds like they're desperate," Jaks said in a too-sensible tone.

They stopped and waited for the farmers to catch up. "You talk to them. You're nicer," said Meila.

The woman had a weathered but kindly looking face with crows-feet wrinkles at the corners of her blood-shot eyes. Two of the lads puffing after her were plump and looked so similar they could only be twins. Trudging behind them came a stocky young man with wide nostrils opening out straight from his face. All the young men lugged sacks over their backs.

"Hello. Sorry to bother you, citizen. You're heading to the muster? Could you take my boys with you?" the woman said between breaths, leaning with one hand against her hip. "We only heard this morning when a herald came through."

"Muster?" Jaks asked.

"You didn't hear? The Voros army landed. The king has issued a call to arms . . . I thought you were heading to the muster point." The woman frowned. Her boys caught up with her, panting.

Meila and Jaks exchanged a glance.

"We're not going there," Jaks said—not knowing where "there" was—and looked to Meila for help. But she didn't meet his eyes. "We're going back to the capital."

The woman weighed his words and replied, "All right, my sons will just go with you to the main road, then. The muster is at Lohort village, a league from there. My husband would have taken them, but he . . . passed away recently."

Jaks looked at Meila again, who just nodded to him. "I'm sorry to hear about your husband," he said.

"Yes, well, he fell and hit his head last week. Dead and

buried. Nothing I can do about that now." The woman's shoulders slumped, and she pursed her lips tightly. She then turned back to her young men and said, "Off you go, boys."

The woman—their mother, she guessed—grabbed the twins, one arm around each, and hugged them tightly. Her shoulders shuddered as she let out a loud sob and held them for a long minute until one of them pushed her away. "We'll be okay, Ma. We'll be back soon—don't you worry. Ma Kendall will help you with the harvest," the lad said to her.

She reached for the third son, but he brushed past her and patted her on the head, saying, "See yah, old bag."

The twin brothers, Meila learned, were actually twenty years old, a year or two older than Jaks—their rounded faces made them appear younger than they were. The oldest brother was five years older and lacked in wit but had a sly demeanor about him. They had been walking slightly behind Jaks's horse for just a few minutes when one of the twins asked, "How come you're not going to the muster? You must have done your conscription by now."

Jaks followed the burly youth's gaze to his upper arm covered by the sleeve of his leather armor. Self-consciously, he slapped a hand to where the conscript brand lay beneath and rubbed at it. "I'm . . . we're . . . on the king's business. We're on an errand."

The other twin looked back and forth between Jaks and Meila, one eyebrow raised. "What is she? Someone important or something? She looks foreign."

Meila pivoted in her saddle to look back at Jaks and asked in amusement, "Yes, what *am* I?"

The twins stared at her, as though astonished she could speak, or perhaps surprised at her accent.

"She's a, she is a . . ." He fumbled for an explanation for a moment. "She's a master from the Academy. And I'm her guard. We're on a secret mission—"

"All right, that's enough," Meila said, glaring at Jaks as though scolding him, and then turned away.

"Ooh," the twins said simultaneously.

Jaks flicked his horse reins to distance himself from the brothers, but heard the eldest brother say to the twins, "She don't look like she'd be from the Academy. She looks like a dancer. I bet she's one of those dancers. You know." He sniggered.

"Shut up, Harold, you're an idiot," the first twin said, and they all fell silent.

Meila felt anxious to be rid of the farm boys, mixed with a little guilt that their father's death was related to her captors' actions.

Several minutes later, she swiveled around in her saddle—not confident to turn her horse at a sharp angle—and called back to the young men, "Our paths part here. We're heading over the field. The main road is not far; I'm sure you can get there on your own." She used her imperious tone.

The farm boys shrugged and dragged their feet down the dirt path past Meila and Jaks. One twin muttered as he passed by, "Dunno why you just don't take the road."

Ignoring the comment, Jaks waved as they departed. "Bye, good luck . . . You're very brave."

Meila laughed when the twins and their brother were out of earshot. "'You're very brave' . . . what was that?"

"I felt bad that they have to join the conscript army. Technically, I should be going to the muster as well. I don't really have an excuse not to. If we run into a muster sergeant, they'll take me in." He nudged his horse to follow Meila, directing her horse again to follow the edge of the cornfield.

"All the more reason to avoid any further contact with people. Wouldn't want to be hauled off as cannon fodder," she said.

"Cannon fodder?"

"On ancient Earth, they shot enormous guns, cannons, at the front line of charging soldiers. So, the generals would send in the most poorly trained troops first as 'cannon fodder,'" she explained.

"Did your ship have a gun like that?" asked Jaks a minute later, probably having toiled over the idea since she'd mentioned it.

"No, nothing that large. It wasn't a warship. We only had weapons for protection if we were boarded or landed somewhere hostile."

"Could you design one? Something that Grandmaster Mulgrave could build with the runic forge?"

She turned to him and saw a boyish grin. "Possibly. But if we retrieve darkcore rifles from the wreckage, they'll be almost as good and ready to use. Whereas a cannon of whatever design would take months or years to build. And, we would need to obtain an energy source—gunpowder, most likely. All hypothetical. Best just to focus on getting to the wreckage in good time."

They picked up their trail on the other side of the cornfield and continued their journey in silence.

Finally, they crested a hill and Meila spotted the rivertown, where they'd been kidnapped, several miles in the distance. With their goal clearly located, they took a direct route, rather than trying to follow the tangential one their captors had taken them that night.

Several peasants tended the wheat fields as they approached. Meila's augmented vision distinguished them as two women and three men with shovels—all wizened and old—no young helpers visible, perhaps sent off to the muster as well. One put a hand to his brow and squinted at them but soon returned to his digging.

"Well, it appears that Ranger Cromer didn't pick up our trail," Meila said. "Hopefully, we can find out where they've gone." Meila's horse broke out of the field and stepped over a ditch to surer footing on the road leading into the town.

Drear and gloom hung over the buildings, vastly different from the lively cheer of a few days ago. The few people on the streets were twitchy-eyed at the storm clouds overhead and similarly at Meila and Jaks riding into their village. An elderly woman, pushing a cartful of wood beams, yelled at them as they passed, "The muster is the other way." She stopped and scowled when they ignored her.

They dismounted at the traveler's stable beside the Drover's Inn, and Jaks greeted the stablemaster.

"They been looking for you. The Ranger and all. Disappeared a few days ago—didn't yous? Caused them quite a kerfuffle. They thought you'd run off together . . ." His face then cracked into a knowing grin and he tapped his nose. "Yous done banging your bits together and back now, eh?" He winked at Jaks.

She didn't understand half of what he was saying but understood his lewd insinuation and ignored it. "Where has the grandmaster gone?" she asked, handing the weathered man the reins to the mare.

"Out looking for yous. I expect he'll be back soon." The stablemaster gathered the reins of all three horses in his hand.

Jaks pointed at a horse already settled into the stable. "That's Vixhana's horse. She must be here."

"Yep. They go out during the day looking for yous and come

back in the afternoon. The captain and the ranger been back an hour already." The man nodded at the inn and led the horses to the stalls inside.

Jaks rushed up the outside stairs of the building to the sleeping rooms and rapped knuckles hard against his sister's door, already grabbing at the door handle. It didn't budge, but he heard a loud thump inside the room. "Vixhana. Are you there?" he called through the door.

The door opened to a dark room, and his sister's powerful frame filled the doorway. Naked but for a bedsheet clutched to her front, sweat glistened on her skin, and her dark hair was tousled and loose. She stepped forward, pushing Jaks into the hallway, and closed the door.

"What the hell, Jaks. Where have you been? We've been looking everywhere for you two," she said, barely controlling her anger. She turned her glare on Meila and then down to her holstered pistol. "Did *she* put you up to this?"

Meila stared back wide-eyed at the muscular, strong-boned woman who, in her nakedness, radiated with primal energy. Together with the scent of passion, she suspected they'd interrupted Vixhana and a companion in the throes of lust.

"Ah, oh, I'm sorry, Vix. I'll go wait for you to get changed," Jaks stuttered and bumped into Meila, trying to retreat past her.

Vixhana grabbed her brother by his arm. "Stay here. Tell me, where have you been?" she said. "If you two just wanted to go and grind, you didn't need to run away to do it."

Jaks's face colored in a second, ears red as beets. "It's not anything like that. We were kidnapped." He stared at the wall, unable to meet her nakedness or her glare, and then explained the events of the past four days as quickly as he could.

Vixhana released him and her face softened as she listened;

by the end, she was studying the purple bruises on their faces and nodding in approval at their fight to escape.

The door to the bedroom then opened and the lean figure of Ranger Cromer walked out.

Jaks's mouth fell open, and he stared at the man.

The ranger leaned casually against the doorframe, exposing a mess inside the room with Vixhana's discarded nightwraith armor and weapons around a barren mattress.

"Now, let me get dressed and we'll go discuss this some more while we wait for the grandmaster to return. He should be back soon," Vixhana said.

Jaks looked uneasily back and forth between Vixhana and the ranger, clearly not liking what he saw. Meila nudged him in the back, rousing him from his bewilderment, and turned to go downstairs to the communal washroom.

Vixhana called out to her, "Wait. Wait here until I'm clothed. I'm not letting you out of my sight for the time being." The nightwraith retreated to her room and began hopping around in the shadows, donning clothes and armor.

An hour later, Mulgrave and Tavis burst into the tavern, surprising the few diners sitting around eating and drinking, and stormed up to the round table where Meila sat with Jaks, Vixhana, and Cromer. "What's this all about?" the mage asked in an irritated voice.

This time, Meila explained the kidnapping, describing the events of the past several days in greater detail than Jaks had earlier, and attributing their escape to the electromancy invocations that Jaks had conjured.

Everybody stared at Jaks, and his face reddened again until he murmured dismissively, "It was nothing."

Tavis folded his arms and scowled, staring at the center of the table.

Mulgrave rubbed his chin, then looked over at Ranger Cromer. "Do you remember seeing the men?" he asked the arrow-bearded man stabbing a chunk of meat on his plate.

The ranger paused the fork halfway to his mouth. "Don't know who they were, but I remember the bald one and the fat one." He nodded his head at the back wall of the tavern where the men had been that evening. "I asked around for them, but no one knew who they were or saw them leave the village."

Mulgrave clasped his hands in front of him and said to Jaks, "Sinister, but I doubt your father would have any hand in this. I'm sure he has better things to do than organize a kidnapping. As you say, the pair were most probably slavers on the prowl for fresh meat." He nodded to himself. "I think our captain should keep a closer eye on our ward from now on."

Vixhana nodded briskly in response and settled her gaze on Meila.

The mage pulled a chair to join the table and then waved his hand at the innkeeper for more food.

From there, their discussions turned to the Vor invasion and speculations about the numbers and location of the enemy horde—and what King Silas would do to defend the country.

All the while, Meila listened and ruminated, aware that she was becoming dangerously entwined in the lives of these people —far more than she wanted. If she weren't so reliant on the escape pod back at the Academy for planetary rescue, if she had another transponder to signal her location off-planet, she could escape all of this to some isolated haven and wait for evacuation. *Damn these people and their problems.*

She contemplated toggling off her emotions, but then realized she was feeling something she hadn't for many decades —she was starting to care.

Chapter 30

Apprentice

Jaks–Jurn Lowlands, Ascoria

F or one of them, it was going to end badly.

Jaks and Tavis stared at each other, rain beating a staccato on the tin roof of the open-walled shelter and dripping through rusted holes to the packed dirt floor beneath their feet.

That morning, they had gifted Bako's captured horses to the stable master as payment for stall hire, and resumed the journey interrupted several days before by the kidnapping. They followed Ranger Cromer out of the rivertown, pausing at the next village for Grandmaster Mulgrave to display the king's emissary letter to the soldiers at the border cordon, and then broke out onto the roadless riverplains of Jurn.

The horses forded countless streams and rivers—the namesakes of the delta plains. Often flooded and impassable by foot during the spring, in summer and autumn they were lush, fertile pastures for shepherds with their herds of cattle and sheep.

Midafternoon brought storm clouds rolling over the plains

with raindrops falling fat and heavy. When visibility began to diminish under the downpour, the drenched ranger directed them off to a cluster of buildings in the foothills of the mountains nearby. A complex of old mining buildings crowded around an abandoned iron mine that, according to Cromer, had been exhausted and caved-in several years before. Only the tin-roofed shelters and warehouses in ramshackle condition remained.

With six humans, six horses, and one pack mule to shelter, the ranger commandeered the largest building in the abandoned site. The tall structure was simple but sturdy with steel beams propping up a rusted roof; it looked built to shelter heavy machinery and had no need for walls of any sort. Indeed, a rail track led from the mine entrance out to this very building and ended at a rotten wooden barrier with several wrecked ore carts marooned nearby.

It was here that Grandmaster Mulgrave had clapped his hands to summon Jaks and Tavis beneath the leaky tin-roof. They came together and stared at each other as the others settled at the other end of the warehouse.

Jaks knew this test was due.

Mulgrave had learnt that Jaks had successfully invoked electromancy when he had cut ropes and then fought Bako and Jop. Now, the grandmaster wanted to see it for himself.

If he failed to show it now, it would disappoint the mage, and Jaks's powers could be justifiably dismissed as chaotic manifestations that were as uncontrollable as the rain outside—unreliable, untrainable, and a waste of his time.

Then, Jaks reckoned, once they returned from their quest, the Academy would release him to be conscripted to the battlefront and likely suffer a meaningless death at the hands of a horde of axe warriors.

But even if he did successfully manifest electromancy, would it be enough to dislodge Tavis from his apprentice position?

Despite Meila's reassurance that the Academy would find Jaks a master if he showed electromancy potential, he wasn't so sure. Tavis, a dual-mage commanding gravmancy and pyromancy just like Grandmaster Mulgrave, could pursue a legacy to create powerful runic-forge weapons and artifacts, whereas Jaks, with only electromancy, had no creative potential, only destructive power.

"Show me what you can do, lad. I really hope your powers have matured," Mulgrave said, resting a hand on an upturned ore cart. Tavis moved to stand behind the mage and kept a wary eye on Jaks. "Something small. One of the first exercises I use with an apprentice is palming an energy ball—in your case, a lightning ball. Do you need a trigger . . . another spider, perhaps?"

"Um, that won't be necessary," Jaks replied, wishing to go and dry off by the fire that Vixhana was trying to start with a flint and tinderbox.

He raised a cupped hand in front of him and visualized a ball of brilliant white sparking to life. Nothing happened. Tense under the close observation of the grandmaster and the smirking Tavis, he had forgotten the other two aspects of invocation; without them, he wasn't invoking magic, he was simply imagining things. Under such scrutiny, away from the urgency of life-and-death, why was it so much harder to invoke magic?

Frustrated with himself, Jaks took a deep breath and began the invocation as he had been taught. He closed his eyes and recalled the memory of his father. Bestial and sneering, looming over his bed with a giant hand descending to crush his face—had it been a dream, as he had always thought it, or was it a genuine memory?—his body trembled, and his mouth curled unconsciously in fear. Forgetting the reason for summoning the memory, a haze descended and his mind fell numb and empty. *Dammit. Not this again.*

He cursed inwardly, kept his eyes closed and tried again, this time holding the fear. *Paper tigers. Thoughts are just thoughts, they are not real.* He then concentrated on willing the lightning into life.

His closed eyelids flashed red, and an odd humming sound grew in front of him. He flicked open his eyes and discovered a sphere of blue-white light in his outstretched hand. Feelings of delight surged through him—and the lightning ball extinguished. Out of the corner of his eye, he glimpsed Mulgrave's disappointed look at the fleeting demonstration.

Without hesitation, Jaks invoked the lightning ball again and resolved to sustain it for far longer. This time, the lightning ball sprang to his palm, and he carefully balanced the fear and his consciousness, teetering like a seesaw.

After a few seconds, the ball grew larger, stretching outward. Suddenly, it flashed up a column and struck the rusted roof. A loud explosion blew a man-sized hole through the corrugated tin, blasting chips and slugs into the sky, adding metal castings to the rain.

Surprised by the explosion, Jaks lost the invocation, and the warehouse went silent and dim. Rain poured through the hole and soaked him to the skin.

Laughter boomed from the other end of the warehouse, where the normally straight-faced Vixhana pointed at the hole in the roof and slapped her leather-encased leg. "You'll be the death of one of us one day," she called out.

Only Meila joined in the laughter, while the men stared with a mixture of fear and dismay on their faces. Tavis cowered behind an ore cart covering his ears, while Grandmaster Mulgrave swore loudly and started musing aloud about the magical properties he'd seen. Ranger Cromer's initial look of surprise quickly faded, and he turned to calm the horses still startled by the explosion.

"By gods, what a spectacle," Mulgrave said with a grin peeled to his face. "You've got potential, but you're going to have to work on reducing that volatility. At this stage, you will need to focus on sustaining a small invocation for as long as possible. That will get you used to channeling magic until it becomes as natural as breathing."

The mage looked at Tavis, who had recovered from his fright and had a pinched expression on his face. "How long can you sustain a fireball now, Tavis?"

"Two hours, Master," the apprentice proudly replied and invoked an oblong flame in his hand, recovering his display of cowardice.

"Well, go be useful and help light that campfire." Mulgrave gestured at Vixhana, who had returned to working a tinder at a smoldering pile of wood.

For the next hour, Mulgrave coached Jaks to maintain a pearl of buzzing energy in his hand. He could sustain it for a minute at the most. Maintaining the invocation drained his concentration quickly, until his head felt heavy and thick.

"That's good for now . . ." The grandmaster nodded and stroked his chin. "There's enough here to convince me to take you on as an apprentice—your gift is rare and needs much training. I'll keep you both on for now, but once we get back to the Academy, I'll need to decide which of you to continue with." He looked at Tavis, at the other end of the warehouse, drying himself by a crackling campfire, and back to Jaks.

Jaks grinned. "Thank you, grandmaster. I won't let you down."

The rain eased overnight, and by the morning, the clouds were mere puffs of white. Only puddles and mud remained as evidence of the rainstorm of the previous day.

Ranger Cromer rode out to scout the surroundings while the rest of them broke up camp.

Jaks felt a lighter mood while the ranger was gone. His anxiety about his survival instructor had taken on an additional layer of confusion since seeing the man walking out of his naked sister's room at the rivertown inn. He felt betrayed by Vixhana. How could she share a bed with the cruel man who had belittled him so often? Surely, it had been a one-off dalliance. He'd heard of soldiers having "pre-battle" relations with each other—the threat of death stirring febrile urges to seek company —but he couldn't stomach the idea of Vixhana and Cromer being together.

As they finished packing and began to wonder at the ranger's whereabouts, he returned. "The area from here is notorious for wulverions, but I didn't see any signs or tracks of them around. We'll need to remain alert for them, however," he said.

"Wolves, did you say?" Meila asked, vaulting onto her saddled mare.

"Wulverions," corrected Cromer. "They run together in packs of much greater numbers than wolves and can turn into shadows. Only the sound of their pounding feet will alert you before they attack. We should keep double-watch and a fire burning through the night."

"Fascinating beasts," Mulgrave remarked. "One of the few species that use illumancy in that way. A few other species, birds mainly, use it for attracting mates or to ward off predators, but wulverions use it to stalk prey. Truly, one of nature's assassins." Mulgrave looked at Vixhana in nightwraiths' armor as though comparing her to the wulverions.

"Well, if a pack of shadows starts tearing me apart—I'll know what they are." Meila laughed, trying to lighten the mood. "How long will we be riding amongst these land piranhas?"

"About four days to the Jurn Highlands. From there, there'll be different kinds of predators to watch out for," Cromer replied.

Now clear of the riverplains, a road led away from the mining camp and took them to the south—mountains to their right, and a grassy ocean of brown to their left.

The savannahs of Jurn were renowned for their savage wildlife and rugged nomads with their tent villages who once roamed the sweeping plains. However, exiled decades before, the plains folk had been forced by King Silas's armies, in his great land grab, into the wild mountains to the south and the great forests of Strock to the east.

Now, ranches of longhorns and fortified towns attempted to tame the wild expanse—their success thriving and failing on keeping out the lions, wulverions, and other predators that not only kept the humans corralled but also the immense stampeding herds of wild ponies and antelope under control. Of all Ascoria, the province of Jurn was the most lush but also the most wild.

As the group followed the dirt road skirting the edge of the savannah, they established a riding formation with Cromer leading, followed by Mulgrave and Tavis (with the pack mule), then Jaks and Meila, tailed by Vixhana, always at the rear.

Mostly, they rode single file, but when he got bored, Jaks would ride up beside Meila and make small talk.

He enjoyed her company, even though she talked down to him like a child at times. He again pondered her rebuff of his declaration of love for her. Could she not see that he was a grown man of eighteen years, that they had a real connection? He kept his muddled feelings to himself and stared at her lovely, slender neck, confusing himself even more.

Midmorning, Ranger Cromer pointed at a large group of figures approaching through the plains from the west. Jaks saw several were on horseback, but the other hundred or more were on foot and carrying rucksacks. By their snail's pace, he guessed they would cross paths when their road met up at an intersection ahead.

When the group joined the main road, they headed straight toward Jaks and his party. As they neared, he recognized the king's pike and shield crest on the lead rider's chest plate and saw the people on foot dressed in conscript armor similar to what he himself had worn only weeks before. They all had spears, while a few had crossbows across their backs.

"Ho!" The lead horseman rode forward, the markings of an army captain visible on his shoulder. "Greetings, citizens. You going to the muster?" The gray-haired man—probably a garrison captain from one of the remote towns—eyed Cromer and Vixhana appraisingly, then fixated on the crest, like his own, imprinted on their saddlebags.

The column of male and female conscripts stopped and dropped their rucksacks to the ground, eager for a rest from their march. Most of them appeared fit and healthy, but some looked long past their peak fighting days. One elderly man wheezed, leaning heavily against a stick, and then dropped to the ground with his rucksack still attached to his back, resembling an upturned beetle.

Ranger Cromer sat forward on his horse and pulled at his beard. "No. We're on private business. You can be on your way."

"But we're at war." The guardsman licked his lips and straightened in his saddle. "*Everyone* is called to arms. You're not deserters, are you?"

Jaks admired the man's courage to challenge the dangerous-looking ranger with the even more lethal-looking Vixhana behind him.

Even though any of the three—Cromer, Vixhana, or Mulgrave—could have intimidated the guardsman into submission, the grandmaster saved the man his pride and rode forward. "We're on the king's business," he said, pulling out the letter stamped with the king's seal.

The guardsman's eyes bulged as he read the letter. "Right you are, my lord. Sorry to bother you." He quickly handed the royal decree back to Mulgrave and saluted awkwardly. "I had to check—we've had some trouble with muster dodgers along the way." He glanced at a group of young men casting resentful looks around at the others. "Let me clear the road for you to pass."

"That won't be necessary. We'll go alongside. Your people are weary. It must have been a hard night under the rain."

As they rode past the conscripts, Tavis drew alongside Mulgrave and spoke in a loud voice that Jaks heard, even from several yards back. "Grandmaster, perhaps we *should* return to Dunberrin with the muster? With the Vors invading, surely our efforts would be better directed to producing weapons and such to aid the defense. We're maybe wasting our time chasing after artifacts that may not even be there," the apprentice said. "Even if we can find this wreckage, bandits or wildmen may very well have pilfered everything." Tavis's face creased with concern. "What if there's nothing there . . . and we've wasted all this time?"

Meila interrupted before the mage could reply, trotting up beside the apprentice and mage. "No one can get into a weapons locker without the ability to unlock it. Only one of my crew or I could do that. If there's a locker in the wreckage, the weapons will be there."

Tavis grunted. "Truly, what difference would they make against tens of thousands of Vors, anyway? We should be building proper siege machines back at the Academy."

"You moron. One of these"—Meila held up her darkcore pistol—"stores over a million megajoules of dark energy. On automatic fire, I could kill a couple hundred of your Vors in a minute. What could your stupid catapult do?" She waved the pistol around in the air. "And any one of the rifles on my ship could sight and kill your Vors from over ten miles away. If you think some piddly siege weapon would do better—go ahead and build your wooden toys."

Tavis scowled and mumbled, "They'd be iron and steel . . ."

Jaks grinned as the woman verbally cut down the apprentice. Mulgrave simply laughed.

Meila sighed, and shaking her head, holstered the pistol.

Tavis conceded defeat with a flap of a hand and grumbled quietly to himself. After a few minutes, seeking some other target for his agitation, he leaned back over his saddle to look at Jaks and whispered, "You should be with those conscripts. You'll never be a mage," then turned away.

Jaks's ears colored, and he glared at the back of the apprentice's head, wishing him dead. Then, in a surge of anger, he drew up behind Tavis and whispered forcefully, "The grandmaster took me on as an apprentice yesterday—so there. I bet he's going to get rid of you when we get back."

Tavis glared at him. "I don't believe you," he said, then flicked his reins to veer toward the grandmaster.

Jaks watched the apprentice confer with his master and then smirked when the older apprentice's shoulders slumped and his back sagged. Not long until he would be rid of his opponent.

Chapter 31

The Wulverions

It was two nights later that death stalked them from the dark.
Jaks huddled under a blanket with his back to the bulbous lower trunk of a dardan tree and flicked his eyes open for the fourth time in as many minutes. *Wake up, I can't fall asleep on watch with Ranger Cromer.* He looked at the tents and sleeping forms of his companions and found Cromer standing in the shadows near the tethered horses. The glow from the campfire flickered against the veteran's cloaked back as he stared out into the darkness surrounding their glade of trees.

His back tingled as though something was watching him. However, flashing his lightstone torch beyond the edge of the trees revealed nothing but the emptiness of night—nothing but lack of sleep playing tricks on his mind.

He shook his head, shed the wool square from his shoulders, and lurched over to the crackling campfire. He scrunched his eyes several times, then threw more branches onto the fire and rubbed his hands over the flames. He yawned. Not long until the change of guard shift and he could get some more sleep.

The last couple of days of traveling had been tiring—sitting in a saddle for ten hours a day—but not dull, since Jaks had taken up a new hobby: zapping flies and insects, a fun, distracting exercise that required fast reactions and grew his invocation skill.

Grandmaster Mulgrave highly approved. Even more so since it reduced the swarms of biting gnats around them.

However, Vixhana hated Jaks's newfound skill; the sharp cracking sound and trail of fried bugs irritated her. She would snap at him, ordering him to stop. Jaks would, but then renewed with vigor each time a fresh plague assaulted him.

Jaks grinned, feeling he'd mastered the small, basic invocations. It must be time for more potent ones.

A tingling sensation suddenly ran up his back again. He looked around the camp and noticed the horses shuffling and grunting. *There is someone watching us.*

Vixhana's stallion let out a whinny and thumped at the ground. A loud whistle followed, and Ranger Cromer turned to him with his fingers dropping from his lips. "Get everyone up, we're surrounded." He held his bow in his hand with an arrow on the string and jerked his head back to the dark fields.

Jaks took up the call. "Wake up, wake up, wake up!" he shouted as he ran back to the tree where he had left his repeating crossbow, snatched it up, and ratcheted the first bolt into its groove with cold and trembling hands.

"What is it? What's going on?" Vixhana rose from her sleep mat, having refused the comforts of a tent, and pushed her way to her feet. Fully armored, she was ready in an instant, sword bared and into her hand before the others had even appeared.

Mulgrave and Tavis scrambled out of their tents. Tavis was in a cotton gambeson, his mélange of armor parts still piled up in his shelter. He looked about wildly and rummaged around for his sword somewhere back in his tent.

"Wulverions. They've surrounded the campsite," the ranger called to them without turning from the outward danger, an arrow nocked to his bow and ready to draw.

The horses snorted and shuffled, their dark eyes wide and searching. Jaks's palfrey, a brown gelding, pulled at its tether and came loose from the tree it had been bound to—finding freedom, it twisted about as though unsure where to run to.

Her longsword in her right hand, Vixhana stretched out her left and invoked illumancy. A bright beam of light shone from the end of her fist.

She took charge and shouted out commands to defend. "Secure those horses," she ordered Jaks. Then, directing her illumancy beam at Meila—standing by a tent with her darkcore pistol in one hand and a lightstone torch in the other—she said, "You, watch the road." She instructed Mulgrave and Tavis to watch a section each. They all faced outward with their backs to the campfire.

Jaks crouched as he approached the loose palfrey. He caught its attention, and then, whispering to it, stroked its mane. He placed his crossbow on the ground, keeping one eye on the trees as he retied the horse's tether to the trunk. Despite his presence, the animals continued agitating, and Vixhana's stallion snorted and pawed at the ground.

Jaks caught glimpses of eyes reflecting his torch beam.

"Looks like hundreds of them," Tavis said, having finally pulled on a steel breastplate and found a sword and shield.

Meila corrected him. "More like about fifty of them . . . I can see their heat signatures. Most of them are circling—makes it hard to count," she said, brandishing her pistol two-handedly in the direction of the road.

"Are they going to attack?" Jaks asked, having returned to the defensive circle. He gripped his crossbow tightly and considered whether he should use the weapon or attempt his electromancy if the wild animals pounced at them.

"Huh, the eyes just disappeared . . ." Tavis said, his voice rising higher. The apprentice unconsciously stepped backward, only stopping when the campfire flicked at his backside.

"They're circling closer," Meila said.

The sound of dozens of pounding feet surrounded the trees, but Jaks couldn't see anything beyond the tree line, despite the probing beams of the rune torches and Vixhana's invocation.

He tensed himself for an attack. He would use the crossbow, he decided, admitting to himself that his control of lightning was still largely untamed and might harm his companions or the horses close by.

With a roar, an enormous ring of fire sprang to life and encircled the entire glade. Raging, neck-high flames resembling a burning fence filled the darkness. Grandmaster Mulgrave held his arms widespread with an expression of intense focus on his face as he channeled the magical barrier.

Several wolf-like forms burst into flame. Ablaze, they leapt out of the ring of fire, howling, and writhed about on the ground. The curved trunks of the dardan trees were silhouetted by the fire, and several of the lower branches caught on fire. Smoke and the smell of burning wood, flesh, and fur wafted through the glade.

Several more shadows dared the flames and leapt through, but then vanished amongst the tree trunks as soon as they penetrated the ring of flame.

"A few came through," Vixhana yelled. "Near you, Jaks." She ran toward him while he looked about wildly.

Meila's mare squealed, and the other horses thrashed at

their tethers. Hooves flew about dangerously, and Jaks backed away from the muscular animals.

The back legs of the mare collapsed, dragged down to her rear haunches by some unseen attacker. Its whinnying turned into an agonized squeal.

The other horses broke away except for the pony, which heaved about still on the end of its restraint.

Vixhana swung her longsword at a dark shadow attached to the leg of the mare and was rewarded with a howl as an injured wulverion lost its camouflage and was revealed with its spine cleaved in half and blood spurting from its severed aorta—it collapsed to the ground, spasmed, and died.

An arrow hissed across the glade and pinned another wulverion, causing it to expose itself as it twisted to snap at the arrow in its back leg. Even before it fell, Ranger Cromer had another arrow flying toward another shadow bounding toward the struggling pony.

"Look away from me. Look away," Vixhana shouted. A few seconds later, light erupted throughout the woods from where she stood.

Jaks dared a glimpse at her and saw her magnificent, as he had never seen her before. His sister radiated brilliance, looking like a warrior angel descended from the heavens. Her face, skin, and armor emitted pure white light. In her left hand, she had a struggling wulverion by the throat, held up in the air like a ragdoll. In her right hand, she held her sword above her head, about to strike at a blinded wulverion stumbling at her feet.

Awed but almost completely blinded by his sister's illumancy, Jaks immediately regretted his glance. Howls and brays of animals surrounded him. Snarling jaws attacked and pounding hooves sought escape.

He pointed his crossbow at something growling, a blurry

shape moving toward him. He pulled the trigger, and the weapon shuddered. The bolt thudded into flesh.

Then a weight rammed into him, the blow spinning the crossbow out of his hands.

Within a second, something clamped his left elbow and crushed it painfully. *Jaws of a wulverion.* Even wounded, it wanted to kill him. The fangs, unable to penetrate the rune-forged armor, bit down several times more until they eventually found the unprotected flesh of Jaks's hand and sank in.

He screamed and tugged away desperately, but it held fast. Although his vision was clearing, he could only see a black shadow tearing at his arm. He fumbled for his dagger.

"Get down, Jaks!" Meila yelled from behind. He fell to the ground, kicking at the shadows with his feet.

The hiss of her darkcore gun sounded, followed by a sickening squelch.

Wet, warm globs of flesh pasted his face. The clamping force fell away around his arm. He scrambled backward and collapsed onto his side, holding his left hand up with his right.

A few seconds later, Jaks's burnt-out vision cleared. Pain agonized his hand, but he dared not look down, fearful of the damage he would see.

Vixhana was still glowing but not the blinding radiance of before; three furred beasts lay broken around her, while a fourth hung impaled on her longsword.

A dardan tree was ablaze, its lower trunk burning and flames creeping up, and scorched brown leaves tumbled through the air. Tavis was pointing his sword at a wulverion at the base of the burning tree and channeling a torrent of fire at the squirming beast.

Mulgrave shouted, "Apprentice, stop. That's enough. You'll

burn the whole area down," while still holding out his arms, steadily maintaining the protective ring of fire.

Horses still lunged about the glade, running up to the fiery barrier and then turning back when the grandmaster flared the flames in front of them to keep them inside.

Meila's mare lay several yards from Jaks, with several chunks of flesh torn from its rear and its throat ripped open. Somehow, it held onto life as blood frothed at its neck wound.

The pack mule had suffered similar wounds but was already dead, lying near the western side of the glade by the magical barrier. Two dead wulverions lay near it, one punctured by arrows and the other with its head blasted off—presumably by Meila's darkcore gun.

Quiet settled over the glade except for the roaring flames of the protective barrier and the crackling flames consuming the burning dardan tree. And nothing moved.

A dozen wulverions lay dead around the campsite. Without their arcane camouflage, the beasts looked like common wolves.

"It's safe now. They're gone," said the grandmaster. He dropped his arms, and the flaming barrier vanished with a rush. Then, striding to the burning oak tree, he thrust his hands into the flames, and again, there was that rushing sound—like a door thrust open into a sealed room—and the blazing tree extinguished from the bottom up. The only light remaining in the glade was from the dying campfire and from Vixhana's illumanced sword and armor.

Meila holstered her darkcore pistol and surveyed the darkness beyond the tree glade. "They headed out west to the hills," she said.

Finally, Jaks summoned the courage to look at his ravaged left hand.

In addition to the finger chopped off by his father as a child, the rest of his hand was a mangled mess—torn skin and exposed muscle with a couple of fractured white bones jutting out of the bloodied meat. Blood streamed from the end of his arm.

"Grafuk, Jaks. Get something on that," said Vixhana, sheathing her sword and stomping over to grab his injured arm.

Meila ran to her tent and returned with a waterskin and a small bag of exotic packages and bottles.

"This'll numb the pain," she told Jaks, giving him a small white pill that dissolved in his mouth; within a minute, he felt nothing but a numbness in this injured hand and a tingling sensation all over his body.

After Meila splashed water over the wound, she patted it dry with a torn cloth and instructed Vixhana to hold his wrist firm. She grabbed his fingers and pulled on them, using her other hand to push the extruding fragments of bones in Jaks's hand back into place.

Vixhana swore aloud, her face creased in anticipation of Jaks screaming in pain.

Jaks sucked in a breath, also expecting excruciating pain— but when he felt only a slight twinge at her manipulations, he began to giggle.

Light-headed and slightly euphoric, he said, "That pill. I feel invincible."

Meila nodded. She studied his hand, and satisfied with her intervention, slapped a gel pad on either side and wrapped a bandage to hold them in place. "The medigel applies particulates that'll accelerate the healing," she explained.

Vixhana shook her head. "Nasty wound, Jaks. I've seen similar bites from warlions, and most go on to lose their hand— sometimes even the entire arm. It's mauled pretty bad," she said with a note of sympathy in her voice.

Meila frowned. "It'll heal fairly well with the gel there.

Although, it'll probably be deformed and impaired in function. Sorry, Jaks." A shadow of doubt then swept over her face. "Hmm, that is, as long as the gel is compatible with your physiology . . ." She gnawed on her lip and furrowed her brow. "Damn, I didn't think of that," she said, suddenly looking conflicted and torn. "Your genetics could have diverged from ours over the past few thousands of years. The healing gel might confuse your body's cells and see them as foreign."

"What does that mean?" Vixhana's eyes narrowed.

"The particulates could attack his body. Instead of assisting his cells in the healing, they might kill them . . . maybe we should take this off now, just in case."

Jaks hadn't seen Meila so void of confidence before. "If it was attacking me, what would it feel like?" he asked.

"Pain, swelling, hot. They will also distribute throughout your system. If it attacks your organs, the reaction could kill you." Meila gave him a fretful look. She then tugged at the bandage and unraveled it, undoing her handiwork to fling the material aside. "I'm sorry, I don't know enough about the differences in our immunology to know if it will help you or harm you. Here, I'll get some more water to wash the gel off." She strode off to the saddlebags lying by where the horses had been tethered.

The euphoria of the pill lingered, blurring Jaks's attention until it was drawn to the other side of the clearing by a horse's scream. There, Ranger Cromer had stabbed Meila's dying mare with his sword and watched as the horse shuddered its last breath.

He wrenched his sword from the animal's chest and said, "They were after horse flesh. But I doubt they'll be back tonight; I think Vixhana killed the alpha." He pointed his blade at a large beheaded wulverion at the nightwraith's feet.

Mulgrave appeared, having made a circuit of the fields outside, and wandered over to Jaks, who leaned against a tree. "How's the hand?" The mage placed a hand on Jaks's shoulder.

Meila returned with a water bladder and poured it over Jaks's outstretched hand until the blood and gel washed away. "It's about as raw as you can get." She wrapped Jaks's hand again, but this time without the sticky gel.

Under a quarter-moon, the dead wulverions and equines were dragged into the field and heaped into a pile. Once the mass of bodies reached chest-height, Mulgrave held his arms wide as though to embrace the corpses and spoke a single word: "Burn."

A dome of flames roared to life and smothered the bodies with incinerating heat. Tongues of fire leapt into the night sky and roared a crackling descant.

Jaks cradled his bandaged hand and wrinkled his nose at the odor of burning flesh. He stared, fixated on the cremation.

The next day's travel saw the road end at a village built around a ruined tower, surrounded by a palisade of sharpened logs.

Several farms, mere plots of pumpkins and cabbages bounded by rocks, and a piggery—that they smelled before they saw it—huddled close to the primitive settlement. A few peasants toiled at the soil but dropped their tools and ran for the settlement on seeing their group approach.

"I wonder how those pigs survive with wulverions around?" Jaks asked to distract himself from his throbbing hand. Although Vixhana had slung his left arm up around his neck that morning to keep it from knocking about, it pained him with every sway of his horse. He had accepted another of Meila's pain-dulling pills that morning, but he didn't want to ask for another, not wanting to seem weak.

"You just smelled their natural defense. Wulverions detest the stench and squealing. I expect the villagers can barely put up with the pig sty themselves," Vixhana said as she screwed up her face in disgust. She was marching alongside her stallion, holding the reins, with Meila sitting astride her warhorse; the two of them had been taking turns to walk, following the loss of a horse and the pack mule to the wulverions.

At first, Vixhana had ridden with Meila behind, but the warrior woman had grown uncharacteristically flustered with the smaller woman's arms wrapped around her; within a few minutes, she'd stopped abruptly and dismounted the horse to allow the other to ride alone.

Whatever the villagers' feelings were about the pigs, their feelings toward strangers were very clear.

"There's a body hanging from the wall," Meila said, her eyesight even sharper than the ranger's.

As they approached the gates, a horn blasted from within the settlement.

A thin woman peered over the palisade and trained a crossbow on them. A few minutes later, three more men and women appeared behind the wall with crossbows and spears.

"What do you want?" the first woman shouted, almost shrieking, at them. "If you're wanting conscripts, you'll be getting none here. This here is *our* land. We don't bow to no king."

Jaks gasped as he distinguished features on the hanging body. "That's the tabard and uniform of a royal herald," he said, hoping that it wasn't Minto's body hanging there.

"Pigfuckers," Vixhana spat, glaring fury at the fortified settlement and the mounting number of armed peasants bristling the wall. "How dare they kill a king's representative. I'll massacre the whole lot of them." She loosened the sword at her hip and then looked at the great axe strapped to her horse.

His sister's zealous patriotism was inflamed. She looked as though the assault on the herald was an assault on her personal being. He had not seen her so riled up since Karisa told them of their father's abuse on her.

Her form dimmed and her features lost definition.

"Vixhana, stand down." Ranger Cromer trotted his horse toward her.

She ignored him and completed her transition into a magical shade: a black blotch that bewildered the eye. Was it a shadow cast, a stain on the ground, or a trick of the light? The shade swept the axe from its holster and absorbed it into its magic. "Darkness, night. I will murder every one of the traitors," it said.

"Captain. Stop. We have no business here." Mulgrave backtracked toward them and stared at the shadow. "You will not attack." His face was stern and voice commanding. "The king will be notified, and he will deal with these rebels in due time—now is not the time. We have a task to complete."

The shade raced toward the village anyway, but then halted. Moments later, Vixhana snapped out of the blackness and back to her true form; the massive double-bladed axe was in her right hand and the bastard sword in the other.

She glared at the villagers, as though daring them to attack her.

The villagers cried out in alarm at her sudden manifestation. Their crossbows trained on her, and a single bolt hissed through the air and struck her in the chest. On anyone else, it would have pierced the leather armor and critically injured the wearer, but on Vixhana, it bounced off like a twig striking a stone column, then tumbled to the ground. An invisible shield of gravmancy protected her.

After what seemed minutes but was only several seconds, she turned and stomped back to her horse and slammed the axe back into the holster—the stallion sagged slightly with the weight. She slapped her palm against the leather scabbard and turned to Mulgrave.

"Apologies, Grandmaster. I forgot myself in the moment. As you say, the king will deal with these traitors," she said in a measured voice, but with eyes still fired with menace.

With the villagers watching from the fortifications, the ranger took the lead again and rode a wide arc around the settlement and crops.

Several miles to the south, the plains became rugged with brown and gray hills, and bare but for only tufts of limp grass and brush. And beyond that, the land rose into a wide mountain range that eventually joined the crags far off to their right.

"The Jurn Highlands," Mulgrave said. "Last time I was here, decades ago, we only reached as far as these hills. We'd broken the nomads and chased the remnants this far before they melted into those mountains. Silas decided it wasn't worth chasing them any further, and the army turned around right there," the grandmaster explained to Meila like a child. "Who knows what's going on in those mountains now."

They had lost their riding formation by now, with no road to follow and their only landmark the mountains in front of them.

"I mapped the wreckage to the northeast, still some miles that way," Meila said, pointing up into the rough peaks. "A few days from here, perhaps?"

"Could be weeks, depending on the terrain and weather. Since we abandoned those saddlebags"—a further consequence of losing a horse and the pack mule to the wulverion attack—"we have fewer options for routes with no ropes and less cold-weather clothing."

"Needn't worry, the grandmaster and I can keep us warm." Tavis rubbed his hands, and pyromantic warmth radiated around them.

After a few hours into the barren midlands, they made the surprising find of a tiny, still lake—mirrorlike at the bottom of a wide basin of rounded, basalt hills.

A trio of goats startled when Ranger Cromer crested the hill overlooking the body of water. The wild animals bolted for the other side of the basin and clattered over the edge into the stony terrain.

"As good a place as any to stop for the day," the ranger said to Mulgrave. "The horses can water at the lake, but we camp up here."

Jaks walked his palfrey to the edge of the lake. The water was fresh from the recent rain, and he was amazed to see tiny, silver fishes flitting in shallows of the crystal-clear lake. His horse then dropped its mouth to the water and slurped, disturbing the surface and causing the fish to flit into the depths. It was a beautiful place: secluded, raw, untouched, with the wind pinching with every gust. Although tired from the day's ride, he daydreamed of living in a little house overlooking a lake.

With a couple of hours of daylight left, Grandmaster Mulgrave took his apprentices to the far end of the basin. "Even injured, every mage needs to be able to invoke magic to defend himself," he said, and then standing back from them invoked a suit of fire that enveloped his body from head to toe.

Tavis mimicked the grandmaster's invocation without hesitation and smirked a superior grin at Jaks through the flames.

Jaks concentrated on an invocation, but the best he could do was summon a halo of electromancy around his uninjured hand —far from a full shield of magic. The only point of redemption was, he kept it channeled for a minute longer than his previous record.

"Keep trying, lad. It'll come," Mulgrave said. "The second defense that you'll have to master, of course, is the wall. It will be beyond your capabilities at the moment, but you should at least start practicing."

"Like this," Tavis said to Jaks as though talking to a child. He stood back and invoked a chest-high barrier of flame two arm spans around himself. "I could push it out further, but I wouldn't want to burn you."

Mulgrave nodded. "Well done, Tavis. I'll spend some time with Jaks now. Run along and go keep watch with the master ranger." The mage perched on a flat ledge and ran a hand over his bald head. When the first apprentice had disappeared over the ridge, he said, "Try again. His presence probably wasn't helping."

"Yes, he's a distraction."

"Tavis is the most promising apprentice I've had for many years. His mastery of pyromancy is well beyond what I had at his age, and his gravmancy boons well in the smithery." The grandmaster spoke, but all the while scrutinizing Jaks closely. "I don't know what it is between you two, but you obviously antagonize each other to no end."

"He started it—" Jaks began.

"Never mind. You'll need to sort it out." The mage hopped onto a stone ledge overlooking the lake and sat cross-legged. "Now, let me see how you perform without distractions in the way. Go over there and try again."

Jaks retreated to the lake's edge. Reflected rays from the sun cast his shadow against the side of the stone basin.

Without Tavis sneering at him, Jaks settled easily into the three aspects of invocation with a level mind. In fact, the lightning armor came so swiftly that he laughed aloud, and it echoed around the bowl of the lake as he stood encased in a yard-thick suit of sizzling electricity. He stared at his body with white and blue arcing between his torso and limbs and leaping outward to threaten anything that came near him.

Grandmaster Mulgrave stood up on the stone ledge—a distance of twenty yards—and pointed a hand toward Jaks. "Hold steady. I'm going to test it," he shouted above the sound of crackling sprites.

A bolt of fire shot from the mage's hand toward Jaks's crackling armor.

An explosion met the firebolt on striking the outer limits of the invocation.

Several more bolts of increasing size battered the armor of lightning, each fusing and exploding before they could strike Jaks.

With each attack, Jaks felt the invocation losing power and his concentration wavering. With the sixth fire bolt, the armor shrunk and then abruptly dissipated. In fear that the mage would attack again, Jaks shouted, "Stop!" and held out his hand.

Mulgrave appeared in front of him, smiling, and slapped him on the shoulder. "That's it, lad. You have great potential," the mage said. "I think it's when your thoughts are contaminated by petty anxieties that your control is the poorest. Trivial threats make you indecisive and cloud your will."

Jaks nodded, finding truth in the grandmaster's words.

"Yes, that's enough for today. You can stay and practice if you like, but I need to talk to your sister again—I thought she was going to go off like a fireball at those villagers. I don't want her going back there in the middle of the night." Mulgrave shook his head, then wandered up to the camp.

Alone by the lake, Jaks invoked the electromancy armor again. A familiar acrid odor filled his nostrils, and the hum of electricity filled his ears.

Nothing could touch him inside his shield. Cocooned, he was invincible.

Tavis might have both pyromancy and gravmancy, better magic control, and greater endurance, but Jaks was catching up fast. With the rarest of magic, he had no doubt the grandmaster would choose him over that other self-conceited smartass of an apprentice.

His smugness, however, was shattered a few seconds later when his armor of electromancy snapped out of existence and left him with only the lingering bitterness of metal in his mouth.

Chapter 32

The Jurns

That night, the group were forced down into the lake basin to shelter from the chill of howling winds.

Jaks swore they were the calls of wulverions and fought sleep throughout the night. But weakened from weeks of travel, invoking magic, and the pain of his mangled hand, he nodded off and cried out in his sleep as nightmare beasts chased him through a forest, caught him, and ate his hands and feet. And leading them was a hideous monster with the head of a wulverion on the body of his father.

In the morning, the winds stilled and left gray clouds to hide the mountain peaks of the Jurn Highlands before them.

Up to yesterday, the distant rocky titans had held Jaks's attention as they rode closer to their wreckage of Meila's ship. But today, riding one-handed, the midlands enraptured him with its great plateau of stone stretching in every direction.

Curious swaths of green trees peeked out of gorges, flowing like rivers of forest through this vast bed of flat, gray rock.

With no way to cross the ravines—some so long, one

couldn't see where they started or finished—Jaks concluded they would need to descend into one and hoped that it would take them to the base of the mountains.

He gritted his teeth against the pain of his freshly re-bandaged hand and regretted refusing Meila's offer of her pain-dulling pills.

Earlier that morning, he'd barely stifled a scream of agony when she removed his bandage and examined his crippled hand. "Looks like the healing gel might have helped, although I washed most of it off the other day. This part here"—she pointed at puncture marks on his wrist—"probably didn't get the gel and is worse off than the rest of your hand."

A chunk of meat from the palm below the stump of his little finger was missing, and the wound was sloughed and red, looking like the side of his hand had been sliced off. Thankfully, the two bones that Meila had pushed back into place remained where they should, and the overlying flesh was a reassuring but messy red.

"Good. You didn't suffer any ill effects from the medigel," she said, peeling open a new pad of the stuff. "Let's put some more on. The skin and muscle should heal up, but without a surgeon to fix the bones, those fingers will probably be next to useless." She pointed at the two closest to the stump of his little finger. "Sure you don't want a pill?"

Jaks shook his head, resolving to be strong.

That had been an hour earlier, and he decided he would continue to suck up the pain. He was getting used to it. Besides, it was a fitting punishment for his failures. He had spiraled into moodiness that morning.

He thought of Karisa and how their lives could have been so much happier if they had sailed away to Faucony as she had wanted to. He ruminated on how he had failed her and his mother, lived in a state of denial at the evil his father had perpetrated on them, and had done nothing about it. Yes, he deserved this pain for what he had failed to do for the two people he had loved the most—now both dead because of his weakness. He needed to toughen up, be stronger, or forever be a weakling.

"There's someone over there," Meila said. "Ranger—someone there is watching us," she repeated louder to the wiry hunter several horse-lengths ahead.

They all turned to her and saw her raise her finger and point to their far right. "Female human with some animal-skin headdress and facial markings."

Jaks squinted against the sun, but only saw the rocky expanse dotted with boulders and sheer ledges.

"Can't see anything, except those bronzes over the mountains," Tavis said, pointing at a pack of dragons flying into the distance. "Probably nothing."

"No, she's still there. About eight hundred yards out. Peering over that outcrop." Meila pointed again.

"Are you sure? How can you see that far?" Cromer asked, as he pulled out a metal-tubed spyglass that telescoped out as he pulled it up to his eye. The telescope ranged over the landscape and then froze as he focused. "I think you're right—there is someone there."

"Bandits?" Mulgrave asked, loosening the mace he carried at his side but never used, even when the wulverions had attacked.

The ranger shrugged and collapsed the spy glass, thrusting it into a saddle pocket. He fingered an arrow to his bow.

Over the next few hours, many more watchers appeared,

surreptitious stalkers, none coming closer than the first. On this open plateau, Jaks wildly imagined he and his companions stood out like savories on a platter.

"Best you all prepare for a fight. This doesn't look good," Vixhana said, securing her shield and placing a hand on the pommel of her sword. "Unless we descend into one of those great ravines, we have no cover. What say you, mage?"

"We could put a ravine between them and us, if we grav-jump across. We'd need to leave the horses and provisions behind," Mulgrave replied, speaking through the raised visor of his battlemage helmet adorned with a firebird with red wings. "Last resort, though. Let's find out how many there are."

Tavis was the only one of them that looked unconcerned, seemingly ignorant of how outnumbered they were. He grinned as he arranged his shield and hotchpotch of armor and flexed his hand as though ready to invoke a maelstrom of fire magic.

Jaks also craved a chance to test his newfound magic, but his experience with bullies and kidnappers had taught him to fear the unexpected, which in this case could come from a dozen fronts. With his crippled hand, he couldn't handle a crossbow, so he had only his rune-forged sword and his magic.

Ranger Cromer pulled his horse to a halt. "Here's a greeting party."

A figure emerged on a ledge overlooking them and leaned casually against a carved bone spear as several more figures with shortbows arrayed themselves behind. The man wore a horned goat skull over his head and a goat-skin cloak on his back. Bronzed and leathery with age, Jaks thought he looked like some wild medicine man.

"What are you doing here?" the goat man asked in a heavily accented voice.

The ranger, with his ironwood bow and an un-nocked arrow

at his lap, narrowed his eyes at the man and then addressed him in a guttural flow of words in a language that Jaks had never heard before.

The goat man's face changed from wariness to puzzlement, and then he replied in the same heavy-syllabled tongue. His attendants stared at the ranger and lowered their weapons.

Again, Cromer replied to the leader and gestured at Mulgrave. The goat man examined the mage intently.

Mulgrave then spoke out several of the foreign words. Jaks was amazed. The grandmaster knew some of their language too, whoever they were. Partway through his sentence, he looked lost for a word and reverted to Ascorian. "Forgive me, my Jurn is very basic. I am Grandmaster Mulgrave from the Academy of the Arcane."

"You travel dangerously. Lucky we find you first. You will come. The Uwama will instruct you," he said in an inarguable manner, then pointed his bone spear to the east. "You must follow."

"Is *he* the Uwama, or is taking us to him?" Meila asked.

"Uwamas were the Jurn nomad chiefs before we drove them out of the plains . . ." Vixhana kept her shield raised but removed the hand on her sword. "They were all women, so I would guess this man is not one."

Thirty archers and spear-carrying men and women inched out of crevices, nooks, and from behind boulders to accompany them at a distance.

An hour later, a wide ravine yawned before them. A cliff wall dropped twenty yards from where Jaks overlooked the edge, and its far side was shrouded from view by conical tips of a forest rising from the bottom.

For the horses to descend would have been impossible had it not been for a narrow path carved into the cliff side. Jaks and the other riders dismounted for the walk down, each leading their horses with caution.

The goat man, who had introduced himself as Witabu, waited for them at the ravine floor beside one of the tall pines. Along with the small forest, a pebbly stream meandered along the ravine and babbled quietly with the whispers of the pine needles releasing their sharp, refreshing scents. The overhead sun revealed the lush valley for a rich paradise hidden within the barren midlands.

"The waters from the mountains run through the ravines all year long," Witabu, the plainsman, said to Mulgrave, as Jaks made the final few yards of the descent in front of them.

"The ravines are gouged by water—surely, there are floods?" asked the grandmaster.

"At times. But, as you will see, our village is built to withstand the greatest of storms."

Witabu spoke an order to the youngest of his entourage. The boy dashed down the ravine ahead of them. As the last of their horses, led by Tavis, caught up with the group, the plainsman lifted his spear and continued along the wooded ravine.

They came upon a clearing with a corral of pregnant goats, bleating as they gorged on a pile of food scraps; a goat herder nodded at Witabu and stared at Jaks and his companions as they passed by. A hundred yards more, and the forest opened up to a field of carrot, pumpkin, and potato plants, on both sides of the stream. The fields were joined by a flat wooden bridge and tended by tribe folk with hoes and wooden wheelbarrows. Fearful, despite the old plainsman's assurances, they stopped their work and watched on in silence.

As woods again filled the ravine, Jaks noticed rope bridges spanning the trees above.

A little girl gazed at them from ten yards overhead and giggled as she dropped winged seed pods that spiraled toward the ground in a blur and whirled amongst the riders. Witabu barked a reprimand at the child. Nonplussed, she made a face at him, sped off on bare feet along the swing bridge, and with laughter trailing behind her, vanished amongst the treetops.

The rope bridges became more numerous further on. Eventually, they were shadowed by a giant wooden platform the width and length of the Academy's main dining hall.

A raised open-sided structure, it stretched between at least twenty trees and was secured to each with braces and frames to support expertly placed joists and planks. Ropes hung from the underside for a variety of purposes—dangling lanterns, hanging deer carcasses, and benches bearing pots, pans, and cooking utensils.

Below the raised platform, a deck at ground-level mirrored the one above. A hole at its center accessed the running water. And around it, a group of women loaded kindling into several stone ovens and firepits. One dome-shaped oven, however, already spouted a trail of smoke while a sweaty man thrust a flat-bladed shovel into its small opening and retrieved flatbreads to cool on a nearby platform.

Witabu beckoned to a pair of spear-wielding sentries, who watched uneasily as they neared.

"Leave your beasts here. They will be guarded. We go up." He gestured to a set of wooden stairs on the side of the structure and ascended. The guards appeared delighted with the horses and began inspecting each one as though they were at a market: stroking manes, lifting tails, checking teeth and ears.

Vixhana looked down at the tallest guard, a half-foot shorter than her. "Watch out, he bites," she said, and then released her battleaxe from her stallion and gripped it in her hand as she stomped up the stairs.

Jaks followed his sister and paused when he reached the last step.

Several children ran and skipped about the immense wooden platform playing a game of chase, whilst a few even younger ones sat playing make-believe with toys of exquisitely carved wood, stone, and bone laid out on a brown animal hide. On the other side of the platform, a dozen women crafted as they knelt or sat cross-legged amongst rows of low tables near a woman seated on the only chair in sight. Four armed guards stood at attention beside her and cast wary eyes on the strangers.

Jaks jolted out of his wonder to see Witabu, Mulgrave, and Cromer bend and bow to the seated woman. He scurried over to Vixhana, Meila, and Tavis behind the tables and was followed by several of Witabu's hunters, who ranged themselves about the deck and shooed away the children. They scampered away over rope bridges to other platforms suspended throughout the forest.

"Welcome, Grandmaster," said the woman, who then looked at one of her attendants and spoke a few words.

The young woman rose and glided on slender legs to another set of stairs. Jaks swallowed and drank in her sharp features and long, auburn hair elaborately coiled around her head. She was beautiful.

"Uwama, I did not know your people flourished here," Mulgrave addressed the seated woman, taking his helmet from his head and holding it under his arm.

She placed her hands in her lap and rested green eyes on the mage. "We do not flourish, Grandmaster, our people survive by the grace of Hodrin and this oasis that He created for us."

She cast her eyes upward momentarily as she spoke the name of her god.

It was the second time Jaks had caught himself staring, but he couldn't help but be enchanted by the Uwama. The chieftess was a gray-haired counterpart to the young woman who had fled down the stairs. Beautiful, the two shared grace of movement, slender long limbs, and intense, deep-set eyes that commanded attention. And she spoke in fluent Ascorian with a silky alto. Her voice reached into his heartstrings and plucked a desire to be near her and just listen to her speak. Unconsciously, he walked closer to her and stood behind the grandmaster to stare over his head.

"Can you tell me of the Highlands?" Mulgrave said. "We are just passing through these parts to reach them."

The Uwama frowned. "Truly, only a fool or a braveheart ventures into the mountains. There is little to be found other than wild beasts and monsters. Is that not why your king chased us here a decade ago, hoping we would expire against those cruel spires?" She rested a finger on her flawless jaw. "Tell me, what do you seek there? You are treasure hunters?"

The mage locked eyes with her for a moment and then removed his gauntlet and reached under his breastplate to extract a folded piece of paper.

Meila suddenly strode up to the grandmaster and grasped his wrist, preventing him from unfolding the map that she had marked with the location of the wreckage. "You can't show them. How do you know we can trust them?"

Mulgrave looked from Meila to the Uwama and back, then addressed the seated woman. "Uwama Xandu, Chieftess of Jurns, are your motives pure? Can I trust you to do us no harm?"

The Uwama laughed. "Of course, you cannot trust us." Although her words were antagonistic, Jaks yearned for her to keep speaking, that he could continue listening to her rich tones. "But even though your armies drove us from our pastures and plains, we know that we were only there because of the grace of Hodrin, and we bear you no ill will."

At that point, the young plainswoman reappeared bearing a tray of chiseled stone mugs and walked around offering one to each of their group. As Jaks took a mug, she studied his face and then his injured arm. "Are you sick?" she asked in accented Ascorian.

Jaks's face flushed as he searched for words, not wanting to embarrass himself while talking to this attractive woman. "I fought a wulverion."

"Oh," she said, scrutinizing him up and down, and then stared at his teeth.

He closed his mouth, wondering if this was how his horse had felt while being examined by the guards earlier.

She walked to Tavis and offered him a drink. "How about you? Are you healthy?" She leaned forward to examine him closer as the apprentice took a mug. He nodded and returned her brazen stare before coursing his eyes over her figure.

"Yes, you are better," said the beautiful plainswoman.

Tavis looked at Jaks and smirked.

Jaks sensed a burning in his stomach and clenched his teeth. There had just been an unspoken competition—and Tavis had won.

Meila had removed her hold on Mulgrave's wrist by then but continued standing between him and the Uwama.

"The Jurns have welcomed us into their village, my cautious *ward*," Mulgrave said, stressing Meila's subordinate status. "That alone is a great trust." He waved a hand, gesturing for her to move aside.

Meila frowned but allowed the mage to unfold the map and

hand it to the chieftess, who merely gave Meila a curious look as she received the paper.

"We seek a wreckage fallen from the sky. It has landed at this location." Mulgrave pointed a finger at a point on the map. "We seek to examine the debris."

"From the heavens? Is it an omen?" the Uwama asked, holding the map into the light.

"A magical skyship," said Mulgrave, glancing sideways at Meila and coughing, "that could unravel important wisdom and knowledge to us."

The Uwama interrogated the grandmaster for several minutes, probing his knowledge of the ship's origins and nature. Jaks was impressed with his master's disingenuous replies that avoided any revelation of the unworldly origin of the starship. Eventually, she exhausted her questions and sat for a minute, tapping elegant fingers on the chair arm.

"You seek this relic for knowledge? Through such peril?" she asked.

Mulgrave pulled a second paper from his pocket and passed it to the Uwama. "For the king. I am but his emissary."

The gray-haired woman leaned forward and examined the grandmaster closer. "An emissary. You are of status within your country. The king listens to you?"

Vixhana stepped forward. "The grandmaster is held with great esteem in Ascoria. His actions and words are of legend," she said.

The old mage laughed. "She exaggerates. I am but an old magesmith doing the king's work."

"But the king would bend his ear to you, if you asked?"

"Yes, of course."

The chieftess was quiet for a minute and then looked back at the map. "Dragons and other wild beasts roam the area that you search. Also, the terrain changes often because of landslides and rockfalls. Wandering there without knowledge of the Highlands, even with your mighty armor—especially with your mighty armor—could be a death sentence."

She then lowered her voice, as though telling a secret. "We know of this 'wreckage' you seek—"

"You have seen it?" The grandmaster's voice rose a half-octave. "You know where it is?"

"My hunters have seen it but most of it was buried beneath much rubble." She turned to one of her guards, whispered a command, and watched him run off over one of the rope bridges. "It is one of the areas they hunt rarely. As they described it, they saw a star fall from the sky and found their way to it the next day. It had struck a mountainside and slipped down, causing a great slide."

"Could these hunters take us there?" Mulgrave asked, excitement showing on his face.

The Uwama leaned back and accepted a mug from her attendant, sipped, and returned the vessel to her tray. She looked fondly at the young woman and said, "What is that phrase you always say . . . how does it go, my flower? 'I do something for you, and you do something for me'?"

"So wordy, Mother. It's just 'I help you, you help me.' Everything must be fair," the young woman replied, and walked back down the stairs with the serving tray.

The Uwama stood up from her chair. Diminutive, she was the same height as Meila, but where the gray-haired woman was wide-hipped and elegant, the outworlder was slender and graceful.

"Yes. If you help me, I will grant you my hunters to take you to your relic."

"What is it you want?" Mulgrave asked, stepping back as she came toward him.

The Uwama motioned for him and the others to sit with her cross-legged around a knee-high table.

"You must ask your king to allow us to live back on our lands. We were once a tribe of over a thousand, but now fewer than six hundred survive and lessen with every year." She sighed. "When the tribes fled the plains, most continued deep into the Highlands. Some survived, but most perished in the cold, starving, and savaged by beasts or bands of evil men. Hodrin led us to this abandoned village. But even here, we too slowly perish." The Uwama squeezed her eyes shut for a moment before she continued. "Hodrin created our people for the plains. The mountain gods are merciless toward us, their mountains and plateaus yield barely enough for the few of us living to survive, and they curse us with weak infants that die before they take their first breath."

Mulgrave's face took on a look of concern and he rubbed his scalp briskly. "Your tribes were offered peace, but they refused to submit to the king. That is why you were—"

"Were chased out," said the Uwama. "Yes, we fought to remain on our plains. Would you not have done the same? But, clearly, we had no chance against such an army. We chose to flee rather than submit." Her eyes flared for a moment, then dulled with sorrow. "But now we are a different people. Languishing, dying, barely surviving for over two decades, I would rather have my people back on the plains with our herds and ponies than slowly expire in these ravines. Even if it means bowing to your king."

"You would come under King Silas's rule? You would give up your chieftess rights?"

"Our people would still need a leader, but yes, we would

submit to his rule in exchange for the right to roam the plains once again."

Mulgrave nodded his head. "It saddens me to hear of your tribe's struggles, and I bear some of the guilt of harming your people. In apology, I would be pleased to bring your plea to King Silas."

The Uwama and the grandmaster settled into a long discussion, with a plan for the mage's party to escort a representative back to Dunberrin once they had completed their salvage quest.

Bread and dried meats were brought to the table by the chieftess's attendants. But as the shadows lengthened over the ravine, Jaks ignored his pangs of hunger, wallowed in the pain of his hand, and suffered the gloating grin of Tavis while Xanra, the chieftess's daughter, doted on him.

Eventually, Jaks made an excuse to check on the horses. He found the palfreys and Vixhana's stallion resting by the rivulet, downstream from the lower platform, with the same two guards fussing about them.

As he approached, the tallest one lifted a small child to sit on Jaks's gelding. The brown-haired boy squealed in delight and thrust his face into the horse's mane and hugged the animal. Three other children bounced on their toes, waiting for a turn. Jaks shrugged and left the children to their entertainment and went to explore the surrounding woods.

A minute of wandering and Jaks came to the bottom of the ravine's cliff face. He gaped at a web of rope bridges and smaller platforms above him that spanned from the chieftess's deck to the walls of the ravine, where scores of open cave mouths dotted the cliff.

He flinched when a whirling disc whizzed past his face. A giggle erupted. On a bridge stood the rapscallion, the little loner girl, staring cheekily down at him. She threw another winged seed pod and dashed into one of the cave mouths, laughing.

He grinned at the girl's impish behavior and examined the cliff for a path up to the caves—which he guessed were where the villagers lived and slept—but the rope bridges appeared to be the only entrances.

A male voice startled Jaks from his study of the cliff face.

"You come see?" said a youth about Jaks's age standing behind him in the tree line. Wild-looking, he was attired in leggings and jerkin made of animal skin and wore a wolf-hide over his shoulders.

Pointing to the cliff caves, the youth repeated, "You see? You come?" He turned and beckoned over his shoulder.

Jaks was curious to see where the caves led. Were they just shallow alcoves or a deep network? Were they furnished? These people seemed to live like primitives, but could they have comforts within?

The young man seemed friendly enough. A knife dangled at his hip but his movements, gesturing and hopping like an excited child, lent him the role of an enthusiastic host keen to show a stranger his home.

Jaks hurried after him and caught up at the bottom of the stairs.

"I'm Jaks." He tapped his chest and examined the short tribesman, appreciating a grubby yet rugged, handsome face.

The youth pulled himself as tall as he could and grinned back. "Rakiyura . . . Raki. I show you village." His eyes fell on Jaks's bandaged hand and he frowned. "You are . . . a cripple?"

Jaks explained his injury but found no judgement in the youth's response, unlike the young woman's dismissive tone before.

"Hodrin bless you," Raki replied and then leapt up the steps in threes.

The two young men slipped across the Uwama's wooden platform, evading the chieftess's tables on the other side of the platform. Meila and Vixhana threw him quizzical looks, but he ignored them and dashed after his new friend onto the wooden planks of a bridge.

The two of them could have run side by side, but Jaks's head spun when the bridge started to sway, and he stopped to grab the waist-high guide rope with his good hand as the rocking continued.

Raki paused and returned to place a small hand on Jaks's elbow and muttered soothing sounds to encourage him across the planks; at one stage, the tribesman tipped Jaks's gaze up with a chin lift to jar him out of his contemplation of the fall to the ground below. In that moment, the youth reminded Jaks of his friend Minto, when they were young, coaxing him along a high wall to a hiding spot where they spied on pretty girls next door.

At the end of the bridge, Jaks found the little whirler girl standing there in the cave mouth, watching him and rolling her head from side to side while batting her temples.

The tribesman barked a few guttural syllables at her, "*Suli, oto bargen.*"

The girl slapped her forehead one last time and high-tailed into the cave mouth.

Jaks followed the tribesman and ducked into the cave. As the sunlight faded behind him, his eyes adjusted to a glow at the other end of the tunnel.

An excavated room with a wooden floor and a couple of knee-high tables greeted him. Light radiated from lightstone lanterns, revealing furs and skins blanketing the wall. Three similar rooms connected through short tunnels.

Raki ducked into the next room and beckoned Jaks along. Inside, two gray-haired men bent over a table taking turns to shuffle colored stones over a checkerboard; they greeted the young tribesman and stared astonished at Jaks. Raki spoke an explanation to the elders, at one stage miming someone swaying, at which the two men cracked toothless grins at Jaks.

Knowing he was the brunt of a joke, he mimicked wobbling on his feet, and then joined their laughter as he felt some gate of acceptance opening to him.

They left the old men to their game, and Raki led a path through the cave complex, passing scores of tunnel offshoots blocked by hanging hides and skins. Jaks restrained an impulse to peer into the rooms, guessing them to be the private chambers for families and individuals.

Dozens more tribe folk greeted and gaped at the pair as they dashed by, with Raki proudly introducing his guest to each.

Jaks sighed in relief when, finally, he could stand straight in a tall, rounded cavern. A slit of sunlight cut through motes of dust from a long, narrow crack in the ceiling, and beneath it, a craggy hole fenced off with ropes occupied the center of the cave. In the closest corner, boxes of spears stood with iron tips upright. In another corner, unstrung shortbows were similarly stored with bowstrings draped over wooden spikes in the wall. Quivers of arrows lay stored nearby. Along with piles of animal hides, coils of rope, boxes of nails, and hundreds of other miscellanea, the cavern was a massive storeroom.

A staircase hewn into the wall climbed up to an open hatch filled with sunlight. Jaks blinked against the brightness at the top of the steps and found himself in a wooden shack with an open door.

"High village," Raki said as he stepped out of the hut.

Once Jaks's eyes adjusted to the midafternoon sun, he discovered himself in a settlement atop the plateau.

Dozens of stone buildings with black slate roofs covered the tableland. Tribe folk toiled outside the buildings, darting in occasionally to access a tool or material, and settling back outside to complete their handiwork. Animal hides stretched over drying racks next to a woman scraping a fresh skin with a sharp blade. A circle of men chipped at stone blocks fitting together a new hut. Cooking pots boiled delicious odors as cooks stirred and commanded attendants busy at preparing vegetables and meats.

They strolled through the village and soon amassed a small following of gawky children who chattered and stared at the tall Ascorian invader. Soon, Jaks found himself holding a tiny hand and looked down to see the whirler-throwing girl parading alongside him, looking down her nose at any who dared to try and steal her prize. He smiled at her and squeezed her hand, eliciting a sparkle of eyes and a flash of teeth.

Raki was a popular youth. Adults greeted him warmly from their chores as they walked by, and he replied to each with a word or two and a nod. Jaks nodded his head congenially at each villager and repeated their greeting, *"Hodrin uhsaga,"* which Raki assured him meant "God's blessing on you."

At the edge of the village, Jaks looked out over another ravine full of pine trees, and then turning about realized the plateau was a tower of rock in the center of a single enormous cleft in the midlands with rivers of trees surrounding the village on all sides.

"It's like a castle," Jaks said. "No wonder they settled here."

Raki picked up his words and replied, "Caves here . . . before us. We find caves and build here." The tribesman led Jaks back to a pair of stone buildings where several women were sewing animal hides together as clothes and mats.

"Jaks, there you are," called out a voice from behind. Vixhana was staring at him and the circle of women and children. Grandmaster Mulgrave trailed several yards behind her and was gazing around the village in a group with Tavis, Cromer, and Meila led by the older tribesman Witabu. "I was wondering where you had got to. New friends?" his sister said.

The grandmaster called out, heading toward a small tower presiding over the village, and summoned Vixhana and Jaks to follow.

Jaks grasped Raki's hand and thanked him for the tour.

That evening, the Uwama dined with their party under the moonlight and lightstone lanterns on the platform in the ravine. As they ate, a tribeswoman danced before them to a flautist's melody. A gifted illumancer, the dancer weaved spirals of color through the air with her hands and entranced them with magical images of two forbidden lovers and their tragic story.

After the dancer finished, a dozen older tribe folk joined the Uwama's table and spoke politely with Mulgrave, Cromer, and Vixhana in stilted Ascorian that they'd learned to a greater or lesser extent. In the past, the Jurns had extensive trade with merchants and even welcomed the occasional outsider to settle with them—often having fallen for a beautiful tribeswoman. The Uwama's perfect fluency, she explained, came from having lived in Dunberrin learning the healing arts decades before, when King Irin, "the Roadmaker"—father of the current king— had ruled. Now, the only contact the Jurns had with outsiders was with fur merchants from Ellipta and the nearby villages in the plains.

From the plateau above, the sound of more revelry drifted

down to Jaks's ears. Wilder, with chanting and beating of drums, he imagined villagers bouncing and swaying to the music.

After Witabu directed them each to a sleeping chamber at the conclusion of the evening, Jaks crouched inside the small room hewn into the rock, bare except for a hanging lantern with a thick, burning candle and a raised alcove with furs and goat hides laid out as a bed.

Several minutes later, Meila brushed through the animal-hide door-cover and smoothed out her sleeves. She was all business. "Let's change your bandage. Change your dressings now and we'll have one less to make later when the surroundings will be far less hospitable. Go on, sit down," she said, patting the ground next to a bowl of water and a cloth she had prepared.

A sweet odor permeated the room as Meila peeled off the wound dressing and gently cleaned the wound. "Pretty good. The granulation tissue is excellent." She pricked the tip of his fingers with a wood splinter. "Feel that, sharp?"

"Blunt." His thoughts were elsewhere, though. He stared at her shoulder.

"We should get the chieftess, or one of her healers, to splint your hand properly, though. Get those bones healing straight." She spun a dry cloth dressing around Jaks's hand and tied the end off at his wrist. "The particulates in your system will continue to assist your muscle and skin regeneration until they're all used up. In two or three weeks, the soft tissue should be done. A month, and the bones should be fully knitted." She forced a smile, then picked up the bowl with the used bandages and stood to leave.

Perhaps it was her proximity, or the enclosed space, or the dangers of the Highlands that would invade their life the next day, but a heady desire took hold of Jaks's senses.

"Don't go." Words spilled from his mouth before he knew what he was saying. "Stay. Share my bed tonight?" The words were so brazen, he almost regretted them.

She froze, her face turned away from him.

He had said his desire. He couldn't take it back, didn't want to.

Her hand jerked away from his grip, and she remained facing the door-hide. "No. You need rest. To heal . . ." Then she fled the room.

The rejection stung like a crown of nettles. He could not have been any clearer in his feelings for her, yet she had dismissed them again. Without even looking him in the face.

So, it was not disappointment that festered this time, but anger and indignation that left a sourness in his mouth. His heart turned cold.

Meila stood a little way down from Jaks's room, back to the wall, panting. An uneasy feeling cut through her with a saw-toothed blade. An emotion stirred that she had not felt for years, if not decades. Lust.

The last time she and Anton had been passionate, some anniversary or other, the act had been robotic and unsatisfying, and not attempted again since. But at this moment, propositioned by a tall, attractive man, her desires were ablaze.

But she couldn't succumb; she was loyal to her vows of betrothal.

She hurried through the tunnel, out onto the swing-bridge. The bowl dropped into the ravine below as she grabbed the sides and welcomed the night air nipping at her face and arms.

She shook her head clear and lowered her heart rate, then

stared at the silhouettes of swaying treetops and considered the irony.

She laughed aloud, not caring who heard. So ridiculous that she should be so confused by a young man, a fraction of her age, with annoying curly hair that demanded to be straightened, and a painfully handsome face that she wanted to slap or caress or both.

How had she become so cold and neutered that she had forgotten what it was like to have feelings unmodulated by cerebral implants—to be human?

Desire and affection enlivened her. The entire planet made her feel alive with the wonder of its unmarred landscapes, magical forces, mythical creatures, and the fight for life and liberty.

Alive again, after decades of deadening herself to the genocides that she and the *UWFS Mendhelsson* crew had brought to other Old Colonies. Guilt, yes. Regret, yes. She couldn't save those worlds, but hopefully, maybe, she could save this one.

Meila heaved the rope-bridge left and right, swinging and laughing. Caught up in the struggles of this world, she had been delivered from her own, unknowing that she had broken a heart in doing so.

Chapter 33

The Wreckage

They departed the village the following morning beneath a gray and foreboding sky. Witabu and three tribesmen led the way into the forest ravine and toward the Highlands of Jurn.

The tribesmen hunters were sinewy, hard men born to scramble over peaks and mountains. Outfitted with satchels over their backs, they were armed with stabbing spears and horn bows and dark-fletched arrows. The grandmaster was pleased to have the mountaineers with them, but Jaks merely felt indifferent.

Earlier that morning, the Uwama had expertly set the fractures in his hand properly in place and splinted them with wood. However, the effects of the pain-dulling pill he'd coldly accepted from Meila had worn off, and now both his hand and face were throbbing in pain—and the artificial sense of invincibility had wilted to a sense of annoyance.

Carrying on regardless, he rolled his shoulders beneath his backpack laden with provisions and essentials and picked up the pace to catch up with his sister at the back of the group.

Vixhana cast him a sidelong look. "What's with you? You look as glum as a pickle."

"Nothing," he muttered and stared at the path.

"Hells above, Jaks. You're a mess to be sad for."

He shrugged, unsure whether she referred to his appearance or his mental state. Whichever it was, he agreed with her on both counts.

Vixhana's concern, however, was brief, and she scolded him. "No excuse to dawdle. Don't fall behind." She had been snappy since giving up her great axe. Witabu had laughed at the oversized weapon. "You won't need that; there are no elephants for you to butcher here." Reluctantly, she'd left it at the Jurn village, along with their horses, and hitched her sword and shield.

Mulgrave and Tavis, sacrificing armor for agility, had abandoned their plate armor—gauntlets, boots, pauldrons, helms, everything except their breast plates. In their place, they wore borrowed leather boots, leggings, and furs from the Jurns.

Around midday, Jaks was tiring, and Vixhana prodded him repeatedly to keep up with the others. He hadn't realized how much stamina he had lost since conscription. Thankfully, the group stopped a half hour later, when the ravine floor rose and the cliffs fell away on either side to deliver them to the base of the Highland mountains.

Behind and below them, the plateau spread out, a cracked table of stone, and ahead of them, the Highlands were close enough for Jaks to see a thunder of dragons, or perhaps just a flock of large birds, circling one of the peaks. Pine trees hugged the mountains and a cap of white topped many of the higher peaks.

The terrain steepened from there on and enveloped them in mountains all around. Witabu and his men blazed the trail and assisted the less experienced adventurers over sliding shale slopes, narrow canyons, and at one time, over a makeshift rope bridge that traversed a short crevice that yawned between cliffs. Fortunately, the wind was mild and one less hazard to worry about, certainly a boon as Jaks tight-rope walked across the rope with only one good hand to stabilize himself over the two-yard length.

The tortuous landscape afforded no lack of concentration. A misstep here or there meant slipping to his death or sliding into injury. So, for the rest of the day, the trek forced Jaks to clear his mind and forget his aches and pains. There was nothing better than danger to focus his head.

That evening, they stopped beneath a rocky outcrop to camp. Although lengths of slimy algae dripped from the overhang, underneath it was dry and sheltered from the wind. A fire crackled, and the food was passed around the hard shelf, barely capable of fitting all nine of them.

Meila approached him and made idle chatter about the day. Still hurting from her rejection the night before, he moved away as though he hadn't heard her and warmed himself with the tribesmen around the campfire.

The next morning, a crashing boulder on the other side of the valley startled awake most of those who slept. The startled screech of several dragons echoed high above, and a subsequent rockfall of stones and pebbles followed for a couple of minutes and then settled into a pile of debris.

Jaks clambered to his feet, heart pounding at the sound of the avalanche and the dragons.

In the dim dawn light, the hunters yawned and stretched without a care. Reading their calm as a signal of safety, he settled back to his sleeping mat and stilled his pulse with a breathing exercise.

Once the sun had risen enough to march safely out of the valley, the group trekked until they came to a rapid, white river—heard well before they saw it. Jaks sighed in relief when Witabu declared they would only need to follow its length and not attempt a crossing.

The river remained their deafening companion for the rest of the morning, a leviathan desperate to slither through the mountains and carve a channel to the sea. If it had been calmer, they could probably have sailed right back to the lowlands, but even Jaks—with his lack of boating experience—could see that a boat would soon be smashed to pieces by the chaotic, watery maze of boulders.

"The site is over the ridge in the next valley," Witabu translated from one of the hunters to Mulgrave as they veered away from the river and began ascending a steep hill.

The sun hid behind rolling clouds, and a brisk wind howled past them as they crested the ridge. The next valley lay between three mountains and had yet another river coursing through it; however, this one was a calm cousin to the monster that had humbled them earlier that day.

The valley floor was flat and the easiest terrain they had walked for the past day. Lone skeletal trees and small bushes struggled to grow even near the river.

"Around the side of that mountain," Witabu again translated for a hunter pointing at the largest of the three mountaintops. Nothing grew on its sheer slopes, and vast tracts of loose and broken stone marked the surface. Even the top was cracked, resembling the shape of a horn.

Daylight faded as they reached a point where the hunters told them they would see the wreckage.

Witabu was the first to reach the rock—a giant extrusion

from the side of the mountain. He suddenly crouched and waved his hand downward.

"There are people there!" said the head tribesman, pulling back behind the rock.

Ranger Cromer, Mulgrave, and Vixhana pushed their way to the front, pressed against the stone, and carefully peered into the valley beyond.

After a few minutes, they withdrew, and Mulgrave swore. "Hell and damnation—they're excavating."

In his place, Jaks poked his head out to spy on the interlopers.

A mile away, at the bottom of the horned mountain, humanoid figures toiled at the base of an avalanche; this rockslide, however, at its base, had a large alien structure. Ragged walls and twisted pylons stood out of the stones, looking like part of a ruined house made of metal. The figures appeared to be carrying stones away one by one to deposit them in a distant pile that, by its size, Jaks guessed they had been working on for at least a couple of days. One of them appeared to be giving orders to the laborers, while a couple of others—near several lean-tos and tents—tended a spitted animal over a cooking fire. Three sentries stood listlessly around the perimeter of the excavation.

"Who are they?" Jaks asked when he turned back to the whispering group behind him.

"Vixhana will scout them once night falls," Mulgrave said. "Could be wildmen curious for loot, but we need a closer look."

"It's definitely the *Mendhelsson* . . . a sizable fragment," Meila said quietly as she crouched at the rock, watching the excavation. "No instruments operating. Only the emergency beacon is functioning." She looked away, and Jaks saw her face downcast and eyes moist. "She was a beautiful ship."

Vixhana peered around the rock again. "They're finishing up for the day and look to be settling into the camp. I'll wait until a couple hours past dusk and then move in. The rest of you should find cover—"

"No cover. It is very open." Witabu waved a hand at the darkening valley.

Mulgrave made a decision to withdraw back to the ridge overlooking the valley, an hour's trek under the moonlight. No fires were lit, and a fearfulness kept everyone in hushed voices and whispers as evening fell. Thankfully, the grandmaster channeled pyromancy to warm the air and remove the chill as they waited.

"Is there going to be a fight?" Tavis said to Cromer, within earshot of Jaks.

The ranger ignored Tavis's question but could be seen running wax over his bowstring and counting his arrows.

"Damn, I wish I hadn't ditched my armor," Tavis said to no one in particular, his voice sounding high-pitched and thin.

Vixhana had stayed behind at the observation rock, dropping her backpack and securing her black leather armor against stray straps that could create any noise. That had been two hours ago, and Jaks imagined her nightwraith form now slipping through the darkness toward the excavation camp.

The wind piped an eerie harmonic as it coursed over their heads; fortunately, on the leeward side of the ridge, they were spared a direct battering. Waiting seemed an eternity.

A whistle and then a voice called out a few hours later—the tall warrior woman returned from her clandestine task. She materialized suddenly in their midst, breathing heavily. The hunters scrambled away in fright and brandished their spears at her in the dark until Witabu rasped a command.

"Well, what did you find, Captain?" Mulgrave stepped

closer to Vixhana, who seemed to have forgotten her backpack on returning. He invoked a yellow flame that hovered in the air to illuminate the night.

"Warriors of Voros. I counted twenty-four, armed with swords and at least a dozen crossbows. Probably a half-torgue." She hunched down and looked around until her eyes fell on her brother. "Pass me something to eat, Jaks."

"What are Vors doing here?" Tavis asked from somewhere in the dimness.

"I'd say they've been here two or three days excavating that wreckage. I was going in for a closer examination, but somehow, I was spotted." Vixhana then swore uncharacteristically. "I've never been uncovered before like that. They sent out search parties, but I outdistanced them and misdirected them to the other valley."

"Maybe they had a dog that caught your scent or a trained dragon that heard you while you were 'manced?" Mulgrave suggested.

"No. I had a clear view of their camp, and they didn't have any guard animals."

"How do you know they're Vors? Could they just be bandits?" Jaks asked as he handed his sister a handful of goat jerky and a waterskin.

"I know my Vors, Jaks," she said in a cold voice. "I see one every time I look in a mirror. Besides, the ritual tattoos on the face and neck give them away."

"Mages?" Mulgrave asked.

"A firemancer and at least two grav warriors with them."

"Do they know what they're digging out from the avalanche?" Jaks asked.

"Ten leagues from the closest coastline, in the middle of a

mountain range . . . of course they know, stupid. Right, Master?" Tavis replied.

Anger inflamed Jaks's face, and he resisted an impulse to punch the other apprentice.

"Someone must have told them about the wreckage . . . and the weapons," Meila said in a hushed voice.

Mulgrave turned and the magical flame followed to illuminate Meila, deep in thought. "I thought we were the only ones who knew about this?"

"Apparently not," Vixhana said, looking at the smaller woman suspiciously. "What else is she not telling us . . . what are you not telling us?"

"No one else knows. I'm telling the truth. I have told no one else of this location. There must be someone else with an implant and access to a scanner—"

"Like who?" Vixhana challenged her.

"I don't know. Maybe someone else did survive . . ." Meila grabbed the warrior by the arm and spoke quickly. "If someone else is alive, we have to rescue them. I have to know if one of my crew is there."

Ranger Cromer spoke for the first time since Vixhana had returned. "If they are there, he or she is on *their* side—not ours. That makes them the enemy."

"No. My crew wouldn't side with the Vors. We saw the atrocities they committed against their own people. Their culture is vile and evil—"

Vixhana placed a hand on Meila's wrist. "How do you know that?" She tightened her grip. "You are a spy. What lies are you hiding? You are no traveler—you have been watching us." She pulled Meila until their noses almost touched.

Meila struggled against Vixhana's grip but stopped when her other hand was equally pinned by her side.

"What is this all about? What is your mission here? Did you lie to us about the weapons?" Vixhana asked in an acidic tone.

The outworlder slumped against the warrior's grip and her gaze fell as her energy fled. After several seconds, she looked up to meet Vixhana's interrogating eyes. Despair painted her face. "The old worlds are dying. Trillions of people have ravaged dozens of planets over the millennia." Meila sighed heavily. "My ship has been searching for lost colonies, like this one, for recolonizing."

"Recolonizing?" Mulgrave said, frowning.

"Hundreds of millions of new colonists." Meila turned to face Mulgrave, while Vixhana maintained her vice-like grip on her wrists. "The truth is, your people arrived here as a fringe-world colony over seven thousand years ago. But soon after it was established, the supercluster colonies and the origin worlds descended into a century-long intergalactic war that destroyed the wormholes that allowed us to travel between galaxies. The fringe worlds were isolated and forced to sustain themselves. A few thrived. Most collapsed and disappeared. And some, like yours, regressed to primitive remnants of humanity."

"You didn't answer the mage. What do you mean by *recolonizing?*" Vixhana said through gritted teeth.

Meila wilted under the anger of those around her, but drew in a breath and continued, "The first wave of ships come to cleanse the planet. If the old colonists have been classified as 'peaceful' and unwarlike, they are corralled to a less desirable part of the planet. But if they are not . . . the world is 'depopulated.' Battle fleets remove the old colonists, clearing the way for the second wave of ships and their burden of new colonists."

"That is outrageous, monstrous." The grandmaster's eyes protruded, and his teeth were bared.

"That is recolonizing," Meila replied weakly. "Much like how your own country was subdued under one rule."

"That's completely different. Every territory had the opportunity to submit and continue under Ascorian rule. None were eradicated for mere convenience." Mulgrave wrung his hands in agitation.

"And what is your part in this?" Vixhana jerked Meila's wrists. The smaller woman flinched in pain.

"My ship was scouting your planet, collecting information about the condition of the surface—how survivable and sustainable it is—and the well-being of the original colony. We would have then returned to Earth and submitted a report to the Ministry of Colonies."

She then looked to Mulgrave, who was rubbing his head in agitation. "Look, I'm sorry I didn't tell you the full truth—I didn't think it would help for you to know. If they do decide to repopulate this planet, it wouldn't be for decades or possibly centuries. But it changes nothing about why we're here, right now. If anything, it makes it even more important that we get those weapons before the Vors do."

Surprisingly, Jaks heard his own voice pierce the night. "She's right." He coughed and then continued, "We still have to defend our country from the Vors, regardless of what is coming later."

"So, there are weapons here?" Vixhana's voice leveled, and she loosened her grip.

"Yes . . . I'm almost certain there are. If I'm correct, that section of the ship is rear-portside and housed part of the engine and shielding. There was a weapons locker in the engine room. It's partially covered in rocks, though—so I can't be a hundred percent sure."

No one spoke for several minutes. Thoughts churned and

glances were exchanged; Mulgrave and Vixhana stared at Meila as though attempting to read her mind. The hunters and Witabu watched on, uncomprehendingly, sitting on the rocks near the crest of the ridge.

Eventually, the grandmaster folded his arms, anger abated. "Jaks is right. We can only deal with one invasion at a time. We need those weapons to repel the Vors, and then we can worry about the greater foe from there."

"I can help. I might be able to persuade the Ministry to preserve Maya—your world—or at least ring-fence the continents that you are living on. I want to help you," Meila said. Her eyes flicked around them all and settled on Jaks.

"You can let her go, Captain," Mulgrave said after a long minute and placed a hand on Vixhana's wrist. "She withheld information from us, but she did not lie. Disingenuous, but not malicious. Just doing her job, so to speak."

"Yes, in the beginning, but not anymore. I've seen your world for what it is—beautiful and pristine. It deserves to be protected." Meila rubbed her wrists and stepped back from Vixhana. "Your civilization is backward but verges on an industrial age, and it has something that needs to be preserved that no other colony has."

"What's that?" Jaks asked.

"Magic." Meila smiled wryly, then raised her hand and opened her palm; in an instant, a tiny green dragon danced lightly in the air, and she smiled, holding out her illumancer invocation for everyone to see. "I'm one of you."

Chapter 34

Ambush

Meila—Jurn Highlands, Ascoria

Meila did not sleep that night but instead directed her cortical implant to run a thirty-minute rejuvenation protocol that replaced her need for sleep. Alert, she sat guard—with one or another of the others who took turns sleeping—and gazed down into the valley, wondering which of her crew could be alive.

Now more than ever, she regretted the absence of a long-distance communicator in her cybertronics. On the *Mendhelsson*, her home for the past three decades, it had been unnecessary; the starship comms had been built into the ship, surrounding her, always close enough to allow her to talk with shipmates and the AI in any part of the vessel. Outside of the starship, she had no way of sending out a signal to find out who might be out there.

Because she was sure someone was there.

And that someone must have used a UWF scanner to locate the starship debris, just as she had. There was no other way a large, organized group could have found their way here, so determined to spend days excavating an avalanche.

Her heart lifted with hope that it was Anton, her eccentric biologist husband. But it could also be any of the seven other scientists who had been aboard the starship.

Except Stefan.

Stefan Knight, in hindsight, had been poorly equipped for life aboard a starship. Although highly qualified as a Planetary Actuary—one of the geniuses who analyzed and calculated the overall worth of each Old Colony world—his claustrophobia and anxiety had grown with each year they spent in space. In the last months of their orbital mission around planet Maya, it had seemed that he was improving—keeping to himself more but complaining less about the suffocating, confining starship.

With their return to Earth soon coming, Meila had missed the man's deteriorating state. He had become suicidal.

With a darkcore pistol, he had blown his head off; in doing so, he'd triggered a critical fracture in the hull of their ship. Whether the Actuary had been trying to kill all of them along with himself, Meila had never found out. They had only had a few minutes to reach their escape pods and evacuate the ship.

But one of her crew was alive.

She had to find out who.

She scanned the desolate valley again, her visual implants adapted to the darkness with night-vision augmentation. A nocturnal bird—an owl?—circled in the distance, outstretched wings buffeted by air currents. It swooped toward the ground, several hundred meters away, near the river cutting through the valley. She magnified and focused her vision on a movement dashing below the flying predator. A small animal bounded in a zigzag toward some unseen escape. Left, right. It didn't reach its bolt-hole fast enough—the predator snatched it from the ground with great talons and plunged a saber-like beak into the helpless creature and then flew off with its prey.

On the *Mendhelsson*, she'd had an overvalued sense of invulnerability, protected by millions of tons of synthmetal and shielding. But now, with death as common as a pair of talons from above or a spear through the back, she felt scared but also exuberantly more alive than ever before. Decades of leading lost-colony missions had turned her hard and remorseless. It had taken danger and threat to her life for her to rediscover her humanity.

She patted her legs and the reassuring lumps of her knives and darkcore pistol.

A quick glance at the sleeping forms, and she snuck over the ridge and down into the valley on a scouting mission of her own.

Alone with her superior vision and nimble feet, Meila made it back to the massive rock within half an hour. There, she found Vixhana's backpack and left it hidden in a crack.

Peering around the rock to the Vors campsite, a mile away at the base of the horned mountain, it was too far to discriminate faces. She crouched and crept behind boulders and scrawny bushes, stalking toward the campfire where three guards kept watch over the campsite. Hopefully, whoever or whatever had alerted the guards to Vixhana earlier on wouldn't see her skulking now.

She stopped behind the skeleton of a lone springfell tree, a half mile from the Vors camp. Here, she could see several sleeping faces beneath the lean-tos. Although partially obscured, she easily recognized them as localized humans—not one of her crew.

One figure, though, caught her attention: a long, thin individual curled by the fire with a coarse blanket pulled up to his neck, asleep. Not a typical Vor male, too delicate of bone and muscle. Although full-bearded, like the guards, the man was unkempt and had what appeared to be a collar around his neck and a chain trailing away from him.

A prisoner.

She stared for a long time. Magnified her implants to their maximum resolution. Her mouth went dry, her breathing quickened, and the hairs on her neck stiffened.

It was Anton.

She emitted a sob at the condition of her husband. He was even gaunter than his usual leanness, and his face looked as though he had aged a dozen years since she had last seen him several months ago. Scars crisscrossed his face and over his eye. Patches of hair were missing. *An ear missing?* His decrepit condition caused her heart to lurch. Although their passion had gone, she still loved him at his core. He was a pitiful sight.

An impulse to rush into the camp took ahold of her. She had boasted to Tavis that she could kill a hundred Vors in a minute, but that was if they were lined up waiting to be shot—not under battle conditions. There were twenty-five of them. Could she guarantee the high degree of accuracy she would need with the pistol to kill enough of them, forcing them to abandon their hostage? Some of them were mages too, and she'd seen what a firemage and gravmancer warriors could do in a fight. No, she couldn't take the risk of a rescue attempt by herself.

She'd need to go back for help.

A while later, just as the valley took on the amber hue of dawn, Meila scrambled over the ridgeline back to their resting point.

"See, she didn't run away," Jaks said, a relieved look on his face.

Ranger Cromer grunted as he stared at the dark-haired foreigner.

Meila walked to Vixhana, who was sharpening her dagger, and dropped the nightwraith's backpack at the warrior's feet. "Here," she said, breathing hard.

"Where did you go?" Jaks asked, offering her a waterskin, which she waved off. "I knew you wouldn't leave us."

His icy demeanor toward her since they left the Jurn village was gone, and he seemed genuinely eager to see her return. A stab of guilt reminded her she would need to make amends with him—her rejection of his invitation to his bed had affected him harder than she'd thought it would. But now that she knew Anton was still alive, she did not regret that denial.

She flashed a small smile at him and then leaned against her knees to catch her breath. When she looked up, it was to focus on the grandmaster, who had just woken on her return and was rubbing his eyes.

"They've got my husband. They have Anton prisoner. I saw him shackled and injured. We have to rescue him," she said, stepping over to the mage as he stood.

"Were you seen?" Vixhana asked.

"I didn't go as close as you probably did . . . and I think the person who saw you was Anton, but he was asleep the whole time I observed them. Listen, we need to rescue him, we need to change the plan."

The previous night, Vixhana, Cromer, and Mulgrave had decided on a strategy for the following evening. A daring ambush that required them to creep into position and then have Meila snipe the firemage—who they assumed was the leader— and the two gravmancers, while Ranger Cromer shot the regular guards. Subsequently, the grandmaster and Tavis would enfence and blast the Vors with fire magic as Vixhana leapt into the killing zone to finish off any survivors.

Jaks had looked aggrieved at being told his only task was to stay with Meila and protect her if things went wrong; he had glowered when the grandmaster told him that his electromancy powers were too unreliable and unrefined to be involved in the coordinated attack.

The four Jurn tribesmen initially refused to be involved with the assault, worried about the aggression involved. "We only bring you here," Witabu said. "This is not our fight." However, after Vixhana pointed out that their efforts in fighting the Vors would greatly assist the Jurns' plea to King Silas, Witabu and the hunters agreed to join Meila and Jaks as reserve fighters.

"Impossible. Too dangerous," Cromer said. "The plan relies on complete surprise. If we make a rescue attempt first, we lose the initiative."

"What if we begin the attack as first planned, taking out the three mages and guards, but then in the confusion, you"—Meila nodded at Vixhana—"go in and snatch Anton and carry him away? I take it your magic would allow you to get in and out quickly. Then we carry on with the rest of the plan?"

Jaks wrung his hands together. "That would be dangerous for Vix."

"This prisoner, is he worth it?" the nightwraith asked flatly.

Meila looked appalled, her small nose wrinkling and her eyebrows creasing to a point. "He's my husband. Of course, he is *worth* it." After a minute, her scowl dissolved, and she continued, "He is an expert in biology and medicine . . . healing, what you would call it. He could advance your planet's healing arts by centuries, millennia. If you're wanting something tangible out of it."

A clatter of rocks and several animal-like snorts interrupted them. A crowned stag and three does skittered out of thick brush below them at the bottom of the hill. Before anyone could say anything, a bowstring twanged and an arrow from one of the tribesmen streaked over the top of the deer. Meila heard the hunter swear as the animals leapt back into the bushes and trees. Witabu and the other hunters laughed at the embarrassed man.

"What do you think?" Vixhana turned to Mulgrave, her face revealing a conflict of emotions.

"Certainly, we should try to keep him out of danger. If we don't extract him first, it will be difficult to avoid harming him with fire area-magic in the main assault. Tavis or I could attempt to grav-jump in and then out with him . . . but you have greater experience in that sort of thing."

Vixhana nodded. "All right. Let's go with that plan. As soon as the first targets go down, I'll retrieve him and we carry on with the plan as before. Is there a way to stop him ratting us out if he sees us with this super-sight you have? Tell him that we're attempting to rescue him?"

"Sadly, no. The most I could do is try to get his attention in the dark at a distance that no un-augmented human could see— and hope he recognizes me. But if that failed, he would probably alert the guards. I doubt he has any hope of rescue out here in this wildland." Meila sat down to rest her legs. "It'd be best if we just wait until late enough that Anton will be asleep like the rest of them."

The day passed with the group waiting and watching the Highlands unfold around them. The roar of a mountain lion echoed later that morning, perhaps announcing a successful kill, perhaps one of the deer they had seen earlier. That afternoon, clouds roiled overhead, threatening rain, but passed by with just a brief shower and then cleared to a peaceful, blue sky.

Meila marveled at a thunder of dragons that soared over the valley episodically; she invoked miniature illusions of them in her palm and crafted the tiny figures to amuse and calm herself against the excitement of being reunited with Anton—and the anticipation of the necessary violence to free him. She thought she should feel guilty about plotting murder, but she couldn't help but think the Vors deserved what they had coming to them for torturing her husband and attempting to steal her starship.

Two hours after a stinging, chilly night fell over the Highlands, a wedge of moon slunk over the clouded peaks.

Meila and the group of nine men and one other woman took only killing implements and snuck down to the junction of the three valleys. There, a bend of the river meandered from the Vors' vale and into the other valley. A journey that would have taken one hour in the daylight took three in the dark.

The riverbed had the advantage of being the lowest part of the narrow valley and allowed the ambushers to inch their way beside the tinkling waters to within a half mile of the Vor camp.

"Tell me what you see from here," Mulgrave whispered to Meila as they lay against the stones of the riverbank, finger-streaked mud across their faces and exposed skin.

Meila peeped over the riverbank and spotted the closest Vor guard exactly 641 yards from her position—indicated by the rangefinder built into her visio-cortical implant. Only he and two other guards appeared to be awake.

A score of almost motionless bodies were sprawled under lean-tos and tents protecting them from the cutting wind. She tensed when she saw Anton curled, as he was last night, in the open near the fire, but relaxed upon seeing him asleep.

The previous night, she had observed a heavily tattooed firemage using the largest tent; the fierce-looking woman had pushed open the tent flap and invoked a bright flame as she wended her way to a makeshift latrine on the outskirts of the campsite.

Meila's other two primary targets, she guessed, were the two men lying next to huge double-bladed battleaxes. No one but gravmancers like Vixhana could wield such mammoth weapons in combat. No one had told *them* there would be no elephants to butcher.

Reminded of the nightwraith and the others waiting for her reconnaissance report, she shuffled backward on her belly and then informed the others of what she had seen.

Mulgrave gave the order, and they dispersed to take up their ambush posts.

"*Hodrin uhsaga,*" Witabu said, invoking the Jurn blessing as Mulgrave slipped away with Tavis, cautiously treading up the riverbed with just moonlight guiding their steps.

Ranger Cromer cast a quick look at Vixhana and then, with quiver in hand and recurved ironwood bow in the other, hunched low and started his stealthy advance to the north side of the camp—opposite where the grandmaster and his apprentice would be positioned.

"Let's go. Keep quiet. Secure your weapons. Watch where you step," Vixhana warned and then crested the riverbank, followed in single file by Meila, Jaks, and the four tribesmen. The nightwraith invoked an illumancer shield in front of herself, an eerie impenetrable black wall hiding them from the guards, two arm-breadths to either side and as tall as she. Meila switched to an infrared visual filter and confirmed the heat signatures of the Vors still blissfully unaware of the ambushers closing in to set their trap.

At a hundred yards from the closest guard, Vixhana signaled a stop and carefully lay down amongst the scattered stones and boulders that peppered the valley floor.

Meila mimicked her action and listened to Jaks and the Jurn hunters shuffle for several seconds until they all lay in nervous wait. Thankfully, the whistling wind covered the sound of any stones that clattered with their movements.

Cromer was to her distant left. Her respect for him leapt a level at seeing him hidden a mere sixty yards from the Vor guards who sat around the sputtering campfire. Anton's pitiful form lay a few yards behind the guards.

On the far side of the Vors' fabricated shelters, Mulgrave and Tavis hugged the ground, unmoving.

Minutes seemed to stretch for hours as she waited for the ranger to trigger the attack. Sweat moistened her grip on the darkcore pistol, but fortunately, the diamond-hatching kept it firmly in her hand. Jaks was muttering nearby but quietened at Vixhana's low shush. What was going on with the young man? He seemed troubled since leaving the Jurn village—friendly one minute and then glowering and moody the next.

Her thoughts returned to the present as her attention was drawn to the slowly rising figure of Cromer lifting his bow and drawing back a strung arrow.

"Get ready," Meila said in a low voice, then rolled into a kneeling firing posture and pointed her weapon with both hands at the firemage's tent. The handgun's low-temperature aiming beam pierced the fabric and rested on the enemy leader's chest. The wonders of her visual implants would make it an easy shot.

Vixhana dropped the illumancer shield and pulled herself into a crouch, fists to the ground, looking like a giant panther ready to pounce.

As soon as the ranger's first arrow hissed through the air, Meila pulled the trigger, and the buzz of the pistol firing was immediately followed by the firemage's torso exploding inside the tent. The canvas billowed outward with splatters of flesh and bone, collapsing the shelter on top of her mangled corpse.

Meila looked back to the campfire and saw a guard slump to the ground with an arrow through the back of his head.

The other two guards stared in astonishment at the dead man and rose to their feet.

The tribesmen's bows twanged around Meila, and four more arrows hissed through air to pierce and stagger the remaining guards.

The closest gravmancer stirred and rolled to his side under the lean-to he shared with three other warriors. Meila blinked and then traced the targeting beam to his chest and squeezed the curved trigger again.

Pzzt . . . the blast blew the man's chest apart and exploded into the ground behind. Dirt, rock, and viscera pelted his sleeping neighbors.

There was a pounding of feet as Vixhana ran forward eight paces, leapt into the air, and hurtled toward the middle of the camp.

Meila needed to find her third target quickly.

Confused voices called out around the Vor camp, and several figures sat up and looked around.

The second gravmancer sat up, looking around, confused. His hand rested on a giant battleaxe beside him.

Vixhana landed gracefully on the far side of the campfire, a few yards from Anton.

The aiming beam flicked to the single remaining enemy mage, and Meila squeezed the trigger as she kept the beam focused on the gravmancer's chest.

He stood at that moment and the darkcore bolt struck him in the belly. The effect was the same as with the previous shots —flesh and organs burst out of his back, removing a quarter of his body mass and folding him in half. The wooden lean-to collapsed as the follow-through blast splintered and smashed the crooked branches that supported the structure.

Shouts and alarmed voices cried out all over the camp. Men and women staggered and lurched to their feet, throwing aside the furs and blankets that just a few minutes before had been warm havens of peace.

Meila stood for a clearer view as Vixhana lifted Anton in her beefy arms. His neck lolled back abruptly as a chain attached to his iron collar yanked against a heavy boulder rolled onto the distal end of the restraint. Meila gasped, fearing his neck broken by the sudden tug; however, relief came when Anton's hands grabbed at the chain, indicating him alive.

Vixhana deposited Anton and stepped toward the boulder.

Suddenly, there was a thud and the ground near the campfire erupted into a cloud of earth and rock.

A second later, another explosion blew Vixhana off her feet. *Darkcore blasts.*

Meila had the only such weapon in sight—but something else, powerfully explosive, had just detonated a half-ton of earth and rock in front of her eyes. Her eyes darted around for the source.

Vor warriors stumbled out of their lean-tos toting swords, axes, or crossbows; a few more clambered out of the largest canvas tent at the far side of the camp, calling out orders, or perhaps demanding explanations, from the confused mass of men and women.

Vixhana lifted and threw aside the boulder that only a gravmancer—or three men—could move, freeing the end of the chain restraining Anton.

At the flap of a small tent, thirty yards from the nightwraith, partly hidden by lean-tos, a warrior with a face tattooed in geometric symbols aimed a sleek-looking weapon at Vixhana.

Meila targeted the tattooed warrior with the hand weapon, but the man began to dart toward Vixhana, firing off shots as he moved. They landed randomly, creating bursts of dirt and rubble.

The explosions caused the nightwraith to stumble, and she fell to a knee.

Meila's heart pounded and her hand jerked as she attempted to track the gunner's loping movements.

She fired the darkcore pistol, despite the fleeting, intervening blurs of other Vors obscuring an accurate shot.

She missed.

Instead, a Vor warrior moving in front of her target took the shot in the hip. He spun forward and smashed his head against the stony ground.

The Vor gunman—unknowing that he was now a target himself—fired another couple of shots in Vixhana's direction, steadily approaching her. If he knew how to use the weapon properly, he would have stopped for a more accurate shot; instead, he used the foreign weapon bluntly, pelting his target with blasts. One shot hit the campfire and slammed the stack of burning wood into a spray of embers and flaming branches. Other shots further disrupted the earth and scattered debris everywhere.

Further chaotic shouts sounded as the campfire faded and left only the moonlight for the Vors to see by.

Vixhana scooped Anton into her arms a second time. He sagged into her like a child, and she flipped his loosened chain over her shoulder.

The gunman drew up directly behind the two. Meila couldn't target him; Vixhana stood in the way.

The next blast from the gunman ruptured the earth

underneath Vixhana's feet and heaved the two of them forward to smash against a heaped pile of rocks.

Time slowed leadenly while Meila could do nothing but stand paralyzed in shock and watch the horror unfold.

Jaks cried out a moment later, only grasping Vixhana and Anton's dire position as the two crumpled together in a heap. This could not be happening. His invincible sister.

"Get up, get up," Jaks yelled at Vixhana and started loping toward her before he knew what he was doing.

An arrow sprouted out of the Vor gunman, who was lining up another shot. The missile penetrated his leg up to the fletching, with the arrow-shaft emerging from the other side. The man twisted in agony and fell.

"Get up," Jaks called out to his sister again as he ran.

"Stop, boy," Witabu shouted after him. And, just as the words left the tribesman's mouth, a wall of fire roared to life just a few yards in front of Jaks.

Jaks skidded to a halt, the heat of the flames drying and stinging his eyeballs as he stared through the fire wall for glimpses of his downed sister. *I need to help her.*

Despair and fear swamped him as he looked for an opening around the burning, neck-high barrier, but it encircled the camp.

He gulped. His only way was *through* the flames.

Jaks hesitated for only a moment, before running forward and leaping into the fire. But blinded and deafened by the roar of the surrounding inferno, he faltered and fell within the flames, his momentum too weak to reach the other side.

Flames lashed at his face and hands as he lurched, not

knowing what direction he faced. He screamed in pain, fearing he would burn to death.

Jaks's panicked thoughts leapt to the lightning cocoon—his one protection. He rammed his emotions into the image and willed it into reality.

Lightning crackled to life and enveloped him in a ball of white and blue pulsating energy. Where the electricity sparked, the flames withdrew, as though intimidated by the greater power. The familiar metallic smell filled his nostrils, and the pain of his exposed skin retreated.

With the flames driven back, his vision returned, and he focused on Vixhana.

Like a rolling storm cloud, Jaks erupted out of the fire wall just in time to see Vixhana staggering back to her feet with Anton still in her arms. He breathed a sigh of relief and dropped the magical armor.

However, the gunman, too, rose from the ground, having broken off the arrow penetrating his leg and then pulled out the shaft. He knelt on his uninjured knee and pointed his darkcore weapon once again at Vixhana, grimacing as his aim wavered back and forth.

"Get down, Vix," Jaks shouted and raised his arm for an invocation. But his sister continued to stumble and lurch as blood streamed from her scalp and over her face.

Her movements blocked a clear attack on the gunman; however, he couldn't wait a moment longer, he had to kill the man before he fired another shot.

An attacking pulse of bright white and blue arched from Jaks's hand toward the gunman with an ear-splitting crack—but instead of striking the Vor, the lightning pulse forked toward Vixhana and Anton.

In the split second that he realized the deviant path of electricity, he snapped out of the invocation, but it was too late.

The energy pulsed through Vixhana and Anton in an instant. Limbs stiffened, bones snapped with the powerful involuntary contraction of muscles, neck muscles corded, and eyes bulged.

Anton's body flew out of the nightwraith's grasp, his weedy figure tumbling amongst the rocks.

Vixhana's muscular mass dropped heavily on top of him and crushed him.

Facedown in the rocks, neither of the two moved again.

Meila's horrified scream registered in Jaks's periphery, but he was too shocked to do anything but stare at the bodies splayed before him.

If he had had greater awareness, he would have seen Mulgrave and Tavis at that same moment—attacking the Vors with fire and flame—and Tavis felled by a blow to the head by a maniacal hammer-wielder who in the next instant received an incinerating blast to the face from the grandmaster.

But, for Jaks, nothing existed other than the aftermath of his lightning strike on Anton and Vixhana. She couldn't be dead. Not his invincible sister. Frozen in place, not knowing what to do, he yelled at her to get up. *Don't be dead. Don't be dead.*

The Vor gunman, seeing his targets taken down, grinned and sought a fresh target; Jaks found himself staring back at the black metal of the hellish darkcore gun.

In that second, an arrow sang through the dark and thunked into the gunman's chest. He stared at the foreign object incredulously. Moments later, another of the ranger's arrows joined the first and slammed the Vor into the dying embers of the campfire. He flopped about for several seconds more and went still.

Stung with grief, Jaks ran to his sister's side, fell to his knees, and rolled her off Anton's body.

His hands came away sticky with blood. Her skin was hot and her leather armor smoked where it touched metal. The smell of cooked flesh assaulted his nostrils.

Despite vigorously shaking her by the shoulders, her mouth lolled open, and her eyelids remained shuttered and unmoving.

"Vix, I'm sorry, I'm so sorry." He collapsed beside her and sobbed.

Time passed in a haze with Jaks lost in grief, oblivious to the panicking Vors running around him and the torrents of flame and waves of arrows that ended their lives.

A while later, Grandmaster Mulgrave placed a hand on Jaks's shoulder. The wall of fire had smoked out, cries of the injured had silenced, prisoners were secured, and the dead were being counted and laid to rest.

The fight was over, and Meila staggered forward with her darkcore pistol held limply in her hand.

She stared at her husband. His skull was crushed against the rocks. And similar to Vixhana, the skin of his hands and face was blistered and dark. Where the iron collar had touched his neck was burnt and raw. As Meila rolled him over, his eyes stared back dull and lifeless. She murmured quietly over the body and closed his eyes.

"Did you see that?" Jaks said suddenly.

Vixhana's chest rose and fell almost imperceptibly.

"She must be alive." He grabbed her by the shoulders again and shook her.

"Stop, lad, you'll just injure her more." Mulgrave knelt beside her and pressed two fingers against her blackened neck, then peeled her eyelids open. A magical flame hovered over his shoulder to illuminate a face marred not only by charred skin but by many cuts and grazes. "Yes, she breathes, but her mind is not there," he said.

Relief flooded Jaks, and he cleared her hair from her bloodied face. "I'm sorry, Vix," he said. "I'll stay with you."

Although she was not dead, she was not truly alive. No one knew if she would eventually recover or be cursed to remain in a coma and slowly die.

Tavis, too, having suffered a blow to the head, was incapacitated. In a mumbling stupor, however, his breathing was steadier and stronger than Vixhana's, so he seemed more likely to live. A day earlier, Jaks might have felt happy at seeing his adversary for the apprenticeship crippled, but today, all he could feel was overwhelming guilt.

Jaks and Meila stayed with Vixhana and Tavis that night; unfortunately, there was nothing in her healing bag to bring either of them out of the darkness. But they did what they could for them. And fortunately, his sister's burns were less significant than they had originally looked. Bandaged with medigel, Jaks hoped Vixhana would pounce back up and scold him, but that she did not.

The next day, they cremated the dead bodies. The Vors went in a single heap, but Meila created a separate pyre of sticks and branches for her husband. When the grandmaster channeled flames to consume his body, she stared expressionless as the wind scattered smoke and ash across the valley.

Then, with the ashes cooling, the group—except for Jaks, who stayed to monitor Vixhana and Tavis—turned to the avalanche and began clearing the shale and rock from the wreckage of the *Mendhelsson*.

After several hours, Meila scrambled over the blackened and twisted starship debris, eager at first, but then sagging when no weapons were found. But as the day progressed, she brightened again at the discovery of other relics, and ordered their removal, sometimes requiring the elder mage's smithing magic to cut away objects and parts.

The reality, though, was that after all this effort, at the cost of Vixhana and Tavis incapacitated from injuries, the only weapon they gained was pried from the fingers of the Vor gunman.

Two darkcore pistols were not enough to repulse an invasion force.

Ranger Cromer fumed over the wasted time and risk.

Mulgrave said nothing.

Chapter 35

Consequences

Jaks–Jurn Midlands, Ascoria

The Uwama of the tribe folk frowned at the wounded man and woman being carried toward her.

Jaks and the able-bodied members of the salvage party had arrived at the canyon village of the Jurns. Mulgrave and the ranger carried Vixhana on a makeshift stretcher, and a couple of tribesmen carried Tavis on a second.

"Put them down over there." The Uwama pointed to the platform below the wooden deck spanning the canyon trees. "Xanra, fetch my tools," she directed her elfin-faced daughter, whose bare feet skimmed her up the steps in response. The chieftess then nodded to the grandmaster, but her greeting turned to a frown as she saw Witabu and Meila leading a group of Vor prisoners.

Tavis moaned, and the Uwama turned her focus to the injured apprentice. "What happened to him?" she asked.

"A hammer to the head and a blow to the back on falling." The bald mage pointed at Tavis and then, having noticed her expression at the Vors, said, "We ambushed a group of Vors.

Needn't worry, they'll leave with us in the morning." He gestured at the three miserable-looking men and one woman who had been hauling a long metal object and now thudded it to the ground.

"And her?" She looked at Vixhana, immobile on the canvas between two long branches.

"I electrocuted her," Jaks said in a toneless voice. Head hung low, he then stood mute.

Meila stepped up and continued Jaks's explanation. "She's been unresponsive since then. Four days now. I got a naso-gastric tube into her." Although they had not found the weapons they wanted from the wreckage, they had uncovered medical supplies that Meila had used to help treat Tavis and Vixhana. "So, we've been able to keep them hydrated, at least," she said, and picked up the refillable bag of water to allow the fluid to drain into Vixhana's stomach. "Keep her lying on her right so the water doesn't backflow into her throat."

The Uwama nodded, then bunched her long, silver hair into a bun and stabbed it into place with two carved sticks whittled for the purpose. She knelt to examine Tavis and then Vixhana with expert hands.

Jaks stepped away from the platform, offloaded his backpack, and slumped against a tree. Footsteps padded up to him, and Meila knelt in front of him.

He glanced at her warily, readying himself for the outlash he expected from her. They hadn't spoken since the night of the ambush. She hadn't yet taken an opportunity to wail upon him for his dangerous use of electromancy. It would probably be now.

"I killed your husband. I tried to save him, but I killed him. And maybe Vixhana, too," he said in a rush and then hung his head between his knees. He had to confess to her and endure her anger. It was what he deserved, for her to shout and rage at him, or worse—to show her disappointment in him.

Meila grabbed his arm and pulled him up. "Let's get away from here. I need to say something to you." She shoved him toward the pine forest darkened under the overhead bridges and platforms that were the Jurns' connection to their plateau village.

"Stop," she ordered once they were out of sight, the trees their only witness.

He hung his head low and gritted his teeth.

"Stop it," she said in a harsh tone. Her hand gripped his arm again. "Yes, you fucked up. Fucked up badly. You made a huge mistake, and if it wasn't for you, they might both be alive and walking." She scowled at him and shook his arm. "Isn't that what you want to hear?"

"It's what's true. It was my fault—" Flashbacks of Vixhana and Anton as lightning pulsed through them, faces contorted and eyes bulging, tormented him.

"Be quiet and listen to me." She released his arm. "Wallowing in your self-recrimination and self-pity isn't going to bring them back. Harboring this blame will only fester and rot you inside like an abscess."

"It's what I deserve."

"Deserve? What about the blame I deserve? I'm the one who asked Vixhana to rescue Anton. I pleaded to have her risk her life. If she had refused, if she just said it was a bad idea, maybe Anton would have just laid low the entire time and survived. I don't know. All I know is that other people had a hand in his death too, not just you. The Vor gunman, for one." She chewed on her lip and leaned against the rough bark of a pine. "Maybe they would have died anyway? Maybe his death and her sacrifice saved others of us from dying?"

"I'm going to give it up," Jaks blurted, interrupting her. It had been in the back of his mind ever since the incident, and now that he had said it, it made perfect sense. "I'll never use the electromancy again. It's just destructive and evil. All it does is kill. If I keep using it, all I will be is a cold murderer like my father . . . I can't live like that."

"You're not listening to me, are you? Nothing you do is going to make amends. Giving up your power—"

"If I didn't have this power, I wouldn't have electrocuted them." He felt a weight lift from his shoulders. It was the right thing to do. He needed to tell the mage. Then it would be done. "I need to find Grandmaster Mulgrave."

"Jaks, wait," Meila called after him, but he loped off unheeding.

He found the stocky mage and Cromer with Witabu and the Uwama, seated around the low table on the elevated wooden platform. When Jaks appeared from the stairs, the wiry tribesman beckoned to Jaks and pointed at the bread, fruit, slices of meat, and cups on the table.

The Uwama gestured to a cushion at the end of the table and addressed Jaks. "*Hodrin uhsaga*, apprentice. Come and eat. Your sister and the apprentice have been taken up to the village, where I will attend them again later. There is little more I can do for them. They need time to heal," she said.

"It is kind of you to help us, Chieftess," he replied stiffly.

"Sit, lad." Mulgrave patted the cushion. "Vixhana and Tavis will stay here with the Jurns to recuperate while we return to Dunberrin," he said. "She is a trained master of the healing arts."

"A long journey would hinder any recovery," the Uwama said. "Even worsen their injuries."

Jaks nodded. If Vixhana and Tavis were staying, it would make his next words easier to say.

"Grandmaster." Jaks had remained standing and now inclined his head to the mage. "Since I came to the Academy, my wish has been to become an apprentice, and I thank you that you gave me the opportunity." He licked his lips and screwed his hands together. "However, I do not want the responsibility any longer. This power I have . . . I will never use it again. I must relinquish my apprenticeship to you." He heard footsteps behind him, and Meila came up beside him.

"Did you tell him to do this?" Mulgrave asked the outworlder.

"I had nothing to do with it."

"What are you talking about, lad?"

Jaks repeated the explanation he gave to Meila earlier, and with each word, he felt more certain it was the right thing to do. "I can't live with this unpredictable energy; it's like a viper inside me that, if let out, strikes at anything around me. It killed Meila's husband. It put my sister into a coma."

The bald mage stared at Jaks for a long minute, after which his face softened and he pushed himself to his feet. "It was a dangerous mission with a bad outcome. But your country still needs you. Needs *us*. No one is going to force you to use your magic until you're ready again. Once we return to the Academy, we can restart your training."

Jaks shook his head. "No. That's not it. I'm not going back." He then turned to the Uwama, who was watching expressionless. "Uwama, would you allow me to stay and live with your tribe? Your people are peace-loving and gentle—how I wish to be. I would help in the village in whatever way I can. I can help look after my sister. And, maybe I could teach. Teach the children numbers and how to read, write, and speak Ascorian."

"Of course. The Jurns welcome all who desire our simple life. For, are not we all one under Hodrin? However, I would not wish to *steal* you from your master."

"He is no slave. He goes about as he wills." The grandmaster turned to Jaks. "Think on it, lad. You have a power that no one else has had in almost a century. Our understanding . . . your understanding of it is so little. If you can learn to control it, there are incredible things we might discover. You could be the master of great power one day." He toiled with his beard for a moment. "Do you remember the story I told you, when I burned down my friend's house and his brother died in the fire?"

Jaks nodded.

"It was not my friend's house. It was that of my family. And the boy who died was my brother." Mulgrave locked eyes with Jaks. "Our mother was distraught and drove me away into the woods, decrying me as a sorcerer. However, what I told you about my father was true. It was he who arranged a new start for me—although I couldn't stay with them any longer—he forgave me for my stupidity."

The mage's words gave Jaks some small comfort but did little to soothe his guilt.

"My father forgave me, but it took me years to forgive myself. No one blames you, lad. Don't waste your years like I did—especially in a time like this, when your country needs you." Mulgrave's voice fell to almost a whisper, and he looked reluctant to say his next words. "Choose wisely. If you stay, there may be no turning back."

"I know this is the right thing to do. I'll stay here with the Jurns. Help look after Vixhana and Tavis."

"Well, that's that, then," Ranger Cromer said, dusting off crumbs from his legs as he stood from the table. "There's a war to finish. If he's staying, he's staying. We've been away too long chasing . . . scrap." He waved a hand at the piled backpacks, sacks, and the metal tube they had salvaged from the starship wreckage. "We need to be on our way tomorrow." He then turned his attention to Jaks. "I should drag you in for desertion, but out of respect for your sister, I'll leave you to find your peace." Sadness marred his face, the first time Jaks had ever seen any sensitivity from the ranger, but it was gone as quickly as it came, replaced by a laugh. "However, if she does recover, I wouldn't be surprised if she, herself, charges you with the crime and drags you in by the ear."

That evening, Jaks stared around the carved-out cave that would be his new home with the Jurns. He hung up the lantern he had used to navigate the dark and slid down against a wall. Was it the right decision? Should he have just kept following the grandmaster blindly, growing his power so that he could kill more people faster? Kill legions at a time?

If he'd had any of the other energies, he could have used it for some good. Crafting, smithing, or art. But electromancy was so raw and ruinous, like the lightning that fueled it. He had to discard this power in the same way he would have tossed away a dagger, had it been that he'd injured her with.

Not only was the electromancy a reminder of his mistake, it dishonored her to keep using it. Abandoning it was a repentance.

He had a chance at a new life here with the tribe folk. A peaceful, simple life.

A voice startled him out of his thoughts.

"You're giving up so easily?" Meila stood in the entrance from the cavern hallway. "I thought you were better than this."

He lurched to his feet. "I'm not—"

"Do you think she would want you to give up? Run away? Was Vixhana one to quit anything?"

"I'm not her. It's not that simple. It's everyone I've loved . . . My mother, Karisa, and Vix, all dead, or almost dead, because of me. Whatever I do, or don't do, people die around me. I'm a curse. The best thing is for me to keep away from anything that matters. At least here, I can't do much harm."

"These people, they're not just things. They matter too." Meila paused, drawn into her thoughts. Tense lines in her face suddenly softened. "This world matters. It's worth fighting for."

"There are many thousands who can fight, all better than me." Jaks waggled his bandaged hand.

"And what about us?" she asked in a hushed voice, staring into his eyes.

"Us?"

Her face abruptly hardened. "You're supposed to be my guard, aren't you? I'm the ward. You're the guard."

"Anyone could be your guard . . . you don't even need guarding," he said, confused.

She huffed loudly. "You're impossible," she said, then turned and stormed out of the room.

It was done, his decision made.

The next day, she cornered him again as he watched from the Uwama's platform while the grandmaster and the ranger prepared the horses for their journey back.

Meila approached Jaks from the stairs. "You may have given up on yourself, but I haven't," she said. "Take this, it's a long-range comm." She pressed a gray disc with a floppy strap into his hand.

"What is it?" Jaks said, turning over the coin-sized object.

Although it was hard and inanimate, he had the uneasy sense that it was alive in his palm.

"You wrap it around your wrist." She took it back from him and folded it over the wrist of his uninjured hand, where it tingled on his skin. "It lets us communicate over great distances. It'll reach across the entire realm. I've got one too from the salvage." She pulled up her sleeve to reveal a similar contraption on her arm.

"I don't need it. I'm not going to change my mind, if that's what you're thinking."

"Look, Jaks. I owe you. I would still be in prison if it weren't for you, and I can't imagine what would have happened if you hadn't rescued me from Bako and Jop." She looked up at him with tender eyes. "This village may be where you want to be now, but if you change your mind, you'll be able to find me and let me pay my dues." She slid her hand down to his and held it for a moment. Then, at the sound of Mulgrave calling up to her, she turned and strode over with a flick of her raven hair.

Jaks watched the travelers depart. The ranger, grandmaster, and Meila followed by Witabu and two other tribesmen—the Jurns' representatives to petition their union to the king of Ascoria.

A pang of guilt stabbed at him as they walked into the trees of the distant canyon. But once they had gone from sight, he shook away the unwelcome feeling.

With them gone, so was the burden of responsibility. With them gone, he could live peacefully.

"It will not be the last you see of them." The Uwama appeared beside Jaks at the wooden railing. "Although you are welcome to live among us, the *energies* will not be denied. You cannot refuse the call for long." She arched her brow. "This, I believe."

Jaks turned to refute her but stopped when she shook her head and walked back to her entourage.

He would stay with Vixhana and pray that she would live.

As Meila nudged her mare through the canyon, leaving the Jurn village, she cursed Jaks's stubbornness. Like a mule, he had refused to go on, but she wouldn't give up on him yet. The long-range communicator would keep them close. She nodded to herself. *He'll come out of it.*

But meanwhile, she could not lose time waiting for him, eager as she was to return to the Academy with the grandmaster. A horde of these damn Vors needed dealing to.

She grimaced as she looked at the innocuous synthmetal tube the prisoners carried in front of her. Yes, there was no time to waste. She would need all of it if she was to design and construct a super-weapon.

Chapter 36

A Viper in the Wheat

Lord Sicaro—City of Irin, Ascoria

The crippled man sagged in the saddle, teetering on an angle that threatened to tip him from the back of his black stallion. Rain soaked a blood-tinged bandage that covered his head and left eye. Fat droplets fell from an elbow slung to his chest, low enough to display the torn insignia of Sanford Province to the guards ahead.

Sicaro grimaced beneath the hood for using the mummer's trick. Although distasteful, it was necessary for his plan-within-a-plan to work: for two kings to die, and he to rise in their place.

A score of hobbled and drenched Ascorian soldiers trailed behind him, scattered along the road for a mile, bent and trudging in mud-caked boots, with the most depleted riding tandem on bedraggled horses. The stronger ones assisted their comrades, who limped on makeshift crutches and picked up those who fell. A group of battle-weary survivors, four days after the horde of Voros first bloodied Ascorian soil.

The horseman straightened as the road ended at a stone-walled city, hedge-hogged by a palisade of sharp wooden logs.

Ascorian sentries lined the wall, and a guard captain called down from the tower gate to confirm them as more of the same casualties that had been trickling in over the morning. Horrified at the pitiful state of his fellow soldiers, he called for the gates to be opened and hurried men down to assist the injured.

Despite his obvious wounds and weakened state, the leader, recognized by the guard captain as the Castellan of Castle Sanford, entreated to see the king, vowing vital news of the Vorosian horde that the monarch needed to hear.

The castellan's men slumped into the cover and warmth of the gate tower. The injured castellan, however, waved away offers of assistance and followed the captain and two escorts through the town, over a giant stone bridge, toward the palace on the northern banks of the Irin river.

Even through the pouring rain, it was clear that the city prepared for war. Lines of sodden soldiers with shovels marched the streets. Horse-drawn carts laden with bricks and planks splashed through puddles. Humans and beasts alike headed toward the south city wall where, no doubt, their burdens were delivered to strengthen the Ascorian defenses.

Pity their labors. They will cry in terror when they see the gargantors leap even the tallest of their walls, thought the castellan.

At the palace stables, he slid off his horse and threw the reins to a stable boy.

As Sicaro shuffled toward the basalt staircase that fronted the building, the guard captain followed and quietly said, halfway up the stairs, "My lord, are you sure you would not freshen before you present yourself to the king?"

The castellan shook his black-bearded head and continued the climb.

An entrance hall, a long corridor, and several pillared guards led to a pair of doors traced with iron leaves.

Two sentries encased in steel and embellished in platinum issued a last challenge. The castellan and his escorts then waited as one of the two whispered through a grilled windowlet.

Finally, a door clunked open to the inner sanctum of the Ascorian king.

"Lord Sicaro," said King Silas. In simple robes and the royal collar of shields around his neck, he left a wide table surrounded by military men to meet his loyal subject limping into the throne room. "My friend. I feared you lost to the invaders."

The guard captain bowed at the foot of the dais. "My king. The Lord Sicaro arrived just this hour through the storm with a score more of injured soldiers."

Silas thanked the soldier and dismissed him with a nod.

"My lord, come warm by the fire. News of Harek's damnable horde is surely welcome, but first tell me of your ordeal." The king gestured to a raised fire pit crackling at the side of the room with an inverted iron funnel suspended above.

At his signal, guards scraped over a pair of chairs from an audience area, empty but for two restless messengers. Sicaro slumped into one of the offered chairs and studied the king's retinue.

The Ascorian king was not without considerable protection; in addition to a dozen King's Guard on sentry duty, four nightwraith warriors, a pair of silver war dragons—tongues flicking the air—and two hounds with armed handlers were in attendance. Even the eight old generals at the war table could probably put up a fair fight.

Sicaro recognized them all. He had argued, strategized, and commanded with each of them during the Uniting Wars in his previous commanding post. However, they had all kept their military ranks while he had lost his for a peacetime role as a caretaker. He withheld a frown at the frustration that had long dogged him and brought him to this point. Although he officially outranked each of them, his true sphere of influence was small and his command over armed forces insignificant. He needed to rectify this inequality.

Sicaro slid to his knees in front of the king. "My king, I am at your mercy. I failed to preserve Sanford. They swept over Commander Lytton's regiment and the castle by surprise—"

"No need. Sit, my lord." Silas assisted Sicaro back to the chair. The castellan's wet clothes squelched as he sat. The king sent for a blanket and then sat in the opposite chair.

It could all end here. A flash of a dagger through Silas's neck and the Ascorians would be leaderless, kingless. However, Sicaro estimated his chances of escape as low, and besides, there were other ways of subduing this enemy.

As though reading his mind, two nightwraiths took up positions behind their monarch, and he cast the thought from his head. A white-haired clerk then joined them from the shadows and waited on his monarch's needs.

The warmth of the firepit and the wool were a welcome comfort as Sicaro selected words to continue. "I should have followed my intuition . . . but I knew Lytton's men would have lost respect for him if I had countermanded his orders. Having been in his place, I humbled myself to allow him his poor choice rather than belittle him." He looked to the tiled floor and shook his head.

"What orders?" the king's clerk asked. Sicaro turned to study the man and took a moment to place the man as the king's senior civil magistrate, Lord Jor Hummerford. The ring of hair around his bald pate had turned white, but his eyes were still bright, mirroring his razor-sharp mind. A dangerous man, despite never having borne a blade to battle.

"Lord Hummerford." Sicaro inclined his head to the king's childhood tutor promoted to run his courts and treasury. "The commander spread his troops thinly along many miles of coast. When the Vors landed in the late of night, they cut through so swiftly that we only learnt of an attack as the first raiders leapt and scaled our walls at the break of dawn. It was then that I saw the extent of the invasion, my king." He shook his head slowly, with a tormented look to his face. "Thousands upon thousands of Vors . . . it was clear this was no simple raid. Spread far down the coast were plumes of smoke from Lytton's fractured encampments and our damaged signaling towers."

"Why Sanford, of all places? There are hundreds of miles of coastland closer to Voros than there," Hummerford asked.

"Strike where least expected?"

"How did you escape?" the king asked, leaning forward with wide eyes.

"Yes, my lord, how did you escape?" Lord Hummerford repeated, eyes narrowed and lips pursed.

Sicaro sensed the bald man's suspiciousness but ignored him and looked to Silas. "Your majesty and I have fought many battles together in the past—and I know an impossible fight when I see one. They had already taken the gate and were pouring through. The castle was lost. As soon as I saw the odds, I rallied my garrison and fought a retreat pursued by the Vors' for many leagues."

Lord Hummerford opened his mouth to speak, but Sicaro pushed ahead with his next deceit. "After our pursuers fell behind, we hid, and then I returned with two of my best men to gather more information on the invading force. It was an opportunity no good commander could waste." He adjusted the bandage around his head and winced.

"You went back?" the magistrate interrupted, only to be ignored again.

"It goes, my king, that I am born of Vor parents but am your loyal servant; however, I still bear the appearance of my ancestors, and when we came across a dead warrior near an encampment, I took on his armor and markings to slip into the enemy—"

"You dressed as one of them?" Hummerford asked, eyebrows rising.

"Keep up, old man. That's what I said."

"Let him finish, Jor."

Sicaro stared into the king's eyes in his best attempt at earnestness. "I slipped into their midst amongst their drunken, wretched rejoicing. It took all of my resolve not to reveal myself and stop their rapes and defiling. But in my subterfuge, I infiltrated far enough to glimpse this Vor who calls himself king. But in poor fortune, I never got close enough to make a chance on his life."

Silas shook his head. "A pitiable shame."

"His warriors speak of him in great fear and respect. Respect not for his personal prowess or politics, but for his cruelty and cunning. His person is plain, however. Tall, not of a warrior's build, but slender like his lordship." He nodded at the frowning Lord Hummerford. "Sharp jaw but clean-shaven like a boy, the little that I saw."

Silas looked enthralled, so Sicaro pressed on, "However, that night as the camp slept, I returned to Castle Sanford through tunnels made for escaping the keep but accessible if one knows the riverside exit. Halls heavy with sentries, I sought the Vor king a second time but was again thwarted by guards.

Maybe a nightwraith could have gotten to him, but God did not design me for sneaking and creeping in shadows."

"That he did not. Go on."

He grinned and leaned in close. "Luck found me in another way, though. In the chamberlain's office, a guard slept at his post over a table of maps and papers. After I disposed of the man, I discovered a trove of the enemy's information. I studied their plans, examined their maps, and learnt of their strategies. However, before an hour was out, I was discovered and fought my way out of the castle while suffering these wounds." Sicaro lifted his injured arm and touched his bandaged forehead.

"Incredible, my lord. Your courage is heroic." The Ascorian king nodded and inclined his head.

"Yes, incredible . . . almost unbelievable," the magistrate said, his hands clasped in front of him with a forefinger tapping a knuckle. "I beg your forgiveness, but how can we know the truth of this? Perhaps, my lord, you were knocked unconscious, and a memory formed from a dream?"

Sicaro froze his expression before a scowl could form. He itched to strangle the man right there. "Your concern is touching, Lord Hummerford. But you do not think I would chance upon the enemy's map horde and leave without one?" He reached into the recess behind his chest plate and extracted a tattered, folded map.

Silas accepted the Vor map and held it to the light. "By God, I had thought they would immediately move on us here at Irin. But they are splitting their forces to Cerik and Hera. There may be an opportunity here."

"Exactly, my king. If we strike quickly, half of Harek's army will be to the east and half to the west—we could cut them right down the middle back to Sanford. We could retake the province and then pick their forces apart bit by bit."

"The war council must see this map." The king stood, glancing at the gathered generals where one of them was ramming a finger emphatically onto the table as he spoke over the others, and turned back to him. "Lord Sicaro, I would be grateful if you would join my war council and advise me as you have in the past, my friend. I have grown battle-weary, but dragging you—and that other lot—back into this makes it easier, and maybe then I can finally retire in peace."

Sicaro repressed a smile at the words he had been waiting to hear. "Aye, my king. I am but your servant."

A viper in the wheat.

Blade of Lightning

Book 2

Chapter 1

The Edge

Karisa–Castle Sanford, Province of Sanford, Ascoria

Karisa Rauhalik gasped for air and rolled to her side, away from the Vor king. His hands had loosened around her neck just as her life-force had begun to slip away. Each time, death edged a little closer; each time less narrowly escaped.

So cruel, was this king of the Vors. Since raiders captured her, after ambushing her company a few months before, Karisa had been a slave in King Harek's harem. And in that time, he had already murdered two other courtesans.

She had to escape before he killed her, or worse—handed her to her father. She would flee tonight.

"Why do you not beg?" the king asked. "Why do you not struggle? Do you not fear death?"

He could not have been further from the truth. She woke some nights, drenched in fear and sweat from nightmares of dying.

"Are you so terrified that you do not even fight for your own life?"

"I wish only to serve you." Her throat could only manage a

whisper. She knew that if she rewarded his cruelty with fear, more would follow. She had seen the other women. Women who trembled under his gaze, who screamed and thrashed under his ministrations, only to splutter and die in his hands. She wouldn't be one of them—she knew what he wanted and refused to give it to him.

"I think you enjoy it. I think I pleasure you very much."

"Yes, your highness," she replied, her voice raspy.

"Liar," he said. "I'll break you one day. I'll hear you wail and cry. Now, get out—I have a massacre to attend."

The guard, who had been standing at the tent entrance all the while, parted the flap for Karisa to leave, but not before clamping an iron collar around her bruised neck.

Clutching a blue silk wrap to her chest, she walked out into the nipping cold, ignoring the snarling hound and its handler stationed outside.

Under a full moon, thousands of armed figures had assembled in an open field on the forest's edge nearby.

Guided by flaming torches, eager but hushed voices boasted and chided one another in the semidark while *torgue* leaders and commanders ranged between the armed warriors, calling out orders.

"They're moving out already?" Karisa asked her harem guard.

"We expect the Ascorian column to march through the pass in the morning," said the man. "The king commands all units to be in place before the sunrise."

"God have mercy."

She trailed the guard back to the tent she shared with the other two women. Karisa was the longest serving. They called her the king's favorite, but it was only because she had outlived the rest.

"Boe," she said the guard's name, once they had reached the warmth of the tent and he had attached her chain to the central pillar. Silina and Gertrid stared wide-eyed at her from under a blanket they shared, fearful and thankful that the king had chosen her that night instead of one of them.

"Boe, you are so kind to me." She looked from his bulbous nose up to his uneven eyes—one always squinty. But even so, he wasn't an ugly man, just plain, a face who might have come to watch her on stage a dozen times but whom she wouldn't remember.

During the walk between tents, she had illumanced her appearance subtly. Over the past weeks, she had noted that Boe eyed her longingly when her hair was back-lit gold and loose around her bare shoulders.

She shook her hair out, and it glistened in the candlelight. Her face illuminated with magic to hide her bruises and highlight her cheek and jaw angles, blue eyes, and plump lips. She passed him a tip of the silk wrap.

"Wrap me." She spun and swayed in front of him, covering herself yard by yard, as his breathing hastened with desire. Of course, he had been watching when Harek touched her. They all did. But unlike the rest, Boe would look away, pinch-faced, when the punishment grew harsh.

When the length of silk was gone, she touched his arm and placed her lips close to his ear. "Tonight . . . it must be tonight we run away."

Boe breathed fast and an artery pulsated on the side of his temple.

"Loosen my collar? My neck hurts terribly." Wincing, she pulled at the restraint. The plain iron device wrapped in leather was the first barrier to her escape.

Mesmerized, he keyed the lock open, then shot a glance over his shoulder.

Karisa tailed a second bolt of silk around her neck and over the collar. "An hour after you are relieved, I will meet you at the latrines. Bring the uniform," she whispered into his ear. The final act of a month of whispers and promises to him had now arrived.

Nodding, he retreated to wait for the rest of his duty outside the tent entrance with his fellow guard.

Seeing the other girls' shocked gazes—a guard would be fed to the *gargantors* for unlocking a girl without permission—she lay between them and pulled them close.

"I'll come back for you when I reach help." She promised she'd find her sister, Vixhana, a captain of an elite warrior unit called the Nightwraiths, and lead Vixhana and her unit back to assassinate the Vor king and retrieve the two women. She was sure her detailed observations of the Vor guards' routines would help them return unobserved. The hounds and dragons, with their sensitive ears and noses, would be their only concern.

"Take us with you," Silina said, eyes pleading. Her once proud and haughty face quivered, a tapestry of purple and blue bruises.

"I won't be long. I promise. Now hush, you must try to sleep." She blew out the candlelight and waited.

An hour after she heard the changing of guards, Karisa unhinged her collar and began an invocation—one with which she had little practice. She knew well the illusions that drew focus and attention to herself; however, the light-annulling invocations that the nightwraith warriors used were more complex—they absorbed light so they wouldn't even cast a shadow. When she had been a child, Vixhana had instructed her in the technique, but because it hid rather than beautified her, she had never used it again.

She drew on her memory of Ella, her little dog. On that evening in the castle, a few days earlier, during the banquet of celebration, she had seen a dog that looked exactly like her Ella cowering in a metal cage. It was a delicate, tiny-boned dog and had been protected by bars from the slavering war hounds that had paced nearby. She had ached to hold the trembling creature and had found herself conflicted when her father finished talking with the king and approached her to say, "You left it behind. Be a good girl and you'll get it back."

Despite the fear for her pet, she basked in that joy of knowing Ella was alive and used the emotion as fuel to nullify any light that touched her.

At the rear of the tent, her shadow hands tugged at the canvas until there was enough of a gap for her to slip through.

Since she had last been outside, the horde of warriors had filtered into the trees, leaving only a scattering of tents and a bare garrison of guards and camp followers.

She would have to escape through the Vor army in the surrounding forest—or around, if she could find an "around." She chewed her lip. *Damn, I should have fled yesterday.*

Boe, poor lovesick Boe, waited by the latrines wrinkling his nose. It was a perilous place to walk in the dark; a misstep meant a bootful or two of excrement. She found him at the furthest trench.

He startled and almost dropped the package he held when Karisa whispered in front of his face. "Don't be frightened. I'm going to take your hand and you will be invisible, like me."

"How—"

"Shush. Into the tree line, so I can put on the clothes."

Several yards into the forest, she dropped the lightvoid

invocation and pulled the puffing harem guard into an embrace behind a dense of shrubs. She kissed him lightly on the lips. She owed him that, at least.

"We must keep moving," Karisa said breathlessly, pulling on the oversized Vor warrior outfit and boots he had brought as best she could, then threw away the ridiculous silk wraps.

"Give me your dagger," she said, and then tucked the sheathed weapon into her belt. "Which way do we go? Which way is the pass?"

Hesitantly, she invoked a stick-thin illumancer beam to light their path through the forest. Boe stared at the brightness emitting from her hand and up into her face.

"It's just light magic. I can't turn you into a toad or anything, silly."

"I don't know about this. Maybe we should go back," he said, his voice a higher pitch than normal. "They'll send hounds after us."

"Don't worry"—she cupped his hands with hers—"everyone will be too distracted by the battle to notice us gone. By then, we'll be safe. You're my hero, my rescuer—my brave, strong Boe."

They inched through the forest, neither knowing for certain which way to go, except that glimpses of the moon through the branches told them they were heading away from the camp.

After what seemed like an hour, they froze at the sound of a voice ahead. Karisa dismissed the lightbeam, dropped to a crouch, and channeled a light-nullifying cloak around them both.

"Is it them?" she whispered, fearing they had crept up on the back line of Vors waiting in ambush of the Ascorian army column that was expected to pass down the forest road in the morning. She swore silently, having hoped somehow with luck, prayer, the grace of God, that they would stumble out of the forest into an Ascorian sanctuary—an abbey or monastery perhaps—or at least get a clean run to a village or town.

"This way." Boe pulled her toward a direction perpendicular to the path they had been walking. She gave his hand a grateful squeeze. Her shoulders were aching with tension and her neck was painful to turn from the choking the king had given her.

A few minutes later, she tugged on Boe's hand to pull him to a stop.

The dimmest of lights ahead.

More warriors.

Again, they adjusted their course but only to stumble into more close encounters: the clank of a weapon, muffled speech, looming silhouettes—requiring changes to their path almost every few hundred yards.

"Stop," Karisa said finally. "We're going in circles." They were huddled behind a fallen tree after a voice had challenged them and cued them to scramble away for several minutes. It felt as though they were surrounded. She continued to cloak Boe and herself with lightvoid magic until the mental effort was too much to continue and counted her breaths until the woods went silent.

Boe's insecurity returned. "The king will be furious when he finds you gone."

"Doesn't matter. We'll be safe back with my people."

"Your people are about to be ambushed and slaughtered. We could still go back."

"It's too late . . . we don't even know which way 'back' is." She fumbled in the dark and found his shoulder. "Do you hate me so much that you'd abandon me now?"

Boe's hand clasped hers. "I would die for you, but the king is even worse than death . . . you weren't around when he flayed alive Iain just for groping one of his slaves. He tolerates no insult to his crown."

"Then better to die together than suffer that sadist." Her fingers found his face and stroked his cheek. "Let's rest. I'm tired."

Curled in Boe's arms for warmth, she succumbed to the fatigue from a day of abuse and a night of flight and fell asleep, numb to the surrounding danger.

Sometime later, she startled awake to sounds nearby: a hedgehog nuzzled through leaves a few yards away, and a lark sang a hesitant morning melody in the distance. The forest canopy had brightened with yellows and reds, while white boughs stood like the legs of lithe dancers.

"Wake up." Karisa shook the wonky-eyed guard awake. "We have to be away from here before the fighting starts."

Under the golden hue, they walked and mostly avoided the Vor warriors lying in wait. The two times they stumbled across hidden men and women, a hasty lightvoid invocation cloaked them and they vanished into the trees—careful to make sure they didn't betray their presence with the movements of bushes and branches they brushed past.

"Did you see that? A ghost . . ." a fearful voice trailed away.

The trees and undergrowth thinned until tan hills undulated ahead. Encouragingly, there had been no sign of humans for the past hour, and Boe had spotted some wild berries that were tart and seedy.

"Ugh, they're gross. Sure they're not poisonous?" Her face twisted into a wince.

"Dunno . . . at least we'll die together," he said, copying her words from the previous night, then smiled at her with the blackberry juice dribbling into his beard. At least he was trying;

thankfully, the big-nosed guard had grown bolder since their rest, quelling some of Karisa's misgivings about bringing the man along.

The guard squinted at the sky and reasoned that they were heading north because the sun had risen to their right. If he was correct, they had skirted the massed armies and could break out straight to the Reynford River and follow it to the City of Irin. "How far is it? The city?" he asked.

She shrugged. "Four, five days, maybe?"

"And you will vouch for me when we come across soldiers?"

"Of course. As long as they don't kill us on sight. It'll help if we can replace these outfits with some regular clothes. And we should cut that hideous beard off." She mimicked a snip of scissors with her fingers and flashed him a smile to lighten the mood. She then scanned the empty hills before setting a brisk pace away from the edge of the forest.

It was midmorning when they first smelled smoke. Behind them, pillars of smoke rose from the direction of the forest and carried with the breeze. Signs that the ambush had begun.

"Glad I'm not near those damn firemages, they burn everything in sight," Boe said.

The hills soon flattened to a tan, grass-swept expanse. In the distance, a road cut north with a few homesteads nestled along its side, each surrounded by farmlands of brown, dug earth. And on the horizon, a signaling tower stood like a lighthouse overlooking the sea of toiled dirt. Karisa heartened at the sight that promised a return to true freedom.

"We must hurry to one of the buildings and borrow some clothes," she said, pulling tight the oversized trousers and tossing her hair to cover her neck.

It was then that they saw dozens, scores, and then hundreds of figures emptying out of the line of hills that they had just abandoned—running and tripping along the road or through the fields and plains. Some so close that she recognized the pigeon-chested chest plate, steel cap, and brown leathers of Ascorian conscripts. Some bore swords or spears but most were empty-handed. They threw desperate glances over their shoulders.

Enemy horsemen followed and swept through the fleeing troops with axe and sword, cutting swathes through the men and women crisscrossing the open ground, unable to escape the murderous mounted warriors.

"Run, Boe!" Karisa yelled, her gullet rising. She turned from the routing mass and ran.

Pounding feet and frightened cries sounded faintly in the distance. Several Ascorian soldiers hurtled out of the hills toward her and Boe; then, like frightened fish, they veered away and scattered.

A minute later, four or five horsemen crested the hills and shouted excitedly as they chased down the fleeing soldiers. They were Vor skirmishers, whose usual task was to harass the flanks of a battle. But now that their enemy was routing, their bloodlust transformed them into merciless cutthroats.

"Faster!" Boe shouted at her, grabbed her hand, and propelled her along.

The skirmishers could cut them down in an instant. She had to do something. She steadied her mind and forced her fear aside to summon an inkling of joy to channel into her illumancy. Ridiculously, a childhood memory returned to her—she and her mother prancing and laughing through meadows similar to the ones around her. She hung on to it and plunged into a lightvoid.

She and Boe vanished from sight, leaving two small flickering pools of black on the ground, as though the sun were directly above but with no substance to view.

"Keep running . . . we need to get to some cover. I can't keep this cloak up for very long," she said. By now, the horsemen had run down the soldiers and were casting about for more victims; a couple stared in their direction for several seconds. One then shouted a command, turned in the opposite direction, and kicked his horse into a canter toward another group of fleeing Ascorians.

Several minutes later, exhausted from the lightvoid magic but within the cover of some bushes at the base of a hill, Karisa and Boe stopped to catch their breaths as she dropped the invocation and watched her hands and arms reappear.

From their cover, they could see that the routing Ascorians were thinned out over the plains, and the road and farms were littered with bodies. However, at the head of the road coming out of the hills, an organized group of Ascorian soldiers fought a thin-lined retreat against a mass of Vor warriors. A small cloud of red and green spiraled over the battle. Sleek draconic forms swooped down to rake talons across heads and shoulders, then circled around for another attack.

Armored horsemen and footmen on both sides thrust and chopped at each other. Firemages roamed the battle line, with the occasional burst of flame to engulf the occasional soldier or two. Pillars of smoke trailed their paths from the forest out onto the plains.

"Hideous beast," Karisa said, watching as a huge four-legged beast bounded into the fray and tossed bodies aside like sticks, ripping through the brittle flank. "Sickens me to my core."

The monster, a gargantor, was a favorite of the Vor king. Some days before, she had been forced to watch as the animal—almost the size of an elephant—tore apart and devoured a prisoner with its daggerlike claws and serrated maw.

Minutes later, the Ascorian line collapsed under the combined fury of the gargantor and Vor warriors. A few

Ascorian horsemen turned their mounts, threw down their banners, and galloped for their lives. Their cowardice was infectious, and others followed in panic.

Distracted by the battle, neither Boe nor Karisa noticed the Vor skirmishers until they were already upon them.

Six blood-splattered riders surrounded them, axes or chipped sword blades held menacingly at their sides, and snarls etched into their faces. A broad-shouldered woman, with blue tattoos around her short neck, cantered forward and tipped her head to examine them. "What have we here?" she asked. Her face then turned to curiosity. "Wait . . . deserters? Deserters from our own ranks?"

Boe stepped in front of Karisa with his hand on the pommel of his sword.

"Tell them I escaped and you're taking me back," Karisa whispered to the outmatched guard.

"She escaped and I—"

"Is that so? What I know is that she's the king's pleasure. I've seen her around." The woman slid from her horse with her blade in hand.

"I caught her. I'm returning her," Boe finished, his voice shaky.

"I don't think so. Holding hands like lovers and hiding like thieves. I know what's going on here," she said with a smirk. "You've been letting your trouser-snake do your thinking."

"I haven't touched her."

"You should start thinking with your head. Now, thinking of brandishing your sword at me . . . that's not good thinking either."

Boe removed his hand from the pommel of his sword.

Opportunities were streaming away. Karisa had to act. All the skirmishers were looking toward her. It had to be now.

She thrust her hands outward and invoked a blinding lightburst—light flared in the hills like a blast of sun.

Horses neighed and reared, tipping their riders up, and the warriors lifted hands to eyes. Two men fell to the ground, one dangling with his foot caught in a stirrup. The thick-necked woman cried out in alarm, and her hand darted up to cover her eyes.

"Quick, with me." Karisa grabbed Boe's hand and invoked the lightvoid cloak, disappearing into a pool of black. She pulled the guard to the top of the hill, then ran down the other side. They needed to find more cover, but scanning as she ran, she found there was little to help except low bushes and the occasional tree.

"Where did they go?" a male voice shouted from the other side of the hill.

"The whore's a lightmage, you idiot. Get back on your horse," the female warrior's voice could be heard shouting back at him. "Spread out and search for them."

At the bottom of the hill, Boe tripped, and his hand slipped out of hers. His body snapped into sight just as one of the horsemen crested the top. "Here's the man," the skirmisher shouted.

Karisa heard thundering hooves as the riders descended on them. She reached down for Boe's hand, but in her panic and inexperience, she lost focus on the lightvoid completely.

"Here's the woman."

In fear, she turned to the charging horseman and gasped in horror as a battleaxe cleaved through Boe's head. The blade emerged through the guard's face with blood and brain tangled through thick, dark hair. He stood for a second, then his legs crumpled and he collapsed to the ground, blood pumping out of the ruinous gouge in his head.

"Tie her up before she vanishes again," the woman warrior commanded, trotting down the hillside. However, the fight had left Karisa. Exhausted, unable to fuel another lightvoid, she slumped to the ground, defeated. Her dagger was knocked out of her grip and a rope looped around her hands and neck.

Months of hope, thwarted. She growled a curse of frustration. Now more than ever, freedom seemed so distant.

She would try again. But she needed greater help.

She prayed that Vixhana and Jaks would keep their oaths. No one else would come for her.

Chapter 2

Desperate Times

Jaks—The Village of the Jurns, Ascoria

Jaks squinted against the morning sun as he reached the plateau-top of the village of the Jurns. He examined the ancient huts of gray stone surrounding the staircase that led up from the caves below, uncertain which was the infirmary that housed his sister. He had a debt to repay her.

It had only been a day since Grandmaster Mulgrave and Meila had departed on their journey back to the Ascorian capital. A day since Jaks had abandoned electromancy for its part in critically injuring his sister Vixhana. And a day since deciding to self-exile.

Guilt weighed heavily on his mind. He would do whatever he could to keep her alive.

Around him, villagers garbed in skins and furs of wild animals busied themselves at all manner of tasks. Three *kaikushkas* spun flaxes into baskets, and several more of the elderly women tended cooking pots over firepits. A crew of men chipped away at a pile of rocks; a neat stack of rectangular blocks sat next to them, the product of their craft. And at the edge of the village, a band of young men hauled on ropes as voices shouted up from the canyon below. When the carcass of a black bear finally breached the top, the group cheered, then dragged the dead animal over to an awaiting butcher.

A hunched woman, as though reading his mind, raised a crooked finger and pointed at a nearby building with a sloping slate roof.

He nodded thanks and hurried past.

As he opened the door, he saw he was in the right place.

Two figures lay in separate wooden cots. Furthest away, Vixhana faced him. But only her closed eyelids, nose, and mouth were visible; the rest of her face was covered in bandages. A thin, narrow tube trailed into her nose through to her stomach. Tavis lay on the nearer mattress of animal furs, and a bench of healer's tools and shelves of stoppered stone jars lined the far wall.

The windows in the hut were shuttered to the chill, and a cheerful hearth, flued to evacuate the smoke, warmed the building. A woman, with her back to Jaks, wiped the brow of the enfeebled apprentice.

"How are they?" Jaks asked, hoping the tribeswoman understood the Ascorian tongue.

She turned, and he found himself staring at Xanra, the chieftess's daughter.

Intense green eyes gazed at him from beneath slender eyebrows. Delicate ears peeked out from beneath a braid of auburn hair wrapped around her head like a crown, and soft lips pursed at the sight of him.

"Close the door. You're letting out the heat," she replied in Ascorian. In the warmth, she was dressed only in a light leather tunic and leggings.

As Jaks obeyed, the woman continued. "Your sister is stable.

But Mother says only Hodrin knows what will come of the lightning damage and the fall on her head." With her words, guilt stung at Jaks again.

"Will she live?" he asked.

Xanra shrugged. "Perhaps. Perhaps not. She barely moves other than to sigh and twitch." She wrung out the used cloth in a clay bowl filled with water. "Your friend, though, has a better chance. At times, he murmurs and his eyes flutter as though ready to wake."

"He is not my friend. To be honest, we've traded a lot of ill feeling between us. I don't know whether to be sad or happy about his condition. I came to see Vixhana."

"Oh, is he a bad person?" She put the bowl aside and directed her gaze at Jaks.

"Not exactly," he replied, then explained how their rivalry had ignited: Jaks gliding into the grandmaster's service with the threat of displacing Tavis from an apprenticeship that he had worked hard to attain. Their hostility seemed petty now, with the apprentice lying comatose.

"You people fight over the smallest of things. Come help me roll your sister to her back. Ease the pressure off her side," she directed him.

"An apprenticeship with the Academy is not a small thing." Jaks kneeled to assist the young healer with Vixhana. "People often pay huge amounts of money to gain a master. If you don't have money"—realization struck Jaks that Tavis's family probably had very little—"you have to prove yourself through tests and feats."

"Would you end him to win this apprenticeship? He is vulnerable . . ." Her eyes flicked over to the incapacitated young man.

Jaks was aghast. "No, I'm no monster," he said. "Besides, I

don't wish to be an apprentice anymore. There is no reason for us to continue our conflict."

They then rolled Vixhana to her back. He grimaced with the effort but was grateful he could help her in some way.

"You speak Ascorian well," Jaks said as he retreated to the other side of Tavis's cot. The attractive woman made him nervous, and he wanted to please her.

She cast him a scornful look. "Mother says we will need to speak your language if we are to join your empire. She regrets our people tried to fight your king instead of submitting and blames herself for our exile." Xanra poured clean water from a stone jug into a tiny cup, then dripped it into a funnel and tube feeding into Tavis's nose. She did the same for Vixhana.

"She is wrong, though. We Jurns must have freedom to rule ourselves—we would never fit in with your aggressive ways," she said as she finished her task and sat on a chair before the fireplace.

"King Silas is a just and generous ruler," Jaks said in a defensive voice, and explained how he was nicknamed the "Breadgiver King" by the commonfolk. "Our country has prospered greatly since he united it. Before him, it was a dozen small kingdoms and realms. We were forever at war with one or another for the past couple of hundred years."

At that moment, Tavis groaned loudly on his cot. He flailed his arms and kicked off his fur covering in one motion. Xanra rushed to replace the fur, but it was then that he began to retch and shudder.

Jaks froze, unsure how to help.

"Go find my mother," the young woman commanded, and leaned over the big-eared apprentice to hold him on his side. "Go. Don't just stand there."

There was little that Jaks could do to help either Tavis or Vixhana after that—that day or anytime over the next week. He visited and helped turn them each day, but other times, he stood by uselessly as the tribesfolk attended dutifully to the patients.

Fortunately, there were other distractions as Jaks sought his part in the Jurn village. He was greeted and welcomed throughout the plateau-top by the tribesfolk. The few children amongst them traipsed after him and scattered with laughter when he drew up his arms and chased them in mimicry of a giant. There seemed to be no one parent or mother to each youngster; instead, all of the adults showed fondness for every child in some communal form of parenthood. For a population of several hundred, the eight young children were starkly few. Perhaps that was why they placed such prestige on fertile women, and particularly those who were pregnant—glowing mother-goddesses who were always with a young aide and doted upon by men and women alike.

Everyone had a duty in the Uwama's village, and Jaks's was to hunt.

Partnered up with him was Raki, the youth whom he'd met on his first day in the village. Bushy-haired and bright-faced, he beamed at Jaks and handed him a hunting spear.

"We get meat," the young man said. The grinning hunter walked over to a weapons rack and picked up another spear, along with a shortbow and arrows, then beckoned for Jaks to follow him down to the gully floor.

With that, their friendship rekindled. Over the following days, Raki and Jaks roamed through gullies and plateaus with weapons in hand and talking. Jaks became an apt student at both tossing the short throwing weapon and learning the Jurn language. Without the judgmental and harsh criticisms of Ranger Cromer that'd had Jaks doubting his every action during survival training, his hunting instincts naturally flourished. But even with the addition of Raki's deft tracking skills, the pair only brought back about half as much meat as the other hunters each day. "Too much talking and not enough stalking," the older men would admonish them.

But despite his gradual insertion into the Jurn village, Jaks thought increasingly of Meila. He missed the easy, free talk he had with the raven-haired outworlder about anything and everything. He missed her childlike delight, as raw as someone discovering vision after being blind. Yet, it was clear that Meila did not want the intimacy he wanted with her. She had rejected him twice already, and now she was far away.

And the more he thought of her, the greater a question burned in him: Why was he here?

He had thought his self-exile was an atonement for injuring Vixhana and killing Meila's husband. And he had thought that by staying with the Jurns, he could help his sister recover, but there was little he could do—anyone could do—to bring her out of her helpless state.

So, Meila's challenge haunted him: *"Do you think she would want you to give up? Run away? Was Vixhana one to quit anything?"*

The thought nagged him that maybe he had got it all wrong.

Tavis broke out of his unconscious state several days after their return from the wreckage site.

Jaks's first exchange with Tavis did not start well.

"Here's the hero," Tavis said sarcastically from his bed as

Jaks entered the healer's cottage. "I heard you were still around."

Jaks had come on his regular afternoon visit to help turn Vixhana and was surprised to see the apprentice sitting upright and alert. He had hoped Xanra would be present, as she often was, but only a toothless kaikushka sat with the still-comatose Vixhana and the thin, pale-looking Tavis. The old woman ignored him and lanced holes around the edge of a tanned hide with a bone needle.

"You're awake." Jaks ignored Tavis's jibe. "You look better."

The apprentice snorted. "For someone half-dead," he said. "What are you doing here?"

"I came to see Vixhana."

"But why are you here at all? Why aren't you out saving the world?" A sneer crossed his face. "No other family members to try to kill? Xanra told me this morning what you did." His eyes flicked to Vixhana lying on the neighboring cot.

Jaks's right fist clenched, and his left spasmed like a claw now that it was healed and no longer bandaged. The jibe pierced like a spear. He took a deep breath and spread his fingers. "Things have changed a lot since you were injured."

"Yes, I can see that." Tavis looked pointedly at Vixhana's unmoving form.

"Look, there's no need for us to be enemies—"

"Enemies? Are we enemies? You're the one who's trying to cut me out of the Academy—" Tavis began, but stopped when the elderly crone tapped his shoulder, having lowered her needle to her lap.

She raised a finger to her toothless maw and made a wheezing sound that bubbled a glob of spittle at the corner of her mouth.

Jaks silently thanked the old woman for the interruption

and continued. "I'm not an apprentice anymore. I live here with the Jurns now. I vowed to never use my powers again and have left the grandmaster's service."

Tavis stared at him as though he had sprouted horns. "What? Why? What really happened? I can't remember anything from that day."

Jaks recounted the ambush at the wreckage in detail, starting from Meila's first shot with her darkcore weapon, followed by the Vor gunman's startling and explosive retaliation, and finishing with how his lightning attack had accidentally struck Anton and Vixhana. Describing the clash felt like a confession: Tavis the Pardoner, and Jaks the sinner. By the end, he was grim-faced and mired in grief.

For several minutes, the only sound in the cottage was that of the kaikushka's needle punching holes in the leather.

The ashen-faced apprentice looked away and fumbled with the edge of the fur covering his legs. He appeared lost for words, and another emotion—ashamed. "I'm sorry, Jaks. I shouldn't have taken that cheap jab at you. I admire Vixhana. She's like one of those heroes you read about in children's books. I hope she comes out of it."

They both stared at the once mighty nightwraith.

Jaks sat down on the wooden stool next to Tavis. "I've said some nasty things to you as well. I've thought some even viler things," he said.

Their eyes met for a second, and they looked away, embarrassed by the rawness of the moment.

"We're good now, Tavis," said Jaks. Saying the apprentice's name felt alien, but somehow declared his change of heart toward the frail young man. "Let's just move on. There's no point dwelling on the past. We shouldn't torment ourselves over what we can't change."

Jaks stiffened as his own words echoed through his mind. Something twisted in the guilt-laden, troubled space between his ears. Some truth seemed to emerge like a gleaming gem unveiled in the rubble. Had he got it wrong? Were his actions forgivable, just as he had forgiven Tavis?

Although the magnitude of his own wrongdoing was at the heavier end of the stick, did it mean he had to keep beating himself with it forever? No amount of self-flagellation could bring back Vixhana. This self-exile served no purpose. It did not remedy the wrong; it was just a punishment, plain and simple. He had to honor Vixhana in deeds, not sacrifices. She wouldn't want him to quit and hide away. *She would want me to be like her—heroic.*

"Sometimes, you're not as stupid as you look," Tavis said, his face cracking into a cheeky grin to interrupt Jaks's thoughts. "Yes, let's put aside the past."

Jaks spluttered a laugh, and the kaikushka shushed him for his outburst, causing both young men to snicker. She then glared at them both until they quieted, but mirth still brightened their eyes.

Over the following weeks, Tavis continued to regain his strength and drive. And for several days now, Jaks hadn't heard the apprentice complain of pains at all. In fact, the only noise he had made recently was to plead the Uwama to clear him fit to attempt the journey back to Dunberrin.

***

Jaks's life with the Jurns changed with the return of Witabu.

A month after the elder tribesman had departed with Mulgrave and Meila for Dunberrin, he thumped up the stairs to the Uwama's platform on a cool, brisk evening.

Witabu leaned on his spear, puffing. *"Hodrin uhsaga, Uwama."* He inclined his head to the chieftess as the other two tribesmen who had accompanied him appeared.

The woman replied in kind and gestured for them to sit at the low table where Jaks regularly joined her and other villagers to eat.

She laid long fingers on Witabu's forearm. "The ponies still run the plains?" she asked.

"Few. The dark wolves roam fearlessly and in packs of many dozens. Much has changed there. They are not the same grasslands we left behind."

"Maybe so, but I am glad to see that none of you were injured on the journey." She leaned forward. "Tell me. You met the Ascorian king?"

"I did, but it was a poor time to have taken him the request, Chieftess. Their enemy conquers province after province, with rumors of entire towns turned into slave camps. He says these Vors have taken all the south and threaten to burst into the north . . . if they haven't already—it's been two weeks since we left."

"But what did he say to our request?"

"Sacrifice. If we want to subserve to his rule, he demands we join this war now. All of our fighting men and . . . fighting women. Although I explained our women do not fight, he demands we provide five hundred warriors."

The Uwama slumped back and looked to the night sky. "I feared there would be a price—but not one so great as that."

Xanra leaped to her feet. "Mother, we cannot accept this. The children and kaikushkas would be left with no one to protect them," she said. "We don't have to fight some foolish war for a tyrant who drove our people from our lands. We have no duty to him. We should cheer for his death, not laud him."

And so the debate began.

The rest of that evening, arguments fired back and forth over the Uwama's deck, but with doubtful progress. It seemed to Jaks that the Uwama had already decided and was merely allowing her daughter and others a chance to voice their feelings before she declared her predetermined choice.

When Xanra eventually thundered across the rope bridge to the plateau caves, and the other dissenters lost their vigor for debate, the Uwama vowed to deliver her decision the next night, then dismissed the tribal court.

As Jaks departed for his chamber, the wizened Witabu grabbed his sleeve and pulled him aside.

"Your friend *Mee-la* said to give you this," the old man said in the Ascorian tongue. He held his horned goat's helm under one arm and extended a waxed envelope with the other.

"Is she well?" Jaks asked, accepting the crumpled package with a nod.

"I saw only a little of her after we arrived in Dunberrin. But she gave me this to give to you. She seemed bothered—pushed it into my hands and then dashed back to her forge." The man yawned. "Now, these bones must get some sleep. You should rest too." He then stepped onto the closest rope bridge and left Jaks staring at the envelope.

He extracted a parchment and studied the words under lantern light:

Jaks,
I have been trying to contact you on the communicator I gave
you. I have information you will want to know.
We need you. Desperate times.
Meila.

It had been a month since he had dropped the wrist device into a basket, along with his armor and sword, somewhere in a chamber deep in the plateau fortress. Although he had thought of Meila daily, he had never retrieved it. He hadn't wanted to talk with her until he had something good to say. But what was this information she wrote about?

He tucked the letter away into a cloak pocket, turned to the rope bridge, and gripped the sides with white knuckles. Even after traversing it hundreds of times, it still seemed to buck like a wild horse every time he walked across. Once within the caves, he wound his way through the tunnels to a storage chamber and his old possessions.

The basket stood out from the many others. The only one with a sword hilt poking above the rim. And there was the other thing, the alien device, lying under his leather armor, intact and quiescent.

He placed the gray disc against his arm, and a strange tingling prickled his skin as it had done the first time Meila placed it on him. It caused him a moment's pause before he folded its brown binding around his wrist. He marveled at the beauty of the molded metal—unlike anything he'd ever seen crafted on this world. Her planet must be beautiful if it were filled with things like this.

That first time he had worn it, though, he had pried it off within an hour of Meila riding away. She said it would keep them connected, but at that time, he had only wanted to punish and exile himself for the damage he had done, including killing her husband, Anton.

He frowned at the uneasy sensation of the alien device alive against his skin. The tingling progressed to a chill until the disc felt cold to touch.

The rim of the device lit with a copper glow and an image of

Meila formed abruptly in front of him. Her oval face and almond eyes wrinkled as she frowned. Incredible. Some form of illumancy was projecting her image through the relic. She looked perfect. He gulped, not realizing how much he had missed her face.

"Damn you, Jaks. There you are. Did it take that stringy hunter all that time to get back to the village?" Meila said.

He dropped to the floor cross-legged and stared at her image, gaping and agog.

"Have you lost your voice?"

A familiar metallic odor permeated the air and filled his nose. Electromancy thrummed close by. Not the lethal lightning that he'd vowed never to use again, but something else.

He looked at his wrist and fixated on the disc, and found it was no longer an inert gray. Tiny copper-colored lines, circles, and squares glowed over the device's surface and dived into its interior. However, it wasn't his eyes that he was seeing with. Even when he closed them, he could still see the intricate paths. He was sensing them with his electromancy.

"Jaks?" Meila's voice rose with some concern. "Are you alright?"

He thought he had better say something and planned a reply that he was fine and was simply amazed to see her—but before he could even move his lips, she replied as if he had just spoken aloud.

"I was worried there. I forget you've never used a comm before. You sound strange, though. Your voice. It's different . . . sharp," she said.

"But I didn't say anything." He looked around the cave, wondering whether someone else had spoken, but his only company were baskets and shelves.

"Huh? Never mind. How are Vixhana and Tavis?" she

asked. After Jaks declared the latter recovered but the former still unconscious, she shook her head grimly. "It doesn't sound good for her. If Anton had survived, he might have been able to help." She stopped, only then seeing the fault in her words. "Let's hope she recovers soon."

"Listen up," she then said. The image swayed for a moment and the background to Meila's head lit up. Workbenches and hanging lightstones of the Academy behind her gave a warmth of familiarity. "The tube we salvaged from the *Mendhelsson* was a magnetic shield generator . . . I've modified it to build a velocity cannon. I won't get into specifics, but it could be a game-changer against the Vors. Think of my darkcore pistol, but thousands of times more powerful." She paused for a breath. "The only thing is, I need you here to try to make it work. It needs an electrical generator and you're the only power station that I know of on this planet. We need you to come back to the Academy."

She wants me to kill people with a weapon she built. Is this all I'm good for? Jaks clasped his hands together and wrung his fingers. He opened his mouth to reply, but she spoke again as though he had already voiced his thoughts.

"It's not the only thing you're good for, but at the moment, it's the best thing you can do."

"You can hear my thoughts?" He brought the shimmering wrist device to his face and gazed at it, astonished.

"What do you mean? No. I just hear your voice, although it sounds sharp at times . . . and sometimes I don't see your lips moving, but I thought that was because the lighting is poor around you—"

"You *can* hear my thoughts. You responded to me twice now when I had only been thinking about what I was going to say.

Or else this thing is sending my thoughts to you and turning them into speech."

"Interesting." She narrowed her eyes and scratched her head. After a few seconds, she began to nod enthusiastically. "This could be a passive effect of your electromancy."

He had an idea. *Let me test this.* He opened his memories of the past few weeks and focused them into the communicator.

"That's astonishing," he heard Meila say but continued to concentrate on piecing the past together and projecting it through the device: Learning the Jurns' language, hunting with Raki, tribal life, and images and memories of his conciliation with Tavis. His sad last thoughts were of Vixhana, comatose on her cot. He stared at Meila's unwavering projection as he transferred his memories to her.

"The comm device works as though it's an extension of you. It must be through your electromancy," she said, her face intense in thought. "I think it allows you to sense and interact with the electrical components inside the device. Although it's just a machine, your affinity to electricity must be allowing you to connect with it as naturally as the neurons in your own brain. I wonder what you can do with other devices?" She rubbed her chin in a manner that reminded him of Grandmaster Mulgrave.

Despite their fascination with this new discovery, the urgency in Meila's written note cued him to change the topic. "You said in your letter that you had some information I would want to know," he said.

"Oh, yes. We'll have to explore this other power another time." Her expression turned from curiosity to concern as she continued. "Yes, your friend Minto came looking for you a while ago. He was delivering messages to the Academy."

"He's alive? Thank God. I was worried it was him that rebel village hung from their palisade."

"I know. That's why I'm telling you. He came to the grandmaster's lab looking for you. I told him what happened with you and Vixhana. He was quite concerned about her injuries."

"He's adored her ever since he first laid eyes on her." A memory of six-year-old Minto staring googly-eyed at sixteen-year-old Vixhana flashed into his memory.

"She looked so normal back then. Probably because she wasn't dressed like an assassin," Meila commented on Jaks's projected memory from his childhood.

"You saw that? I better be careful what I think." He was amazed his thoughts were transferring so easily to her.

"He's a pleasant fellow. Anyway, he wanted to tell you he saw your *other* sister recently . . . Karisa?"

"No, he couldn't have. She disappeared after the raid. She's dead." He shook his head, confused. If she were alive, he was sure she would've been discovered by now.

"Apparently not. There was a parley between King Silas and the Vor king, where they were supposed to negotiate a truce. Turns out that damn tyrant just wanted a stage to demand our surrender."

"But what has this to do with Karisa?"

"She was standing behind the Vor king. I'm sorry, Jaks, but she was shackled by a collar . . . like how Anton was." Her gaze fixed on him, but the corners of her eyes dropped, betraying her sadness. "He said she looked well, though—glowing, in fact."

"All this time, I thought she was dead. Her body in some ditch or sunk in the sea." *She's alive?* As realization sank in, his neck tingled with joy. *She's alive!*

"A slave, though. Some would say she might be better off dead," Meila said, not as enthusiastic about the situation as he.

Jaks clambered to his feet, steadying himself against the

pommel of his sword jutting out of the basket. "I've got to rescue her. It was my fault she was even at that raid."

"You can't just go up and get her. She's surrounded by an army of axe-wielding barbarians," Meila replied as she walked to another workbench, whereupon lay a long metal contraption attached to numerous wires and coils. But he was too distracted to take much notice of Meila's surroundings, let alone his own.

"But I can't just leave her. I have to do something," he said, the glimmerings of a plan forming in his mind. "I have an idea. We can meet up and use your illumancy to sneak into the enemy camp with a lightvoid invocation and rescue her."

"That's ridiculous!" Meila exclaimed. "For one thing, my power is very limited, and I can only conjure little fantasies—not major invocations like that. Second, you can't just wander around the Vor encampments searching for her. We'd have to interact with them to find where she is kept. And third, she's the king's prize. She'll be highly guarded."

"You're right. Both of us going in wouldn't work. But alone, I could melt into their camp as one of them. I speak Vor and have Vor blood in my veins. I just need outerwear to complete a disguise."

"You're talking suicide, Jaks."

"I need to do what's right. Karisa needs me. I made an oath both to her and my mother." As the words spilled from his lips, his resolve to fulfill them grew. "You were correct—what you said last time. Vixhana wouldn't quit. She wouldn't turn away from someone in need. If she was conscious, she'd be the first to go. I might not be a hero like her, but I can take on her courage."

"Courage or foolishness? You're so impulsive sometimes."

"I've been a fool all my life, but now I'm taking a risk that's worthwhile—it's time to be courageous and stand for what's right." Not just for his sister, but his mother, too. "They were all strong. I'll show that I can be too." He gritted his teeth.

Meila's lips pressed into a thin line, and she turned to place a hand on the contraption behind her. Jaks recognized the metal tube from the salvage site. Squares and chunks of newly forged steel sprouted from its side, but the ship part in the center took prominence. "I really need you at the Academy to help me get this thing working. It could radically change the balance of firepower in this war. You might not have heard, but we're not doing well. If Irin falls, the coasts of Finstaf will follow, and then Dunberrin."

"What does it do?" He squinted at the image of the device. The length of a ballista, but without moving parts, it gave no clue to its workings.

She lectured him on the design of the weapon—what she called a velocity cannon, or a "velocannon" for short. The barrel was the metal tube they had salvaged in the Highlands. A magnetic radiation shield. Electricity energized an electromagnetic field inside the tube, and when a darkcore pistol was fired at full power through the barrel, the plasma bolt would be accelerated to almost the speed of light. When it struck something solid, she explained, the deadly bolt would explode and destroy everything within a half mile.

"It uses the darkcore plasma and layers an additional force on top of that technology," Meila summarized. "This velocannon is the weapon that can turn the tide of war, but it needs energy."

"From what?"

"You." She smiled and held out her hand. "Watch this." A tiny figure spun to life on her palm. Jaks's eyes widened at the fine details of her illusion. The figure was him! Despite her reservations about her illumancer powers, her skill with what little she had was impressive.

Miniature Jaks stood on a stone battlement beside the velocannon mounted on a heavy steel frame. Sparks scintillated around his hands as he gripped sides of the cannon. A moment later, the weapon spat fire and shuddered in its frame. "The batteries and capacitors that I built can't generate enough electrical charge . . . but I think you can."

Although puzzled by her unfamiliar technical terms, it was clear what she wanted. "You think I have the power to use it. You want my electromancy."

She nodded, and the illusion blinked out. "We were all disappointed there wasn't a weapons locker on the *Mendhelsson*, but this velocannon, if it works, could be more powerful than a thousand soldiers armed with darkies." Her forehead creased as she implored him. "Come to the Academy and help us win this war, and then go find your sister."

"I vowed to abandon electromancy after that day—"

"Mulgrave and I have been talking. He says that you can't abandon magic—just like how you can't give up breathing. It's part of you. You might hold your breath for a while, but it'll claw its way out when you're at your most desperate."

It made sense. All those times the lightning had risen unbidden, defending him against danger.

"So why didn't he tell me this before he left?" If the old mage had known he couldn't abandon his magic, why had he let him banish himself to the wilderness?

"He knew you needed time and space to grieve. That rascal can be pretty wise sometimes. Besides, he didn't want to tear you away from your sister's side." Meila then held up a piece of shining steel in front of her chest. He recognized it from the illusion she had generated. It was the handle-piece through which his miniature self had imbued electromancy. "So, will you come back to Dunberrin now? We really need you."

"I want to help, but I'm going to trust my instincts and go after Karisa. If I wait, there's no knowing what will happen to her. If I hesitate, I could be too late. I couldn't live with that."

Emotion stormed Meila's face for a long minute, until she slowly nodded her head and grimaced. "Just stay alive. You're the only person who can power this velocannon. Promise me you'll come back in one piece?"

Jaks nodded, his thoughts already racing to the mission ahead. He'd never contemplated such a bold mission before. It would test the extremes of his abilities, requiring skills his sisters possessed in abundance—and hopefully ones he could similarly employ: disguise, determination, courage, and strength. He dismissed an unbidden mental image of the fearsome Vors from the salvage site and steeled himself to do whatever was needed to rescue Karisa. It was what Vixhana would do.

"Promise me?" she repeated.

"I promise."

Chapter 3

Crossing the Mountains

Mud splattered Jaks's leggings as he trudged alongside the engorged stream flowing through the gorge below the Jurns' plateau village. Three days earlier, a storm had rolled down from the mountains, on the same day the Uwama declared her people would go to war, like some portent of the journey to come. The mood of the village had turned grim but resolute. For despite their reluctance to fight, the Jurns were loyal to their charismatic leader. Now, at last, the rain had stopped, and the tribesfolk assembled to leave.

Could they survive the journey? Even the toughest of them feared the predators and harshness of the Highlands.

At least one villager, however, was enraptured by the promise of adventure. Jaks caught sight of the boyish face of his hunting companion, Raki, excitedly bobbing amongst the throng of tribesfolk waiting to ascend the narrow path up the cliff face to the warband's congregation point above. Hitching his backpack, he bumped and nudged his way toward Raki. Arrow nocks, spear ends, leather shields, and travel baskets of the hastily armed tribesfolk caught on his own protruding scabbard and travel gear along the way—he apologized at least a dozen times before he caught up with his friend.

"I thought you would stay here with your sister?" Raki said, his expression shifting to one of puzzlement on seeing Jaks outfitted with sword and armor.

With the hasty preparations over the past few days, Jaks had not had the chance to tell the ever-cheerful youth of his new plans. "Vixhana will be cared for, whether or not I'm here."

Although her condition had improved in the last several days—eyes opening, and making garbled sounds for a few minutes before relapsing into a deep slumber—her long-term prospects were still uncertain. *"In a few days or a few weeks, Hodrin may restore her. But she may not be the mighty warrior she once was,"* the Uwama had said during her last bedside visit to Vixhana.

"Xanra will stay, and others, too. They will continue to care for her." Sixty tribesfolk, from what he saw: children, the elderly and crippled, and a dozen hunters and helpers to protect those left in the village.

Jaks clapped a hand on Raki's shoulder as it came to their turn to ascend the cliff path. "Besides, I have a task to do. I received word that my sister Karisa survives. I am going to rescue her from the king of the Voros," he said. Raki's eyes widened. The quest sounded heroic to Jaks's ears, but likely foolhardy and grandiose to others.

Raki grinned. "Adventure, my friend."

"Yes, adventure." Jaks returned a weak smile. "Come, let's join the rest of the warband," he said before his friend thought to question his sanity.

As Jaks had told Meila over the wrist communicator the day before, calling them a warband was a gross exaggeration.

Although half of the five hundred making the trek could throw a spear or shoot an arrow, the rest—mainly the Jurn women, who were gatherers and crafters—had never handled weapons except in whittling, decorating, or ceremonial dance. And none had experience fighting in formation as part of an army. Witabu had told him that after the last of their ponies died over a decade ago, the Jurns had lost their greatest advantage in fighting: mounted archery. So, without their beloved animals or army training, this warband, Jaks realized, no matter how brave and committed they were, marched toward disaster.

An hour later, the warband had assembled on a stony expanse. Apprehensive faces sought last glimpses of their near-abandoned village on the other side of the gully through the treetops, and Jaks could hear scattered weeping and sobs that were quickly reprimanded and silenced.

The chieftess, bedecked in boiled-leather armor, dragon-scale helm, and bearing an iron-tipped quarterstaff, stood on a boulder to address her warriors. "My loyal Jurns, when we return, the grasslands will welcome the soles of our feet again. Our journey will be hard and fraught with danger, but one that our children, grandchildren, and later descendants will thank us for. Be proud and take courage that we walk this path together." Her voice boomed over the stony flat; Jaks had often suspected that the Uwama possessed sonomancer abilities after being spell-bound by her sonorous voice, but now, her voice projecting to him—hundreds of yards away—and to each individual as though she stood right beside them, was a clear feat of magic.

As Jaks watched the mass of tribesfolk straggle across the plateau—a sea of animal-skull headdresses and spears—he shook his head and jogged to the Uwama where she stood offering words of encouragement to passing tribesfolk. "If I may suggest, Chieftess, perhaps we should organize the warband into marching columns. And split them into smaller sections with a leader for each. It would be good training for the warband before we get to the more treacherous parts of the traverse. They will pass through the mountains far easier if they are in lines." He was thinking of the narrow gullies and cliff paths that they would surely encounter as they took the route directly west across the mountains, a shortcut that could cut weeks off their trek to join the main Ascorian army in the river city and deliver Jaks to find Karisa.

The Uwama looked down at Jaks, lifting one eyebrow. "Indeed. Your father was a famous commander, wasn't he? Maybe you've inherited something from him? You could help me with your ideas."

He nodded and stiffened from a chill that ran down his spine but decided the chieftess had no malicious intent on bringing up his father—she had no way of knowing of the evil the man harbored in his soul. If he did have some of the strategic aptitude of his father, it was the only similarity they shared. Her suggestion appealed to him. He had always fancied himself an excellent Stratega player—a board game he would play against his schoolmates and resoundingly win—and although an unexceptional swordsman, his conscript unit training and love of battle lore could be something he could use to help the Jurns.

She commanded a halt in her powerful voice, then with the help of Witabu and Jaks, selected five respected hunters as leaders. She directed the warband into sections and assigned a leader to each. "Anything more?" she asked Jaks.

"Balance the groups to have equal numbers of experienced men. The less experienced should then pair up with them to shore up their morale. I doubt they will get any preparation once you get to Irin, so I wonder whether we should begin each day with drills and training?" Some practice fighting in formation might improve their chances on the battlefield.

The Uwama nodded appreciatively and, as the first column started marching, she beckoned for him to walk alongside her and Witabu, where they discussed the transformation of the Jurns from a bunch of wilders into a proper fighting unit.

Hundreds of humans marching through the Jurn Highlands would never go unnoticed. A multitude of eyes, mostly bestial and hungry, but some human and cruel, prowled the high tops and cliffs overlooking the columns of Jurns—which were sometimes four-person wide but at others just single-file as the terrain demanded.

Snow carpeted the higher peaks and melted into mountain streams to join rivers already swollen with the rain of the past few days. Rockslides, crashing boulders, and towering overhangs whistled with biting winds. Not a place that Jaks really wanted to return to, but now, with a purpose and goal, the trek was simply the first of the barriers between him and Karisa that he was determined to overcome.

He shivered and thrust his balled hands under his armpits as he marched. A pair of mountain lions hunched on a vantage point halfway up a mountain overlooking their passage; he felt as though they were watching him alone, spying him out as the likeliest morsel. *Ridiculous*, he thought, *no lion would attack such a large group of armed humans.* He tore his eyes away from the carnivores.

The danger that day, though, roved even higher above. Like ice demons crystallizing from the clouds, a flight of white dragons circled the warband. Fewer than their lowland counterparts, they were larger—Jaks estimated the size of a small man—and their wings thundered episodically when they scooped the frozen air. Three times so far, the winged predators had swooped at individuals at the rear of the column—one time, talons successfully grabbed a woman by her shoulders and lifted her off her feet, only releasing her when her fellow tribesfolk fought off the screeching beast with spears and staffs. Shaken but tenacious, the injured woman bit on a stick as the Uwama stitched her lacerations and bound her wounds, then got back on her feet to march again. But, unfortunately, only to succumb to the cold a few hours later.

After that, Tavis volunteered to rear-guard with a couple of experienced hunters, and the boom and flash of the apprentice's firebolts eventually sent the dragons winging off to find some easier prey.

By the afternoon, the valley widened into highland turf dusted with snow and wide enough that the center was clear of rocks and shale. The Uwama ordered a halt, and ancient hide tents that the Jurns had once used on the lowland plains were pitched against the elements.

Campfires burst to life with Tavis's fiery touch, generating heartfelt applause from the shivering tribesfolk. The apprentice found himself the hero of the day and received the first offerings of hot soup and dough sticks of the evening. And once the Jurns learned of his ability to conjure a dome of warmth around himself, his tent overflowed with bodies clambering for a spot near this living furnace.

Angry shouts woke Jaks from a fitful sleep. His tent—the size of that of the traveling acrobats that used to visit the city once a year—was crammed with men snoring, groaning, and talking in their sleep. As the voices continued, a few light sleepers like Jaks roused and peered around the darkness.

"What's going on out there?" someone asked in a croaky voice. The flickers of a campfire outside the tent greeted Jaks as he stumbled over a few sleeping bodies and slipped out into the icy night.

Curiously, he saw no sign of the duty watchmen near the fire except a couple of mugs—one tipped over, its warm contents steaming slightly—on the ground, forgotten.

He pulled his fur cloak tight with one hand and placed his other on the pommel of his sword and walked toward sounds of commotion on the outer edges of the camp. A few other men and women angled out of other tents and joined him in his investigation.

Behind a supply tent, they discovered several Jurn tribesmen surrounding three cowering figures. The watchmen poked spears and burning torches to keep the figures on their knees and barked questions and orders at their captives so quickly their responses were jumbled blatherings. A large cut in the back of the tent suggested the thieves intent, as did the scattered packages of food rations strewn on the surrounding ground. Bagfuls of dried meats, seeds, and nuts had been crushed beneath the struggle that appeared to have led to their capture. A dagger and a couple of clubs were their only weapons.

Witabu arrived and soon anger leached from his pores. "Bandits. There are probably more of them." He interrogated them in Jurn and then in Ascorian when the thieves responded in kind. They claimed they were remnants of a larger group who had ranged the Highlands for years—one of the many wild men the Jurns called "highland devils." They took whatever they could from wherever and whomever. "Thieves, in other words," Witabu declared.

The men were bound and brought before the Uwama in the

middle of the camp. The sky had tinged to a steel gray of morning and the screech of a dragon echoed from some distant valley.

Jaks warmed by a campfire. The capture of the bandits had ousted what tiredness remained from the day before; with no further need for sleep, he toyed with the long-range wrist comm and explored its channels and machinations with his magical senses. The device fascinated him. Tiny rivulets of power coursing through a miraculous artifact that could transfer his voice and image thousands of leagues away to another person— and he could see and control it through a nascent sense as though the comm were a living extension of himself.

He yelped in surprise when Meila's image unexpectedly manifested in front of him. She lay on her side, only her face illuminated, tendrils of hair draped over an eye. "Jaks . . . so early. What is it?" she asked.

"Sorry, I didn't mean to wake you. I was just playing around with this thing."

"What's going on? Where are you?" She sat up in what he assumed was her bed.

He updated her on the first day of their mountain traverse and the overnight incident with the bandits.

Out of the corner of his eye, he watched the three captured thieves—pitifully thin and haggard—kneeling in front of the chieftess. She was saying something to them. Too far away to hear, he saw the men shake their heads. Then, without warning, one of the wild men slumped to the ground with a spear piercing him through the front. One of the Uwama's personal guardsmen stepped on the man's chest and tore the weapon out without hesitation. The body arched and shuddered. The other two bandits followed. Their executions were simultaneous and without ceremony. He looked to the chieftess, expecting some shock or disgust at the brutal executions, but found only an icy disdain etched across her face.

"What's wrong?" Meila asked. She drew curtains in her bedroom and a golden hue seeped in.

"She just executed those thieves. I thought she'd just cut a finger off each or something . . ."

"She's a tough leader, Jaks. I wouldn't expect anything less of her. Executing a bunch of thieves isn't going to bother her. She knows how to make tough choices and is probably leading her people to certain death." Meila bent down to pull on her boots then stood and stared directly at Jaks. "Promise me you won't fight alongside them—you'll be killed too. In fact, you should just come straight back to Dunberrin with Tavis once you get across the mountains—it's a fool's errand you're chasing to the south."

"You know I can't. I've told you. Karisa needs me. Without Vix here, it's up to me alone," Jaks said. He tore his gaze away from the dead bodies, now being dragged away for burial some distance from the camp. "I better go. We're running field drills this morning and I have to help the Uwama with instructions. I'll talk to you again soon." She said a farewell and the comm image dissipated to leave only the memory of her worried face.

Over two hours that morning, the Jurn warband trampled the valley floor with basic army unit maneuvers that Jaks had learned well from his conscript training and now taught his Jurn peers: a spear-and-shield formation and a tactical front-line retreat—the latter often yelled at him by his conscript sergeant, as being the single most important skill of a soldier—allowing the front line, as it tired, to fall back for fresher soldiers to replace them. The last thing they wanted was for the formation to flee in terror as their front row collapsed from battle-fatigue.

The tactics, and others Jaks knew of, had brought many

victories to Ascorian armies in the past. Superior discipline and confidence from drills and practice translated to greater morale and lethality on the battlefield. In particular, the Ascorian victory led by Jaks's father himself during the legendary "Battle of Skulls"—the defining combat of the last year of the Unifying Wars when the Skull Clans of Cerik banded together—owed much to the ability of the infantry to hold their lines in the face of the terrifying foes while warlions and horse cavalry tore the clans apart.

The Uwama had a natural gift for command and used her sonomancer-enhanced voice to call out orders to the five sections of her warband. Jaks would instruct her on what was needed, and she would word her commands unambiguously to her warriors and leaders.

However, despite the Uwama's superb orders, it proved far more difficult for the untrained warriors to coordinate their movements. The section leaders did their best, and Jaks rushed about shouting, but learning the tactic fell to a mass of individuals whose only idea of formal movement came from ceremonial dance.

Eventually, the command trio of Witabu, Jaks, and the Uwama held their collective breath as the warband sections completed a last attempt at the drills. One section seemed to have learned the fighting retreat and transitioned their front lines fluidly, but Jaks could only shake his head as the other four groups fell over each other and tangled their spears together. Thankfully, there were still several more days to get this right.

Witabu laughed at the miserable sight while the Uwama boomed out to signal the end of the drill and instructed her warriors to separate into fighting pairs to train individually for another half hour—the first chance that some would ever have to learn how to pit spears against a human foe.

Dragging their boots and spear butts from their morning martial practice, the warband then resumed their march. Pebbles and rocks crunched underfoot. Skeletal shrubs and trees shivered in the whistling wind. Men and women gritted their teeth and shouldered their packs and weapons while staring at the back of the person in front.

Two days of marching mixed with exhausting morning drills delivered Jaks and the Jurns through winding valleys of cliffs and sheer slopes. Those early days seemed easy, until the valleys tapered away and Witabu was forced to lead them over high mountain paths.

Narrow, steep trails demanded they snake in single file. One mountain, one day, and then another.

Two of the tribe slipped to their deaths in this precarious passage: one youth who larked about—and thudded to his death after a wind gust—and an older man, who stumbled and then rolled down a cliff face, collecting an avalanche that buried him and stifled his cries. And yet another four tribesfolk, easy pickings on the cliff-side paths, were plucked away by predating dragons. Pragmatic and stoic, their fellow Jurns mourned as they shuffled onward.

Finally reaching what Witabu estimated to be halfway across the craggy range, Jaks stared down a ragged cliff overlooking a raging white river.

"Someone's going to swim *that*?" Jaks shouted to Witabu, who leaned over the precipice and kicked a loose pebble down into the deafening thunder of the rapids.

Earlier that day, Jaks had overheard the wizened hunter and the Uwama arguing about where to cross the river. She had favored the narrowest point to send their strongest swimmer across, for him to tie a rope and establish the first parts of a rope bridge. Witabu had countered, his deep wrinkles furrowed to dark lines, arguing that no one could safely swim this frothing barrier and that they should follow the watercourse a few days north until it calmed enough to swim safely. The Uwama, the more obstinate debater, had got her way, however, and a broad-shouldered man named Tahnn was stretching his arms and staring dubiously at his watery adversary.

"What if there was another way for someone to cross?" Jaks approached the Uwama. "Wait. Don't let him swim yet. I have an idea, but I have to talk to someone." He searched the crowd massed along the riverbank and found the sandy-haired head he needed.

"Tavis." He tapped the apprentice mage on the shoulder to get his attention. "They're trying to get someone to swim this thing."

"I heard. It's insane."

"Could you gravleap it? With a rope?"

"Me? I'm not battle-trained in gravmancy. I apprenticed to learn to make artifacts—not jump and bound into battle."

"It can't be that hard, can it? It's only about thirty yards across. Vixhana could gravleap four times that. And if you run at it from up there"—Jaks pointed to the cliff where he had been standing with Witabu—"you'd have a better chance."

"But if I don't make it, I'll get pulled under and smashed to a pulp. I don't like water, you know. I don't like dying, either."

Jaks reminded Tavis about the debt he had to the Jurns nursing him back to health from his injuries.

The apprentice yielded. "Alright, then . . . I'll give it a go," he said, all the while shaking his head at his folly.

The Uwama nodded acceptance and gratitude to Tavis's

offer—the nominated swimmer slapped the apprentice on the back, grinned with relief on his face, and hastily untied the rope from his waist.

The Jurns cleared a space along the riverbank for the apprentice to practice the gravleap before he made the actual attempt. A run, a jump, an invocation of magic to negate gravity and send him into a glide; and finally, a gradual reduction of magic to land. Hurtling through the air while maintaining an invocation was not as simple as Vixhana had made it look. The first time, although Tavis leaped past the thirty-yard kern marker, he landed jarringly and elicited a sympathetic gasp from the watching crowd. The next few times, however, he soared through the air and landed as gracefully as any dove or swan. Onlookers cheered and yelled; Jaks couldn't help but join along—clearly, the grandmaster had selected Tavis for an apprentice, not only for his double-mage powers but also his ability to learn quickly.

The sun dropped behind the mountain peaks as puffy clouds reddened the sky. With a few hours of daylight left, Jaks joined the excited throng lining the riverbank and stood on a flat boulder with several others.

On the cliff ledge, Tavis bounced on his toes, pulled on the rope tied around his waist, and turned to face the rapids. People shouted encouragement, but he didn't seem to hear them over the rumbling of the whitewater monster that blocked his path.

A brief twinge of jealousy wracked Jaks as the crowd surged in anticipation. Tavis had all the attention, and he would get all the glory—if he made it across—with endless praises from the tribe.

Witabu clapped the apprentice one last time on the shoulder and stepped back.

Tavis crouched with arms crooked before him in a runner's starting position.

He rocked back and forth for a few long minutes, then burst from his crouch and dashed toward the ravine.

The clifftop offered him a generous distance to the edge, and he took all of it in rapid strides.

Rope trailing behind him, he looked heroic as he bounded from the cliff edge.

Over the crowd. Over the churning rapids. He appeared to rise even higher.

He hurtled through the air, legs pumping uselessly. Except for a few shrieks of fear, the warband quieted and held their breaths.

The waters tossed up tendrils of froth to snatch at Tavis's feet as he reached the pinnacle of his leap.

An onlooker screamed in fear for the apprentice.

He descended in an arc to the other side of the river.

Within seconds, Tavis landed on his target: a circle of smooth rocks devoid of boulders.

Jaks joined in with an eruption of cheers—

Splash.

The rope trailing from the apprentice's waist slapped down into the water behind him.

The rapids grabbed the rope.

The rope pulled at his body.

Cheers turned to cries of alarm and shouts of warning.

Jaks stared uselessly as Tavis stumbled and fell as the river pulled him by the rope across the stones toward its crushing embrace. Fear pounded a tempo in his chest. Had he caused yet another person to take on a risky mission that would end in his death? He panic-prayed and offered his own life instead of

Tavis's, but knew that Death and God could not be bought so easily.

Yelled commands from the clifftop drew his gaze to several men and women pulling their end of the rope taut—they had allowed too much slack into its length and now strained to lift the rope above the raging torrent.

Each foot the rope rose, the nearer Tavis was dragged toward the river that hungered for him.

Almost at the water's edge, his movement halted as though an anchor had hooked and fastened him to the ground. The rope around his waist tightened, but he remained motionless and stuck to the ground like glue.

Half a minute later, the rope sprang free of the rapids, lifted taut, and dripped as it hung suspended in midair.

Jaks breathed a sigh of relief and thanked whatever magic or miracle had saved his friend.

Tavis crawled up the riverbank and wrapped the rope around a tree trunk. Finally, the ordeal was over.

Not until the next day—after a rope bridge had been constructed around Tavis's hard-earned foundation, and Jaks had clambered over—did he discover what had prevented the apprentice's doom.

"Gravmancy. I weighed myself down to resist the rope's pull," Tavis explained. But despite his self-satisfied grin, the magic hadn't protected him from a fractured rib and a flare-up of his abdominal pains where the rope had constricted him. Fortunately for him, he basked in two days' rest as the tribesfolk completed the river crossing. Two days in which Jaks never saw him alone; whether designated by the Uwama or spontaneously adoring, men and women constantly attended him in one of the great tents and plied him with food and steaming drinks.

Jaks contemplated Karisa's rescue mission during those days of waiting. Despite his brave words to Meila, he knew little of his Vor heritage or their behaviors and manners. Infiltrating her prison and freeing her without detection would rely on raw wits and daring he had never tested before. Of all the fields of magic, electromancy was of the least help. A gravmancer had superhuman agility and strength; an illumancer, disguise; a firemancer, fiery distractions; and even a sonomancer had the wrappings of stealth. Regretfully, he had no magic of practical use to sneak into an enemy war camp.

The following day, the warband amassed on the west side of the rapids—less several dropped packs and weapons but thankfully no drownings—and resumed their march. They climbed a hill of shale and then dropped into the valley below. The junction of two mountains provided a perfect drill-ground for the warband's morning training.

"Left face . . . Shield wall . . . Advance," commanded the Uwama.

"That's it, I think they're getting it." Jaks rubbed his hands together. "Can they do a fighting retreat?"

"Halt. Fall back." The front lines of each fighting section danced a retreat behind their comrades.

"Not bad. Still needs some work. A few more days and I think they'll have it."

The paired melee training afterward, however, showed Jaks the enormous steps that the warband had grown over the past days of training. The Jurns possessed a toughness and aggression that surprised him. It needed little to transform, even the female Jurns, into ferocious fighters. Having been thrust into a harsh, merciless wilderness for decades, they were instilled with a strong will to fight for survival. With confident spear thrusts, firm postures, bone-chilling shouts, and ardent battle-scowls, the warband now at least resembled a fighting unit.

A few days later, Jaks gasped as he crested the last of the mountain ridges and glimpsed brown, war-torn plains that were the Jurn warband's destination. Columns of smoke and irregular blotches dotted the flat expanse. Had the battle for Irin been fought already?

The Reynford River plunged down from the mountains and slashed through the plains until it emptied its lifeblood into the sea. Jaks squinted to resolve the City of Irin that was cut in half by the half-mile wide waterway. Two stone bridges spanned the waters, joined by a small island in the middle, and walled city sections on the north bank and south bank capped each end of the vital thoroughfare.

Over two thousand years before, Irin had once been the center of a mighty ancient civilization. The Opodic Empire had ruled the lands that Jaks's countryfolk now called Ascoria and Ellipta. And for nine generations, a lineage of Empress's held powerful sway over a terrified population, using roving priests and slayers to tax heavily and adjudicate often. However, a rebellion flared up in the third century and overthrew the rotten civilization. Now all that remained was the island of earth and stone in the center of the river that had once formed part of the foundations for the Opodic Palace that had spanned the width of the river.

Raki pointed at a wide black blot on the far side of the city. "What is that?"

"That, my friend, is war," Jaks replied, and shivered as he imagined the defenders on the city walls trembling at the enemy horde, braying to rip down every block of stone. "Tens of thousands of warriors, beasts of war, and siege machines." He spotted scores of siege towers and guessed there would be catapults and scorpions aplenty, although they were too far away to see.

"Are they still fighting, or are we too late to help?"

"I don't think they've attacked yet. Maybe the Vors are still preparing for their assault." Jaks shifted his gaze to the nearest side of the city. "Strange. Something is happening on this side of the river as well." He pointed at a dark military scar curving around the city, not as expansive as the horde on the opposite side of the city but extensive enough to blockade the road and any chance of the Jurns marching unhindered into the city to join the king's forces.

The warband came to a halt and Jaks scurried forward to join the Uwama's retinue.

"I'm sending Witabu with some scouts to find out what's going on down there." The Uwama's face had become more pinched and weary since the start of the march, coarsened now as she crinkled her forehead with concern. "We need to know who's enemy and who's not before we reveal ourselves."

Witabu and his men returned the next morning to where the Jurns were encamped in the giantwoods at the base of the mountain range. A soldier in a tidy Ascorian uniform bearing a signaler's badge stitched to his lapel accompanied him.

"The Vors have been congregating on the opposite bank for days, waiting for war groups to arrive from different directions," Witabu said. He then nodded toward the Ascorian signaler. "The sergeant here is from a warlion battalion sent to reinforce the city. They arrived yesterday to discover the Vors blockading Irin."

The signaler, sturdy and muscular, coughed to interrupt. "Signals with King Silas this morning state that Commander Nikor shall take you under his command. Commander Nikor sent me to pass on his order that your battalion is to join us immediately. There is to be a joint assault on the enemy blockade to reach the city, and there can be no delay. The opposite bank might be attacked soon and could fall if we don't reinforce them."

The Uwama shot Jaks a worried gaze.

"Don't worry, your people are ready," he said, but a quiver in his voice betrayed his uncertainty.

Chapter 4

Breaking the Siege

The Jurns emerged from the forest an hour later. Excited babbles and laughs punctuated the air, the manifestation of relief at their escape from the Highlands—even though all knew that battle awaited them on the plains.

Jaks did not share their jubilation. Instead, he rubbed his hands and breathed into his cupped palms to warm them. But no matter what he did, he could not stop shivering. The chill came from within, from the fear that what he had taught the Jurns would amount to nothing, that the Vors would slaughter the tribesfolk he'd grown to love.

As the warband squared off into sections, preparing for the march to join the Ascorian regiments, Tavis farewelled the Uwama and the tribesfolk to begin his lone journey north back to Dunberrin and his master. He pried himself away from several tearful hero-worshippers—his fawning band since the crossing of the rapids—and clasped arms with Jaks.

"I think your followers have said it all, but you made a tremendous difference along the way. If it wasn't for your bravery, more lives would have been lost," Jaks said. "A few months ago, I wouldn't have spoken this, but I have to admit, I'm envious of your powers."

"You shouldn't be. Your electromancy is by far the greater magic."

"No. It's an evil magic. It only kills. Nothing useful like what you did over the river or can do in the forge. I can't trust it. I can't trust myself to use it again."

Tavis shook his head. "Magic isn't good or evil. It's your motives that decide so. Evil intent breeds evil, but righteous intent yields good. You're a good person, Jaks. Even though it pains me to say." He looked embarrassed at the admission.

"We'll see," Jaks replied. Talking about good and evil triggered a recurring question that troubled him: Was his father's evil bred into his being? Did it yearn to escape his self-control, urging him to take whatever he wanted and satisfy any desire that took him? Was that why fear so controlled him? Preventing his inner evil from escaping?

He clenched and unclenched a fist, then hid the hand behind his back as though it offended him.

"You're an odd one," Tavis said.

Jaks laughed at the truth in the words. "Good luck with the rest of your journey. It's a long way home," he said and smiled at the apprentice.

"Ha, you're the one who'll need the luck." Tavis pushed his thumbs into the straps of his backpack and began his trek back to Dunberrin.

The Jurn warband marched onto plains covered with the brown grass of fall. In the distance, wild horses kicked up dust, and flights of swallows darted ellipses. "We once roamed lands similar to these." The Uwama's gaze scanned the horizon. "Prairies and grasslands. They remind us we are fighting for something worthwhile."

Jaks wondered whether she would still feel the same after counting the dead and dying after the impending trial-by-battle. He would assist the Uwama with her command in the Jurns' first engagement. He owed them that much, at least. One battle, of the many that would be in this war. But after this Vor barricade was broken, nothing would stop him from finding a disguise and melting into enemy lines. Unconsciously, he scratched at his two-week beard. Rampant facial hair—a mixed gift/curse of his own Vor heritage, usually shaved away each morning—was a vital aspect of his plan.

A Jurn section leader shouted in alarm and pointed.

Swift movement from the direction of his attention and within minutes, mounted figures dashed in from the horizon and stopped at the distance of an arrow's flight.

Warlions.

Magnificent manes billowed through vests of leather. Iron-capped skulls revealed only the tufts of their ears. Angular jaws snarled their bone-crunching power, and enormous paws hid claws that could rip open steel plate armor. Fifteen hands tall, reaching the shoulder of a warhorse, they were three times more muscular, agile, and deadly.

Riding atop, their human riders—all small and light—were outfitted in riding leathers, steel lances, and equally hardened glares. Cloaks swept from their shoulders and draped the backs of their feline mounts.

The Ascorian signaler accompanying the Uwama illumanced a pattern of flashes with his hands that brought the riders padding toward him.

The lioness-riding leader vaulted off her beast—maneless and sleeker than the males—and saluted before conferring with the Uwama. She would lead them to Commander Nikor's warlion battalion.

The warlions of the second regiment stretched and basked behind a ridge of hills. On the ridge top, sentinels and signalers monitored the Vor blockade—a mile-long stretch of enemy warriors, tattooed, bladed, and waiting—a mere half-hour's forced-march in the distance. Warlion riders readied their mounts, adjusting armor and tightening straps. Tails flicked and furred ears twitched.

Jaks shuddered at his first glimpse of this field aswarm with beasts of war. Astonished chatter, and a single enraptured shriek, burst aloud from the Jurns as they approached their bestial allies. Wary eyes in return, feline and human, however, quickly dulled the tribesfolk's excitement.

Unexpectedly, a wave of embarrassment for his adopted tribe swept over Jaks. Such an ill-equipped rabble compared to these superbly trained warlions and their handlers. Indeed, as they neared, the riders' gazes turned disdainful and wry.

"What! We were waiting for this mob?" a voice called out from amongst the handlers, and was echoed by a lion's snarl. "What a waste of time." The woman turned away and bent back down with an iron file to attack her lion's claws.

Ignoring the outburst, the Uwama called a halt to the warband and set them to rest. Delegating the warband's command to Witabu, she gestured at Jaks to follow as she ordered their seconded signaler to take them to the commander.

Several minutes later, they climbed the central ridge and approached a hard-faced man squinting at a subordinate officer.

"We mustn't delay any longer, sir," the officer said. "The south bank walls have been under assault for an hour now and the last signals from the city plead reinforcements now or the entire city could fall."

Commander Nikor, wiry and with a scar cutting a diagonal down his face, began a reply to the officer, but stopped to face the Uwama as she made final strides to reach him. He glanced over her shoulder down at the Jurn warband arrayed in an infantry square on the field below and grimaced. "Gods above. When they said a 'mountain infantry unit,' I didn't think it would literally be from the mountains. Who are you?" the man asked, his eyes ranging over the Uwama in her ornate armor.

"My lord, shall I prepare the regiment?" the officer persisted but remained ignored.

"Uwama Xandu. I command the Jurn warband," she said in the accent of a highborn Ascorian noblewoman, raising surprised looks from both men. "And my advisor," she said of Jaks, but kept her gaze locked on the commander. "We may not share your fine steel or ride fearsome beasts, but our mutual enemy waits in the distance, and we are ready to fight."

"So you are." Nikor inclined his head. "Apologies, my lady. An ally is an ally. Your arrival is timely. I am sorry we cannot dally for pleasantries."

"Sir. We must act," the officer petitioned again.

"Yes, we have no more time to lose. My lady, your warriors shall assault the left"—Nikor pointed at the distant line of enemy warriors—"my warlions will take the center, and seventh heavy battalion will attack the right." He pointed to the steel-clad mass of infantry, on the opposite side of the warlion meadow from where the Jurns had stalled, that Jaks had only just noticed a minute before as they climbed to this vantage point. The heavy halberdiers and pikemen were as uniform, disciplined, and even more heavily armored than their warlion counterparts—a far cry from the leather-armored and short-speared Jurns.

"Even with your warriors, my lady, the blockaders still outnumber us." The commander ground a thumb to the scarring over his forehead. "Pray that my riders can break their center quickly. If they do, it will be just a short step to flank and attack their rear. If they don't . . . your warriors will need to prove themselves mightily today."

The sun, gray behind clouds, hung to Jaks's right. In front of him, in clear sight of the Vor barricade, the Jurns scurried into three rows on the Uwama's command. Thick furs and cloaks, that warmed their backs in the Highlands, were left behind. With spears and shields, they faced the enemy. Their inexperience didn't show, or so Jaks hoped. It could even be said they looked fearsome with their animal-skull headdresses and lean, chiseled faces. He gripped his oval shield with the lightning-bolt insignia in his crooked hand and palmed the pommel of his stabbing sword with the other. *Here it starts.* He threw a quick prayer upward, wondering if whether some enemy soldier was praying to the same god—who would the deity favor?

A horn blared the attack. Moments later, monstrous roars and the clatter of weapons rang down the line of soldiers and beasts. Boots and paws thumped forward, and officers shouted for a walking pace. No wasting energy until they were close enough to charge.

In response, the black line of Vors grew even darker. Behind them, the city walls of Irin, and the brown waters of the Reynford River, pinned them into a dire standoff. There could be no rout of retreat for the Vors—triumph or die. This would be a desperate battle.

Ahead of Jaks, a tribeswoman—one of the flax weavers he had befriended back in the village—fell out of formation and sank to her knees. She leaned against her shield and retched. She wiped her mouth and with an upturned head met his eyes. He spared her a weak smile as an older tribesman stooped to pull her back into the line. He wished he could go over to her and tell her she would be safe, but he couldn't lie.

"Shouldn't someone lead the charge?" The Uwama marched beside Jaks and forty reserve warriors, in addition to her ten personal guards. "Should I be in front?"

"They will charge when you command them," Jaks replied. "They need their leader to give commands and order reserves to bear up weaknesses. You are the most valuable person here. You cannot risk yourself in front." He stiffened his shaking arms and clenched his jaw. His fear wasn't for himself but for these hundreds he had attempted to train so hastily. Each death would be his fault—would any of them survive? Inexperienced, outnumbered, and poorly armed—the odds were against them.

When the three Ascorian formations marched to within a half mile of the Vors, the enemy's howls and bellows of challenge carried to their ears. Blue-tattooed, scarred, and sneering, they waved axes and swords overhead. Ditches gouged the battlefield between the two army lines, and the defenders rested their shields on mounds of packed dirt.

To signal the start of the charge, horns again blared down the line.

The warlions roared in response and pounced onto the grassy meadow.

The Jurns loped toward the enemy shield wall. But as they approached the ditches, their charge faltered. Warriors veered and pushed to avoid the deep holes, tripping and falling over each other, only to be overrun by those behind. Jaks swore aloud and shouted at his compatriots ineffectually. Picking up his words, though, the Uwama pierced the clamor and din of panic with her sonomanced voice and ordered her warriors to stop, reorganize, and then advance at a walking pace.

The warlions, unhindered by the defensive ditches, leaped the gaping holes with their riders clinging to their backs. To the far right, the gleaming Ascorian infantry maneuvered the ditches with ease well ahead of the Jurns.

Arrows clouded the sky, whistling toward the Ascorian advance. The Uwama, alert to the threat, boomed a "shields up" to the warband and ducked for shelter under her shield-bearer's barrier. Jaks's own shield bucked as an arrow splintered against steel. Wooden shafts thudded around him.

One of the Uwama's guards nearby crumpled despite his upheld shield; an arrow pierced his thigh, eliciting a pained moan from the man. Gritting his teeth, he pulled the shaft through completely. "Flesh wound," he said and grunted. A moment later, another arrow struck him in the belly, and he collapsed.

"Keep them advancing!" Jaks yelled at the Uwama, seeing the Jurns stalled under the shower of arrows. Dozens of men and women had fallen, struck by arrows, and their fellow tribesfolk dropped weapons and shields to assist them.

"Leave the wounded. Keep advancing." She repeated his command and was rewarded with a rapid reformation of an infantry line.

At the center of the Ascorians' assault, the riders of the second regiment leaped from their warlions as they neared the Vor front. Their beasts then surged forward, unencumbered, and sprang at the shield wall—those in the rear bounding off the backs of the warlions in front and then over the armored line. Swords and axes swung desperately, but the mass of muscle and claws tossed the humans aside as they tore apart the defensive wall from front and back. Chunked flesh, dismembered arms, and decapitated heads flew into the air. Following into the gap, the dismounted riders finished the wounded and wedged open the Vor center.

Several minutes later, and a dozen more dead or lame from arrows, the shaky Jurns reached the Vor line. Their spears thrust and jabbed at the Vors' shield wall but found no openings and simply rebounded off metal and wood. Several Jurns attempted to batter the wall down, bashing shield against shield, but sword thrusts from the defenders drove them back.

It was futile. The enemy was too disciplined and the Jurns too inexperienced to penetrate the defensive line. Men and women clambered up the dirt mounds and battered at the defenses, but without any progress. Several more of the warband fell as swords and axes flashed over the shields to slice exposed heads and necks.

"Send up the reinforcements. Shore up the left—the Vors may push the flank," Jaks advised the Uwama as they followed a couple hundred yards behind the warband.

He looked at his feet, stepping around a ditch. His eyes trailed into the pit and a woman's face stared back up at him. An arrow pierced the dead body through the chest. He reeled in shock as he recognized the lifeless features of the flax weaver. *Oh, God. I'm sorry.* Fighting an urge to climb down into the ditch and shake her awake, he bit his lip and continued forward.

The forty warriors yelled in response to the Uwama's command and jogged to the left, but not before the Vors on the flank surged forward and blood-thirsty axes and swords swept into the Jurns from the side. Folding onto the warband, the tattooed warriors cut and cleaved arms and necks. Already brittle, the Jurns, like startled gulls, turned to flee from the brutal counterattack.

"Keep going!" Jaks yelled at the reserves between rapid breaths. They were losing terribly. They were being slaughtered. Even if the warlions came to their rescue, they couldn't defeat this many of them. Should he shout at the Uwama to call a retreat and then run? Darkness shuttered his focus—fear, that forever demon, began morphing into terror.

The mass of flanking Vors welcomed the reinforcements with savage swathes and cut down the first dozen. The following Jurns stopped in their paces—recognizing how outnumbered they were—froze, then turned on their heels to run.

Witabu swore aloud, and the Uwama grabbed at Jaks's arm. "What do we do? I must help them. They are dying out there."

Jaks had been wrong. The warband needed a leader in front —a champion—to stiffen the Jurns' morale and stir their ferocity. Not the Uwama. She was their heart. It had to be him: he was the only one with the power to do what was needed. "Stay back. Stay away from me," he yelled at her.

White and blue flickered around the edges of his sword and shield as he ran toward the charging Vors. Routing, Jurns scrambled out of his path, leaving Jaks facing hundreds of screaming Vor warriors.

The electromancy, suppressed for months, rushed to his bidding. The triple steps of invocation merged as one and crackled around him in a sparking, magical aura. Half-panicked, half-enraged, he willed the magic into a dazzling ball of lightning as he sprinted forward. Grass burned behind him and left a trail of smoke in his wake.

Forks of electricity leaped and blasted arrows that targeted him. The projectiles burst into flashes of fire and banged with every strike.

All eyes on the flank drew to the glowing lightning god thundering across the meadow. The charging Vors faltered and hastily formed a shield wall to meet this new adversary.

A Vor griefmaster, teeth bared and eyes rounded, pushed through the wall carrying an enormous two-handed battleaxe. He took three steps, leaped again, and then soared through the air with the crescent of his weapon bearing down on Jaks.

Jaks pointed his sword at the gravmancer. Lightning lanced down the weapon to strike the enemy battlemage. A brilliant flash splintered the axe and hurtled the charred torso backward to thud at the foot of the shield wall.

"Regroup. Follow me," he yelled at the Jurns behind him.

Jaks frowned as the shield wall parted fifty yards away. A red-robed woman marched through the gap, weaving her arms through the air. Flames appeared in her hands and grew as her arms continued their intoxicating dance.

The visage of a burning dragon flew out of the fire and flapped flaming wings above the firemage.

Jaks shuddered, fearing the powers of this woman who so masterfully conjured this draconic invocation to life. His nerve almost broke when the dragon spat a column of fire into the air and flailed its neck from side to side, hovering above her.

The firemage stared at Jaks and then thrust her arms at him.

The dragon swooped and raced across the field as though to engulf him.

An electric wall crackled in front of Jaks; a bully's sneer, a biting spider, an armored fist, and his mother's crushed skull fueled the shield into existence.

The draconic missile smashed into the shimmering barrier with a conflagration of flames. The detonation deafened and blinded him momentarily, even though he had turned away from the blast. When his sight returned, the wall of lightning stood crackling, but nothing was left of the firemanced dragon except the smoking dirt around him. Jaks staggered, fatigue sapping his concentration and focus—his lightning wall disappeared.

A second fiery dragon swooped into the air above the mage. He couldn't absorb another massive assault like the last. He would have to destroy the source.

As the firemancer's arms snaked the air, the conjuration grew with every motion. The dance focused her attention, building up another magical assault.

Jaks sprinted toward his enemy, jumped over a ditch, and dared to close half the distance to her. His electromancy had not stretched out this far before, but he had to strike now.

The dragon visage continued to grow until it was the width of a ship's sail. The red-robed woman's gaze homed in on Jaks.

He plunged down on one knee and pointed his sword tip at the firemage. Although his mouth was open and his throat shook in exhalation, he heard no sound—and saw nothing other than her scornful eyes.

Her scream only lasted a couple of seconds, before all the air burst out of her chest, and her flesh sizzled and crisped from the lightning channeled into her from Jaks. A curtain of electricity cut the field to her and then forked outward to strike the hundreds of Vor warriors sheltered behind the battlemage.

Lightning vaulted from limb to limb through the enemy flank. Weapons and shields fell from stunned hands, and spasming bodies toppled to the ground. He savored the familiar taste of metal in his mouth and poured energy into the chained lightning until every Vor warrior within a hundred yards lay twitching or still. As he stared at the bodies, a sense of power surged within, and he laughed at the thrill it gave him.

A war cry sounded from behind and a fresh charge of Jurns, stirred on by the Uwama's rally and Jaks's devastation, pounded past him and into the Vor mainline. Drained and depleted, he leaned on his shield and watched the enemy defenses crumble under the warband's renewed assault. Satisfied that they no longer needed his help, he collapsed to the burned ground and closed his eyes as the sounds of battle faded.

Chapter 5

Finding Karisa

Jaks roused to someone shaking him by the shoulders. It was dark. Must be night.

"Wake up," his tormenter said, nudging him again.

Confused, he pushed the shadowy figure away. "Who are you?" His fingers palpated dirt all around him—a ditch?

"Friend, I knew you were around here somewhere. That stubble on your face made it hard to recognize you," the voice said. "It's me, Raki."

"What—"

"It's over." By the light of the moon and a small flaming torch, his friend's forever-cheerful face emerged, smiling despite dried blood marring his features and a bandage wrapping his head. The Jurn youth peeked out of the pit before sitting and leaning against the earth wall.

They reassured each other that their injuries were slight and then grinned at each other in relief. "After you broke the Vors, we pushed them back to the river," Raki said. "If only you could have seen the warlions rip into them! Some drowned trying to swim for their lives, but the rest threw down their weapons and surrendered."

"So, we won?"

"Not quite. Although we reached the city, the other side of the city had already been lost."

"But we still hold this side?" Jaks said.

Raki's face went hard. "The Uwama says the king commanded a full withdrawal and destroyed the bridge. Something about ships coming up the gulf. Our fight has allowed the king's army to withdraw safely from Irin, though."

"Withdraw? But this was our best chokepoint."

"Not anymore. We're all retreating to the border of Dunberrin. They say more allies are coming from Faucony and Strock to help, and then the king will be able to push back at the Vors. Come on. We have to catch up with the rest."

Jaks stood up and peered out of the waist-high pit. A column of flaming torches was snaking out of the city walls opposite to where he needed to go. "No, I've got another task to do. You leave. I have to find my sister." His eyes found what he was looking for—a dead Vor. He clambered out of the pit and dragged the corpse of the warrior back into the ditch. Raki watched him in horror as he stripped the body of armor.

"Too big. Help me find a taller, thinner one." Jaks explained his plan to the youth as they examined different bodies. "I need more than just a beard for a disguise." Minutes later, he settled on a set of armor from a wiry axeman with a gaping neck wound. This second corpse in the narrow ditch was too much for Raki to tolerate, and he scrambled out. Jaks saw his discomfort and said, "Thank you, my friend. You have been good to me. Go join the warband. I'll see you another day."

"*Hodrin uhsaga*, Jaks." Raki's eyes lingered as though seeing him off for the last time and then he fled toward the trail of torches.

Alone with the two bodies, Jaks talked to them in the Vorosian language as though to relieve some tension in the confined space. Although his Vorosian was rusty—Karisa the only person he spoke it with after their grandmother died—his ear for languages was clear and he would sometimes talk to himself just as he did now, savoring the powerful guttural sounds of the western continent. A short time later, satisfied with his disguise, physical and lingual, fatigue defeated him again and he became as still as his grave companions.

A Vor voice and shuffling above the ditch woke him some hours later. "Anyone here . . . help . . . help . . . please?"

Morning sun and cawing crows crashed into Jaks's senses. The voice called again with a pleading, pitchy angst. Jaks shook his head—he had a plan to enact. This was no time to help an enemy, even someone who sounded as pathetic as this. But eventually, his conscience won. After tucking away Meila's wrist device within his borrowed leather chest piece and sheathing his runic-forged sword—his shield lost in the fray—he climbed out of the hole and approached the calling figure.

The Vor crawled through burned grass. Something had torn his nose from his face and turned his eyes into bloodied gouges. Warlion claw wounds—maybe the same claws that had torn off the man's arm below the elbow. Jaks pressed a fist to his mouth to counter a wave of nausea.

"Here, I'll help you." Jaks dragged the man to his feet when he realized this enemy could help improve his disguise.

He crutched the thankful warrior up to the city gates, noting a few other survivors shambling around the battlefield too. A few looted their fellow Vors while several others weaved through the bodies, ditches, and carrion birds toward the gates as well.

Four Vor sentries challenged Jaks but waved him through at the sight of the injured warrior. "Fuck, he'll be dead in a day or two, but take him up to the infirmary anyway," a red-haired one said. "Up by the bridge."

An ironwood side door swung open and Jaks guided the blind man onto the cobbled streets of Irin. The first test of his disguise had been passed with ease.

Scores of warriors roved the streets, smashing down doors into the elegant townhouses and buildings and dragging out the few citizens who had refused to escape with the Ascorians the night before. Now chattel, men and women—most elderly but some not—were tossed onto the street to be assaulted, abused, and then clamped in iron collars. Jaks shivered and willed himself small as he limped his wounded companion to the infirmary.

At the damaged bridge—where workers were already toiling over repairs—he sighted the aftermath of the previous night's battle. A half mile away, on the opposite riverbank, fire and smoke angled over the city. Milling figures smothered the shore as rowboats, rafts, and fishing vessels, filled with Vor warriors, slid across the water. In addition, dozens of ocean-going longboats unloaded at the docks to Jaks's left and right, and more anchored mid-stream awaiting their turn. These must have been the ships that Raki had spoken of.

"Over there," a gruff veteran directed Jaks, pointing to a quaint, steepled church on the corner. Its sacrosanct interior, though, was bared to the elements: doors had been ripped from the hinges and only shards remained of its stained-glass windows. Inside, dozens of wounded lay groaning and mumbling, ministered to by several healers with bandages and thread.

"They'll look after you now," Jaks said to the blind warrior and patted him on the shoulder. He then turned to a medic nearby and asked in his best Vorosian enunciation, as casually as he could, "Has King Harek crossed the river, do you know?"

The healer, a matron with hands nimbly stitching a leg gash, raised her eyebrows and glared at him. "How would I know? What would the king want with you?"

"Nothing. I, ah. Just small talk."

"Well, if you've got time for blathering, warrior, go empty those buckets in the gutter. Then go refill them at the river . . . upstream, mind you, don't want no piss or death in them." She nodded at several wooden buckets filled with blood-soaked rags. "Wring out the rags, too."

Scowling like a scolded child, Jaks grabbed two of the containers, cursed as gore sloshed his boots, and dragged them out into the main avenue. However, once outside, he saw an opportunity in his task. Perhaps this was no annoyance; although not in his original plan to track down Karisa, playing water-boy could at least cloak his true purpose—once he discovered where the king rested, his slaves were sure to be close.

The boulevard paralleling the docks bustled with warriors. Carts, boxes, and fishing lines were shoved into the river to make room for several mustering points. As each group of fifty men and women converged, a coarse shout would stir them to march off into various parts of the city, making room for the next unit to assemble.

Wary-eyed, Jaks toted the buckets along the edge of the buildings, well clear of the bristling masses, until he arrived at a landing where the water ran clear, and an empty rowboat bobbed.

Two oarsmen resting on broad pilings ignored him as he kneeled at the dock edge and dipped the first bucket into the river.

A few minutes later, he leaned against a piling and pretended to rest. He made eye contact with one of the men. "How fares the king? Has he crossed the river yet?" Jaks asked, sweating, but plying a casual tone.

The men exchanged glances, and the burliest coiled a rope around his arm. "How the fuck should I know," he said, then spat into the shushing waters and returned to his length of rope.

Several more bucket trips from the church to different docks—and many more blank faces for answers—left Jaks unenlightened on the king's whereabouts. Surely, the Vor king would travel with his main army? He began to doubt the effectiveness of his plan.

His last encounter raised his doubts even more about his investigation methods. A sharp-faced archer, directing the loading of a cart with bundled arrows, narrowed her eyes at his question. "Hoo, where're you from? That's an odd accent. What's your torgue? Who's your *telsun*?"

Before he could answer, she snatched his left arm, causing the bucket to drop from his hand. Pulling his sleeve, she twisted his forearm to study each surface with painful jerks. Not finding what she wanted—maybe the conscription brand that would have labeled him an Ascorian—she released him, and stood with hands on hips in his path.

"Well, where's your torgue and telsun?"

"Killed at the northern barricade by warlions, they were," Jaks lied, and cringed at his fabrication of a peasant's accent. "The healer sent me to take water for the wounded."

"If they were all killed, I wonder how *you* survived, then. Who was your telsun?" Two other archers carrying arrow bundles rolled their loads onto the cart and stopped to eye up Jaks.

"Rauhalik, Sicaro. Died too . . ." he said, using the first Vor name he could think of, his father's, hoping it sounded common enough to satisfy this suspicious fox.

Her eyes narrowed, but then relaxed. "Sounds familiar, but I don't know him." She turned, losing interest in Jaks. "Go on, then. When the infirmers finish with you, report to the muster commander for a new torgue."

Nodding, he grabbed his buckets and returned to the river to refill the spilled vessel, thankful she hadn't checked further up his arm.

He was drawing too much attention. There must be an easier way to locate Karisa.

Wounded warriors stumbled into the infirmary throughout the day, keeping Jaks busy with buckets while the bleeding and broken-boned were mended. No longer asking directly about the king or his entourage, he took to lingering and listening to loose tongues on the docks and streets: Yes, the craven Ascorians had fled. No, we're not to pursue them. Yes, beer and ale aplenty tonight.

Shoulders aching, and confidence sinking, Jaks hefted buckets for the tenth time that day, and ambled back to the church along a quiet side street. Shadows inched toward the last few hours of sun.

"Hey, get back here!" A shout and running footsteps thumped up behind him. For the second time that day, a bucket of fresh water was knocked from his hand as a tiny figure ran past him. Two more youths, scrawny and dirt-smeared, quickly followed the first while throwing furtive glances over their shoulders.

Jaks shrank against a wall and clamped hands around his last bucket.

A blond-haired Vor ran after the youths, leading four other warriors. "They're going down the alley," he yelled.

The smallest, lagging on the heels of his mates, turned too late and skidded into the bricks of a battered storefront. He let out a cry and fell to the pavement, but his companions vanished down the alley.

"Got you, lily-boy," the first man triumphed under a hanging sign of a gem-encrusted ring. "Find those others and clamp them in irons," he yelled at his compatriots and lifted the stunned child up by the arm.

A minute later, the men returned empty-handed, and Jaks—bucket retrieved and about to return to the river—overheard talk of the waifs escaping over a wall. "Go search the buildings. I'm taking this one inside for a while." The blond man leered at the boy, picked him up bodily, and carried him kicking into the ransacked store.

The words chilled Jaks. The boy was no more than six years old, and his captor's intent was vile. He stood for a long minute on the empty street, lips curled and jaw clenching. An unbidden memory scratched at a scarred door, stirring an inner vigilante that howled at him to act.

He might not save every child, but he could save this one. Vixhana would have.

Buckets rolling to the ground behind him, Jaks stormed into the store.

His boots crunched underfoot. He paused for his eyes to adjust to the gloom within. A mess of glass shards surrounded him, as did smashed display cases with tiny wooden drawers torn from slots.

A hallway darkened the back of the store. *Down there?*

A deep laugh came from a staircase to the right. *No, up.*

He leaped steps, three at a time, up to a room illuminated by a window presiding over a table, chairs, and three wooden cots. The boy was sprawled on the floor. The hulking frame of the warrior stood over him.

At the sound of Jaks's entrance, the Vor looked over his shoulder. "What the hell do you want?" he demanded.

Jaks drew his sword. "Leave him alone."

"Bugger off, pisshead. He's mine." The man turned and swept out a dagger with his giant paw. The boy scuttled away to hide under a cot.

Months ago, he might have wet himself and flinched from this man bulking over him, but anger, not fear, was now his prevailing current. Besides, the sword was not his best weapon by far. With an innocent in the room, his only worry was not harming the boy.

Jaks's sword crackled to life with filaments of electricity racing over the engraved steel.

"Your little tricks don't scare me." The man sneered and swung the dagger in arcs, his longer arms making up for the shorter blade, and forced Jaks backward.

Another step back and Jaks would stumble down the stairs. He jabbed back with his scintillating sword.

His opponent darted right, nimble for a big man, evading the blade—but not far enough—lightning surged between the gap to his face. He yowled and staggered a retreat.

Jaks wasted no time and grunted with a two-handed cross-swing of the sword. The blade struck the man's wrist and sliced through skin and bone as easily as paper. Although brandished in battle before, it was the first time this rune-forged sword had tasted blood—it followed through the slash and spat blood over the floor as though appalled at the flavor.

The severed hand and dagger thunked to the ground, and the knifeman screamed as blood pumped from the stump, splattering Jaks's face and further decorating the room in crimson.

Worried the noise would attract attention, Jaks switched to a one-handed grip on the weapon and lunged at the man, spearing him through the chest.

Electromantic energy seethed through the sword; sizzling sounds and smoke seeped through the man's leather tunic. The blade rammed down to the hilt.

He pulled the blade out, pushed the Vor with his crippled hand, and said, "No more little boys." The man crumpled onto a blanket-covered bed, gurgling froth and gawping wordlessly.

A moment later, short limbs scrambled out from under a neighboring cot. The scrawny boy stared at the dead body for a long moment, then his face soured and he kicked its lifeless leg.

"You got him good," the boy said in Ascorian with a squeaky voice. Eyes squinting, he edged away from Jaks. "You're not going to kill me, are you?"

Jaks forced a smile, wanting to reassure the lad. "No, I don't want anything from you . . . except don't tell anyone what happened here."

"You're not one of them." The boy stepped a foot closer. "You're talking Ascorian, like me!" Barely coming up to Jaks's ribs—and about just as thin—the lad grinned under his mop of brown hair.

He had relapsed automatically into his native tongue in response to the boy's usage. He smiled, but now glanced back at the door at the top of the stairs. "We've got to go. His friends are around and will be back soon."

"Are you a spy?"

"In a way. I'm here to rescue someone."

The boy's eyes shone, and his mouth dropped open. "Like Gilgat!"

"I don't think so," Jaks replied, recalling popular stories of Gilgat the Great: Mighty warrior and hero from the Dawn of Steel some four hundred years before. Whereas Gilgat had no fear, children's books told—even when he fought for thirty days to defend the walls of his Empress's fortress—Jaks had much to spare.

"Yes, yes, you just saved me, and you're going to save someone else . . . is it a princess?"

Jaks laughed as the boy bounced on his toes with awed eyes gazing at him.

A shadow flipped onto the balcony outside the window; the movement caught their attention.

"It's Hugh. I knew he'd come back." The boy flicked a catch and swung open the balcony door for the youth. "Hugh . . . he saved me already."

Hugh, a pimply teen with a strong physical resemblance to the younger boy, stared warily at Jaks and leaned through the door as though to snatch the boy out. He froze when he saw the dead Vor on the bed. "Oh, God. Come on, Davey, we've got to go."

"But we have to help him, Hugh. He's going to save a princess," Davey said.

"Horseshit. This is no time for make-believe." Hugh grabbed the boy by the arm.

"He's not one of them. He's Ascorian, like us."

By this time, Jaks itched for his own escape from the building.

Too late.

A booming voice sounded from the shop below. "Krayas— you finished with the sod? Didn't find any more of them. Krayas? Ship's heading out. We gotta get back to the docks . . . Krayas?" Footsteps thumped the lower steps of the stairs.

"Follow us," Davey beckoned.

Footsteps at the top. He could stand and fight—in a narrow stairwell, he could electroshock easily—but the copious blood painted across the room dampened his enthusiasm to shed more. There had been enough violence today. Time to run away.

Hovering over a narrow alleyway, the balcony promised an ankle-breaking fall to the ground. The alternative was even less desirable: ancient vines climbing a wooden trellis.

"Come on, it's easy," Davey called down, peering over the copper spouting from the rooftop.

Thick though the vines looked, the trellis appeared dry and brittle.

"Fuck! What the hell happened here?" A tall Vor stood at the door, staring at the blood-splattered corpse.

Jaks had to jump or climb now. He gripped the woody vine strongly with his good hand but could only gain a tenuous grasp with the thumb and two good fingers of the other. Cursing his choices, he swung out and scrambled for footing on the trellis.

"Out there. Get him." The warrior began to squeeze through the balcony door as a second shadow appeared behind him.

As Jaks pulled himself onto the tiled roof, Davey grinned at him and scrambled up the sloped roof. Swearing and curses flew from below, but the Vors made no attempt to follow other than to rattle the trellis and vines.

For several vertiginous minutes, Jaks trailed the boys up and down cracked clay and over greened spouting, surrounded by brick chimneys and ever-higher rooftops. Eventually, he joined them, crouching atop a round parapet presiding over the district.

The river cut through the city below and tracked out to the distant river-mouth where the sun touched its brackish waters. Boats and ships continued their ferry work, and armed figures filtered through the main roads and boulevards. A haze of smoke blanketed the city on the opposite bank, but the fires and tall plumes of that morning were gone.

He had only visited Irin two times before, accompanying his mother, lead actress, and Karisa, child prodigy, as they toured the country with an acting troupe over a decade ago. This, the oldest city in the kingdom, and third largest—after Dunberrin and then Finstaf—contained buildings that were from an era of their own. Red-brick edifices with ornate wooden trimmings were sprinkled with towers, statues, and minarets. Jaks scanned the magnificent vista of manses and houses, and sadly reflected that stately, beautiful Irin had been subdued by a barbaric king.

"It's a princess, isn't it?" Davey craned his neck at Jaks as though wishing him to do something heroic right there.

"I came for my sister. She's no princess, but—"

"Family's everything. Our ma used to say, didn't she, Hugh? That's how I knew Hugh would come back for me. If we had a sister, we'd rescue her too—wouldn't we, Hughie?"

The older brother shrugged, staring at Jaks's deformed hand. "You climb pretty well for someone with that." He shuffled uneasily. "Thanks for rescuing Davey. We were just looking around the boats and they started chasing us. Bastards.

We're going to have to hide for a while. Hopefully, our food stash will last up."

"You should have fled the city with your parents last night," Jaks said.

Hugh laughed, and Davey's face drooped. "Our ma died a couple years ago, and our da . . . well, he left to dig diamonds," Hugh replied. "Nah, us lot run the streets—well, we did before today."

The brothers were street urchins, from a gang of orphans and runaways who had gravitated to this city of wealthy merchants to leech off the rich and fancy. A naïve few, like Hugh and Davey, remained despite the siege, thinking they could blend in just as they had before, and perhaps prosper from the chaos brought by the Vors. What they hadn't counted on was for the entire city evacuating and leaving the thieves with barely anything to steal—and little food to pilfer.

Jaks listened that evening to the anxious reports of nine scruffy boys and two girls in the stained-glassed loft of a long-abandoned and partially collapsed mansion a few blocks back from the docks.

"I heard from Winny about some turnips she says were left behind in Frothton's basement. Her lot took a heap, but there's still plenty that we can have," said their leader: eldest girl, Hanna. She was stick-thin, and if not for her voice and flat neck, Jaks would have thought her a boy ripe for conscription.

Unfortunately, she didn't like Jaks.

"Why did you bring him here?" she had demanded of Hugh and Davey when they brought him through the rooftop door as the sun set behind them. Although mollified by Davey's account of Jaks rescuing him from the Vor, she wouldn't look Jaks in the eye when she said, "He has to go in the morning."

Too tired to care how a common thief felt about him, he

sought some rest but dismissed the tattered mattresses and even more ragged-looking sofas, and slumped onto some cushions in a corner. Dozing, he half-listened to the urgent chatter of the youths about their encounters that day. It was several minutes later that his ears perked up when an older boy said something that triggered his attention.

"'. . . she was lovely as that statue outside Dor's Brothel,' I says to Dunny," a dark-headed youth, named Tim, was saying. "Then Dunny goes and yells at her, and everybody on the boat stares at us standing on the wall of the governor's palace. The lady and the other ladies was laughing, but the guards looked so pissed. When their boat gets to the dock, theys come after us."

"Wasn't my fault . . ." said the boy, presumably named Dunny.

"We start to run along the wall, but Dunny then goes and trips over. Feet caught in the vines, he's hanging upside down like a bat. The bastards below jumping up and down trying to grab him."

"Only fell because you were going too slow—"

"Then I see the lady bring her hands up in front of her eyes and suddenly it's like the sun landed in the middle of the governor's docks and I can't see anything, so I kneel down on top of the wall. When my eyes clear up, the lady has knifed one guard, and another is sinking into the river." The dark-haired boy continued with a grin across his face. "Two ladies chained at the neck run away through the palace gardens. But a couple other ladies just stay behind crying."

The other boy finished his friend's story. "Stupid here didn't help, so I pull myself back up, and the guards that're trying to get me see what's happening and go off after the runaways."

Jaks stood and towered within the loft. "This woman, this lady. Was she tall, like me? Slim? Did she have golden hair?" He advanced on the boy, Tim. Too aggressive—the boy and the other youths startled toward the windows and doors. "Sorry. I didn't mean to frighten you, but that lady—she could be my sister, Karisa."

He extracted more information from Tim and Dunny. Details of the slave woman and the illumancy attack convinced him it was Karisa: what other woman, so mesmerizing to men and boys, showed such daring while wrapped in nothing but silks? But despite the heartening sight, the encounter ended sadly with the two chained women recaptured on the street and forced back inside the palace.

"I bet they'll still be there," Tim said. He had quickly warmed to Jaks, like Davey, and was entranced with the idea of rescuing a damsel from an evil king.

Two accomplices for his quest. Maybe he did have a bit of Gilgat the Great in him?

"How brave are you lads?" Jaks placed his hands on Tim and Davey's shoulders and drew them in. "Here's what we're going to do."

Chapter 6

The Palace

From a rooftop nook, Jaks and his two young conspirators sheltered from the stinging weather and studied the governor's palace. Suspecting that Karisa was inside of it, they had to find out where.

Davey and Tim sought him out each day and brought turnips and keen eyes to help him locate his sister within the enormous building. He drank rainwater from jars he set on window ledges and slept in abandoned attics, never setting foot on the streets below, keeping to the "thieves' highway" and safe from confrontation.

Autumn had favored the Vor invasion, but days of hail and howling wind had now wintered down the invaders' advance and sent them into hibernation. The City of Irin was transformed into a Vor fortress as the invaders settled in: residential districts converted to barracks and slave quarters; open marketplaces to rallying grounds; and the fields outside its walls to roaming grounds for their massive gray monsters.

For three days now, they had changed vantage points,

straining for glimpses of life through the hundreds of windows in the palace.

"She must be in an inner room. I'm just going to have to go in," Jaks said to the boys one afternoon. The three of them huddled in the alcove of an ornate manse as the rain eased to a pitter-patter.

Davey roused from dozing against a gargoyle carved from stone. Impishly, the small boy yearned to break into the palace himself and wander the corridors and staircases—searching, he said, but probably more likely for food or valuables than for a human slave. He would often jiggle his legs and pick his nose when forced to sit still, so Jaks usually sent him to spy from various other windows, or trees in the neighboring park. Now, though, the mop-haired boy had had enough climbing for the day.

Tim, the pimply other boy, had at first seemed as air-headed as the younger, but Jaks discovered that beneath his idealism, he simmered with anger and sought retribution on the invaders of his beloved city: heroic revenge. Jaks's mission struck at the enemy king's treasures and seemed as good a cause as any to the youth.

"I'll come too," Tim and Davey said simultaneously.

"You're too little," the older boy said. "We can't have you to worry about."

"I'll look after myself."

Jaks folded his arms. "No. I'm going in alone. There are scores of guards in there. If I have to fight, I don't want you near me. However, I do need your help to get inside. Go home, get some rest, and I'll tell you my plan when you come back in the morning." Not for the first time, he wished for Vixhana's powers, desperately. As a shadow, he could have simply leaped into a window and flitted through the hallways until he got to Karisa and then escaped just as easily.

Later that evening, after the boys had returned to their gang hideout, Jaks climbed through the attic window into his nightly hideaway. He extracted the wrist communicator from behind his chest piece and strapped it to his wrist. It chilled his skin as though stealing his heat. After a second, the alien artifact hummed alive, and offered its inner electrical pathways as it had several times before.

He sat for hours absorbed within it: following, exploring, and changing channels and corridors for no reason other than marveling in finding out how it worked.

Eventually, he reached out for the patterns of Meila's communication device with his electromancer sense. There was no response. Was she too busy to answer? Although she didn't respond to his initiating signal, Jaks smiled on discovering that he could access her device through his own.

This time, he explored the inner workings of Meila's communicator. He infiltrated the device's storage space and found recordings of recent transmissions—not to him but to yet another device, a third communicator device.

Playing through the stored transmissions, Jaks felt a twinge of guilt, as though spying on her through a window. And well he should, because the bearer of the third device was none other than King Silas, monarch of Ascoria.

The communications were military and political: often Meila relaying messages for an advisor such as Grandmaster Mulgrave, or some other military official from Dunberrin, to the king. An apt messenger, she and the king seemed to have an easy relationship at first. The messages themselves meant little to Jaks but conveyed a picture of sound strategies that seemed to fall apart at the last minute. What should have been decisive military strikes or defenses were repeatedly subordinated by the Vors with always greater maneuvers or deceit.

But as the messages progressed, and the war had continued against him, the king's paranoia had sharpened to an edge, and he had—as of a few days ago—banned any further communication of strategic information using the device on suspicion that their transmissions were being intercepted. Indeed, Meila had barely escaped a return to prison on a charge of leaking secrets to the enemy. In the last transmission, only Mulgrave's directly spoken promises and pleadings to the king had kept her out of severe incarceration.

Playing the recorded messages, Jaks succumbed to an odd longing while he watched Meila. That opinionated, hard-willed woman had some hold over him that he couldn't stifle.

"Jaks." Meila's image materialized in front of him, startling him out of his thoughts.

"I was just trying to contact you." He sat upright and drank in her features. Raven hair tied back, she wore a tan tunic open at the neck. Her surroundings placed her in one of the Academy's workshops. Benches groaned under machinery and gadgets, and forges clanged in the background.

"Are you alright? I heard that Irin fell in the last battle. Last I heard from you, you were spouting off some nonsense about infiltrating the Vors—"

"I have. I'm in hiding opposite the palace where I think Karisa is being held. Trying to find a way to rescue her."

"What palace?" Her eyes widened. "You're in Irin? Is that where you are?"

"Yes, but I think the Vor king is in residence and the place is heavily defended."

"Oh, God, Jaks. It's far too dangerous. You can't risk getting caught. Get out of that city. I need you here at the Academy."

"She's so close. I can feel her nearby. Some boys from a local gang saw her just a few days ago." Jaks thought the words rather than spoke them. *Still works. Best to keep silence.* He recalled the dull thuds and muffled voices that had trickled up to his ears from deep in the building earlier that evening. There might be a few people stationed below. Officials, officers?

"What boys? Never mind, you'll never get into a fortified building with the Vor king inside. Do you really think you can just skip on in and steal his prized concubine?"

Blood rose to Jaks's cheeks, and he spoke out loud. "She didn't choose to be where she is. She's clamped in irons and chains. I didn't come this far to run away now." His anger dissipated as he remembered Meila's husband had been in a similar situation.

"I'm sorry, Jaks. I know you feel responsible for her, but you and I have had terrible results from attempted rescues . . ."

"I rescued you in the forest."

"This is on a whole different level compared to two thugs in the forest." Meila frowned. "Look, I need you. *We* need you. Your electromancy may be the last chance we have to fight off the Vors. I have a velocannon ready, but we don't have a strong enough power source—we don't have you."

"I'm not turning back now," he repeated, biting his lip, remembering to only think the words this time.

"You're doing that thing again." Meila's image stilled for so long that he wondered whether his device had broken, but then she continued. "Alright, if you're being so stubborn about it, I'll send you some help."

"Huh?"

"You think you have the correct building, but you don't know where she is precisely inside?"

He transmitted a silent *yes.*

"I'll send you some eyes. A droid. Do you remember those eggs that we salvaged from the *Mendhelsson?*"

"Eggs? I didn't know they were eggs."

"They're not actual eggs, you idiot. They're Hammond-Zhang Droids. I call them zingers. I'll send one to you." Meila walked to a drawer in a workbench and held up an oval-shaped gray object that she had correctly described as the size of a chicken's egg.

The device sprang up into the air in front of her and hovered. A small fin popped out of the top and two round discs folded out of its front. A flying metal fish.

"You control it with the comm device." She showed Jaks by flitting and jigging the zinger around the workshop. "You need to place your wrist on a flat surface, like a table or desk, and the control panel will open up from its lateral port. You use your other hand to maneuver it and activate its functions."

"But why?"

"It can see through walls, amongst other things. You'll be able to fly it over the palace and see whether Karisa is actually there. And if she isn't, promise me you'll leave the city and come back to the Academy."

"But how are you going to get it here?" The zinger sounded useful, but not if he had to go back to Dunberrin to retrieve it.

"I'll send the droid to you. I'll transfer an Ascorian language file to it first. Then, it'll take . . ." Her eyes flicked up for a second. ". . . four hours and seven minutes, give or take, depending on the wind and weather. It's designed for planetary atmospheric studies, so it's made for traveling long distances. In fact, that's all it's for, really; its sensor and sampling array is pretty basic compared to some of the other droids we had."

An hour later, satisfied with her instructions to Jaks, she rubbed her eyes and yawned. "Been up two days straight. I need a few hours to rejuve. Let me know what you're going to do before you do it." With that, the zinger droid sped out of the workshop, and Meila disconnected her comm, leaving Jaks alone in the attic.

Sometime later, Jaks awoke to a presence in the attic. Too dark to see anything except the frame of the open window. Then something hovered above him; his electromancy sensed an oval object glimmering in his magical eye, dense with silver and gold. *Has it been four hours already?*

He sat up and grasped the flying device in his hands. Like the wrist comm, it chilled his skin to touch. Jaks examined the device under the moonlight at the window. The same gray metal as Meila's ship, a similar ovoid shape except for the dorsal fin and two eyes that seemed to return his stare. *It looks curious. Does it blink?*

He frowned. Meila had said something about giving it orders. He delved into the droid's electrical interior and lost himself to his magical senses as the device lay in his hands. Vastly more sophisticated than the wrist comm, many pathways and compartments made no sense to his naïve brain, and he withdrew confused and astounded—the device seemed alive.

"Standby. Awaiting instruction," the zinger messaged into his thoughts.

"Fly around the room," Jaks whispered. It flew a circuit of the room so quickly he barely registered its movement.

Touching the droid's cold exterior, he repeated the instruction wordlessly, activating the device's circuitry through his electromancy. Again, it darted around the dark attic, dodging the pile of furniture atop the trapdoor leading to the lower floors.

Next, Jaks manipulated the wrist-comm device with his powers. Far more effective: he could control the droid directly.

And in addition, by doing so, he found he could look through the droid's eyes. Amazed, he saw an overhead view of his body, unconscious on the attic floor—a quick lesson that diverting his mind to the zinger rendered him senseless to anything but the device's sensors.

With electromancy, he didn't need the control panel as Meila had; instead, he could communicate with the droid through the wrist comm as though controlling an extra eye—an incredible one that could fly around and spy.

Dawn light filtered through the window when Meila interrupted him from his experimentation with the zinger. Her image materialized in front of him, refreshed but for her mussed hair.

She quirked an eyebrow. "Well? Have you found her yet?"

"I haven't sent it out yet. I've never used this thing before, remember."

"You're not using the control panel? Damn. What I'd give for that ability. Mental manipulation of tech."

"At least it's useful for something other than just killing people," Jaks said.

"Here, let me . . . the building over the avenue? Impressive-looking place." Meila had her arm planted on a desk in what looked like the grandmaster's library.

The zinger droid sped out the window. Jaks closed his eyes and followed the device's path through its sensors. Mind-locked to the droid, his forehead bumped down against the attic floor as his body fell senseless.

"I'm switching to a gamma scan. Then we can look inside for biologicals."

Jaks's mind reeled as images returning from the zinger swirled and distorted. Colors vanished and the facade of the palace building dissolved into a depth of grays and whites. He cast his thoughts to Meila. *"How can there be so many people in there?"*

"If it's the Vor king's residence, you don't think it'd just be him and a few women to keep him entertained, do you?" Her voice sounded in his mind, but his vision remained focused through the zinger. "Also, some guard dogs."

Jaks grimaced. *"Only way they can detect nightwraiths."* Even so, Vixhana would still have had far better chances of infiltrating this place than him, judging by the number of soldiers he would have to elude.

"I'd say most of those we're seeing are guards, although many on the lower floors are probably servants. I don't know what your sister looks like, but if we sweep through the building, tell me if you see anyone who resembles her, and we can focus in on the face."

"How about you let me have the droid back? It's easier for me to see if I'm controlling it," he said.

He directed the droid in a circuit of the palace, achingly slow, stopping to zoom in on tall, slender figures, not that there were many of them, and the ones he saw—each time his heart lurching in hope—were all strangers.

"Get an angle from inside the courtyard," Meila said. "We'll get a better view of the inner rooms."

Jaks soared over the five-storied palace and into the central garden. Nausea rolled in his gullet for a moment but was soon replaced by exhilaration. *"It's like I'm flying. Is this what it's like in your ship?"*

Meila laughed but didn't reply. "Hover in the branches of those trees there. Best to keep hidden as much as possible." A bird fluttered from a tree as the device descended into the leafless branches.

The palace was well awake now. The bottom floor,

especially the kitchen, teemed with figures, while the grand hall was busy with servants and guards. And in a chamber on the third floor, yet another gathering assembled. All the while, dozens of armed silhouettes roamed or sentried the building. But it was on scanning the top floor, in a room overlooking the gardens facing the river, that Jaks thought a triumphant, *Yes!*

"It must be her. I need to get closer." Within a few seconds, Jaks had the droid hovering outside the balcony window, peering through a slit between closed curtains. Could he make the droid talk if he could get close enough? Inside the room, two figures lay side by side. Although he couldn't see furniture well with the droid's special vision, he guessed they lay on a bed.

"Is it her?" Meila asked.

Jaks studied the angular face, turned toward the window. Her eyes still closed, she breathed steadily, as did her female companion behind her. A gem-encrusted collar connected to an iron chain tethered her to a granite column at the center of the ornate bedroom. His heart skipped a beat as his sister's features resolved in the faint morning light and his shuttered eyes squeezed out tears.

It was her. He had found Karisa.

"Can I talk through this?" He directed the thought to Meila.

"No, it doesn't generate sound."

"What about a light?"

Activating the droid's light beam, Meila highlighted the internal pathway for Jaks's attention.

Directing the zinger's light through the part in the curtain, he focused the beam on Karisa's closed eyelids. He switched the light on and off several times.

Her face crinkled, and she rolled away from the light.

Not giving up, Jaks directed the beam to the back of her

companion's head and weaved it around, hoping the moving light would wake his sister.

A minute later, Karisa stirred again and lifted her head as though watching the bright dot weaving over the bed.

With one hand grasping the chain dangling from her neck, she sat up in the bed and turned to the window.

"I'll try some basic signaler's code." Jaks directed the beam to her chest—too bright to shine in her eyes—and flashed the droid's light in a sequence that he racked his memory to recall.

J . . . A . . . K . . . S.

Was that right? Would she realize the short and long flashes were a code?

Karisa squinted, as though confused. She walked to the curtain, her slave chain taut by the time she reached an arm to pull the fold aside. She stared in astonishment at the device with silver eyes flying outside her window.

Again, Jaks flashed the signaler's sequence at her, hoping he was doing it right. At the same time, a few distant thumps registered on the edges of his hearing. Something out of sight of the droid's vision—unimportant.

Her astonishment turned to surprise. She mouthed something back to the droid through the glass. It looked like she was saying his name. "Jaks?"

Another face appeared beside her to stare at the device; a shorter, buxom woman, wrapped in similar colored silks. The two women looked at each other and back to the zinger and spoke energetically.

He watched as Karisa stretched out a hand toward the droid. The chain around her neck kept the window latches out of her grasp. She then held up her palm and illumanced a light at the droid. **J.A.K.S.**, she signaled back his sequence, and then mouthed his name again—but instead of her voice, he heard a boy's. It sounded familiar, but not Karisa's.

"Jaks!" a boy's voice cried out again.

And then pain. His eyes flicked open.

The attic was full of people.

Chapter 7

The Thieves' Highway

Jaks grunted and rolled to his side, dazed as he transitioned back to his surroundings. A shadow stood over him, the whites of its eyes menaced him, and a huge paw reached down to grab his arm.

"Stay down or I kick you again, fucking roof rat. Got you now," the shadow yelled at him. A Vor voice. *How did they get up here?*

The attic door, inlaid with the floor, gaped open. The piled furniture he had thought would hold it down was shoved aside. Their hideout had been discovered.

"Jaks," Davey shouted. It must have been he who had yelled before. The boy was standing half out of the attic window. The older boy, Tim, had a hand on Davey's shoulder, looking as though trying to pull him along. They must have arrived while Jaks was senseless. Before or after the Vors pushed their way up through the attic door?

A second shadow stomped past Jaks, boot barely missing his head in the narrow room. "Come on, lads. We're not going to hurt you. Just want to talk." The shadow stepped into the light streaming through the window and revealed a greasy-haired man trying to sculpt a reassuring smile despite a mouthful of rotten teeth.

The hand clasping Jaks yanked him to his feet, aggravating the stabbing pain in his ribs. He cried out as his captor, a heavyset warrior, ripped open his collar and exposed the Ascorian conscript brand high on his arm. "A spy. Thought so," the warrior said in the guttural tones of Vorosian.

An open palm smacked him across the face, and Jaks fell stunned to the floor.

Angry voices, deafening in the attic, shouted and yelled at each other, and stirred Jaks out of his mind fog.

Thumps and thwacks of a frantic struggle threw chaos into the confined space.

Jaks pushed himself up on his arms, but a body bounced against him and knocked him back down. Wetness splashed his face.

"Fucking runt stabbed me." Greasy Hair said as he clutched at his bleeding leg. He pulled himself up and staggered into a corner of the attic.

Little Davey trembled at the other end of the attic, brandishing a thin stiletto blade that looked as long as a sword in his small hand.

Tim stood behind him, also flashing steel but displaying annoyance rather than the obvious fear of the younger boy. "Shit, why'd you do that? Come on, Davey, we got to get out of here."

"No." The mop-headed boy continued to bear up his stall at the two Vor warriors. "Jaks needs us."

The heavyset warrior rounded on the two street urchins. His bulk dominated the triangular room, and a shortsword

appeared in his hand. "You're the little runt that face-planted the wall the other day. You're too small to have killed Krayas . . . was it your bumtoad here who killed him?"

"Kill him, Stug. The fucker stabbed me. Just kill all three of them," the injured Vor said.

Fear paralyzed Jaks. He couldn't risk a lightning bolt. Tim and Davey were too near; a lethal invocation could kill the swordsman, who was an easy target with his back to Jaks, but could as easily transmit through him and kill the boys as well. It had to be a shocking touch, hopefully stunning the man until he could draw his own sword to stab him. Restraining the electromancy was the hardest part.

"Put down your knitting needle, boy." The Vor named Stug dipped his sword tip under Davey's nose and grinned as the stiletto blade fell from the boy's trembling fingers. Neither boy understood what he had said in Vorosian, but they understood his meaning. "You, too, bumtoad." The sword moved toward Tim.

Jaks reached out with his good hand, dimly aware that the other Vor was shuffling up against the wall behind him. Grabbing the left leg of the swordsman above his boot, he dampened his fear with thoughts of angrily stabbing the man to death and then invoked a jolt of lightning to his fingertips.

"What the fuck?" The swordsman kicked away from Jaks's grasp. Underpowered, the jolt had merely stung the warrior. Half-turning to look down at Jaks, he said to the wounded Vor, "Finish the spy. We'll keep these other two."

Jaks rolled onto his back to look up at the greasy-haired Vor. A fresh wave of panic urged Jaks to retaliate as harshly as he could. Electrocute these damn Vors to a crisp. No, he couldn't. Davey and Tim were still too close.

Greasy Hair snarled and flourished a long knife. He bent

down on his good knee, one hand tipping Jaks's chin to expose his neck as though to shave his beard; however, the tip angling toward his throat told otherwise. "Hold still. Won't take long."

Jaks grabbed the attacker's wrists. His crippled fingers were weak around the man's knife-hand wrist, but his good hand grappled the man's other hand away from his chin. The evil tip of the blade wavered over him in the struggle—

The knife plunged through the outer part of his left shoulder, piercing skin and muscle. Jaks screamed in agony.

As it had done only a few times before, his power surged to his defense without thought.

Boom! A lightning blast launched Jaks's attacker upward and threw him against the tiles of the slanted wall and breached a hole through the roof. Slate fragments clattered through the attic and light poured through the shattered lining.

The Vor lay broken across the gap; he twitched for a few moments and then went still.

The pain in Jaks's shoulder forced his attention to the knife impaled there. He grabbed his arm below the wound and groaned.

Pain clouded his vision, but out of the corner of his eye, he saw the remaining Vor, still with his back to Jaks, suddenly drop to the floor with a thud.

A small, gray ovoid object clattered to the wood next to the swordsman's head. The zinger droid. Had it attacked the Vor?

Davey's small face appeared over Jaks. "Don't die! You can't die." He stared at the knife.

Voices shouted from below.

More Vors on the way. They had to get away from here, but he couldn't bear to move with the steel in his shoulder. Jaks knew from his conscript training that he should wait for a trained medic to remove the knife—someone who could stifle the torrent of blood that might follow. However, more warriors were coming for them, and he needed to run and maneuver to escape. Wild movements would grossly widen the knife wound —especially if he knocked the blade or handle. The risk of worsening the injury by extracting it now was less than stumbling with it in place. Besides, even now, the slightest movements were like shards of glass grinding in his arm.

"You've got to pull it out of me, Davey," Jaks said, staring into the boy's terrified eyes.

Davey wrapped trembling hands around the handle and hesitated.

"Pull it. You can do it," Jaks said, gasping between the words.

His shoulder lifted slightly as the boy heaved on the weapon and rolled onto his backside with the effort of pulling out the knife. Jaks let out an involuntary yell at the spear of agony.

He clapped his hand to the shoulder wound, squeezing blood through his fingers despite the pain. Thankfully, the blood seeped rather than gushed. Gritting his teeth, he staggered to his feet.

"Come on, Davey. We've got to go. Through the hole." Jaks flicked his head toward the jagged opening he had blasted. It would be faster than running to the window, where Tim had already disappeared.

Davey scampered over the dead Vor and out the makeshift escape route, slowing only to tear off the man's coin pouch—too much of a temptation for the little thief to resist even in the height of danger.

A steel-helmeted woman's head popped up through the attic door opening. "Crap, Stug. What a mess." The new Vor planted her elbows on the attic floor and pulled herself up.

Too pained to focus an invocation—although it would have

been an ideal opportunity to take her down, without either boy in the way—Jaks squeezed himself through the opening behind Davey.

Tim was on all fours beside Davey on the sloped slate roof. The two boys pulled on Jaks as he clambered up to join them.

Thankfully, the slope ended in a gutter that joined with the adjacent building rather than a steep drop to the road below. The gutter gave them a flat surface to follow. In fact, knowing the rooftops as well as Tim and Davey did, a thief could travel for entire blocks of buildings without pause.

Under a clear morning sky, Jaks scrambled after the fleeing boys as fast as his damaged body could take him.

Minutes later, the helmeted Vor climbed up onto the roof after them.

Jaks's neck itched under her glare. When he dared a glance back, he swore as several more warriors appeared next to her. He had hoped all Vors were as phobic of heights as he had been —before those months of crisscrossing the Jurns' rope bridges— however, these ones seemed to have no fear of the vertiginous terrain. They followed Jaks and the boys, slowly but steadily.

"They're chasing us," Davey shouted. He had a habit of stating the obvious.

Slate to clay tiles, sloped and flat roofs, around chimney stacks and lightning rods, Jaks climbed and shuffled as Tim led them across the Thieves' Highway.

The wind felt fresh and the sun warm on his face after the confines of the attic; however, there was no time to appreciate it in this snail-and-slug pursuit.

He would have laughed at how ridiculous their pursuers looked—lumbering warriors swearing and cursing as they slipped on and cracked tiles underfoot—if the stakes had not been so serious. Blood oozed between his fingers, and every movement clouded his mind. At that moment, he wished he had some of Meila's pain-dulling pills.

In a mere three-quarters of a mile, the buildings changed from majestic mansions of minor nobility and wealthy merchants to workers' lodges and boarding houses that teetered upward like children's blocks. Each floor slapped haphazardly on top of the last, with little thought to aesthetic or safety.

"In here. No one's lived here for years. It's condemned," Tim said, dropping to a rickety balcony that creaked under his weight.

It was clear why the building was uninhabited. It was so poorly constructed that misaligned floorboards gaped wide while rotted ones bent underfoot of even the malnourished boys.

"Can't stop here. They would've seen where we went," Jaks said, despite wanting to pause to apply some first-aid to his bleeding.

"Careful, the stairs here have collapsed in places. I'll lead. Follow in my footsteps," Tim said and took to the poorly constructed stairs.

One flight down and Jaks stared through a raw hole where the steps had collapsed in a fragmented mess to the flight below.

Foot over foot, he reached for jagged remains of the steps jutting out from the wall. His head spun and vertigo flared for a moment. He froze and breathed deep breaths for precious seconds while he recovered his nerve.

Deep voices sounded from the top floor, where they had been minutes before. A sharp crack was followed by voluminous swearing. Would the heavy-footed oofs dare this death-trap? No sooner had the thought framed in his head than a plate-sheaved leg crashed through the ceiling above. The steel-capped boot on the end of the foot dangled pathetically as its owner cursed, and rotted wood thunked around Jaks's head.

"Keep going," Tim called to Jaks, from where he stood on the landing below.

The leg pulled up and out of the hole, and a face glowered back down. "Damn runts. Stay where you are," the woman yelled at him.

Jaks breathed in relief as he made the last step and joined Tim on the landing.

"Look out!" Tim cried out and pushed Jaks to the side.

Thud. A wooden shaft quivered in the floor where Jaks had been standing. The vanes of a crossbow bolt glistened green and brown. His gaze flew to the hole where the warrior's leg had smashed through. A pair of eyes peered through it over an expended crossbow.

"There's an entrance to the sewers in the courtyard. Let's go." Tim pushed Jaks toward Davey, who was already fleet-footing down the next flight of stairs.

The last two sets of stairs groaned threateningly as they continued their descent, but eventually released them to the ground floor with nothing more than a few blisters from gripping the railings too hard.

"Do you think they're still chasing us?" Davey stared up the staircase.

Jaks listened for a few seconds, but what voices he heard were remote. "They're persistent, but I don't think they're coming down this way. They'll probably look for another way down. It'll give us time to get some distance. Where are these sewers?"

They stumbled out of a doorless entrance into a courtyard. In a distant past, the square space might have been filled with carefree voices of children circling the tree at its center;

however, the only residents now were lizards and crawlers, and the only things that grew on the skeletal tree were cobwebs.

Tim shuffled along the wall to the bush-covered northeast corner of the courtyard. When Jaks joined him, the boy pointed down at a stone-lined hole edged with brown algae and slime.

"Davey, you go first. I'll go last," the older boy said. The smaller boy slid down the sewer hole as Jaks looked on with open disgust. "It's not so bad down there. Use the holes in the side as you go down."

Jaks wanted to clutch his shoulder to prevent it from scraping the sludge, but he needed his good arm to climb. He gulped and swung his legs into the hole, poking his foot around for purchase. Although his boot found the first hole, the next failed and his planned descent turned into an uncontrolled slide. He yelped in panic and landed with a splash. Pain shot through his buttocks and shoulder all at once, and he lay in the ankle-deep water, not daring to move.

A presence brushed up to him in the narrow tunnel. "Are you alright?" Davey asked, barely visible in the semidarkness.

"I'm okay." When the pain subsided, he palpated his legs and was relieved to find no lasting injuries. A broken ankle would have been disastrous. "Let's go," he gasped. His strength was fading. He needed to rest, but Tim dropped down beside him and urged him along.

"Not here. We have to keep moving," the youth said.

The sewers wormed away in every direction: stone tunnels and drains filtered away the city's filth and kept it from drowning in the storms. If he had been alone, Jaks was sure he would've been lost within minutes. Fortunately, Davey was as knowledgeable of the network beneath the city as he was of the one above it, and he led them without faltering for over an hour. From time to time, marching boots or coarse Vor voices echoed from above, but they encountered no one and nothing other than the occasional scuttlebug or rat.

"We need somewhere to stop for a while. I have to tend to my arm," Jaks said eventually, guessing that they were nearing the river. The air was brisker here, and a seagull cawed through an iron grate overhead.

"Almost there," Davey replied over his shoulder. "This is the timberyard. It has the best hideaways. It's huge."

Indeed, he was not exaggerating.

The three fugitives scanned the expansive timberyard from atop a long wall. Their tunnel had opened out to a walled stone channel that sloped down to the main river some yards distant. From there, they had climbed green-stained steps to their current observation point.

The timberyard stretched a mile along the riverside, right up to the outer city wall. At its busiest, Jaks imagined it would have been a miniature town within the city. Hundreds of workers, ant-like, would have unloaded logs from river barges, cut and prepared planks in deafening sawing sheds, and swung them on cranes to their store piles. At the moment, thankfully, the complex of buildings and yards was as still and silent as a graveyard.

"I think they took most of the wood to the south city to build up the walls and barricades," Tim postulated after Jaks remarked at how little lumber there was around. "But even before that, they say the yard was low on logs trying to supply the army's weapon smiths and armorers. The foresters couldn't keep up."

"To the big storehouse?" Davey fidgeted as he quizzed the older boy.

"The old bargehouse is better. It has running water, and there might be some dried fish hanging up there."

Several minutes later, Jaks stood at the door of a sturdy bargehouse. The wooden building stood low over the water on heavy columns, with its rear section resting on solid ground. He stopped at the entrance, his gaze drawn out to the river. Anchored ships and boats bobbed against the current but showed little life onboard except the occasional guard. The city bridge, arcing from south to north, on the other hand, teemed with activity; even at this great distance, light glinted off shields and blades under the late-morning sun.

Shoulders slumped, he entered the building. A refuge. But was it a place to recoup for another rescue attempt, or a place to launch an escape from the city?

Chapter 8

The Bargehouse

In the bargehouse, a walkway surrounded three boats and two flat barges floating in the middle of the building. At the top of a ramp, out of the water, another barge rested on wooden supports. A pair of river gates, lower edges rotted, were all that separated the building's wet-space from the river.

Empty workbenches lined the walls of a workshop that filled the dry end of the building. Loops of hessian rope lay in coils whilst others stretched across the ceiling, from which hung dried husks of cod and trout.

It was a good space to recoup and decide what to do next.

With a sense of relief, Jaks walked to the solid ground of the workshop and sat cross-legged before peeling off his leather tunic to examine his shoulder wound. Pain returned afresh as the adrenaline rush of escape faded.

Davey stared at Jaks and wrung his hands, while Tim paced about the walkway.

Blood clots and smears obscured the wound. Although it was less alarming without the knife sticking through, he couldn't trust that it would heal without further treatment. It could fester. Vixhana had told him about a dragon handler she knew that died several weeks after one of his beasts nipped his wrist. Infection had set in and they didn't amputate his arm in time. If only Meila were here; he needed her able hands, miraculous bandages, and pain-dulling pills.

As if his thoughts had summoned her, the wrist communicator vibrated against his skin and a yellow light swirled around the disc edge. He electromanced the device with the tiniest of invocations, barely requiring a thought, and accepted the connection.

An image of Meila's annoyed face materialized, hovering over the comm. "You've got to stop giving me such frights. I saw what happened after I flew the zinger back to your attic," she said.

"I'm sorry, I thought the attic was secure with the furniture holding the door down—"

"Clearly, it wasn't." After a pause, her voice softened. "You have to get out of that damned city. It's far too dangerous to carry on with this fool's task. I got the droid back into the air after I used it to knock that warrior in the head. And I can tell you, there are hundreds of Vors searching the buildings and rooftops around the palace after that fiasco. Guards have doubled. Your sister isn't getting out of there any time soon, even with your help."

"I've got to try again." Jaks's stubbornness persisted, even though he knew the truth of her words.

"You tried, and you have to accept you've failed. Come back to the Academy and we'll win this damn war. And *then* we can rescue Karisa. She's probably as safe there as anywhere." Then, as a consolation, she added, "At least you know she's alive."

He chewed on his lip. He'd discovered his sister's prison but couldn't get near it. Frustration tore at him like clashing tides. Damn the Vors who'd found his hiding spot.

A minute later, air swished through a cracked window high up in the bargehouse. The zinger darted inside, its owl-like eyes homing in on Tim and Davey. The boys squealed in panic and took refuge behind the dry-docked barge.

Jaks laughed despite it aggravating his shoulder pain and called out to the boys, "Don't worry. It's not dangerous."

"This is the gang you were talking about? They're just children. Where are their parents?" Meila asked.

"They're orphans," he said, then grimaced in renewed pain.

"Jaks, I didn't realize you were wounded. What happened?" She maneuvered the zinger to hover by his shoulder. The boys crept back to Jaks and ogled the flying wonder.

Jaks described the desperate fight in the attic to her, what little he remembered of the chaos. Although she had observed part of the standoff through the zinger's sensors—after she had flown it there to investigate his abrupt communication loss—the zinger had shut down temporarily after smashing into the Vor's head.

"No telling how deep it is with these scanners. The zingers aren't designed for wound analysis. Pity we didn't recover a medical droid. Anyway, you need to open it up and wash it out." She fumbled about her workshop bench and drew out a second droid identical to the other. "These zingers have a compartment we usually use for drawing environmental samples. Let me see if I can fit a gel bandage inside and fly it to you. It'll take a few hours, like last time. Stay put."

Her image blinked out.

"I need some water and rags for this, boys," Jaks said, clutching his arm below the oozing shoulder wound. He'd be lucky if anything were remotely clean here, let alone approvable by a real healer.

"I'll find a bucket." Davey padded off to search the workshop.

"I'll look for some rags," Tim said, heading for stairs leading up to a second level of the building.

Jaks blinked away a tear at the boys' loyalty; the bond bought on the promise of heroism was shattered, but persevered now in friendship. An even more valuable attachment, given the help he needed.

His thoughts drifted back to Karisa. She had been so close, just a glass pane away. He fought further tears at the memory of her face, beautiful even without her illusions, and of seeing her shackled by the neck like a common criminal. They had connected through the droid: she had recognized his signal and responded. So close.

He kicked his heel in frustration against the side of a nearby boat, rocking it on its supports. In this wounded state, he couldn't climb, couldn't fight effectively, and couldn't attempt any semblance of a rescue. But could he hide here until his shoulder was healed enough to try again?

The boys returned with water and rags, and despite their squeamishness, they helped Jaks clean his wound. Davey pried the skin edges apart while Tim tipped water from the bucket into the wound.

Stars circled Jaks as the pain ravaged his arm. With gritted teeth, he watched the bloodied water wash away. When it ran clear, he grunted for Tim to stop.

Tim handed him a ragged piece of sailing cloth he had found in an upstairs room and helped Jaks crudely wrap his shoulder. Hopefully, Meila's second zinger droid would arrive soon with her miracle bandage. The last one had saved his hand;

if this one had similar effect, his shoulder would be healed in just a few weeks—or even just a few days. They could stay holed up here in the meantime and then make another attempt to rescue Karisa. He perked up at the thought and even forced a smile for Tim and Davey.

"Thanks, boys, you've been good to me. You're real heroes in my eyes," he said, eliciting a grin from both.

Remembering a sentinel function that had intrigued him during his previous explorations of the zinger's internal circuits, Jaks glided his hand over the droid's sleek fin and activated the pathway to *guard and watch*, centered above the bargehouse for any intruder larger than a mouse. The metal owl turned and flew back out the cracked upper window. It glowed green around the disc edge and would continue to do so as long as the perimeter remained "safe." It boggled his mind to think of how anyone, even Meila, could create something so incredible.

He frowned, remembering her comment from months ago, about her people following after her—that she was just the first of an entirely new colony. If they controlled such powerful artifacts, like this droid and the darkcore weapons, was this war just a roach fight before the victor was squashed by an invasion of invincible flying machines? He shook the thought out of mind. Regardless of the distant future, it didn't change his resolve or immediate goals. Life could not stop because of ifs and maybes.

Tim had chosen well. The old bargehouse was an ideal hideout. Jaks learned that, except to dry fish, it was long disused since two newer, larger bargehouses had been built further upriver. The only things left upstairs, where a couple of boat-repairers once dwelt, were damaged sails, dirty mattresses, mugs, rat traps, candles, matches, and a single laceless boot. Boys and girls from the street gang would occasionally visit to "borrow" dried fish and sometimes hide if chased from other thieving activities around the timberyard.

Jaks sat restlessly as he waited for the other droid that Meila had sent, imagining it flying across the plains at tremendous speed.

"I wonder if Hughie is okay," Davey said, as daylight dimmed outside, obviously worried about his older brother. "He was going to check out some of the travelers' inns today. Yesterday, he scavenged a bag of dried mushrooms and reckoned there could be more stuff around there. He was mad at me 'cause I kept coming to help you and said I wasn't doing my share."

Tim, the older boy, was asleep upstairs—the morning's escape had taxed him to exhaustion. So, it was up to Jaks to reassure the younger boy. He shot him a smile and ruffled his mop-like hair.

"Let's check on him, shall we? I'm sure he's okay," said Jaks. He flicked an electromantic instruction to the zinger, via the wrist device, and sent it skimming toward the gang's den, a mile and a half away through the evening sky, and angled the projection of the wrist-comm image for both of them to see.

The zinger arrived in less than a minute. If only he himself could fly like this, his quest would be over in minutes. He would fly into the palace window, grab his sister, then return to Dunberrin in hours . . . but all Jaks could do was sigh in envy of birds and dragons.

Outside the old mansion, he instructed the droid to circle and survey the building. It was oddly bereft of activity. He had expected some activity on the top floor at least; however, only one human-sized biological object inhabited the building. But staring at the gamma scan returning through the wrist comm, it looked like nothing he had seen before.

The droid zipped to the balcony doors at Jaks's command. Heart pounding, he realized the twin doors lay shattered and broken. He switched the scan to regular vision and activated its light beam. He wished he hadn't.

Davey gasped and whimpered beside him.

Transfixed by the zinger's image-feed display, Jaks felt his breath freeze in his throat.

The object was a streak of blood. A dark rivulet smeared the floor and ended at a pair of glowing red eyes. Rat eyes reflecting the light.

The vile creature was hunched on the chest of a body. It stared into the light for a moment, then leaped away and scurried into a dark corner. A dagger protruded from the body's neck. The slender neck of Hanna, the leader of the gang.

The zinger continued its survey of the room. Blankets torn from cots were strewn about. Shelves, once laden with the gang's loot and forage, lay askew with their contents scattered over the floor. Bloodied boot prints, too large for any of the youths, tracked out of the balcony doors. There had been a struggle here. Hanna hadn't gone out without a fight.

"They killed her." Davey sniffed and ran a sleeve across his face.

Jaks wrapped his arm around Davey and held him close. "Well, Hughie's not there. He might be alright." He couldn't be sure, though. The mess around the room looked far more than just one orphan's fight. "I'll search around for any sign of the others."

The droid circled widely for a couple of hours, gamma scanner penetrating buildings, searching for survivors.

Disappointingly, Jaks could only conclude that the Vors had brutally combed out all the buildings in the palace's vicinity. No sign of Hughie, the street gang, or any free civilians whatsoever—only dead ones and a few dozen chained up in a warehouse by the docks.

It was true, what Meila had said. Around the palace, troops garrisoned every building, inside, outside, and on rooftops. Guards manned nascent barricades blocking the streets, and several neighboring buildings were being pulled down for materials—it appeared that gravmancers were even better at demolition than construction. Anything to separate this fortified area from intruders. They might even dig a ditch and flood it for a moat, Jaks mused. The Vor king had reacted strongly to discovering a spy so close to his residence. The chances of rescuing Karisa were bleak.

One last sweep of the palace took the zinger back to the courtyard, even though it was dark now. He had to know.

Again, the droid hovered outside the curtained room that was Karisa's prison and revealed the inhabitants of the room, but only the buxom slave woman from that morning was present.

As he squinted at the wrist comm, about to instruct the droid to scan the rest of the palace for Karisa, the image feed spun wildly and then blacked out.

A few seconds later, the image returned, revealing a sleek head and talons raking the zinger's sensors.

"Damn. A dragon attacked the zinger," Jaks said to Davey, but the boy, distraught after seeing his gang leader dead and left to the rats, was curled at his feet on a thin mattress and sucking his thumb, eyes closed.

The wrist-comm image flashed a red light and strange letters appeared. And then, just as he was fearing the droid had been destroyed, the images revealed the zinger speeding upward, faster than any dragon could fly, directly toward the night sky—as though escaping into the stars.

A minute later, he sighed with relief as the droid continued skyward without further attack. As it pivoted its sensors down to the city, streetlamps and firepits appeared as tiny dots far below.

But relief turned to disappointment as he realized the zinger couldn't be risked near the palace anymore. He instructed the droid to return to him and resume guarding the bargehouse.

Turning away from the wrist comm, Jaks squinted into the dark interior of the building. He should go find a candle upstairs, he thought. Instead, however, he stayed seated on the steps. Succumbing to fatigue, he nodded off beside the younger boy.

A buzzing noise woke Jaks from a nightmare of his father's giant hand looming toward him through the dark. Eyes flicking open, sweat soaking his garments, he found the sky outside the window as dark as midnight.

In the few seconds it took him to shake off the specter of his father and orient to the shadows of the bargehouse, his wrist comm buzzed again and flashed red.

Sentry warning.

He activated the image feed from the zinger and smiled as the pictures highlighted an incoming droid similar to the first. It could only be Meila's delivery. If it was midnight, as he was guessing, this delivery had taken thrice as long to get here as her estimate.

A few seconds later, the delivery droid flew in through the cracked window. It was encumbered with a bulky package, making it look like a flying ball of string. No wonder it had taken so long to fly here.

He cut and pried the bindings away from the droid to reveal one of Meila's medigel dressings half-stuffed into a cavity in its underside. A few green pain-dulling pills accompanied it within a stoppered vial. He popped one into his mouth and welcomed the immediate dismissal of pain and the sense of invulnerability that followed.

Davey sat up on the mattress beside him, rubbing his eyes.

Feeling guilty that he'd woken the boy, Jaks nevertheless enlisted his help to peel the medigel from its protective wrapper. Then held against his shoulder, it clamped over the wound like a limpet. A wrap of bandage and it was secure. He thanked Davey and patted him fondly on the head.

The next morning, Tim received the news of their gang headquarters' discovery by the Vors and Hanna's murder with difficulty. He blinked rapidly for several seconds, then, with veins thick in his neck, stormed out into the timberyard. On his return, although his eyes were red, he seemed otherwise back to his usual self and toted a sack of loot that he had scavenged from nearby shacks. He then disappeared upstairs to sort his find.

For the next two days, they stayed in the bargehouse, pondering their next steps. Should they remain in Irin hoping for another opportunity to rescue Karisa, or stay to spy on the enemy army, or flee this wasps' nest and return to Ascorian lines?

As Jaks monitored the timberyard and city around them with the zinger droids, Davey and Tim wandered the timberyard, looking for supplies abandoned by workers to fill out their rations beyond just dried fish.

Jaks, however, only traveled outdoors in those days through the eyes of the zinger droids; his electromantic connection with them became second nature. He flicked between both devices, sent them instructions, and received image feeds with minimal conscious thought.

Although directly receiving droid images into his mind gave him the most clarity—as though he were the droid himself—he dared not fall into the trance the electromantic connection required. Instead, the wrist-comm projection sufficed. Projected against the wall gave the best view; otherwise, the image hovered in midair—great for depth, but poor for detail.

An endless influx of Vor warriors and beasts of war trickled into the city from the south. The many thousands repaired damaged buildings and moved in as though to settle for a long while. Beautiful mansions and estates became military outposts, market squares transformed into distribution centers, and gardens and fields were stomped over as practice grounds.

And as more Vors arrived and space within the city diminished, incoming torgues moved into buildings closer and closer to the abandoned timberyard. Within a few days, they would surely move into the site itself, and Jaks and the boys would need to find a new hiding spot.

Other than to spy on the enemy—though valuable in itself, feeding information to Meila and King Silas's advisors—the next days did little to aid Jaks's personal quest. Indeed, the longer he spied on the Vors, the more he realized how impossible it was to reach Karisa.

Stubbornly, he lingered in the captured city despite Meila's forceful pleas to leave while he still could. Eventually, they devolved into angry commands.

And in the end, she was right, as usual.

On the third morning in the timberyard, Jaks startled awake as his wrist comm vibrated and constricted his wrist. Immediately, he identified the electromantic alarm of the droid he had renamed "Slasher"—marked by the scratch on its side from the dragon attack—signaling down from its patrol circuit two miles above the bargehouse.

The disc flashed red, but before he had time to project Slasher's image feed, a series of coarse voices yelled to one another outside the building's river door. From the number of verbal exchanges, it sounded like a large ship coursing along the river. However, bending his neck to gaze under the rotted wooden barricade, the closest ship was moored a half mile distant.

Frowning, he returned to his wrist comm and flicked on the image feed. The bird's-eye view clearly showed the bargehouse —familiar from days of examining the city from above—and the timberyard as still as always. But there in the river was a small ship, crewed with warriors.

Impossible. Nothing had been there a few seconds ago.

Davey came running down the stairs, his hair crumpled where he must have been lying on it, calling Jaks's name in a panicked voice and rubbing one eye at the same time. "Ship . . . ship, there's a ship in the sky!" He pointed toward the cracked-glass window above them.

"It can't be—" Compelled by the waif's fear, Jaks arced his neck up to stare and gape as the prow of a gray-colored mass edged into view several yards above the building.

More shouting sounded through the window, and he caught a glimpse of a wide-browed woman leaning over the side of what he could only describe as a "skyship." She pulled on a rope until a metal pulley clanged against the side of the vessel and looped it several times around a mooring bit.

The ship continued to pass over the bargehouse, a wooden hulk with patches of red and many more ropes dangling off the side.

Hairs on the back of Jaks's neck rose. He felt tiny under the massive object, fearing that at any moment it would fall out of the sky and crush their bargehouse.

Seconds later, Tim leaped down the stairs, three steps at a time. "Do you see it? Are my eyes playing tricks on me?" His voice trailed off as he followed the gaze of his two friends and confirmed the reality of their shared vision.

"It *is* flying," Jaks reported as he examined the pictures from his wrist comm. The vessel resembled the timber barge in the workshop behind him that he had slept in over the past days. Rectangular and flat-hulled, it was built to carry heavy loads, but more than that, this magical object—for it had to be magic to fly—was three times larger, bore a couple of small sails, and brimmed with warriors and weapons. Scorpion bolt-throwers, crossbows, spears, and crates of square blocks with no obvious purpose.

The fore-and-aft sails seemed too small to guide the giant ship, but when Jaks magnified the droid's sensors onto the deck, he suspected that its actual propelling force came in the hands of four people seated beside large sourcestones at the corners of the ship. Indeed, when the ship changed course and glided downward, a communication seemed to transpire between these navigators that only finished when the warship settled on a central lumberyard a few hundred yards from the bargehouse.

"Alright, that's it. We've got to get out of here," Jaks said to the boys and looked around the building for an escape route.

"We could go back to the sewers?" Davey suggested.

"No, you rat-brain. That ship is between us and the entrance." Tim screwed up his face, then turned his back as though looking through the walls.

"Are there no other ways to the sewers?" Jaks asked.

"Sure, there are, but we'd have to hunt around for them. I

only know the big one because that's the only one I've ever needed."

"They're too close for us to sneak out and start searching around . . . I've got another idea." Already, Jaks thought he could hear the coarse shouts of the crew getting nearer to their hideout. Glancing down to his wrist comm, his pulse quickened as the overhead view revealed warriors spreading out from the skyship to enter nearby buildings.

Davey spluttered another suggestion. "I could run out and get them to chase me through the yard while you and Tim sneak to the sewer entrance? I know the place real well and they'd never catch me." The boy held up his head, lip trembling but bearing an otherwise courageous face.

"Brave, but unnecessary, Davey." Jaks patted the smaller boy's shoulder. "No. There's a better option." He nodded toward one of the rowboats moored just inside the river gate. Missing a rudder, oarlocks, and thwarts, the thing was nothing but the husk of a boat.

"That wreck? It's so bare, it doesn't even have anywhere to sit."

"We're not going to sit. Quick, go upstairs and bring down those old sails. Davey, you help me open this river gate."

A couple of minutes later, they had cranked the wooden gate up a yard, and Tim had dragged down a tattered sail.

"Grab some food and we're out of here." A glance at his wrist comm showed warriors at the building next door. "Forget it. No time. Get in the boat. I'll cover us and push us out."

He threw the rotted sail cloth and a bargepole onto the rowboat and beckoned for the boys to climb down; the old boat rocked wildly as they clambered in one after the other. "Tim, untie us. I can't do it with one arm."

Once the boat drifted free from the mooring, he needed

Tim's help again, this time to maneuver the bargepole and push them out into the river while half-covered by the sailcloth. As they slid under the partially raised river gate, a light breeze swept over them. Feeling exposed, Jaks hastily pulled in the pole and then tucked the cover over them, hoping their rowboat looked uninteresting and abandoned.

Holding his breath, he listened for the outcry of anyone who might have spotted them. Daring to slip into an electromantic trance, he accessed Slasher's sensors. Back on shore, there were no efforts to chase them, nor any sign that the warriors had even seen the rowboat.

But on the other side of the river, something else seized his attention.

Several more skyships skimmed the buildings of the south city, gliding toward the river. Swarms of dragons accompanied the flying ships; some perched on the railings, while others flew in a multitudinous cloud of red, bronze, and silver.

Not just the one skyship, but an entire flotilla.

The odds against Jaks's countryfolk seemed abysmal. The gargantors dominating the ground war were bad enough. But they had nothing to match these marvels of the sky.

Something jabbed him in the chest, and he snapped back into his full body senses.

"Wake up." Davey poked him again in the chest. His worried face then softened as Jaks's eyes regained focus. "You looked like what you did in the attic."

"It's not good, boys. But we got away just in time. There were lots more ships on their way." He grimaced at the two pairs of eyes looking back at him under the sailcloth.

"The princess . . . we're not going to rescue her?" Davey whispered over Tim's head.

"Sorry, Davey. We can't. It's impossible. Our opportunity, if we ever actually had one, is truly lost. I think we were lucky to have remained hidden for as long as we did." Jaks sighed as the river sloshed their boat downstream and beyond the city's borders. "No. There's no way we can get back without getting caught. We're going to Dunberrin."

"Dunberrin? Never been there." Davey paused for a moment, then added, "Maybe me and Tim can find a new gang there."

But Jaks was already lost in thought and didn't reply. Did he regret entering Irin on a quest that, in hindsight, was a disaster? No, he had to attempt that rescue, for Karisa's sake. The regret would've been if he had not tried at all. Should he damn himself for failing? He snorted. He had tried his best but had been a fool to think he could rely on his wits and a magic so volatile that he still feared it like a tempest inside of him.

Yes, he had been wholly unprepared, but his only regret was not having the grandmaster's training. Strangely, he felt more focused now than ever before: he needed to master this electromancy; he needed to return to Mulgrave—and Meila. Although it was a curse and a gift, he was determined to tame it, especially now that he saw a use for it beyond just lightning bolts and destruction.

He grimaced as his thoughts returned to Karisa. *Sorry, Karisa. I'll come back when we win this war.*

Chapter 9

The Engineer

Meila—The Academy of the Arcane, Ascoria

Meila Tahn ran her thumb over the runestone of her welding torch and blinked as a thin, white flame shrieked from its nozzle. Sweat beaded her brow as she flipped down her welding mask and crouched behind the steel frame of her latest build. Although she hid any outward excitement at Jaks's imminent arrival—following his escape from the City of Irin three weeks ago—she welcomed the distraction of uniting steel to steel to calm her anticipation. Bemused by a childlike giddiness, she attributed the feeling to relief at finally being able to trial the velocannon using the young man's electromancer powers. If it worked, it could destroy thousands of Vors in an instant; if it failed, the Ascorians would remain greatly outnumbered.

The runic furnace, at the center of the square courtyard, roared at her back. *Hell, it was hot here . . . and noisy.* The only reprieve was a constant cool breeze blowing in through the ocean gate and out through the main gates leading to the land bridge and the main city. With the slightest of thoughts, her auditory implants selectively dampened out the sound of dozens of other magesmiths and their assistants hammering and welding. She sighed with relief, wondering why she hadn't thought to muffle the sound earlier.

High above, the underside of the bronze dome of the building curved around the furnace's chimney like the hand guard of a thrusting sword. Sparrows and other small birds flitted about and nested in the corners of the high ceiling.

Built over six centuries ago, when the city outside was burgeoning as a shipping hub, the Academy was an imposing castle. Besieged several times, it had fallen only once when Duke Dunberrin's griefmasters gravleapt onto the walls from assaulting ships. The victor had renamed the locality after himself, built a gravity-defying palace on the peninsula nearby, and was then invaded by the Ascorians a day before the last blocks were about to be laid. Out of respect for the overwhelmed Duke's valiant attempts to lay the last stone before he died, the Ascorian king allowed the city name to remain unchanged. Now, the castle was The Academy of the Arcane—the kingdom's center of magical studies and the forging of sorcerous weapons and devices—and the palace housed the Ascorian throne.

Focusing now, Meila returned to her task. Other than her protective visor, she wore little more than a leather apron over her sleeveless top, shorts, and boots—similar to the men assisting her: Grandmaster Mulgrave and Apprentice Tavis. Anything more and it would have been intolerable working so close to the two-thousand-degree heat source for so long.

She nodded to the apprentice, trusting him to gravmance the heavy steel tube into place while the older man steadied the base.

"Righto. It'll just take a minute." Unlike the plasma-welders she had supervised during her spacecraft-manufacturing days, this dual-runestone device amalgamated fire magic and grav magic into a supra-heated torch as efficient as any welder she had seen. That it was being used to create an even cleverer device of her own design, a gravfire mortar, brought a smile to her face.

Meila the engineer, once was, was again. It had been over forty years since she had designed and built anything lasting. Too long . . . the pleasure of creating. Why had she ever abandoned her engineering career? Invention had been in her essence since the engineers' playground of the UWF orbital factories where she had begun her working life. There, she had refined quaternary engines and stardrives until her promotions peaked with designing fighter-craft and atmospheric flyers. But for a born "engine head," it was the decades of building starships that had sparked her desire to fly the damned things.

It had seemed natural back then to submit to the implant modifications, flight school, and years of scraping her way up the UWF hierarchy in pursuit of snagging her own command. Although her lack of aggression kept her from a Juggernaut, or any of the other coveted military helms, they had never been her goal. Instead, a tiny science vessel, like the *Mendhelsson*, had been ideal for her.

And although she still grieved the destruction of her ship, the past few months of engineering devices for the Ascorians had revived a childlike thrill of design and construction. These war machines were not the sophisticated starships she had once built, but magic certainly led to innovative designs under the guidance of crafty magesmiths like Grandmasters Mulgrave and Hazeldine.

Several minutes later, she set down the welder, lifted her visor, and signaled for the mages to stand aside. As the metal cooled from yellow to gray, her eyes traced over the completed weapon.

Her visual implant calculated each exterior angle of the weapon. The measurements didn't need to be exact, but she would have judged herself harshly if the tolerances deviated by more than a quarter of a percent from her blueprint. Finally, she grunted and nodded to herself. Almost perfect.

In twenty-four hours' time, after it had cooled and then passed her second inspection, the weapon would be ready for battle—its embedded runestones channeling compressed air through a variable-angle tube to lob incendiary bombs onto enemies up to two miles away. A powerful weapon, of which they had built ten after experimenting with different-sized prototypes.

"That's the last of them, lass," Mulgrave said. He still spoke to her like she was a girl. Of course, it didn't help that she looked half his age. She couldn't help but smile back at the mage, withholding a chastisement over his error, unable to rebuke a man who resembled her great-grandfather's age: five centuries old.

"When Jaks gets here, we should trial the prototype," she said.

Tavis shook his head. "Not that again. It doesn't work. We're wasting our time on that thing. Jaks doesn't know smithing; he can't do anything that we can't."

A week ago, Mulgrave's big-eared apprentice had staggered into the Academy one midwinter's eve. Unkempt and stinking from his journey, having left the Jurns behind in Irin, he spoke little of his travel except to mention accompanying one of the many convoys bringing stores of food and grain back to the capital. Of the recovery from his head wound, he also made light explanation. But to Meila's surprise, when the grandmaster asked after Jaks, instead of the dismissive reply that she'd expected, Tavis slumped and made a sincere confession to the old mage. He begged forgiveness for the antipathy and maliciousness he had subjected Jaks to in the past. What had triggered this change of heart, she didn't know, but she appreciated that he was less prickly and snarky than before.

Ever graceful, the grandmaster had granted his apprentice the forgiveness he pleaded. And since then, the two had returned to master-and-apprentice; together, the three of them were a constructive force spitting out weapons and inventions at a pace second to no other Academy workshop.

As such, Tavis's turnaround against her velocannon, and dig at Jaks, surprised her. Perhaps Jaks's imminent arrival had rekindled the apprentice's fears of being usurped. "Sure, Jaks doesn't know the workshop or forge as well as any of us," Meila replied, "but it isn't his knowledge that we need . . . it's his electromancy. You only saw the velocannon when I tried to energize it with the sheet-metal capacitors. They weren't anywhere near powerful enough. But I've seen what Jaks's electromancy can do and I think he can easily generate enough voltage to make it work."

Mulgrave interrupted as Tavis stared at the floor moodily. "She knows what she's talking about, lad. Why don't you go assist Master Doeg and Shazair this afternoon while she and I meet with the Lord Defender? It doesn't need all three of us to discuss the best locations for these mortars and organize training for the crews."

"Sorry, master. You know best." The junior mage bowed and shuffled off after draping his leather apron over a nearby bench.

"Let's clean up before visiting his lordship. Meet me in the library in a half hour," Mulgrave said, as he arched and pressed his hands against his back.

Waylaid, as he often was, it was two hours later that the bald magesmith appeared again. Shaking his head, he jabbered some excuse involving Grandmaster Hazeldine and her "flying-ship folly."

"Ever since those images of the Vors' skyships came back, she's been obsessed with getting her version to work. I've told her we don't have large sourcestones to spare, like what those blue-stained barbarians have. But that stubborn mule is going to use Doeg and Shazair's sourcestone packs instead," Mulgrave said. "They're still quite unstable."

Meila nodded. "I did offer, months ago, to help her out. Maybe I could have a look at her plans later on. I've a lot of experience in engineering systems to compensate for poly-drive concepts. Math can solve a lot of things."

Mulgrave stared at her for a few moments before his brow unfurrowed and he laughed. "If only I could steal your brain for my own."

"Your brain is fine. It's my memory implants you want. Come on, the lordman awaits." Returning his laugh, she took his proffered arm, and they exited the library into the main corridor.

As they crossed the land-bridge from the Academy to the city, dodging horse-led wagons clattering under loads of coal and timber, Meila gasped as a tall, bearded man lunged into their path.

Mulgrave reflexively thrust a hand in front of Meila, but she pushed past and cried out, "Jaks!" Although his face was weathered and his clothes disheveled, she knew the figure was him. She grabbed his wrists. Cold to touch and thicker than she remembered.

He looked a decade older than last time she had seen him in the flesh. She plied her memory for anything that had happened over the past weeks that could account for his appearance.

After Jaks and his two new wards had fled Irin by boat, they drifted until nightfall, then poled their vessel to the river's edge and continued their escape on foot. Through vales and copses of trees, the zinger droid had traced a path that evaded the episodic Vor patrols. And after two days of sneaking north through wine country, surviving off charred rabbits that Jaks would zap, and sleeping in abandoned vineyards, they finally left the Vors behind.

Once in this neutral zone, Meila and Mulgrave had cajoled the sullen Cromer—in Dunberrin, training ranger apprentices—to order a ranger patrol to bring the three escapees into safety. The wiry hunter had no love for Jaks. Pity and anger, yes, and at least enough loyalty to Vixhana to have stirred him into arranging a signal transmission to the frontline.

From there, rangers had found and escorted Jaks and the boys back to the border of Dunberrin and King Silas's encampment: a little village transformed into a defensive line between two mountain ranges. Comprised of a hastily built fortress and two miles of wall, it was the last barrier between the invaders and the Ascorian capital.

Tim and Davey had been reunited at the border camp with Hughie, the latter's older brother. The older boy had escaped the raid on their gang's hideout. Hanna, sacrificing her life for her gang, had slowed the Vors long enough for Hughie and a few others to fleet-foot to the sewers and eventually to safety. Jaks had insisted the boys rejoin their friends, who had been repurposed from their light-fingered work to running errands for soldiers in exchange for food and shelter. He had departed for Dunberrin days later, sad at losing Tim and Davey's cheerful banter but also relieved at not having to worry about two dependents.

"You look terrible," Meila said, releasing his wrists and restraining an impulse to stroke his cheek. "You look like a Vor. That beard, I'm surprised no one has tried to cut it off you . . . head attached."

The intense look didn't shift from his face. Instead, he took her shoulders and tipped his head down to her face. This time, she didn't resist. Couldn't resist. The hunger in his eyes was unstoppable. Their lips met with such electricity, she feared his magic had stirred. But it wasn't electromancy—it was passion that flowed from his lips to hers.

"Enough, enough," Mulgrave's voice clamored behind them, a few seconds later. "Every carter and his horse is staring."

Opening her eyes, she pushed away from Jaks, and her breath steamed between them in the cold, still air. His eyes still pursued her. She stiffened her back and shook her head. "What's got into you?" she said, then laughed lightly. "That was some greeting. Come on, let's get off this bridge before we get run over."

She pulled him to the end of the bridge and found a space on the busy wharf. In the distance, a coal freighter groaned against the dock and poured dark nuggets down an iron chute into a bin. Dockworkers, blackened with dust, shouldered shovels up and down, as they transferred the load to awaiting carts. Closer, though, a merchant eyed Meila from the prowl of his ship as his crew rolled empty barrels up a gangplank.

Ignoring the stare and the activity behind them, she turned to embrace Jaks briefly, then inquired after his shoulder, hand, and legs, frowning as he responded. She then palpated his arms and chest to assess his health.

"He's fine. Stop acting like an old ma'am," the grandmaster said, shaking his head imperceptibly.

Her face turned hot, and she stared up into the air.

Stealing the opportunity, Mulgrave interrogated Jaks. "Any news from the highway? Anything of the thaw?" he asked.

"A ranger with my caravan thought the chill will stay awhile yet. He said he'd been in the mountains a week before and the iron mines were laden with snow, and the ice dragons were bolder than ever—a sure sign of a long winter, he reckoned."

"The weather could side with us, then. Let's hope for at least another month before the Vors shake off their winter crust." The grandmaster then smiled, as though he had just remembered who he was talking to. "It's good to see you, lad."

"And you, Grandmaster." Unkempt, sour-smelling, Jaks clasped the mage's extended hand.

Mulgrave then nodded to the avenue of workshops leading toward the inner city. The ringing of iron on anvil sang throughout the district. "Come. We're going to visit the City Lord Defender. We need to discuss training up crews for a new weapon we've invented, as well as other matters to discuss. You look like a felon and stink like a beggar's blanket, but you should attend all the same." He exchanged a glance with Meila.

"Lord Defender? I've not heard that title before," Jaks said.

"One of King Silas's most trusted generals. The king designated his lordship to review and tighten the capital's defenses. But most significantly, the Lord Defender was tasked with raising mercenaries from the Pact countries. Indeed, he has been quite successful in his negotiations with the embassies, and apparently, a few legions are already on the march as we speak." Mulgrave paused and shifted from foot to foot as though weighing his next words. "You've met him before, his lordship."

"Lord Castias? Welsford? I don't know that many lords

personally. That was . . . my father's thing. He rarely took me to functions and usually sent me away when he held them at our estate." Jaks lowered his gaze as his voice trailed off.

"Yes. It was your father's thing." The grandmaster placed a meaty hand on Jaks's shoulder. "The king's delegate *is* your father. He's asked for you to attend him personally on your return."

Chapter 10

City Lord Defender

Jaks—The City of Dunberrin, Ascoria

Jaks sagged under the mage's hand. Lord Sicaro Rauhalik, City Lord Defender, and the dark hand of his nightmares. Here in Dunberrin. Tiny claws scratched at the sealed door in his mind, tearing at the edges, threatening to release the terror it hid.

"Are you alright, lad?" Mulgrave asked as he gripped Jaks's arms.

"It can't be so. My father?" Jaks reached for a dock post and slumped against it. "He was down south when the Vors landed. They started with his province and castle. I thought he was dead." Or so he had hoped since first learning of the invasion. Never voiced, but strongly wanted.

"As alive as can be."

"He should be dead—"

"It is said he escaped wounded with a handful of his garrison. Lost an eye to the cause. You do know he was one of the king's staunchest supporters during the Unifying Wars. He's been here since the fall of Irin," Mulgrave replied. "Done an excellent job scaling up the industrial district's production and bolstering the city's defenses. We've had little to do with him so far, but with the gravfire mortars completed, we need him to give us soldiers to crew them."

"I can't go. I can't see him—not now."

A gentle hand took his and Meila crouched into his view. "I know it's a lot to take in. It'll be okay."

"You know what he did. What he's done. I told you about him."

Taking both of his hands this time, she drew closer and locked his gaze. "He's highly stationed now, the king's man. Has done a lot for the city. People can change. Maybe he regrets his past?" She took a breath. "He seeks you out. Perhaps he wants to make peace with you?"

He glared at her as though her words dripped with poison. How could she side with him? Make peace with the man who beat his mother to death in front of his eyes?

"You don't know what you're asking," he said, and yanked his hands away from her.

Meila's face furrowed in worry. "Sorry, Jaks. If it's just going to churn up bad memories, don't come."

Jaks gritted his teeth and muscles corded his neck as he girded himself against the storm of anger and confusion inside. Maybe he should see the monster? Publicly expose the past, demand he admit his crime and face the executioner's blade? No, it would be futile. He had no proof. His father wouldn't admit a thing.

However, the least Jaks could do was confront him and show that he was not afraid of him any longer. The past months proved he could be courageous: fear no longer defined him.

He made a decision. "I'll come." Jaks flipped a nod and

stood. Not because his father requested it but to prove to himself—"I'm not scared of him."

The City Lord Defender held court on a floating fortress moored in the naval yards. Accessible only through the Army District and down a lengthy pier, it was gated and guarded as though protecting the king himself. The giant ship, bedecked in painted carvings of sea sylphs and tritons, bristled with guards.

Around midafternoon, Jaks followed the grandmaster and Meila up the ship ramp, wishing he hadn't come. He was flustered from the last checkpoint, where the guards had removed his sword and dagger and left him with only his coin purse and the zinger droid—a harmless bauble to them— treating them like criminals being brought before a magistrate. They forced even the grandmaster to spreadeagle like a common thief.

A man sneered down on them from the floating fortress and motioned for them to walk up the gangplank onto the ship. Onboard, yet another contingent of guards awaited. A gesture from the man allowed them to pass without challenge.

"Grandmaster, apologies for the inconveniences," said the man, hands concealed beneath his cloak, and the sneer unshifted from his face. "One can never tell from appearances alone, with illumancers and disguises all about."

He looked familiar to Jaks. Similar of age to Ranger Cromer and cast from the same craggy mold, the man triggered some memory from the past.

"Understandable," Mulgrave replied, his face unreadable.

"I am Lord Sicaro's humble servant, Master Kyle Halwoth. His lordship has been waiting." He pivoted and walked to a tower below the quarterdeck of the ship.

Halwoth. Of course. One of his father's veteran retainers. Often slinking after his father and staring at the children, licking his crooked lips. However, it was by a different name that he recalled him—Sneer.

They entered the ship's tower, passing beneath a doorway carved with cavorting sylphs and mermen.

The door closed behind and Jaks's eyes struggled with speckled beams of red and green within. As his eyes adjusted, and he dismissed the kaleidoscope projecting from the colored-glass bricks along the outer walls, a chamber unraveled before him, and he discovered it partitioned by shadows and curtains.

Several guards he mistook as statues, until one turned his head, dotted the vast room and at its center stood a giant of a man.

Sneer tiptoed to whisper in the man's ear and then swept a hand at the awaiting trio before retreating into the shadows.

"Mage, how many years . . . was it at the scorching of Trillian Castle?" the giant boomed.

"No, my lord, I was not at Trill when it fell. Master Iver, perhaps?"

Behind the grandmaster, Jaks couldn't move—his limbs rigid, then trembling, as a thieving darkness rose. His father's voice alone, enough to seize him with panic. Frozen in place, he could only listen, even though his core screamed to run and hide.

Lord Sicaro laughed. "Of course . . . it couldn't have been you. That one died inside the castle with the rest of the traitors."

Mulgrave tensed but continued. "Three years past? Our king's jubilee. His highness shared his table with us. We sat left and right, if you recall. The day his highness named you Castellan at Sanford, I believe."

"So, it was. Well-remembered, Grandmaster." Sicaro stepped into the light. A patch tied with a string covered his left eye, but nothing else had changed. Black hair and beard bordered features that would have befitted a bear as much as a man. Penetrating eyes lifted over the mage's head and fell on Jaks.

To his astonishment, the Lord Defender surged forward, nudging Mulgrave and Meila aside. His hands gripped the sides of Jaks's head as he studied his middle child. "Who is this? My son? Mirror of my image. The beard makes a man of you."

Locked into the bear's grip, fearing the hands would crush his skull, he gaped at his father wordlessly. Skeletal flashes, like hands clawing out of a grave, tore through the door of his memory and unleashed a flood. Jaks's eyes glazed over as the past rushed back—

He trembles, brandishing a knife at his father. On the hallway floor beside him, mother shields her bruised face. She scrambles for the stairs. His father bats the knife out of his hand and shoves him aside. She descends the stairs on the threshold of escape, but the giant snatches after her. He must be stopped. In an instant, a snap of light and a thunderclap splits the air: lightning sparks from his hands and strikes his father and his mother—their bodies spasm and tumble. Her head strikes a step, then another. Hard. She slides to the bottom of the stairs, neck at an unnatural angle.

"Shocked to see your own father?" His father laughed, releasing him and disrupting the deluge of memories. His one eye then fixed on Jaks's crippled hand. "Seems we have much to catch up on."

Finding his voice, Jaks whispered, "I killed her—"

"What's that? Speak up."

"I killed her," he murmured.

"Master Halwoth, bring my son a drink. He sounds parched. Traveled far today. Bring him a stool to sit."

The grandmaster coughed. "Yes, apologies, my lord. He

arrived just this hour. I should have sent him to rest and present himself later."

Sneer led him to a three-legged stool. Behind it, a man with twin daggers at his waist slipped further into the shadows, but not before Jaks glimpsed rings of tattooed ink around his neck. Surrounded by his father's men and reeling from the flashback, sweat beaded his face, and fear—he had thought conquered—gripped him hostage.

Had he remembered true? Doubt seized him. Who was the monster here? His father or himself?

Unheeding of Jaks's turmoil, his father returned to the center of the room and looked at Mulgrave and Meila.

"So, this is the so-important prisoner I've been hearing about." Sicaro traced his gaze over her. She crossed her arms in response. "Silas is beguiled by her, it seems. But what is to stop her from escaping?"

"Ward. Not a prisoner. She is promised her freedom in exchange for passing her knowledge to the Academy," said Mulgrave. "As to her running away—"

"I have nowhere to run to," interrupted Meila. "You may have heard that I have no way of returning to my home."

"Indeed, the king himself believes you're cast here from another dimension," replied Sicaro.

"Planet. But for all purposes, it may as well be another dimension, as I cannot travel to either."

"Remarkable. Perhaps you would stay and tell me more of this 'planet' after we finish our business today? Master Halwoth would return you to the Academy this evening."

Meila's face creased, and she firmed her lips, but she was saved by the grandmaster.

"A shame, my lord. I cannot spare my ward today," Mulgrave said. "Even now, Grandmaster Hazeldine awaits her otherworldly knowledge to assist vital calculations in constructing a skyship. A most critical counter to the Vors' own —if we can master its flight."

Darkness clouded the Lord Defender's expression fleetingly. "Another time . . . let us tend to your petition then, mage."

Their discussion faded from Jaks's ears as the grandmaster and his father retreated to an oak table recessed in an alcove. Meila dragged her feet after them until only her back was visible to him. Left alone to his thoughts, even the lurker behind him fell from his consciousness.

He bent forward and stared at the floor.

How that memory had shuttered itself away for these past years, he could only guess. It was that day when he had faced his father with Vixhana and Karisa at their family estate, that his shield of self-delusion had begun to peel away. At the bottom of the very stairs she had died on. And it was today, when his father had held his head as though to crush it, that it had collapsed.

It was guilt he had barricaded himself against, deceiving himself into blaming his father for the murder to cover his own guilt. His rampant imagination was an escape, a guardian against horrors that threatened to drive him insane. Perhaps this was how he dealt with secret pain. What other memories had he lied to himself over? Bolted doors to secrets he hid from himself. Too painful to open.

The stairs. It was an accident.

Electromancy, maybe the first time ever, had risen in the panic to save her—but had instead killed her, just as it had injured Vixhana. Twice now to his family. Would there be another? Would he end up killing Karisa? Or was he destined to kill his father? Weren't these things fated to occur in threes? He needed to escape the situation. Leave the city.

No, not again.

He had descended this spiral once before after he injured Vixhana. He'd fled responsibility for months. No, it couldn't happen again; guilt and self-blame wouldn't smother duty again. He would not flee. He had debts to pay. Still had to rescue Karisa.

His father's muffled voice crept into his ears. "Ale?"

Jaks's eyes rose, and he flinched from the bear of a man standing in front of him, holding a mug in each hand.

"Ale?" his father repeated. Perhaps misinterpreting Jaks's horrified look as puzzlement, he continued. "I sent them off. The mage and the girl. Give an old man time with his son."

Indeed, the grandmaster and Meila were silhouetted against the reddening sky at the door and then vanished as it closed behind them. How could they have abandoned him?

"My thanks, my lord," Jaks said, accepting the drink as though the head of froth might turn into acid.

His father gestured, and a guard brought him a chair. He sat and drained his mug, his one eye never leaving Jaks.

Jaks sipped the ale, then realizing how thirsty he was, downed the remaining liquid with one long draw. A small boy appeared and hastily removed both of the empty mugs, bowing as he disappeared back into the shadows.

"I brought you up the way my father raised me. And his before that," said his father. "The rod and the fist are the best teachers. Your warriors will only respect you if they know you can beat them down at any time."

Jaks stared, not finding words to respond. The realization that he himself had caused his mother's death made his father's beatings and abuses seem almost trivial.

"You're the same as me. We've both done what others call evil." His father pulled his chair closer. Jaks resisted the urge to lean away. "I covered for you . . . when you killed her. Using magic to kill your own mother—it would have been a witch trial."

Jaks kicked the stool back and stood. "I didn't mean to. Didn't want to hurt her. I was trying to . . ." He could hear his voice rising, but couldn't finish his sentence.

"Sit down, boy." Lord Sicaro nodded, and a firm hand from behind guided Jaks back to his uprighted stool. "Your sister, too. I hear you killed her, too. That oversized bitch."

"I didn't kill her . . ." Jaks replied in a voice barely a whisper. Indeed, Vixhana was still alive; he had sent a droid a week ago to check. Although he had seen her only for a short time through the zinger's owl-like sensors, he had shouted with joy at finding her conscious and hobbling around the Jurn village on crutches. However, to tell his father that would not remove the fact that he had nearly killed her.

"It seems this power of yours is a rare one, my sources say." Sicaro loomed over Jaks, who sat on the stool like an obedient schoolchild. "Perhaps it's time you did something useful with it."

"I was apprenticed to Grandmaster Mulgrave before—I think he will have me back. Then I'll be able to learn the magic properly."

"Nonsense. I heard about how you broke the barricade at Irin. Defeated a gravmancer and then a firemage. Summoned lightning to decimate a formation of warriors." His father raised a finger and Halwoth the Sneer materialized to receive a private instruction. The henchman then departed, and his father continued. "You don't need further tuition. You need a role that befits your ability. And a mentor who will grow your power, not stifle you in some forge, turning you into a smith."

"Ever seen a gargantor, son?" Sicaro asked abruptly, his gaze drilling down into Jaks's.

Without waiting for an answer, he continued, "Monsters! Big as a house, with claws and tusks like sabers, and the head of a tiger with teeth like daggers. The things can leap as high as they are tall. Few places they can't get to. We fought one in the Unifying War when the Heran rebels brought it over from Voros. Routed an entire regiment before it could be brought down with ballistae and fire." His father's eyes gleamed with almost worshipful intensity.

Jaks nodded, wondering how the topic had changed so quickly.

"Born killers. Like you." His father leaned forward in his chair. Jaks leaned back, intimidated by the huge presence. "When gargantor pups are ready to be whelped, they don't wait for the mother to push them out. They tear at the birthing sac and claw their way out. The mother falls into throes of agony as her newborns rip up her insides. She eventually collapses from the savaging and the pups tear their way out and take their first feed off their mother's corpse."

Jaks felt sick. "I'm no gargantor. I didn't tear her apart."

"Alas, you are a born killer, boy," his father persisted. "Born with the power to kill anything in your way."

"I don't enjoy killing people," Jaks began, but then stopped as he remembered the exhilaration he had felt on seeing the field of dead Vors he had killed. He had laughed with the thrill of exerting his power.

His father grimaced. "The world is changing, son. The old ways don't work. Uniting Ascoria under one crown was a start, but Silas lost his way. We need to start anew."

"But it means nothing if the Vors win—" Jaks's head spun with the turn of topic from gargantors to crowns.

His father stared at him as though waiting for him to understand something.

The back of Jaks's neck tingled. Something significant had been said, but he couldn't grasp its meaning. There were too many thoughts and emotions clattering in his mind.

The Lord Defender continued, "Started but stalled. That's why Voros invaded. Ascoria had gathered a great harvest but failed to protect it. Instead of solidifying Ascoria's might, that fool Silas disbanded the armies and allowed good warriors to soften and lose their edge."

"Why are you telling me this?" Jaks asked, fearing that the more he heard, the more he would sink into some trap.

Sneer appeared at that moment and passed an object to his master before settling back into a shaded alcove.

His father weighed the object in his hands and then presented it to Jaks. "Here, take it," he said.

It was a rod of cold metal. His arms sagged under unexpected weight in the three-foot-long object. At its midpoint, steel twisted around an octagonal, black stone that he would have mistaken for a cylinder of coal if not for the engraved runes. Similar spiral cages at each end of the rod bound equally dark runestones. A sense of doom radiated from all three—danger dwelt in each. He clenched the artifact around the grips between the runestones.

"What is this?" Jaks's voice took on a high edge.

"It was crafted by the last electromancer in known history, a Grandmaster Vinton. You heard of him?"

He nodded, recalling a copy of the personal account left by Vinton in the Academy library. The electromancer had embodied the spirit of a true battlemage and was a legend. Jaks often marveled at the power the mage must have commanded, such as summoning a storm that sank half of the Ranilan fleet a century ago and thereby ended their religious crusade. Yes, he even remembered mention of Vinton's rod of lightning piercing the clouds to draw down forked tentacles of electricity.

"I thought you might like it—a loan from me to you."

"Me?" Jaks stared slack-jawed at the artifact and trembled at the thought of what power it contained. Unable to form a sentence, jumbled words fell out of his mouth. He couldn't recall his father ever giving him anything of value in his life before, certainly nothing as valuable as this.

"On one condition," the enormous man said. "Join my retinue. Develop your power under my tutelage. With the rod and my guidance, you might eventually be as powerful as Vinton himself."

The idea both appalled and appealed to Jaks. Fame like Vinton? Ever since the siege of Irin, he had felt a strong desire to weave electromancy once again. What if he could do far more? Alter weather and summon clouds of lightning? What a spectacle. No one could dismiss him any longer. They would lower their eyes in respect and beg favors from him.

Jaks studied the rod and felt a thrum of power course through the artifact as though welcoming its new owner. "I can sense its power," he said. He knew he wanted it. But could he accept it at the cost of kowtowing and submitting to his father, who, up until this day, had been the person he most feared and despised?

"Other things, too, of course—wealth, women." He snapped his fingers and Sneer pulled back a curtain to reveal a recessed alcove. Three thinly clad women lounged on settees and cushions. The henchman stroked the braided hair of one; she arched her exquisite neck like some exotic creature.

Jaks fumbled for words, but nothing other than mumblings came out of his mouth. Of course, he wanted power, money, and companionship. Didn't everybody? His eyes connected with a particularly curvaceous woman. He turned away, painfully aware of his aching need, worsened by Meila's casual dismissal after he had kissed her that afternoon.

"Go and think about it. I return south within the next few days. I would have your response by then. Son. The world is changing faster than a swift on the wing. What you see is only the tip of what all that is happening, and you would do well to be at the center of it all—with me."

"Yes, my lord . . . Father. I will think on it," Jaks said. He stood and reluctantly dropped Vinton's Rod back into his father's extended hands.

The tattooed man stepped out of the shadows and guided Jaks off the ship into the dark of evening.

At the end of the jetty, beneath flickering torches, the swordsman looked at him sideways. "Your father is a great man. Many of us have followed him for longer than you are old and would die for him without pause. You would do well to accept his offer. If you did not, an offense would be created that could not be ignored." He then turned and simply vanished as only an illumancer could.

Chapter 11

Firing and Testing

Jaks shuffled through the city, savoring the solace of the darkening streets despite the nip of winter at his face. Hours later, as bells rang the night curfew, he arrived at the Academy and a familiar guard bid him through the night door. Although he glimpsed Meila and Mulgrave with a few others in the ground-floor laboratory, he slipped past unseen and found his old room. Collapsing onto the bed, he fell asleep and was haunted by black hands proffering a glowing bar of red-hot steel.

"Come on. Wake up. We've got lots to do today." Meila's voice pierced his slumber. The light of dawn silhouetted her against the doorway. "*Blah.* Go and wash first, though. I've lived for decades in tight spaces, but this is the worst I've smelled for a long time. Come down to the lab after you're done."

"Wait." He threw his legs over the cot and rose unsteadily. "What did my father say to you yesterday?" He had awoken confused, not from the tendrils of sleep but from a dilemma. Perhaps she could help.

"What? He didn't say anything to me. First time I've met him. Stared at me as though I were curio at the museum. Even when I explained the firing process for the mortar crews, he wasn't really listening."

"Nothing about big changes taking place?"

Meila quirked an eyebrow at him. "Well, there is a war going on. So, something will change . . . win or lose. What are you on about?"

He shook his head as he sifted through his thoughts. His father's invitation had not been a peace offering to a neglected son—it had been a bribe and a threat. It was becoming clear now, with fear and fatigue no longer buffeting his mind like a pair of mad ravens as they had the night before.

Lord Sicaro had not changed at all since the days he had frothed at the mouth as he beat his son and his wife. *Mind games. I'll not have any more of this.* The death of Jaks's mother from panicked electromancy was his father's fault, not his.

He clenched his jaw and moved toward the door. Meila stepped back, her nose crinkling.

"He's planning something. He's *always* planning something," Jaks said. "I don't know what, but it's always about power. He must want more—"

"More than he has now? He is in charge of the largest city in the kingdom. The capital, nonetheless. What's more?"

Realization crept across her face. Jaks nodded at her. The unspoken inference thrummed in the air between them like a hideous portrait that should be trampled and destroyed.

"But if he wanted the Crown, why would he do it in the middle of an invasion?" Meila said, thinking aloud. "The disruption would allow the Vors to just walk in while the kingdom reels in chaos."

"I don't know. It's just some things he said . . ." He trailed off, unable to pin hard evidence to his suspicions.

"Do you have any evidence?"

"Nothing I can show someone."

"Then we have to leave it be. There's no point slinging around accusations without proof. It would do more harm than good." Meila stood back from the doorway as though ending the conversation.

He nodded, seeing that he needed more proof before he could convince anyone with enough power to do anything. He might possibly even need to go to the king himself. "I'll get evidence. He's not just a danger to me, but to everyone."

"Just don't do anything stupid. I'll see you downstairs when you're not stinking like rotted tripe." Meila wrinkled her nose and left.

An idea gathered momentum as he grabbed clothes from the shelf and then went to wash in the water room at the end of the corridor. The beard came off with flicks of a shaving blade and was flushed down the drain. Dashing back to his room, dripping and slapping wet feet, he retrieved his carry pouch and extracted the zinger bot.

Minutes later, the droid sped off to carry out its orders. The plan now in motion, Jaks went downstairs to find Meila and the grandmaster.

"Better," Meila remarked when he came across them in the downstairs lab. She slid a hand over his clean-shaven chin and slapped it lightly. "Follow us. We're doing the rounds."

The morning shot by in a haze after he joined Meila and Tavis traipsing behind the grandmaster like subordinates tailing a general. Keeping to some schedule that only he knew, Mulgrave attended meetings with other grandmasters and roamed the lab and workshops, inspecting and barking instructions at his journeymen and master magesmiths. Everywhere within the massive building, in whatever corner or room they could find, men and women found space to work magic and muscle on all sorts of weapons, armor, and contraptions.

By midday, Jaks was ready for their primary task of the day. They stood at the Academy's sea gate, the huge iron barrier leading out to the abandoned wharf. Ocean air whistled between the gaps of the gate to counter the immense heat of the runic furnace.

Inside, off to one side of the sea gate, a large object lay beneath a ragged shroud. After they peeled away the canvas, Jaks gazed upon the creation that had been awaiting his return.

Sturdy steel legs and frame grasped a long metal cylinder with a metal box capping off one end. Jaks realized he had seen the device before—back in the Jurn caverns when Meila had projected her nascent illusion of the device. It had looked smaller then. What stood in front of him would not be easily carried on a battlefield.

"The barrel is the magnetic radiation shield that we recovered from the *Mendhelsson*. It used to generate a constant double field, but I've modified it with parts from the escape pod and one of the darkcore handguns to create an old-school velocity cannon."

"Looks interesting," he said, intrigued by the weapon's eclectic manufacture.

"Velocannon for short. The finish is rough, but the principle is sound. Darkcore particles become unstable as they approach the speed of light. In a normal darkcore weapon, the plasma bolt is limited, so it doesn't damage the weapon. But in a velocannon, as soon as an over-charged bolt leaves the primary weapon and enters the magnetic field inside the secondary barrel, it is accelerated to a point that hyperexcites the particles—but all the while keeping it from contacting the interior. It's bloody marvelous." She then smiled as though he should be equally impressed by her explanation. Seeing that he wasn't, she continued, "An agitated darkcore bolt is so powerful that they are usually only fired from space where the target is hundreds or thousands of miles away. It can vaporize anything within a half mile, while the blast will carry even further."

Now Jaks's eyes widened. "Is it safe?"

"Don't worry. It's *old-school*," she replied dismissively. He frowned at her peculiar phrase.

A loud clank drew their attention to the sea gate where Tavis had been hand-cranking a cog and chain. The gate racketed to a stop and the passageway to the old stone wharf stood wide open. Out in the open, a couple of dragons screeched overhead. A breakwater, a half mile out, whisked up ocean foam as it buffered the sea's incessant pounding. Several dinghies and fishing boats bobbed in the waters of the harbor and a frigate flying Ascorian colors sailed past and made its way to the city's naval yard.

The grandmaster walked along the slime-coated wharf with a fan of fire spewing from his hands, searing the slime until it was blackened and devoid of its slippery growth. Both gravmancers then carried out the velocannon and positioned it facing the open sea. "Let's hope it works this time," Mulgrave said and stepped back. Tavis shot Jaks an irritated look and followed the grandmaster back under the archway.

Meila withdrew a handgun from a satchel she carried and inserted the weapon into the steel box from the bottom. Her hands inside the device, Jaks couldn't see what she was doing, but it was a quarter hour before she finished and called him over.

"I've unlocked the darkie to your neuronal signature. Don't trigger it more than once. There is only enough ammunition for perhaps six or seven of the hypercharged shots."

Jaks nodded. "How do I use it?"

"When I tell you, take the left grip and hold on to the gun inside. Aim it above that breakwater." She demonstrated by placing her left hand on a metal handle on the side of the box and sticking her right hand into a hole at the back. "Then you're going to have to channel your electromancy through the handle."

"That's it?" Jaks stood behind the weapon as its creator stood aside.

"See the fins on the end of the barrel?" She pointed at short, thin pieces of metal lying flat. "If you generate enough field, they'll spread out like flower petals, telling you it's charged enough to fire. That's when you pull the trigger."

Suddenly aware of the power in his hand, Jaks released the weapon, fearful of accidentally firing it.

"Okay, I'm going to go hide in the archway. Listen out for me to give you the go-ahead." She darted away and left him gaping as she went to join the grandmaster semi-hidden in the archway. After a minute, she shouted out for him to proceed.

Palms sweaty, it was hard to keep a firm grip. He looked at the velocannon and then back at Meila several times. She waved him on. Was this how Karisa and his mother had felt on stage, pressured to perform exactly how the audience demanded? Sweat beaded his brow.

Emotion. Visualization. Will. The chain of power was second nature to him now. It took little effort to trigger the spiral of fear: always violence, the threat or memory of it. Today, he drew on the memory of seeing his father the day before, heightened at knowing he would have to answer to him, worsened with imagining the consequences of denying him his fealty—the fist and backlash that would surely follow. Shaking with the emotion, he imagined lightning coursing through his hands and then furrowed his forehead to will the magic to life. He closed his eyes to concentrate.

A loud humming sound startled him back to the present. The metal fins at the end of the barrel vibrated erect. Strangely, their tiny movements reminded him of little fish dancing rather than of the flower petals that Meila had described.

"Now, Jaks. Aim with the scope over the breakwater and fire," Meila yelled from behind.

Sighting down the magnified lens tube, he inched the orange dot in the center over the top of the wave-swept outcrop. A few seconds later, he squeezed the trigger.

The weapon shuddered and emitted a coarse scream. A white line seared his vision but was gone in an instant. In the distance, the horizon disappeared as the ocean was tossed into the sky and became a billowing cloud folding in on itself.

Another cry sounded behind him, but it was one of delight from Meila as she ran up hooting and calling out, "Yes!" and, "That's it!" repeatedly.

Her excitement contagious, he caught her up, and the two jumped up and down, staring at the cloud that seemed even now to be growing.

A roar grew from the ocean, killing the laughter on their lips. Moments later, a booming gust of wind and water blew Meila and Jaks to the ground. And as they struggled to hands and knees, a giant wave crashed against the harbor's seawall and swamped it from view. Broken but still angry, the wave slapped at the boats on the other side and threw itself against the Academy's dock with one last effort.

The pair watched uselessly as the wave surged against the velocannon and knocked it off the dock into the water.

Meila swore aloud in a foreign tongue.

The mist blew away minutes later, and the harbor settled into choppy waves. Thankfully, most of the larger boats were still afloat, but Jaks was certain there were fewer rafts and dinghies than before.

Meila ran to the edge of the dock and stared down at where the cannon had disappeared. Seconds later, she sighed in relief, touching the side of her eye socket. "Thank God, it looks mostly intact and is just a couple of meters under the surface. Shouldn't be too hard to retrieve."

"It'll work again?" Jaks asked.

"I hope so," she replied. "Once we fish it out."

Mulgrave and Tavis appeared beside her, the old man shaking his head, muttering and cursing at the harbor as flotsam bobbed to the surface. "Gods, there's going to be a lot of explaining to do."

Sure enough, dismayed faces soon jammed the archway and shouted a hundred questions. Grandmaster Hazeldine, clutching a forge hammer, stomped out to the dock. "What the hell, Mulgrave?" She stared out at the harbor as it sloshed like a bowl of water in a toddler's arms.

Sheepishly, Mulgrave pointed first at the seawall, then at the patch of harbor where the velocannon lay submerged, and then shrugged as he spread his palms.

Chapter 12

The Bribe

The rest of that afternoon, Jaks clung distractedly to the slippery ropes that Tavis—grumbling and spluttering each time he resurfaced—tossed up from where he ducked and dived to bind the velocannon in its watery grave. Despite the apprentice's protests, Mulgrave had decided the task was a great opportunity for a lesson in gravmancy and ballasting. But despite the shouts and splashing of the pair in the water, Jaks gnawed his lip, thoughts fixated on his father. Should he vow allegiance to him or risk creating an enemy of him?

"What's going on?" Meila stared at him from where she stood holding another set of ropes several feet away.

"What—"

"Yesterday, you grab me on the bridge, and since then, you've barely said anything except to ramble on about some conspiracy. And now, after we've successfully trialed a weapon that could change this stupid war, you're as glum as if you were at your own funeral."

Jaks returned her gaze, as the two gravmages gulped and

dived again. "I'm sorry I grabbed you yesterday, but I was so excited to see you . . . although it may not seem so, I've missed you more than anything. You know how I feel about you."

"I thought you'd be over that by now," she said. Did he catch a glimmer of affection in her eyes? She then shook her head, and her face was unreadable again. "We've no time for that sort of thing at the moment. We need to focus on our mission," she said with finality.

It was best not to press the issue. She did know his feelings, but he couldn't pressure her into reciprocating his love.

The divers resurfaced with a splash, then sunk away again, thankfully breaking an awkward silence.

Jaks stared at the ripples they created as his thoughts returned to his original dilemma. "He wants me to join him," he spurted out, in a sudden impulse to share his problem with Meila. "My father, that is. He wants me to go into his service."

"Your father? Is that what's stirred you up?"

"There's this artifact. A true magical artifact—I could sense the raw power it held. He's going to give it to me, if I vow fealty to him and join his retinue."

"Sounds like a bribe." She paused.

"Isn't that what I should do? Forgive and join him—like a proper son should?"

"That's taking it a bit far." Doubt clouded her face. "Maybe it wasn't such a good idea for you to have seen him on such short notice."

"But if I get the rod—I could kill him. I'm sure of it."

"What? I can't believe you'd even think of that. What sort of person would you be? Vow loyalty to your father—even for a bribe—and then murder him with the very thing he entrusts you with?" Meila shot him a look of disbelief. "That is vile. I thought I knew you better."

Jaks's shoulders slumped. He wrapped the rope around his hands, not knowing what else to do with them as they waited. "You're right. It'd make me a monster as much as him." He sighed and shook his head. "You're right. I wasn't ready to deal with him so soon."

"Say no to him and stay here with us. You know the old mage will do anything to keep you around," she said, looking down to where Mulgrave submerged. "I know nothing about the artifact your father offered you, but I doubt it can affect the course of this war as much as the velocannon. And because you're the only one who can power it, you're more important than anyone else in Ascoria at the moment. Even more than your father."

Jaks eventually nodded, seeing some truth in her words. "Do you think Grandmaster Mulgrave will take me back as an apprentice—after I said I'd given it all up?"

She chuckled. "He knew you would come back eventually."

"Did *you* think I would?"

"Probably . . ." Her face was blank and unreadable again.

At that moment, splashes and splutters signaled the divers' surfacing. Tavis paddled to the dock, swearing between breaths, as the half-naked grandmaster stroked to the wharf with rope in tow. Their conversation interrupted, Jaks and Meila bent to grip slippery arms and assisted the swimmers back up the ladder. The velocannon resurfaced too, soon after, dragged back to dry land. Meila sighed in relief and ordered the gravmancers one last task: return the device back to the lab. Once back with her tools and bench, Meila tended to the velocannon as though it were an injured and long-lost child—chastising it for its scrapes and blemishes.

Chapter 13

Father and Son

That evening, Jaks stood on the rooftop of the Academy, gazing over the city. Dunberrin was renowned as a cultural center in the Pact Countries. Opera houses, theaters, and festivals drew merchants and visitors from faraway lands to see talented performers like Karisa, and their mother before her, on stage. Colored lanterns, illumanced skyworks, and street performers had once festooned the streets, celebrating the city's brilliance. But now, shadowed with war, it looked nothing like the multicultural oasis of that past era. Instead, it was dull and lifeless.

The winter sun had fallen to dusk and cast a red-rimmed haze over the horizon lined with building tops. As vestiges of sunlight vanished, a full moon illuminated the rooftops and streets. Heralds sounded the curfew with horns and cries, and the last remaining citizens dashed home to avoid a fine or a night in jail. But throughout that eerie transcendence, Jaks thought of nothing but his father.

He was somewhere out there. On his capital ship, or in

some hall within the army district, or perhaps visiting some official. There had been more to Lord Sicaro's words yesterday than mere arrogance or wishful thinking—they hinted to disaster within a spiderweb of subterfuge and deception. Or so he thought. Just as well he had a spy that might help him refute or confirm his suspicions.

Hugging his cloak tighter, he ignored the twinge in his shoulder—thankfully healed, with only an occasional pain to remind him of the knife wound that had sunk to the bone.

He plodded past the huge bronze dome and descended a corner tower to spiral his way down to the hallway and finally into his little room. Mulgrave and Tavis were nowhere to be seen, nor Meila.

He closed the door and lay on his cot, wrapped in darkness, eager to meld with his droid and see what it had discovered.

During the weeks returning from the river city of Irin back to Dunberrin, Jaks had become well acquainted with the zinger. Within the safe confines of the Academy, while he tranced out, it was second nature now to subsume the circuits of the wrist comm: to see and hear through the droid's sensors, while flying it like a bird. And in the inner workings of the device, he had discovered how to instruct it to complete certain tasks.

Circling a hundred yards up, the zinger scanned the Lord Defender's ship. Under lightstone lamps lofted about the vessel, dozens of sailors scurried about the deck as though preparing for sailing the next day; working into the evening surely meant an early departure. Perhaps, Jaks hoped, his father was being called away and he might not have to encounter him again. Of his lordship, though, there was no sign—even with the droid's gamma sensor to pierce the deck and walls of the ship.

Fortunately, the zinger had not wasted the day. Deducing that his father's business revolved around the ship's tower, Jaks had had the droid record hours of images and sound. It only needed Jaks to review them—and surely, he would find evidence of his father's traitorous machinations.

Barely sensate to his body lying on his cot, Jaks spied on ghostly recordings of his father from earlier that day. Images played through his mind as voices accompanied the figures and revealed their secret discussions. However, after the first hour of a dull meeting with the royal quartermaster, he fell asleep.

Sometime later, he awoke to a shout nearby—but a few minutes of quiet dispelled that idea. Slightly refreshed, he returned to the zinger's memory bank.

Picking up the replay, the quartermaster finally departed with a dour look. Next, a flurry of courtiers and messengers proceeded before the Lord Defender. A late shipment of coal from Zura; Strockian mercenaries delayed; Fauconian allies questioning a request to sail east instead of west; the merchant union begging for tariff reductions; and a city physician reporting a cluster of disease. Hints of trouble, but unclear of what.

Around midday in the recording, the flow of visitors halted for a notable character: his father's man, Craeg Vesenira. The blue-tattooed swordsman from the deviant island of Ellipta sauntered in from the deck and bowed. And Kyle Halwoth, with a sneer—as always—plastered to his face, lingered by the Lord Defender's side to complete the sinister trio.

"My lord," Vesenira began. "The woman reports that she could not access the nightwraith barracks last night."

"But the rest?" Sicaro asked.

"Except for that one, all the packages have been delivered."

"Plenty enough. Three-quarters of the nightwraiths are down south, anyway. The few remaining will make little difference," Jaks's father replied to the Elliptan warrior.

"We have done all we need to do here. You've messaged the king, Master Halwoth?" Sicaro queried.

"Yes, my lord. The tower signaled the report this morning. As you say, the capital is as well-prepared as it can be. A competent commander of the Guard has been appointed. And now that your role here is complete, you return to his majesty's presence forthwith."

The Lord Defender nodded, then strode out onto the middeck with his two lackeys behind. "One last inspection of the city, then our final task tonight, and our time here will be done." A squad of soldiers clicked to attention and turned to break a path for the Lord Defender. A whistle sounded, and sailors ceased their tasks to stand and salute.

As his father walked out of the droid's scanner focus, Jaks pondered what he'd heard. What were these "packages" they spoke about? Where were they delivered? And to whom?

He had to find out more.

Jaks refocused on the zinger and sped through the rest of its memory banks. As the shadows stretched and the sailors tired around the quarterdeck, Lord Sicaro finally returned to his ship.

The bearlike man walked without hesitation to a curtained alcove. Opening a chest with a velvet lining, he wrapped a huge paw around an object and slung it to his belt. A weapon with three runestones bound in steel spirals—Vinton's Rod.

"My lord," Sneer said, as his master shuttered the curtain and returned to the main chamber. "My man in the Academy reports that the foreigner and your son have not left there this full day. Apparently, they have been causing a great disturbance in the harbor." As he spoke, he assisted his master out of his fur coat and into a black leather jerkin.

"How so?"

"That king wave that struck this afternoon? Not some freak

phenomenon but a result of a weapon that the magesmiths and the woman built. Fired out to sea, it created enough of an explosion to send a wave rushing back. Said to be made from parts created on her world."

Jaks's father stood motionless for a moment. "That mage mentioned nothing of the sort. How could he keep this from me?" His tone was more melancholy than angry.

Sneer shrugged.

"Large weapon? Siege or hand?"

"Said to be the size of a ballista. It was thrown off its perch into the harbor but was retrieved. Maybe damaged."

"The woman is the main prize, but if the weapon is not too sizeable, we will bring it back. Otherwise, I'll destroy it. Stay here. We'll be back soon." Sicaro swept out to the ship's deck, and with Vesenira behind him, vanished into the night. *The bear and his shadowdancer.*

His father's last words stabbed a sense of dread through Jaks. It must have been his father who had sent those men to kidnap Meila at the river town. He was after her again.

She was in danger.

Jaks flicked a return instruction to the zinger and then snapped out of communication with the droid. His father might even be in the Academy now; the recording was several hours old. He sensed it was near midnight; Meila would most likely be abed already.

His mind spun as it recovered from the prolonged connection with the droid. Groggily, he threw his legs over the edge of his cot, stood up in the darkness, and stumbled to the door.

Thumping noises in the hallway outside his room. Scattered light under the door. Someone was out there.

He trembled as he reached for the handle, but then pulled

away, fearing what he would find. Unbidden, electricity sparked along his fingertips. His subconscious was readying his defense; electromancy had awoken like the talons of a guardian owl.

The light under his door flickered as though someone stood outside.

Jaks stepped backward until his legs struck his cot and stopped his retreat.

The door swung open, pushed inward on well-oiled hinges. A giant stood silhouetted in the doorframe.

"Here you are. I've been looking for you, boy," his father said.

More thumps sounded from the hallway, but his attention was only for the intruder looming over him, a mere two strides away, as though he were a child again cornered in his room.

"Put it away. There's no need for that. It's just your old papa," Sicaro said. No eyepatch covered the older man's eye as it had on the previous day. Both eyes, intact and undamaged, stared at Jaks. Of course, the eyepatch had been a ruse.

As though suddenly ashamed of being found out, the crackling energy at Jaks's fingertips disappeared. "Why are you here?" he said. "What's going on out there?" He squinted into the glare of the hallway but couldn't see any sign of what was making the sounds.

"So full of questions. But I asked mine first, remember. Only yesterday—surely, you've not forgotten." His father hefted the artifact that was Vinton's Rod and waggled it toward Jaks like a chew toy to a dog. "You owe me your life, son. If I hadn't covered for the foul murder of your mother, you would have hung by the neck. Everybody hates a mother-killer."

"That's a lie . . ."

"A lie that everybody hates a *mother-killer*?"

"I didn't kill her on purpose." He stared at the long shadow of his father, unable to look into his face. Meeting his eyes would shatter his nascent courage. "It wasn't my fault. You were beating her, and I tried to defend her . . . the bolt stunned you both. It was an accident. She fell down the stairs."

"Yet, still the same result." Lord Sicaro thudded the tip of Vinton's Rod against the stone floor and planted both hands on the top. "She was an adulterer, you know. By rights, I could have had her tried and imprisoned—you just did the job first."

"More lies. Lies, lies!" Jaks glared at his father, angry enough now to look at him directly. His fists clenched into balls. How dare he malign her like that—his mother, who had given everything to raise them. "She wasn't like that. You twist everything. She used to be famous, and you couldn't bear the attention she got. But she never strayed from us . . . or you."

"How the pup loved his mother," Lord Sicaro quipped. "She was a pretender. Deceitful and lying, like them all. If only you could see through the masks she wore. Not like you and I, boy."

"I'm not like you. I would never be a tyrant." Jaks needed to unveil this beast. How could his father wrap himself in so many deceits? "I know what you used to do to Karisa . . . she was just little . . . your daughter, of all things. You're the monster. You beat your wife, you tortured me, you abused your daughter—*you* are the liar here."

Lord Sicaro stood rock steady; the air seethed with tension —ready to burst into fire. But when he spoke, his tone was level and calm. "If we're talking monsters, son, you need only look at yourself, boy. It was you who killed your mother."

Jaks panted for several breaths, ignoring the accusations, true as they were, and then continued, "I also know you're planning some treason. I don't know what it is, but I heard you conspiring with your men. I will tell the king."

Lord Sicaro shook his head slowly. Then, as though disappointed at Jaks's outburst, he said, "This little room is far too small for this. Come out into the hallway." He turned and walked out, still clutching Vinton's Rod.

Jaks balked, swaying and grinding his teeth as his anger dissipated, to be replaced with fear. Despite his earlier bravado, he saw no way out of this situation. Cornered and desperate, his electromancy was his only ally, but his fright spiraled tornado-like, sucking away the focus and imagery needed to invoke the magic. He just wanted to slide under the bed and hide.

An exchange of voices in the hallway, out of sight, refocused his attention. His father and his henchmen? Did they have Meila? Or were they still searching for her? Maybe she had worked late into the night in the maze of labs downstairs. She had little need for sleep. He had to find her before they did.

Jaks fumbled for his sword where it lay nudged into a corner and pulled it from its sheath. He sidled out of his room. The doors were all closed down the hallway, except for one.

Outside Meila's room, three figures faced him. And there she stood, immobile.

A blindfold, a gag, and ropes around her wrists bound her, while a muscular Vesenira clamped thick fingers around her arm. Blood trickled from a split in the shadowdancer's lip; he spat and smeared red over his chin. Meila, too, showed evidence of violence: grazed knuckles and a severe lean as she held her weight off her bare right foot.

In her lightweight flightsuit—that she still often wore, swearing it kept her warmer than any other garment—she cast a tiny figure against the two warriors detaining her.

As Jaks stepped out of the doorway, Lord Sicaro tapped Vinton's Rod to Meila's chest. "Your friend here is quite the battler." She twisted against Vesenira's grip and shook her head as though to rid herself of the blindfold and gag.

Jaks stopped in the center of the hallway. "Leave her be . . . I don't want to fight you. But I will if I have to." His knuckles whitened around his sword. "I won't let you hurt her—not like every other person I've loved."

"He loves her? Isn't that nice," Vesenira said, then laughed.

"Let her go."

"She doesn't need your help," Sicaro said.

"Let her go." Jaks raised his sword an inch. To fully brandish a blade at his father would be unreconcilable.

"Who is in the right here?" Sicaro asked. "What is she really, son? . . . nothing but a ward of the state. I am merely taking her back into custody. I have rescinded her captivity and am taking her under the king's protection."

Jaks faltered. It was true. His father would bear all rights in his position to do what he wanted with prisoners in the city. Blocking him was to impede a royal agent. It might as well have been the king standing here. The tip of his sword dipped to the floor.

"Now, put it away." Sicaro lowered the rod from Meila's chest.

But Jaks wasn't finished. He looked at the stump of his missing finger—one of the many "punishments" from his father. "But this isn't about *your* privilege. This is about right and wrong." Anger burned like a naked flame. "Your twisted words bare your corruptness. You cannot confuse me with them any longer. I know what you are. And I won't stand for it." He raised the sharp point of his sword at his father. "Now, I'm telling you again, let her go."

"Take the prisoner. Go find the device." Lord Sicaro half-turned to Vesenira. Wordlessly, the swordsman tossed Meila over a shoulder like a sack, opened the door at the end of the hallway, and vanished into the darkened library. "Uh-uh," his father said when Jaks took a step toward them.

Sicaro's eyes then drooped. Sadness etched his face like lines of bark.

Jaks's sword tore away from his hand, suddenly heavier than a block of granite. When it struck the floor, it didn't bounce or rebound, but clung as though glued by an extraordinary force. Then, Jaks sagged uncontrollably to his knees, succumbing to a weight that pressed down on his head, his shoulders, his arms—the over-bearing heaviness of gravmancy.

"I never hated you, boy—you just had nothing worth taking notice of. A thready runt with no backbone," his father was saying, as Jaks's face remained plastered against the cold stone floor. "But after hearing about how you broke the siege at Irin, I thought you might finally have something worth bringing in."

Jaks fought for breath, barely hearing his father's monologue crushed beneath the tyrant's gravmantic invocation. Too much longer and he would suffocate.

"But it's clear your backbone is as stiff and inflexible as that of your bitch sister. Obsessed with rules and lacking ambition. The two of you have been of no use to me. If only you were more like your little sister—such a pleasing and progressive creature."

Jaks growled in this throat but emitted little more than a mewl. Intolerable, to hear this monster spewing more lies, talking about Karisa as though she craved to please his vile whims.

Although he hoped Grandmaster Mulgrave might come to his rescue, he needed to regain control, himself.

Immobile under his father's gravmancy, he reached for the

only thing he could think of—remembering how Meila had distracted the warrior in the attic.

The zinger droid was hovering in the freezing night outside Mulgrave's library, awaiting instructions. At Jaks's command, it smashed through a painted glass panel and zipped through the bookshelves toward the light of the open door. It centered on a giant, silhouetted figure and darted forward—its tiny but powerful motivator transforming it into a dangerous projectile.

"What's that?" Sicaro said, a few moments after the glass broke. He inclined his head to listen.

A thud, followed by a grunt, granted Jaks release from his father's control. Like a marble slab lifted from his back, the magical weight dissipated and once again Jaks could lift his head. His father was bent with one hand on his knee: stunned by the zinger's blow.

The giant reached down to the droid lying inactive by his foot and picked it up. Inspecting it, he grunted again, and then dropped it to the stone floor and crushed it under his heel.

Jaks felt a pang of anger and loss, as though his father had murdered his pet. He pushed up onto his hands and knees.

Another object lay in the hallway, halfway between them—Vinton's Rod.

The zinger's strike must have sent the artifact flying from his father's hand. Whichever of them possessed it would have an advantage. Jaks had felt its dormant power; he didn't know if his father could use that power, but either way, he needed to get to it first.

Jumping to his feet as his father continued to grind the zinger underfoot, he sprinted for the rod.

But, with his hand almost on one of its runestone spirals, his father was already there.

Sicaro landed from a leap of jaguar speed—that, as a human, only a gravmancer could achieve—and kicked aside Jaks's hand.

A gauntlet followed, an uppercut that smacked into his forehead and sent him flying backward down the hall.

Stunned from the blow, his vision clouded, Jaks staggered, pushing against the wall. A framed painting of a past grandmaster lay fractured nearby, knocked down by the fracas.

"Too slow, son—"

A hesitant voice called from behind his father's back. "My lord . . ." The voice came again, in an even higher pitch. "My Lord Sicaro, is that you? What is going on?" The speaker stood in the doorway from the library. Tavis, wrapped in a nightgown. "A noise awoke me . . ." His voice petered out. Jaks hoped it was because the apprentice had comprehended the violence before him.

"You should have stayed in your bed," Sicaro said.

Jaks's head cleared in time to witness his father turn and strike the blurry-eyed Tavis with the end of the rod. The apprentice's head crumpled. Blood and brain splattered the wall as his body fell to the floor. *Oh, God, Tavis. I'm so sorry.*

"You shouldn't have done that. He wasn't involved," Jaks heard himself say, astonished that his voice held up despite his bowels twisting like snakes. Tavis's corpse continued to trickle blood from its shattered skull. Blood dripped from the tip of the deadly rod. Did it seem to glow in his father's murderous hand?

"You're all involved. Sadly, that's what you don't seem to understand." Sicaro kicked aside Tavis's body, imprinting the pooling blood with his boots. "If you are not my servant, you are my enemy."

Face still throbbing from the earlier slap, Jaks backstepped two paces from his father. Fearful of being gravmanced to the ground again, he had to use the advantage of distance.

Sicaro strode toward him, rod half-raised, face curled as though he regretted the violence to follow.

Jaks punched the air at his father and threw his fear along his arm and transformed it into lightning. He yelled as jagged lines of electricity cracked through the air. Metallic odor filled his nostrils. The hallway erupted with brilliant light.

And lightning struck Vinton's Rod.

Silence spanned the distance between them in the corridor. Lord Sicaro and Jaks froze and stared at the magical artifact that the older man held in front of him. Two of the once dark runestones glowed emerald green in their steel spirals after absorbing Jaks's lightning bolt. Dreadful realization stabbed at Jaks. Vinton's Rod stored electromancy, just as a common lightstone stored an illumancer's power.

Sicaro sighed as the rod dipped to the floor. "Such a waste," he said. The runestones colored the giant's face in a sickly green glow. The rod then angled toward Jaks. "How does this go?" Electricity then scintillated the cages of the runestones as though seeking an escape.

Anticipating his father's next move, Jaks invoked the one defense he knew. Electromancy sprung into a cocoon around him, dancing and circling in a protective shield. Over the past weeks, he had refined the invocation to a point where he could now see through this shield while keeping it reactive enough to repel any regular weapon. Although confident it would shield him from an elemental power of his own creation, he was uncertain whether it would repel the attacks of a gravmancer.

The tip of Vinton's Rod leveled. His father, unperturbed by the scintillating shell around his target, mouthed words and thrust the glowing artifact at Jaks.

The rod blasted out lightning, filling the hallway, probing the walls and ceiling. Drawn to Jaks's shield, as though thirsting to rejoin its source, the power returned. The shield pulsed and absorbed the electricity, but his doubts grew as his cocoon grew hotter and brighter—blinding him to anything outside his invocation. Over the sounds of the crackling magic, another sound—deeper, more ominous—drew his sightless eyes upward.

Then the shield exploded.

Hard fragments peppered his head, and dust filled his throat. The overhead noise became an aching groan.

His shield overpowered, and his vision clearing, Jaks gasped at the sight of tremendous blackened cracks in the curved ceiling. They riddled the stonework from above his head down the hallway to where his father still stood.

"I'm still here . . ." Jaks croaked in defiance.

Stone fragments fell around Lord Sicaro, repelled by a cocoon of his own gravmantic power. With a snarl, the giant raised Vinton's Rod to the ceiling—and *pulled* it down.

Chunks of granite, placed by gravmasons and supported for centuries by mortar and sheer weight, tore from the ceiling. His last glimpse of his father was of the man turning away before disappearing behind the veil of falling rock.

The ceiling buckled toward Jaks in an avalanche. Panic spurred him to scramble backward. He turned and ran, one arm above his head, as though he could hold back the massive blocks of stone.

At the end of the hallway, he flung open the door to the water room, but the small alcove yielded no exit. A dead end.

Jaks climbed up on the washbasin, feeling the press of the brass tap against his back, and turned to face his doom.

A wave of dust blew over his face and all light blinked out. Half-deafened by the smashing of stone, and blind to approaching death, he held his breath until the burning in his lungs forced them open again.

Several more breaths . . .

He coughed. If not for that spontaneous act, he could've believed himself dead, such was the quiet and darkness around him.

With extended hands, he probed the alcove's walls and traced the surface to the door. But instead of open air, his fingers found only rough, unyielding hardness. Cupping his hand, he concentrated, and a tiny ball of lightning spun into life with flickering light.

Blocks of granite piled against the doorframe. Bizarrely, amongst the settling dust lay broken lengths of wood and leather-bound books. The Academy's main library had rested above the hallway; now, parts of it lay within. Although alive, Jaks couldn't budge anything but a few torn volumes and small rocks from the debris.

He was trapped.

An hour passed and, with each minute, Jaks felt fragments of his soul go with them. Meila was in the grips of his father and Vesenira, bound and restrained. Each second seemed to seal her fate as much as he was sealed in this veritable tomb.

With nothing else to do but wait in hopes of rescue, Jaks sought to make sense of the events. What did his father want with her? An object of desire? He had seen the gleam of interest his father had in her; that, he could understand, but not the lengths his father had taken to kidnap her. It could not be a salacious need. He must have another reason to possess her. They said knowledge was power. Perhaps that was his motive. But for what ultimate purpose?

He wondered whether he should be sad that his own father had tried to kill him. Perhaps in a different lifetime, but not this one.

He had never doubted the man could murder without

remorse—whether it be a warrior on a battlefield, or his own son in his bedroom. The attempts today merely consolidated Jaks's suspicions of a monumental deceit cranking in the hands of an evil man. Although he had no grasp of his father's plan, he had to convince the king that he was in danger from his most-trusted nobleman.

After another period of shouting and useless shoves at the rubble, he finally heard voices yell back at him from above. Another half hour passed before Grandmaster Mulgrave and several other Academy gravmancers found him and lifted away enough debris for Jaks to scramble up to what was left of the main library.

"It was my father—" Jaks began as soon as he clambered up beside his rescuers. Several incredulous faces stared at the dust-covered Jaks, not at his appearance but at his accusation.

"Come away," the grandmaster said, pulling him to a desk and chair away from the collapsed pit of shelves and stone. All the Academy staff seemed to be in the library, helping with the damaged floor or hindering with pointless instructions. "I found Tavis dead. We haven't found the lass. Tell me."

Jaks recounted the confrontation and fight with his father and then described the suspicious conversations he had witnessed in the zinger's recordings. He left nothing out, and by the time he finished, he was out of breath, having spoken so quickly. "We might be able to save her. We have to go after her."

The grandmaster rubbed his chin and then his head. A habit of the mage when mulling over a hard decision. Eventually, he shook his head. "It's been over three hours. If what you say is true, and I do believe you, he'll have her wherever he wants by now. If it was to his frigate, it would be impossible to get to her without a fight. You must remember that he has all the city garrison on his side." Mulgrave's face sank with a sadness that Jaks had never seen in him before. "The Lord Defender marches to his own beat. I do not doubt your suspicions about him, but there is nothing to evidence his actions or intent except your word."

"If we can prove he has Meila, it would show that he came here and killed Tavis . . . and tried to kill me."

"But would not prove that Lord Sicaro intends to kill the king or contest his crown—which is what you're saying. Alas, your father is a powerful man. Not one at which you can casually point the finger of treason. I'm sorry, Jaks, but thin accusations from an estranged son will convince the king of nothing."

"I have to do something." Jaks hammered the desk with a fist and several books bounced. "I snuck into a captured city. I can sneak into the docks. That has to be where he's taken her."

Mulgrave shook his head. "You'll get nowhere until the curfew lifts. Your father has turned the night guard into militant thugs and the gate-men into prison keepers—all in the name of keeping the city safe." He paused as Jaks's agitation sidled into desperate futility. "Once the curfew lifts, I will see what I can do. Besides, I will need the time to rally Grandmaster Hazeldine and the rest of the faculty. I'll need them to accompany me as witnesses. From what you say, I dare not audience with him alone."

Jaks nodded as though to join him.

"Yes. But *you* must stay behind. I would not risk what might happen if he saw you still alive, even with us all there. There cannot be a fight," Mulgrave said. "Based on your report, I will confront the Lord Defender at his naval yards and demand he explain himself. Although, I don't think he will willingly give up Meila. Considering the efforts he's made to take her, we can at least confirm the situation. And after that, we can seek the king's favor for her return." The grandmaster then sighed and rubbed his eyes. "But first . . . I have a dead apprentice to take care of."

Jaks followed the grandmaster down to the Academy morgue—nothing more than a small basement—and stood next to Tavis's draped body for several minutes. Responsibility for his death dragged like a millstone around his neck. Although they had clashed over apprenticeships, his tears for the big-eared youth were as genuine as any he had wept before. Tavis's life would have been so much better without Jaks around.

"I am in need of a new apprentice . . ." Mulgrave raised his eyebrows inquiringly at Jaks.

"I'd be honored, Grandmaster." He bowed awkwardly, all too aware of the proximity of the dead apprentice he was replacing. "I shouldn't have abandoned your tutorage in the first place. I hope I can serve you as well as he did."

"I'm sure you will. Maybe not in the same capacity, but I'm sure you will."

Leaving the morgue, they passed through the lab, looking for Meila's velocannon, checking on his father's threat to steal or destroy the weapon. Jaks sighed in relief, finding it standing untouched where he had last seen Meila working on it, although now covered by a sheet and tied with rope, as when he had first seen it.

However, what was out of order was an over-sized prototype of a gravfire mortar that Meila had decided was too cumbersome to use. Flattened and crushed to pieces, its tubing and frame were destroyed. Meila had outsmarted her captors on at least one thing, fooling them, at least temporarily, into believing the lesser weapon was what had upended the ocean. Jaks smiled at her cleverness.

"Not all is lost. At least we still have her inventions."

Mulgrave nodded. "Get some rest. Use Tavis's room if you need," he said, reminding Jaks of the demolished hallway leading to his own room. "I'll go round up the faculty now."

Jaks returned to the grandmaster's library and slumped into a chair. He sent an instruction to the droid above Irin City to return, and then, still wide awake, drummed his fingers over the central desk as he awaited the rising sun.

Hours later, the horns blew an end to the curfew, and dawn colored the lead-lined window.

Seeking to examine the weather, he walked over and peered through the break in the windowpane made by the zinger that last evening.

But at a sight that drained his last hopes, he stiffened and bellowed a cry of anguish.

Too late.

At full sail, Lord Sicaro's frigate was far out at sea.

He thumped his fist on the windowsill, mindless of the glass fragments, and emitted a sob.

He knew exactly where Meila would be. There was only one place. And that ship was sailing.

Chapter 14

Ascension

Meila–Sicaro's Frigate, City of Irin

The sound of chanting roused Meila from a restless sleep. The chain attached to the iron cuff around her ankle scraped against the floor of her prison. Unnecessary because of the locked ironwood door and guards outside, but Lord Sicaro, she had learned, insured his cargo several times over. And, it seemed, she was his most precious.

Even after a fortnight of sailing, and the ship having docked two weeks ago, she remained confined to the brig with only a thick, smudged portal to tell her day from night. And even then, her knowledge of the blurred, but majestic, buildings through the glass came only from overhearing the chatter of her prison guards: they were docked in the Vor-conquered City of Irin.

To combat hours and days of tedium, she sought comfort from her memories over the past weeks. She called on visual and auditory recordings of her daughter, engineering school friends, Anton, and, strangely, Jaks.

No opportunity for escape had presented, but she would not give up hope. She had escaped worse situations before.

They knew nothing of her implants or illumancy. Those and her wits. She would use them to escape, somehow.

She pushed aside her blanket and sat up on the thin mattress—the one piece of furniture they allowed her, other than the chamber pot in the corner.

The chanting and shouting continued, and she bolstered her auditory implants to clarify the distant voices. Thousands of voices. Adulatory and excited.

"Trumpus, nai garn. Trumpus, Garn Sicaro!" enthusiastic crowds repeated throughout the city. Whoops and yells accompanied the mobs.

"What are they saying?" Meila called through the bars in the door at a guard, who also oriented her head to the noise.

"Glory, the new king. Glory, King Sicaro. Or something like that," the pig-nosed woman replied. "Our leader is finally at the station he deserves," she stated without any lick of sarcasm. An idolatrous smile and insane glint twisted her face—clearly one of the many sycophantic minions who infested this ship. She cuffed one of the other guards on the shoulder and pulled him into a circle-dance as they both laughed in delight.

The words, however, burned like molten lead in Meila's stomach. Disbelief dissolved into dismay. What dominoes had fallen in the past weeks to dispose of the previous Vor king? So quickly? Her captor was even slyer than she had ever imagined. Jaks had thought it was the Ascorian king who was in danger, but it was the Vor king who had been dethroned.

Later that evening, several Vor warriors led by Sicaro's head minion, Sneer, clanked into her prison cell. He motioned and the largest of the goons kicked Meila in the shin until she stood up.

She said nothing, ignoring the pain, and stared daggers into the man's head.

"Put this on her," Sneer said. The warrior obeyed without hesitation, snapping a leather-lined collar with a chain around her neck and cuffs around her wrists. The female guard then sidled past and unlocked Meila's leg-iron.

"I understand congratulations are in order," Meila said to Sneer as the man tugged on her chain, leading her up through the ship. She was glad to escape this floating prison but couldn't resist a jab at one of her kidnappers. "Your esteemed leader . . . now a king. Who would have thought? It seems these barbarians will follow any hairy swine."

Kyle Halwoth paused mid-step and stiffened at her taunt. He tugged on her chain, snapping her head back, and glowered. "Behave," he chided her, wagging a finger. He resumed the climb up the stairs that opened to the middeck and moonlit night.

The Vor thug behind her planted a hand on her backside and shoved her up the hatch.

The buildings of Irin, lining the river, flickered and wavered in the light of thousands of torches, pulling away as if horrified at the riotous celebration seething through the streets and avenues below them, their grandeur mocked by warriors and followers drunkenly vomiting and pissing over centuries-old fences, porches, and hedgerows. Bookshelves, paintings, tables, chairs—anything that would burn—were dragged from mansions to fuel great celebratory pillars of fire.

Meila, thankful for the clearance given her by her armed escorts, trudged behind Sneer through the chaotic corridors of the city. Her experience of Vor natives was limited to her interactions with the captives they had taken at the wreckage of the *Mendhelsson.* Their behavior, albeit as prisoners, had suggested none of the potential for the debauchery that raged around her now.

Despite the chill winter night, nakedness danced with abandon around bonfires, and lust humped and grunted within the doorways and recesses. Fights broke out with fists thrashing in the semidark. And everywhere, barrels poured out mugfuls of froth and ale to sate the staggering crowds of merrymakers.

A barricade of stone blocks ended their march through the wild night. Sentries ushered them through to a makeshift courtyard that, in contrast to the streets outside, was disciplined and tense. Vor warriors and ex-Ascorian soldiers—presumably traitors from Sicaro's retinue—stood guard together. They eyeballed one another as though, at any moment, this armistice would fragment.

Before her, the palace, for it could not be called anything less, wore the majesty of the surrounding city. Several stories high, it was crowned with palisades and fronted with towers at each corner. The upper windows were punctuated with flower racks beneath each, but no balconies were to be seen.

And inside, all glittered with gold. Statues, orbs, vases, and even sitting furniture glistened with luxurious yellow under lightstone chandeliers.

Meila balked at the opulence. Back on Earth, such waste of precious elements was rare on the homeworlds. The United Worlds had dealt with such class-bound maldistributions of wealth many millennia ago. Here on Planet Maya, despots, dictators, and their nobility still hoarded their riches—while their peasants scrapped the ground for sustenance. At least the UWF were good for some things.

Sneer tugged on her leash again, snapping her head back and yanking her from her thoughts.

They arrived at an antechamber before an ornate pair of doors. Two guards, both tough-looking women, straightened to attention as the trio approached. A hound behind them growled menacingly.

"This is King Rauhalik's new prisoner. She is to join the others," Sneer addressed the tallest guard. Although he spoke in the Ascorian tongue, the woman comprehended his instructions. She nodded and turned to the doors while extracting an iron key hung from a pocket.

Sweet scent and perfume escaped the doors as they swung open. The guard captain vanished into the chamber beyond. Seconds later, the room flooded with light; a central lightstone sconce reflected light off mirrors and golden surfaces and illuminated the far reaches of the room.

Her heart raced; her senses absorbed the sensuous fabrics, languishing settees, and the fragrant air. Was she to be a pleasure slave once more? A rare creature to expand a collection? A flashback from her year of slavery returned to her —defiled and hopeless on an orbital station, an object of a depraved cult—filling her with panic until she stamped out the fear with a tweak to the implant in her amygdala.

"What do you want at this time of night, captain?" a young woman's voice called out in Ascorian. Several figures, tucked under fine blankets and lying prone on stacks of velvet and sateen, were scattered around the chamber. A few stirred and groaned in their bed-places, covering eyes with a hand or a cushion.

However, the woman who spoke was already on her feet next to a long, plush settee against a pillar in the center of the room. Wrapped in red and white silks, her limbs were naked and her hair tousled and wild.

Meila stared, wide-eyed. A tingle of déjà vu unsettled her as she regarded the woman's face. Thick locks of yellow hair framed a face of cosmic beauty. High-cheeked, wide of eye and mouth, and plush of lips. The type of face that would draw stares from men and women, no matter which planet they colonized. Meila squinted, as the initial sense of recognition—she would not have forgotten this face if she had ever seen her before—shifted to envy. She snorted back a laugh at herself. She was losing her mind. Jealousy? Ludicrous in the circumstances. How could she begrudge a courtesan for her attractiveness in a harem?

"And who is this?" The woman stared back at her while tightening the impractical silk shifts around her torso and waist.

"Ah, lovely Karisa," interrupted the rat-faced Sneer. "You must remember your father telling you of our new guest?"

Looking Meila up and down, she replied, "Your new prisoner, you mean."

"Karisa . . ." Meila said, choking back her surprise. The woman's gaze narrowed in return. "You're Jaks's sister."

That was the source of familiarity. The doe-like eyes, high brow, and straight-edged nose. Like brother, like sister. But what cast him handsome for a man, sculpted her celestial as a woman.

"You know my brother?" Karisa turned to Sneer. "Is this some sort of trick?" she demanded as she stepped forward until a chain halted her. She hooked fingers under a slave collar wrapped in soft leather around her neck.

"No tricks. Why would I play games with you?"

The guard captain interrupted, "My lord, is the new one to remain collared and chained?"

"Release her. She is no mage," Sneer replied, tearing away a wolflike gaze he had fixed on his master's daughter.

Not that you know of, thought Meila.

A few minutes later, with the restraints removed and both Sneer and the guard captain retreated from the harem, Meila rubbed her neck where the collar had chaffed.

"Turn out the light," a woman's voice croaked from the shadows, its owner a figure lying on a mass of cushions.

Karisa slid a hand over the lighting sconce, and the room plunged back into darkness. Seconds later, dim yellow and red flames danced along the top edge of the centerpiece settee as though it were on fire—illumancy, for the fabric remained unsinged.

The blonde-haired courtesan sat down on the settee, heedless of the flame illusion behind her head, and pulled a blanket around her shoulders and knees. She looked at Meila. "How do you know Jaks? Does Father keep him prisoner too?" Pushing aside a cushion, she patted an empty spot beside her.

Knowing the risks and dangers that Jaks had taken in attempting to rescue this young woman, and knowing the abuses she had suffered as a child—and presumably now—Meila brushed aside Karisa's contained manner and was overwhelmed with a need to comfort her. She reached for Karisa and wrapped her arms around her, pushing aside iron links hanging from her slave collar. Her eyes moistened, and she replied, "No, he's no prisoner."

Karisa stiffened at the embrace but soon relaxed into her arms.

Meila broke the hold and sat back with Karisa's hand in hers. "They fought. Your father and him—Jaks was trying to stop him from taking me. There was violence. Thunder. The inside walls of the Academy collapsed. It couldn't have been anything but his electromancy . . . but then your father emerged with no sign of Jaks."

"I'm sure he's alive. I would know if he was gone." The young woman looked uncertain, as though trying to convince herself of the denial.

"I hope so. He would have fought his hardest."

"What is he to you?" Karisa asked, her blue eyes turned down at the outer edges, reminding Meila of Jaks's face when he spoke of his mother. "I haven't seen him for a long while. Were you lovers—"

"No. Nothing like that," Meila cut in. Guilt twisted her gut at the memory of how she had spurned his romantic advances. How it must have shattered his heart. "He tutored me in prison and helped petition my release to the Academy under Grandmaster Mulgrave."

"I can't place your accent. Is it from the south . . . the Isles of Ranila? No, that's not right. I've never seen your like before. And one thing I know is faces."

"I'll tell you, but keep an open mind . . ." Meila began, and then shared with Karisa deep into the night, trusting that this sister of Jaks and Vixhana would keep her secrets from their captors. She described her homeworld and her flight career. Conjured scale-model images of the starship *Mendhelsson* and pictures of a dying Earth to an intrigued and wide-eyed Karisa. And finally, she recounted the journeys and encounters that she and Jaks had endured.

It was the first time she had spoken so fully of her exhilarating adventures on this planet with another person. It was cathartic. Enthralled by Meila's origins, the young woman was an attentive audience and, unsurprisingly, saddened to hear about her sister rendered unconscious by Jaks's electromancy.

Meila ended her story and said, "I don't know what your father wants with me. But I didn't think it would be for this kind of thing." Her eyes darted around the chamber decorated with colored silks. "He went to a lot of bother to kidnap me, but I haven't seen him since that day. Just that sniveling minion of his eyeballing from time to time."

"Everything he does has a purpose. You are pretty . . . he

takes what he wants," Karisa said, wringing her fingers together until she looked down to them and smoothed out her palms.

"I'm sure I'll find out soon enough," Meila said. "Unless we can find a way out of here before then. But first, tell me what has been happening here."

Karisa folded her legs on the settee and described the recent events. A week before Lord Sicaro's frigate had docked, the Vor king had fallen ill with a mysterious ailment. By the morning her father arrived, King Harek had been dead for two full days. "I'm sure my father had something to do with it . . . probably some plan to coincide with his arrival. He must have planted an assassin close to the king," said Karisa.

"The king had no heir? Isn't that how these dictators plan their succession?" Meila asked.

"A child the age of seven. Back in the Vor capital. But she's of no consequence, apparently—the Vor way is only through combat."

"I should have guessed."

"It was chaos out there. The one time I was glad to be locked away safe. We could hear clashing in the streets, and a few times, even in the palace corridors. Continuing even until this morning. One challenger would win, with peace and quiet for a day; then another would arise the next."

"So, what's different about your father winning today? Won't there just be another challenger tomorrow?"

"Possibly. But he has already eliminated two other contenders, even before they challenged him. The last had been Voros's most powerful pyromancer. A legend, so the chambermaid says. Thought to be undefeatable. I didn't witness the duel, of course, but apparently father easily bested him with speed and lightning."

"Lightning. I thought Jaks was the only one around who could do that?"

Karisa shrugged. Chain links rustled with her movement. "Perhaps it runs in the family? Maybe . . ." She stared wishfully at her hands. The next moment, tiny lightning bolts sparked to life and danced around her fingers—but without the crackle or presence of real electricity. Disappointed, she folded her fingers into a fist.

Their discussion turned to details of the palace, from what little information Karisa had garnered from her shackled excursions to the gardens and to and from King Harek's bedchamber before he died.

The courtesans' chamber itself comprised three rooms: the lounge where they lived and slept, a bathing room with a pool of flowing, warm water pumped around the building, and a toileting closet that the women used—except Karisa, always chained, forced to use a lidded pot that a chambermaid would empty and scent daily.

There were several entrances and exits around the palace. Kitchen-workers, servants, and guards accessed various doors and gates around the building, while the main entrance was only open to guests and officials. However, escape would not be easy, for even the lowliest of portals was highly guarded.

"Rope these silks out the window?" Meila speculated.

"No. Guards on the ground and dragons in the air. We wouldn't get far."

The outworlder continued thinking out loud. "Jaks escaped the city through sewers to the river."

"The chambermaid complains about odorous sewers," Karisa said.

"Can you find out if there's a connection from the palace?"

"Yes, if anyone knows, Rasish will know. I'll find out from

her. Even though she has to empty my waste, she says I'm the only person who talks to her."

"It's a start. Getting rid of that collar is going to be a problem, though. Does it nullify your magic as well?"

Karisa shook her head. "Just plain iron. It's all it needs to be." She sighed, pulling at the device futilely.

"If only we could get a key," Meila said, wondering who else other than the guard captain could unlock the padlock on the collar.

"Do you know how to pick locks? None of us know. Maybe you do?" Karisa's eyes lit with hope as she fingered the metal restraint.

"We don't have mechanical locks like that where I come from. Our neuronal signatures are our keys." Meila bent closer to examine the device. "I could try to figure it out."

Sunlight edged the window curtains, and a few of the sleepers stirred. A woman on a plump sofa nearby propped herself up on an elbow. She yawned, then her face wrinkled as she studied Meila. "You must be the new girl . . . what is that you're wearing?"

The topic of her flightsuit, worn for almost a month, and her unwashed state became the focus of the five women who comprised the late King Harek's harem—and so presumably the new king's—as they each awoke and descended upon their new companion.

Meila needed little encouragement to strip off her flightsuit and sink into the steaming waters of the harem's bathing pool. Three of the courtesans, including Karisa, scrubbed her back and lathered her hair. Meila laughed in surprise when one woman, a buxom brunette named Takola, bucketed water over her head. When the last drops trickled down her face, they teased her about the layer of scum that her bathing had left in the pool. Fortunately, a ready supply of hot water replaced the first, gushing from a bronze tap shaped like a lion's mouth.

Refusing to wrap herself in one of the ridiculous silk swathes that the courtesans wore, Meila hand-washed her flightsuit and slipped it back on, knowing that its advanced material would leech out moisture and be dry within minutes.

The following two days passed with no further challenges to the Vor crown, and Meila learned every detail of her ornate prison. In their daily routine, the courtesans—except for one girl, prone to spontaneous weeping, torn from her family's farm only a few weeks before—would craft a joint fantasy of courtly grandeur within their prison: serving tea to one another, reading out poetry, and singing. In efforts to keep up the illusion, Karisa would illumance away the chain around her neck, even though its weight could be seen to drag on her. "We know it's a farce, but it's the only way to not end up like her," Karisa explained, glancing at the timid, red-eyed girl clutching a cushion to her chest. "Harek had her only once, but she was a virgin up to then. She has the curse."

"Curse?" From afar, Meila studied the girl's face for flaws but found only perfection.

"She has the look of an angel. For as long as she possesses beauty, she will be pursued by men driven to own it."

Meila laughed ironically. "Yes, this world and every other. Only where women are treated the equal of men, is it curtailed. And, even then, it is only by wafer-thin layers of civility that keep men from falling to their desires."

"Not Jaks, though," Karisa defended her brother.

"All men," Meila asserted.

During those two days, Meila made many attempts to unlock the padlock around Karisa's neck, kneeling beside the young woman as she lay on a divan patiently. She guessed that as a start, the pins inside the device needed to be manipulated exactly to activate the lock. However, the hairpins that they had were too stiff and broke at any attempt to bend them into a helpful shape. They needed something more flexible.

The only people to visit the courtesans were the harem guards, who delivered food and drink twice a day, and the chambermaid. The girl, Rasish, visited each morning and completed her duties, cheerily carrying an empty chamber pot when she arrived, and still smiling even as she left with a used one.

Despite her unenviable job, the girl's joy was constant. "Only when I come here, miss," Rasish said, when Meila commented about her demeanor. "The princess is so lovely, and she is always nice to me."

She looked at Karisa, who smiled back at her and replied, "Thank you, Rasish. You're beautiful too. I hope that one day, we can all be free and happy like you."

Then, on the second day of their frustrated attempts to manipulate the padlock, Karisa leaned to the girl's ear and asked, "Will you bring us some nice hairpins, Rasish? Ones that will bend and won't break."

The girl agreed with a nod.

That afternoon, Sneer was back with his personal guards. Without explanation, they escorted Meila by the arm along the corridors and stairways of the palace until they stopped in a round chamber.

A pair of guards stood before a single iron door.

With no other exits, whatever lay behind that portal must be important. Was this her new holding cell? A few minutes later, Sneer's guards clattered to attention. *"Trumpus, Garn Sicaro,"* they chanted in unison, as a giant figure with several more Vor warriors approached.

King Sicaro claimed no adornments with his new title, looking much the same as how Meila had first seen him on his frigate and every time after. His dark eyes pierced into her soul from within his bearded face. He wore a black bearskin draped over his shoulders, a black steel chest-piece, and banded armor over his arms and legs. A sheathed sword hung at one hip, and a twisted spiral of iron at the other.

Sicaro approached the door and pressed a dimly glowing runestone to a panel; the slab of iron then slid into a slot in the ceiling, revealing a tunnel beyond.

"No interruptions," he said to his men and disappeared inside. Sneer nudged Meila into the room.

A lightstone flared to life in its sconce. Three doors, similar to the first, awaited. The king paused before the furthest and again applied the runestone key to the door.

Another lightstone ignited within a chamber filled with shelves that sagged with gold and silver bars, golden ornaments, and chests that, too, must be filled with riches.

"I have heard stories of your kind," Sicaro said to Meila. Without waiting for a reply, he strode to a steel chest and bent to manipulate its lock. He continued, "Someone had Harek believing your people fell from some distant star."

Meila stilled herself, a sense of dread rising into her chest. It could only have been Anton who informed the late Vor king of their origins. Her dead husband might have volunteered the information at first, but their subsequent treatment of him—enslavement—suggested they wanted more. And, that their last meeting was at the crash site of the *Mendhelsson*, told her he had most probably bartered the promise of high-tech salvage in exchange for his life—just as she had.

"What you're wearing seems to reinforce your oddness. However, fanciful myths don't draw my interest, and frankly, I don't really care where you come from," Sicaro said. "What does interest me, though . . . is this." He reached into the chest and lifted out a beautifully engineered object. Familiar to her eye and training, it was a darkcore rifle.

"What is it?" Meila played dumb. She knew exactly what the UWF12MW Standard Darkcore Rifle was. She just didn't know how he had acquired one.

He pointed the barrel at her.

She flinched. *Damn.*

"You know very well what it is and what it can do." With the weapon still pointed at her chest, he pulled the trigger. This time, she forced herself not to react. She knew it wouldn't fire. Only she, as the ship's commander, had authority to unlock a rifle—whether it be to a specific individual with implants or to a specific neuronal signature as she had for Jaks. Only *in extremis* would she remove all the protections that prevented it from firing by the pull of the trigger alone.

"This is my disappointment," he said, releasing the trigger. He sighed and lowered the weapon barrel to the floor. "However, I was told that, similar to how a key unlocks this vault room, you know the key to unlocking this artifact."

"I don't know what you are talking about," Meila replied, frowning.

Ignoring her reply, the giant moved in front of the steel chest, nudging it closed with his leg, and continued. "Some trickery, I presume, to unlock it. The previous one of your kind, with great confidence, said that you could do so. You being his superior and such."

Meila scowled at the mention of Anton, but then swiftly relaxed her facial muscles, reprimanding herself for revealing her emotions so openly. She couldn't feel antipathy toward her dead husband for revealing the information. She wouldn't have been surprised if they had tortured it out of him.

"Whoever said that was wrong. I know nothing about unlocking that thing." She would never authorize the release of a darkcore rifle to this tyrant. However, if she could gain control of the lethal weapon, she would gain the upper hand. All she needed to do was get ahold of it.

Pain smacked the side of her head as something hit her.

"Lies," said Sneer. "Liar. You will obey the King." His gloved hand slapped her a second time.

Her head hung limp and stars spun as she sucked up the pain. She had forgotten about Sicaro's rat behind her.

"This doesn't have to be difficult," Sicaro said. "Simply do what I ask and then you can go back to the women's quarters to stay in luxury. Then, after everything settles down, I'll free you. All you have to do is activate this—along with the others in the chest behind me."

Of course, there were more. Since the first moment she had set eyes on the rifle, she had assumed that Anton had brought the rifle down with him in his escape pod; just as she had assumed of the captured pistol at the salvage site. The pistol was a standard survival weapon in every pod, but the rifle was not. He would not have brought the rifle, would not have brought something he could not activate.

There must have been another wrecked section of the *Mendhelsson* that had made planetfall. Untracked. And the Vors had found it first.

A few seconds later, the pain subsided. "Maybe if I have a look at it, I can figure out how it works. I have a knack with mechanical things," she said in a quiet voice, with an obsequious look fixed to her face.

Sicaro held the rifle up sideways to her, firm in his massive hands.

As though curious to inspect the weapon, she stepped forward. "Can I hold it? To see the other side?"

"Don't take me for a fool." He glared at her but reversed the rifle in his grip to display the other side.

Doubting that she could wrest the weapon away from the giant—at least twice her body mass—the steel chest was her only other choice. A locker held eight darkcore rifles and four pistols. With any of them, she could blast her way out of this place.

Unfortunately, *he* was in the way. She tensed to leap past.

But before she even moved, he shoved the point of the rifle muzzle into her chest.

Her body crumpled to the floor, overwhelmed with a sudden heaviness—just like the time Sarah, her tech assistant when she worked as a design engineer, had accidentally dialed the gravity in their orbital lab too high. *Damn him. Damn this gravmancy.*

"You disappoint me," Sicaro said, then moved back to the steel chest and lowered the weapon inside. As the gravitational pull normalized, his sneering henchman pinned her arms behind her. "Judging by your intention, it's clear that you could grant my request. It is saddening, however, that you would instead concoct a deception to use one against me."

"What do you expect? Kidnapping me from my bed and dragging me into the center of a barbarian horde? Into a damn harem!" Her anger boiled over, quashing the rational part of her mind that told her to shut up and keep quiet. "I will never help you, you evil bastard."

"'Never,' can be a fickle word. You'll come to your senses. Better the *Queen's Quarters* than a dungeon, don't you think? I am a generous man—I'll give you a day to change your mind,"

Sicaro said placatingly. "And you need not worry. I'm not like Harek. I have no need for doxies. I won't be spreading your legs anytime soon." He looked her up and down as though to do that very thing. She had never felt so naked within her flightsuit. "My daughter seems rather taken with you. Think on this. 'Tis a better option than being stretched on a rack. Karisa will need handmaids once she is queen at my side."

After a moment to unravel Sicaro's words, a surge of revulsion struck Meila—his intent too obscene for her palate. Her fists clenched involuntarily. Sneer tightened his grip on her forearms. Although Jaks had talked of Karisa's past abuse at the hands of their father—to hear him speak of its resumption was as offensive as the smell of a rancid pit. "You are sick. Karisa is your daughter, not your wife. You disgust me," she hissed through tense lips.

Sicaro smiled while shaking his head. "Such old ways of thinking are why Voros and Ascoria need a new regime. Soon, once I am formally coronated, I will declare my queen," he said, and then leaned down to her eye level. "I will give you a single day back in your warm and cushioned chambers. When I see you again, I expect your full cooperation. Anything else, and it will be to the dungeon and a torturer to help you see reason. One way or the other, you will give me these weapons."

From the palace vaults, guards escorted Meila back to the harem. With an ultimatum coming the next day, she needed to hasten the escape she had planned with Karisa and the other women.

But Sneer had orders, additional to returning Meila to the room. Karisa was unlocked from the pillar by the weaselly henchman and led past in chains. Her face turned ghostly white, and her shoulders slumped.

Meila grabbed the younger woman's arm. "Leave her alone. You can't take her to that beast."

A guard rushed up and pried Meila's hands off Karisa and shoved her to sit on a velveteen sofa while Sneer dragged the girl out of the chamber.

"Stay strong," Meila called to Karisa, in a weak effort to empower the cursed woman-child.

Without her main conspirator, the once starship captain contorted her mind for hours, computing an achievable escape plan with her cognitive implants and gray matter. There had to be some way out. If she had had access to her wrist comm and one of the zinger droids, she was certain she could've found a route. But, the last she knew, the wrist comm, along with her darkcore pistol, was hidden under her bed back at the Academy.

One critical piece of information, which they had drawn out of the chambermaid Rasish in the past two days, was a way out of the building: a sewer dump beneath the palace, in a room carved out of the rock substrate, and blocked by nothing except a rusted grill.

But getting there, past the many palace guards, was a problem that even this human-computer could not solve without more information about the guard movements, palace layout—or a bunch of armed fighters. The only real possibility was if they could remove Karisa's slave collar and slip past the guards under the cloak of her illumancy. Then they could seek out the sewers.

Finally, late that evening after the other consorts had retired to their plump sofas and cushion beds, the harem doors opened and Karisa flowed into the chamber.

With head hung low and with red, puffy eyes, she was garbed in a traditional Ascorian gown, the kind Meila had only before seen on Dunberrin noblewomen. It was crimson and stitched with golden thread, embroidered with patterns that curled and wove around her bodice. Karisa's golden hair spilled over her shoulders, freshly combed, and as majestic as the clothing she wore. A stark contrast to the silks and ponytail that she had left the room with that afternoon.

A guard followed and locked her slave chain to the central column.

Meila stepped forward to grab Karisa's arm. "Tell me this is not what it looks like."

The king's daughter ignored her demand and shrugged off the touch.

"Talk to me, Karisa. Say you haven't made a deal with that beast," Meila spluttered in her eagerness to break into the other's consciousness. "We can escape together, all of us. We'll figure a way to get that collar off you, then we can get to the sewers, to the river, just like Jaks did. We need you."

"Leave me alone," Karisa murmured. She picked up the slack in her iron chain and flowed to a wide, round divan. There, she collapsed into the piled cushions and tunneled her head beneath.

Shocked at the transformation in Karisa, Meila muttered a curse at the woman's father—what threat or tainted thought had he planted in her head, for her to agree to this madness? Surely, she could not willingly consent to becoming his queen?

She sat on the divan and placed a hand on the girl's shoulder.

Karisa turned away, dislodging the touch once again and, before Meila's eyes, illumanced into nightwraith dark, retreating even further into her hiding space.

Several hours later, the grim light of dawn slashed through a gap in the curtains onto Meila's face. She hadn't slept, but instead had activated a rejuvenation protocol to replenish her neurotransmitters; normally, a process she would only do while navigating a long and complex flight path. Lying beside Karisa's sleeping form through the night, she had needed to stay alert in case the girl woke clear-headed and willing to talk.

Yet, Karisa remained withdrawn, and the countdown ticked away. At any moment, the doors would be thrown open and Meila forced to decide her fate. Release the darkcore weapons and bear the shame of mass murder? Or deny him and face torture and death?

Escape was the best path, but she needed Karisa. Without her, the alternatives were futile or suicidal. Meila gritted her teeth and looked at the seam of morning light.

A rattle at the main doors, and Rasish the chambermaid entered the chamber. She smiled, with her empty chamber pot in hand, then frowned when Karisa didn't respond to her greeting. "I was going to give her these," the girl said, holding out several small hairpins.

Meila grabbed them, and once the girl had left, she bent down and pushed the tip of one pin against the floor to bend it. She sighed with relief when it held its shape.

She climbed onto the divan beside Karisa and pushed the cushions aside. She shook Karisa's shoulder and repeated her name, louder each time. "Come on, wake up. I've got new pins." Without waiting for her to wake, she grabbed the padlock.

Karisa awoke at the first pull on her neck and sat upright. She stared at her crumpled gown and then at Meila. "I thought it was a bad dream . . ."

"He's coming for me this morning. We might never get another opportunity," Meila said, holding up the bent hair pin to show Karisa. "Let me have a go at the padlock. We can get out of here."

"I can't," Karisa interrupted. "I have to stay."

"Why? You don't owe him anything."

"It's better for everyone if I cooperate."

"Don't be stupid!" Meila leaped off the divan and glared at her. "No one benefits from this madness. No one except *him*. And it's just wrong. It's sick." She steadied her breathing and calmed her voice on seeing Karisa's face crumple under the burden of truth. "Look. If I can unlock your collar, we can start a fire to distract the guards—"

"He'll kill them." Karisa looked at the other women in the chamber, who were rousing at the sound of Meila's raised voice. "All of them, and you . . . if I disagree." She lowered her legs off the divan and rose to her feet. "It's not such a hardship, being a queen. It's normal in some countries, Father says."

"Abhorrent countries. Countries that kill their babies at birth and become so inbred that the children become malformed and feeble-minded." It was impossible to restrain her anger while trying to drain the poison that Sicaro had injected into Karisa's mind. "Your father is manipulating you, just as he did when you were a child. Blackmailing you. You're an adult now. You can't let him use you like this." But Meila could see the fatal despair behind the girl's eyes. Desperation driven there by loyalty to save the people she loved—as it had been with her mother.

"There's no point. We can't escape. There are guards everywhere, hounds, dragons . . . we would never escape. If I try, he says he will kill all of you, one by one, in front of me. It's the only way I can stop him." Tears flowed from Karisa's eyes.

Takola wrapped her arms around Karisa and pulled her to sit, then kissed the top of her head like a mother to a child. The three other courtesans hastened over and added their embraces.

With Karisa lost to her father's blackmail, Meila turned to her last resort.

She grabbed several silk shifts from a basket and began tying them into a makeshift rope. After the final knot, she pulled back the curtains to the bay window and arched her neck to examine the grassy courtyard below. The window slid up only enough to reach an arm through. She would need to go *through* the glass.

As she weighed her options again and questioned her sanity, a rattle at the chamber doors announced the too-early arrival of guests. The doors swung open, and a guard shouted, "Stand for the king." She then stood aside for Sneer and the hulking figure of the Vor monarch.

No time left.

Meila ran back several steps and turned to the window. Someone shouted at her, but she ignored them.

Bounding forward, she pumped her arms and sprinted for the window, aiming for the center pane. She would likely injure herself, but it was her last chance for freedom. She had to reach the river.

"Stop her!"

A yard from her target, she leaped. Her head shattered the glass.

But as she hurtled forward, a weight whipped around her ankles like the tentacles of an octopus.

Her body slammed to the floor under the influence of gravmancy. A bleeding deadweight, she slid back into the room.

Her escape was denied.

Chapter 15

The Bear King

King Sicaro—The City of Irin, Ascoria

His new subjects called him the "Bear King." Not simply because he towered over them in his black plate armor and furs, but that King Sicaro's sudden appearances at the barracks of his warriors and dens of his beasts-of-war subdued both men and beast equally with fear. Vor warriors fell to their knees and hounds nuzzled the floor as he neared, compelled by his power whether they willed it or not. His first task was to make sure all bowed to his throne.

The dark rod always in hand, he strode at the head of his contingent of twenty and seized the attention of all until the room or hall or courtyard was hushed. As he inspected each man and woman, they would breathe, "Sire," and lower their eyes. Those that displeased him met the ground with force, unable to inhale or expire, their chest or throat crushed in the grip of an invisible titan. The Bear King was no trivial nickname, for all were torn down to their knees.

Gone was the gentleman lord of Sanford. Done was the

comradely general of Ascoria. These Vors respected none of that. All they respected was a king of power.

Even when Karisa had been coronated at his side—not as princess, but as queen—none dared challenge this revolution in Vorosian monarchical law. Only the Ascorian Bishop of Irin—who had remained in his cathedral after his flock had fled—had said a word. He decried it a moral corruption, a violation of nature, and a sin against God. The man had died in seconds.

King Sicaro displayed her frequently—removing her collar for those occasions only. And despite any reticence his subjects might have carried about the relationship of the new queen to the king, her astonishing beauty swayed them all in his favor. Not that he cared what they felt, as long as it boosted their loyalty to his crown.

And such was his climb in popularity, aided by rumors of this glamorous new queen back on mainland Voros, that over the winter, shipfuls of colonists dared the seas to see their new king and queen, and receive an allocation of land to toil in the spring. Then, as the lands warmed, Vor farmers brought breed stock to greening meadows, and gardeners and orchardists plowed and seeded fertile soil in the conquered southern provinces.

But now that summer was coming, it was time to stir.

Hibernation was over, and the Bear King hungered for Ascorian blood.

Chapter 16

The Battle for the Border

Jaks—Border between the provinces of Irin and Dunberrin

Jaks's left eye twitched as the horizon darkened with the arrival of the Vor horde. He shivered, despite the warmth of the late-afternoon sun, unable to dismiss his growing horror at the sheer numbers of warriors and beasts of war that he and the Ascorian army would face.

He was standing atop a fortress at the center of a two-mile-long palisade wall closed in on either side by mountains. It was here that King Silas had rallied his army after the defeat at Irin and awaited reinforcements promised from the Pact Countries —but they never arrived, and so the Ascorians stood alone.

Jaks had spent the last few months under Mulgrave's instruction, cursing himself for not blocking his father from kidnapping Meila. Focused to master his lightning, one could find him on the pier or the roof of the Academy—when not assisting the grandmaster—practicing his electromancy and reliving the fight from the day she was taken. No longer a slave to fear, he channeled the emotion into his magic, and honed his skill until he could reliably channel lightning into the ocean and

604

the skies like a blade. And today, he would use that power to fight an army. Only then could he hope to reach Meila and Karisa.

His hand rested on Meila's velocannon where it sat on its steel frame. The barrel gleamed brightly as the square case with the darkcore gun inside weighed down the back and tipped the weapon skyward. One or two successful shots with the weapon and Jaks could change the course of the invasion.

Two scorpion bolt-throwers and their crews shared Jaks's tower top with barrels of spears waiting to be loaded and fired. And amongst them, a squad of soldiers in steel cuirasses and armed with crossbows stood ready to fend off dragons that might attack from above.

On the palisade below, along a raised walkway, more of the deadly siege weapons waited, stationed every hundred yards for the entire two miles. And alongside them, thousands of Ascorian soldiers and conscripts waited to defend this hardened line across the valley. The Jurn warriors and the Uwama, too, he was sure, were here somewhere. He'd caught glimpses of some tribesfolk but had not lingered to engage them. Jaks was sure they would be staring out now, as he was, wondering how their enemy had arrived so quickly.

As soon as summer flowers had sprinkled the meadows, the enemy had poured out of the City of Irin. The Ascorian generals had expected the invaders to pillage the less well-defended provinces first; however, they marched directly for the border and King Silas's main army.

On top of fears of overwhelming Vor numbers, disturbing rumors had circulated for months that a *new* and even more brutal king now led the armies of Voros. But no one knew for certain.

Even Jaks's spying, using the zinger droid high over the Vor-held City of Irin, had found no certainty of a coup. And, although he had spotted his father's frigate moored in the river, he could not trace him from the clouded altitude that the droid flew to avoid another scrape with patrolling dragons. And of Meila or Karisa, he could not see them directly, but he knew in his heart they were there somewhere.

"It's those skyships that worry me," said Grandmaster Mulgrave, standing beside Jaks and holding a magnifying scope to his eye as he examined the distance.

"And the damned gargantors and their warriors do not?" King Silas replied to the mage, standing on the other side of the grandmaster.

"Of course, they do," Mulgrave said patiently. "But unless we can counter their ships, they will have a free hand to rain down missiles and explosives. There is already disquiet amongst the troops; it won't take much to shatter their resolve."

"Yes, yes, we should retreat to the capital. It is much safer there," the king said, in a sudden swing of mind that revealed the taint in his character following an immense betrayal some months before.

After his father had kidnapped Meila, Jaks had sent a message to the king to warn the monarch of his father's treachery; however, the warning had been dismissed as the rant of a disgruntled son.

So, when Lord Sicaro returned to the king, Silas had welcomed him with a hearty handshake. It was said that Jaks's father, with a poisoned knife in hand, had then attempted to stab the king. If not for the sharp eyes—and sacrifice—of a nightwraith guard, Ascoria would have lost its king. But Jaks knew in his heart that it was not his father who had wielded the tainted blade, but his father's assassin, Craeg Vesenira. A tapering blood trail was the only trace of the assassin after he escaped.

But despite the killer's failure to plunge the knife into Silas's chest, a nick of the blade had been enough to sicken his target and leave him bedridden for weeks with delirious sweats and shakes. After he'd recovered enough to walk unaided, the poison's toll became clear: the king quickly spiraled into a debilitating paranoia. For months after, he locked himself away, refusing visitors, and communicated through a slot in the door.

Subsequently, in the uncertainty of the king's mental state, morale plummeted, and soldiers deserted their posts. Whole bands of soldiers and conscripts stripped their insignia and slipped away into the mountain forests—preparation to repel the invaders began to fall apart even before the enemy arrived.

Only in the last few weeks had the king been coaxed out of his tower and returned to a semblance of leadership.

"Not what I meant, sire," Mulgrave gently countered Silas's anxiety. "If Grandmaster Hazeldine can get her experimental skyship stable in the air, it will increase our strength in the skies. If we could delay the enemy until her ship could fly here from the capital? Perhaps consider sending out nightwraiths to sabotage the building of their siege weapons, or raiders to attack their supply lines? With the skyship, we could raise our velocannon high enough for a clear shot."

Jaks nodded. Even up here, at the highest spot of the fortress, they were still not high enough to get an accurate shot and ensure they wouldn't destroy the Ascorian defenses with the back-blast of the velocannon. Meila had said the explosion could destroy anything within a half mile. If they could get the weapon onto Hazeldine's experimental ship, *that* would be the ideal vantage point to fire it from.

However, the king would take no risks and refused to do anything other than shore up the defensive walls.

There would be no delaying the Vors.

The next morning, a fur-coated figure rode out of the enemy line up to the Ascorian fortress gates.

The rest of the Vor forces, camped two miles back, stained the far hills and fields. Overnight, siege towers had started to rise, assembled from wood and materials their army had carted from Irin. Similarly, the giant frames of trebuchets under construction stood out amongst the tents of the enemy encampment.

The Vor rider stopped at the main gate of the palisade wall.

Ascorian sentries trained crossbows and scorpions on the enemy warrior as though she might attack them alone.

From his station beside the velocannon, Jaks studied the woman. Except for a blue motif tattooed on her cheek, she reminded him of Vixhana. Tall, muscular, and with eyes that glinted steel.

"A message from the king of Voros for your pathetic leader," the woman called out to the sentries on the wall above her. She held up a leather scrollcase.

A liveried herald dashed out of a side gate to retrieve the scrollcase. For a moment, Jaks thought it was Minto, but the official was far too old to be his childhood friend. He wondered where his past companion was in this chaos of war. Although he'd kept a watch out for him, Jaks had not sighted him even once since returning from Irin. He had heard rumors that Minto was on some secret mission for the king. Wherever he was, Jaks hoped for his friend's sake that he was somewhere a lot safer than here. As Jaks's thoughts wandered, the older herald returned through the same gate from which he'd approached the Vor messenger and pounded his way to the king's tower at the opposite end of the fortress.

Several minutes later, to Jaks's surprise, the herald, accompanied by two guards, puffed his way heavily up the tower stairs toward him. After a few seconds to catch his breath, the official instructed him, "Go with the guards to the king." Jaks dutifully followed the pair back, wondering whether they would have manhandled him if he had refused. His neck tingled with a sense of a foreboding.

Panic and fury echoed in the king's tower chamber as Jaks entered. "There he is. Son of the viper!" The silver-haired king pointed at him and strode up. Then, just as quickly, he backed away as though frightened. "Your father. Your father! How can this be?" the king spluttered. Although armored in embossed steel plate, he lurched in dramatic steps as though struggling with its weight.

"The lad has nothing to do with it, Silas," Mulgrave said in a controlled voice. "The son doesn't control the father any more than the cub controls the lion."

Jaks gaped in confusion. The words of the king and the grandmaster were falling like missing pieces around a puzzle.

The brunt of King Silas's erratic rage then diverted to a piece of paper he held in his hand. He waved it as though it were on fire and threw it to the ground. He then slumped onto a heavy oak chair, shaking his head and muttering nonsensically to himself.

"Look at it, lad." The grandmaster inclined his head to the letter on the ground, lying beside the discarded scrollcase.

Jaks uncurled it and read. In beautiful cursive writing, the document demanded the immediate surrender of all lands of Ascoria to the king of Voros.

However, it was the name of the king that caused Jaks to sway on his feet and grip the paper tightly—*King Sicaro Rauhalik*, Ruler of the Burned Lands, Chief of the Clans, Lord Commander of Voros.

"It can't be . . ." Jaks began, then stopped. It was starting to make sense. The invasion landing in Sanford. His father's heroic escape and return to King Silas's folds. The assassination attempt. And ultimately, his father's frigate in the center of Voros-controlled Irin. His father's hunger for power and control had never let up. It had festered into a grandiose scheme to dominate *both* realms, Voros and Ascoria. If Jaks hadn't been so distressed that his father had caused his country's collapse, he would have nodded in appreciation at the clever timing and alignment of wheels and cogs to bring the devious plan to bear.

Silas unfolded from his chair with the aid of a young squire. "Surrender? Mulgrave, is it the only way? His army is far greater than mine. We have already lost every battle. Yes, I must surrender! We cannot win." Silas grabbed the grandmaster's arm. The king's face pleaded for the wisdom that seemed to have fled him.

"Out, out! I will speak to the king alone," Mulgrave ordered the guards and servants from the chamber. He looked at Jaks and flicked his head for him to leave as well. "Word of surrender mustn't reach the ears of the troops. Go now." The mage's words trailed behind them as they left: "Pull yourself together, Silas. Your words are poison to the ears of your soldiers . . ."

As Jaks teetered along the palisade wall back to his tower, he maneuvered past dozens of soldiers. Half were armed with spear-and-shield, whilst the other held bows and carried quivers filled with bodkin-headed arrows. Seeing him leave the king's tower, a few grasped his arm as he went by and asked anxious questions.

"Is it a request for surrender?" "Does the king hold his courage?" "How many warriors do they have?" "Is he going to retreat? If we do, I bet half will run for the mountains."

He brushed past them without replying. His mind was elsewhere.

If his father now held the Vor crown, it meant he held its prisoners. A shudder jolted Jaks's shoulders as he despaired at the thought of both Karisa and Meila within his father's vile hands. Perhaps he had dragged them in chains to the battlefield? He wouldn't put it past his father's controlling ways. They could be as close as a field away.

Another thought horrified him. If Meila and his sister were in their midst, and he fired the velocannon at the Vor forces, the blast would kill them. The very two people he had vowed to rescue.

He shook his head. If he used the destructive weapon, he'd make sure it would be against the distant flanks, away from the center or rear, where any hostages would be held.

On his return to the velocannon, it seemed to Jaks that the Vor siege towers had grown even taller, and the ridge of warriors thickened even darker along the horizon. *Were their siege weapons finished so soon?* Vor dragons circled the ocean of enemy warriors, and behind them, several masted skyships hovered as though waiting to dive forward. The sun continued its morning ascent as the two armies waited and stared at each other across the hills and fields that now seemed as narrow as a garden path.

A quarter hour later, Grandmaster Mulgrave appeared on the palisade wall with the royal herald.

The Vor messenger standing beside her horse, with the sun

to her right, scowled up at them. "Where is your cowardly king? Why does he not show himself?" she called out.

Ignoring her questions, Mulgrave glared down at her. "Go back to your kennel and tell Sicaro that he shall find nothing here but pain and death," he said. His words were addressed to the surrounding troops as much as to the Vor messenger. "Tell your compatriots that your new king cares nothing for your country and thinks nothing of destroying it for his own greed and power."

Bits of paper scattered in the wind as Mulgrave tore the letter of demand apart above the messenger. The empty scrollcase followed, thudding to the soil at the forehooves of her horse.

"To the ashes with you," said the tattooed woman. She spat, then mounted her stallion.

Jaks watched the messenger ride away, the certainty of battle sealed with her departure.

He tugged on the chest straps of his torso armor with trembling fingers and rubbed the pommel of his shortsword to calm his nerves. To replace his original armor—abandoned in a pit outside Irin—he'd acquired a new set of finely crafted fighting leathers embedded with steel plates from the Academy's armory. However, his sword was the same as he'd carried since the start; albeit its blade was now rippled and warped with black lines left by the lightning that had coursed through it several times now. Although it couldn't hold an edge like it once did, its true deadliness, in the hands of Jaks, was far greater than its maker could have ever imagined. Little comfort to Jaks, however, as he contemplated the tens of thousands of Vor warriors thirsting for blood a mere few miles away.

As the sun reached its zenith, horns blasted from the Vor line.

The siege towers rolled forward, and trebuchets slid, the latter lifted by gravmancers and pushed by warriors from behind.

More horns blasted up and down the frontline. The wind carried their shouting and chanting to Jaks's ears as the horde advanced.

"The flanks . . . The forest!" a signaler called from his post behind Jaks. The man, holding a telescopic lens in one hand, pointed left to the central mountain range where the palisade wall curved away.

Within the woods that lined the valley, a mile from the Ascorian wall, a jet of flame blasted through the green canopy for a moment. Two pillars of smoke rose nearby, and battling figures spilled out of the woodland onto the edge of the plains.

The battle had begun.

Jaks stood behind the velocannon, gripped the left handle, and stuck his hand in the back for the darkcore gun. The metal barrel appeared dull, as clouds masked the sun above, and the fins at the far end lay limp and lifeless. He tilted the barrel up and down, then left and right. Well-oiled on its steel frame, it moved easily. Avoiding the central mass of Vors, he squinted through the targeting sight at the west flank. He shivered at the formidable, undulating mass of warriors that blacked out the tubular lens as he panned across the horizon.

As ready as he could be, palms sweating, Jaks looked around for Grandmaster Mulgrave. The veteran mage was nowhere to be seen amongst the Ascorian soldiers dashing around the towers and walls and readying the scorpions, ballistae, and mortars. Jaks frowned, needing his master's direction for when to fire the weapon—the responsibility for the first shot was too much for him to take alone.

An Ascorian signaler from the king's tower blared three notes from his warhorn.

In response, the thump of Meila's gravfire mortars sounded as they fired flaming bombs. The missiles sang as they arced through the air and landed a mile away within the Vor lines. Tiny explosions marked each as they struck a hapless warrior or exploded between their ranks.

"Too far. Aim for the center-most tower," a woman wearing the winged helm of an Ascorian general shouted from the wall further down from Jaks.

The two mortar crews within earshot redirected their weapons, and the following bombs landed closer to one of the siege towers. "Thirty yards left," the general shouted, correcting the teams again.

Much further down the line, a lucky mortar crew hit a tower to the right flank. A cheer broke out as the top burst into flames; however, their glee sank a few minutes later when a figure leaned out of an arrow portal and the flames magically extinguished.

"Damn pyromancer . . ." a conscript muttered nearby.

The tidal wave of Vors surged toward them.

They were close enough now that ladders could be seen carried and dragged. The warriors were eager to scale the walls even before their siege towers could catch up.

Ascorian scorpion bolt-throwers thudded along the wall and from the two towers as the enemy finally marched into range.

"Take that, you fuckers!" shouted a soldier from behind a bolt-thrower he'd just fired, several yards from Jaks's position. His spear and others slammed into the Vor frontline, impaling many, but doing nothing to slow their march. If anything, the leading edge sped faster.

Jaks looked around, desperate for someone to tell him what

to do. Mulgrave was strangely still absent, as was the king. He leaned over the tower crenel and looked at the general, hoping she might give him direction for the velocannon. But she was preoccupied with sending reinforcements along the wall and did not even hear his shouts above the cacophony of war.

Anxiously, he wiped his hands dry on his leggings for a surer grip on Meila's lethal weapon. He'd have to decide on a target and make the call himself.

He squinted at the east and west flanks. Ascorian reinforcements had engaged with the ambushing Vors. Warlions pounced onto the tattooed axe warriors, their riders lunging with spears from their backs, preventing the Vor flankers from skirting around the far ends of the long wall. He couldn't fire near them for fear of killing fellow soldiers. The center he wouldn't risk either, not with Karisa and Meila possibly there.

Fretful, Jaks's sweaty hands slid on the velocannon's steely grips as he swiveled it back and forth.

There.

A pair of trebuchets, a mile from his tower but only a half mile from the wall to the west.

Surrounded by ranks of warriors clattering axes and swords against shields, the great throwing arms of the siege weapons bent down to receive their massive, rounded missiles as huge counterweight blocks rose at the other end. Normally, a trebuchet could only throw its projectile a hundred yards further than an arrow, but with gravmancers multiplying the power of the weapons, they could reach over twice that distance. Soon, the deadly boulders would thunder like meteors at the Ascorian defenses.

Jaks's breathing grew faster. The closest Vors were well past the trebuchet line. *Grafuk! They're so near already. I should have fired much earlier.*

"Wind your crossbows! They'll be in range in a few minutes," yelled a captain of the bow, on the wall below. The man then swiftly wound the ratchet on his own weapon.

Phooom!

An explosion rocked the tower.

A hot wave of pressure staggered Jaks into the velocannon and pivoted it wildly. Dazed and confused, his hands slipped from the weapon.

The rear edge of the tower was covered in a pool of flame and two soldiers stumbled around within it. They slapped at themselves, yelling in pain and fear.

"Get it off me!" screamed one flailing man whose shield still clung to his arm uselessly while his other arm and his legs burned.

Several other soldiers rushed to help but could do nothing but kick at them, trying to push them out of the spreading fire.

Dozens more explosions of red and yellow flame burst around the tower and walls. Some engulfed soldiers, but elsewhere, they just ignited the wood or stone surfaces they struck and burned with black, oily flames.

Fire was falling from the sky.

Far above Jaks, a Vor skyship sailed overhead. A few seconds later, flaming balls plummeted to the ground behind the tower and splattered a line of soldiers waiting as reinforcements. Each explosion burst with the same sticky substance and created new blazes. Burning, shrieking men and women ran and collapsed amongst the flaming buildings and tents of the camptown.

And further along the Ascorian defenses, even more skyships on short sails floated over and rained down hellish fury.

The only airborne defenders they had were caught in a maelstrom of talons and fangs halfway up to the flying ships.

The Ascorian war dragons swooped and screeched in mighty clouds of bronze, gold, blue, and red, fighting for the skies against their Vor cousins. Streaks of breathed flame and globs of black acid were traded back and forth. The dragons, preoccupied with their own grim battle, left the skyships free to deliver whatever devices they wished to deal.

A hand grabbed Jaks's arm. Grandmaster Mulgrave pulled him to his feet.

"The king has lost his mind. He is calling a retreat! I cannot convince him otherwise," the bald mage shouted at him above the clamor of explosions, roaring flame, and screaming men and women.

Jaks's face contorted in surprise.

Mulgrave released him and began deftly unbolting the velocannon from its frame. "We must get this back to Dunberrin. The wall here will hold long enough for us to make an escape. Damn the man, he has turned utterly spineless."

Jaks shook his head in frustration. The velocannon could have helped, or maybe not. He wouldn't ever know. They'd lost the battle for the border before it had truly begun.

"Shoot the bastards. Fire!" a voice commanded from somewhere. Ascorian crossbows twanged as the enemy charged across the last few hundred yards of the battlefield.

The Vors thrust forward oval shields whilst those behind turtled beneath shields held overhead. Iron-tipped bolts sank into and glanced off shields. However, some of the deadly missiles found gaps in the shield wall and pierced the fleshy targets behind them. But even as the victims were trampled by their comrades, shields shifted to close the gaps.

The grandmaster shouldered the velocannon. Although the weapon was as heavy as a pot-bellied merchant and as long as the cart he might drive to market, the gravmancer carried it as easily as a broom. "See you below," he said, then jogged to the rear of the tower. With a glance at Jaks, the mage leaped over the side.

A cry of surprise formed on Jaks's lips at his master's seeming suicidal act. But his frown then eased. Despite the chaos and panic all around, he laughed at his unnecessary worry —of course, a gravmancer could control his fall without danger. Jaks regretted his own powers couldn't do the same.

Forced to the stairs instead, he picked up his shield, palmed his sword pommel to keep it still, and ran past several crossbowers and a scorpion crew.

At the rear of the tower, he winced at the sight of the two burned corpses of the soldiers caught in the first explosion—the pool of fire had been extinguished but clearly too late for the men.

At the bottom of the tower, Mulgrave waited, studying the disorder around him. Jaks caught his breath beside him and followed his master's gaze. More than a quarter of the canvas tents and buildings burned fiercely.

Regiments that had been waiting to reinforce their comrades now rushed about, whacking down flames and throwing precious water onto the fire—but their efforts were of little use and the blaze continued to spread.

"Follow me. Hold the end so it doesn't get damaged." Mulgrave tilted the finned muzzle of the velocannon to his apprentice. "Hopefully, the draft horses haven't taken loose."

The pair of Academy mages jogged through the ranks of a sword regiment battling fires and wound their way through the camp. Flaming tents and buildings reddened Jaks's face with their heat as they passed.

Halfway through the camp, a warhorn pulsed out a five-note rise from the fortress behind. The motif was repeated into the distance by other signalers.

The order to retreat.

Jaks glanced back, concerned for his fellow countryfolk. Hundreds of ladders peeked over top of the palisade. Faces filled with bloodlust topped the scaling devices but were stabbed and chopped down before they could clamber over. The top of a square siege tower neared the fortress where he had been stationed minutes before. A ramp fell forward to bridge the gap to the wall. Vors charged out of the tower, screaming defiantly even as spears and bolts knocked them off the ramp.

"We'll take this cart. Go get two of those draft horses before they bolt, lad," the grandmaster said, pushing the velocannon onto the back of a cart as they reached one of several on the far side of the camp. Fortunately, the fires hadn't reached this far yet.

Jaks coaxed two stocky, long-maned horses out of the corral. The other beasts, thirty or forty of them, stamped and snorted. An eye on the approaching fire, Jaks left the gate open for their escape.

An entourage of mounted soldiers in the Ascorian king's purple livery galloped past their cart as Jaks and Mulgrave hitched the horses to it. At their center, King Silas rode unhelmeted and without a glance sideways or back. Behind him, his army appeared to be holding back the Vor attackers at the wall. Jaks couldn't make out whether they retreated or not, despite the order to do so.

When their cart reached the hilltop, Jaks looked down on the valley. The consequences of the king's panicked withdrawal were apparent. Thousands of Ascorian soldiers darted through the flames of the burning camp—fleeing in a chaotic swarm. Clouds of smoke veiled the battle at the wall, but through breaks in the hellish swirls, brave defenders remained to stave off the attackers. Enormous boulders pummeled the fortress and palisade, some flying over to smash into the burning encampment. Vor skyships yawed, escaping the pillars of smoke, and turned languidly to the flanks. Exhausted of bombs, they descended as though to swoop on the remaining defenders directly.

"We must hurry from this disaster," Mulgrave said. He shook his head and flicked the reins at the horses from the cart they sat upon. Jaks, at the back of the cart, stared at the defeat in futility.

Fleeing the border, the Ascorian army fought as they retreated. Entire regiments that had been ordered to remain and hold back the attackers were slaughtered. But even with those sacrifices, thousands more were massacred as the Vors took up the pursuit.

Only when night fell on that terrible day and the nightwraiths were in their element did the Vors stop their chase. Even the most blood-thirsty brutes couldn't fight through the deadly shadows that ambushed them in the darkness.

Over the night and the next several days, the Ascorian survivors—half of what had first manned the border—limped back to their last refuge.

The Battle for the Border was lost. Only one Ascorian hold remained—the City of Dunberrin.

Chapter 17

Unrelenting Storm

Jaks—The City of Dunberrin, Ascoria

Six days after escaping the border, and three since arriving at the ivory-white walls of the capital, Jaks stood atop the battlements beside Ranger Cromer. The last of the Ascorian army—those that hadn't deserted—had straggled in the day before, and now the city locked down for its final defense.

"Do you believe in evil?" Jaks asked the master ranger. "Is it born into me?" He glanced at the veteran's hawkish profile and immediately regretted spilling his worries to the man who had once been his harshest trainer.

Ranger Cromer fixed his gaze on storm clouds darkening the horizon, pausing so long that Jaks was sure the man hadn't heard him.

Cromer surprised Jaks with a reply a minute later. "Evil? It's not something you believe in, it just is."

"So, it could have been passed to me." Jaks rubbed his arms as though to expel the curse within. Since the revelation that he had caused his mother's death, and denied his own hand in it for years, he had to know what else he hid from himself. Perhaps an evil equal to his father's?

"We all do evil deeds from time to time. There's no denying. But nothing is black or white," the ranger said. "Your sister saw things that way. And it is what probably near-killed her." His jaw tensed as he spoke of Vixhana. During earlier travels, the two of them had shared an intimate attachment. "Heroes and villains, good and evil. She thought she always knew the clear path."

A moment of guilt stung Jaks at his part in injuring her.

"But is she free of evil?" Cromer said, while still glaring at the brewing storm. "You know she has killed more men and women than most soldiers would in an entire lifetime of war? Many in cold blood. Could a person do that without taking some satisfaction from extinguishing another?"

Guilt twisted Jaks again. This time at the thrill he'd felt personally after he had channeled the wave of lightning through the Vor warriors at the siege of Irin. Hundreds had died and dozens were burned into cripplement. There was no question he had reveled in killing them. Evil, then, *did* seed his core.

But, as though to counter his thought, the ranger continued, "Yet, there is no *force* of evil that compels you against your will. It is always your choice how you act when the sun rises or the blade swings." The man straightened as though finished with dispensing his wisdom.

Jaks swayed against a wind gust that blew over the battlements and eventually nodded in agreement. The ranger was right. No matter how much his father's blood indwelled him, his path was his alone to carve.

Minutes later, lightning speared the horizon and danced across the distant plains. Thunder boomed in response, as though to applaud the furious spectacle.

"It's heading away from us, toward those damned Vors. Hope it drowns them," said the ranger. "The trial flight can go ahead. Let's go back down to the others."

Reminded of their actual purpose for scaling the battlements, Jaks cleared his head and turned his attention to the mustering fields in the military district. There, below, prepared their last hope against the enemy invaders and his father: the velocannon bolted onto Ascoria's one and only flying ship.

Chapter 18

The Skyship

The skyship, Grandmaster Hazeldine's invention, would have been a pitiful sight stranded in the middle of the dirt field, had it not bristled with scorpion bolt-throwers, and been armored with steel plating along its sides. A decked, flat-bottomed galley, it measured forty yards long. However, with oars removed, the only feature its past crew might have recognized was its central mast. Its crossbeams and boom, though, no longer flew a sail but instead carried a squad of war dragons, the size of wolves, assigned to protect it.

Although gravmancers from the distant nation of Zura had mastered flyers over two hundred years before, the chariot-like vehicles with their small sail—like the one stored in the Academy's museum area—could only levitate the mage alone and relied on the wind for propulsion. Hazeldine's masterpiece, in comparison, held up to fifty crew, a dozen dragons, and cut through the sky on the power of runestones and mages.

Jaks needed to get to his station on board the ship. A reeking squirt of dragon excrement lay in his path. He screwed up his nose and stepped over it to catch up with the ranger. A ribbed gangplank led up to the deck of the ship nicknamed, by its crew of gravmancer engineers, "the *Kingfisher*" for its tendency, during earlier test flights over the harbor, to dive unexpectedly, bow-first into the water like its bird namesake. Although the eight gravmancers who gave the ship the ability to fly had since learned to synchronize their levitations and declinations well enough to glide the skyship wherever the captain directed, Jaks had crouched and gripped the railings with whitened knuckles during the one previous time he had flown on it.

Grandmaster Mulgrave met them at the top of the gangplank. "Good to fly?" he questioned the goateed man.

"Aye," Cromer replied. "Let's take this god-forsaken deathtrap for a ride." The grimace on his face suggested he regretted Mulgrave hand-selecting him for the skyship crew.

"How about you, lad? Will you hold your guts in this time?" The mage raised an eyebrow.

"I skipped breakfast, and I think dinner is too far past to return. I'm ready." He patted an empty leather pouch at his hip —just in case—remembering the previous day when he had skidded over his own vomit and ended up teetering over the ship's edge.

"We haven't fired the cannon since Meila was taken. I think we had best make sure it still works while we're up there this time," Mulgrave said. "Once we're clear, Master Cromer will spot a target area in the mountains . . . make sure you hit it."

Jaks nodded. A missed shot could destroy the buildings of a mountain village or a mining settlement. That was assuming the potency of the velocannon on water translated into an equally devastating effect on land.

Only Meila could have told them what to expect. His heart sank at the thought of her. He twirled the strands of hair he had recovered from her pillow and kept coiled in his pocket. Her medikit, clipped around his waist, was the only other thing of hers he had saved—it could only be useful.

An ear-splitting whistle broke the air and snapped Jaks's focus back to the deck.

Well-trained to the commanding blast, the thunder of war dragons leaped from their perches on the ship and buffeted the air with their wings. Hisses and screeches added to the momentary chaos, and Jaks flinched as a red wing brushed past his head.

Seconds later, the dragonmaster—with no weapons but her whistle and illumancy signals—blew two more bursts in a code, and a swirling conjuration resembling a hurricane appeared above her head. With further screeching, the deadly beasts split into a multi-layered patrol above and around the skyship.

With the galley lightened of its draconic load, and expecting the captain to call out the skyship's own take-off drill, Jaks jogged to his assigned position at the prow of the deck and clipped a rope dangling from the railing to his belt. Just in time.

A horn blew. High pitched, then low. *Prepare to fly.*

"Cast off the anchors, you damned slouchers," the skyship captain shouted.

Captain Gant's voice was never less than a shout. The cantankerous seadog had been Grandmaster Hazeldine's choice to command her flying ship, and a better one, she could not have found. After decades of commanding a three-masted cruiser, chasing and sinking pirate ships along the trading routes of the northern seas, his maritime prowess was the glue that bonded the skyship crew into a tight-working unit. That he was also a master gravmancer able to comprehend the complex machinations of the mages below deck—responsible for harnessing the gravity-wells and grav-floats that moved the vessel—uniquely granted him authority to command this unusual fighting platform.

The world swayed beneath Jaks's feet as the ship lifted off the ground. His stomach heaved, and he ducked below the railing and held on. Laughter boomed behind him. The veteran crew were clearly amused at the antics of this dirt-footed novice.

"Damn you, idiots, secure those shafts," Gant shouted as several scorpion spears rolled across the deck. Two sailors fleet-footed over to grab the wooden shafts and secured them point-down into an ammunition barrel.

Thirty sailors, drawn from Gant's cruiser, bore crossbows and stationed weapons around the ship. They were unrequired for the regular duties of sailors, such as rowing oars or rigging sails, so their role was simply to repel boarders and defend the ship—as well as Jaks's skin.

Everything rested on him and the velocannon. Despite all the gravfire mortars, flamethrowers, blinding barricades, and other devices that the Academy had invented, Meila's velocity cannon was the only one that had a chance of stopping the relentless advance of the Vors. Although he had charged up the cannon twice yesterday, he had not pulled the trigger. In fact, he hadn't since the day they tested it at the Academy. But today he would.

Once the skyship cleared the highest building of the city—the flute-glass-shaped royal palace—the deck tilted and wind rushed through his hair as the ship sped forward. Jaks leaned away from the invisible force of the gravity-well, pulling him toward the prow of the ship. He had little understanding of the magic involved but knew that once they reached the captain's desired speed, the gravmancers below would cease the conjuration, and only then would he stand with ease. Compared to the Vor flying ships he had studied through the zinger droid's sensors, Jaks was confident the *Kingfisher* could out-fight any that his father commanded; however, theirs was only one, to the several or more that it might have to engage in combat.

Jaks looked to Grandmaster Mulgrave and Ranger Cromer, standing mid-ship, also tethered to the railing by braided ropes and iron clips. The mage wielded a staff capped by a red orb the size of his fist, and the ranger carried a composite bow and a quiver of arrows.

"You remember the mountains," said the ranger, who had slid his way up behind Jaks. The pull of the gravity-well relented, and Cromer wobbled on his feet as he adjusted. "Different view, but the same that we trained in."

Jaks didn't need reminding of those awkward days as a conscript, but he nodded, recognizing some of the distant contours several miles ahead of them.

"Draper's Peak, then north." The ranger's finger pointed at a barren mountain face. "Nothing around there but rocks and goats for miles. Won't be any patrols either—at least not ours— too exposed to hide anything. Let's see what this thing does."

Thankfully, not a place the dryads would visit, either. Although he didn't know how far the velocannon's effects would reach, the forest dwellers' habitat was on the opposite side of the mountain range and surely well beyond anything the cannon would damage. Jaks's heart warmed. He hadn't thought of the tiny creatures and their hidden orchard for a long time.

All eyes were on him; his back itched from the attention. The skyship was gliding a mile above pasture lands, green with springtime, but dotted with cattle and sheep—ready to be herded into the city streets at the first sign of the invaders. Grasping the handle and grip of the cannon, Jaks swung its long barrel and aimed at the pale outline of the mountain face.

"I'll line her up for you, boy." Gant manipulated steering rods at his helm. The ship yawed port-side, straightening Jaks's aim onto his target. The gruff captain then yelled at the dragonmaster, "Get your damned pets out of the way."

The handler sent a withering look back at the pirate-chaser and then signaled her dragons with a series of whistle blasts; the winged beasts of war swooped into the wake of the *Kingfisher*—safe from the danger at its prow.

The air pulsated around Jaks. "Stand back!" he yelled over his shoulder, fearing that the ranger or one of the crew might stray close enough to attract the electrical current to themselves.

He checked again that the orange dot overlay the target. The pale mountain. He willed lightning through his hands. The familiar smell of metal filled his nostrils. The steel fins hanging at the end of the barrel flipped erect, as though standing at attention, and the velocannon whined a high-pitched buzz. His finger hovered over the trigger.

Shouting erupted behind him, so loud and desperate that it broke his concentration. The fins of the barrel flopped as the electromancy dissipated, and he twitched his finger away from the trigger.

Several sailors, leaning against the ship's railing, yelled and gesticulated back at the city.

Smoke clouds billowed up from the capital, too thick and wide for workshop furnaces, too many for an accident.

"The city's under attack," yelled Gant. "Bring her about, you apes." The captain came into his own at that point, as though preparing to chase down a pirate ship. His bellowed orders commandeered the flight-plan from a mere exercise to battle stations. "Recon for attacking force."

The *Kingfisher*, its gravmancer engineers over-eager to turn the ship about, spun on its mid-point, pivoting from bow to stern in less than half a minute. At the abrupt movement, Jaks grabbed at the railing with one hand while desperately holding onto the velocannon with the other.

Shouted curses and swearing erupted around the deck as sailors fell and bashed against hard points around the ship. Tethers snapped on some of the heaviest sailors, but fortunately, tall steel plates balustraded the sides and kept any from being tossed overboard.

Reeling from the maneuver but now facing the city, Jaks had a clearer view of the devastation ahead.

A dozen huge fires, each the size of a city block, spewed smoke and flames from locations all over the peninsula. As the ship reversed its rearward travel and accelerated toward the city wall, an explosion blew a cloud of debris and smoke up from the market district, starting a new fire amongst the stalls and shops. But there was no horde of invaders, nor enemy ships, in sight—only tens of thousands of people panicking in the streets.

Captain Gant steered the *Kingfisher* in a loop around the city, and every eye aboard searched for attackers. However, no one, not even the master ranger, could spot a source of assault.

But Jaks knew. Months ago, he had observed through the zinger droid a hooded agent on his father's frigate reporting on sinister deliveries. The information had been far too vague to identify the locations or the corruption that would hatch at each. But now he knew. Now, they all knew, and could see it for themselves.

The barracks of the Hog Legion and the Royal Pikes spewed smoke and flames over the military district. A half-dozen residential blocks were smothered in choking clouds. And outside the city walls in the industrial sector, a cotton mill and two oil distilleries layered black fumes and exploded to spread fire to surrounding buildings. Scores of pump-carts with firemen spraying water at the flames looked pathetic against the fiery monsters they fought.

"At least the Academy and the Royal Palace are undamaged," Jaks said to himself. But he shivered at the thought of how the Ascorian king might react to this new threat. Already a brittle shard, the monarch, he feared, could easily shatter and throw the remains of himself and Ascoria at the feet of the Vors, pleading for mercy against insurmountable odds.

As Captain Gant sought a landing site amongst the smoke and flames, Ranger Cromer called out another unexpected sighting. "Ships to the west," the hunter said. "Tracking the coast. Can't be our fleet. We don't have that many left. Vor, I think."

Indeed, an armada of ships filled the sea off the distant coast, visible at this distance to Jaks only by the sheer number of them. Unable to distinguish their affiliation, he trusted the master ranger's sharper, more experienced eyes. But Captain Gant, wanting to confirm the identity of the ships for himself, barked orders to reconnoiter the approaching fleet.

"Bastards. It's too much of a coincidence they turn up at the same time as these fires," the captain of the ship spat.

"A signal? Or a distraction?" Mulgrave shouted above the rushing wind. "Get closer, Gant."

"That's what I'm doing, old man," the captain shouted back and scowled at him, clearly not liking being ordered around on his own vessel.

An idea flashed into Jaks's mind. He slid his clip along the railing, detaching and reattaching it to bypass those of other crew members, and approached the trio of Gant, Cromer, and Grandmaster Mulgrave.

"Captain, I can scout out those ships before we get too close —if they have dragons, they might attack us." He dug into his belt pouch and drew out the zinger droid, Slasher. "My droid can stay well above them and show us what we need."

With the dented and scratched droid as the last of its kind—the other destroyed by his father—he kept the device close and reserved it for essential tasks. The last time, yesterday, for the king's generals, it had darted over the Vor land forces closing on Dunberrin—confirming their location, three days' march away. Similarly, scouting out this flotilla of likely enemy ships equally warranted sending the droid into danger.

"Go to it, lad," Mulgrave replied. "Hold off, Captain. Our best weapon could be surprise."

Gant scowled again at Mulgrave but nodded to Jaks and pulled on the ship's controls to return it to circling the smoking pillars of the troubled city.

Jaks sat cross-legged and propped himself against the ship's side. Closing his eyes, he merged his mind to the droid through the wrist comm, commanding the flow of circuits with pulses of electromancy. It sprang out of his hand and sped toward the gathered ships.

The droid returned images as it flew over the ocean. As the first ships came into view, Jaks watched in dismay as Ascorian flags heaved at full sail ahead of the main mass of vessels. Fleeing, pursued, remnants of the royal Ascorian fleet cut through the waves to escape the wooden sharks at their sterns. Two hundred ships streamed the Vor naval flag—a tiger and an elephant fighting each another on hind legs. They tossed and rolled on the high seas behind the ten Ascorian ships. Dragons circled the pitiful survivors: blues and bronzes, bodies the size of dogs and talons the length of daggers. The winged beasts dived at the Ascorian sailors. Exposed heads and shoulders were slashed, and an occasional sailor lifted bodily off the deck and dumped screaming into the churning sea.

The ships of the pursuers teemed with sailors and warriors and appeared so overloaded that their decks were dark with jostling bodies. Jaks wondered whether the invaders intended to land these thousands of screaming fighters directly onto the docks and pebbled beaches of Dunberrin. The only downside, for the overburdened Vor ships, was that they could not catch up to their prey, despite the dragons harassing the Ascorian crews.

Jaks sent Slasher spiraling above the clouds, gave instructions to circle and evade, then broke his connection to it. Opening his eyes, he hurriedly reported his findings to the expectant captain. "Couple of hundred Vor ships chasing a few of ours. Scores and scores of dragons." He stood, rocking on his feet for a second. "Their ships are heavy with troops."

"Damnation." The grandmaster shook his head. "No warning. They must have taken out the signaling tower at the Point," he said, referring to the northwestern tip of Ascoria where the fleet had been holding off the invader's ships.

"How many left?" Gant questioned while pulling at his beard.

"Ten? But they're slowly getting away."

The captain's proud shoulders slumped, and a pained look overtook his face. "Not good, not good. Even added to the score of ships in port and patrolling the rest of the coast, we haven't near enough to fight off that many of the bastards."

"Unless we reduce the odds," Mulgrave said, slapping a hand on the captain's shoulder. He pointed at the velocannon. "There could be some danger to our fleeing ships from a wave surge, but if we target the ships at the rear, they might be far enough ahead to escape undamaged."

Ranger Cromer stepped between the two men and pointed to the master signaler at the aft of the ship. "We should signal Dunberrin and ask what the king wants us to do."

Gant shook his head. "No time. Even if the Dunberrin tower is still in action and monitoring us, it'll take hours for them to get Silas to respond . . . if they can even get through to him at all. When we chase down pirates, we don't ask permission first." He pointed to Jaks and ordered, "Get to your station, mage. I'll take us close enough to sight your target . . . the rear-most ship. Smash 'em up good, you hear."

Jaks unclipped from the railing, staggered to the prow of the ship, and re-secured himself next to the velocannon. Then, shaking with both excitement and fear, he took hold of the weapon, then angled the barrel down at the enemy armada. Still a splotch on the ocean at this distance, dots against an immense green-blue expanse, he waited until the *Kingfisher* flew close enough for him to single out his target—a galley boat lagging the fleet by three hundred yards.

Every few seconds, the skyship sliced through tufts of cloud, blanking out Jaks's view through the aiming scope. He turned to the captain, pointed to the deck, and shouted, "Down." He hoped the man would comprehend his request to drop below the cloud line.

To his relief, the *Kingfisher* descended, and the air cleared of the pockets of moisture. But even with a clear line of sight, the aiming scope at this distance—a dozen miles—swung wildly back and forth over the galley. A dilemma. Wait until the skyship nears enough for a steady aim and risk becoming the target of enemy dragons, or shoot now and risk missing the galley, wasting a precious shot?

Captain Gant yelled at him across the ship to shoot; sailors shouted, relaying their captain's order.

Jaks waved off their demands—and waited.

A few minutes later, as the *Kingfisher* overflew the first of the fleeing Ascorian ships, Jaks's aiming dot was finally steady on the laggard galley.

"Do your fucking magic now, mage, or else I'll come up there and squeeze it out of you," Gant yelled, so loud that he must have been invoking sonomancy to project his voice. The old seadog clearly had many gifts.

The dragonmaster, leaning over the railing, also looked at Jaks and shouted to reinforce the captain's message, "Now, boy. Their wings have spotted us. They're flying up toward us." The woman then blasted her whistle and pointed below. A cacophony of screeches and shrieks responded, and their own multi-colored cloud of winged beasts dived to meet the enemy dragons.

It was time. Aware that it would be the first time he would fire the velocannon in combat and unsure whether it would even work, Jaks rested his finger on the trigger and gritted his teeth. Electricity sparked around him, and he channeled it into the cannon. The weapon sang a high-pitched whine and its metal fins sprouted outward, trembling as if with the same anticipation coursing through Jaks's shoulders.

The bustle of the ship, the shouts of the captain and crew, all faded to nothing as Jaks's senses needled down to the two things that mattered: channeling the lightning and keeping a steady aim.

He squeezed the trigger.

The velocannon shuddered, and a scream tore from its alien throat.

An enormous white mountain erupted from the sea like a fist of God punching an uppercut from the salty depths. Seconds later, the *Kingfisher* bucked and a mighty rush of air roared past. Jaks's feet lifted from the deck and thumped back down.

Holding onto the velocannon kept him from a heavier fall, unlike several of the sailors, who soared and then plummeted to the deck. Screams and anguished shouts cried out.

Focus disrupted, Jaks's magical channeling cut out, and the velocannon's power died away as quickly as it came.

As the skyship leveled, the shouts of Captain Gant drowned out the curses and swearing of the crew as they recouped. He bellowed orders for reports of ship damage—none.

Jaks stared down at the tsunami caused by the velocannon blast. Having reached its apex, the mountain of water crashed back down and radiated out immense waves, further adding to the waves already pushing ahead from the initial explosion. Ships at the rear of the armada, like tiny pieces of driftwood, were swamped; some, the lucky ones, rose back up, but scores vanished forever.

As the leviathan of water rolled beneath the closest of the Vor armada, ships rode the surge. Several more vessels overturned with the watery assault, but many—still more than a hundred—survived. Pushed and pulled by deranged tidal currents, they swirled in disarray.

Only two of the Ascorian ships faltered. Hostages of the hostile sea, they toiled within the chaotic currents. The remaining Ascorians, however, hastily recovered and continued their escape.

"Damn good work. That's given our ships time to gain some distance, mage," Gant roared. "The opportunity is ours to take."

Grandmaster Mulgrave nodded agreement from where he stood surveying the carnage.

A few hundred yards below the *Kingfisher*, the air was filled with swooping and thrashing wings. The Ascorian reds and greens, with the advantage of height, slashed down upon the

Vor dragons with razor-sharp talons, ripping the wings and bodies of their enemy brethren. A dozen blues and bronzes fell to the onslaught, spiraling or plummeting to the ocean surface below.

But, despite the Ascorian dragons' initial advantage, the aerial fight was far from over. Pairs grappled in midair, falling as they fought, slicing and biting at one another. Others broke off and pumped their leathery wings for height, only to swirl and dive again at an enemy below.

The battle was too fast to follow and figure out which side was winning. Jaks hoped that if Vor dragons endangered the *Kingfisher*, his mastery of electromancy would be nimble enough to catch the darting beasts.

Even now, the velocannon's aftermath left the sea churning and swirling unnaturally. Jaks stared at the weapon in awe, barely believing that this hunk of metal could cause such devastation and destruction—a quarter of the Vor ships sunk and many more limping and crippled.

"Now, son," the captain shouted at Jaks several minutes later, the Ascorian ships now well ahead of the pack. "Fire it again. Get the rest of the buggers."

If Jaks had been close enough to see the faces of the enemy sailors and warriors reeling from the mammoth assault, he might have felt pity for them. If he had been close enough to hear their terrified screams, he might have felt guilt for his second attack on them. But he felt neither.

The armada, having lost interest in their prey, had slowed, with many ships at a quarter-mast. *Regrouping*, Jaks thought. And perhaps puzzling together what had caused this oceanic eruption.

The second velocannon blast engulfed the center of the Vor

fleet. A three-masted frigate disintegrated, and a watery monument towered in its place, filling the air with vapor.

The sea surged once again and pulverized the surrounding ships. Jaks laughed with glee even as the *Kingfisher* was buffeted by the blasting wind again. Heady power pumped through him. *Damn them, they deserve that. Destroying our peace.* Once the skyship stabilized, he grinned as hoots and cheers sounded behind him—the sailors of the *Kingfisher* celebrating a win.

Once the vapor cloud cleared, he finally relaxed his grip on the velocannon and gazed down on the angry ocean and the few Vor ships that were left afloat. He thumped the side of the weapon in awe.

Only then did his euphoria dwindle, replaced by worry, on seeing that the metal fins had melted to gray lumps and tiny lines marred the surface of the barrel. It was destroying itself with each shot. He had fired it only three times in all. How many more could it handle? Could it even do one more? And then, would it just fall apart—or explode, destroying him and everybody aboard? He looked around and, seeing no one else had noticed the damage to the weapon, kept the secret to himself. No need to cause alarm.

Mulgrave appeared and pounded Jaks on the back. "Well put to the squids, lad!" Only a handful of ships remained below, drifting directionless amongst the fragments of their smashed allies. "Shan't worry about the remnants. We'll turn the tide of this damned war with this. Bless the lass—she would have been happy with the results." He beamed a smile.

Jaks had never seen him so excited. He'd tell the grandmaster about the lines later.

"We've done well today," said Mulgrave. "Today it was their navy, soon their armies." The rest of the crew were similarly joyous. Untethered but locked together with crooked elbows, they jigged around and hollered with pride—their little skyship was far deadlier than anything they had sailed before.

The Vors' dragons had suffered a similarly brutal defeat. The aerial battle had thinned their numbers and savaged the remaining few so severely that they dove with fearful screeches for the mainland. In a stretch of mercy, the Ascorian dragonmaster sounded orders for her beasts to break off and return to the skyship. She clucked proudly and threw chunks of meat to the monsters for them to snatch out of the air.

Despite the chain of defeats and losses across the country since the Vors invaded, this one struggle, at least, had been won, Jaks thought. Perhaps a small win, but surely enough to dent his father's gathering forces. And certainly enough to foil whatever plan they had destined this armada for.

In the distance, smoke still plumed over Dunberrin. Jaks shuddered at the thought of the carnage that would have resulted had the naval invaders ambushed the city in the midst of that chaos. For now, though, he could only pray that they would bring the fire under control before the main force of the Vors arrived at the walls. And hope that the *Kingfisher* and the velocannon would hold together long enough to challenge his father's armies in battle—the ultimate battle that would decide the fate of Ascoria.

Chapter 19

A Horde at the Gates

King Sicaro–Province of Dunberrin, Ascoria

The Bear King gestured impatiently for a signaler to attend him as he stared at the thin white line that was the city wall of Dunberrin. A seemingly impenetrable peninsular city to a casual observer, but not to him. For, standing on a grassy hill with his retinue and personal guard, the fields he saw below were not the green of the cultivated meadows and farms that had surrounded the road leading to this rally point, but the black and brown stain of his Vor army. So vast it was that, even from this elevated point, his eye could not distinguish the furthest flanks; thus, he depended on a chain of signalers to organize this seething sea of foot and mounted warriors, hounds, dragons, a few captured warlions, and gargantors.

Sicaro's greatest wish was that he could have crushed Silas once and for all at the border battle. But the coward had made a habit of slithering away at the last moment. And, as he should have guessed, the Ascorian and most of his army had bolted at the first engagement, with the loss of several thousand who stood courageously and died as their craven compatriots fled.

Like a dog with its tail between its legs, Silas had run until he could run no more and was now holed up in the city before him.

The signaler arrived and saluted to him, then quietly awaited his orders.

"Send a message for the supply wagons to stop here," he said to the signaler, who fidgeted nervously with her polished-steel signaling cone. "Except for the siege wagons and arrow carts. Each torgue and regiment should carry enough food and water for the last few miles."

The woman nodded, then retreated to message her counterpart at the supply battalion a mile to the west.

"Craeg," he addressed his personal assassin, standing at his side. The scar that split Vesenira's ear and reddened the right of his face had paled over the few months since his failed attempt to kill the Ascorian king. Disguised by illumancy to look like Sicaro, he had got close enough to stab his victim but was foiled by one of Silas's personal guards. Shamed, Vesenira had snuck back to Irin and materialized at the gates to have himself presented to the newly crowned Vor king. Sicaro, despite his disappointment, had ushered the shadowdancer back into his fold—but not before extracting a death-promise from the man.

"Sire? Shall I seek out the Ascorian now?" Vesenira replied, his hands palming the pommels of his swords, as was his habit.

"That faux king is still holed up in his palace, my eyes report. Although the fires didn't come near his hideout, the damage to the city was extensive and as much as could be desired." Indeed, two days of fires had destroyed much of the market district and dozens of residential areas. But best of all, a few of the incendiary bombs had burned down several barracks and storehouses of the Army District, leaving only charred stones and the skeletons of hundreds. "But without the armada follow-up, the opportunity has been lost to end this battle tidily." Sicaro's face flickered with anger for a brief moment. "Much of the city could have been ours by now, and we would be preparing for the final blow, but for the betrayal."

"Uncertain, my king," Vesenira reminded him. "They say it was a giant wave—"

"Impossible. Two hundred ships. By a wave! They were not rafts and barges. No mere wave could sink such deep-hulled ships." Sicaro spat out a bitter taste in his mouth. "Mutiny is what it was. That traitorous bastard."

He should not have trusted that pot-bellied pillager who was always with a flask in his hand. Captain Narler had been Harek's best and most reliable raider, or so he had been told. "Who knows where he's led them . . . or defected to? Damn him to his pirate hell."

Rumors of the fate of the missing fleet had been sent by his spies in Dunberrin. The most ridiculous reported destruction by a freshly erupted underwater volcano and the most believable stated that the fleet admiral had mutineered the armada to foreign waters. If those traitors ever neared these shores again, a volcano would be an apt description for his retribution on them, Sicaro thought.

The Vor king returned to his original reason for summoning his assassin. "A change of mind, Craeg. Rather than have you slink into the city to finish off Silas, I will save that pleasure for myself. Over the wall and through the city, I will climb his fluted palace and crush his head in my hands."

Vesenira nodded assent. "Sire, as you command. I shall remain at your side, your shadow where there is none."

The Vor army trampled farmland and orchards as it approached the enemy's capital city. Mounted scouts ranged ahead, while legions of axe-wielding warriors and crossbowmen marched in columns of thousands. Teams of horses followed, dragging great wagons of timber and parts that would be used to reassemble their dismantled trebuchets, ballistae, and siege towers. Gargantors trailed even further behind; their handlers kept them distant from the main army to prevent the beasts from becoming overstimulated and attacking their own side. Overhead, a dozen skyships with billowed sails glided with their loads of bomblets and bolt-throwers. And all around them, dragons spiraled and looped.

Ceaseless, the sea of invaders marched to within a mile of the outer district of the city. There, standing empty and abandoned before them, lay the smoking ruins of factories, warehouses, and residential slums that had, over the decades, outgrown the limits of the city wall and spilled out into the plains.

As he stood surveying Ascoria's last refuge, the acrid smell of smoke wafted over Sicaro. The firebombs that his agents had planted months before had incinerated three-quarters of the mile-wide industrial area, leaving rubble and ash—many still smoldered and trailed strings of smoke. He shrugged. No great concern. The slave camps were crammed with plenty of hands to rebuild it once this business was resolved.

A nearby white-washed farmhouse, the last before the city, collapsed as a gargantor leaped onto its roof.

Sicaro's horse, a seasoned destrier that stood several hands above common mounts, flicked its head and flared its nostrils at the menace—a whirlwind of claws—a hundred yards ahead of them. Nearby warriors varyingly responded with laughter or fearful cries.

He shook his head at the mindless destruction; the monsters had a predilection for smashing human constructions, as though buildings and other man-made structures offended their senses. Another reason the destructive beasts were usually kept distant from cities and towns. That they could be tamed enough to fight was a miracle—and he had a dozen of them at his command. A leathery head reared amongst the ruins and, as though swatting a child's block tower, a massive paw smashed through a wall and sent splinters of wood flying into the field outside.

"Why isn't that thing with the others?" Sicaro yelled at the cluster of generals and commanders behind him. They were debating over a table of maps that had been brought up and placed beneath a tattered pavilion. Several of the gray-bearded generals jerked upright at the king's voice and looked at each other.

"They should all be on the coast flank, readying for the water. The damned thing needs to be kept away from the siege towers," he finished. He raised a finger toward a distant paddock where workers hastened to build one of many fifty-foot-tall wheeled constructions.

Arlo, the man who had infiltrated the Vor council, and risked his life to poison King Harek—paving Sicaro's path to the Vor crown—responded to the command. Recently promoted to a full general, in reward for his loyalty, the square-faced Vor gestured at a junior officer and sent him jogging off to the beast's agitated handler.

The king swung down from his horse and approached the open-sided war tent.

"Sire, all looks in order for attack, come morning," Sneer reported as Sicaro strode in. "Regiments from west to east are all in place, sealing off the peninsula—ready to take their final positions at dawn. Trebuchets and tower-bridges are on time to be completed this evening for the gravmages to advance them under the cover of dark to their final staging points. Two torgues will stay with each to guard against any sabotage attempts by nightwraiths."

Sicaro nodded and leaned over the map table. "The outer district still provides good cover, despite the fire damage. Silas should have let it all burn down," he said. "Our center attack will have plenty of cover in the streets."

"You will remain at the rear during the attack, sire?" A general with a tattooed bald head raised an eyebrow.

"Indeed not. I will be where needed," Sicaro replied. Vor tradition required a leader to lead from the front; hence, the importance of a king who was the fiercest of warriors. "Where the threat is most high."

"As to that, sire. A private word, if you wish. You won't like this . . ." interrupted Sneer, touching the king's elbow.

"What is worse than the loss of a fleet of ships?"

"Your son, the younger Rauhalik, breathes. Sighted this week within the city, traveling to and from the Academy of the Arcane." Sneer's eyes narrowed as they often did when he delivered ill news to the king, unsure whether it would trigger an outburst of anger or days of furious activity to attack the issue; however, laughter was not what he expected.

"Ha. Tough little shit. Harder to kill than I would have thought. The boy has more of my blood to him than I would have guessed." The king rested a hand on Vinton's Rod resting at his hip, and the glimmer in his eyes faded to dark coals. "Although his lightning is a dangerous weapon, he has little experience on a battlefield. With my mentoring, we could have routed entire battalions with strikes to strategic points. But as it is, I doubt he can do more than kill a few dozen here and there. No great loss to our superior numbers."

"That's not all. The Ascorian flying ship. It is to *that* he has been traveling, along with his master."

"Yes . . . their ship." The Bear King stared at one of the Vor equivalents landing on a trampled cabbage field nearby. "And what has he to do with it? Is it he who makes it move so quickly?"

"I can't say what the boy does for the ship. Highly guarded. Even to Helena. She cannot get close enough to study the secrets of it." Sneer steepled his fingers as he mentioned the city-guard sergeant they had paid with a kingly coin and promise of lands of her own.

Sicaro stroked his beard. "Nevertheless, there is no need to delay our plans due to one ship. It's time to grind Silas into the gravel. The boy, I'll deal with, if he shows up. He will present no problem." Vinton's Rod sparked as he ran a massive hand over its caged runestones.

Chapter 20

The Battle of Dunberrin

The next morning, a skyship flew below the cloud line, so small in the distance it looked nothing more than a bird. If it hadn't been pointed out by a marksman, gesturing at it with the end of his crossbow, Sicaro would not have noticed it.

"Can only be the Ascorian skyship, Sire," the man—one of his personal guards—said to him. "Ours are but rising just now." He tilted his head to the fields where the Vor flying ships had rested overnight and where the first had just parted the knee-deep fog.

The dawn sun blinded Sicaro momentarily as he looked out over his army to the east.

Columns of his best warriors assembled. The swirling white of fog around their legs steamed off, while the glint of steel from their weapons and armor reflected their menace. Trebuchets were already throwing boulders against the city wall, and siege towers were rumbling toward the edge of the canal. Although Ascorian mortars—their only weapon with enough range to respond—lobbed explosives back, they were few and did nothing to dampen the Vor army's final preparations. Dunberrin was sure to succumb quickly.

In the first assault, the gargantors would swim across the bay and gain the granite walls under the assistance of their skyships and dragons. Once underway, the distraction would open the way for his siege towers to extend their gravmancy-aided bridges across the waterway and for thousands upon thousands of his warriors to stream onto the walls. He knew the defenses better than any man. Strength of numbers, guile, and surprise would take the day. Nothing could stop him.

He gestured at a signaler as he looked up at the Ascorian skyship roving above the city walls—its captain likely too scared and out-numbered to venture any closer. "Send a signal to Commander Fritchar and his skyships to deal with that. Five should be adequate to corner the thing, or at least chase it away from the battlefield." Though only seen from afar, Sicaro's skyship captains had reported the Ascorians had succeeded at building a faster, fleeter ship that was twice the size of theirs and undoubtedly more heavily armed. However, even the largest of gargantors could be brought down—as could the largest of ships. Feints, maneuvering, and superior tactics would overwhelm any enemy, no matter how quick or strong.

Continuing his orders, he spoke: "Five more of the skyships are to go defend the gargantors during their crossing." He expected little resistance from the Ascorian navy—the few ships they still had remained moored along the opposite edge of the city, leaving just ballistae and bowmen to protect the commercial docks where the monsters would set ashore. "The last two ships are to stay in reserve at my command." The limp-faced Sneer, nearby, nodded, then gestured to the signaler to begin his task.

Black steel plate, the same he had worn in the campaigns to

unify Ascoria over a decade ago, covered Sicaro from neck to toe. Said to have been crafted in an ancient volcanic furnace from a metal rock found in a lost subterranean city, the articulated armor was invulnerable to physical weapons swung by anyone other than another powerful gravmancer. Many times, he had carved his way through a melee, blades and points glancing off him unnoticed, leading the charge to victory.

Sicaro grasped the warhammer Sorrow in his right hand and Vinton's Rod in his left. With his weapons and his gravmancy, he feared nothing.

It was with some surprise, then, that a brilliant flash drew his eye to the west flank of his army.

In less than a blink, the meadows that had lay under the smear of Vor warriors disappeared in a blinding explosion.

BOOM!

Sneer grabbed at his king's arm and screamed in his ear, but his voice was drowned out by a groan from the earth itself.

Sicaro staggered, then fell as a blast struck him like a cart of rocks.

All around, warriors were thrown to the ground. Horses toppled like toys, and war dragons tumbled through the sky.

For several seconds, he lay stunned by the blow. Blood streamed from his unhelmeted head where something had struck him hard. Gray cloth lay across his legs—a tent torn from its pegs. He pushed it aside and rose to his feet, pushing on the shaft of his hammer for support; even under such duress, he never released his grip on either hammer or rod.

A stone thudded to the ground next to him, followed by a shower of pebbles and dirt. The air clouded for as far as he could see—thicker toward the source of the explosion. He invoked a gravmantic shield, warding aside the falling debris. An uprooted tree smashed to the ground nearby. Rocks the size of melons slammed about while stones and pebbles rained down in a freakish hailstorm.

Eventually, the downpour of detritus ceased, and the dust began to settle.

To the west, where the explosion had originated, it was devastation. Nothing stood, not even the ancient oaks and ironwoods that had dotted the landscape only minutes before. Of thousands of warriors, there was nothing left but crawling figures and corpses on a pitted wasteland.

He found his voice and shouted at one of his generals nearby, struggling to his feet. "What caused it? Did you see?" The man, however, still confused, tripped and fell away.

Another man, a thin man holding a dented round shield over his head, edged his way closer. Sneer peered out from under the dome. "My lord, you are injured," he said, staring at the king's face.

"It is nothing," Sicaro replied, wiping the blood on his brow into a smear. "What is the source of this chaos? I've never seen anything like this."

"The last thing I saw before the explosion was the briefest of flashes on the Ascorian skyship. I was looking up at the craft and saw a bright light at the exact time of the explosion. Perhaps this was the purpose of your son on the ship?"

"It cannot be. He doesn't have enough power to do this . . . no one does."

"No one of this world," Sneer offered.

Sicaro froze as realization struck. "That bitch. She has made a fool of me."

"Who?" Sneer dropped the shield to the ground. "The woman?"

"The weapon at the Academy. I shouldn't have believed her. She deceived me to destroy something lesser. I should have destroyed the entire building." Sicaro spat a curse, then lifted his gaze to search the skies. He must get to the Ascorian ship and destroy the weapon. If it fired again, it could end his assault, end his army and his hold on Ascoria.

Several men and women, finding their king, scrambled to attend him and begged for orders, unable to make sense of the devastation surrounding them. Desperate fear swirled in their eyes, reflecting the screams of the wounded in the fields.

Sicaro gazed around. The west flank was decimated. Fifteen thousand fighters gone. Almost half his army destroyed in one earth-splitting attack from the Ascorian skyship.

He had grossly underestimated the outworlder woman and her creation. He gripped his weapons tightly as anger threatened to cloud his mind—he quickly stifled the emotion and assessed what he had left to work with.

The east flank remained—albeit disarrayed for the moment, fear obvious in the disordered lines of assembled troops, but mass panic had not yet taken hold. A quick assessment and he gauged there were still enough warriors to take the city once the gargantors assaulted the flank and the siege towers were uprighted.

"Deal with this," Sicaro ordered Sneer and several commanders stumbling toward him. "Rally the troops. We continue the attack."

"Sire, perhaps we should retreat and regather," said a torgue captain with a trembling voice.

A tiny voice at the back of his mind cried out in agreement to the captain's plea. Perhaps the best course was to retreat his army? Gather more warriors—form a slave army to command from the thousands that had been captured—and attack another time? He grimaced at the thought. No, he couldn't show the slightest weakness, even after such a sudden turnaround of fortune. He would see Silas crushed before him today.

Sorrow smashed into the side of the captain's head, pulverizing it to mush. The decapitated body tumbled several feet into the dust.

"We continue the attack," Sicaro repeated with his bloodied warhammer held at the ready for another dispute. No one challenged his command. "See it done," he directed Sneer.

He lowered his weapon and stalked toward a mired Vor skyship in the distance as his shadowdancer appeared behind him. "I have a bigger problem to deal with."

Chapter 21

Skyward

Jaks—Onboard the Kingfisher above the City of Dunberrin

Jaks stared in disbelief at the savaged earth below. From a second after he had fired the velocannon, he had lost sight of the ground as the *Kingfisher* bucked ferally and sent him flying until his tether snapped tight and he fell to all fours. Dust had then obscured everything as it billowed up around the skyship, quickly followed by a pounding of flying rocks and stones to the underside of the vessel.

But now, several minutes later, as Captain Gant and his gravmancers finally leveled out the ship, and the air cleared, the destruction was vicious and raw. But was it enough to turn back the invaders?

Visible through the tainted haze, a massive crater had hollowed out a segment of the cultivated farmland. What had been a patchwork lined by hedgerows and thin cart roads was now a black gouge surrounded by a brown stain for miles around. And where, minutes before, Vor columns had inked the countryside, multitudes of dust-covered bodies and body parts lay scattered and unmoving amongst the churned earth.

He blinked his watering eyes and coughed dust out of his throat. His stomach churned, and he expelled its contents—whether a result of the rolling deck, the elation of conquest, or the excise of guilt for many thousands of murders, he felt it all.

"Get yourself together, lad," said Grandmaster Mulgrave, pulling on the railing up to Jaks's position. "A better result than I could have imagined . . . but we need another. Many of their legions on the other side of the field still stand and are regrouping."

Jaks wiped his mouth and followed the mage to the velocannon. He pushed the guilt aside. It was either the Vors or his countryfolk.

"The barrel looks damaged. I'll cool the metal and examine it closer." Mulgrave laid hands on the metal shaft and a frigid breeze spiraled around him. "Not too quickly or it might worsen those cracks," he said.

A minute later, he spun the weapon on its holding bracket and gazed into the dark barrel. Wide enough to reach inside, he thrust his arm into the round opening and felt around. He frowned and pulled his arm out, then ran his hand over the exterior as though to smooth the cracks on its surface.

"How does it fare?" Jaks asked. It had only been fired four times. Surely, it could do more. Then he remembered it was just an improvised contraption made of wreckage. They were lucky it even worked.

"The cracks threaten to strike all the way through the barrel." The grandmaster shook his head.

"Just one more time and it'll all be over!"

"Another time might destroy it." The grandmaster grimaced. "It would kill all of us with it. No, we need to return to the runic forge. I can weld steel bands around it for reinforcement."

Distracted by a movement below, Jaks staggered a step. His voice pitched high. "We don't have time, Grandmaster." He pointed at several flying Vor ships and a cumulus of draconic forms.

The bald mage squinted over the prow. "The fiends just don't give up."

"Their ships soar our way. Coming for us. Coming to stop us," said Jaks. The hairs on the back of his neck rose. He sensed an angered grief rising toward him, seeking revenge for the tragedy of thousands killed.

A whistle pierced the air. The dragonmaster sounded her device twice more and illumanced a commanding rune into the air. Red and green beasts leaped and dove from their perches on the masts and railings of the *Kingfisher* with a flurry of wings and bursts of breathed fire. Having overcome his initial fear of them and becoming accustomed to their contained ferocity on the ship, Jaks found pride at seeing the powerful creatures once again leaping to the ship's defense.

Captain Gant bellowed for his sailors to prepare for battle. Ballistae clanked as they were ratcheted tight and loaded with quick, light spears. Heavier spears and grape-shot canisters waited nearby in case the Vors neared for ship-to-ship combat.

"Five of the devils!" Gant shouted for all to hear. "Outnumbered, but we're more than their match. Their tubs are nothing compared to our lady. Let's show them how we fight in the Ascorian navy!" Bold words, but ones that the veteran seadog doubtlessly believed.

The crew, emboldened by his words, cheered and shouted as one, "*Kingfisher!*"

Jaks's reports of the zinger's recordings over the past weeks supported that confidence—as long as his observations of the enemy ships were accurate. Although half the size of the

Kingfisher, his father's ships took twice as long to change direction and generally flew half the speed; however, with raised sail and wind to fill it, the longboats could speed like an eagle on the wing.

Yet, both the strength and the weakness of the Ascorian skyship was in its human engine. Designed by Meila and Grandmaster Hazeldine to allow eight gravmancers to coordinate their magic, it relied on the skills and control of those eight gravmancers who sweated in the gloom below deck.

Captain Gant relied on a set of four levers to signal his course adjustments to the gravmancers. Each lever manipulated ropes and springs to adjust dials in front of each of the eight mages seated with knees around a large runestone. According to the dial instructions, they would alter their gravmantic "well," and the combined gravity fluxes then resulted in changes of speed, direction, and/or elevation of the skyship. Sometimes all at the same time. It was a delicate dance of gravmancy that had taken many hundreds of hours for the captain and crew to master. Mastery now tested to the extreme.

"Hold on!" Jaks shouted to Mulgrave as the ship jolted and pressed him against the side rail.

"We take the fight to the enemy. Target the rightmost ship. Toss firebombs when we pass over," the captain cried out from the helm. With a height advantage going into this fight, his sailors could rain down oil flasks like flaming meteors with impunity.

The air ahead and below exploded into a hurricane of red, black, blue, and green. Dragons dived and swooped, screeching and slashing with razor-sharp talons, biting and snapping at all within reach. How they distinguished friend from foe, or whether they even knew, Jaks wondered at the terrible spectacle.

The *Kingfisher*'s ballistae thunked and clattered as the crews reloaded and fired spears into the fray. Either the sailors had a clearer idea of which dragons were theirs or did not care which of them they hit.

"Protect the ship," Mulgrave said to Jaks. "Do what you can. I'm going back for my runestaff." He waved a thick finger toward the ship's stern, where the ironwood staff was gripped in a weapons stand, its fire gem glimmering a life of its own.

As the mage retreated, a flicker at the edge of Jaks's vision and a deafening screech caused Jaks to flinch. If he had been the target, the slight movement would not have saved him, but the black dragon's prey instead stood at middeck, lifting an armful of spears. The dragon hurtled toward the sailor, first spitting a glob of dark liquid at him and then raking claws over his astonished face. Thrown back and screaming, the man's blood misted the air as his jaw parted from his skull. He thrashed on the ground, clutching his mangled face. Black acid bubbled where it splattered his exposed skin and armor. Spear shafts clattered to the deck and rolled chaotically around the dying man.

More screeches. Several draconic figures swooped in from all directions.

Abandoning their ranged weapons, the sailors picked up fighting spears and sabers, and poked and slashed back at the dragons in defense.

Another sailor was lifted and dragged until his rope tether tightened and tore him out of the dragon's clutches, only for the man to collapse with blood spraying from his ragged neck.

The captain's second mate, a haughty Fauconian, speared a blue dragon as it dived. But even with a shaft through its chest, the winged monster fell onto the hairy-chested man, slashing and biting at him as it died. Wings and arms entwined, the duo convulsed in a death match until a red-faced sailor stabbed the dragon several more times, but not in time to save his shipmate from disembowelment.

Bolts of fire spat from the rear deck. Grandmaster Mulgrave, with a dome of fire over his head and shoulders and runestaff in his hands, invoked fiery projectiles left and right at dragon shapes harassing the captain's helm. Backed up to the mage, Captain Gant held up a round shield and a stabbing spear at the swooping figures. The pair danced a defense to clear the ship up to the central mast.

Jaks fell into his battle training. He diverted the terror of the situation into an invocation and created a web of electromancy, thick and deadly with lightning. He drew his sword.

Several yards away, a red dragon and another midshipman fought. The beast flapped in midair with talons grasping the edge of the man's shield. It hissed and then breathed fire at the sailor. The man screamed as the jet of flame blinded him and burned his face.

"Let go of the shield!" Jaks shouted.

Whether in response to Jaks's command or the agony of his blistered face, the sailor released the shield and fell to the deck. And, as Jaks anticipated, the dragon gained height with the shield in its grip—high up enough for the electromancy to spare the man below.

He swung his sword. Lightning flashed through the gap from steel to dragon, snapped like a whip, and filled the air with brilliant white. Where it struck, it exploded and blasted the beast into a starboard arc over the ship's side.

But no sooner had he lowered his sword than another of the hell-born creatures plunged toward him. His reflexes too slow to react, he could barely twitch his sword to the new threat when his mage shield reacted and burst with a blinding light.

Outstretched talons exploded, and the dragon's electrified body thudded to the deck. A wing knocked Jaks's feet out from under him. Head striking the deck hard, his surroundings blurred into darkness.

Jaks roused to a woman's face close to his and her hands gripping his shoulders as she shook him. "Get on your feet, mage. No time to nap. The battle isn't done," she yelled and flopped his arm over her shoulder and pulled him up.

He groaned and stood, thanking the sailor before she stepped back to reach for her spear and shield. His waist feeling unusually free, his gaze trailed down to his rope tether—blackened and smoking, it dangled, burned to a wick by his electromancy.

A distant shout followed by several thudding noises about the ship raised Jaks's dazed attention. Through gaps in armor plates at the prow of the ship, he saw only clear skies ahead: no dragons or skyships.

"Below," Ranger Cromer shouted from the middeck. "Ships below. Prepare to repel boarders!"

Leaning through the gap, wind stinging his eyes, Jaks's gaze fell on four flying longboats below. The fifth Vor ship spiraled wildly in the distance, clouded with Ascorian war dragons. On the nearer skyships, he could see battle-enraged faces sneering from the deck and their bearers flourishing axes and knives, their blades begging for blood.

A manic web of ropes spanned the air between the Vor ships and the *Kingfisher*. A second later, yet another of the strands hummed through the air on the tail of a whaling harpoon, disappeared beneath the skyship, and thunked.

Several bearded Vors pulled on the rope and reeled in their catch with beefy arms. Spiders entrapping a wasp.

"Cut the ropes." Gant gestured with a falchion in his hand. "Climb down if you have to."

Jaks watched incredulously as five sailors unquestioningly obeyed the captain's order and clambered over the sides, sure-handedly clinging to mooring ropes and hawsers. He shook his head, admiring their bravado and loyalty.

But soon after, the first of them screamed as he plummeted into the vast gap below. Missiles pelting the underside of the skyship sent one after another of the sailors to their deaths. Their lives sacrificed for only three of the many harpoons to be cut free.

With crossbow bolts pinging off shielding along the rails, no other sailors dared follow their mates over the edge. Instead, they turned to hurling oil flasks topped with flaming rags at the Vor ships.

Most missed their targets, but a few scored hits on two ships below. Glass smashed and splattered over warriors and wooden decks. Oil ignited and burned black as it consumed screaming men and women—several became so confused, they jumped from their burning ship into the abyss.

Ruthless flames engulfed a canvas sail on the Vor ship closest to them and the captain's helm on the furthest.

At the other end of the *Kingfisher*, Grandmaster Mulgrave pointed his runestaff and projected an immense blade of fire. Scorched by the intensity of his magic, ropes binding the ship fell away, braids burned to charred ends within seconds.

Chaos. Burning deck, panicking crew, and flapping ropes sent the first enemy skyship wildly adrift.

The second damaged ship, too, tiller ablaze with its captain unable to approach the burning controller, lurched and then rolled upside down. Its crew and warriors, untethered, tipped out of the ship and fell screaming with arms flailing uselessly.

"Enjoy the view down!" a red-headed sailor shouted at the rolling ship and laughed.

Jaks's eyes dropped to the farmlands and city below. The skyships, bound in a tangled web, drifted above the main battlefield.

The battle for the walls of Dunberrin raged, with tiny dots of infantry and beasts of various shapes marring the landscape. Plumes of smoke and roaring fires smeared the already demolished outer city; siege towers and bridges forded the canal moat. From this height, Jaks couldn't discern the sway of the battle. Disappointed, he realized that if he fired the velocannon at the Vors now, the blast would most likely demolish the city wall and its defenders as well.

Shouted warnings from the crew behind him renewed Jaks's focus on their battle for the skies.

The last three skyships pulled level with the *Kingfisher*, pulling in their harpoon strands. The two ships to Jaks's left were lined with terrifying, bearded demons, gesticulating with wicked axes and swords. They balanced on the edge of their longboat, vying to be the first to leap the quickly narrowing divide. And to his right, the third ship rose. Warriors hurled grappling hooks. All fell short, but it wouldn't be long until they could secure their prize.

Teeth gritted, arms trembling, and fighting an impulse to run away and hide, Jaks turned to the dual ships on the port-side.

Warriors, from the land of his father and his ancestors, but as different from him as Zurans, Ranilians, or any other barbarians from a far-off land, jeered and yelled across the gap of only forty yards. "Rip off yer arms," "Tear off yer head," and

"Fuck yer skull," they screamed. No doubt they would if they boarded. But they wouldn't get that far if he could help it.

"Take cover, mage, you'll get shot!" shouted a sailor, himself winding back the cord of a crossbow to fire back at the enemy.

At Jaks's command, filaments of electricity warped around him. Seconds later, a Vor crossbow bolt seeking to lodge in his chest struck the elemental shield and exploded, its fragments repulsed and impotent.

With their snarling faces and burning hatred still piercing his shield, he gathered the pool of fear brimming in his head, feeling oddly confident yet utterly terrified, and visualized a scenario for the Vors' destruction. Another minute and the ship would be within range of the invader's grappling hooks.

Clouds swirled and brewed above the pair of skyships, darkening and pulsing brightly several times. A sound like whips cracked the air.

The skin on Jaks's arms prickled, and the smell of metal invaded his nostrils.

With palms stretched toward the clouds pent up with crackling energy, he drew them down.

Forks of lightning barraged the Vor skyships in a storm of electromancy.

Wooden masts detonated, timber decks erupted, and bodies exploded.

White flashes, faster than the eye could follow, danced across the ships, lightning bolts seeking anything they could lash at.

"Get the fuckers," yelled the Ascorian crossbowman, who a minute before had been fearing for Jaks's safety. "Take that, fucking squidbait!" The sailor twanged off his weapon, but it was a needless effort.

Under the blasts of the lightning storm, the pair of skyships splintered apart. The prow of the nearest broke loose and tumbled as though falling off a cliff—men and women aboard uselessly grabbed for anything that could stay their descent; several seconds later, the flaming remains of the fractured skyship followed, leaving a trail of smoke and tumbling crisped bodies. Storm clouds lathered the second skyship with sheets of lightning, each bolt smashing parts off even as it plunged out of control.

The debris of the two ships falling smaller, Jaks clapped his hands together and broke off his invocation. The arcs of white energy disappeared in an instant and the clouds receded and dissolved.

He slumped forward, gripped the rail, and gasped for air—unaware he had starved himself of breath throughout the storm.

"Mage." The crossbowman clapped a hand onto Jaks's shoulder. "Master, their last ship is upon us. You must help." Though still light-headed, he turned to the sailor's gesture as the last of the Vor skyships, grappling hooks grasping, crunched into the side of the *Kingfisher*.

Dozens of warriors aped over the sides of the Vor skyship. Sailors stabbed and slashed to repel the boarders, but those who fell were ruthlessly trampled by their eager comrades pushing up from behind. Jaks prepared his sword, the melee too close for broad strokes of lightning.

"Boy," a familiar voice cut to Jaks's soul.

All else fell away as King Sicaro, black steel from neck to toe, descended like a dark angel from some hellish aerie. With arms outstretched, left hand gripping a triple-stoned rod and the other a giant warhammer, he alighted the deck.

"There is a reckoning to be had for what you have done."

Jaks fell, compelled by his father, to his knees.

Chapter 22

The Duel

Jaks—Deck of the Kingfisher

"Demon child," said Sicaro to Jaks. "I always thought it would be the older one who would be the thorn in my side . . . but it turned out to be you."

Jaks stared at his father, his cheek pressed, paralyzed, against the deck, gravmanced with invisible slabs like everyone else he could see from the corners of his eyes. Warriors and sailors, Ascorian and Vor alike, lay sprawled and unmoving under the warrior king's magic, groans and gasps for mercy barely heard above the howling wind.

The dark clouds above grew smaller as the *Kingfisher* hurtled uncontrolled toward the ground, dragging the Vor skyship down with it.

One of the three runestones on the spiral rod that his father bore pulsated gray and midnight black—no doubt fueling or magnifying his gravmancy—the red and green glow of the other two stones simmered, waiting.

"First mother, then sister, and no doubt craving to murder

your father and king as well," he continued. "And how about the other sister? Slit her pale throat and make it complete?"

The words burned in Jaks's mind. The truth being, more than anything, he did desire to kill him. No one had brought greater pain or suffering to him than his father. No one more shame or guilt. But unable to even breathe, his chest crushed by the gravmantic giant, he could not shout his rage nor focus his power to invoke a stroke of lightning—he could do nothing but strain his lungs for air.

"Enough!" Grandmaster Mulgrave shouted.

On the edge of Jaks's dimming vision, the stocky mage pushed to his feet on the middeck with the timber of the central mast at his back. Leaning on his staff, he pointed the orb atop its shaft at the Vor king. "Enough, Sicaro. Destroying us all will make no difference. The battle is lost. The invasion is lost. You have lost."

Fire burst from the grandmaster's orb and enveloped the steel-encased bear. Heat so intense, ironwood decking warped and blackened beneath the roaring flames. Bodies beneath the path of flame caught fire; if they still lived, they made no sound as they burned.

Abruptly, the weight lifted from Jaks. Chest heaving, he sucked in the sweetest-tasting air. Released. He rolled flat on his back, with his vision sharpening and strength replenishing.

The upward rush of air around the *Kingfisher* slowed and the sounds of humanity returned with gasps and then groans of pain.

"Ancient fool," Sicaro bellowed from within the raging cone of fire.

Forging to his feet and backing up to the skyship railing, Jaks groaned as the flames retreated, revealing his father unharmed by Mulgrave's pyromancy except for his beard and hair scorched to stubble and his face an angry red.

"Your fire is pathetic, old man." The Vor king held Vinton's Rod before him—the red runestone within its spirals glowed brilliantly, having absorbed the grandmaster's pyromancy. "Once I destroy this ship along with the two of you, Ascoria will be mine." He made a peculiar gesture with the rod, pointing at Jaks momentarily, although his eyes remained latched on his veteran adversary.

Mulgrave called out to Sicaro, "Look . . . your army is breaking. The few legions you have left will soon dissolve into a rout." Jaks followed his father's gaze to the battle on the land below. The *Kingfisher* had leveled out from its plunge over the Vors' rear line. Low enough that the cries of both humans and beasts rose to his ears. "Your towers are destroyed. With no passage across the canal to aid your monsters, they fall one by one." As though cued by the mage's words, a gargantor, prickled by pikes and engulfed by unnatural fire, toppled from the wall and splashed into the canal below.

A clamor of bells then rang from the city walls.

The canal frothed, but it was not the great, gray monster returning; instead, several of the city bridges broke the surface, returning to their peacetime positions. Was the grandmaster mistaken? Had the Vors taken control of the vital bridges and city gates?

The truth manifested when the gates crashed open and armored warlions bounded out of the giant portals—the beasts roared as they sprang into the midst of the Vor legions. Bodies were torn and tossed aside. Catapults and trebuchets were abandoned as the invader's panicked and fled.

Warriors and sailors aboard the skyship, many limping or pained from Sicaro's paralyzing assault, had retreated to opposite sides of the deck to recover. But at the sight of the turning tide of battle below, the Vors dismissed their injuries, began chanting, and raised their weapons in defiance.

The Vor king lifted his hammer and howled a war cry, signaling his warriors to attack.

A coiled snake, Sicaro lunged across the deck, the spike of his warhammer swinging at Mulgrave's skull. The mage's magical staff lashed out to counter the blow. A ball of raging flames erupted around the pair and obscured them from view.

And all down the skyship, the melee renewed as both sides roared and met with a clash of steel on steel.

At the stern, Captain Gant hefted a saber, leading five of his sailors as they defended the steps into the belly of the ship. Middeck, the fight degenerated into a brutal bloodbath of axes, knives, and fists; the combatants wrestling and stabbing at whatever enemy they could.

Movement flickered on the edge of Jaks's vision. He twitched toward it. There it was—a pool of shadow with no source—a memory from the night.

Confused, he scrambled back from the darkness slithering across the deck. Were his eyes failing? Was he hallucinating fragments of Vixhana?

Then it lunged.

Pain stabbed through Jaks's belly.

He stared incredulously at a steel blade sprouting from the front of his leather doublet.

A hand materialized around the dagger's handle and continued to sink the blade up to the hilt.

"That'll do you, whelp." The rest of Craeg Vesenira materialized in front of Jaks, cords of muscles protruding on his tattooed neck and down into his arm. His father's assassin did not smile or grimace at his deed; instead, bitter sorrow shadowed his face.

Jaks fell to the deck, dagger embedded in his front and blood seeping from the wound.

The bare-chested Elliptan stood over him with a second dagger in his hands, readying a deathblow.

Jaks raised a hand against the blade. Electromancy responded to his fear.

Serrated lightning and a deafening clap tore between Jaks and Vesenira.

The assassin was hurtled backward, lifted into the air by tendrils of white. His body crumpled against the far railing, smoldering and spasming for a few seconds until finally going limp, a grotesque mask twisting his face.

Jaks gasped, sickened at the sight of the dagger protruding obscenely from his body. No one around to help—the clashing sailors and boarders showed no sign of abatement and the fiery ball surrounding Mulgrave and Sicaro flared even greater than before. He spilled Meila's medikit around himself, groaning with every movement . . . weakening with each second.

He had studied the contents earlier that day and racked his memory for what Meila had instructed each was for. It was the medigel bandage that he needed right now. The miraculous healing particulates that would stop the bleeding.

He gritted his teeth and yanked the leather-handled dagger from his gut. He screamed, almost passing out in pain. Breathing heavily, a minute later, he lifted the edge of his doublet and slapped the bandage to the seeping wound. The doublet fell in place, and he pressed the pad to his skin. Despite the agony, he didn't seem to be bleeding much. Hopefully, there wasn't much internal bleeding either. Perhaps, off-center, Vesenira had missed his vital organs and vessels.

Pain—there was something for it. Meila had shown him before.

The green bottle. Tiny pills to numb the body. He threw several in his mouth and slumped flat on his back. A dozen breaths later and the pain had receded to a dull ache, and his energy slowly returned.

He pushed himself up onto his hands and knees.

His father stood with chest heaving on the middeck, staring at the grandmaster, his warhammer and Vinton's Rod held to either side.

Mulgrave, his back to Jaks, panted heavily with his mage's staff raised to his opponent.

Their fiery shield had extinguished, but its aftereffects smoked and burned around them. Several human forms twitched on the deck, charred and disfigured. Flames ran up the central mast and out along its beams.

On the far side of the burning ship, the remaining warriors and sailors continued in a whirl of stabbing and swinging blades.

Where the Vors had boarded, their skyship now drifted free from the *Kingfisher*, its tethers and grappling hooks hanging loose.

"Apprentice . . . how bad is it?" the grandmaster shouted to Jaks but without turning his head. The veteran battlemages appeared at an impasse, fatigued and swaying heavily. Mulgrave stumbled, almost falling, but caught himself by leaning on his staff. His right leg was awkward at the knee; his arm, on the same side, fell limply; and blood poured down his brow.

The Vor king grimaced, also showing wounds—chest plate cratered inward and the left side of his face blistered, red and raw.

"Fine, Master. I'll be fine," said Jaks, wincing as he rose to his feet, never taking his eyes off his father. Injured, the man looked even more dangerous and terrifying.

The Vor king tossed down his fisted hammer and tore off the dented chest piece. He cast it aside, and his breathing eased. Vinton's Rod thumped into his palm and he met Jaks's eyes.

"Your master is nigh dead." Sicaro flared a disdainful look at the bald mage leaning on his staff. His eye blazed through the ravaged side of his face. "And you will soon join him, frightened little boy."

Jaks placed a trembling hand on the grandmaster's shoulder and pressed him to retreat.

It was time to face the source of his greatest fears.

He paced to within three arm-lengths of the man he had once called "father." His lips thinned to a line, thinking "torturer" would have been more apt. The quivering fear of a minute past pivoted toward a shaking anger.

"You don't intimidate me. My powers are far greater than yours." He raised his crippled hand. Sprites of lightning jumped between the remaining fingers. "You cut me, you beat me, you deceived me . . . but you have not conquered me." His other hand lifted, and sparks danced back between his palms. "I have made mistakes, but the blame is on you. You are right, there is a reckoning to pay . . . but it is *you* who will pay it."

"Enough," snapped Sicaro. "Time to finish this—" Two strides and the giant vaulted toward Jaks with Vinton's Rod swinging in an overhead arc at his head.

Energy surged through Jaks's hands. Bitterness tainted his mouth.

A brilliance of lightning caught his father in midair, focused on the artifact swinging in his hands.

The blast reversed the weapon's descent, sending both attacker and weapon flying in separate directions.

Sicaro hurtled backward. He struck the charred center-mast and slid to its base. Vinton's Rod, torn from his grip, spun through the air and disappeared over the side of the skyship.

The Vor king slumped, wheezing through blistered lips, his chest visibly labored through the gap in his armor.

Jaks searched for a weapon. He reached down for a long-bladed rapier in the cindered hand of a dead sailor. Still weakened from his belly wound, possibly bleeding internally, he hefted the weapon with both hands and walked toward his father.

Sicaro groped for the closest weapon—a spear with a blackened haft and tip. Leaning against the mast, he stood to meet his son.

"No magic . . . sword against spear," the giant declared.

Jaks shook his head and electrified the blade of the rapier. He would not trust his father to honor any arrangement. Jagged lightning rippled along the steel. Wisps of blue flickered off the tip.

Sicaro lunged. Jaks's arms sank, encumbered with an unnatural force, dragging the rapier blade to the deck. With speed belying his injured state, Sicaro drove the spear at his son's undefended chest.

But Jaks needed no shield to defend, nor blade to attack.

A column of white and blue surged from Jaks's arms. Lightning enveloped Sicaro mid-stride and paralyzed him statue-like as forks of electricity raged over his body.

The gravmantic weight vanished and Jaks raised the rapier in front of him. He double-stepped, knocked aside the spear, and plunged the electrified sword into his father's chest.

The blade pierced the gambeson and slid between the ribs. Realizing he had been screaming as he did so, Jaks took in another breath and then pushed again until it went no further.

Sicaro groaned, spitted on the end of a sword and broiling at the hand of his son.

Shuddering uncontrollably, a glob of blood ejected from his mouth. His eye bulged in its socket and gray vapor fled his skin.

Dead weight then pushed against Jaks's hands. He released the rapier and stepped aside for the body to fall to the deck.

Tendrils of lightning fizzled out, and he collapsed beside his father's corpse.

As consciousness slipped away from Jaks, a sense of great evil disappeared with it. He had overcome and destroyed that which he feared the most. Sicaro was killed and Ascoria was saved from his tyranny and deviant visions.

Jaks fought to uphold his failing strength. There was one thing left to do, an oath to fulfill, but the darkness couldn't be denied—it enfolded him in its grasp.

Chapter 23

Sisterhood

Karisa—The Palace of Irin, Ascoria

Muffled voices from outside the chamber doors woke Karisa from a troubled sleep. Her head rose from her pillow to listen closer.

The voices grew louder. A moment later, the rasp of steel escaping its scabbard cut through the dark. A shout, right outside the doors, was followed by the unmistakable clash of sword on sword. A hound growled but then went silent. Grunts, thumps, and more yelling grew louder.

Karisa pushed aside the silk veil surrounding her canopied bed and slid out barefooted, ignoring the chaffing slave collar around her neck. She gestured and a hovering globe flicked into being to light the room. She had to find out what was happening.

"My queen, what is it?" said Takola, the eldest of the handmaids—not so long ago a courtesan. She rose from the other side of the grand bed, grabbed a long, elegant robe, and held it out for the wife of King Sicaro with trembling hands.

Karisa donned the garment in a swift motion. "I don't know.

Quickly, gather the others and hide in the steam room." She gestured at the four other handmaids, also staring terrified at the guard-room doors.

No sooner had the women retreated than the chamber doors burst open; a couple of them screamed as light from the guardroom sliced through their quarters.

Karisa stood in front of the door to the steam room, her arms spread wide as though to protect her servants. The chain to her neck was stretched to its extreme. The hovering globe vanished to be replaced by a curtain of darkness that enfolded her, the chain, and a yard in every direction.

"My queen. Queen Karisa. Are you safe? Where are you?" The silhouette of a warrior holding a broadsword stood in the doorway from the guardroom. "Deserters attacked us," the figure said.

Recognizing the captain of the guard, Rachella, but uncertain of the danger still about, Karisa spoke through the veil of her illusion. "What do you mean, deserters? What are they doing here?"

Sheathing her sword, the captain scanned the room but seemed unable to pinpoint Karisa's location. "They're saying the king is dead. The garrison has turned to looting. I am afraid the situation has become dire."

"Dead . . .?" Karissa's voice trailed off. She lost focus and the veil of illumancy fell away. She stumbled against the wall.

Captain Rachella saluted her bewildered queen but then glanced back to the chamber doors as though wary of more intruders. On the other side, four bodies lay dead: one female guard, the hound, and two heavily bearded men. The fight had been quick but deadly. "A signal message from the front says the king was killed. At least half of the assault force was destroyed, and the rest are in full retreat."

"Gods be thanked!" Takola strode out of the steam room and began a tiny dance. She raised her hands and jabbed at the air.

"No time for rejoicing, handmaid," admonished the captain. "The queen is in great danger." She placed a hand on the pommel of her sword.

"What was the fight about?" Karisa walked to the door and stared at the blood-filled room. Far away, shouts sounded from the central staircase of the palace.

"You." Captain Rachella followed her and kicked the largest man's body. "Forgive me, my queen, but you are nothing but chattel to them now. You and your handmaids are treasures for the rapists. We must flee before more appear."

"Thank you for your loyalty, Captain." Karisa touched the female guard on the arm. "Will you release me from this collar?" Much relied on the guard's goodwill toward her. To her relief, the sturdy woman extracted a key without hesitation and freed Karisa from her binding. There were still some good people, even amongst the Vors.

A small figure dashed into the guardroom from the outer hall and skidded to a stop. Captain Rachella swept out her sword and pointed it at the intruder. "No further!"

"It is only the chambermaid, Captain. She is no threat." Karisa touched the small girl's arm. "Rasish, are you harmed?"

The girl stared in horror at the blood and dead bodies but shook her head and stammered a reply. "My lady, you must hide. There is chaos outside. They say the king is dead."

"Yes, so I have heard. It is hard to believe."

Deep inside, a tone of pure joy sang in Karisa's soul. Her father was dead. The spider that entrapped her, the leech that drained her, the monster that used her, was dead. She could not prevent the smile that slowly creased her face. She knew she must look like a madwoman with the danger lurking the hallways around them, but she could not shed the release she felt. Even if she died tonight, she would die satisfied knowing that the devil had died before her.

"Listen to me," said Karisa, taking command of the group, enacting a plan that she and the chambermaid had prepared for such a day. "Rasish will lead us down through the servant's stairs to the dungeons. There, she will give us torn and dirtied rags to disguise ourselves." She looked at the young girl.

The twelve-year-old girl nodded, pulling her servant's tunic tightly around her shoulders.

"Captain Rachella, if you are loyal to me, you will come and help us escape. If not, please leave me now. Take what you want from my chambers and know my thanks for protecting us from these two." Karisa shifted her gaze to the would-be rapists and bent to pluck a sword from the hand of the closest. She had never seen the man before, but then again, they all looked the same behind their matted beards.

The guard captain, without a pause, bent to help and replied, "My lady, I would follow you to the ends of the world."

With the help of the captain, Karisa removed and then donned the dead guard's leather jerkin, holding back her nausea as the cold, congealed blood on the inside of the armor pressed against her skin.

With a glance in both directions down the hallway, they slipped out into the darkened palace. Six ex-courtesans, a chambermaid, and a guard.

At the grand staircase, voices rose from the lower floors, accompanied by the sounds of stamping boots, scraping furniture, and doors being slammed open and closed. Episodically, muffled screams would break through the sounds of looting—palace servants caught and exploited for sport.

Following the chambermaid—zipping through palace shortcuts like mice in a barn—they bypassed a trio of Vors carrying sacks over their shoulders by sneaking through side corridors as the warriors brazenly trashed room after room. "Queeny, oh queeny, which room are you in?" one of them called. Not guards who knew the palace layout, but simple axemen on the prowl.

They similarly evaded two more groups of looters until Rasish opened a small door leading to a narrow spiral staircase.

The escapees inched down the cramped and creaking stairs, lit only by globes of light that Karisa illumanced in front and behind her. Joslyn, the timid ex-courtesan, only a year older than the chambermaid, wept quietly as they descended.

A tomb-like chamber hewn into the rock foundations of the palace claimed them at the bottom. Then, after a few more twists and turns through a labyrinth of storerooms and tunnels, they arrived at Rasish's stash.

"Change into the most ripped and torn clothes," said Karisa, poking about a pile of stinking clothes in a corner of the room and pulling on a ragged robe and a tatty brown scarf over her pilfered armor. A box of unburnt incense and censers resting beside the garments scented the air with a heady spice.

"But they stink," complained Takola, holding out an ambiguous garment.

"The worse you stink, the better the ruse. You are no longer a queen's handmaids. You are Plague Sisters." Ascorians and Vors all avoided the Sisterhood, who on every continent had nuns traveling through towns and cities to take in anyone ostracized for their deformities or chronic illnesses. Associated with sickness and disease, they were paid to then move along as quickly as possible. A perfect disguise for a group navigating through dangerous lands.

Karisa continued, "You, too, Captain. Cover yourself. But hurry, I need you and Rasish for one last task before we leave. I need to access the dungeon."

The prisoner lay curled in a corner of the cell, facing the wall. A woolen blanket covered the childlike form, and a single finger clutched its edge.

They had burst into the prison guardroom minutes before, Captain Rachella and Karisa, with bared swords ready to incapacitate or kill the guard, but the man was nowhere to be found. Now, they and the others stood at the end of a corridor of iron-barred cells.

"Is this her?" Karisa asked of Rasish, her voice rising in horror as she clutched the bars and stared inside. "What an awful place."

Inside, the figure stirred.

"Meila, it's me. It's Karisa." She cast a globe of light through the bars and into the stone cubicle.

After King Sicaro and his armies had forged north, leaving just a small garrison to guard the city and his queen, Rasish—on Karisa's instruction—had bribed the prison guard with one of the queen's ruby rings to allow the young girl to attend the tortured and abandoned outworlder.

The Ascorian king had banished torture many years before —bringing an end to the barbaric practice in the realm—but the new Vor king had no qualms about reintroducing it; as such, a cell had been modified into a dungeon to extract cooperation from the resisting foreigner.

Meila had been welcomed by iron chains dangling from rings hammered deep into the stone walls, and by a wooden bench with a tidy row of instruments and tools. Shackling her in irons, her torturer—a silent, thin man with long fingers—had wasted no time in taking to her with his emotionless eyes and steady hands.

His pliers crushed her fingers, toes, and any fleshy part he could find; his hammer shattered the bones of her hands and feet; and his scalpels carved lines into her back and torso. Her grunts and groans had echoed the depths of the prison for days. But she did not relent.

Each morning, Sicaro and Sneer visited and offered her release from the attentions of the gaunt man in exchange for unlocking the darkcore weapons. But each morning, she would reply with the same—a shake of the head.

What they did not know—Meila had told Rasish in the days after—was that she could dampen the pain and fear with secret devices inside her head. So, although fractured and mutilated, she persevered and never released the weapons.

Only when the thin man began amputating fingers and toes did her resolve erode. The sight of her bloodied stumps and her digits lying on the dungeon floor agonized her. Even special implants could not prevent the mental anguish of their loss.

But the memory of two people fueled her tenacity, she had told the chambermaid. A brother and sister. A girl who sacrificed her freedom for the lives of first her mother and then her sisterhood of slaves; and her brother who sacrificed his freedom and safety for the lives of little boys, honest tribesfolk, and her. Heroes who made no claim to heroics.

Then one day, the silent man entered her cell, but instead of taking up his instruments, he hunched in front of her and stared. After an hour, he stood and said, "God, take you now." He scooped up the ten withered digits he had removed from her hands and feet, dropped them into a pouch, wrapped his instruments, and left the cell.

Sicaro had then returned one last time. "No matter, I have power enough. The rats can have you," he said and departed.

For days after, Meila drifted in a morass of grief and despair. Hunger and thirst tormented her. Darkness smothered. Even the prison guard stopped visiting.

So, the chambermaid had been met with a cry of relief when she had first appeared. Rasish had unbolted the irons, wept with her, and then fed her, beginning her restoration.

But even knowing the horrors of the torture submitted on Meila, through the chambermaid's reports, Karisa was not prepared for the pitiful vestige of her friend.

Meila pushed herself up. Twisted, deformed hands, with torn cloth threading the stumps, dropped the blanket from a wasted body. Bandaged feet appeared at the ends of thin legs as they unfolded before her. Red and purple lines etched her chest and arms in a lattice of scars. Only her face was untouched, one of the few graces her torturer had granted her.

"It's not that bad," said Meila. She grasped the top of her gray cotton shift to conceal her chest. A weak smile forced its way to her lips.

Tears rolled down Karisa's face. She addressed Captain Rachella. "Does your key open this?"

The cell opened and Karisa swept to Meila's side. They embraced, and the younger woman's tears flowed into the other's hair and down the scars on her back.

"He's dead. The Vors are routed and are retreating," said Karisa. "We must escape before they return."

The "Plague Sisters" bore Meila through the city. Karisa and the loyal captain carried her on a stretcher while the others swung incense burners and chanted as they shuffled along the avenues in the mists of early morning. As they passed, Vor warriors reeled away with their sacks of loot, covering their faces and scowling, eager to avoid these harbingers of disease.

The city gates were abandoned. They passed through a side gate swaying open in the wind and began their journey to Dunberrin.

Chapter 24

New Beginnings

Jaks—The Academy of the Arcane, Ascoria

Jaks and Mulgrave gazed over the rooftops of Dunberrin. A late afternoon breeze swept in from the ocean, cooling the scorch of the day.

In the three weeks since the Vor horde had been rebuffed at the city walls and routed through the fields and farmland to the south, the city had lost no time in rebuilding.

Although sections of the city still lay in rubble, much of the ruins had been sorted and cleared by a worker army of citizens and refugees. Construction crews had re-dug foundations, and now, block after block, buildermages steadily regenerated the city. Buildings rose, and excited chatter spread amongst the homeless crowded into the parks and squares.

A pain spasmed Jaks's belly and distracted him from his survey of the city. Leaning against a merlon, he winced and cupped a hand over the spot.

"A wound like that, you'll carry for the rest of your life," said Mulgrave, standing at his left.

The bald mage's own injuries—smashed bones and black-purple bruises from his confrontation with Sicaro—however, were healing far slower than Jaks's. One arm in a sling and one over a crutch were markers of how close the grandmaster had been to death.

"You're lucky to even be alive," said Mulgrave. "We both are."

"Thanks to the Uwama," Jaks replied, recalling the blurry days in the Royal Infirmary under the care of the Jurn chieftess. "She and the medigel. Without both, I'm sure I would be ashes in one of those giant pyres."

Even now, two weeks since the last of the enormous mounds of dead had been cremated, whiffs of smoke and scorched flesh lingered in his memory. Their ash now covered miles of farms and pastures, and their charred remains lay buried in pits that would fertilize the soil for decades to come.

And the land to the west, where the velocannon had split the earth and killed tens of thousands of Vors, was a giant crater —a half-mile wide, and deep enough that the sea seeped through cracks in the bedrock and was reclaiming it as a lagoon.

"You would have had your own pyre—" the grandmaster said.

"Such a privilege," said Jaks, half-heartedly. He straightened as his abdominal pain receded.

"I would have cremated you myself," said Mulgrave with a glint in his eye.

No such honor had been given to his father, though. The head of the Vor king had been removed for presentation to the Ascorian king and the body thrown onto the first of the funeral pyres. It should have been joy that Jaks had felt when he watched Ranger Cromer decapitate his father's corpse and drop the head into a sack; instead, it had been intense sadness.

"So, what of your research, Master Jaks?" the grandmaster said, addressing him by his new title.

"You shouldn't call me that. It makes me sound old." Jaks shook his head but was secretly delighted at the sound of it. With the surety of position, the permanence of a role, and a purpose to fulfill, he had found his security as a Master of the Arcane. The council of grandmasters had decided that the title of apprentice, or even journeyman, did not befit Jaks's manifested power. A conjurer of lightning and a manipulator of storms, his mastery of electricity had turned the tide of war. So, they had said, he would be Master Jaks, electromancer.

"You'll get used to it." Mulgrave laughed. "Being *named* master is just the beginning."

Jaks frowned and wrung his hands together. "As for that . . . re-examining Grandmaster Vinton's writings has been little help," he said. Searching for a focus for his research at the Academy, Jaks had pored over the work of the last known electromancer. "It's clear he was obsessed with destructive power; hence, the rod he created." He thought of the artifact, blasted from Sicaro's hand during their confrontation, that had been found and now rested in an Academy vault.

"You think there is a better use of your magic?" said Mulgrave.

"I know there is." The electromancer reached into a pocket and brought out the egg-sized zinger droid. It hovered in the air, circled his head, and then returned to his palm. "Devices such as these. You used to say that knowledge is a power greater than sourcestone. You were right. It is knowledge that created this droid and the velocannon."

"You think you can make these things?"

"Not yet, maybe never anything as extraordinary. But I can study Meila's devices, dissect them, and see what I can learn from them. Maybe technology we can use in other things—new signaling devices, skyships, or those engines to replace waterwheels that she talked about." Jaks brought the zinger up to his face and squinted at the familiar dent it had received from the dragon's talon. "I'd not damage this one anymore, though. Perhaps I will start with the salvage at her workbench."

Mulgrave nodded. "Aye. You might as well take her things. Take over her workstation . . ." The silence that followed left unsaid what they both suspected—Meila was dead.

For days, as he had lain infirmed, he had sped the zinger back and forth over the governor's palace in Irin and the rest of the city for signs of Meila or his sister. His gut told him they were there, but the eyes of the droid denied success. Instead, he found looting, savagery, and chaos as the Vors took what they could and fled—some to the south, but many sailing back to their motherland. If either of them was still alive, he could find no trace.

The grandmaster yawned and rubbed his face. "I've been up on this crutch for too long. I need to straighten out for a while." He bade his leave and hobbled away.

Alone on the rooftop, Jaks walked to the far side near the family of blue dragons that made it their home, coiled up around one of the turrets. They hissed at him when he approached but quieted as recognition set in. They were no threat. The beef chunks he threw them when he visited had placated them to his presence. Beautiful creatures. He toyed with the idea of adopting one of the baby dragons for a pet but doubted the adults would simply allow him to snatch one of their young.

He stood for a long while, staring at the sea and the yellow globe dipping on the horizon. His mind drifted, ruminating over the past year and a half, from when he went from being a conscript tormented by bullies to a master who crafted lightning and storms. He commanded power that none other had possessed for almost a hundred years. He could kill and disfigure. He could demand fear. But he could not abandon the oath he had made to his mother. In a few days, now that his wound was healed enough to travel, he would take to horseback and take his search in person southward for signs of Karisa, and Meila too.

"Hey there, Sir Hero," a man's voice called across the rooftop. One of the dragons screeched at the newcomer. It leaped off the tower and beat its wings until it soared around the towering runic furnace.

Minto's familiar face rounded the brass dome, and Jaks dashed forward to greet his childhood friend. Time had worn his face thin; however, the amiable grin and impish sparkle in his eyes were unchanged.

"Who let this rabble in?" said Jaks, smiling. They clasped arms, and Minto punched him lightly on the chin, raising a laugh from both.

Along with a yellow cap sporting a rakish red feather, the herald's attire presented him as someone of importance. Jaks looked him up and down. "God, it's good to see you, Minto. I thought I would've seen you at the King's Triumph. I asked around, but no one seemed to know what had happened to you."

Minto tapped the side of his nose. "Secret stuff. I wasn't dressed in this foppery for the entire war, you know. Tell you later. But I am disappointed that I missed seeing you paraded around like a trophy. Rather spectacular, I heard. Mister 'Defender of the Realm and Hero of Ascoria.' I heard the king has even commissioned a statue of 'The Stormcrafter' for his halls. I'm surprised they didn't make you a grandmaster straight away."

As his friend was enjoying the ridiculous-sounding titles the king had awarded him, Jaks reddened and waved them off.

A wry smile then curved the side of Minto's mouth. "But you'll have to spill the details later . . . I'm actually here on official business."

"Official?" said Jaks. Minto held no document bag or scroll that a herald might present on royal business. It was then he noticed two guards, bedecked in the king's purple, at the turret door. A cloaked figure appeared at the stairwell and limped toward him, supported by a third guard.

"His majesty commanded a royal escort," replied Minto. He stepped aside and made an elaborate flourish to introduce the important personage. "Master Jaks, may I present—"

"Jaks, you wretch," interrupted the figure as she turned down her hood.

His jaw dropped, and his knees threatened to fold.

Meila.

Incredible, clever, *alive* Meila. Sunken eyes and hollow cheeks distorted her face, but despite those features, Jaks would recognize her anywhere. His heart pounded at the sight of her. She reached out for him, and he swept her up in his arms and laughed.

Alive but not *whole*. Scars crisscrossed and puckered the exposed skin of her arms and chest below her neck. Fingers were missing on each hand, the stumps at odd angles to the remainders, and the hands themselves contorted and twisted as though they had been mangled by the wheel of a wagon.

"Meila," he said. "I'm sorry. I thought you were dead. There was no trace of you—" He spluttered an excuse about the futility of his search and the limitations on him imposed by his belly wound. Tears of joy welled in his eyes as he realized his mistake.

"Shut up. Come here. I've missed you." She wrapped her arms around his waist and pressed her face against his chest.

Dropping his arms around her shoulders, he pulled her tight. He closed his eyes and kissed the top of her head. "I'm glad you're back." She looked up at him, and his tears dropped onto her face.

A look of resolve crossed her face. She crooked a hand behind his neck and pulled him down until their lips met. Passionate and needy, they pressed together with urgency. Murmuring to each other between kisses, they continued until an embarrassed cough interrupted them.

"Our duty is done here. Please excuse us, my lady." Minto bowed to Meila. Then to Jaks, he addressed, "Master," and tipped his cap. Turning, the herald nudged the grinning soldier back along the walkway.

Then alone, with the horizon a lingering glow, Meila pulled him by the hand to sit together on the battlement between a pair of merlons.

Even in the dim of twilight, the deformed hands and scars on her arms were stark. Jaks frowned in concern at her wounds.

"Who did this to you—was it my father?" asked Jaks. He touched her cheek and placed a hand gently on her thigh. "What happened?"

"His man," she replied. She told him of her imprisonment and Sicaro's intent to torture her into submission. "I couldn't give up the weapons. They weren't as powerful as the velocannon, but used well, they could have countered it. Don't worry—after a couple of years, the scars will fade. You know how fast I heal. Once you have medigel particles in you, everything heals fast." She placed her right hand over Jaks's maimed left. Two cripples holding hands. "My fingers, though . . . what is done, is done."

"I'm glad I killed him. Had I known he had done this to you as well—"

"What would you have done? Killed him again?" said Meila.

He shook his head at the confused emotions his father's death had left him with and changed the subject back to her story. "How did you escape?"

She told him how Karisa and Rasish had freed her and how their commune of "Plague Sisters" had escaped the city. "They carried me north while I could not walk. Your sister is a fine leader, Jaks. Resilient and smart, as seen in few. You should be proud of her."

"I am." Jaks smiled. Few people talked of Karisa well, except for her appearance and grace. It pleased him to hear someone acknowledge her other attributes.

"I bet you *didn't* know that she wields a swift blade as well?" She quirked an eyebrow. "We crossed paths with hundreds of Vor warriors fleeing south. Most chose to leave us alone. Incense burners and her illusions of boils and pox were sufficient to warn most of them away, but she could not cover all nine of us. Several of the predators needed a sharp sword. Reflexes of a snake, Jaks. One blackbeard, she pierced through the throat as soon as his eyes glazed over with lust, staring at our little Joslyn. Another, a tattooed monstrosity, she dodged as he went to grab her, and her dagger was in his kidney three times before he could even turn."

Jaks gawped, wide-eyed at the description of Karisa's martial feats. If it had been Vixhana, he would not have been surprised, but his little sister? "Hells, it sounds like I've been short-changed some fighting skills," he said, and then chuckled.

Meila responded with a laugh, then continued. "Then, two weeks ago, we spotted riders flying the Ascorian flag. Your sister signaled them, and they took us in," said Meila. "We arrived today. I wanted to come straight here, but the city guards took us to the king instead."

"How did he receive you?" asked Jaks. Rumors held that King Silas was temperamental even following the defeat of the Vors. Although the paranoia that had afflicted him during the latter days of the war was less, the Ascorian king was a shadow of what he had been.

"Must have felt sorry for me. Discharged me from duress of the court."

"He freed you?" Jaks laughed. "It wasn't as though we were holding you, anyway."

"Didn't want me wandering off, however." She winked. "Say hello to your new Royal Science Advisor." She bowed her head with faux humility as Jaks congratulated her. "Nothing much changes, though. I'll live and work here like before, except I'll be paid for it." The evening enveloped them, and Meila twirled a finger in a flourish and conjured a yellow globe to bob in the air beside them.

Jaks clapped his hands. "We can work together. Make things. Like these wrist devices. I was thinking that if we could make more, they could be helpful for fleets at sea, or merchants making trades, or people lost in the mountains. That sort of thing." Although the ideas came out of his mouth, his imagination dwelt on Meila and him being together like the magesmiths Doeg and Shazair—working and living together. Jaks looked hopefully at Meila.

"On this planet, without the infrastructure, we couldn't produce anything as advanced as the wrist comms, but there are alternatives," she replied, appearing bothered by a concern.

"There is still this problem of the United Worlds Federation returning. They would make the Vor invasion seem like a mere distraction in comparison. Eventually, a starship, or an entire terraform fleet, might appear. Maybe years or decades. But we'll have to be ready. I'll have to convince them that this world is worth preserving . . ."

"Still?" asked Jaks. Meila's previous life was puzzling and mysterious to him. The threat presented by what she called the UWF was almost incomprehensible.

"Of course." She looked at him as though annoyed. "It's why I was sent here in the first place. To assess the planet for repopulating."

"I mean, you still think it's worth saving? After you've seen how we live compared to your world? Wouldn't it be better if your people came and we could have the flyers, giant buildings, and all of those amazing things you showed us?"

She shook her head. "They cleanse the planet of whatever is leftover of the old colony. Indigenous populations cause problems, claim rights, start riots and wars."

He frowned. "We could fight them, then."

Meila laughed. Then, seeing he was serious, stroked his hand. "No, we couldn't. It would be like trying to dig a hole in the ocean. Every scoop would be refilled with water and would drown anyone that tried."

She leaned forward and kissed him lightly on the lips. "Don't worry, we'll think of something. But let's not worry anymore of it today."

Jaks nodded and would have been content to fold her in his arms for the rest of the night, but one last question burned in his mind.

"Karisa. Where is she?"

Meila looked at the darkened rooftops. "She had some

business to take care of. Had a message for you, though—meet her tomorrow at noon at the usual place. I assume you know where she's talking about."

He did. There was only one place.

The next morning, Jaks tiptoed out of the room, leaving Meila asleep in his bed where they had lain together. She had not refused the offer to share his bed this time. Although the pains of their wounded bodies kept them from anything other than taking comfort in each other's company, they had slept curled together.

At a brisk walk past the Academy gates, he roamed the city streets, restless in the time before he would see his sister again.

It had been several days since he had last witnessed the rapid pace of the city being rebuilt. At a couple of building sites, he stopped briefly to marvel at gravmancer builders floating massive stone blocks and huge timbers into place. Construction crews then hammered and screwed each into place before the gravmancers returned with the next. Dunberrin healed from its wounds as quickly as Jaks and Meila did.

He paced the walls outside of the Army district. Although the guards would have welcomed and saluted the "Hero of Ascoria" into the military zone, he had no formal business there that morning. However, he could not completely escape his newfound fame.

A trio of off-duty conscripts recognized the famous "Stormcrafter" and ran toward him with awed faces. One waved a drawing of Jaks that had been recently printed by a local news press. After zealous salutes, the recruits assailed him with questions about the fight with the Vor king: "Was he really your father?"; "Is it true you fried him to a husk?" Jaks's annoyance grew, as did the size of his audience, when they begged him to summon a lightning storm for their entertainment. At the limit of his patience, the storm in his eyes, however, subdued their excitement. Muttering excuses to leave, he pulled the cowl of his cloak to shadow his face and parted the circle of adulators as he strode off.

The bells of the Cathedral of Dunberrin tolled midday, and Jaks walked onto its sacred grounds.

The ornate building had survived the war unscratched and had served as an infirmary for the wounded during the final battle. Today, the grand monument continued to house hundreds of refugees still fearful of returning to the southern provinces from where they had fled from the path of the invaders. Eventually, they would go back, but only after their farmlands had been secured and rid of the deserters from the Vor army who still lingered.

Children ran and played around the gray headstones and trees of the cathedral's green spaces. A groundskeeper admonished and waved them off, but it was apparent to Jaks that the man fought a losing battle—quicker than he, they treated him as much a part of the game as the hideouts and treehouses they had built.

He arrived at their mother's gravestone and discovered a single white rose resting there. He looked about for his sister, but only an old man with a tattered bag and a scruffy, gray dog wandered the rows.

Alone, Jaks bowed his head and whispered, "Oh, Mother, it could have been so different. If only it had been *him* who went down those stairs that time. If I had never been such a coward. If I had stood up to him. You would still be alive. And this war might never have been. They think I'm some sort of hero, but if only they knew."

"We can't change the past, Jaks . . ." For a second, he thought it was his mother answering. But the voice came from behind. He turned, and it was the old man.

"Who are—" Jaks began.

The man continued, ". . . but we can change where we are going." The illumancer mask then fell away and revealed a familiar face. "And you did," said Karisa, in her pure form.

Jaks smiled, and so full of joy, he hugged her, lifting her off the ground. She squealed and laughed, squeezing him back. He had practiced what he was going to say when he first saw her, but all that came out was, "You haven't changed!"

She shared the same timeless beauty of their mother, and seeing her face caused his heart to ache for the past. The same haunted eyes stared at him, scarred with unspoken pain, but even deeper now. But, in contrast, her blazing smile and golden hair, as always, lifted his spirits with delight.

"Still picking up strays, I see," said Jaks, as the scruffy dog sniffed at his leg. Unimpressed, it wandered off.

Brother and sister then jabbered at each other for a minute until they broke off laughing. Their joy of reunion shared, they sat at the foot of their mother's grave to talk less hurriedly. Jaks had worried that Karisa would be cold and accusing—blaming him for her capture and enslavement, and then failing to help her even when he had come so close. However, his fears were dispelled. He should have known that his sister's resilience would take her through those dark times, attributing blame directly to those who captured her. In the end, she did not want details of Jaks's last fight with their father, only assurance that her abuser was truly slain.

"I made an oath to look after you—" Jaks began, his lingering guilt forcing its way to his consciousness.

"You and Vixhana are obsessed with oaths."

Jaks shook his head, reminded again of his broken oath, and continued, "I failed in my promise to you, Karisa. You ended up kidnapped and enslaved. I couldn't rescue you—"

"As I see it, you killed the one who has enslaved me all my life. That is the promise fulfilled." She parted her cloak and revealed a longsword and dagger at her hip. The dagger slid out, and she pricked the end of her thumb. A red drop formed.

"What are you doing?" said Jaks.

Karisa pressed her thumb against Jaks's cheek and smeared the blood down his face. "No more oath. I am marking you free of the promise you made to Mother. I can look after myself and don't need you worrying about me anymore."

He nodded as she sheathed her dagger. She was the weaver of her own fate. "But what will you do? Where will you go now? Will you return to the stage and live in the manse? You and I are its only heirs."

"I burned it down last night," replied a stony-faced Karisa. "I couldn't bear to know that the place stood with everything that had gone on in it."

He nodded a second time.

"I saved this for you, though." She swung her bag around and reached inside. She revealed a rolled canvas. Holding the top edge, she let it drop open.

He gazed at the family portrait she had cut out of the frame —four of them but not Father—when they had last visited the estate with Vixhana.

He smiled tensely at the last visual remnant of their mother, knowing that it meant as much to Karisa as to him. "You keep it," he said.

"No. I won't be in one place for long enough to hang it up." She cast him a side-long glance. "I am back with the troupe. We've booked a ship leaving tomorrow. We're going to Zura."

"Zura! It's so far away," he said. A journey of several months, sailing from port to port. He might not see her again for years—if ever.

"I can't stay in Ascoria. It's different now. People were talking about me even before I arrived." Karisa's face flickered with worry. "People will learn that I was 'the Vor Queen.' There are rumors already. I can't stay here. I need to restart my life, somewhere far away." Her eyes then flickered with excitement. "I hear there are provinces where they only allow illumancers to live. Imagine the mystique!"

Jaks knew he could not stop her, that he should not, now that his oath to her was retracted. She was a survivor and just as capable—*no, more capable*—than he. If she had been the one gifted with electromancy, their father would never have been able to propel the invasion to the last walls of the kingdom.

Karisa rolled the portrait in her hands and tied it with string. Her eyes took on a mischievous twinkle and a wry smile edged her mouth. Curiously, as she proffered the canvas to Jaks, it *floated* from her hand.

The rolled painting levitated in the air between them.

Jaks grabbed for the canvas, fearing it would fall to the grass, but as he wrapped his hand around it, the familiar lift of gravmancy met his fingers: gravmantic lift he had known aboard the *Kingfisher* when it ascended into the sky. "You, too? You could become a nightwraith, with Vixhana," he said as the weightless painting regained its slight heft.

She laughed. "I'll leave that to her. Where is she, anyway?"

A breeze swept over them, and a voice spoke from a shadow in the row of gravestones behind them. "Here . . . barely. After my little brother almost killed me." A tall figure materialized from the puddle of darkness.

"Vixhana!" Karisa cried out with joyous surprise tinged with horror, for the once imposing battlefield assassin was a skeletal, pale remnant of her former self. Her black armor hung loosely on her body. Where muscles once undulated and bulged beneath leather and hidden steel plates, her limbs were thin; where her face was once handsome, it was gaunt. However, although her eyes were sunk deep into their sockets, they still glinted with steel. She resembled what Jaks imagined a mythical wraith might look like.

But despite her muscle loss, Vixhana stood tall and straight with her longsword at her hip, just as she had a year and a half ago at this very spot.

"I'm so sorry, Vix. I don't know if you ever heard my apologies back in the Jurn village. I sat by your bed—" Jaks began.

The eldest sister laughed and strode over to her younger siblings. Her voice was thinner but still held its commanding tone. "All forgiven, Jaks. I have no memory of the incident, but Cromer explained it all as we traveled back from Jurn." She looked to the avenue running alongside the cathedral's grounds and nodded to the ranger, who was waiting there with two horses. "What happened, happened. I'm just glad that the three of us survived." Opening her arms wide, Vixhana gathered Jaks and Karisa into an embrace. They leaned in and affectionately pressed their foreheads together for a celebratory minute.

"I'll recover," Vixhana then said. "I have to. I still have a duty to uphold and a country to protect . . . thanks to this one." She winked at Jaks, who gave her a small, humble nod.

"You're tough. We're all tough," Karisa said as she looked at the last surviving members of their family. "We're lucky to be alive after what all we've been through." Jaks and Vixhana nodded in solemn agreement.

At the foot of their mother's grave, hours passed by as they shared their ordeals of the past months and spoke of old times.

Even after his father's death, Jaks had still felt laden with a sense of unfulfilled duty. But seeing his sisters both here, the disturbance finally lifted. They were all safe and free to make their own choices. The kingdom needed to be restored, and there was still the threat of Meila's people returning to claim their world. But for now, he had a sense of arrival. A job completed.

Vixhana departed first. She would return to the nightwraith barracks and rebuild her strength until she could return to her military duties. Dependable and loyal, Jaks knew she would most likely serve the kingdom with the elite soldiers for the rest of her working life. In the distance, Ranger Cromer rested a supportive hand on Vixhana's arm and handed her the reins of her horse.

"I need to go gather some clothes and provisions for the voyage tomorrow. It'll be a long trip. Take care, Jaks," Karisa said and threw her arms around him one last time.

Sadness engulfed him, knowing he might never see her again.

Their farewell was interrupted by laughter as a little boy ran down the cemetery row next to them, chased by an equally small girl waving a ragdoll in front of her.

"Good luck, sister," Jaks said as they parted.

"Farewell, brother." Karisa turned away, her face transforming back into her old-man's mask.

Her canine companion sprang to its paws, stretched on front legs, and shuffled to her side.

Jaks watched Karisa and her dog exit the gates of the cathedral grounds.

This chapter of his life was sealed.

An evil king, a cruel father, was torn from power, and a brutal invasion repelled.

He would only look forward, for he had clearly chosen his path. No longer submissive to fear, he was its conductor: controlling and manipulating the very emotions that once chained him.

He had chosen the path of courage—a warrior in the face of fear.

He was the Stormcrafter.

The End

Don't miss out on future books by J.T. Moy
Signup to J.T. Moy's mailing list to receive special offers and
updates about upcoming releases.

Website: jtmoy.com

Mailing list: https://linktr.ee/jtmoy

About the Author

J.T. Moy is from Auckland, New Zealand. A medical doctor and careers consultant, he changed careers himself in his mid-40s to write scifi/fantasy novels. He is married and has two children.

www.jtmoy.com